# Unleashed

Erica Chilson

A Mistress & Master of Restraint Novel

**Copyright © 2012 by Erica Chilson**

Wicked Reads
PO Box 29
Nelson, PA 16940

www.ericachilson.com/wicked-reads

Printed in the United States of America

First Printing, 2015

ISBN-13: 978-0692429549
ISBN-10: 0692429549

# Dedication
**My parents**. Unconditionally.

*If you want to feel worthy, have worth. If you want to be useful, have a use. If you want to be loved, accept the love that is given freely.*

Katya Waters has finally made peace with her past, but the present and future are becoming a never-ending nightmare.

At the end of Restraint, Katya fled back to her hometown, seeking solace from Ezra's constant micromanaging while hiding from her true feelings over what had happened to her at the hands of the men she had grown to trust.

Before Katya can come to terms with the catastrophic events she had endured in Dominion, she is whisked away from the comfort of her safe haven. Never getting a moment to reflect before being thrust back to Dominion, Katya's defenses are down. Ezra's controlling and manipulative ways know no bounds when it comes to Katya and their daughter. Vulnerable and susceptible to his influence, Ezra forces Katya and Ava into The Edge Building's fortress of a gilded cage, where Katya fears she will never get out.

Hanging onto her sense of self and moral code is difficult for Katya, as Ezra influences every aspect of her life, leaving her feeling powerless and lost as she falls deeper under his spell. Unsure where she fits into the lives of the men who impact her so deeply, Katya seeks direction from an unlikely source to regain her power.

Katya's intuition screams that she is in danger, which is why she allows Ezra to keep her caged safely within the world of his creation.

*...And then* the threatening notes are delivered– written with the words only the monster ever whispered.

# Chapter One

What a whirlwind my life has become. After years of being the master of my destiny, being the head of my household even though I was an adult-child living with her parents, I'm now thrust into a role I don't want. A role I don't understand. A role so tentative, it's like staring into murky water, not knowing what lurks beneath the surface until you dive right in.

I am Katya Waters.

Clarity is an absolute must. For without it, I am lost– set adrift in a world of Ezra Zeitler's creation.

Max and Clara Waters are agreeable, malleable yet set in their ways. My parents, Ava, and I had a simple life of structure and well-formed boundaries. We all had a role we played within each other's lives. Our roles were set in stone, and we never deviated. This was a source of great comfort, to know what was expected and when it was expected of us.

Our roles were tailored to our strengths: My father and I worked to provide for the family, while my mother was the consummate wife and mother, who knew when to step back and allow me to take charge of my own daughter. Ava was the child who tried to rule the roost but was easily thwarted.

I moved back home after two months of mental gymnastics, manipulations, torturous therapy, and bitter truths. I returned home to reach a level of clarity and to make peace with the reality of who ran me down, felled me to the ground, and raped me. I had a few days to sink back into the harmony of repetition before I was yanked back into the hell I left behind in Dominion, by none other than my past and present victimizer– Ezra Zeitler, the father of my only child.

The larger part of my personality is furious, fighting with claws and fangs to return to her parents, return to a place where she is in charge and knows exactly what is expected of her– a place of safety and comfort. A place that is easy yet unfulfilling.

The smallest part of my personality is thrilled with the challenge of taking on Ezra Zeitler and all of his baggage, but the larger part is winning.

I thought myself a cold-hearted bitch.

I was wrong. So very wrong.

I'm the opposite of cold-hearted.

I'm stupid. So very stupid.

The easily led astray part of me is slowly infecting the intelligent, dominant part with her addiction to Ezra– with her love for Ezra, her infatuation with Cortez, and her affection for the rest of the residents of Dominion, New York.

The intelligent woman wants to run back home to her parents. The compassionate mother wants to stay in Dominion for her daughter, so father and daughter can form a bond. The stupid girl wants to seduce the love of her life.

Compassionate mother is winning.

The intelligent woman is smothering the life out of the stupid girl. She will relent for Ava, but she will not lower her moral code by being a man's dirty little secret.

Without self-respect, I am smart enough to know Ezra will walk right over me, rule my life and everything within it, and that would be a travesty of the highest order. Being smothered would kill something vital within me.

I've been at the mercy of others before, and there is always a price to pay. The price is always your self-respect, your moral code, and your dignity.

Ezra means well by everything he does, with his stalking, his constant surveillance, his manipulations, and his overlording. He means well for his *own* ends. There aren't many people on this planet such as Ezra Zeitler. There is something infectious about him. No, he doesn't take no for an answer, because you are at his mercy, unable to say anything but yes.

I hate how my love, adoration, and respect for Ezra makes me powerless and weak-willed. He doesn't empower me; he makes me feel dependent, and I loathe it.

Like the most potent of drugs, being in Ez's presence removes all clarity, leaving me to trudge through murky waters with my only beacon being Ezra. The only way to survive my life in Dominion is to be at Ezra's complete and total mercy. My biggest problem, like with any drug, is that this is only an issue in the absence of Ez. Otherwise, I don't notice how skewed I've become.

Last night I was subjected to hours upon hours of 'convincing', as Ezra, Cort, Aaron, and Ava pled their cases to my parents, who ultimately pushed me back to Dominion. Then the trio left to exorcise their demons at the Lakeview, but refused to elaborate. I was then trapped in a moving SUV for three hours, being indoctrinated by Ezra while Cort sat beside me. Cortez kept rolling his eyes and chuckling underneath his breath at the level of lunacy Ezra displayed, all the while Aaron kept elbowing Cort in the ribs for disrespecting their messiah.

I'm only here for my daughter, or so I lie to myself. Ava has been glued to her father's side, sitting next to him as he drove us back to Dominion, sucking up his rhetoric about our future as a family.

Now I sit in my living room in The Edge Building, watching my life unravel as if from a great distance. I have no idea what is expected of me, how I fit into this group, or if I'm even wanted.

I thought the older I got and the more healed I became, the more in control of my destiny I would become. I was wrong. Just as Ezra manipulated me into surviving my attack, he's doing it right now as well. At this point, I'm not sure if I want to hug him or kill him because of it.

We arrived less than half an hour ago, only to find Roarke and Kayla waiting for us inside my old apartment. I would have been furious, but by all accounts, I did turn in my key and leave, making this place no longer mine.

I'm not a social person, so having Kayla, Roarke, Aaron, Cortez, Ezra, and Ava all packed into my old apartment is making me feel batshit crazy. I was used to this compact space only having me in it.

I cherish my privacy.

The apartment was just an illusion of ownership and privacy anyway. It was just a swanky prison Ezra trapped me in during my therapy: ever-watched but with expensive surroundings. As much as I love the space and long to find comfort in it, I resent it more.

The tighter Ezra's fist is wrapped around my life, the more eager I am to escape his clutches. The only way any of us are to survive whatever the hell our life has become, is with some well-placed boundaries.

I'm a control-freak without a plan. Where do I fit in? Where will Ava and I live? Where will I work? Who can I trust? Can I even trust myself when clarity flees the moment I sink into Ezra's presence?

"Katya, I would like a moment to speak to you in private. Please." Ezra's smoky voice flows into my ear, shocking me senseless to the point that I thought I was imagining it at first. His lean figure is casting a shadow over me as he stands next to my chair, impatiently glowering at the current occupants in my apartment.

"Why?" flows from my parted lips as I try to rein in my rising panic.

I don't want to be alone with Ezra. There is too much to say and not enough words to say it. I need to set some boundaries before I'm under his influence. No, I'm not ignorant enough to believe that Ezra will actually abide by whatever mandates I lay down.

"I believe we have some arrangements to make regarding our living situation. I would also like to discuss how you left Dominion without my counsel." Ezra's voice is stiff with formality, as if he's unaccustomed to not having his way immediately.

"Pull up a chair," I offer with false enthusiasm, gesturing to my dinette set. "We can hammer out the details. Right here. Right now."

"Why are you avoiding me? I haven't been alone with you since..." Ez trails off, sounding wretched and repentant. He glances at our daughter, finding her chatting with Kayla. "My punishment," he breathes out softly so his voice doesn't carry. "I need to talk to you. Alone," he orders, used to being obeyed.

Ezra's command tugs the invisible leash tying us to one another– the tie I've now come to despise as much as find a comfort within. I watch his back disappear through the open panel between our apartments, knowing he's completely confident I'll obey.

My feet itch to follow, which is exactly why it's not a good idea for me to speak privately with Ezra. I'm weak-willed when it comes to his manipulations and head games.

I quickly look to Cortez, finding him staring at Ezra's retreating form. His eyes flick to mine, and we share a moment of perfect understanding. Cort nods in agreement, flashing me an expression laced with immense compassion because he's been in my position too many times to count. I follow after Ezra, knowing that Cortez will have my back and will keep me from making a huge mistake. It's a welcome comfort to have someone on my side for once.

The worst privacy violation known to man is the hidden panel between our two apartments, acting as a doorway from my living room to connect to Ezra's bedroom. I was gutted when I first made the discovery, and every time I thought of it my stomach twisted in knots. It's worse seeing the evidence in person than in my memories– the betrayal cuts deeper.

I wince, heart beating in my throat and pounding in my ears as I step over the threshold to walk through Ezra's bedroom. I don't dare look anywhere but directly ahead, even though every inch of this space is imprinted in my vivid nightmares. I stride past where a solemn Ezra is sitting on the edge of his bed, no doubt waiting for me to join him. Without a backward glance, I make my way to his living room.

It wouldn't be a brilliant idea to sit on a bed with Ezra while engaged in a deep discussion with intimacy riding our emotions. Plus, I'd rather be skinned alive than to ever touch the spot where Ezra had made love to his fiancée, much less sit on it while pouring my heart out and bleeding my soul dry.

My stomach is roiling with the visage of Ezra and Adelaide's tryst playing out in my mind, their song of passion and adoration destroys me from the inside out. Just the thought has me rubbing the ache between my breasts and blinking away unshed tears.

Heartbreak: proof I'm not a stone-cold bitch. Also proof that I'm an idiot.

Sensing rather than hearing Ezra follow me, I curl up in the first chair I locate, putting distance between him and myself. I've never been in Ezra's private space before, other than his bedroom via the portal to my living room– a memory I long to forget.

I try to ignore the creepy factor when I note our apartments are almost identical, right down to the furnishings, appliances, and color schemes. If the room wasn't a mirror image of my own, with masculine personal items scattered about, then I'd swear I was sitting in my living room instead of Ezra, Aaron, and Cortez's.

I take a deep breath and tuck my shaking hands between the sides of the chair and my thighs, stilling my movements while restraining all temptation to reach out and touch the man hovering nearby.

Ezra settles himself on the sofa opposite me. A look of confusion and hurt mars his handsome, stern features as he tries to catch and hold my gaze but fails. I'm using every tactic in my self-preservation arsenal not to be taken up with what Ezra is emoting. He's already beneath my skin, and we've yet to begin. If he were to unleash all those emotions he's holding back, Ezra would roll right over me and destroy everything I am until I cease to exist as anything other than his puppet.

"Why are you avoiding me, Katya?" Ezra asks softly. The quiet serenity of his voice is holding back a dam of volatile emotions.

"I'm not." I swallow hard on the lie. Thick and toxic, it gets stuck in my throat.

Silent, Ezra just looks at me– looks through me –and Master Ez flashes behind his eyes. I stifle a shiver at the revelation. I've noticed this phenomenon before. It's like Master Ez is a separate entity within Ezra, and I seem to respond to anything that part of him wants from me. I can't allow Ezra to unleash Master Ez, because with absolute certainty, he will get me to talk. I need Ezra to stay in control so I can fortify my self-restraint.

"I know we need to talk about many things, Ezra. But I also know you didn't cull me from the herd to chat about our living situation and Ava's custody agreement." I pause, trying to formulate my thoughts into words. "Maybe. Just maybe… I'm uncomfortable talking about what you really want to talk about because it's beyond complicated."

I squeeze my eyes shut tight, avoiding the inevitable. If I can't see him… if I can't hear him… I don't want to be here. I don't want to have this conversation. I don't want to feel what I'm feeling. I just want to go home to my parents and hide.

HIDE!

Ezra Zeitler is everything to me: everything I want, everything I long to have, and everything I can never have. Not only does he hold the power of where I live, where I work, and who my friends are, he's also the father of my only child.

When I look at Ezra, I do *not* see my boss. I see the man who was my therapist, my best friend, my confidant– my lover. Aaron was right; Dr. Jeannine, Kimber, The Boss, Master Ez, and Ezra Zeitler are all one and the same. I can't mourn over the loss of them, not when he's within arm's reach, sitting across from me, with his need for affection and acceptance bleeding from his eyes.

Goddamnit! Ezra Zeitler makes me weak-willed and dependent, and I can never afford to be either.

Without question, I want to give Ezra everything he needs, and that is a path which will lead to my ultimate ruination.

Head falling into his hands, Ezra can no longer look at me as the silence stretches on. His shoulders are taut as he bows forward with his elbows resting on his knees. A violent ripple rolls through his body. Instead of eliciting his patented sigh, Ezra stifles a sob.

"Are you angry with me?" he whispers in a tortured voice.

"No," I breathe just as softly, tone mirroring his.

Still covering his face, speaking through his spread fingers, Ezra sounds defeated. "I haven't seen you, nor spoken with you, since directly after my punishment. We haven't spoken since you remembered– you didn't even tell me the memories resurfaced. You just left me..."

"I had to go," I gulp out, loathing how Ezra can make me feel horrific with just a word or a glance. Not only is he disappointed in me, I hurt him. "I can't think clearly with you nearby," I speak the God's honest truth. "I'm not angry with you, Ezra, and I didn't mean to worry you or hurt you in any way. I just had to see our daughter, and I needed the comfort of my own mother."

"What else am I left to believe, other than that you blame me? You blame me, don't you? Just admit it. I can handle the truth." Ezra's voice breaks, and I realize I'm not the only one who is confused, nor am I the only one who's feeling powerless at the moment.

But unlike me– a person who is used to feeling powerless – Ezra isn't, and the emotion is killing him.

I get up from the chair to settle next to Ezra on the sofa. Tugging his hand away from his face, I clasp his palm in mine, interweaving our fingers. I focus on where our hands connect, because all I want to do is to curl up on Ezra's lap and bury my face into the side his neck and inhale his smoky masculine scent, and then forget the world. I long to allow Ezra to suck me into his fantasy land, like taking a toke from the most potent of drugs. Once the euphoria takes hold, all else ceases to exist.

Minutes alone with Ezra, and I'm being stupid again. Without fail, unintentionally and involuntarily, I turn into an irrational woman who thinks love means every-goddamned-thing in this world.

Treading carefully, I begin. "I'm sorry. I didn't even think about how you would perceive my leaving, how you would see it as if I blamed you or harbored ill-will toward you. In that moment, all I could think of was myself. I was being selfish, but I had to go. I know how you operate, Ezra. I'm just not ready to talk about all of this just yet."

Ez leans into me heavily while squeezing my fingers. "You needn't be apologetic. I understand. But I have to have some reassurance, or else I will find little peace. I need to know that you and I are okay."

"We're okay," I utter quickly before I realize Ezra is manipulating me while acting like a martyr. The bad things is, he not even trying to do it. It's just inherently who he is.

"I've been insane since my punishment. You have no idea how difficult it was for me to leave you be, to not stalk you and pressure you. At first, I was just trying to give you space because I knew I didn't deserve your attention. I knew you were disappointed in me, not wanting to be around me. But then I figured out Cort was lying to me, how he wasn't taking care of you as he said he was. I should have realized it sooner since he's always up to his conniving bullshit."

"I trust Cort," I say emphatically, defending him. "I trust him to know what I need, and he knew I needed time alone to get my head on straight.

"You wouldn't have left if I had been paying closer attention." Ezra's arrogant voice resonates with his god complex. "I will remedy that from this moment forward."

"Jesus Christ! You can't smother me to death, Ezra," I warn, exasperated. "Your stalking is one of the many things we have to discuss. It's the main reason why I find it so difficult to be around you."

Obviously backtracking, "That isn't what I meant by a remedy," Ez mutters sheepishly, head turning to the side so I can't even see his eyes in my peripheral vision. "I just meant we'll talk our issues out like mature adults."

"Uh-huh…" I mutter, not buying into his bullshit for an instant. "Yeah, that would be a welcome change." I take a deep breath, and spew out what's really bothering me. "Ezra, you must realize how you're creating what you fear most. You feared me leaving, so your controlling actions pushed me back to my parents' home. As one of your father's victims, I would think you'd understand how the need to feel in control of your own life is what makes surviving endurable."

"See, you *do* blame me!" Ezra stresses, trying to yank his hand from mine. But I hold on tightly, not allowing him to manipulate the situation to suit his own needs and wayward emotions.

Ezra Zeitler may be my addiction, but I've been raising our daughter for well over a decade, and she acts and thinks just like her father. If I can deal with Ava, then I can manage Ez.

"I don't blame you, Ezra. I don't blame anyone except for Ray Hunter." He flinches when I say the name of his father– the monster.

"My father is Marcus Zeitler, at least in all the ways that count," Ezra bites out fiercely. "Marc is a good man, whereas my mother's *rapist*– your rapist –is not. If I could tear the Hunter from my blood, I would." Ez scratches at his thigh viciously, as if he can physically remove his genetic makeup. "Learning my conception and my true identity ruined me," he snarls in misery, somewhere lost inside his own head.

I don't allow either of us to spiral down into Ezra's passive-aggressive tantrum. "Ray Hunter is a bad person, but that doesn't taint an entire family. Our daughter has that same blood flowing in her veins as you do."

"Exactly," Ez breathes, wincing. "Even God hates my bloodlines. Besides Ray, the only other Hunters in existence are within a few hundred feet of my person right this very second. Just as my mother's family; the Holden line is dying out, with only me and any children I create. Anything born of me will never be normal. Trust me on this."

"Nothing is wrong with our daughter," I defend, reaffirming my belief that you can never love anyone while suffering from self-loathing. Ezra the martyr will never truly love his children until he can love himself. He blames himself for everything.

Turning from me, looking green as if he's about to be sick, Ezra whispers so quietly that I almost don't hear him. "Nothing is wrong with Ava, except for the fact that she is the reincarnation of my mother with my exact, same personality."

"Well, I've never met your mother," I mutter wryly, hinting how Ezra likes to keep me in the shadows like his dirty little secret. "So, I can only assume your mother is as beautiful as Ava– just as intelligent, I suspect. Somehow we managed to get a blue-blooded WASP for a daughter, even with my poorer than dirt, mutt ancestry. As for our daughter's personality, I'm rather partial to how her father's mind works–"

Cutting me off, "No, you're not," Ezra snarls, never believing the truth, even if I were to smack him in the face with it.

"Ez, you're a twit," I grumble, beyond annoyed by his insecure, bullshit routine. "Are we going to talk, or are we going to spend all of our time reassuring your bent pride? I'm the woman here, lest you forget. Shouldn't it be me who's fishing for compliments?"

Not even cracking a hint of a smile over my teasing, Ezra spirals further down the rabbit hole. "You don't understand. I've done horrific things. I'm *still* doing horrific things on a daily basis," he spews the truth I already suspected. "Even now, my mind is spinning ways to maneuver everyone into position to get me what I want, and I'm completely unrepentant and shameless in my efforts. I make excuses that I can't help myself because of my past and mental illness, and whether or not that is true remains to be seen."

"Ez," I try to stop the litany of his failings. Nothing is odder than having to reassure a freakishly intelligent, sensitive and giving, painfully handsome man. It baffles the mind, it does.

"My children are born of a rapist, and I'm not only speaking of my birth father. I *am* a rapist," Ezra stresses, squeezing my hand for emphasis. "The legacy I will leave behind for my children isn't the vast amount of Holden and Zeitler money, enough to sustain twenty generations if none of us worked another day in our lives. My DNA infects any child I beget with mental illness."

Ezra has a way of working his way beneath my skin, making me forget all about my own malfunctions, and the only thing I want to do is heal him. I shift on the sofa until we are facing one another, still holding hands. I force Ezra to look me in the eyes, to see the truth radiating out.

"I want to be very clear with you. I mean it, Ezra." I squeeze his hand to get his full attention. I can tell he was hanging out somewhere in the past. "I've had almost twelve years to come to terms with my rape. I've never blamed you, or Aaron and Cortez."

"You should," Ezra rasps out, looking at me like I'm the one who's insane. "I raped you, Katya. I raped you, put my seed in your belly, and then I ran like a coward while I left you with a monster. I didn't find out whether or not you survived until Marc told me while I was raging in a fit of despair. I spent the better part of nine years searching for you, even though no one would tell me who you were or where I could find you." Ezra leans forward and whispers the truth as he knows it directly into my face. "No one would tell me for *your* own good."

Startled, I realize everyone was right. "I'm glad you found me for our daughter's sake. But I'm also relieved it took you so long to find me. It gave me a fighting chance by allowing me to grow stronger so I could survive you."

Ezra flashes me a sardonic look. "I finally found you at the monster's parole hearing, but only because Marc fucked up and didn't get us out of the hallway in time. Not only did I bribe the judge to appoint me as your therapist, I threatened to bankrupt his entire family if he didn't. I then spent the last three years stalking you as several different entities, and thankfully you've revealed them all."

"W-o-w," I breathe out in a gust from my lungs. "Thinking it, and having you say it, are two very different beasts. The truth sounds even more disturbing in your voice."

With his features twisted and tinged green, looking thoroughly disgusted with himself, Ezra leans back away from me. "You should blame me, Katya. Lord knows, I do."

I release Ezra's hand, only to grip his face in my palms. I force him to look at me. "I may have not remembered your face or name, but I never blamed you– not for anything in the past, that is. It's your actions starting now that matter. The only difference between a few days ago and the past decade, is that I have a face and a name to put with the memory. You did what you had to do to in order to survive and to protect Cortez and Aaron, and no one will ever respect that as much as I do. I was a stranger to you, and in the same situation, I would have chosen them too. I was only one person, and there were three of you. Three lives should always trump one. Always."

"I shouldn't have had to choose in the first place!" Ezra cries out between quivering lips. His pale face turns lifeless as tears spill rapidly down his cheeks. As sick as it is to think, a visual representation of Ezra's pain makes me love and respect him even more. "I shouldn't have been in the position to have to choose one life over another. I shouldn't have had to witness what Cort was forced to do in the days prior. Poor Aaron," Ezra groans from deep within his chest. "It was even worse for Cortez. If it wasn't for this vile DNA in my body, I would be normal and none of us would have been harmed."

"It's over," I bite out, shaking Ezra's head between my palms. "It's time to move forward to the future. We need to figure out how to make a life, to make the most of the life we've been given. We didn't die at the hands of Ray, and the biggest 'fuck you' we can give that man is to live this life we've been gifted with to its fullest."

"You don't get it, do you?" Ezra whispers, breath tickling my cheek. "What I told you as Kimber was fact. Ray didn't do anything to me. He had me sit in a chair and watch as he tormented two of the most important people in my world. I had a bed to sleep in, and food and water to nourish my body, while my father forced Cort to rape and starve for days on end. I was exempt, and the comfort I was offered was a double-edged sword. It made them hate me as they went without, even as it tormented me with its warmth and kindness… a punch to their flesh hurt me more than if I had been physically harmed."

"It's over." Judging by Ez's glazed expression, he's not hearing me. I shout into his face, "It's over! You are not your father, just as my daughter is not hers. We are individuals, Ezra. What happened to you and the guys is no more your fault than it is mine for what happened to me. Do I need to repeat everything Dr. Jeannine ever typed to me?"

"Tell that to my victims," Ezra grumbles, looking like a lost child. "There is no way you are okay after all I've done to you. I always know what I'm doing is wrong, but I just can't seem to help myself. I also never feel bad about it later, and I know I should. I feel guilty for never feeling guilty. Not unlike a sociopath, except for the fact that I do feel emotions. I just need you with me, whether you want to be or not, and I'll do anything to keep you. *Anything*," he warns.

"I'm here," I sputter, exasperated. "See me?" I gesture to my body. "Here I am," I say wryly, because we both know I simultaneously don't want to be here but I do. "I'm also fine. I'm one of the most resilient people you'll ever meet."

"Are you sure you're okay?" If I wasn't already heartbroken, Ezra's crestfallen facial expression would do it. His smoky eyes hold unshed tears and his pale face is flushed red. I can feel his shame and guilt wafting from his pores, and it's unwarranted

"We're wiping the slate clean right now. Everything stays in the past, but the bullshit you pull from here on out is all on you," I warn, meaning it. "As for me, I'm fine. Truly. This is going to sound strange, but I've always said this to my family in the past, and they've always looked at me like I've grown a second head. Ava, she has given me a reason to live, to not dwell in the past. Yeah, I know it's weird, saying that the product of my rape is what brings me the most healing."

"It doesn't sound crazy to me," Ez says with a wry grin. "And not just because I've heard it all from my patients."

"Ha! Stop the lunacy act, Ezra," I demand, sick of his self-deprecating bullshit. His waffling between broken and domineering is giving me a migraine.

"I wish I could," Ez whispers wistfully, thinking I can't hear him.

"I know when you found me again, you expected me to be completely broken. I have issues. Hell, Lord knows, we all do. But I'm not broken, only bent. I've never given up, and I never will, because I have way too much to live for."

I draw Ezra into a hug, consequences be damned. I squeeze him with all of my might, while breathing in his masculine scent. I allow his warmth to soak into my being as I hold him while he silently weeps– heals.

This has never been about just me, or even the boys. Every violent event has far reaching consequences. Our families, my daughter, our friends, and our daily lives are affected by a few torturous hours of time.

"I'm sorry," Ezra breathes into my ear, voice showing his regret more so than his apologetic words. "If I could change the past, I would. I would take your pain away. I would erase all of our misery."

Voice thick with every emotion one can feel, I have to swallow to get the words out. "I wouldn't, Ezra. I wouldn't change a damn thing. This has made us into who we were meant to become. Wanting to change the past means you haven't let it go, and you need to. I would forgive you for our mutual torment if it meant you could move on, except there is nothing to forgive."

With a moan of intense longing, Ezra's lips seek mine. A soft caress, a feather light brush of lips that press until I give a response. His breath is hot and moist as it huffs against my mouth. His intoxicating taste is delivered by the slick swipe of a hungry tongue. The feel of his strong body enveloping mine, wrapping around me in a protective comforting embrace, has me shuddering in his arms.

This is exactly why I was so petrified over being alone with Ezra. I'm in love with this impossible, domineering man, and I have no self-control where he is concerned. Regardless, it's wrong to touch him so intimately when he's involved with someone else, in love with someone else. I'm better than being someone's dirty little secret. I deserve better than second place, and I won't disrespect myself by continuing to torture us both.

I find the strength to pull away, but Ezra's fingers tangle in my hair, holding me immobile. A sound– the most delicious sound in existence –dissolves all of my reservations.

Ezra moans into my mouth as he slides his tongue against mine. My name whispered reverently from Ezra's lips has me giving him everything he wants from me and more.

All Ezra has to do is control me, kiss me, and moan for me, and I am rendered thoughtless. Not only does Ezra take me, I give myself to him freely.

Strong hands grip me under my armpits and lift, abruptly yanking me from Ezra's arms– from his lips. I cry out, wanting more– needing Ezra. I struggle to get back as Ez's hands slip free from my body in an effort to keep me with him.

Suddenly cold, eyes blurred with a wash of lust, I look around in confusion as I'm dropped unceremoniously into a nearby chair. I blink several times until I can focus on the perfectly formed ass standing between me and the object of my desires.

"Cort, why the fuck did you do that?" Ezra's growl holds the sharp, bitter edge of fury. "I wasn't hurting Kat. She was sitting on my lap, not the other way around. She was kissing me back, you jealous bastard!"

"Jealous?" I can hear Cort rolling his eyes just by the tone of his voice. "Twit, I'm protecting all of us from your spoiled need for instant gratification. If anything, seems like you would have learned how in the heat of the moment I forget my shit. But once rational thought returns, I'm meaner than a feral cat and hold a wicked grudge. If you keep this manipulative bullshit up, you're the only one Kat will blame. Just as I always do."

With the partners in a standoff, all I can do is stare at the back of Cortez's t-shirt, unable to see around him. That damn sigh echoes throughout the living room, and the sound has my breath hitching in my throat, waiting for an epic fight to erupt. I have no idea what the origin of the word 'twit' means for these idiots, but clearly Ezra doesn't appreciate its usage applied to him.

"Katya wants me in a way you don't," Ez grumbles, nearly whining, and then his tone takes on the note of gloating. "She's not mad at me anymore, and she doesn't blame me like you do."

"I'm a goddamned consolation prize?" I mutter underneath my breath in disgust. I close my eyes and shake my head, trying to clear it. "Un-fucking-believable." I inhale and exhale to slow the rhythm of my breathing as fury meets arousal.

I wish I had a bucket of ice to dampen the fire raging in my hormones. If Cortez hadn't stopped us, I would have gone along with anything Ezra wanted. Anything. Except I would have hated myself afterwards.

"Wow, everything you both just said was wrong," Cort mutters in disbelief. "Katya has absolutely no self-control when it comes to you, and you exploit it," Cort defends me, sounding on the edge of physical violence. My eyes dart to his clenched fists. "We have important shit we have got to get settled. I don't think fucking Kat is a good idea right now, do you? Your daughter is within earshot."

In a single lunge, Cortez is looming over Ezra's seated form. Not touching, their glowering gray eyes clash in silent struggle. We all recognize how when Cort sounds rational, our own sanity has fled. Ez visibly relaxes, nodding an apology at both Cort and me.

I blush in mortification when what Cortez said permeates my lust-fogged brain. I try to remember if I made any sounds loud enough to carry into the other apartment. Finally getting my shit together, I have to swallow several times before I can even speak.

"Cortez is right. We have a lot of things to settle: living arrangements, Ava's schooling, where I'm working, schedules and shit. Plus, under the circumstances, I wouldn't think you'd want to touch me like that," I state firmly, getting angry with myself now that I'm no longer within the noxious cloud of pheromones Ezra releases– his decadently addictive scent that injects images of warmth and safety and twisted sheets into my brain.

"What circumstances?" Confusion replaces Ezra's anger.

Eyes connecting like perfect partners in crime, "Adelaide," Cortez and I say in unison. We huff a laugh at how ridiculous Ezra makes us behave. No doubt that goddamned perfume Ezra is releasing is why Cort has an epic bulge in his trousers

"What about Adelaide?" Ezra looks back and forth between Cortez and me. He scowls at us, sulking, and then his eyes light on the tent in Cort's pants and a funny little smirk twists his lips.

With sarcasm so thick you could choke on it, Cort flings his words like projectile weapons. "Adelaide, you remember her, don't you? Your *lovely* fiancée?" Cortez wrinkles up his face, as if her name on his tongue leaves a bitter aftertaste.

Ezra just shrugs and looks at us like '*so?*'

Cort mumbles quickly, "Kat has informed me how she will no longer touch attached men. She also said that if we respected her, we would respect her decision."

Ezra's smile widens, giving me a hint that he has no intention of respecting my wishes. In anything. Ever. Because he doesn't respect me, and he never will.

Heart breaking for the billionth time, "I hate the both of you so much right now," I snarl, getting angrier by the second. "I swear to God, I could tear your nutsacks from your faithless bodies."

"Whether or not I'm faithless remains to be seen. I believe it depends on who you ask. Perception is a wicked mistress." I didn't think Ezra could be any smugger. But then he smiles brightly, as if silently saying, "*I win. You lose.*"

"Knock it off, assfuck," Cort threatens his partner. "This is all your fault to begin with. I'm on the '*no touch*' list because of Divina, which is also *your* fault. You're off limits because of Adelaide. Again, *your* fault, as is Aaron since he was added because of his attachment to *you*. Ezra can do no wrong," Cort twists out, lifetimes of resentment flowing in a torrent. "I'm just the whipping boy."

Ignoring Cort's bitterness, Ezra flashes me a look, as if he's thinking, '*Kat is fucking batshit crazy if she thinks we give a shit about what she thinks, just as no one cares what Cortez thinks.*'

It was Cort and Kat against Ezra, but then they turn their stormy gazes on me, both sharing identical looks of exasperation, as if I am the one being utterly ridiculous.

"This is *not* up for negotiation," I demand, so done with the both of them. "I've already explained my reasons to Cortez, and he said he understood. I'm not going to demean myself by being anyone's mistress. It doesn't matter if you don't respect me, because I'm going to respect myself."

I'm starting to get really pissed off, especially with myself. How can the man before me make love to his fiancée and declare his undying love to her, and then days later kiss me while telling me he never wants to let me go. I feel disgusted, and not just with Ezra.

"Yeah, like Cort won't chase after you, anyway." Ezra snorts, sounding more like Cortez than himself.

"Oh, damn straight. We've come to a mutual understanding." Cortez winks at me and smirks. In an instant, I remember him chasing me around my apartment. A wicked blush creeps up from my chest, staining my cheeks and kissing my forehead.

"Enough!" I order, waving my hand about, cutting off this insanity-filled thread of conversation. "The answer's no. If you keep fucking with me like this, it's going to piss me off more, and then I'll leave."

"NO!" is shouted in unison, as both Ez and Cort lunge toward me, like I'm going to evaporate into thin air.

"Respect me, goddamnit!" I whisper-shout while warding the pair of them off with my upraised palms. "I realize you guys have never raised a daughter before, but I've been doing it for eleven years. Being a mistress is not the example I want to set for Ava. This isn't up for debate. You're both in relationships, and I'm not your in-house whore," I seethe, gasping for breath. "I'll earn my place in your lives, and not with my cunt."

"I would never think of you in that way," Ezra says, trying to convince me with his sincerity, yet that is exactly what he's making me out to be.

Cortez says, "I'd like you to act like a whore for me. That could be a lot of fun. I'll even play the pimp, and Ezra can be your John. I'll kick Ez's ass for being mean to my lady of the evening." Leave it to Cortez to defuse the situation with snarky humor. I huff a laugh at his serious expression. He waits a heartbeat before he winks at me.

"All right, prankster–" I start to speak but Cort cuts me off.

"I was being serious. It would be a lot of fun," he grumbles underneath his breath. "I like playacting in the bedroom."

"Not happening," I drawl out, trying to be angry but failing miserably. "We just got back. I need to make arrangements for Ava. Where are we going to live? Where is she going to school? I need a job. I have a lot to figure out, and my sex life isn't even on the list."

"That's all been taken care of, Katya. You've nothing to figure out," Ezra says calmly, ever the consummate politician. "Especially your sex life– all taken care of."

"What do you mean? I'm not your goddamned mistress, Ezra! I plan on taking care of Ava as I have for the past eleven years." My voice rises as anger engulfs me. I will not be Ezra's pampered pet, waiting for him to call on me. I earn what I have. I will not eat from Ezra's hand out of misguided guilt.

"Katya," Ezra sighs loudly, exhausted by the fact I won't just kneel at his feet in subservience. "Ava is my daughter as well. I want to know her. I need her in my life. Your feelings of possession toward Ava, I feel them toward her, too. You have an apartment, a job, friends, and us. This is your home. The only reason Ava wasn't with you for the past two months is because you were saving for her schooling. Any father, whether coupled with the mother or not, pays for their children's schooling. You speak of setting a good example for Ava, don't make me out to be a deadbeat dad. Please allow me to provide for the both of you. I want you and Ava to be happy, safe, and secure. But more so, I want you both close to me," he says in a tone filled with aching longing, and it softens my heart.

"I can't go back to Edge Publishing," I mutter stubbornly, chin rising in defiance. "I didn't earn the position."

"Will you agree to the rest of my offer?" Ezra asks, hope strongly lacing his voice.

"Yes, but I will pay for our living expenses, just as I have been for the past two months. I have some money saved that I will use to pay you until I get another job." I cross my arms over my chest and stare him down. "I also want privacy. I don't want my every move monitored like I'm some kind of convict. I don't want that for my daughter, either."

"Katya, we will negotiate on those points at a later date," Ezra says, causing Cort to snort loudly. That overbearing, domineering man has no intentions of stopping his stalking.

Ever.

"Katya, have you ever wondered why I run a publishing company? I'm a doctor, so why would I do that?" His eyes dart to Cortez.

When I shrug at Ezra, he looks at me like I'm completely daft. It's pretty much self-explanatory; I'm simply too frustrated to answer Ezra.

"Cortez was always highly creative. As children, we would live out his fantasies. There was never a doubt of where his passions lie. I became a psychiatrist, not only to heal others but to heal us– to heal myself. I had the money and influence to make any company I wanted, so I created Edge Publishing for Cortez. I would have done the same for Aaron, except his passion is caring for us, and later he came to me after the conception of Restraint, and told me he wanted full-run over the business. This provided the perfect opportunity for the three of us to partner in business as we do in our personal lives. Cortez writes the story, I heal the mentally ill, and Aaron takes care of Restraint. It doesn't matter whose money financed these business ventures to begin with. It's Cort's imagination that sells the books, and Aaron's innovative thoughts that have made Restraint what it is today."

I swallow a lump in my throat the size of a bowling ball as I rub the aching spot between my breasts. I knew it would be difficult to join the pack. I don't know if I can ever be an equal to them, because there is way too much history for the trio. I will forever be an outsider.

"Three years ago, when we finally found you, I was thrilled to learn you had the same passion as Cortez. My greatest joy in life is providing for those I love and care deeply for. I need to be that source of comfort for you, too, Katya. We can all be together– a true partnership."

"Ezra, your manipulative powers hold no bounds," I grumble, getting annoyed at myself for leaning toward him like a plant thirsting for the sun.

Cort flashes me that sympathetic look again, while Ezra just talks over me. "You've earned your position at Edge. Even if we weren't connected, I would have given you the job if you had applied. You are highly qualified, and you've completely turned Edge around in less than two months. Your job is waiting for you. Your staff is still in place. *Yours*," Ezra stresses. "Edge is *yours*."

"Ez–"

"Don't punish me because of my power and money. I can provide all of us with the stability and comfort only monetary security can offer... so let me." Ezra sounds oh-so reasonable. But it's like trusting the Devil; there is always a steep price.

I don't trust this side of Ezra– the side that will do anything in his considerable power to get whatever he wants. It's terrifying when what he wants right now is me. I know that he's pulling out all the stops to keep me under his thumb.

I will concede that I did do a good job at Edge Publishing. My clients trust me, and my staff works well together. I don't want to leave my home and job just to be stubborn and spiteful; it would solve nothing.

"Okay," I mutter, still unsure but knowing Ezra does have a valid point.

"Okay?" Ezra sings as his eyebrows meet his hairline. He smiles hesitantly, as if fearing I will change my mind. "Okay," he nods his head yes, more sure this time. "Good, I thought you'd argue more." Ezra chuckles to himself.

"Sucker," Cort mouths to me. "You didn't stand a chance."

"I think this qualifies for a group hug." Ezra pulls Cortez and me into a huge hug, arms curling around our backs, pressing Cort and me to his chest. His scent invades my nostrils, fluttering my eyes shut, and I notice the same drugged expression on Cort's face.

Ez is alight with pleasure as he squeezes us giddily. "I'm so happy all of my family is finally with me." Ezra's bliss and relief is etched in the tone of his voice. I smile at the glorious sound.

Ezra grips Cortez's neck in his palm, drawing Cort's forehead down to his lips. As Ez plants a large kiss on Cortez's forehead, Cort's lips arch into a contented smile– a smile I've never seen before. It's a private one that he only shares with Ezra.

I feel humbled that they allow me to witness their affection. While appearing innocuous to an outside observer, you can feel how intense it truly is.

"I know you said no sex, but affection is permissible, correct?" Ezra gazes down at me with hope and a lingering question in his eyes.

I shake my head. I lick my lips a few times to moisten them, allowing me to speak. "Y... es," I stutter, but it comes out sounding more like a question. Ezra is a sly bastard; he'll somehow find a way to trap me with my answer. "But only with a chaperone," I tack on for safety purposes.

"A chaperone?" Ezra sounds amused. He smirks at Cortez, arching an eyebrow at his partner. "And Cortez is to be our chaperone?"

I shake my head yes again.

"Very well, then." Ezra gives us an innocent look. He palms the back of my head as if he's going to kiss my forehead just as he had Cortez's. But instead of an innocent touch of affection, he takes my mouth in a searing kiss that is just this side of violent. Ezra's teeth sink into my lip, and then his tongue invades my mouth. He palms my breast and squeezes as his thigh parts my legs, knee rubbing against my sex in a brutal rhythm.

Stunned stupid. All it took was two seconds. I had no time to process, let alone push Ezra away.

Surrendering, all I can do is melt and whimper. I release a strangled sound from deep within my throat as I lean into Ezra for more. As soon as I kiss Ezra back, he stops abruptly. Stepping away, he's wearing the biggest, cockiest grin I've ever witnessed.

"Knock it the fuck off, Ezra!" Cortez roughly shoves Ezra out of my orbit. Still stunned from the blistering kiss, it's an acute loss to be standing alone. But I'll be eternally thankful to Cortez for saving me from myself.

Standing forehead to forehead, the partners confront one another: Ezra is visibly relaxed and pleased with himself, and Cortez is furious with fisted hands and clenched muscles readying for attack.

"I mean it. Katya said no, and for once you're going to listen." Cortez's voice holds everything left unsaid.

"I can do a lot of damage before Cort can stop me." An arrogant laugh rumbles up Ezra's throat while his stormy eyes pin me in place. "I could be inside your body in less than a minute, and not only wouldn't you protest, you'd beg me for it. You'd beg," Ezra mouths salaciously.

"Ezra, goddamn it!" Cort shouts, shoving Ezra further away from me.

Smile dimming, Ezra asks me, "Why all of a sudden are you afraid to be alone with me?"

"Are you high?" Eyes bulging, I just stare at an unrepentant Ezra. "Did he seriously just ask me that after molesting me?" I look at Cortez, silently asking for help. We share a secret, and he promised to keep it.

"Ah, Kat's just so in love with you that she can't help herself," Cortez says sarcastically. "You make her throw her moral code in the trash, and she'll hate herself later. You do to her what you do to me."

I watch Ezra's amused expression, and relief hits me. Cortez wasn't being sarcastic. He only wanted it to sound that way. This way he wasn't lying to his partner.

"Hmm… I'm not an idiot. I'll figure it out eventually," Ez purrs while tapping his temple like an evil genius. "But right now, I have to see my mini-me about décor and a contractor about removing a wall," Ezra says as he makes his way toward his bedroom.

"What do you mean– a contractor?" I mutter, at a loss at how quickly Ezra can flip a conversation or escalate a situation.

"The portal between our apartments isn't exactly ideal. It's my bedroom for heaven's sake." Gesturing like he owns the world, "I'm going to make one large apartment. No need to tell me what you like, Katya, for I already know. We will have a huge suite for the three of us,–"

"Three of us?" I gulp out, confused. Cortez's insanity filled laughter is answer enough.

Ignoring the fact that I interrupted him, Ezra just continues to speak as if I hadn't. "And a home office for you and Cortez to share. Plus a pair of suites for Ava and Aaron. That's if Aaron's still staying here." Lips spreading wide enough to make the Cheshire cat proud, "Aaron's been sneaking off to Kayla's apartment at night."

"I'd say you're getting ahead of yourself," Cort grumbles, but leaves his statement dangling.

Again, Ezra keeps on talking at Cort and me, ignoring any protests we have. "Ava can stay with Kayla until the work is completed."

"Hey, just a second, mister!" I stride forward in a rush. Fingertips gripping Ezra's shirt sleeve, I yank him back into the living room. "We need to discuss this. I don't want to live in a construction zone forever. I want my privacy. I don't want cameras trained on me twenty-four/seven. I'm a grown woman. I should get a choice in whether or not I live with you fools." I don't stomp my foot, but just barely. "What the hell will your fiancée say about a shared suite?"

"Privacy is but a state of mind, Kitten." Cortez says in annoyance, eyebrows pinched together. "Wait until you meet Ezra's adopted father. Marc makes Ezra look passive. I haven't had privacy from Ezra since I was in my mother's womb. You best prepare your daughter. She'll have a bunch of overprotective idiots around her." Cort's demeanor screams that he doesn't agree with the way Ezra stalks.

"I'll *try* to be good," Ezra says innocently, barely keeping his giddiness in check, and then he flashes the wickedest of grins ever to grace his handsome face.

Cort and I groan, accepting defeat, because if you deny Ezra anything, what he comes up with next will always be a billion times worse.

"You suck at lying," I grumble.

"Do I, now?" Ezra muses. "Do you honestly think it will take long to complete the apartment? It is me we're talking about, in case you've forgotten. Do you honestly think I'm planning this on the fly? What do you think I've been doing for the past three years?" He sighs at me, as if silently saying, '*Katya, you forever exhaust me.*' "A week– tops. Money may not buy everything, but it can buy a lot of reliable craftsmen, especially when I've had the blueprints ready and waiting for months."

"I'm not even going to comment on your bullshit," I mutter in disgust while raising my hands in defeat. "As for the rest of what you said, I don't know if I'm comfortable with Ava staying at Kayla's place. They just met, and I don't even know where Kayla lives. I'd rather Ava slept with me. It's not that I don't trust Kayla. I've just missed our daughter for the past few months."

Cortez laughs, looks at Ezra and me, and laughs some more. Emoting a volatile cocktail of amusement, disgust, and exhaustion, Cort says to me, "Uh, Kitten, when will you ever learn? Ezra does as he pleases."

"Apparently never," I grumble a reply to Cort's rhetorical question.

"You live next door to the three of us. Don't you think Kayla would be very close as well? You only need to know one thing about Ezra, he controls the lives of everyone under his power." Eyes popping, lips twisting, Cort sings, "Shocker! Kayla lives directly across the hall from us."

"That's it!" I stomp, furious with myself for not getting a clue sooner. "I've had enough of the lot of you for one day. You go see our girl about the décor," I say to Ezra. "You go do something nefarious or write something truly wicked," I say to Cortez. "I'm going to see a man about anger management. I'll be back when I don't want to beat the living shit out of all of you," I say to both of them over my shoulder as I storm out of their apartment.

I glare at Kayla's door on my way by, picking up a tail before I even make it ten feet down the hallway.

# Chapter Two

Roarke follows me down the hallway and gets into the elevator with me, all the while his hands never leave his cell phone. Suspicious that he's texting his Lord and Master, I lean over to see what he's doing.

"*Farmville 2*," Roarke says with a grin, showing me his budding digital farm. "Most addictive game ever. This is the *Country Escape* version. I play this on my tablet, too. I stay away from my laptop at all costs, or else I get too engrossed in the real deal."

"I bet," I mutter in disbelief as a two hundred pound bodyguard shows me his cartoonish pigs, cows, and chickens.

"It's so fun." Roarke's beyond excited as he clicks on a miniature corn field, and his avatar immediately obeys by harvesting it. "I'll send you a game invite. Don't worry; I know how to find ya. I'm already following you on Facebook." And the '*everywhere else*,' goes without saying.

"Uh… So, you're never actually paying attention, then?" I raise an eyebrow as I ask, secretly thrilled that Roarke is with me and not eagle-eye Aaron.

"Oh, I'm paying attention, all right," Roarke mutters as he continues to play on his cellphone, never looking at me as he speaks. A second before the elevator opens, he steps forward and to the side, ready to vacate after me. "I'm a retired police officer. I can scent bullshit and oncoming danger on the air, and everything I do is repetitious." Following me off the elevator, "I could go through life blindfolded because Ez is as reliable as a Swiss Clock."

I mull over what Roarke said about Ezra being reliable as I walk through the lobby and out the main doors of The Edge Building, popping out onto the sidewalk filled with people going about their day.

"What do you mean? Ezra always seems to be making up shit as he goes along." Unlike Aaron, Roarke allows me to walk down the sidewalk toward Restraint without dragging my ass back into the black SUV from Hell.

"Once you learn all of Ezra's eccentricities, he's predicable, even in his insanity. Cause and effect. It's when something doesn't go his way that shit hits the fan. So, do us a favor and do as he asks."

"I'm living my own life," I snarl, walking faster, getting angrier with every step I take.

"You can lie to yourself if it makes you sleep better at night. But as a man who has dealt with Ezra's bullshit since grade school, you should heed my warning. I had to quit being a cop because of the lunatic. The shit I was witnessing and perpetrating was a conflict of interest. When it got to the point that I should arrest myself, I had to reevaluate my career."

Interest piqued, I slow my walking. "What'd you do?"

"You don't wanna know." Roarke answers with a giant grin, but it doesn't mask the shudder of revulsion that flows through his enormous body. "I have no life. Aaron has no life. None of us do. Even Ezra is fighting to live his own life. None of us are immune. Including you," he says pointedly.

"You make absolutely no sense," I grumble, moving faster the closer to Restraint we get.

"You're an oddly moral person, Katya," Roarke doesn't sound impressed. It's more like he's sad for me. "I used to be as well. I suggest you never make sense of what I'm trying to impart, because I'm not sure you'd ever be able to live with yourself if you knew the absolute truth. Just saying, Dominion is a cesspool of deception, and Ray Hunter and his merry trio of fucked-up-ness dropped a pile of shit at your feet that you will never escape. Better just deal, girly."

"I'm dealing," I mumble grudgingly.

Just not very well.

Restraint looks different in the light of day with no crowd lined up, flowing down the block as they wait for admission. There are no bright lights blinding your eyes or deafening music pumping into your eardrums. Restraint looks very sedate and dreary during the day.

Roarke leads me to a side door, not the main entrance. "How did you know I was coming here?"

"Predictability," Roarke says with a smile. "You're a bit like Ez in that regard. I've also been following your every move for the past three years. Who the hell do you think tells Ezra what your next moves are before you even think of them?" A warm, brown eye winks, clearly amused. "I might've lied and told him you were hunky-dory when I knew you were turning tail for Pennsylvania. I bought you a few days to get your shit straight."

"Thanks, I think." I pause, staring at the '*Employees Only*' painted on the door in front of me. "You have no idea why I'm here at Restraint," I grumble, hating how the big guy next to me knows me more than I know him.

"You feel out of control because Ezra is controlling every aspect of your life. Since you've been in Dominion, you've barely left The Edge Building, except to go to Restraint. You started down North Avenue in this direction. I didn't have to use my super-sleuthing skills to deduce you were going to Restraint to get your power back."

Roarke opens the door, stepping to the side to gesture me through first.

"Thanks," I say as I step over the threshold to enter a quiet Restraint. A burning sensation crawls up the back of my neck, a feeling of being watched– pure instinct.

After my violation, I trust that gut feeling that overcomes me from time to time. I call it self-preservation. I turn slowly to look at my surroundings. I see no one and nothing out of the ordinary.

"What's wrong?" Roarke looks around as he asks.

"Does it feel like someone is watching?" My voice quakes with paranoia.

"I don't see anyone or feel anything, Kat," he mutters in confusion. "But I'm so in tune with Ezra, that unless it's a threat to him, I don't feel it anymore."

I shake my head at Roarke as I try to scratch the sensation away. I let it go. I've had quite a few emotional jolts in the past few days; my imagination is just playing tricks on me. The inside of Restraint is a shock as well. The dance floor is empty, the lights are bright, and it's so quiet that every sound echoes.

"C'mon, Dexter is this way," Roarke says, taking my arm.

"What?" I gasp. "How'd you know that?"

"I'm not a mind reader." Roarke chuckles huskily. "Don't be so surprised, Katya. I told you I was a police officer. I'm highly observant, even if I don't look like I'm paying close attention."

Roarke leans forward, keeping one hand on the small of my back while typing in the code to the door to the dungeon with the other.

"You feel betrayed by Queen, so you're not visiting her. That only left one other person who could give you what you're seeking, as you've yet to be properly introduced to the others. Dexter's a perfect choice for you, by the way."

Roarke walks me through the dark and desolate dungeon, toward the hallway at the back. "God, this is so bizarre," I mutter as we walk through the darkened dungeon with its larger contents looming in the shadows like prehistoric animals.

"Any advice?" I meep out, hating how unsteady my voice is.

"The first thing you need to know is that Dexter Hayes is Marcus Zeitler's cousin– Marc is Ezra's adoptive father. Marc and Dexter were raised as brothers by their grandmother."

"Shit," I whisper, already feeling like a moron for coming here. "Of course, Dexter would be related to Ez. Why am I not surprised?"

"Second piece of advice," Roarke says without missing a beat. "Never be surprised by anything in Dominion. If it seems normal, then you're not seeing it clearly."

"Jesus Christ," I pray.

"So you need to realize whatever you say to Dexter will more than likely reach Marc's ears, but will undoubtedly never reach Ezra's. In fact, this is perfect." Roarke laughs at some private joke I'm not privy to. "Dexter pisses Cortez off something fierce."

"Why?" I mutter, realizing this is why Ezra always gave me Aaron and not Roarke. Roarke's loyalties do *not* lie with Ezra. I'm not sure where they lie, but he's not Ezra's little bitch for damn sure.

"Oh, piss Cort or Ezra off while using Dexter's name, and they will fight in front of you. You'll get more info while watching them throw tantrums, than by trying to have an adult conversation with either of them."

Curiosity piqued, I ask, "No shit?"

"*Really*," Roarke stresses. "If you ever want to know something, just pit Ezra and Cortez against each other by bringing up Dexter or Ade. Words will flow like lava from an erupting volcano."

"Cort's the volcano in this equation, right?"

Chuckling loudly, Roarke shakes his head no. "Ez is the volcano and Cort is the lava. Together they destroy everything in their path."

"Ah... huh? Come again?" I stammer out, confused beyond words.

"Don't try to reason that out," Roarke says with a hearty laugh. "You'll see what I mean soon enough. They don't go long without erupting. So, Dex is right in there," Roarke says, pointing a few doors down.

I take a step forward, unsure if I want to do this or not. Nervous, my voice quivers as badly as my hands. "I... maybe this isn't such a good idea."

"Don't be scared, Kat. Dexter's a sadist, but only for those who need relief through pain. Otherwise, he's the most patient person you'll ever meet. So speak freely with him– you can trust him. I promise." Roarke turns to leave me alone in the hallway outside of Dexter's private room. "Oh, I won't tell Ez where you are. I was on my way to work when you popped into the hallway at Edge. It was just a coincidence we were headed in the same direction. Honest."

I fist the center of my chest, suddenly feeling warm because I can sense Roarke's sincerity. "Thank you."

"Anytime, little lady," Roarke says with a big grin. "Maybe we will have some peace now that Ez has you here. Maybe Cort will stop rampaging and Ez will act sane." Shaking his head sadly, "I'm dreaming, but it's got to be better with you here than with Ez worrying about you."

"I'm confused," I mutter, hating how it's the sad truth.

Roarke pauses, like he wants to say something but is unsure if he should. He runs his palm over his wavy brown hair, and takes a deep breath.

"Another word of advice, never ask why anyone does what they do. It shouldn't matter to you, because even if they say they're doing it for you, they're lying. It's human nature to be egocentric. Kat, you need to do what's best for you, what protects you, and what makes your life worth living."

I realize Roarke is trying to warn me, but I don't know of what. "It's a hard concept for a woman– for a mother –to put herself first. We think we're supposed to care for everyone while sacrificing our needs."

"It ain't selfish to take care of yourself first, girly. It's smart. You'll need your strength to survive. So, if Dexter can make you stronger, go for it. If Ezra throws a shit-fit because of it, don't let him get away with it."

"Boundaries, that's why I'm here," I admit.

"Ah, perfect," Roarke purrs. "Dexter will teach you how to handle Ez, if that's the type of boundaries you're looking for. Dexter taught Ezra the art of BDSM, so he'll know exactly how to get Ezra to behave. Honest. Good luck; you'll need it," is Roarke's parting remark. Then he disappears back down the hallway, and into the dungeon and beyond.

# Chapter Three

I step forward on shaky legs toward Dexter's private room, my resolve dissolving without Roarke's supportive presence. With a deep breath, I bridge the gap, and I'm surprised to find Dexter's door ajar.

I know it's still daytime, but I assumed that if Dexter was at Restraint, he'd be entertaining a submissive. I lean on the doorframe and stare gape-mouthed at the sight that is Dexter Hayes. He is small for a man, maybe five and a half feet tall. But what he lacks in height, he makes up with lean muscle.

My eyes glue to Dexter in avid fascination as he cleans his flogger. He's shirtless, since the room is above comfortable temperatures. I watch, completely rapt, as a bead of sweat creates a path down his back, gliding around all those perfect, striated muscles. The drop disappears beneath his low-slung, leather pants. A shiver rocks my body at the thought of the bead sliding down the crack of his biteable ass.

"Katya, snap your mouth shut, close the door, and have a seat," Dexter commands, and I listen. He must have felt my eyes devouring him, or perhaps he has incredible hearing and caught Roarke's and my conversation out in the hallway.

A blush sears my flesh as I obey Dexter's command by sinking into the nearest seat.

I sit on the corner of a brocade chaise lounge. My eyes flit around the room, taking in every detail as I try to avoid looking at Dexter. The room is nothing like I would expect.

Surprisingly, the sadist's private space is very warm and inviting. You'd assume a pain-dealer's domain would have a slaughterhouse feel. Yet the space is reminiscent of a French bordello: soft, velvet draped Victorian-style furniture in deep hues of red and purple. It's very royal, with the exception of the BDSM torture devices scattered around the room, which are all a shiny, lacquered black. Overall, I'm as impressed as in awe.

"Does Ezra have the rooms pre-decorated, or do you guys get creative license when you're given a room?" I wet my lips several times with my tongue, mouth suddenly feeling parched.

I'm a ball of roiling nerves because of the conversation that's to come.

"Kat, is that really what you came here to ask me?" Dexter asks knowingly as he glances at me from over his shoulder. A little ringlet of dark hair caresses his forehead.

*There was a little girl, who had a little curl right in the middle of her forehead. When she was good, she was very, very good, and when she was bad, she was horrid.*

Well, Dexter isn't a girl, but I'm sure he can be horridly spectacular. His deft fingertips pull the curl back into place as he looks at me with patient, amber-colored eyes.

Yes, I am stalling. I take a fortifying breath, and then expel it as words. "I have something to ask, but for once I need some foreplay. Just a little bit of small talk." I look down at my hands and twist my fingers together.

Dexter shakes his head yes and turns to face me. Any pretense of not looking at him evaporates. My mouth dries up as my jaw unhinges, and my eyes bug-out at the sight of him.

Dexter is shirtless and shoeless. All he wears is a pair of tight, black leather pants that fit him like a second skin. I'm not entirely sure how he pulled them on without copious amounts of lubrication. The leather was made to fit him, as if Dexter was poured into the fabric when he got dressed this morning. His belt is created out of round, metal rings, loosely sloped around his narrow hips and doing absolutely nothing to hold up his pants— pants that have no belt loops, and are so tight they would never fall, even if they are low enough that I can count the pubic hairs trailing downward to his evident arousal.

I try not to stare at the bulge pressing against the leather, and fail miserably. It's a sick compulsion I cannot help. It has absolutely nothing to do with Dexter the man, but my own morbid curiosity as my sexuality awakens. This must be how a man feels when a smoking hot, half-dressed young woman walks by. You just can't *not* look. It's an impossibility.

I close my eyes to the sight of all that bronze flesh glistening with sweat and the appetizing bulge pressing into the straining zipper. I know exactly what that cock looks like when it's unleashed from that tight leather— long and thick, and able to wrench a scream from an arched throat. My blood boils beneath the surface as my mind conjures up images of what it would be like to unleash that swollen, throbbing flesh myself.

Unbidden, a shuddering breath releases from my parted lips.

In challenge, Dexter looks me straight in the eyes as he rubs the heel of his palm against his cock, moving the bulge into a more comfortable position. His groan elicits an indescribable sensation in me. It's like I just took a toke of pure lust– a dangerous narcotic shot directly into my veins to make my cunt weep.

I wipe at my mouth with the back of my hand, hoping to find it dry. Dexter is sex personified, and I hope to God I'm not drooling from anywhere but between my thighs.

This was such a bad, fucking idea. Whether it's the stupidest or the smartest of my life, remains to be seen.

"Those are some spectacular–" I clear my throat "–pants ya got there, Dexter."

"I can give you the number to my tailor," he deadpans. "Although, he's rather expensive."

"Yes, please," I say enthusiastically. "I'll need two pair."

Without a trace of humor, Dexter murmurs, "If Ezra ever donned leather, Cortez would swoon. If Cortez ever wore leather… God, help us all."

I can't help it, the entire situation is so ridiculous that I burst out laughing. "Sorry. So sorry," I say as a few more giggles bubble up.

"Really, what do you need, Katya?" Dexter gives me a genuine smile as he settles himself on the spanking bench he was using as a worktable.

"I want you to train me," I blurt out.

"As a submissive or a dominant?" Curiosity and worry war across Dexter's features.

"Both," I answer. "I need an outlet to channel how powerless I feel right now. I need to regain some control in my life. But at the same time, I need to know how to give into Ezra without losing myself in the process. I don't want to resent him."

"Understandable but… nah… No. Not a good idea, Kat. I mean it," Dexter answers quickly, shaking his head left and right, as if wishing he could clear away what I'd just asked.

"Why not?" My mood plummets. I hadn't expected Dexter to disagree so fast. I thought he'd at least think it over for more than a split-second before he rejected me.

"I don't think you realize what you're asking, Katya." Dexter stares at my face, reading me. "It's not that I wouldn't enjoy any time spent with you. Trust me when I say I can see why Ezra is so intrigued by you."

"I wish I understood it," I mutter. "Maybe you could explain it to me, and while you're at it, explain why you won't train me."

"I refuse to delve into the inner-workings of Ezra's mind. No one should ever bother." Dexter shudders. "I bet Ezra wishes he wasn't even in his own head. As for why I shouldn't train you, it's the deep connection. A bond between the trainee and mentor forms, causing intense feelings to develop, which are very hard to deny. I'd rather keep my nuts, thank you very much."

"Oh, so humble you are," I mutter flippantly. "God's gift to women with your huge cock, your ability to wield a whip, and your penchant for sadism."

"You're drooling a little bit on yourself, sweetheart," Dexter says drolly, fingertip reaching to wipe the corner of my mouth.

I stare wide-eyed in utter disbelief when Dexter licks the fingertip he just touched me with.

Eyebrow raised in silent challenge, Dexter states unequivocally, "I'm single. However, you are *not*. But Ezra and Cortez aren't my only reasons for denying you. What I do isn't really about BDSM, but it is. We aren't just a nightclub with a dungeon in the back. The Masters of Restraint belong to a group called the Maître du Jeu."

"Huh?" stumbles out my mouth as my eyebrows knit together. "What the fuck?"

"If this was just about getting my rocks off and playtime–"

"And if Ezra wasn't stalking me?" I readily supply.

"That too." Dexter chuckles deeply, as if I took him by surprise. "I'm not sure how much Ezra has said of his family life. But I feel I should formally introduce myself. I'm Dexter Hayes, Marcus Zeitler's cousin."

Grinning, I lean forward to shake Dexter's hand. "Katya Waters, and it's a pleasure to meet you. It's also a pleasant surprise that you're willing to be honest with me, because the only reason I know about the familial connection is because Roarke just warned me."

"As I suspected," Dexter murmurs as he pulls his hand away.

"You should also know tenacious is my middle name," I warn teasingly. Sobering, I ask, "Now, why won't you train me?"

"Tenacious?" Dexter releases a laugh unlike any I've ever heard. My God, it's pure sex. "Good. You'll need the will to survive."

"No shit," I grunt out.

"My cousin, back when he was around twenty or so at the most– I think Ez and Cort were fifteen at the time –Marcus left Dominion for well over a year, and then when he returned, he spread the word of BDSM like an infectious disease."

"Ah," I breathe, feeling enlightened.

"Mind you, I love every demented second of it, so I understand your need to regain your power. But you have to realize, once you join the Maître du Jeu, you can never quit."

"You sound so dang ominous, Dexter," I tease, but my voice wavers with fear.

"For me, it's about BDSM, and I don't ask any questions otherwise. I'm just a low-level flunky who does as he's told, and they leave me alone. I have no idea how deep their shit runs, so I pretend it's a twisted membership of masochists beneath the ultimate sadist. But you belong to Ezra, so I'd say it doesn't really matter, anyway."

"I do *not* belong to Ezra," I snarl, sick to fuck of having to repeat that same line. I say it so often that I'm starting to not believe it myself anymore.

"Sure you do, or else you wouldn't be seeking me for some solace from Ezra's domination. I understand why you are here and what you need from me. I really do. We all need BDSM for different reasons. But yours are no different than Ezra's, believe it or not. Cort, that lazy fuck, he isn't interested in anything but getting available pussy with his master status. Training him was like pounding myself with a hammer. Repeatedly. To the nutsack. Finally Marc just said Cort was a master to save our sanity."

"If Cort didn't want it, why did he do it?"

"Ezra will forever be the answer to any question you may ever ask about Cortez," Dexter states unequivocally– his tone betraying an underlying resentment.

"So I've gathered," I mutter. I blurt out before my brain registers the thought, "Do you think I'm strong enough to train– mentally, that is?"

Dexter tilts his head backward and releases the most intoxicating sound I've ever heard. He laughs so loudly it reverberates down my spine to coil in my belly. Eyes magnetized to his skin, I watch as his throat convulses with laughter. Calming, it takes several tries before Dexter is able to speak.

"Fuck, yeah," he belts out, eyes still glittering with mirth. "You didn't hear this from me, but I think you should know. Ezra is terrified of you– terrified that someday you will realize you're stronger than he is. Petrified for the day you realize you're not a switch. All dominants rely on others to get through life. It's just a fact of life, but it doesn't make them a switch. It just makes them human."

Floored, all I can do is stammer, "I... I..."

"Maître du Jeu is a BDSM group, which I can only assume is some kind of front for the mafia. I don't know if Marc picked up their bullshit in Las Vegas, or if he went to Las Vegas because it originated in Dominion. But it doesn't matter either way, because it's just another fact of life around here. So I just go about my business and pretend I don't find anything out of the ordinary."

My name is Kat, after all. Instead of warning me off, my curiosity is piqued. "Do they ask anything of you?"

"Nope. Not a thing other than giving us rules and regulations on membership, how to run the club, who can and cannot join. Basically, it all centers on BDSM. Whoever the hell is in charge, they get off on power and control while reveling in our submission."

"And you don't think they will have me?" I venture a guess.

"Kat," Dexter murmurs sadly. "You're the mother of Ezra Zeitler's daughter," is his confusing explanation. "So, there are only two trainers in the area if you want to join our little group:

myself and my cousin. Marcus handpicks his students, and I train the rest. You can do the math of who Marc has trained by reading the doors on your way down the hallway, minus those I've trained: Ezra, Cortez, and Syn."

"Is there a difference between the two of you?" I ask, voice cracking. "Not that I expect either of you to take me on, ya know?" I mutter, suddenly overcome with insecurity.

"Well, I'm a sadist, and since that's Syn's passion as well, I mentored her. I trained Ezra for Marcus, because undeniably sexual energy is released during the training process, and that's too disturbing to contemplate, to be honest." Dexter shudders. "As for Cortez, if Ezra experiences anything, that cocksucker has to as well. Even if Marc was hard-pressed to train Cort himself. Even though, I'm pretty sure Cort was trained by Marc unwittingly as a helper monkey."

"Helper monkey?" My lips quirk up. Good God, I want to call Cort that to his face.

"Cortez is Marc's little bitch while he trains other baby masters. Occasionally Marc steals Aaron for sessions, since Cort rubs people the wrong way. I'd hoped Cort would learn by example. But," Dexter parts his hands as if to express how Cort is a lost cause. "Anyway, I'm more cerebral, whereas Marcus is more hands-on. I make sure you know your shit, while my cousin tortures you as a submissive for his own entertainment."

"Um… scary. I've heard so much about Marcus that I'm petrified to meet him."

"Don't be," Dexter says to pacify me. "Marcus is your only line of defense against Ezra. The choice of who to mentor you is taken out of your hands, since Ez would murder his father before he allowed Marc to train you. Cort will enjoy the symmetry of me training the three of you."

"Three of us? You just said Aaron is with Marcus?"

Smiling sadly, like I'm a moron, Dexter explains color to the blind. "The three of you, as in Ezra, Cortez, and *you*. I will take you under my wing for dominance training, but only if Ezra agrees. I'm sure he will, but I will have to hear it from him first," Dexter stresses.

"Thank you," I murmur quietly, suddenly feeling uncomfortable because doubt is slowly creeping in over my decision to seek Dexter out.

"But I cannot train you for submission. First, I don't think you have a submissive bone in your body. You're just addicted to Ezra like the rest of the fucks around here."

"I'm *not* one of Ezra's zealots," I defend.

"R-i-g-h-t, sure you're not," Dexter draws out like I'm a dumbass. "I'll turn you into a strong dominant who can withstand Ezra's aura of persuasion. Second, I can't put you in a position where I have the ability to abuse my power over you. You have no idea what the training entails; how you'll throw your morals, your sexual orientation, and your promises in the trash."

"I think I can resist you, oh humble master," I tease.

"Yeah, go home and ask Ezra or Cortez what happened during Ezra's training, and see how they react. I guarantee there will be bloodshed." Dexter stares me down, eyes bleeding remorse.

"Ah, Roarke said that would happen." My mind alights with possibility. The next time Ezra pisses me off, I'm going to bring up Dexter to Cortez and see what happens in reaction.

"I don't trust myself around you," Dexter admits, blowing my mind. "There's something in you which calls to me. I know you can feel it, too. It's like our needs complement one another. It's beating in the back of my brain, giving me a goddamned migraine and blue balls."

"I've been avoiding Ezra's temptation. I'm pretty sure I can overcome yours," I say cockily.

"Yeah, that's not what I've heard," Dexter says with a grin, like he's been chatting in the locker room after practice. "No matter what misconceptions you're feeding yourself, I can't go against Ezra like that unless he invites me. He's more likely to share with someone who isn't a thief."

"There was so much wrong with that statement that I can't even fathom its hidden meanings." I shake my head to and fro, trying to clear it. "Is Ezra being your BFF why you pulled your hit during his punishment?"

"No, I pulled the hit because it was Ezra being punished, not Master Ez," Dexter says cryptically. Either to distract himself or me, he reaches over to grab a bottle of leather conditioner. He squirts some on a rag, and then rubs the conditioner along his leather flogger.

"I don't understand." I scrunch my face and peer up at Dexter. I refuse to be distracted by his aura of sex and power, or the tease of toys.

"Ezra isn't like the rest of us. We are who we are at all times. No, I don't go around hitting people all day long. That's not what I meant. I follow specific rules every minute of my life. Self-imposed rules. Take yourself for instance; when you punished Ezra, you blossomed. You became who you, in essence, truly are. You bloomed into a strong, assertive, confident woman. You are always these things, but more so during a scene. The scene caused your confidence to grow. Ez is either Master Ez or Ezra, and on very rare occasions, he's both."

"I understand what you mean about how I felt dominating Ezra. But I don't see what you're getting at in reference to Ezra," I say in confusion.

"Think about Ezra– remember him. Try to remember the way he is with you. How mercurial he is at times, going from a tantrum to martyrdom in seconds flat. He's either Master Ez or Ezra. You've never seen him as both, I doubt– not so soon, anyway. Not many have seen him as both. I don't mean to imply Ez has multiple personalities or anything major like that. It's just that Ez hasn't fully meshed the two together. He is better now that you are with them. Before…" Dexter trails off.

"I think I understand. I noticed something like that this morning. It was like Master Ez flashed in the depths of Ezra's eyes." I shrug because I don't get it. But, at the same time, I do.

"That's why I pulled the hit. That is why Aaron was angry with you. If Master Ez had been strung up for the lashing, we all would have participated happily. But it was Ezra hanging there," Dexter says sadly. "Even if it was Ezra who did the deplorable acts, none of us can harm a blond hair on his perfect, goddamned head."

"Shit," I hiss with feeling. "Are you saying I did the wrong thing? I mean, I could feel Ezra's deep need to repent." Tears prickle my eyes as I try to thwart their descent.

"No. No, you were spectacular. I mean it, Kat." Dexter leans forward and pats my knee. I stare transfixed at his hand; it's not much bigger than my own. "Ezra needed it. He needed to be punished by *you*."

"You know what happened, don't you?" I ask, and Dexter tilts his head in reply. "Just so you know, I don't blame Ezra, or Aaron and Cortez." I wipe away the tears that began to fall at the mention of our shared painful past.

"I know everything," Dexter admits, sympathy etching his voice. "I needed to know all the details in order to train them, avoid their emotional triggers. But I knew long before that. I was with their family during the abduction, trying to comfort Marc. I've known Ezra and Cortez since they were twelve-year-old boys, when my grandmother brought Marcus to meet Diane for their betrothal. I met Aaron when he moved to Shadow Haven."

"So Ezra sees you as his family?" I ask, unsure since Ezra keeps everything so close to the vest.

"Um… you'll need to ask Ezra that question, because if I say yes and you find out some private shit, you'll think it's pretty fucking twisted."

I huff a laugh. "You know you're intriguing me, not pushing me away, right?"

"Oh, no doubt." Dexter grins mischievously. "So believe me when I say not to worry. Ezra needed to be punished. He's lighter since then, like he can finally take a deep breath. You didn't know him before– intense wasn't an accurate enough word to describe Ez."

"You keep saying before as if it should be capitalized. What do you mean?" Even as I ask, I already know deep down what that '*before*' means. It's life before Ray Hunter, and '*after*' is every minute since we all survived the attack.

"No, Kat. *Before* is before Ezra found you again. Before you came back. Before Ezra found you, he was a disastrous mess, lost, dwelling in his pain and mental instability. When he saw you three years ago, he found a purpose. Now that you are with him, he is content. I was with Marc when Ezra rushed in with news of Ava. I wish you could have seen how he looked in that moment."

Heart beating out of my chest, I don't know how to swallow Dexter's comment, so I spill the absolute truth. "I have to admit something. I'm petrified of Ezra right now. Petrified."

"I'll help you channel those fears, which are mostly about you, *not* him. You fear how Ezra makes you feel, and you need some semblance of control when one cannot control their baser emotions. But I'll give you some tools to use."

"Good God! I could hug you just hearing that, and I'm not a hugger." We laugh together– Dexter's chuckle is clearly amused, while my laugh is uncomfortable and strained, edging on hysterical. "Okay, so what do I do now?"

"This is going to sound insane," Dexter mutters, shaking his head. "First, when you speak to Ezra this evening, make sure you're not talking to Ezra– find a way to get Master Ez to erupt. I know that sounds odd, but you need to explain to the part of Ezra who believes he is your master, why you wish me to train you."

"Uh… Ez is kind of just who he is, but I've learned I can bend him to the point he loses his shit."

"Yeah, that would be who you need to speak with," Dexter says with a funny, little laugh. "Ez will most certainly contact me the second he's away from you– with threats of bodily harm, no doubt. If he says yes, he'll give you a time to meet me."

Leaning forward, I hide my face behind my upraised palms. Releasing a combination of a groan and a sigh, I voice my biggest fear. "I really have no control over my own life at this point, do I?"

"No." Dexter shifts on the table, and the movement distracts me.

My eyes follow every masculine curve of Dexter's body, and he ripens before my eyes from the appreciation. I can't blink as his bulge swells, straining the leather.

Dexter clears his throat huskily, gaining my undivided attention. "Katya," he commands, but it's breathy and lust-filled.

"Sorry. Sorry, you distract me. Um–" I try to order my thoughts. "Can you at least advise me in the ways of a submissive? After all, that is what I will need with Master Ez. I mean, can you tell me what the submissives are doing right or wrong, and then I can learn from their example? I'll need that information, whether I'm a switch or a dominant."

"Yes," Dexter sounds relieved. "Yes, I can absolutely do that," his voice is husky yet soft. As if physically uncomfortable, he shifts again. "You need to leave, sooner rather than later," he warns.

"Why?" I nearly whine, enjoying my time with Dexter. My tone is filled with hurt and rejection. I want to build a friendship with him, find an ally amongst all the chaos. It's why I chose him to mentor me. Can you be someone's friend when they dismiss you so easily?

"Katya, I know you're not doing it on purpose, but you're calling to my needs. I refuse to break an eighteen-year friendship with Ezra, but you're making it extremely difficult." With every second that ticks by, our needs are thickly cloying the air, making it difficult to breathe through the lust. "Plus, I really need to get back to work."

"I'm sorry. I don't mean to," I whimper, blushing bright red from embarrassment. "I don't even know what I'm doing to trigger it."

"No, it's fine," Dexter brushes off my apology. "After I speak with Ezra, we will find a way to release this pressure without breaking any rules. But, if he says no, you must keep your distance. I mean it, Kat," Dexter roughly commands.

"Agreed," I state, hopping to my feet, preparing to leave. "Where do you work, anyway?" I say to change the subject, but I am really curious as to where the sadist is employed.

"I'm an IRS agent," Dexter admits, yanking a laugh from my throat.

"How apropos. Death and taxes." I snicker over my shoulder as I escape Dexter's plush den of sadism. I listen to Dexter's resulting chuckle flow down the hallway as I exit to the dungeon.

# Chapter Four

I enter my apartment, still reeling from the after-effects of the creepy crawly sensation that was trilling down my spine. I always trust my intuition. It hasn't failed me yet. No matter how hard I looked around on the walk to The Edge Building from Restraint, I couldn't associate a person with the sensation.

Needing some more time to myself before diving back into Ezra's world, I spent a few hours in my office, creating a game plan for tomorrow's workday. When I began to contemplate working on the next day's tasks, I decided I was being a coward. I pulled up my big girl panties and rode the seven floors down to our apartments.

I'm surprised when I enter my apartment to find it empty of occupants. Even more shocked by the workmen mulling around like worker bees in a productive hive. The sound of their hammers pounding, the hum of their air compressors, and the revving of their saws is a song I know all too well after being raised by a contractor.

I'm half-tempted to pick up the *Sawzall* and take my frustrations out on the walls. I wonder if Ezra knows Ava and I can do most of this on our own.

I chuckle to myself as I envision the stunned look on Ezra, Cortez, and Aaron's faces if they witnessed us girls wearing tool belts while wielding drills in our hands. I'm sure they have some wicked fantasies. But what they don't realize, real construction girls are not ripped from the pages of calendars.

I had doubted Ezra's claims about creating a large apartment from our two and how it wouldn't take long for the reconstruction. But I was gone less than four hours, and I see at least five workmen wandering around my home, with my kitchen's contents removed, including the appliances and cabinets.

While in awe, it still angers me, makes me feel as if I have absolutely no control over my life. Even though I rented this space, I didn't own it. The owner does as he pleases, just as he does in everything.

I hope quitting time is soon, because this could get old– fast. Not only is it deafening, it's grating on my nerves how strangers have invaded my private space with my personal belongings. This is my home. It's where I go to relax and just breathe, which I'm in desperate need of at the moment with how my life has been going as of late.

It's not just the workmen, but how Ezra and the gang will now take up residence in my private life. But I guess they were already stalking the fringes of it unbeknownst to me anyway.

I need a few minutes to myself, a sense of normalcy after all that I've been through these past few weeks. I think I've earned it. I sit on my sofa, but the whirrs of the saws and the poundings of the hammers are hard to deny. I may have grown up around construction, but at the end of the day, I went home to a quiet house.

There is no relaxation to be had in my apartment. No place for me to go and hide. Nowhere to find my center in an otherwise chaotic world.

Just as I'm about to hunt everyone down, I hear my daughter's girlish voice flowing in from Ezra's apartment. "Make sure you order a Hawaiian pizza for Mom. Oh, and add green peppers. She loves those."

The portal from my living room to Ezra's bedroom is now eight feet wide where the wall has been cut away. I lean near the large hole the workmen created between our apartments, gazing straight through Ezra's bedroom and into the living room/kitchen combo beyond.

Feeling like Ezra must feel as he spies on all of us, I watch the scene before me. Aaron and Kayla are sitting on the sofa, heads bent close in deep conversation. Aaron's arm is slung across Kayla's shoulders, while her hand is resting on his thick thigh.

Hope springs in my heart as I remember bits and pieces of conversations Aaron and I had, how I was a stumbling block he had to hurdle before he could heal and move on. While it hurts to know I was an unavoidable obstacle in his path, perhaps Aaron was longing to move on to Kayla. While bittersweet, that knowledge lessens the sting of rejection. They are perfect for one another, both holding an infectious childlike innocence and an endless supply of patience.

Ezra is clearing off the dining room table, humming to himself as he completes his task. The more I'm around Ezra, the more I can read him. When he's happy and content, he hums. When he's upset or exasperated, he sighs.

Ezra keeps casting covert glances at the new couple. He tries to hide a smile and fails– impressed with his own matchmaking skills, no doubt. Seeing Aaron and Kayla happy expands my heart, but nowhere near as much as the amount that little smile on Ezra's face can bring.

"What kind of pizza do you want, Ava?" Cortez asks as he holds his cellphone at the ready so he can place the order.

"I'll just eat whatever you get for Mom," Ava says from her perch at the kitchen island. Her feet swing happily as she sits on the stool.

Seeing my daughter content and at ease around people who were strangers to her up until yesterday afternoon is a relief. I'd worried about her transition. But some people are embedded in your soul; you instantly feel the connection as soon as you meet them.

"Are you sure it's your mom who loves Hawaiian pizza, and not you?" Cort replies with obvious suspicion.

Cortez is a smart man for not trusting the word of an eleven-year-old, especially one who is the product of Ezra and myself. Almost thirty years of practice with Ezra's diabolical ways will come in handy with how Cortez handles Ava.

"Cort, who do you think makes me eat that?" Ava gives attitude. The bitchiness is all me, but the firmness is her father. She chucks a pen at Cortez's head. It flies by him and hits the table, rolling to a stop near Ezra's hand.

"Behave. Both of you," Ezra orders lightheartedly. "I can give out spankings," he warns while softly chuckling underneath his breath. Mouthing the words, but I can read his lips, "And only one of you will enjoy it."

Cortez must have overheard Ezra or read his lips, because he releases a naughty chuckle that is loaded with years of shared sexual experiences. The sound is so seductive that it trills up my spine and curls my toes.

I can't help the smile that engulfs my face at the scene before me. It's an unconventional family, but everyone has their rightful place. It gives me hope for the future– hope that we can work out a comfortable arrangement and live peacefully.

As if he senses me watching from my hidey hole, Ezra looks up, eyes connecting with mine. He mirrors my grin as he strides over to me, shutting his bedroom door on his way by, offering us some much-needed and much-feared privacy.

"Hi," I whisper shyly, blushing for some unknown reason as I back away from him.

"Hi," Ezra echoes back as he walks up to me, using his body to force me into my apartment– forcing me to be alone with him. Without touching me, his presence backs me up against the wall.

Slowly, as if waiting for me to protest, Ezra leans his tall form into me. The weight and warmth of him has my eyelids lowering in pleasure. Ezra's gaze searches my face, reading me, trying to discern my emotions. His expression relaxes as if he's satisfied with what he sees.

"Did you find what you were looking for?" Ezra tries to hide his worry, but I can feel it in the tension of his body from where he's pressing into me, as well as the emotions flavoring the air.

"Yeah, I did," I draw out. I rest my hand against Ezra's chest, feeling his heart beating steadily beneath my palm. I try to push him away with both my strength and my words. "Listen, can we talk about that later? I really want to see Ava for a few minutes before dinner. I need to relax without going into things that require therapy."

I try to dismiss Ezra, because the feel of him next to me, combined with the fucked up Norman Rockwell scene playing out in the next apartment, feels too damned good. Ezra can't be that man for me– the head of my family –if he's attached to someone else. I don't want to lower Adelaide or myself by allowing it. Ezra wouldn't be the man I want or need if he'd truly cheat with one woman while being committed to another. You can only be faithful to so many people before that connection is rendered meaningless.

Ezra nods his head as his hands trail up and down my arms in a soothing motion. Whether its purpose is to calm him or me is anyone's guess.

"May I greet you?" Ezra breathes across my cheek, the heat of it making my knees weak and my hands tremble.

My body shudders in remembrance of that kiss on the sofa and the sneaky one that followed. My body doesn't want to be denied when the object of its lusty affection is doing the offering, no matter the moral ramifications.

Ezra's expression is so serious that I bark out a laugh to break the tension. "Greet me?"

I watch as a grin plays over Ezra's stern lips, a slight curve at the corners. Hypnotized by that smile, I notice too late that his smoky eyes are moving closer and closer. His lips softly touch mine– just a mere brush of a touch.

A relieved sigh spills from my mouth, as if I waited all day for this very moment, craved it, and I'm more than satisfied to finally be experiencing it.

Ezra's gaze darts over my face– reading me. As if content with my expression, he slowly leans forward, giving me time to say stop. But I don't, because my body refuses to allow my mind to be in control. A pain-filled moan of long-denied satisfaction bubbles up my throat as his mouth duels with mine.

Without a conscious thought on my part, my fingers tangle in Ezra's white-blond hair. I revel in its silky texture, so fine I can't truly grasp it. If he were to pull back, his hair would slide freely from my fingertips.

My conscience is shouting **STOP**, while my heart is screaming at my conscience to shut the fuck up and enjoy this moment of tranquility in an otherwise chaotic life. I'm not sure who to listen to at the moment, so I shut them both out.

Ezra fuses his body to mine by pushing me against the wall as hard as he can, and something about being truly dominated unleashes my hunger for him. I tighten my grip on his hair, holding his mouth to mine. Both of us are making hungry little noises from the backs of our throats. The impatient sounds are mingling in our parted mouths as our tongues dart in and out in a mating dance. When I nibble at Ezra's bottom lip, my teeth piercing the supple flesh, it's his turn for weak knees and trembling hands.

The reckless, wanton creature buried deep within my recesses resurfaces. I wrap a leg around Ezra's hip so I can press my aching sex against the granite-hard bulge in the front of his pants.

With a grunt, Ez thrusts up, grinding us together while attacking my mouth with his. I eat the sound he releases, swallowing it down and allowing it to ignite the fire building in my womb. With a growl, Ezra tears away from my lips to feast at the column of my neck, teeth sinking in sharply, extracting a yelp of lust-fueled agony from my throat.

"Ma!" Ava calls out from the gaping hole between the apartments. We both freeze, as if we're teenagers caught in the act by our parents. Our daughter blushes at us, but not nearly as brightly as we do.

"We shouldn't be doing this." My voice is thick with guilt as my fingers slide from Ezra's hair and down his back. But my hands vehemently disagree with my statement. My palms settle at Ezra's waist, with my fingertips latching on for dear life. I twist the material of his shirt in my grasp, never wanting to relinquish him.

"Hmm..." Ezra kisses my cheek lightly, lips reverberating from his hum. "I think we should. In fact, I think we should do it often." He kisses me again to reiterate his point. "Several times a day... to completion."

My skin blazes as I look at my daughter. Ava is calmly standing next to us, as if this is nothing out of the ordinary. I don't understand her. Actually, I never have. Ava has never seen me kiss anyone, and yet she watches with absolutely no judgment whatsoever.

"I'll leave my ladies to chat," Ezra murmurs. A peculiar expression flashes over his face, as if he hadn't meant to say '*my ladies*' but he loved the way it slid smoothly from his tongue. Ezra abruptly buries his face in the side of my neck and whispers, "I missed you. Please don't run off without telling one of us where you are going. We were very worried."

Ezra lifts his face from his hiding spot, only to intercept the exasperated look I'm sending his way. He bends back down and nips my neck, startling an inappropriate sound from my throat.

I'm not sure Dexter is correct. Ezra seems to channel Master Ez nicely. There is a definite duality to him, but they are melding before my eyes.

I'm surprised that I haven't fainted from blood loss– all my blood is channeled into a full body blush. I take deep breaths as I walk to the sofa on wobbly legs, and then I drop down onto a cushion with a whoosh.

"It's okay, Mom. You don't have to be embarrassed." Ava looks at me from the gray eyes of an adult set inside a child's face, as she settles onto the sofa cushion next to me.

"No. No, it's definitely not okay, Ava. You don't understand." I scrub my hands across my face, and want to scream bloody murder. Scream for not demanding what I want, what I need, and what I deserve.

Respect.

I want to scream even louder, because if Adelaide Whittenhower was before me at this exact second, I would tear her apart with my bare hands and revel in the sensation of her blood coating my fingertips.

This is why I went to Dexter: I need an outlet for this rage building inside me. This newfound self-hatred because I want what I shouldn't have, what I can't have, and if I'm not careful, I'll do anything I can to steal it.

I want Ezra as mine. I want Ezra to tell the world I belong to him and he belongs to me– just us: Ezra Zeitler and Katya Waters. But I can't have that with a waifish, blonde-haired, blue-eyed, blue-blooded, billionaire princess between us. I want to destroy Adelaide Whittenhower, but rational thought always wins out. I'm scared there will be a time when rationality flees and I'm left with what can only be called possession.

The only reason Adelaide is between Ezra and me, is because Ezra placed Adelaide and me where he wanted us. If Ezra wanted Adelaide, he'd marry her. If Ezra wanted me, he'd break up with Adelaide and be with me. The faithless asshole is using the both of us. Now that Ezra's in the next apartment, even with his goddamned pheromones wreaking havoc on my senses, I can think rationally again.

"It's okay, Mom. It's what parents do. Grandma and Grandpa were always macking on each other, and you didn't bat an eyelash. You and Dad had to do a lot more than kiss to make me."

Ava giggles a sweet, childlike, chiming noise that holds an edge, just this side of sinister. I'm not sure who she gained that from, but I've always found it unnerving.

"Do I need to have the birds and the bees talk with you now, Mom?" Another creepy giggle erupts from my child's mouth. "I don't want to be an only child forever."

"It's not that," I mutter in exasperation. "I don't want you to think parents are cold to each other. Affection and intimacy make happy parents. But your father isn't available."

Ava leans into me, pale face scrunched up in confusion. "What do you mean?"

Voice stiff with reluctance, I mutter out the truth. "I don't know how to tell you this. Since you met your father, I'm sure you've dreamed about how he and I will live happily ever after, together for all eternity, giving you tons of baby brothers and sisters as your faithful minions... but that fairytale isn't going to happen, baby girl. At least not between your father and me."

I don't want to break down, not wishing to place that burden on my daughter's shoulders. But I can't stop the silent tears from splattering my cheeks. I didn't realize the depth of my pain until this very moment. It's been one torment after the next, without a moment's peace to reflect on what I just went through. I begin to cry so violently that the tears dampen my hair.

My heart is already broken, if it's ever been whole in the first place. Playing this game of affection and intimacy with Ezra may feel good as we touch and connect in the moment, but afterward, I feel sick with guilt.

I'm the only one to blame since I make myself feel this way. It's my fault I'm not strong enough to avoid Ezra's manipulations. He continues to pull me in, knowing I don't have the strength to say no. Tainting myself with this level of depravity is one thing; tainting my daughter is another.

Scrubbing at my eyes with my shirt cuffs, I calm down enough to change the subject. "What do you think of your father?" I ask the question that has plagued me since they first met.

"I like Dad." For some inexplicable reason, Ava's voice is laced with wry amusement. "I feel comfortable around him. Dad talked to me constantly today, answering anything I asked. Everyone is so nice. I don't know... it just feels right somehow."

I reach over, taking my daughter's hand, thankful that she doesn't pull away as usual. "I'm so happy for you. Unbelievably happy. These are happy tears for you," I lie while simultaneously telling the truth. I want my daughter to have what I cannot. I'm not jealous at all. My wanting only makes my daughter's having that much sweeter.

"Cort even told me to look at him as a dad, too." Ava giggles, and I know she understands the underlying meaning. Even if Cort and Ezra never touch one another in a sexual manner, their connection is beyond obvious. "Dad said to call Aaron and Kayla uncle and aunt. I want to call them that, but it's up to you, Mom."

The hope in my child's eyes brings tears to mine. Ava has only ever had a small family, just my parents and me. Now this larger world, filled with people who care about her, is offered up on a silver platter. My pessimistic side rears its ugly head. Is it too good to be true?

"A word of advice before we go any further. Never allow anyone to buy your love, okay? It's not their words but their actions that truly matter. I'm not saying that Ezra isn't a great man and father, or that they aren't all great. I just need you to be careful," I warn.

The exasperated expression that flashes across Ava's face screams how I'm being ridiculous. This is my child I'm talking to as if cautious wasn't her middle name. She rolls her eyes at me as I shake my head at her.

"A lady came over while you were gone today. She's from Hillbrook– Ms. Banks," Ava chirps happily. "Ms. Banks helped me pick out classes. Can you believe that? Back home, we just sat in the same classroom all day. Wow! They rotate classes in middle school! Dad even ordered half a dozen uniforms for me. I start on Monday!" Ava claps, thrumming with excitement. Her dream is becoming reality. Who am I to take it from her?

"I'm so happy for you, baby girl. This is what you've wanted for a long time. You have no idea how proud I am of you." I pull Ava into a big hug and squeeze until she tries to wiggle away. I'm not used to her being bigger than me. A few months ago, I could have kept her captured, but now she easily breaks my hold. Ava isn't the cuddly sort anymore– just like her mom.

"Why can't you and Dad be together?" Ava blurts out, like she's been holding the question in since I brought it up by distracting me with good news while she waited for the bad.

"This is difficult for me," my voice wavers as I try to spill the words. "I know it's new for you, but it's also new for me. It's always just been the two of us, and now we have everyone in the other apartment to consider."

I draw in a large breath of air and ease it out. I either speak my piece now, or allow it to fester, potentially harming my child. In all things, Ava's needs come first. I'm not one of those mothers who protects their children from the truth by telling them pretty lies. I don't give out age-inappropriate details, but at some point you have to require more out of your children than forever treating them like toddlers.

"Your father is engaged to a woman named Adelaide Whittenhower." The words wheeze painfully out of my mouth. "I'm sorry. It's one thing to gain a father after eleven years, but soon you'll have a stepmother too. I don't know the details, like when they're getting married or moving in together."

I pause, unable to speak as the brutal reality of our situation sets in. No matter how quickly workmen can transform our apartments into one home, our time is limited as a family. At some point, Ezra will move on, marry Adelaide, and start another family with her, leaving Ava and me alone.

Me. Alone.

Ava will be stressed by a new world she didn't know existed. A world filled with money, power, and influence, and an entire stepfamily who may never accept her as one of their own.

Is this Ezra's way of transitioning me into their lives, so he can easily incorporate Ava into his future?

"Mom?" Ava calls, suddenly scared by the expression of terror that crosses my face.

"Sorry, baby girl." I flash a false smile. "I was just thinking. When your father and Adelaide marry, it'll be the two of us again. Maybe with you splitting your time with your father if he wishes. Which is the biggest reason I'm not complaining about the living arrangements right now. You and Ezra need to bond without Adelaide's outside influence."

Possession and jealousy flash through me like a hot knife. The first time I saw Adelaide touch Ezra, I wanted to bloody her, and that was just a palm on his shoulder. It killed something vital inside of me when I saw them in bed together. But I want to outright kill Adelaide for laying any claim on my daughter, even the title of stepmother.

A thought pings in my head. What if Ezra is planning on keeping our daughter a secret? Are we both his dirty little secrets, being kept locked away from prying eyes? A sob crawls up my throat. The agonized sound shocks me back to normal.

*Pull it together, Katya. This isn't just about you anymore. It affects the both of you.*

Ava just sits, gazing at me with endless patience and understanding, because I am her mother and she knows I will always take care of her and give her anything she needs. Sometimes I think that even at her age, Ava is stronger than me. She holds an inner-strength and calm I can never tap into.

"It's going to be all right, Mom. I know it is. I can feel it." Ava doesn't pat her heart like I would. No, not Ezra's daughter– Ava taps her temple.

"The food's here!" Cortez yells from the hole between the apartments, giving a warning call before he steps foot into my living room through the portal. "Ava, go on and join the others."

The instant Ava is in the other apartment, Cort is on me. His arms engulf me as he sits next to me on the sofa, yanking me into his lap. "Shh… let it out. I've got you." He tries to hold me and I push him off.

"I'm not too proud to admit that I listened to your entire conversation, making sure Ezra didn't bother you." Cortez tries to yank me into a hug again, and I futilely try to shove him off. "Hey, I know you're not about the cuddling and coddling. But I need it right now, just as badly as you."

"I…I can't," I cry out, and then it changes to *I can*. I break down in Cortez's arms, fingers twisting into his shirt as I sob into his chest. I turn into a pitiful mess, sucking up any comfort he's willing to provide.

"I can promise you this, Kitten; that bitch will never touch a hair on our girl's head. Ezra will *never* marry Adelaide Whittenhower. I promise you," Cortez not only professes, he seethes the words. "I know Ezra better than anyone on this planet. But sometimes he does shit that makes absolutely no sense, even for him."

"That scares me," I grumble into Cort's shirt, still holding on to him for dear life.

"As it should, and it's better that it does," Cort warns. "I know Aaron has given you our background, and I'm sure Ezra has spilled some of our history. But Adelaide was the first betrayal Ezra ever dealt me. I've never understood it, because it made no sense whatsoever. So just hearing that cunt's name gets my hackles up. Even though Ez and I haven't been a couple for more than a decade, it was our mutual understanding that every decision we would ever make, we would make it together."

"Including me?"

"Including you," Cort replies immediately.

I ask, hope lacing my voice, "Then you know what Ezra wants from me, then?"

"I thought I did. But what we saw that night, it changed my perception on everything. Just when I was one hundred percent with Ezra's plan, he betrayed the both of us."

I dry my eyes by rubbing my face against Cort's t-shirt, and my tears are renewed when my nostrils register Ezra's scent lingering on Cort's clothing. "How could Ezra being with his fiancée be a betrayal to you and me?"

"It was," Cortez snarls from the depths of his chest. "It still is. It's burning and stinging me, to the point that I want to murder that assfuck in his sleep. Seeing them together, it wrecked me." Voice sounding wretched, "It ruined me, Kat. Not only did you have to witness it, but I had to see Ezra cheating on me in the flesh. There was no way I could talk to him about it, not with everything else going on that was more important than our hurt feelings. That's why I bought us some time, so we could lick our wounds without an audience."

"I'm so sorry," I sniffle. "So sorry."

"Me too... Me too. But you don't have to worry about Adelaide anymore. Leave that pedigreed cunt to me. You and I, we're the same. Adorable mutts sitting at the feet of masters who own quality show dogs."

"Fuck," I breathe, understanding dawning. Cortez had been a young boy living in Ezra's world– a world he didn't belong in, just as I now don't belong.

"You just worry about getting Ava settled in Dominion and at Hillbrook, and most importantly, bonded with her father. Ezra is a good man, with good intentions, and this is coming from someone who is furious with him right now. Ezra does what he feels is right. But he's too arrogant to see when he's wrong, or too mentally ill to admit it. But we all have flaws, so I just deal."

"Did what happened between Ezra and me break you two up?" I don't know where the thought came from, or why it erupted from my throat, but I don't want to be responsible for anyone else's heartbreak.

"No, Kitten." Cortez squeezes me tightly, rumbling his admission in my ear. "It happened a few years prior, back when we were young teenagers. I don't want to explain it; I'm not ready. But we're still committed to each other. I know you see me as a married man and a cheater, but I only married Divina for our family. The only person I'm committed to is Ezra, and I've never cheated on him. Not once. But Ezra has betrayed me many times over, and I've retaliated when I shouldn't. I am a lecher, and we all accept that. Sex is sex, but emotions are different. I find the emotional attachments as the ultimate betrayal… and the lies."

"You guys confuse me," I mumble. But Cortez doesn't confuse me. He's an open book. He does what he does and makes no apologies for it. He will tell you to your face if he plans on screwing you over. Cort's bad behavior is blatantly honest in a strange way.

"You'll get used to us eventually," Cort says, but I'm not so sure I can agree with him. "After how you acted about Ezra's impersonations, I thought you'd kill me when you remembered your rape. I was worried about how you'd look at me when you saw me. I feared you'd never speak to me again."

It's my turn to hug Cortez tightly, arms wrapping around him as I refuse to let go. "I don't blame any of you. I was there, remember? I saw the look in your eyes. I remember how badly it affected you. I only blame Ray," I say with conviction.

"Me too. I remember everything. It haunts me at night. Everything Ray made me do haunts me. I can't even look at Aaron without feeling sick to my stomach. But mostly, sick in my head and heart. Like my soul is tainted by all the depravity Ray Hunter forced me to commit. I couldn't say no, believe me I tried. I should have just let him kill me instead." Cort groans, sounding ill.

I hold Cortez as tightly as I can, and his arms clench around me fiercely. He hides his face in my hair as I rock him back and forth like a mother does a child. I don't know how long we stay like this, but when the air charges with something other than grief and remorse, I pull away.

"I hope you don't feel sick when you look at me," I tease to lighten the mood.

"Oh, Kitten," Cort moans. "That's never going to happen. When I look at you, all I feel is want. There is so much I need and want from you. I look at you how I look at our Ezra, and I didn't think that was possible. I was so frightened that I'd be jealous of you like I was of the others, but I'm not. I want you with us. I never want to push you away."

I didn't like the way Cort sounded when he spoke of jealousy and *the others*. But neither of them are my concern when it comes to relationships and sex.

"Ezra may be *your* Ezra. But he's not *ours*," I tease Cort to wipe the reverent expression from his face. I've never had anyone look at me that way, and it's unnerving in its intensity.

"Sure," Cortez mutters dismissively, discounting everything I just said. "I love looking at your mouth and remembering our time together. The way your hot lips felt wrapped around my cock. How moist the inside of your mouth felt. The rigidness of the roof of your mouth and the softness of the back of your throat, as I stroked against it. How your gag reflex caressed my cock like an eager cunt milking cum," Cortez chants, shocking me speechless.

"You can deny it all you want, but you loved me skull-fucking you to near unconsciousness. I've been there– it's a euphoric plane of existence. It put a fire in your veins that can never be extinguished. It made you feel alive... and you want to do it again," Cort coaxes, grabbing my hand to press it against the bulge in his jeans.

"You're so full of shit!" I hop off the couch with a lunge, trying to flee the truth.

It's hard to deny the flush that creeps over my skin and the thoughts that echo in my mind. The bastard has me pegged. Cort taunts me with that toe-curling laugh of his.

Standing in the middle of my torn-up living room, I turn pensive. "What Ezra does to me, do you consider that cheating on you?" I ask, fearing Cortez's future retribution.

"No. Never," Cort breathes the word like a benediction. "Every touch with that bitch is cheating. We can touch each other. Ezra can touch you. I can touch you. You can touch us. Everything else is a negotiation. Ezra never negotiated with me about Adelaide, so it was wrong… and it wasn't the first time he has done that to me," Cort's voice breaks in anger and betrayal.

"But you're with people all the time, though?" I question their odd agreement.

"*Was* with people all the time," Cort stresses. "And that was negotiated upon a long time ago," he says firmly. Slowly his scowl turns into a wicked grin. "If you won't let me feed you my cock, then at least let me feed you the pizza I ordered. A man has to provide for his family to feel like a real man."

I relent, knowing this night will never end, that Cortez will continue to needle me, using humor and lust to offset uncomfortable conversation, until I finally eat the food Cort provided, and then rest my head in Ezra's domicile.

We all crowd around the dining room table, eating pizza and wings, with Ava gulping milk and the adults sharing a bottle of red wine. Aaron, Kayla, and Ava chat about a recent movie release, A movie I didn't know existed since my head is always stuck in manuscripts for work.

Ezra and Cortez openly stare at me as I watch the single slice of pizza on my plate, as if it's going to eat itself.

"You do like those toppings, don't you?" Cort asks, eyes darting in my daughter's direction. "I'll come up with something inventive for Ava if she's lied to me." Cortez's smirk tells me he is cataloging all the interesting punishments he'll employ against my daughter.

"Yeah, Hawaiian is my favorite, actually. It's just been a long day. Week. Month. Year. Decade. A lot has changed, ya know?" I toss a piece of pineapple into my mouth, but I don't taste it as I chew and swallow out of reflex.

"Do you want to talk about it?" Ezra's voice sounds hopeful that I will open up to him, allowing him to flex his therapy prowess.

"I kind of just want to take a long bath to relax, and then get a good night's sleep to recharge," I mutter, sounding as exhausted as I feel. "I have to get back to work tomorrow, or else I'll never catch up."

"You can take more time. Start back on Monday." Ezra looks at me, hoping I'll agree to everything he ever says without question.

Not happening.

"I'm disrupting everyone. If I don't go back, Kayla doesn't. By the looks of them," I say in the direction of the lovebirds chatting with my daughter. "If Kayla doesn't, Aaron won't. Tomorrow is Friday, so it's just one day that Ava won't be in school while I'm at work. She can sit in my office while I get caught up."

"Okay, but Cortez and I will entertain Ava on and off throughout the day. We'll take shifts." Ezra looks pleased with himself– ever the problem solver.

"Ava's a child, not a puppy," I say with a smirk. "Don't you have some work to do?"

"Being the boss does have its benefits," Ezra says cockily. "I can have Roarke cancel appointments as easily as I had him make them."

"Being a writer does have its benefits. If I don't feel like writing, I don't," Cortez answers when I look at him.

"The pair of you are incorrigible– a very bad example." I give them both a small smile. They really are rather entertaining when I need it.

"I'll see you both in the morning," I say to the Ezes. "Night guys," I call out to Aaron and Kayla. They both look bright-eyed and bushy-tailed. It looks like the beginnings of love to me. I smile widely at them.

I kiss Ava on the forehead, and then leave the guys' apartment in search of my bathtub and some alone time.

# Chapter Five

After two hours of bathroom time, where I ran out of things to shave, pluck, and exfoliate, I wander into my dark bedroom with a calm mind and a patient heart. My entire apartment is torn up already, everything except my bedroom and bathroom. I'm sure by tomorrow that will change. No doubt, it's Ez's way of herding me into his domain– his apartment. I have absolutely no idea where I will belong once he gets his wish.

I see a little lump curled up in the middle of the bed, and I laugh soundlessly at the sight. So much for the sleepover at Kayla's place. I'm guessing Kayla had '*adult*' things to do at bedtime– things even Ezra's influence couldn't convince her to do without. Kayla is so passive, that whatever she wanted to do this evening must have been important to her.

Aaron?

Sliding into bed, I curl around my daughter. I enjoy the closeness, the way she tucks perfectly to my chest, and the fruity scent of her hair as I bury my nose into the nape of her neck. I absorb Ava's innocent girliness. My baby has the softest skin I've ever touched, and until I met Ezra, I thought it was the palest. She is the most unique creature to ever grace this world, and I count my blessings that she is mine every single day of my life. I don't care how she came into existence, I'll do anything to keep her safe and happy.

Anything.

Even if I have to sell my soul in the process.

Neither of us are super cuddly, and as Ava has grown, she refuses the attention more and more. It makes me sad yet proud at the same time. At eleven years old, my daughter is already encroaching upon womanhood– something I entered early at the age of nine. Unlike me, though, Ava is shedding her childlike traits at the same time as she grows into a tall, willowy young woman. I wanted to hold onto her childhood longer, for both Ava and myself.

I wanted my daughter to have what I didn't: years to grow, to learn, to find where her talents lie. Years to play instead of work before she's forced to suffer adult problems. But maybe it wasn't the situation I was born into, but a facet of my personality that had me growing into a young woman too soon– a trait I passed onto my daughter. Maybe Ezra matured early as well, giving Ava a double-whammy.

I lay for a while, holding my daughter as she snores quietly, trying to shut off all thought to my mind. I can't grasp a single thread of consciousness and concentrate. It's like cockroaches flitting away at the first flash of light.

"I can't sleep," I whisper to the shadow in the corner. "How long have you been here?"

"Not long. I just… I just can't stop looking at Ava. You have no idea what the sight and presence of our daughter does to me," Ezra whispers back in a voice teeming with intense emotion. "Seeing how we're both combined in a living, breathing creature. I just…" Ezra's voice turns wry yet with a sweet edge. "Cort just went off on an hour-long diatribe on why Ava is the most fascinating little girl to have ever existed. He's quite the wordsmith."

Taking my interaction with him as an invitation, Ezra creeps to Ava's side of the bed. He gently lifts her arm and pushes a stuffed animal underneath it, tucking it to her chest. Ava cuddles into the toy without waking, murmuring content, happy noises.

"What's that?" I ask of the toy.

Ezra slowly walks to my side, as if fearful I'll kick him out of my room. When I don't protest, he kneels beside me. Curious, I roll to face him. I can barely see the outline of his face in the dark of my bedroom. Not long ago, Ezra would have been upset with this amount of light hitting his features– fearing it would ruin his game, the therapy session from hell. I can see his smoky eyes, the chiseled edge of his cheekbones, and the curve of his mouth, but little else.

"It's a stuffed monkey Cort and I share. I thought Ava would like it. It smells like us." The curve of his mouth tilts into a full smile.

"You have a monkey?" I try to keep my laugh quiet, since I don't want to wake Ava.

"We do, and his name is Monkmee." I can hear laughter in Ezra's voice. "Our mothers took us to a toy store. I think we were four… maybe three," he reminisces, voice light and tender with affection. "We both wanted the same monkey, and there was only the one." Ezra bites his lip as he relives the memory. He flashes me a dazzling smile– white teeth glowing in the night.

"So you share the toy?" My fingers itch to reach out and touch Ezra's face, to follow the curve of his lips. I curl my fingertips into my palm to fight my need.

"If there is one thing Cortez and I do well, it's sharing." Ezra's expression turns serious.

"Do you easily share with only each other, or is it with everyone else too?" I feel like we're no longer talking of the stuffed monkey.

Aaron. Being with Aaron was a gift as much as a torment. While I loved the easiness of our friendship and the youthful innocence Aaron brought out of me, it made me feel rejected by how easily Ezra could give me away to another man.

"Come," Ezra issues a soft demand as he takes my hand in his.

"Where? I can't leave Ava. If she wakes, and I'm not here, she may be frightened." My voice breaks with panic.

"Ava will be fine. She'll do what all kids do when they look for their parents." He sounds amused, and his teeth are flashing as he smiles broadly in the dark again.

"And what's that?" I ask as I tug my hand, trying to get out of his grasp. His fingers intertwine with mine; he isn't letting go so easily.

"They look in their parents' bedroom. Come," Ezra says again as he pulls me harder this time.

"I'm not sleeping with you, Ezra," I warn as I crawl out of the blankets. I turn back to tuck Ava in, not wanting her to catch a draft.

"I just want to talk– nothing else," Ezra promises, twisting his fingers with mine as he tugs me from my bedroom, leaving our little girl all alone to sleep in her strange new world.

Ezra walks us through my apartment and into his, walking past the living room, and down a hallway, until we reach a room I've never been in. I hadn't realized how much bigger the trio's apartment was compared to mine. Mine was a one bedroom/one bath, open floor plan with a home office I've never used. This space is at least five times larger than mine.

The room we enter is pitch-black, but I can sense it's empty. "Well, what are we missing here?" Ezra says to himself, but I can hear a note of amusement and pride.

"What are we doing? This isn't your room," I whisper even though the bedroom is empty. It's nighttime, and you just can't help but whisper as if you're going to wake whoever is asleep.

"You know how you have some OCD issues? Well, so do I," Ezra admits. I just look at him in confusion, and he sighs loudly at my ignorance. "I have to check to make sure everyone is safely tucked in their beds, or else I cannot sleep. Sometimes, I have to check more than once." His voice sounds utterly hopeless.

"Doesn't that make you super tired?" I ask in awe of this man. "Your body needs at least a four-hour block of uninterrupted sleep to remain healthy."

"Yeah, super tired and unhealthy sounds about right... but usually people accommodate me by staying in one place so I can easily locate them. Like, they don't run off to Pennsylvania without telling me first." Ezra's dig hits home, making me feel guilty and angry at the same time. "C'mon, we have to find Aaron."

Being the bigger person because I don't have the energy to fight, I ignore the dig. "I'm pretty sure we know where Aaron is, so why check on him?" I ask as Ezra pulls us out of his apartment to head down the hallway toward Kayla's place.

"Rationally, I know that Aaron is with Kayla, but my anxiety won't go away until I see the truth with my own two eyes. Because if there is a chance I could be wrong about his safety, then my checking on him could have saved his life. I couldn't live with the guilt– not again, anyway."

"I feel like we all need to have this created into a recording. 'None of us are to blame.' Perhaps James Earl Jones will narrate." I tease, trying to change Ezra's mood from brooding martyr to the playful Ez I love. But he's not hearing me.

"Logically, I know I'm not to blame. But very much of it is *my* fault, Katya. Never doubt my culpability in our past and present nightmares." Ezra's fingers shake against mine, betraying his greatest fear. "Yes, I know this is unhealthy behavior. I'm a psychiatrist for Christ's sake. Don't you think I recognize the insanity of it? But I have to see them for myself, or I can't relax enough to get any rest."

"Why do you do this?" I pull Ezra to a stop just outside Kayla's door. "OCD is not unlike any other addiction. Feeding it only makes it stronger."

"I know that." Ezra's pleading twists into a whine. "I was taken from my bed, okay? That's why. Cortez was sound asleep next to me, and that monster put a knife to his throat so I would leave quietly." His voice cracks with intense emotions, and I'd do anything to comfort him in this moment.

I squeeze Ezra's hand, trying to lend him the strength to continue, because I can feel his need to release the words. As a psychiatrist, Ezra listens to everyone's problems, absorbing them as his own, while never dealing with his own very real issues.

"I thought I had saved Cortez by leaving, by sacrificing myself. But three nights later, Ray came back and took Cort and Aaron in their sleep, using Divina just as he had used Cort on me. I had never been as devastated in my entire life as when Ray opened the van door, and it wasn't a whore trapped within but those I had sworn to protect."

Hand flying up to cover my mouth, "Oh, God," I cry out, finding it impossible not to imagine Ezra's terror and devastation.

"Cortez had to make an impossible choice between a fragile nineteen-year-old woman and a skinny fifteen-year-old boy. Ray would have slaughtered my cousin after breaking her, so Cort sacrificed Aaron instead. But it was my fault."

Barely a breath of a sound, I issue a protest. "Ez, no."

"Kat, *yes*. They were mine to protect, and I failed them because my father wanted to give me the gift of my friends so he could torture me into compliance. He couldn't bring himself to lay an angry hand on me, so Cortez was used as my whipping boy. Everything my father wanted to do to me, say to me, or force me to do, he did to Cortez instead, knowing it would harm me worse than anything else. I never gave that ruthless monster what he wanted, no matter what he forced Cortez to do, because I had to beat him in the only way I knew how."

"Rejection?"

"Yes. I don't need my doctorate in psychology to know that, that is why I have to check on everyone constantly. I have to look even when they are in the same room with me. So, please, just make this easier on me by not throwing a fit when I check on you."

I put our joined hands over my heart and try to breathe through the emotions coursing through my veins. I quickly wipe a tear away, hoping Ezra doesn't think it's pity. It's not. I'm empathizing with Ezra's pain, shame, and guilt.

"I'm so very sorry you had to go through that." I kiss the back of Ezra's hand. My face scrunches up when a thought hits me. "You check on me?"

"Since the minute you moved here, I haven't missed a night." Ezra holds my eyes defiantly, waiting for me to argue with him.

"Ah! A few nights ago, you missed when I stayed at my family's home," I challenge smugly.

Ezra arches a pale eyebrow. "Who says I did?" His voice holds smug better than mine.

"You didn't?" I shake my head. "You didn't break into my parents' house." I shake my head no– no way could he have done that.

"You forgot your nightgown here at the apartment, so you slept naked. I laid down beside you so I could get some much-needed sleep, finally knowing you were okay. You snuggled up to me, and we slept peacefully for five hours." The sincerity in Ezra's voice is frightening.

I should know better than to think Ezra a liar. I remember feeling safe and warm, and sleeping better than I had in ages, even with all the turmoil inside me.

Shit!

Ezra is my life-sized, living, breathing Monkmee.

"Do you do that often?" My tone is a mix of awe and anger.

"Usually I check on you a few times during the night. If you aren't sleeping soundly, I'll lay down with you for a few minutes. When I'm desperate for sleep, I'll join you for the rest of the night," Ezra admits without shame.

"Don't you worry about the others while you're sleeping with me?" I pretty much call Ezra a bullshitter. If he's so worried about the others, he's not running off to Pennsylvania to sleep in my bed.

"I join you after my search. As for when *we* were in Pennsylvania, I had Roarke check on everyone and send me snapshots of their sleeping forms. It wasn't as if Aaron and Cortez weren't with us, anyway," Ez says, flashing me a devious smirk.

"Oh. My. God. You are fucking insane," I drawl out in awe.

"Twice, when neither of us were sleeping particularly well, Cortez snuggled up with us. The three of us slept like babies." Ezra grins at the outrage that crosses my face.

I stand utterly speechless, gaping up at the stalking bastard. "I..." I wave my hands about. "I don't even know how to respond to that. It's just so creepy... and so... you." I bug my eyes out at him. This man has no shame. "Never mind. Who do you check on?"

"I check on Cort when he isn't with me. If he's not, I feel crazed. Aaron usually sleeps like the dead, so I check on him once after he goes to sleep, and then I leave him in peace. For a few people, I can't rest until I've witnessed their peaceful slumber. After spending a few minutes chatting about how their days have progressed, it's a comfort how they fall asleep soundly because I'm keeping them safe by watching. I also check on you, and now Ava."

"Not Kayla?" I point to her door as I ask.

"No. I care for Kayla dearly, and she is important to us, but she isn't family." Ezra thinks for a moment. "*Yet*. Kayla isn't family yet. I think Aaron will be changing that in the near future." He smiles brilliantly. "Come– let's see how the kids are faring."

"Ezra, this isn't a good idea. I highly doubt they are sleeping. We'll interrupt them." I dig my heels in and refuse to move.

"So?" Ezra levels me with a look like I'm a twit, and I return it right back at him.

"You really have no boundaries, do you? It's not okay to just enter someone's home and do whatever you want while you visit."

"This said by my Kat burglar?" Ez chuckles heartily, thoroughly amused with himself. "I have boundaries," he poorly denies, eyelashes shuttering the truth lying in the depths of his eyes.

"No, you don't," I argue, flabbergasted.

Ezra grabs ahold of my hair and yanks me to his mouth. He kisses me violently with tongue and teeth, fisting my ass in his hands while rubbing his arousal against my hip like a silent threat. Ezra breaks the kiss before I can react, punch him, kiss back, or release the moan that was building.

"See?" I pant breathlessly as I point at him. "No boundaries!"

"Ah, I see," Ezra drawls, thoroughly impressed with himself. "I have boundaries for all of those who aren't mine. Cort, *you*, Ava, and a few select others are mine, and I have a say in every aspect of their lives. *All* aspects. Always and forever."

Ezra stands before me, arrogant, smug, controlling, and devastatingly beautiful with his halo of white-blond hair and his devilish smirk.

I'm so fucked in the head.

I should be angry, not secretly pleased. But the only thought pinging inside my brain is that Adelaide didn't make the list. Triumph lights me from within, while my subconscious screams that it doesn't want to be owned.

I feel a little high while we break into Kayla's apartment with a key. But is it really a B&E if you own the place? Probably. No surprise, the apartment is laid out exactly as mine used to be. So we don't have far to go to check on Aaron, since he and Kayla are busy in the living room.

I should have turned heel and left the second I heard their song of pleasure. But I'm too fascinated to move a single muscle.

I look at Ezra to find him grinning like a fool. I try to tug out of his hand to leave. Really, I try. Just not very hard. Visibly excited, Ezra pulls us into the living room, bringing the scene before us into clarity.

Aaron and Kayla come into sharp view. I've made love to both of them in various ways, but nothing compares to watching the two of them take each other.

Aaron had hang-ups with Kayla before, because Ezra forced him to take her before he was ready. It's evident by the fervor on Aaron's face that he is totally committed to fucking Kayla into the wall– more accurately, *through* the wall.

Fuck Kayla, he does.

Aaron ruts like a crazed animal, grunting and thrusting wildly. His sweat-slickened muscles coil and clench with every flex of his ass and thighs, causing Kayla's tits to jiggle and swirl in an enticing, moisture-inducing manner.

Kayla's fleshy body is wrapped around the large man's torso, riding him like a mechanical bull. She's giving as good as she's getting. Long, red marks mar Aaron's back; Kayla's nails creating an erotic canvas of ownership.

Suddenly, Kayla glances up at me over Aaron's shoulder, and I try to avert my eyes from embarrassment. I don't want her to be angry with us for interrupting their very private moment. But I should have known better. This is Aaron and Kayla we're talking about, after all. Aaron looks over his shoulder to see what Kayla's glancing at, and he doesn't bat an eyelash at what he finds.

They both smile hugely at us, all proud, like children asking their parents to put their drawings on the refrigerator. Albeit, a perverted display of pride.

With a deep chuckle, Aaron makes Kayla squeal with delight by never skipping a thrust. Ignoring our watching eyes, they return to their festivities.

This time I tug Ezra from the apartment, feeling uncomfortable watching when they are more than comfortable having us watch. Ez follows along, evidently lost in his own thoughts of lust and pride.

Just as I latch the front door closed, I hear Kayla moan, "I love you, Aaron." I can even hear Kayla's resulting scream of ecstasy through the closed door– no doubt Aaron's way of proving his mutual adoration.

Before I can blink, Ezra flings me, pressing me against the wall with his lean body. A protest spills from my lips when he bends his knees for leverage so he can grind his pelvis between my thighs, essentially nailing my ass to the wall.

"Not a good idea in a public hallway," I chastise Ezra, trying to keep my cool. But he's gone– lost in a fog of lust.

I try to move away from Ez, but he just lifts me so he no longer has to bend down. My legs hang limply to the side of his hips, leaving me with two options: I can either wrap my legs around his waist, or I can look like a fucking idiot. Of course, I choose the latter. The former is too similar to the act happening inside the apartment at my back.

"We're the only ones on this floor," Ezra murmurs breathlessly. He reaches down to wrap my legs around his waist, elegant hands proving their immense strength. When he rocks our pelvises together, I bite back a moan. "I own the building. No one lives on this floor except for us," he says with pride.

My eyes flit around, glancing at the huge hallway, thinking it's such a waste of space to lay empty and useless. I can't even wrap my mind around owning a home of my own, much less a high-rise. Unfathomable.

Sensing the direction of my thoughts, Ezra turns into the ultimate caveman provider. "We can build anything you'd like up here. A movie theater for Ava, or perhaps a swimming pool? I know you love to swim. Do you want to raise our family at Shadow Haven? The commute to work would suck, or you could work from home like Cortez?" Ezra's dream of the future is at complete and total odds with his hips gyrating into mine…

And the fact that Ezra has a loving fiancée waiting for him in the tower of her Crestview Castle.

It hurts to listen to Ezra's fantasy of a future, knowing that I won't be in it. It's someone else's future. It may belong to my daughter, but it surely doesn't belong to me. Hearing the words spilling from his throat, and the tenderness and affection lacing his tone, is like twisting the knife in deeper. I don't have the luxury of falling into Ezra's fantasy world, knowing at any time it could be torn from my grasp. Each word uttered is another betrayal on the layers upon layers of bitter betrayals and abuses of power.

Unless this is Ezra's way of buying me off with an expensive cage, to keep me happily imprisoned while I wait to be at his beck and call.

"Hold up there, cowboy." I put my palms against Ezra's chest, trying to pry him off of me. "You're getting a little bit ahead of yourself. Remember how I said no sex? Especially if that sex is in a hallway."

I try to wiggle down, but only accomplish more direct contact with our groins. Wincing, because it feels that damn good, I try to move without grinding our lusty parts together. Not that Ez is helping matters. The more I try to get away, the more eager he is to keep me right where I am.

"Yes, I remember. No sex. But this isn't sex." Ezra unleashes two more circular motions, rubbing his pulsing bulge directly over my throbbing flesh. My eyes roll back in my head and I hiss as if in pain, as my body releases a wash of arousal.

"Stop… please… Stop! It's too much." I put my palms on Ezra's chest again, trying to halt his assault. Hearing the desperation and pain in my voice, he slowly lowers me to the floor. But he doesn't step out of my personal space.

Staring down at me, nearly pouting, sulking, Ezra's expression is a mix of disappointment and need. The disappointment almost has me tearing off my pajama shorts and mounting Ezra to the wall.

Almost.

More than almost.

No, it's definitely not a good idea.

With Ez's intoxicating pheromones wreaking havoc on my hormones– fogging my mind –I'll do anything I can to distract myself from stealing what I want from Ezra.

I'm no thief.

"Don't we have more sleepy-check rounds to make before you pillage my village in the hallway?" I try to bring Ezra back into his right mind. "There could be a homicidal maniac in your apartment as we speak, taking advantage of a sweet, innocent, sleeping Cortez, just as you are me in this hallway."

"You're right as usual, Katya," Ezra concedes, but doesn't look too happy about it.

Ah, guys hate being cock-blocked. That has to be it. I laugh to tease Ezra. I give into his pouting by quickly pecking him on the lips. Ezra tries to make it more, but I shake my head no as I pull away.

I run away from Ezra, skipping down the hallway toward my apartment. I giggle playfully as I prance away, feeling light-hearted from the sensation of those moments which are too far and few in between– those moments that if I could bottle them, I would have more money than Ezra Zeitler.

How could I have forgotten how incredible it was to chase your prey? Ezra's on me in a heartbeat. Before I can release my squeak of surprise, he has me pinned to the wall, his body dominating mine. He's grinding his bulge between my legs before I can even issue a protest.

"Let me make you come. P-L-E-A-S-E." Ezra begs as he rolls his hips against me in a coaxing rhythm. "Just give me that much. I'm a man. We're simple creatures. Just allow us to feed, shelter, and pleasure you, and we'll die happy."

"Ezra," I breathe in warning. "This isn't a good idea." I try to remain sensible, because I need to get the words out before I lose all rational thought. Ezra's destructive scent is wafting into my nose, lighting my cunt on fire while drawing my reckless man-thief to the surface.

"No sex." Ezra groans in my ear, pleading with me. "Let's pretend we're fourteen, and we're just dry-humping as quickly as possible before we get caught." He releases a delicious laugh to accentuate his point.

"Ezra," I try again to bring us back to reality.

"Hey, you teased me. You know better than to run from a man like me. It was your fault. Now you have to suffer the consequence." Ezra manipulates me like a true master.

"Fine," I relent, sounding put out, even though deep down I'm secretly celebrating. "It's just about release. No emotions, okay?" It even rings false to my ears. It's tolling so loudly, it's as if every cathedral's bell in the world is ringing out at once.

*Liar.*

*Katya Waters is a thief and a liar!*

"I'll agree to anything you say," Ezra whispers against my mouth, and that rings false too.

Ezra's lips seek mine, and I fall into his kiss far too quickly for someone who should be protesting. His caress is sweet— tender. The type of kiss you give when you're innocent. But Ezra's not-so innocently pulling his pajama pants down as he kisses me, until he's bare against the satin of my shorts.

Startled, the sensation of his hard cock touching my bare, inner thigh has me crying out in ecstasy. "Dry-humping involves clothes!"

"Katya?" Ezra calls to me, voice shuddering in my ear. "Your reluctance to touch me... is it... is it because the memories haunt you, and my touch brings them back? Are you disgusted to touch me?" He sounds like a lost, little boy, so forlorn it pierces me through the heart.

"God, no!" I shout, shocked that Ezra would ever think such a ridiculous thing in the first place. "It has absolutely nothing to do with that."

"Are you sure?" Ezra implores, gray eyes piercing me, trying to delve so deeply into my soul that all my secrets will be revealed, stripping me bare and raw to his mastery.

"Ezra, you're all I see, hear, feel, or smell when we're together. Nothing exists outside of you," I stupidly admit that I'm in love with the domineering lunatic. Ezra's devastatingly victorious expression has me pulling my shorts off in an instant. "Don't enter me," I warn harshly, words belying my actions.

Ezra traps me, hands gripping the backs of my thighs, sliding my back up against the wall until we're pelvis to pelvis. With a sharp swat to the backs of my thighs, Ez makes sure my legs stay in place. Then his hands move to yank my hair, arching my neck for easier access.

Eyes wide with disbelief, I watch in wonder. Ezra is flushed, feral looking, near to bursting with the hunger of lust riding him hard. His face lowers, and I assume he's going to feast at my neck. But instead, he kisses me tenderly, just a soft brush of lips against lips that leaves me shuddering, as if it had been a violent, melding kiss.

One long, smooth flex of his hips has Ezra's length gliding along my aching flesh. We're so close, I can feel the veins ribbing his cock and the bulbous head teasing at my clit. With a sharp thrust, he pulls back far enough that he almost enters me with every roll of his hips.

"Ezra," his name moans from my parted lips, a sound of immense relief mingled with pure pleasure. "Don't enter me. I'm not on birth control." I groan deep from my throat when he tries to ignore my pleas, cockhead nudging at my entrance.

"I'll behave. I promise," Ezra pants breathlessly in my ear. "I won't break your trust, because someday you're going to let me inside you, and I don't want it to be because of trickery. I don't ever want you to regret it. I want you to beg me for it. Beg me to cum deep inside of you– to make you feel complete. Our future children should be created as you were, not as I was– not as Ava was."

My resolve breaks in the face of Ezra's influence. Some may call it manipulation, but it's just integrally Ezra. This is who he truly is. I can deny him nothing. I don't want to deny him, and I'll undoubtedly regret it when I can think clearly again.

With a fierce hunger, I devour Ezra's mouth, sucking his taste from his lips and tongue. My fingers twist in his silky hair, and his do the same to mine. Neither of us are allowing the other to get away. Both of us fight to control the kiss.

My legs wrap tightly around Ezra's waist as I ride the hard ridge of his cock, gliding as far as his torso, leaving a smear of my arousal behind on his flesh. My fingernails bite into the perfect muscles of his ass for added leverage as I writhe.

A symphony of pleasure rises from our throats, to converge with the rhythmic, wet slap of our bodies sliding against one another, before echoing down the hallway– a sound so filled with longing and relief that it springs tears to my eyes.

I said no emotions, and we both knew that was a bullshit lie. My heart swells and breaks simultaneously. It's a joy I've never known, and an agony I've never experienced. The agonized expression on Ezra's face screams he's suffering through it, too.

Whimpers erupt from my throat from the glorious sensation of Ezra's length gliding as smooth as silk along my folds. I grunt every time his plump cockhead passes my clit. His cock pulses against my flesh, adding to the immense pleasure.

Ezra's body is moving uncontrollably, writhing in jerky stops and starts, which create a jarring rhythm to our coupling. His fingers dig into my ass and thighs as his hips roll relentlessly against mine. Ezra's teeth bite my lower lip, showing me rather than telling me what he wants next.

"Bite me." Ezra's demand is a rolling moan, the sound trembling with a lingering ache. Raw with emotion, Ezra proves he knows how to surrender in order to get what he truly wants. "I'll beg if I have to. Katya, bite me again. Bite. Me."

I arch my neck and curl my toes against my rising release, and then I give Ezra what he so desperately seeks. I sink my blunt teeth into the curve between his shoulder and neck, and then clench brutally. The sensation of my teeth sinking into his muscle forces my climax. My body quivers, and I cannot suppress the words of adoration and moans from slipping past my lips.

Ezra grunts violently while shuddering. He slides his wet cock up my belly, and releases in a hot torrent against the bottom curve of my breasts. Ezra thrusts rapidly, only rubbing the base of his cock and his sack over my slit, guaranteeing his cum doesn't pour out on my fertile flesh.

I'm glad Ezra can still think straight, since I no longer can. I'm positive I was begging him to fuck me just seconds ago, intermingled with the '*I love yous*' I'll pretend I never uttered.

The fact that Ezra is still thinking straight bothers me a bit. I want to be his undoing, but I'm thankful I'm not. If we managed to wreck each other, the consequences would be astronomical.

Ezra's satisfied laughter echoes down the hallway. A masculine, rumbling song of happiness and contentment. My toes curl from the addictively warm sound. Ezra and Cortez's laughter has weight, as if it has substance– a tangible thing.

Ezra gazes at me with the same look Cort gave me earlier. The expression that Cort says is solely for Ezra and me. I can tell that I've got that same stupid look on my face, and it will only lead to my ruination.

Uncomfortable, I inject humor into an even more distressing subject. "I pray that isn't how fourteen-year-olds dry-hump nowadays. Because in two years, I'll be locking our daughter in a tower. Ava's our kid, after all. We should hook her up with birth control the moment her cycle regulates. So… yeah, we're basically screwed."

I laugh out of fear as I wipe Ezra's baby-juice from my belly with his pajama bottoms, and then I yank my damp tank top back down into place.

Wearing a funny, little smile I can't interpret, Ezra shrugs. "Yes, we're Ava's parents, so she will undoubtedly be horrid. My God, I was only a few months older than Ava when I started to have sex with Cort," Ezra reveals, and it seriously freaks my ass out.

"No," I mutter, horrified. "Our daughter is still a child."

"No fear, Katya. Ava may have inherited how our minds matured faster than our bodies, but we're also her parents," he stresses. "With my stalking, I'll know the second Ava tries to be bad, and I'll thwart her before she makes a mistake, and then I'll punish her in the way I should have been. To this day, I wish my mother wouldn't have allowed us to sleep together after it changed into something more than brotherly affection. At the time, though, both Cortez and I would have thrown epic temper tantrums. Ava will never get away with any of that shit."

If any other man had threatened my daughter, I would have slaughtered him. But right now, I'm thankful that I have Ezra on my team. He can be one scary motherfucker. Our daughter's lucky to have him as her father.

# Chapter Six

Ezra leads me back into his apartment, holding my hand while chattering about all the inventive punishments he'll lay down upon our daughter's naughty behind.

Feeling unsure after what just went down in the hallway, I decide to broach an uncomfortable conversation. Might as well be a mixed bag of emotions. "Can we talk for a moment, or do you need to check on Cortez first?"

"We have a few minutes. Cort was sleeping soundly before I went to check on everyone else." Ezra lowers himself to the sofa, radiating patience.

"I have to ask you something. No, not ask. I don't need your permission. I have something to tell you." I lick my lips to moisten the suddenly dry flesh. "I needed guidance, so I paid a visit to Dexter–" I stop short when I notice how Ezra has left the building. Any semblance between Ezra and Master Ez dissolves. They are truly separate and equally pissed.

"Guidance in what area?" Ez asks in a deadly quiet tone.

"Dominance–" I hesitate when Ez fists the sofa cushion, knuckles turning white from the force.

"Stop!" Moving like a predator, Ez is looming over me, seething. Voice as sharp as broken glass, "Don't you dare say the next word that's about to flow from your mouth. You will not submit to anyone but me. Ever. I am your master. Do you understand?"

"Submit? Not likely, as I refuse to ask for permission since I'm a grown woman." I glare up at Ezra, trying to inject this into his brain. "Dexter doubts my switch status, saying I'm confused about what it truly means to be a dominant. So yeah…" I blink, unable to go on beneath the force of Ezra's oppressive aura.

"Continue," Ezra coaxes, sounding reasonable. But his eyes are glacial yet throwing sparks of fury.

"I need Dexter to train me as a dominant, to give me the tools to understand my needs and desires. He said he would never train me as a submissive, because I don't have a submissive bone in my body." I decide complete honesty is the best approach when dealing with the enraged, alpha male looming over me. Ezra visibly relaxes, and then retakes his seat on the sofa.

"Tell me the rest," Ezra allows, sitting primly on his sofa, wearing only a pair of cum-soiled pajama bottoms. He sits with his palms resting on his knees and his back ramrod straight.

This entire conversation is a catch-22. I almost don't answer Ezra, as in doing so, I'm submitting. I'm stubborn, and I used to be a fool, but I'm neither tonight. I relent, knowing by yielding to his demands I'm actually getting what I need in return.

"No matter what Dexter thinks, there is a part of me that longs to please you, and it terrifies me how you'll consume me in the process. So I asked Dexter to point out exactly what the submissive is doing right or wrong, so I can learn by example." I try my damnedest to appease Ezra. "I'll need that information when dominating someone, anyway."

Not a single muscle twitches in Ezra's body– he doesn't even blink. "Why can't Cortez or I train you?"

Ezra is still channeling Master Ez, but Ezra is lurking in the shadows of his eyes. I'm not saying he is two separate personalities. He pulls out traits to deal with certain situations like someone shuffles playing cards in their hand, determining which is better to win the game. Master Ez must be for when Ezra is feeling angry and territorial.

"I can't explain it." I sigh heavily, sounding so much like Ezra that I crack a smile. "It's like you guys are too close to me. I don't want to disappoint you, and I know I will. I won't be able to relax and learn if I feel like it will affect how you see me." I tried to put my fears into words, but I'm not entirely sure I managed it. "I don't want to look like a twit around you, and I won't give a shit what Dexter thinks of me when I fall flat on my ass."

"I will never judge you," Ezra promises.

"I know that," I blurt out. "But I do have some pride, Ezra. Maybe I want you to be proud of me, seeing the finished product, not the bumps and bruises along the way. Maybe I need to have something that is just for me. You've infected every part of my life. Give me a few moments of time that don't involve you. It's just an illusion anyway. I know goddamned well Dexter will tell you whatever you want to know."

"Fine," Ezra relents, not sounding fine at all. "But you have a decision to make." Narrowed, stormy eyes glare at me. His fingertips sink into his thighs, muscles contracting. It's as if Ezra is restraining himself from harming me.

"What decision?" I rasp, throat going dry with nervousness in the face of Ezra's potent intensity.

"I need to connect with you. Right. Now. Connect," he says like it should be capitalized in bold letters. "Either you pick a place and an activity, or I will take you here on this couch."

Ezra's power is frightening. Every muscle in his body is taut, coiled at the ready for attack– to attack *me*.

"I said no sex." I gulp, throat contracting as anxiety overpowers me. "We just got off in the hallway less than ten minutes ago."

"And I don't care," Ezra says flatly. "I don't need downtime to go again. I'm hard again already," he warns, cupping his erection through his pajama pants. As a silent threat, he tugs the fabric down a bit so I can see he's even more aroused now than he was before in the hallway– cockhead swollen purple with blood.

Stammering, "That would be force… and you wouldn't do that to me." I stare at Ezra wide-eyed, scared to even blink. A bunny rabbit captured in the wolf's gaze. He looks back at me with a feral expression– neither Ezra nor Master Ez.

"I've raped you before," Ezra states nonchalantly, as if he's admitting his favorite color is gray. "Once you've crossed that line, it's fairly easy to revisit."

"I would think it would be more difficult now that you know how it feels afterwards. The guilt. The shame. The pain." I mutter, sounding strong and sure, but I still don't dare blink. My eyes are dry and stinging, seconds away from losing the staring contest of my life.

Ezra's breath is sawing in and out of his lungs, rapidly raising and lowering his chest. I can see the artery in his neck fluttering wildly. His fingertips are clutching his thighs, and his toes are curled into the carpeting, as if that is the only reason he remains seated.

"Your choice, or my choice. You have a few seconds before I unleash my true nature. I can't hold out much longer, Katya." His voice is strained, sharp.

"Your nature?" I snort at Ezra, when it's probably the dumbest thing I could possibly do in this volatile situation. "What happened to your views on nurture, Dr. Jeannine?"

Ezra's expression turns rabid in an instant. I'm playing with fire. Not only am I going to be burned, I'm going to be incinerated.

"What happened? This can't be because I asked Dexter to train me. I'm not asking him to be my master. I'm asking him to free me– to teach me how to honor *my* true nature. I'm not going to fuck Dexter, if that's what you're worried about. No doubt the man exudes animal magnetism and bleeds sex. But since I just got done getting off with you in the hallway, I'm sexually sated now. I thought you knew me better than that, Ezra. I hate how you're acting, like you don't trust me. You're off kilter."

"I know that!" Ezra snarls, flabbergasted with himself. "Don't you think I know that? But sometimes the part of me that is Master Ez doesn't give a shit. He wants to mark his territory, even if he just spurted a nutsack worth of cum all over you. Because it doesn't count unless it makes its way inside your cunt to plant a seed in your womb."

"Eww…" I hiss, thoroughly disgusted. "Could you be any more vulgar?"

"Yes, I could," Ezra mutters, shaking his head back and forth as if to clear it. "In fact, I could be a lot worse. The second you said Dexter's name, it took everything in me not to rape you or kill him. You may forgive me for fucking you against your wishes, but Dexter wouldn't be able to forgive me, since he'd be *dead*."

"Ezra," I say calmly, palms rising, trying to show him there is nothing to fear– nothing to fear but himself.

"I get it, Kat!" Ez shouts. Frustrated with himself, the sides of his fists meet his thighs. "Logically, I know that Dexter trained me, and then Cortez, and he would be an excellent teacher for you. But Master Ez's urges aren't necessarily logical."

My face scrunches up as I try to reason out where Ezra's possessive streak is coming from and why Ezra keeps talking of himself in the third person.

Ezra's anger fuels mine, because I always leach the emotions from those around me, rendering it impossible to know if what I'm feeling is my reality or theirs. Being around someone such as Ezra Zeitler is going to put me in an emotional tailspin on a continual basis, and I don't know if I can live through the chaos.

"I'm confused. You were okay with Aaron having sex with me. Hell, you watched the whole goddamned thing! So what's the big fucking deal?" I shout, voice cracking from the pain of Ezra giving me away so easily, only to bitch about it later.

"I gave you to Aaron," Ezra confesses, like he isn't shattering my heart into a billion, unamendable pieces.

"What?" Even in light of the fact that Ezra just admitted to wanting to rape me and murder Dexter, his statement of giving me away disturbs me the most. It makes me feel like a toy he's loaning out to a friend. You don't loan out what you wish to possess. You cherish it, wanting to keep it all to yourself.

"I gave you and Aaron permission to explore one another. If you had said no, that was fine too. In the end, it was your ultimate choice to be with Aaron. I didn't force you to make love to him, Katya."

"Why?" I breathe, hating myself as much as I hate Ezra in this very moment.

"Aaron had expressed a need to connect with you as a way to leave behind the scars of the past, and I thought it would heal you both. You needed to know what it was like to have sex with a friend, without harsh emotions riding you."

"I get that, I guess," I mutter, realizing whether I go left or right, Ezra has somehow manipulated me into going in either direction, because both paths suit his own means. It's when I go directly down the center that throws him off. In this case, Dexter was the center. Ezra didn't see that coming, and it's driving him batshit crazy.

"I may give Dexter privileges in the future, but that is also *my* decision to make." Ezra rolls his head on his shoulders and flexes his clenched fingers, as if the thought makes him furious. "Make a choice, Katya. You're quickly running out of time as my patience grows very thin."

Ezra growls deep from within his chest, the menacing sound petrifies me as much as it excites me. He's peering at me with stormy eyes glazed with emotions I could never fathom, even if I lived to be millenniums old.

My mind reaches clarity, thinking of ways to calm Ezra, as my body ignites at the thought of being taken by force. I shudder at the visual playing within my mind.

*A feral Ezra pounds into me, bruising me with his passion, forcing me to surrender to his whims. He bends me to his will, knowing I will never be whole again when he's through with me. I break with a scream of violent misery, releasing an endless sound from the depths of my soul– terror and ecstasy.*

A strangled sound erupts from my throat, yanking me from my private thoughts. My fantasy bubble pops when Ezra looks at me like he can read the sick depths of my mind.

"We can share a bed, and sleep," I stammer out, racing the clock before Ezra snaps and takes the decision out of my hands. "Is that okay? It doesn't have to be sexual, does it?"

"Yes, we can do that. I have to connect with you, but it needn't be sexual– just intimate." Ezra sounds and looks calmer, but his eyes note my every reaction.

An odd smirk flirts with Ezra's lips as intense heat flashes across his pale skin. "Someday we will play the game riding your thoughts, but only after you agree that I may love you as I'm meant to."

*Huh?* I shake my head to clear it. I'm simultaneously relieved and disappointed. Taking advantage of my confused state of mind, Ezra stands from the sofa, takes my hand, and then tugs me from my seat. Holding my hand, Ezra directs me to another room I've never entered before.

# Chapter Seven

"This isn't your bedroom?" Situated at the end of the hallway, is a large, dark room with absolutely no filtered light. I can't even see my fingertips when I place them directly in front of my eyes.

"No, this *is* my bedroom. I don't sleep in that other room. It has different purposes. I *always* sleep here," Ezra states matter-of-factly.

"Oh. Okay," I stammer, confused.

"Get undressed and get into bed," Ezra commands. I hear the rustle of clothing and the whisper of sheets. "This was your choice. I can always do the other one." Menacing, he threatens me with rape and murder.

Sleeping nude next to Ezra is more of a reward than a punishment, so I quickly strip, and then feel my way to the bed. When I'm crawling midway up the mattress, Ezra lifts me effortlessly, and then places me where he wants me.

I squeak out a very girly sound when a warm, naked body encloses me from the side. "Shh… Don't be scared, Kitten. It's just me." Cortez's voice is slurred, drowsily with the edge of sleep. He snuggles against my back, releasing a purr of contentment. "Mmm… someone smells like sex. I'd know that scent anywhere. Have you been fucking *our* Ezra, Kitten?"

"No," I poorly deny. "I… you sleep together?" I stammer out, trying to change the subject since Cort's exquisiteness is cradled in the cleft of my ass cheeks. I whimper because it feels so damned good and right. I let my conscience rule me, and behave.

"Since the crib. It's a hard habit to break," Ezra says as he cuddles up to me, engulfing both me and Cortez in his embrace. "Just because Cort won't touch me, doesn't mean he won't hug me at least."

"Naked hugs?" I snort. "I don't think it gets any more intimate than *that*."

"That's all the bastard gets from me," Cort growls into my ear, causing me to shiver. Evidently Cort holds a wicked grudge over a lifetime of betrayals. I should really tear a page out of Cortez Abernathy's resentment playbook.

A palm settles on the back of my head, pressing my face against Ezra's warm chest. Ezra and Cort's scents mingle and fill my system. Heady. The strongest drug for someone addicted to the Ezes.

"Go to sleep, Katya. If you stay awake, I may change my mind. I will break your no sex rule for the both of us. You haven't had Cortez yet," Ezra manages to tease and taunt me simultaneously.

But Ezra's suggestion doesn't scare me. I've already thrown my moral code in the thrash tonight– I'll regret it tomorrow morning. A thrill flashes through my body, igniting me, making it impossible to sleep. Cort throbs against my ass as if he can sense what I'm thinking, making the deep ache worse.

I lick my lips, the sound ricocheting around the dark room. "Does Aaron sleep with you, too?" As appealing as it may sound, I couldn't handle it if it were the case.

"No," they state unequivocally in unison.

"Why not?" I grumble.

"It's not like that with us," Ezra replies. "Aaron has some hero worship going on with me. But he's as straight as an arrow; that's why it was so important that he and Kayla connect." Ezra buries his face in my hair and sighs heavily.

"I'd say Aaron's connected with her, all right." I shudder in remembrance of Aaron thrusting like a piston inside Kayla.

Cortez chuckles against the nape of my neck, and then he shifts his hips because he was enjoying himself way too much back there. Cort's hands rub up and down my arms, trying to comfort me, but he only manages to arouse me more.

"When was the last time you made love to each other?" The words are out before I can stop them, and I regret it immediately.

"I can't remember," Cort breathes in my ear, lying his ass off.

"I remember," Ezra speaks up, voice turning husky. He shifts his hips, making sure the result of my question doesn't poke me in the gut. "But it was a very, very long time ago. I believe the blowjob was the last time."

"The skull-fuck punishment?" I ask quickly before I lose my nerve.

"No," they mutter in unison. "The time Ez is bringing up doesn't count either, since it was *not* consensual. It only counts if Ez gets anywhere near my cock," Cort adds. "Which is off limits to faithless, insane bastards."

"What the hell, Ez? Do you go around raping everyone?" I joke, but both men go rigid around me, flooding my veins with fear. "I was only kidding. I didn't mean to pick at a wound."

"Cort was begging for it, and after about ten seconds, he was totally into it. So I wouldn't call that rape." Ez explains his vague rules of consent.

"I'd call being held down by the two people I trust the most in this world, while my partner sucks my dick when he knows I only allow women to have that honor, a violation of the highest order. I don't care if I enjoyed it or not, I've never forgiven any of you."

Ezra just starts humming a concerto in response, completely ignoring how furious Cortez is behind me.

"I'm not gay," Cort mutters, and Ezra starts humming even louder. "There are a few things I keep just for me– things that do *not* belong to Ezra. But some people don't seem to care about how I feel, and they try to force me to do what I don't want to do, just because Ezra wants me."

My voice is soft and intimate in the shadowy dark of their shared bedroom. "You don't want Ezra?" I ask Cortez, and Ezra's humming immediately ceases as he waits with bated breath for the answer.

"It's about who you're attracted to and who you love. I never said I didn't love or want the assfuck. I said I hate his betraying dick, and I have to punish him the only way I can. I've never willingly had sex with another man but him. Ezra isn't so particular," Cortez grits out, vibrating my ear, resentment thickly lacing his voice. "Might as well slap an '*Open for Business*' sign on Ezra's asshole."

Our conversation from earlier this evening pops into my thoughts. Cort kept talking of Ezra's betrayals. I've got to say, this conversation has piqued my interests. I bet if I could get Cort angry enough, or make Ezra batshit again, they'd both blow a fuse and spill all of the sordid details, just as Dexter and Roarke said they would.

"Hey, now," Ez murmurs to Cort, hand reaching out to soothe his partner's hurt feelings. "The two times I've been with someone else, it was awkward and harmful. Don't get jealous," Ezra pleads.

"I'm not jealous. I'm hurt," Cort breathes so quietly I can barely hear him. Evidently Ezra heard Cortez loud and clear, since he releases a sigh in reply.

"Someday you'll forgive me," Ezra whispers back. "Katya won't like being pulled between us like the rope in a never-ending tug-of-war match to the death."

"I'm sorry. I... I just get so angry that I forget I should just deal with it and move on. I'm sorry, Kat. This is the first night you're sleeping with us– well, that you know about, anyway – and I shouldn't be ruining the experience by turning mean and nasty."

I'm sandwiched between both of the Ezes, with Cort fused to my back and Ezra to my front. I don't want to enjoy it, but I do. The one emotion that I'm surprised to feel is safe. I feel safe and content in their arms, as if nothing could ever touch me, let alone harm me, as long as I'm with them.

"Why do you have wives and fiancées? Why do you live here and not with them? Why am I in your bed and they aren't?" The questions keep firing as I work myself up. "Why isn't it just the two of you?"

"That's Cortez's story to tell, not mine. The answer to every question you just asked is Cortez." Ez says the opposite of what Dexter said earlier.

*The answer to all of Cortez's questions is Ezra.*

The truth is, they each are the question and the answer. I can't imagine the amount of power Ezra and Cortez wield over the other, knowing they are the eternal answer to any question you may ever ask about either of them. Where do the rest of us fall where their loyalties are concerned?

"And I'm too tired to tell it right now. I was sleeping until the scent of good sex tickled my nostrils. I'll tell you tomorrow," Cortez says as he snuggles in tighter. "Promise." A few seconds later, his breathing changes, and then it evens out as he drifts off to sleep.

"Thank you for sleeping with us," Ezra breathes against my neck. "We will sleep better knowing you're safe in our arms. Until the morning, my Katya."

"Good night, Ezra," I mumble, my emotional climate a jumbled stew of mass chaos.

# Chapter Eight

Karma.

Karma is a ruthless cunt.

I was a very good girl as a child: working side-by-side with my father in the family business as his little helper, and later on as a skilled laborer. I studied my little heart out from kindergarten until high school graduation, making distinguished honor roll every semester. I was the girl who cried the only time she ever got high honors instead of distinguished, because she knew she'd get grounded when her parents found out, when everyone else was celebrating how they simply passed the class.

I had the American Dream crammed down my throat by a self-made businessman, how this is the land of opportunity, just as long as you had the will to reach out to grab what you earned. I bought the lie that worked so well for my father. That was until the building market crashed and he learned it was all a bullshit lie that sucked your bank account dry as you supported the lives of your employees.

The people who get ahead in life, more than likely did it off the hard work of others, by chance, were lucky enough that Karma hadn't targeted them with her vengeance, or they were sucking the system dry. Yes, hard work will keep you fed with a roof over your head, but if you look to the others around you, you'll just end up bitter.

After striving so hard during my school career, I learned a harsh truth: how much your family was worth was the determining factor on scholarships, grants, and financial aid. It wasn't my community service work, my afterschool activities, my gainful employment, or my impeccable GPA.

Even though my parents' business was not funding my higher education, I was the one who was punished for their hard work. It was as if striving to get ahead should somehow give others a handicap in the game of life. I earned the scholarship, but a girl received it who barely had a C average and spent the majority of her high school career with her thighs spread instead of opening a book. We had the same opportunities from kindergarten on; it was what we did with those opportunities that should have mattered. The individual was attending college, not the parents.

I learned nothing would ever be handed to me, and I came to understand that Karma was just a pretty lie we tell ourselves to feel better when someone who doesn't deserve jackshit– and is a total cunt –gets what should be ours. Only to lose it, because they didn't appreciate that which they didn't have to work for in the first place.

The bitch with my scholarship failed out of college, while I would have made that scholarship fund proud and donated the money back to another well-deserving student after I succeeded. Instead, it was all a waste. I was left to blame the undeserving because the true villain was untouchable– the system.

Even after knowing I had to work my way through college, that I had to earn everything while my classmates sat on their asses, got high, fucked, and drank themselves into an early addiction off mommy and daddy's and the taxpayers' money, I didn't give up.

No matter what, I was optimistic, and I will forever believe in the tenets our great country was built upon, no matter how much her ruling elite fucks me.

Life's not fair. It's a simple truth we all must acknowledge.

I was raped, left with a child, and I'm still optimistic. I deserve better. I've earned my happily ever after… someday my ship will come in. I am far from a dreamer, but I still fantasize about a better life.

I was naïve, innocent, thinking Karma was like a bank account, where you accumulate good to offset any bad you may do in the future. Seeing as how Karma had kicked me in the cunt for the past thirty-two years, and I was undeserving of her wrath, I thought I had a bit of moral wiggle room.

I'd never cheated on tests, never stole candy from the corner store, never got into drunken brawls, or had sex with my classmates. I only told little white lies, like how that pink dress didn't make my mother's ass look fat or the potato soup was delicious when there was too much black pepper in it. I never spoke any of the vitriol that sprung unbidden into my private thoughts, and I always felt bad for thinking it too.

I figured Karma owed me at least one indiscretion. After all, in the bank account of life, Karma was in the red while I was in the black.

So when I woke this morning after an excellent night's sleep, with the scent of the Ezes pleasuring my nostrils and the warmth from their spooning bodies, I didn't feel one ounce of guilt. I looked myself in the mirror this morning as I got ready for work, and I held my daughter's gaze across the breakfast table as we ate like a real family with her father and Cortez. When I called my mother this morning, I told her the God's honest truth, and it didn't even turn my stomach.

I have committed one sin that goes against my personal moral code. My ethics are not built from a religious ideology. They are built on the ability to look my family in the eye, to look myself in the mirror and respect who is gazing back at me, and to be able to sleep soundly at night.

ONE.

I've never felt as if what I did with Aaron was wrong. We were grown adults who found succor in the affection of the other, and I make no excuses for it, nor will I ever apologize.

I could place all the blame on Ezra and Cortez for our fucked up relationship. I could take no ownership for loving either of them, and I do love them. I can admit that much to myself. The level and type of love remains to be seen.

My only sin is trespass– trespassing on another woman's territory. Whether it be Divina Hastings or Adelaide Whittenhower, I am in the wrong, no matter the circumstances.

I could be self-righteous and say since we aren't having penis-in-vagina sex then it's not cheating. But it's so much more than that. It's emotional and sexual. I am building a life on the foundation of someone else's relationships.

I'm in the wrong.

Karma owes me this one. A free pass. The scourge on my soul should be cleared away after all I've suffered. But today I learned another life lesson: Karma isn't a bank account, nor is she benevolent. She is a vicious harpy of a mistress, waiting to prey upon you the minute you feel content, at peace– happy.

You know the feeling, when all is right with the world and a distressing thought pops into your head. '*Something bad is going to happen to balance out all of this good. This cannot last.*' It isn't much later when the bad knocks you on your ass, and you're devastated.

See, I didn't have the comfort of having that ominous thought first. I was still high in the good when the bad dropped out of thin air and shit all over my rainbows and sunshine with its nightmares and devastation, because Karma is a cunt.

A note.

A single, innocuous piece of paper.

As a member of the word-weavers– a wordsmith –no one more than I understands the power of words. It's not the paper they are written on, nor the author, or even the arrangement of letters upon the page. It's the intent. It's the words' meaning that can soothe the savage beast within. Words have the power to teach– to inspire. Words can heal. Words can murder all hope as quickly as your eyes take in the jumble of letters for your brain to comprehend their true meaning.

My punishment for the hallway intimacy I had with Ezra, followed by the good night's rest, is in the form of letters upon a single piece of paper. Of course it is. If you want to break a girl, you kick her where it hurts the most.

Words have power. It's not *'sticks and stones will break my bones, but words will never hurt me'*. Bullshit! The bastards wielding the torturous words know exactly what they are doing, and they use it to inflict maximum damage. Sometimes you don't even know who is targeting you, so you have to blame Karma, or else you run the risk of…

Freaking. The. Fuck. Out.

I've been sitting at my desk all morning long, staring at a scrap of paper as if it holds the mysteries of the universe. If I wasn't terrified to touch it, I'd burn the cocksucking thing.

"We need to talk," Monica says as she barges into my office. I guess a closed door is now an open invitation to enter. But for once, I'm thrilled to see her as a distraction from my problems.

"About what?" My voice shows my annoyance, and it's only tinged with a slight amount of terror. But now is not the time to think about *that*, Katya.

"Before you left, I said some vicious shit to you that I shouldn't have said." Monica hesitantly takes a seat in front of my desk.

"Oh, really?" I arch an eyebrow in her direction.

"I realize that narking on you would gain me nothing." Monica holds my gaze, and not only do I know she's being truthful, I can sense she feels badly about it, too. Her manning up makes me respect her all the more.

"Monica, let's put our shit on the table, shall we?"

"Yes," she breathes out like a sigh of relief. "Please."

"Good," I mutter, quite shocked. See, something good happens, and then something devastating comes next. Now something pleasantly uncomfortable is softening the blow.

"I thought you'd be banging my head into the edge of your desk by now," Monica says with a shudder, finally scared of me, and I have no idea why. Maybe she remembers me dressed as a Kitten while I lashed our resident Mousey.

"What exactly is your issue with me, anyway? Whether I'm at Edge or not, you still wouldn't have this job. You're excellent at your own position, and we don't have anyone else who is qualified to do it. You should feel proud about that. But it's not the job, is it?"

I have a theory about Monica, and even Kristal, and every female I've met since I stepped foot onto Dominion soil, but I just haven't voiced it yet. I'm too scared to admit that I've fallen victim to the same ploy they did.

"No. It was about Cortez. But I'm so over it," Monica draws out, as her big, brown eyes peer up at me earnestly.

"Huh? Why Cortez?" My face scrunches in confusion– all an act to get Monica to explain herself. I had a feeling all roads led back to Cortez Abernathy and his insatiable sex drive. I just needed Monica to confirm it for me.

"Cortez didn't leave me because of his wife. I was never his girlfriend, either." Monica sighs loudly and presses on. "I was Master Cortez's submissive. A couple months ago, he let us all go."

"What do you mean– *let us all go?*" I ignore what the '*us*' implies. How many subs does one man need, anyway? I just can't rationalize the man who held me all night long with the one who fucks shit-loads of women on a regular basis.

"Cortez had a few subs, but not a one of them he claimed. He never really did any scenes with us, either. He just fucked us any way he wanted, and occasionally took us out to dinner and bought us gifts. After more than three years, I thought he was going to formally become my master. At first, I figured it was a coincidence that you showed up a few weeks after he rejected us all. But that was until I saw you at Restraint."

Monica glares at me angrily, shooting pure animosity in my direction, which is odd for a woman who is '*so over it*'.

"The way Cortez looked at you…" Monica shakes her head as she trails off. "Anyway, that's why I've treated you like shit."

"First of all, you treated me like shit from day one. Secondly, Cortez is not my master, and he never will be. I'm not even sure he gives a fuck about BDSM," I muse more to myself than to Monica. "I promise you, not a damn thing about this was about you. You're perfect as you are, and someday, a real master will see how special you are."

I reach over to clutch Monica's hand to lend her comfort, and I'm surprised at how eager she is to latch onto me.

"Do you have a master?" Monica asks me, and I nod yes. "Master Ez?" I nod yes again, and she just watches me in awe.

"But I don't need a master, Monica. I'm a switch, but I think that's only in relation to Master Ez. Not that he let me choose him in the first place," I mutter underneath my breath. "I'm mostly dominant, but I wanted someone strong enough to shoulder the burdens from time to time– release my stress."

"I can relate," Monica murmurs with a dreamy quality in her tone.

"Are you in love with Cort, or something?" I just can't see how Monica could be. Cortez is a hard one to deal with, let alone love. I know how to take him because he's just like me, but others won't be able to understand him as easily.

"No, I'm not in love with Cortez. I just have a hard time finding a dominant because no one will top me. The guys milling around Restraint's club just wanted a quick lay, so I joined the membership. But Restraint's Masters either already have a submissive, or they think I'm too strong and I should just admit that I'm a domme." Monica pulls her fingers through her hair, clearly out of frustration. "I am what I am, dammit!"

"I understand that, Monica. I really do. Maybe you and I could call a truce and work together–" My door opens, and in bounds an eleven-year-old hopped-up on sugar. "I am going to kill Cortez," I hiss underneath my breath.

"Oops… sorry. I didn't know you were having a meeting." Ava looks embarrassed, her pale skin pinking.

"What have you been up to, baby girl?" Ava is covered in chocolate, eyes glazed over, and panting like she's been running through the halls. No shock since it was Cortez's hour to entertain her.

I turn to introduce Monica to my daughter, only to find her mouth hanging wide open, looking like she's seen a ghost. "Monica, this is my daughter, Ava." I gesture with my hand.

"Jesus. Fuck." Monica whispers underneath her breath. "She looks just like her." Monica gazes at me in awe, like I just committed an impossible feat.

"Cort taught me how to hack the security locks," Ava announces proudly, ignoring Monica's strange behavior.

"Ah, yeah. Cort's really good at that," I say absentmindedly, remembering how he broke the code on the chess set treasure box without any problem. "What else have you two been up to?"

"Cort showed me how to hack all the email accounts, too, and the security feeds." My eyes pop out at that. "He thought it would be good practice for when I start at Hillbrook."

"Yeah, and I doubt Cortez means web design class." I'm going to kill him. "Ava, go clean up in the bathroom, and then I need you to locate Cortez and tell him that I need to speak with him immediately," I order.

"You're not going to yell at Cort, are you?" Ava whines at my audacity to scold her new playmate. "We were just having fun. You know how I love breaking complex puzzles, otherwise I get bored." She worries her bottom lip, and I can't help but smile.

"No, I need to see Cort for something else entirely. It's all right. I promise," I placate Ava. "Do *not* leave your father's side until I get home tonight. No more sweets– have a sandwich or something."

"Okay," Ava says with a defiant edge. I can't wait to see what Ezra will do with that attitude. I laugh at the thought. She bounds for the door, and I clear my throat loudly to gain her attention.

"Ma..." Ava whines. "I'm getting too old for that."

"*Getting*, but you're not there yet. Now get your sticky buns over here," I snap playfully.

I point at my cheek, patiently waiting. Ava drags her feet over to me, and quickly kisses my cheek– so fast I doubt her lips make contact. I sigh. She's a little lady now, no longer my baby girl. A little lady covered in chocolate. I smile at the thought.

"Just a minute, Monica. I have to make sure Ava follows through with my orders." I needn't have bothered to warn Monica, since she's frozen immobile.

I pick up the phone and dial Ezra. With a shock, I realize it's the first time I've ever called him.

"Katya," spills warmly from the other end of the line, his smoky voice filling my ear.

"Is Cort with you?" I ask quickly, needing to make this a short call. The longer I'm around Ezra, the worse I have it for him, which means he'll discover my secrets before I'm ready.

Not good.

Not good at all.

"Yes," he mutters, sounding uncertain since he doesn't know what I'm leading up to.

"I'm going to kick his ass. You'll figure out why when tropical storm Ava arrives. Anyway, I need you to keep our daughter close until I get home tonight. I have some errands to attend."

"What did Cort do this time?" Ezra's exasperation flows loud and clear over the phone line.

"Nothing major. Just taught our daughter how to hack everything in the building while hopping her up on sugar. I need to see Cortez. But don't worry, I'm not going to rip him a new asshole. We have some stuff we need to do today."

"Cort's headed your way. He fled the second I answered the phone."

"Damn." I huff a laugh.

"You have an appointment with Dexter at seven this evening. Bring Cortez with you. Please. I'll feel better knowing he's with you."

"Okay, sounds good." A muffled, sinister giggle flows through the phone, and I roll my eyes. "Ava's your problem now, sucker. You can thank your partner for it." I laugh as I hang up, and I swear I heard Ezra growling.

"Sorry, this is new, and we're on a learning curve. I–" my statement is cut short by the petrified look on Monica's face.

"What's wrong now?" I slump forward against my desk, resting on my elbows.

"I'm sorry, Katya. I didn't know." Monica looks horrified, like I'm about to drag her ass off to the executioner.

"What?" I watch Monica's expression, trying to gain access to her emotions.

"I won't lie to you. I've always known Master Ez was Ezra. I saw your bracelet the first time you wore it," Monica tips her chin at my wrist. "I've known all along that Ezra was your master. I've said things to discourage you from being with him– to sabotage you. I was angry about losing three years of my life, trying to get Cortez to become my master. I was jealous, so I didn't want you to have one either. I know that where ever Ezra goes, Cortez follows."

"What does this have to do with anything, Monica?" I ask in confusion.

"Ezra is Ava's father. I need to apologize for my behavior. You obviously had rights to them a long time before I came into the picture." Monica wipes away a tear, and it confuses me even more. "My sincerest apologies."

Monica walks over to me, and puts her hand out for a shake. I take it, not entirely sure what this is all about. I realize she is offering me a truce, but what I don't trust is the why of it.

"No need for a truce. I won't be a problem ever again. Let's start over at square one, Kat," Monica says, sounding genuinely sincere yet scared shitless that I'll reject her offer.

"Why won't you be a problem?" I ask as I finish our handshake.

"Hmm… let me guess. I will lose my job and my membership to Restraint if I mess with you, and those are two of the things that keep me sane. But most of all, we are a lot alike. I just don't feel like fighting for no reason. There are other things to be angry about instead. I also realize that if I could just get over myself, especially the jealousy, then maybe you and I could actually connect. Maybe even be friends someday– who knows. But the alternative isn't worth it. So I'm playing nice."

"I'm good with this as long as you aren't actually *playing* nice, Monica. I need you to actually *be* nice," I warn. "I'm sick of the fakery and lies. I want real, even if it's mean."

Monica drops my hand and looks at the floor. I'm not sure what's going on in that head of hers. She seems broken, and it causes the ache in my chest to throb in response. I stand to comfort her, but Cortez's entrance distracts us both.

"You called for my services, Kitten." Cort nods to Monica, and then kisses me on the cheek. He makes a sour face and wipes his mouth off.

"I see our little monster got to your face first." Cort puckers up his lips and cringes.

I burst out laughing. "Ha! Your own mistakes bite you in the ass. You shouldn't feed children excessive amounts of sugar."

"Ava tricked me into it. We had a bet, and I lost. I should have known better. You and Ezra spawned a very diabolical child, and she has that evil giggle to prove it." Cortez's grin turns to a scowl when he realizes what he just said.

"Hey, it doesn't change anything. It's the truth. Ava will never meet him." I rub Cort's back in comfort.

"I shouldn't have called Ava a little monster, or called her evil." Cort looks despondent.

"Ava is who she is. We are who we are. Never make any apologies for how you were born. It's a version of Ray's laugh, isn't it?" I'd always assumed as much.

"Yeah, it is. His was more of a cackle, though. It's very disturbing." Cort shudders beneath my hand as I caress his back.

"I kind of like the nickname Little Monster. It fits Ava's personality well." I smile to temper the climate of our conversation, but Monica is looking at us like we sprouted a second head anyway.

"How are ya doing, Monica?" Cortez gazes softly at his ex-lover. "That's a lovely blouse you're wearing."

*Awkward.*

"Thanks. I'm good. Better. I should probably go." Monica stammers at Cortez, but doesn't look away from the floor. "Listen, maybe we could have coffee or something soon, Kat." She tacks on, "I really meant everything I said earlier."

"Coffee? Actually, I think I would like that," I say with some surprise. "Maybe invite Queen, too." Monica smiles at me, and it's the first real smile I've ever seen on her face. It brightens her features and makes her rather pretty.

"Is Monica possessed?" Cortez asks after he closes the door behind her.

"Nah– I think we just had a girlfriend moment," I utter in shock.

I punch Cortez in the shoulder, and then swipe his feet out from underneath him. He lands on the sofa in a heap of twisted arms and legs. He sputters curses at me as he tries to right himself.

"What the fuck, Kat?" Cortez straightens his suit jacket and glares at me while sprawled across my sofa.

"That is for teaching Ava very, very bad things. But it was mostly for making several women hate my guts and I didn't know why." I give Cort a hand up off the couch. "So Monica and Kristal? They are interesting choices. They are nothing alike, except for periods of extreme bitchiness." Cort just shrugs at me– the bastard!

"Do I need to worry about any more women hating me on sight? I'd like to know why I'm getting bitch-glares, or being treated like shit."

"You should probably be worried," Cort says in all seriousness, and then he flashes me his patented shit-eating grin.

"Is my office monitored?" I whisper directly into Cort's ear as I pretend to give him a hug. I wrap my arms around his waist and bury my face into the crook of his neck. His arms automatically embrace me back.

"Yeah, everywhere is monitored. Both video and audio," Cort breathes, and then he leans back and gives me a '*what the fuck?*' look.

"Do you feel like taking a walk?" I pull away and pretend to stretch out my back. I groan a bit for added effect. "I could really use some fresh air. I hate being slumped over a desk all day, especially when I'm making up for all those missed days. I just gotta take a break and stretch my legs."

"All right. Sure." Cort nods at me. He's very perceptive, so he catches on to my plan to get away from Ezra's Big Brother eye in the sky.

I take Cort's hand in mine, and as I pass my desk, I quickly grab the letter and shove it into my pocket.

# Chapter Nine

"Where are all the eyes and ears?" I mutter to Cortez as we exit The Edge Building and start heading toward the park a few blocks south.

"Everywhere," he breathes, sounding just as annoyed by the truth as I am. "Ezra wasn't always this way, and neither was Marcus. After we got back from… Well, Marc started it, really. He wouldn't let us go anywhere without protection. That was when Roarke was brought in by my mother-in-law, Pearl. Like Aaron's father, Roarke's was also a guard for the Holden family. They thought it best if we had guards our age, who would blend in as if we were friends hanging out."

"And Roarke was a cop. So that was an added bonus," I add.

"Yeah, but that wasn't good enough for Marc. Alpha males go a bit nuts when the people they think they should protect get hurt, so he started monitoring us via audio at first. It was Ezra who trumped Marc with the video. It's everywhere. Even in our vehicles."

"Ezra's *that* nuts?" I gasp out.

"Yes, but the vehicles weren't Ezra's doing," Cort admits, voice rough with annoyance. "Marc is the one hijacking our lives most of the time. It's a little game he and I play, removing his eye in the sky from my car."

"I couldn't live like that." I mutter. "It's unfathomable. I refuse to live like this."

"Marcus is only five years older than us. Ez and I were twelve when Marc was dropped off at Shadow Haven like an adopted puppy. It was his grandmother's way of a slow transition for Marc, before he married Diane when he reached the age of majority. He was still attending Hillbrook at the time. That shit tends to bond people."

"Fucked up. The elite are just—"

"Fucked up. Yeah, trust me. I get that more than anyone ever would," Cort mumbles, frustration and shame thickly lacing his voice. "Unless it's a property Ez owns or knows someone who owns it, or a vehicle Marc can have Aaron tamper with, we have privacy."

"Except for being followed," I mutter, rubbing the back of my neck. My Chrysalis tattoo is burning, as it always does when someone is staring at me. Since I got back to Dominion, every time I leave The Edge Building, I feel targeted, and now I know why.

"I'm sure Ez sent Roarke after us when we left, but Roarke will leave us be. Whereas Aaron would be holding your hand while texting Ez with the other. Usually I just punch Aaron and tell him to get the fuck off my ass."

"Why is it that Ezra has Roarke and Aaron, and you don't have a bodyguard?"

"I'm not the head of a family," Cort says, and he doesn't elaborate any more.

"With as obsessively safety-conscious as Ezra and Marcus are, I wouldn't think being the head of a family would matter two-licks to them when it comes to protecting you."

"Who says I'm not being watched?" Cort takes my hand in his, weaving our fingers together, and then he gives me a little squeeze. "All I said was that Aaron and Roarke aren't *my* bodyguards."

My eyes dart in every direction as Cort and I walk down North Avenue during the lunch rush. Cars are clogging the street, all going in the same direction, fleeing work for the next hour. The sidewalks are teeming with pedestrians. There is no way I could pick out who is watching us and who isn't. There are too many places to hide, and too many people to hide behind.

"I'm a bit of a recluse, anyway. I don't go many places alone: Edge, Restraint, Whittenhower Estates, Shadow Haven, and I visit James Atwater at his place. All of which are heavily monitored by those idiots. So, when I'm not with Ez or surrounded by his flunkies, Marc usually has someone tailing my ass. I tend to just forget about it, until it blends into the background."

"I couldn't live like that," I mutter, disgusted.

"Sure you could, because you have been, whether you realized it or not," Cort admits, startling me to death. "But I can tell you this, we are alone right now. No trailing Roarke, and my usual companion is at his day job. So we're about as private as we're going to get. So spill why you're acting so fucking squirrelly, Kat."

Cortez and I settle on a park bench a few blocks from The Edge Building. This is where I always go to get some fresh air and to stretch my legs. After three decades of living amongst the forest and lakes and rivers in my area, it's strange to be surrounded by metal, glass, and concrete. I found the nearest patch of green the moment I moved to Dominion.

The park is filled with people eating sack lunches with their noses in books or their fingertips clicking away on their cellphones. No one is paying us any mind, so why do I still feel as if I'm being watched by a malevolent force?

I didn't notice my constant state of surveillance before because it was positive. It was because Ezra was looking out for my safety. My newest stalker is not a benevolent creature, that's for damned sure.

I brought Cortez to this location because it wouldn't look out of the ordinary to my original stalker if I went to where I usually go. Not that my stalker is creating the sensation that is creeping down my neck again. I'm not sure who is watching me, but it's most definitely not Ezra. I try to rub the creepy-crawlies away, but it seems to only intensify the feeling.

"Do you feel that?" My eyes dart around wildly, flicking everywhere but not lighting on anyone in particular. There are too many people to just pick one out of the crowd as the sole source of the sensation. Whoever it is could be hiding in plain sight.

"What?" Cort gazes around in confusion. "I don't feel anything, but I'm desensitized to it after all these years."

"It feels like someone is watching us. My intuition is picking it up, making my skin crawl." My tone holds hints of paranoia, but I can't help how I feel. I rub my palm against the nape of my neck, trying to wash the vile sensation away.

"I don't feel anything, Kat. Maybe you're just stressed out after everything recently. You've been through a lot– more than most people can handle." Cort rests his arm over my shoulders and pulls me into the safety of his embrace. "I mean, it's not like Ezra doesn't have every shit you've taken catalogued or anything." He tries to make light, but for a moment I wonder if he's being serious.

"Yeah, I thought that at first, too, like I was being paranoid. But I felt it twice yesterday. Basically, it's every time I've left the building since I returned to Dominion. I feel it again right now. But hang on… there's more."

I reach into my pocket and pull out the reason I know I'm not losing my freakin' mind. I hand Cortez the note that arrived this morning– the note that has become the center of my universe.

Cort unfolds the piece of paper, revealing the paragraph of handwritten script in precise, masculine cursive. Brain registering the gravity of the situation, Cort meets my eyes with ones filled with terror– terror I've held off since I first read the note.

I retrieve the paper from Cort's trembling fingertips, and read it again and again, until the words blur together from my shaking hand.

*You'll beg for your life, whore! I'll force you to fight back. Your sharp screams and weak struggles will bring me immense pleasure. My son can't save you this time. There is no escaping me, and when I'm finished using your body, I'll dump your broken corpse into the lake like the worthless waste that it is.*

"Do you still think I'm just being paranoid?" I demand, voice cracking.

Cort doesn't respond. He just continues to stare at me wide-eyed with his jaw hanging loose and his tan skin turning pallid. Sweat beads on his forehead to slide in a wet line down his temple.

I don't freak out, because one of us has to stay lucid, logical, and in control enough to keep my ass alive, and judging by Cort's lack of composure, that person is going to have to be me.

"I don't know who sent it. It reads like it's from Ray, but it can't be, because he's still in the penitentiary. It has to be a copycat, someone who wants me gone? The people in your life would challenge me directly– one of your ex-submissives would just punch me in the face. Maybe it's someone from Ezra's life? Do you think it could be Adelaide?" My voice cracks, and I hate appearing so weak. "It has to be someone with knowledge of my past."

I need to have an open mind to figure out what's going on. I can't be blinded by fear, which is exactly what my annoying note writer is hoping will happen. I'll be so distracted by blind panic, thrust back into the past, that I won't notice what's happening in my present. No fucking way.

Cortez draws me tight against his body and squeezes until I almost suffocate. He breathes into my neck, almost hyperventilating. "Let's get the hell out of here. We're sitting ducks. We have to talk somewhere Ezra can't listen in but has four walls, so I don't have to worry about watching our backs. Our room at Restraint has an electronic jammer I installed myself. C'mon, let's go."

# Chapter Ten

I would have bitched and complained when we acquired a bosom buddy on our walk from the park, past Edge, and all the way to Restraint. But Roarke was kind enough not to say a word, and he left us the second we entered the building. I didn't even care that he was probably calling Ezra with our whereabouts. In a way, I was comforted by that knowledge.

My shit is together as we sit in the private dungeon at Restraint, thank goodness. However, Cortez's is not.

"We can't go through this again! We won't survive it this time, and I just don't mean our deaths!" Cort screeches. He grabs a cane from its home on the wall, and violently beats the spanking bench until he's out of breath.

"What do we do? Who do you think it is?" I curl up on the sofa, cradling a pillow to my chest. "Cort, it's going to be all right. Please calm down," I say in a soothing voice. I need him to be able to think, and his temper is amping up my fear.

The cane breaks in half from the force of Cort's hits. He stares at the piece in his hand as if it somehow offends him because it's broken. With slow deliberation, he picks the broken piece up off of the floor, and then whips it across the room, thoroughly disgusted with its existence. The cane spears the wall like an arrow, vibrating with the force. Cortez turns to me with wild eyes, blinking away his tantrum.

When Cort finally sees how terrified I am, he schools his expression and walks toward me. "I don't know who," Cort admits reluctantly as he sits down on the sofa.

"We don't have the luxury of freaking the fuck out, Cort. Self-preservation demands we keep a level head."

"I realize this. I apologize." Cort leans back, settling next to me on the sofa. "First things, first. We need to make sure Ray is still locked up. Second, I think it's best if we don't tell anyone else while we narrow down the suspect list."

Frightened, I grip the pillow tightly to my chest like a comfort object. "Why?"

"Because Ezra and Marc tend to freak the fuck out, and not like my childish display. We'd be on lockdown, without any constitutional freedoms."

"Yeah, I can't live like that," I murmur, shuddering at the thought. "I'd rather be attacked out of nowhere than live a life of fear."

"It's no one connected to me or Aaron. We're not important enough to anyone else. Men like Ezra have their loved ones used as pawns, and I'm untouchable. However, you are not."

The questions stream from my mouth like water. "What do you mean? Why me? Why are you untouchable? Who would target Ezra?"

"Don't ask what you don't want to know," Cort whispers almost too quietly for me to discern the words. "Only two people of interest in our lives would have their bullshit trickle down to affect you, Kat. Marcus and Ezra. Marc keeps a pretty low profile for political reasons, which leaves Ezra, who can never leave well enough alone. So, anyway, this is definitely connected to Ezra, *because* of Ezra."

"Why am I not surprised?" I grumble, disgusted, and then fear washes over me. "What about Ava?"

"Untouchable," Cort uses the word as if it has a different definition than the one found in any of my dictionaries. "Not many know what really happened to all of us, but I know everyone who does."

"Adelaide?" pops out before I can stop it.

"Yeah, she knows," Cort grits out. "I'll try to talk to Ezra to see what's going on with him and Ade without letting out too much. I'll ask around, see what else I can find."

"What do we do in the interim?" I squeeze the pillow and bury my face into it.

"I'll tell Aaron not to leave Ezra's side, which won't be unusual. I'd tell Roarke the same, but the man is too observant not to figure out something is wrong. I can't tell anyone else, because they are either Ezra's or Marc's minions."

"That sounds so fucking odd," I mumble, marveling at how different the lives of the rich and influential are from the lowly nobodies. "This is way outside of my spectrum."

An embarrassed expression flashes over Cortez's face, as if he's not proud of the life he was born into. "It's all I know. You and I need to stick together. So I'm going to go to work with you from now on, which won't be strange since I'm supposed to be writing a book. But I'm blocked."

"What? You're blocked?" I squeak out, worried even more.

"Forget that I said that," Cort brushes it off. "I'll help with the editing, or some shit."

Flabbergasted, I shout, "You suck at editing! I edit your books, remember? You suck!"

"I suck at writing right now, too, but that doesn't mean I don't see other author's fuck-ups. Deal with it," Cort brooks no room for argument. "You're stuck with me, even in your office. Honestly, we need to stay in The Edge Building. No walking outside. If we go somewhere, we need to go from one underground parking garage to the next. I don't trust being out in the open like we were at the park. Edge, Shadow Haven, and Restraint have top-of-the-line security."

"Yeah, so much so that Ava can hack into them," I murmur sarcastically.

"Regina— Queen. She created the system, that's how I know how to run it. I just showed Ava how to play around with the harmless stuff. Trust me. It's secure," Cort stresses. "Shit! What are we going to do?" He leans backward and pounds his head on the back of the sofa.

"Well, we know what we can't do. We can't tell Ezra, or else he'll put us on lockdown. What if this is just some sick prank? I really don't want to spend every second of my life trapped inside our apartment with the workmen. It'd be the same as being in prison. We can't allow whoever this is to change us. They want to frighten me, so I won't let them," I say boldly, but inside I don't feel so bold.

"F-u-c-k," Cort draws the word out. "The workmen. I have to do another background check on them, and make sure it's thorough this time." He pulls my head into his lap and places a hand on my hair, fingertips working through the stands in a soothing rhythm.

"Ah! Been there, done that— it's not happening, Cortez," I warn when his exquisiteness presses against my cheek. I struggle to get back up, but he offers me little wiggle room.

"I've already apologized for taking your mouth like that, Kitten. We're way past that. I just want to hold you. I'm not trying for anything. Honest." Cort starts petting my hair like it's a comfort to him.

Relenting, I snuggle down into Cort's lap for the remainder of our conversation. "Whoever this is, you say they are connected to Ezra, trying to hurt him through me. So, we have to protect Ezra from this, even from himself." I roll my face on Cort's thigh, drying the tears that have escaped.

"Agreed," Cort whispers, suddenly sounding husky. He pulls me farther into his lap, and then crushes me to his chest. "I can't lose Ezra. I can't. There are very few people in my life who matter, and if I lost them, it would kill me. Ezra is one of them; I would never survive his loss." Cortez's voice is thick with unshed tears and unadulterated fear.

"I know what you mean. If I lost some people in my life, it would hurt. Whereas others, it would kill a small piece of me. I think I would rather die than lose one or two of you," I admit, and I'm shocked to realize it's true.

I hadn't realized how much Ezra and Cortez have come to mean to me. I drop all pretenses and just meld myself to Cortez. I bury my face in his neck and inhale. I realize that Cortez and Ezra smell almost identical, a perfect melding of their natural scents mixed with a little bit of mine. It's the scent of home.

"I don't know how to ask this without insulting you, Cortez. So I'll say I'm sorry in advance." With a deep breath, I blurt out, "What about Divina? Would your wife be angry enough at me for being with you that she'd threaten me?"

Cortez's body shakes against mine in silent laughter. "You act as if Divina is the wicked witch." He continues to laugh, but fails at silence. He starts to snort.

Blushing profusely, "What?" I sound as embarrassed as I feel.

"All right, it's time for this conversation. But, first, why do you hate Divina?" Cort bites back his laughter, but just barely.

"Cort, I don't hate Divina at all. I'm trying to respect her. The reason I'm not having sex with you isn't for a lack of wanting. It's because it's disrespectful to the both of us– Divina *and* me. I only asked because the note was directed at me, and I don't know if Divina knows about me or not."

I try to pull away again, but Cort doesn't allow it. If anything, he tightens his hold. The thought of wives and fiancées makes me angry– angry at myself for sharing a bed with them last night. It's emotional cheating, and I would hate the woman who would do that to my husband. I'm a faithless piece of shit and I deserve anything Karma throws my way.

"Of course Divina knows about you," Cort drawls out while shaking some sense into me. "Divina has been begging to meet you for weeks. Do you have any idea how excited my family is over Ava?"

I murmur quietly, not truly wishing for Cortez to hear me because of the underlying insecurities. "No, Ezra doesn't talk to me about these things, so I assume your family doesn't even know we exist, or they do and they just don't care."

"Damn, Ezra's a fucking moron sometimes, Kat. Just remember the lunatic is not infallible. He makes more mistakes than all of us combined."

"I'll remind him of that later," I mutter wryly. "Does your family know about Ava?" I don't ask about myself because I'm a nonissue. My daughter is part of their family now, whether they accept her or not. I'm just the woman who Ezra impregnated by accident.

"Of course, Kat." Cort squeezes me tighter, as if he can feel how tumultuous my emotions are this very instant. "Marc, Dexter, and I were having lunch with James Atwater when Ezra ran in, shouting about his long-lost daughter. We all went to Pennsylvania immediately. We didn't go inside your house, but we all sat inside the SUV, waiting for a report."

"Jesus," I hiss in utter disbelief. "Why?"

"Our family is dinky, Kat, and dying out. Everyone assumed Ezra was gay and would never procreate, completely killing several family lines. Any child Ezra begets will be treated like royalty. So rest assured, Divina is not the one sending you scary notes." Cort wipes tears of laugher from his eyes as he responds to me.

"I don't understand." I squint up at him. "Why would any wife be okay with that? Doesn't Divina have any self-respect?"

"Divina is family, not only my wife but Ezra's cousin. I've known her for just as long as I've known Ezra." Cort's voice is laced with an immense depth of affection. "We were raised with each other by our mothers."

"Do you love her?" My voice sounds small and sad. Upon hearing it, Cort hugs me closer and nuzzles my ear.

"Yes, as a sister and a very dear friend. There are some strange circumstances to our marriage. Think of it as Royal England, and we're keeping the fortune in the family. My mother-in-law, Pearl, is Ezra's aunt. Diane and Pearl knew how Ezra and I felt about one another. They were worried that the Holden dynasty would be lost if neither of us ever had children, especially since it's impossible for us if we were together. With Divina as my wife, their fortunes are secure. Ezra will get the entire Holden inheritance, regardless of what happens."

"I don't understand. Wouldn't Divina want her share? Why is it all Ezra's?" Confusion warps my tone.

"Divina will never have to work a day in her life, and she never has. She will want for nothing."

"Why not require more of your daughters?" Somewhere deep in my depths, my inner feminist is stirring. "If my father had heard you right now, he'd break something."

"Divina has lupus." Cort's voice is filled with so much heartache and pain, that I nearly suffocate beneath the weight of its grief.

Tears immediately spring to my eyes. "I'm so sorry."

"Divina is doing well right now, but she can never have children. We're thankful for every day her health holds out, which is why she is my wife. Ezra is the Holden heir. It's just Pearl, Diane, Divina, and Ezra. None of the ladies can bear any more children– age and disease. It was important that they protected their assets. We aren't talking about some pocket change, here. When your future is dependent on the survival of one individual, you protect him like you do your king in chess."

"Roarke and Aaron," I whisper, understanding dawning on why Ezra has constant surveillance and not Cortez.

"Pearl and Diane are as close as any sisters will ever be. My mother was their best friend, and together they raised us. I was born to be Ezra's companion. Just as Aaron and Roarke were born to protect him. They just didn't anticipate Ezra being gay, or our sick fascination with one another. So Pearl feared for her family line, and my marriage to Divina was insurance for the future."

"Yeah, but Divina's half would go to you," I say, logic twisting my tone. Cort just shrugs as if saying '*yeah, so?*' "I still don't understand," I mutter in confusion.

"Sometimes I think we have to hit you upside the head for you to get a clue," Cort sounds as if he's teasing, but there is an underlying edge of resentment peeking through. "I guess, I need to spell it out. I am married– *in name only* –to Ezra's cousin, to ensure the fortune stays in the family. Diane and Pearl see Ezra and me as partners. They are secure in the knowledge that their fortune is in safe hands."

"I'm confused as to why Divina didn't fall in love and get married. It feels like she's giving her life up to Ezra, like he's a spoiled prince or something." The feminist in me is rising closer and closer to the surface.

"Kat, Divina's disease is *bad*. There are no guarantees for her. She didn't want to fall in love with someone and have to worry about whether or not they were after her money– that if she were to perish, they would destroy everything her great-grandfather, grandfather, mother and aunt had built over lifetimes. Life is too short for that much stress– especially hers if she isn't careful. This is less stressful for her."

"Yeah, but Divina needs to live while she has the chance. I don't get selfless people." I shake my head angrily.

"Trust me; Divina lives just fine." Cort chuckles to himself. "She lives the life of someone who fears they don't have long to live, even though she could live to a ripe old age if she continues to take her medication and keeps her health in check. She's not wilting away at Shadow Haven. She travels the world, taking any lover who strikes her interest. Divina is happier than the rest of us, by far."

"I wasn't talking about Divina being selfless. What about you, Cort? Don't you want to marry the person you're in love with?" Cort shudders beneath me, as if I just struck the most potent of cords within him.

"This is for the family, Kat. The family who took in an orphan boy as if he was one of their own. They loved me, cared for me, educated me, and made me a part of their lives. I have no family except for Ezra, and I'd do anything in my power to protect him. If you can't marry the love of your life, isn't it better to marry for the love of family?"

There is a deep well of sadness in Cort's voice, and I know he wishes he could marry Ezra. Cort and I understand each other better than we realize. We both want the same thing— Ezra all to ourselves, when the man in question gives a part of himself to so many people.

Our state allows same-sex marriages. I'm confused as to why Cort didn't just marry Ezra in the first place. So I ask, "Why didn't you just marry Ezra?"

"I'm not gay," Cort rasps roughly. "Even though Ezra goes around shouting it from the rooftops, the man has been in more vaginas— I don't mean forced, either –than he's had dick. Ezra has never even been inside a dude before. Truthfully, I doubt Ezra and I could be happy without a female in our lives."

"So play around at Restraint," I say like it's that obvious. "You're already married and screwing around, what's the difference?"

"Atop the mountain of reasons of why I hate Ezra as much as I love him, gay marriage wouldn't have impacted my career. But it could quite possibly destroy the highly devout Catholic Holdens and the Jewish Zeitlers. Ezra is the media's golden boy. The more papers the Billionaire Bachelor sells, the more money he brings in for political donations for Marcus and charitable donations for Diane. We feel smothered by Ezra, but he has even less freedom than we do."

"Anonymity," I breathe.

"Yeah, that's also why we can't let anyone at Restraint know who we are, with the exception of the masters and a few people who are in our daily lives. The rest of the members can't know. I don't like wearing that hood. I liked it better when the dungeon was our own personal playroom, but things change."

"Restraint wasn't always like this?"

"No. When it first started, it was just Marcus, Dexter, and Ezra bullshitting. They opened the club, and a few years later, Marc declared the dungeon open for business. It was a good idea until the chaos started. It snowballed, and now we're having a hard time containing it." Cortez pulls me farther into his lap until I'm straddling his hips. "Enough talk of monsters, marriage, and mergers." He grins mischievously.

"I'm still not having sex with you, Cort." I shift off his lap until I'm firmly on a sofa cushion.

"Why not?" Cort's crestfallen tone makes me feel bad for denying him anything. He looks into my face, desperately trying to read me.

"I have to meet Divina first. You could be lying to me. Frankly, I'm just really confused at the moment. I have so much shit going down. I don't think having a relationship with *anyone* is a good idea right now. I need to get my life in working order before I move onto my sex life."

"You're just scared, that's all. Being afraid doesn't make the feelings go away," Cortez says with confidence while projecting an arrogant vibe, like he's thinking about how easy it will be to get into my panties.

"I don't know what you're talking about," I mutter insolently while folding my arms over my chest.

"Sure ya don't." Cortez smirks knowingly. "I'll wear you down eventually. As for Ezra, you're screwed either way. Whether you have sex with him or not, it won't take your feelings away."

"I don't have any feelings for Ezra," I mutter defiantly.

"Uh-huh, riiiigggghhhhtt," Cortez draws out. "Sure ya don't. You don't have to admit it, because I will admit it for you. I know you're in love with Ezra. No one on this planet understands how difficult it is to avoid Ezra as much as I do. I also know you're scared you will fall for me, too. I'm not an idiot, Kat."

"No, not an idiot. You're just fucking arrogant and cocky." I turn away from Cort, refusing to look at him. I'm pissed because he's absolutely correct.

Cortez's hand flashes out to grip the front of my neck. His fingertips tighten to the point of pain– almost bruising. He nips my ear, and I cry out from the sensation.

"We may have a psycho on our hands, Katya. We need comfort. We need each other. You will *not* pull away from Ezra *or* me. You will share our bed, so we all will sleep soundly. I don't like watching Ezra fret all night, wandering from room to room and building to building. You will give Ezra peace, or I will cuff you to our bed. You don't have to screw, fuck, or make love to us– whatever you want to call it. You are one of us, and there's no denying it anymore."

"I'm scared," I whisper as if it's the gravest secret I hold.

"I know that, sweetheart." Cortez lightly kisses my cheek and enfolds me in his arms.

I'm overcome with an insane urge to cry. No, not just cry. Bawl. Howl. Scream. Weep.

I'm so damn scared. I know I'm in love with Ezra. I can admit it. I told Cortez not so long ago that I wanted to be someone's number one. The loves of my life already have number ones– each other. At this point, I don't even know where to place Adelaide. I'm just so confused.

I don't know my place in their hierarchy. But it doesn't matter, because I'll always be someone's number one...

MY OWN.

# Chapter Eleven

Cort and I wait in Dexter's private room for my first lesson. If it weren't for the vicious hate mail, I would be nervous. When you've lived through some death-defying wicked shit, everyday wicked is a cakewalk.

I was vetoed on the suggestion of using our room for the lesson. I felt more comfortable surrounded by Ezra's affinity for the color gray, than Dexter's penchant for Victorian Era furnishings. For the life of me, I just cannot see Dexter, the IRS agent sadist, dominating in a space straight out of a twisted historical romance novel.

I had asked Cortez if Dexter picked out the décor himself or if it was standard issue, and I was shocked to learn that Dexter did in fact pick out everything in the space, right down to the velvet throw pillows.

"I'm not in the mood for this tonight," I mutter out the side of my mouth. Cortez and I lean against the wall, waiting for our sadist mentor to arrive. "I was really looking forward to it, too. Now I just feel apathetic about everything."

"I thought you'd do just about anything for a chance to play with Dexter." Cort winks at me, and a resulting blush creeps up from my chest.

"I just want to be at home where I can see that everyone is okay. We either have the monster, a pissed off ex-submissive, or a rich bitch sending me threatening notes. I need to see with my own two eyes that everyone is all right."

Cort smirks at me like I'm doing something cute. "You sound so much like Ezra right now, it isn't even funny. Spooky is more like it."

"Well, most of the time I act like you," I mutter flippantly. "That's why Ezra and you like me so much. The aspects you love in each other are combined in me– all inclusive with a vagina and tits." I roll my eyes at Cort. But it's the truth. A hard truth I've just now come to realize.

Temper boiling over because he finally has a target for his aggression, Cort shouts angrily at me. "Ezra is right. You're a fucking twit if you believe that shit!"

"How do you know Ezra called me a twit?" Confusion twists my voice, and on the heels of the confusion is hurt. But I expected nothing less than Ezra spilling our sordid tales.

"Wow!" Cortez shakes his head in utter disbelief at my level of stupidity. "You really are a twit, aren't you? Just think for a moment. Do you honestly believe that I wasn't nearby when Ezra was with you– *every single time* he was with you?" Cort's gray eyes bore into mine to drive his point home.

I wince.

"Thanks, Cort." I pat myself on the back while scowling, "Just twist the knife deeper while you're back there, why don't ya? I get that you two are like this–" I cross my fingers and push them in front of his face.

It's easier to be angry than afraid. Cort and I are just alike, lashing out at each other instead of our common enemy. Our fear is so palpable that I'm choking on it. Ultra-sensitive, every emotion and sensation is heightened. Like the perfect storm, our emotions are converging into a stew that could turn catastrophic. Even though I recognize this, I cannot stop myself from being irrational.

"I get that I'm on the bottom of the list. *I get it.*" I croak out the last part. I swallow hard on my unshed tears. My eyes burn and my throat tightens as I fight to stop my emotions from erupting.

*I will not cry. I will not cry.*

"Jesus." Cort tries to pull me into a hug.

"No… don't… please…" Sounding pitiful, I push my fists into Cort's chest, holding him at arm's length. "Please. Don't."

"You can be exceedingly absurd sometimes, you know that? I don't know how your brain spins reality into a nightmare. Shit! It's not like that, Kat." Cort tries to pull me in again, but the door opening saves me from myself.

Dexter strolls in, whistling a jaunty little tune, completely ignorant to the shit-storm brewing between Cortez and me. Channeling all my pain, frustration, and fear into lust, my mouth dries up at the sight of Dexter.

I have a veritable buffet waiting for me at home. But the violence contained within the small package known as Dexter Hayes, still flips a switch inside me.

At the edge of my consciousness lies another fear, one darker than all the others. With all the petrifying information

I've heard of Ezra's adoptive father, I'm terrified of the moment when I finally meet him. If Dexter, with his bronze skin, amber eyes, dark ringlets, and suffocating power does this to me, what the fuck will Marcus force me to feel?

Lips curving deviously, Dexter smirks at me, as if he somehow senses the direction of my wayward thoughts.

My God, I feel like a whore for lusting after so many men. It's like thirty-two years of suppressed sexuality is releasing itself all at once, my sanity be damned. The only consolation is that just because I find them scrumptious, doesn't mean I have to act upon it.

I can fantasize about it, though. No one will ever have to know the depravity in my private thoughts. I just have to accept the fact that it doesn't make me a piss-poor human being to lust after people I don't love... or do love, as the case may be.

I chance a glance at Cort, eyes cutting in his direction, only to find him examining me. I'm struck dumb. I truly am a twit. These two, highly observant men are dominants– part of their gift is reading their submissive. They aren't reading my mind, just my body language.

I try to school the dumb-shit look on my face and slow my breathing as a way of pretending I'm not feeling what I'm feeling. I want my private thoughts kept private. When you have no control over your life, you should be able to own your thoughts at least.

"You need to behave, Kat," Cortez cautions me, proving I suck at pretend.

I flash Cort an innocent look in response, and he snorts at me. I'm pretty sure he whispers '*Lusting after Dexter, how very Ezra of you*' underneath his breath. I arch an eyebrow in question, and he just shrugs.

Dexter stands before us holding a piece of fancy paper with handwriting on it. He clears his throat, looks at the pair of us, and then back down at the paper.

"Here are the rules as commanded by Master Ez," Dexter begins in a deep, resonant voice. "No sex with the mentor or the submissive. You may touch the chest and ass of the submissive. You are here to learn by example with mild instruction on the submissive. You are not to touch the instructor unless necessary for your education. All scenes must take place in private. Failure to adhere to the aforementioned rules will result in punishment by your master."

At the last part about punishment, the sadist smiles to himself as he flips the piece of paper over to continuing reading from the backside. A deep, surprised-filled laugh spills from his lips when he comprehends Ezra's words.

"As a reward for your hard work and your mentor's dedication, a scene of your master's choosing will be performed in the dungeon with an audience. Call it a graduation of sorts." Dexter bursts out laughing. "Is that what Ezra's calling the initiation now?"

"Oh. My. God." Cortez breathes while shuddering next to me. "Katya will have an initiation. Ezra won't know how to handle that. We will witness a level of insanity to the likes of which we've never before…"

"Jesus. Nothing good ever happens at an initiation. Even Pretty Boy's was mildly disturbing."

"Not for me," Cort mutters wistfully. "By far, Syn's and my initiation was the worst."

"I don't know about that. Queen's was rather torturous, while yours was merely a threat with explosive results. Dalton and Alex didn't even have an initiation because we were all too terrified to play witness."

"Nah, Marc just didn't have it in him to harm them in any way. He sent them a cookie cake with '*Maître du Jeu*' in blood-red frosting. I was there when it arrived, and neither asshole would share with me," Cort pouts. "You know how much I love chocolate chip."

"Thank God, we're getting another female. There's been far too much cock around here for my tastes," Dexter grumbles, causing Cort to cackle in response. "If Aaron ever decides to become a master, I fear for that initiation."

"Bloody hell," Cortez whispers, sounding petrified. "Maybe Marcus will take pity on all of us, and send Aaron a bouquet of flowers, or a CandyGram."

I make my presence known. "I'm standing right here, yet it seems you are both speaking a foreign language. Care to share with the class?"

"No," Dexter issues a denial, and then clears his throat, preparing to read more of Ezra's BDSM code of conduct. "Kitty

Kat," he looks at me and actually blushes. "If you behave during your lessons by exhibiting great restraint, I will reward you and your mentor with a no-holds-barred scene between the two of you in our private room, witnessed by Cortez and myself."

Dexter abruptly stops reading. A pained expression flashes over his face while the seam in his leathers strains against the erupting bulge.

"I don't know if I can read this aloud." Dexter groans while shuffling around uncomfortably from foot to foot. "In other words, a free fuck to satisfy your obvious curiosity with your mentor." Dexter chokes out the last part. "It would have been easier if Ezra hadn't told us that until after the initiation. Now the temptation will be far worse with the knowledge of our reward."

I can't help it; my eyes devour Dexter. He exudes something potent– primal. I close my eyes to the vision of him fucking Heidi in the dungeon, all coiled power and unleashed violence. My God, I get to have that if I behave. My pussy clenches so hard that I have to grab Cortez's arm for balance.

I open my eyes and they immediately seek Dexter out. He is staring back at me, panting wildly. His amazing leather pants are a whisper away from popping a seam from the tension of his burgeoning arousal.

Heart beating uncontrollably, pussy pulsing, dripping like a leaky faucet, I feel crazed.

"Breathe and behave," whispers in my ear, and it takes me a moment to realize who spoke to me.

I take a deep breath as I turn to Cortez. I try for innocent and fail. I settle for blushing and covering up my smile with the back of my hand.

"Your fascination with Dexter shouldn't turn me on, but–" Cortez abruptly takes my mouth in a bruising kiss. I either have to open my mouth for his invasion or cut my lips on my teeth. A seductive sound rolls up my throat as he sucks on my tongue.

Unhinged, fed up with the hesitation game I've been playing with him, Cort turns into his version of Master Ez from all those weeks ago. He roughly palms the back of my thighs, fingertips biting into my flesh, and lifts me onto the nearby spanking bench. He's on me in less than a second, leaning into me by wedging his hips between my legs. With a forceful yank to my hair, my head is arched backward. Cort's lips descend on my neck, mouth leaving a path of suction marks in its wake.

I'm surrounded by Cortez: his scent, his taste, the feel of his hard, hot body grinding into mine. Morals scattering to the wind, I make a conscious decision to savor his touch, knowing it will chase the stress and fear away. I lose myself unto him. I know nothing that isn't Cortez...

A throat clears brusquely. "As much as I've enjoyed the show, our submissive is here for our perusal. Plus, I'm not sure how much time you'll need once your post-coital tristesse sets in, as one or both of you is about to lose their shit when Ez finds out."

I blink out of my haze to find myself pressed underneath Cort, who is now missing a shirt and shockingly his pants are unfastened.

When had that happened?

Cort slowly rises off of me, straightening his back. With a wild, alarmed glint in his eyes, he begins tucking his *spent* exquisiteness back into his pants. Cort has marks all over his neck and chest from my teeth and lips– possessive suction and bite marks. Good thing I wasn't wearing my caps, or else I would have bloodied him.

I'm so absorbed by the sight of a panicked Cortez, an amused and aroused Dexter, and the newly arrived Heidi, that it takes me a few moments to put myself to rights.

My blouse is torn down the front– the buttons missing. My bra was either torn or bitten apart, judging by the jagged edges of the fabric. My left breast is completely exposed and decorated with fingertip bruises and teeth marks.

I pull my skirt down from around my waist, noticing my lack of underwear. I find my panties twisted around my right ankle, one leg hole torn out. I try my best to look dignified as I tug my panties past my black Mary Jane shoe. An understated, modest shoe and a very skanky, hot pink panty. I don't even blush. However, I turn a bright shade of crimson as I use said panties to dry my moistened thighs and snatch.

No way is all that juice from me. The look of concern on Cort's face informs me that he had, in fact, contributed to the mess.

Jesus, how did we get so far so fast? I'm tempted to reach down to check to see if Cortez came inside of me. It's like I blacked out from lust. I whimper involuntarily when I brush my legs together, causing a delicious spasm to radiate up from my pussy. Somehow I climaxed, yet I don't remember a second of it. My entire body tremors like a bird settling its feathers.

"You have to take Katya home and fuck her– *both of you*," Dexter stresses. "Every damn night. I can't train her if she's keyed up like this. Kat's needs call to mine, and I want to relieve her of the ache. At least get her off before we train. Cortez, are you listening to me?" Dexter growls while staring at a very confused Cortez Abernathy.

"Yes," Cortez mutters softly to Dexter. "I… I don't know what that was. I… don't know if I was marking *my* territory because Kat was looking at you like she wanted to devour you, or if I was marking Ezra's territory *for* him." Hiding his face in his hands, Cort cries out, "Jesus Christ, he's going to kill me."

"I'm pretty sure you were marking Katya as yours," Dexter laughs out. "Spectacular."

Oozing guilt, Cortez turns to me without looking me in the eye. "Did I enter you? All I remember is kissing you, and then Dexter was telling us to stop. I know I finished– I know *that* much. It's like I blacked out or something." Cort runs his fingers through his short, dark hair, mussing it up.

"I… I… I don't know," I sputter out. Suffering from the fog of lust is my only explanation. "I'll check."

I turn to face the wall for some privacy. Shamelessly, I slide my hand down my skirt to my groin. I'm swollen and tender, and I'm also very wet and slippery. I slip one finger into myself and I'm hit with an intense aftershock. I bite my tongue against the sensation, containing a moan. I'm looser than I normally am. I try two fingers and meet some resistance, but not much.

"You were definitely inside me," I mumble in shock.

I just had sex with Cortez Abernathy, and I don't remember a second of it. How sad is that? It's a travesty of the highest order.

"Ez is going to kill me," Cortez cries out again, hiding his face behind his upraised palms.

"Why? Ezra said we could, not that I should have to ask him for permission on who I have sex with. So what am I missing?" I sound grumpy as all hell.

I wanted to remember having sex with Cort. I'm annoyed at myself that I didn't say no, but more so that I didn't get to experience it firsthand. Such a waste, because my body is screaming that it was epic.

"Kat, you're not on birth control. Ezra doesn't want you on it for obvious reasons, so he has to give me permission to cum inside you."

"Um... there's so much wrong with what you just said. I believe it's me who gets to decide if I'm on birth control, and who, if anyone, gets to cum inside of me. Assholes," I snarl.

"Ezra will kill me," quivers out of Cortez's mouth.

"Ah, there's the post-coital tristesse I've been waiting for," Dexter says cheerfully, a smile evident in his voice. "Nothing is as entertaining as when Cort loses his shit and Ezra gets angry... someone's getting lucky tonight," Dexter sings while rubbing his palms together.

Jabbing his finger in the direction of Dexter's chest, "Shut your goddamned mouth, you ass trespasser," Cortez threatens. "I'm not fucking around this time. Ezra is going to kill me." Cort groans, yanking at his hair in despair.

"Just bend Ezra over the nearest hard surface," Dexter offers helpfully. "That has always worked in the past."

"Kat!" Cort shouts while pointing at me. "Is a game-changer. As in filling her with a litter of calico kittens instead of Siamese."

Dexter and I both laugh at Cortez for that horrific pun– leave it to a word-weaver.

"We're good." I say more to reassure Cort than myself, because I have no idea if we're good or not. Honestly, I'm too terrified to acknowledge it. "You didn't finish inside me. You did on my thigh... and a little bit is on my slit, but not inside me."

"How can you be so sure?" Cort looks so hopeful that I'd tell him anything he ever wanted to hear just to make him feel better.

"I'm too tight for that; I met resistance. No way would I be tight if you had finished inside me. You're way too large for that." I shudder as I remember Cortez ramming his *'exquisite'* cock down my throat. My pussy spasms in need– she wants him back inside of her. "It's not the right time of the month to worry, anyway. I just had my monthly a few days ago."

Cort just levels me with a narrowed stare, not believing my bullshit lie about him not coming inside of me– we both know he did. I know because it's my body, and he knows because I'm not entirely sure he doesn't remember what transpired between us.

One of us blacking out: plausible.

Both of us blacking out: impossible.

Since I know without a shadow of a doubt I don't remember shit, it makes me wonder if Cortez Abernathy is lying to himself.

"I wish I could remember what happened, because by the looks of us, it must've been fan-fucking-tastic." I can't help it, I bark a sharp laugh at the idiocy of the situation. I finally had sex with Cortez, and I can't remember a second of it. The only thing I remember is the sensation of rightness, and that's it.

"It was fantastic to watch," Dexter admits, traces of awe still lacing his voice. "You were definitely fucking each other, and neither of you were quiet about it, either. I heard some interesting things, especially on your part, Cortez." Dexter smirks at us.

"Tell me," I beg, voice quivering.

"I've never seen anything like that in my entire life, and that is saying something." Dexter reaches down to palm himself. "We have to get this show on the road before I spontaneously erupt."

"What did I say?" Cortez grabs Dexter's forearm to stop him.

"You'll tell Katya next time. It will mean more if she hears it from you, and actually remembers it. Right?" Dexter's face and voice are equally soft. "Give Kat your suit jacket– her state of undress is distracting me."

After I'm covered, I decide it's time to formally introduce myself to Heidi. I'm not sure how much she saw, but I'm not embarrassed. Maybe it's because I already watched Dexter fuck her, and I'm pretty sure I'm going to see it again really soon.

"Hi, I'm Kat," I say to Heidi as I extend my hand to her. Heidi's a short, plump woman with strawberry blonde hair, big hazel eyes, and peachy skin. I bet she's as soft as a peach, too.

"Hi. It's nice to meet you, Mistress." Heidi's cheeks pink as she looks to the floor in bashfulness or subservience, it's hard to tell which. Her hand is about the size of mine– small for an adult. I rub my thumb across her palm. She *is* as soft as a peach. I bet her skin pinks up nicely when lashed.

My body is satisfied from the blackout sex with Cortez, but my mind doesn't remember; it thinks it was really good foreplay. Seeing Heidi's downcast eyes and meek demeanor, my body has the urge to dominate her. My nostrils flare as I inhale air at a greater rate, drawing in the scents of the room. I abruptly drop Heidi's hand and step backward. I can't break the rules– no fucking the submissives.

"Assume the position, sub," Dexter orders. His voice is amused, because he's been watching me from the corner of his eye.

Heidi immediately drops to her knees, kneeling before her master. She perches her ass on her heels and widens her thighs. If she were nude, we would have a very appetizing view. Heidi's hands rest on her parted thighs, her chin is pointed downward, and her eyes are gazing at her master's feet.

"Katya, Heidi is demonstrating the submissive kneeling position. Perfection. Study how she is kneeling, as it will be useful for when you control a sub, as well as amuse Master Ez greatly if you were to honor him by kneeling at his feet. Imprint the position in your mind. I will test you on it next time."

"Yes, Master Dexter," I respond as I study Heidi.

Walking around the kneeling submissive in a tight circle, Dexter allows me time to imprint every single detail in my mind.

"Impeccable as always, Heidi. You're a very good girl. You may stand now." Dexter pats her hair, and then steps away. "The most important thing a dominant needs to learn is body language. It will tell you more than a submissive could put into words, more so than a safe-word ever could. Katya, I want you to study Heidi, and then tell me your observations. You have exactly two minutes, starting now."

I watch the beautiful woman for a few moments, and realize that I've been using body language my entire life for my own protection. That untapped knowledge becomes a useful tool to have right now.

"Heidi is pleased with your praise, and she is comfortable in our presence. I think she is awaiting her next command." I hope I'm right, because I can't see anything else.

"Very good, Kat." I want to preen from Dexter's approval.

"Heidi, please remove your clothing, and then approach the bench. I apologize in advance. This will not be a long session, for my patience is very thin this evening," Dexter admits, voice dripping with arousal.

"I wonder why?" Cort muses while shifting uncomfortably from foot to foot, causing Dexter to crack a smile.

Heidi immediately removes her dress, and I notice how quickly she moves when commanded. I like that. I also wonder if Dexter prefers dresses. Heidi wore one last time, too. I watch her every movement, cataloging them. She's comfortable with us watching. I remember that Dexter likes private scenes versus public ones, but engages in public for Heidi's needs.

Heidi has a delicate body, soft, fleshy, and ripe. No muscle definition is visible, just a nice layer of biteable padding. She isn't pudgy, but completely woman. She rests her shins on the padded supports and leans her belly on the bench. The position puts her round ass and the expanse of her back on display.

"Widen your stance, sub," Dexter commands, causing Heidi to slide her knees to the side, opening her sex to our sight. Her soft, pink lips are already swollen and glistening with her arousal. Heidi is definitely a natural, strawberry blonde.

"Kat?" Dexter gains my attention as he extends his hand, silently asking me to join him at the spanking bench. "Touch is another way to read your submissive, just as body language and vocal responses. Whereas people can lie with their words, not many have the talent to school their body's natural responses."

"Thank you," I whisper to Dexter, hoping Cortez can't hear me. "That will come in handy with '*Liar. Liar. Pants on fire.*'"

"Undoubtedly," Dexter agrees. "Katya, I want you to place your hand on Heidi's back, because I need you to learn from her movements as I work her."

I rest my palm between Heidi's shoulder blades, just beneath the nape of her neck. She rises to my hand, and that movement informs me how she welcomes my touch. I circle my palm, massaging Heidi's back, and she relaxes further.

"This is a riding crop." Dexter shows me a black stick that has a floppy piece of leather on the end. "I usually start with this for Heidi. I've been her dominant for the past two years, so I know what level to start her on. If it were just the two of you, I would suggest a soft flogger to start, and work up to more painful means. Beware: not all submissives enjoy pain, so you must negotiate with your submissive before you play. Some may only want restraints, or sensory deprivation, and others may want intense pain. We all have different needs to feed."

Dexter's hand whips back fast, causing the leather to strike Heidi's rear with a sharp '*thwack*' before I can even track the movement. I feel her tense beneath my hand as she hisses out a breath. A light pink mark boils to the surface of her ass.

"Look," Dexter orders in a husky tone, gesturing to Heidi's pussy.

I take a peek, and notice how Heidi is wetter than before because she enjoyed the spanking. Dexter hits her again, this time across both thighs, and she moans as if in ecstasy. I feel Heidi rise to meet the hit. In quick succession, Dexter lashes her several more times in different locations. Each time, Heidi moans louder and starts to wiggle on the bench for some much-needed relief.

"Sub, hold still," Dexter commands, and Heidi immediately stills. "Katya, would you be so kind as to massage Heidi's marks while I fetch another toy?"

I stand near Heidi's head, and lean down to smooth my hands across her back. She breaks out in goose bumps and shivers beneath my touch. I can hear her panting, but the vibration is more obvious to the palms of my hands. When I reach her mounded ass and massage, she begins to rub her cheek against my thigh.

I don't have to be a body language expert to read Heidi. I slide my hands down her rear to her thighs, while trying to avoid her ripe flesh. I notice a red mark directly across her pussy lips where Dexter must have hit her by accident. Even though I want to soothe Heidi's discomfort, I avoid her pussy since it's against the rules. It takes every ounce of my restraint not to rub the pain away.

I quickly massage the marks on Heidi's thighs, and she moans against my leg in thanks. I try not to notice her arousal gliding in droplets down her inner thigh. Unable to stop myself, I quickly swipe one droplet with my thumb, and then lean back feeling guilty.

I gaze up and notice how Cortez is pressed into the corner near the closed door, looking half-crazed. I think he's near the exit in case he has to escape. Dexter stands near Heidi's feet, studying me.

I'm slow tonight. Dexter was testing me. He placed the hit on Heidi's cunny to see if I would follow the rules set down by Master Ez. I can tell by Dexter's pleased expression that I passed with flying colors.

Recklessness overpowers me in the face of Dexter's silent praise. Proving I'm just as dominant, I issue my own test for my mentor. I hold his warm, amber eyes as I lift my thumb to my mouth. I draw my thumb slowly past my lips, and I barely avoid closing my eyes as I taste Heidi's essence on the back of my tongue. The deviant in me wants to watch the men's reactions as I savor the taste of Heidi's pussy.

I gain power through the knowledge that I was strong enough, sensual enough, and cunning enough to unleash their self-control. *I* dominated Master Dexter and Cortez.

The creak of the door opening draws my gaze, and I catch the sight of the back of Cortez's white shirt just before the door closes behind him. The dull thud of something hitting the floor draws my attention in the opposite direction. A paddle lies at Dexter's feet, where he is frozen in indecision, with his eyes wide, mouth parted, and nostrils flaring wildly.

I lick my thumb one last time and savor Heidi's taste. On my satisfied sigh, Dexter tears his leather pants open at the fly, as if he's sprouted claws. I don't even get a chance to enjoy the sight of his arousal before he's sheathing his cock deep inside Heidi with a powerful lunge of his hips.

In less than a second, Dexter screams out his frustrations. Never breaking eye-contact with me, Dexter fucks Heidi violently– spanking bench wobbling on its feet against the floor with each and every thrust.

*Bang.* Grunt. *Rattle. Bang.* Grunt. *Rattle.*

I lean forward and caress Heidi's back during Dexter's continuous onslaught. Heidi mews against my thigh, licking my skin like her name is Kitten.

It doesn't take long for Dexter to reach completion. But the entire time I envision my initiation, where I become a Mistress of Restraint in the mysterious group called Maître du Jeu. I will not break any of the rules Master Ez threw down, because I will not destroy my only chance to change my fate.

I will be their equal. I will be a Mistress of Restraint, standing with my head held high next to Marcus, Dexter, Ezra, Cortez, Syn, Queen, II, Dalton, and Alex. I will have enough power to be in control of my own destiny.

As an added incentive, knowing I could be with Dexter if I behave is a temptation that will be difficult to pass up. Dexter with his bronze skin glistening with sweat, with his tight, black ringlets swaying with his movements, and with his lean muscles using all of that coiled power to propel his every thrust.

Dexter's potent virility enraptures me. But some things are best kept in your private fantasies. I fear Dexter is too much for me to handle.

Neck arching, Dexter screams unintelligible words directly at me as a violent accusation. His orgasm is so powerful, the spanking bench vibrates against the floor in a jarring rhythm. During my mentor's fit of pleasurable frustration, Heidi sucks on my thigh to cut off her moans as she climaxes.

I hold Dexter's warm, whiskey-colored eyes, and I spiral down the descent of release. Even though no one is touching me sexually, a climax is torn from me. I bite my lip bloody to stop myself from begging Dexter to fuck me.

We stay frozen in place for a few moments. Heidi pants against my thigh, with Dexter still deeply rooted inside her. Green and brown eyes locked in silent struggle, both of us trying to figure out what to do next. It's as if either one of us moves—*game over.*

Suddenly, Cortez touches my shoulder, breaking our tableau of indecision.

For thirty-two years, I was indoctrinated with *Husband and wife. Good girls only give themselves to their husbands. No man will ever respect you if you spread your legs for them without saying vows before God first. Self-respect, responsibility, and your worth as a woman hinges solely on whether or not you marry and create children who will become well-behaved, contributing members of society.*

While I still believe in the tenets of my upbringing, my *self*-worth and *self*-respect only hinge upon how I feel about my*self*. No one's opinions matter more than my own. My decisions are my decisions, and only I will have to live with them as long as they don't impact anyone else negatively.

It's time *I* own my needs and wants, and stop allowing others to dictate what *I* want out of *my* life. Just as with self-respect, self-worth, self-confidence, self-reliance, and self-esteem, my power is seated inside me.

No one can steal my power unless I give it away freely, which is the very definition of Dominant, Switch, and submissive.

Power exchange.

Monogamy is another tenet I've had shoved down my throat since birth, one I'm not sure I can swallow anymore. I'm in love with the man whose hand is on my shoulder. That should satisfy any need I may have, but it doesn't. I want the man across from me with a desperation that borders on violence. I have another man at home, who I would give anything to make my own. Yet at the same time, I crave mastering the soft female beneath my hands.

Maybe someday I'll meet the man who will show me monogamy isn't a foreign concept– the man who will win my heart, making me forget all others. The hero who will make me insane with jealousy. But that's forever doubtful. If Ezra Zeitler, with the manipulative powers of a god among men, can't eclipse all others, no man ever will.

For me, monogamy is just an illusion, and I'm not ashamed to admit it. It's freeing– I'm independent in my whoredom. Until my one and only arrives, I'll settle for the mutual respect and adoration of those I allow into my life.

# Chapter Twelve

My confidence in maintaining my own power quickly dissolved with every step Cortez and I got closer to our apartment– closer to the man waiting within. But it was Cort's unadulterated terror that ate away at me until I finally joined him in mutual fear.

The door behind us shuts with an audible snap, inescapably trapping us to our brutal fates. Cortez and I lean against the door, panting breathlessly in fear– fear of Master Ez's wrath.

We both look up to find Ezra standing near the sofa. His eyes widen slightly as he takes in our disheveled appearance. We must look like we've been running from the big, bad wolf haunting the hallway. Both of us are panting, our clothing shredded, bodies bloodied and bruised, with wild expressions marring our faces.

"I'm sorry, Master," Cort grovels as his knees hit the floor with a sharp clack. I grimace at the painful sound. He didn't cushion his fall one iota, so it's going to leave a wicked bruise. That had to have hurt.

"Ava?" I have enough sense left in me to ask if we're alone before the shit-storm that is brewing descends.

"Ava's at the movies with Aaron and Kayla," Ezra answers me, but he's staring at Cortez with a funny little quirk to his lips. Ez's expression turns bewildered the longer he gazes at Cort, who is abasing himself on the floor like a naughty pet. "What's going on with him?"

"I didn't break the rules," I supply happily, and then I release a manic giggle.

We're so dead. We're so fucking dead. From what I've noticed, everyone is petrified of Ezra Zeitler, and as one of his victims– in every sense of the word –I tend to agree with them. Ezra is motherfucking scary when he's in a mood.

"Well, that's good. Since I'd hate to have to kill one of my oldest friends," Ezra deadpans. "What's this?" He points to Cortez, who is resting his forehead on the floor.

I could never be that subservient. Ever. I didn't think Cort had it in him, either. But my current view says otherwise.

"Uh… um… yeah…" I release an anxiety-riddled laugh that sounds borderline insane.

I watch in silent astonishment as Cortez crawls on his belly, using his knees and elbows, until he reaches Ezra's feet, where he rests the side of his cheek against Ezra's bare foot.

With the oddest expression I've ever seen grace his perfect face, almost as if he's in awe, Ezra reaches down and takes a handful of hair to lift Cort's face, inspecting it. The moment Ezra notices the bite marks on Cortez's neck, his eyes widen slightly, but otherwise he shows no other reaction. That doesn't mean anything coming from Ezra– the man is the world's best manipulative liar.

"Ah… I see," Ezra mutters calmly. His eyes track over my body, taking in everything that isn't the same as the last time he saw me: torn blouse with Cort's jacket covering me, splotchy face from blushing profusely, and wild eyes.

"So… yeah… Um–" I try again, but Ezra cuts me off.

"I believe we've covered that already, Katya." Ezra doesn't sound angry, but I can tell that Ezra is hanging on by the skin of his teeth. Master Ez is trying to enter the building. I doubt Cort's submissiveness is helping matters– seeing your partner abasing himself on the floor must call to whatever fucked-up-ness is dwelling deep inside Ezra Zeitler.

"I didn't break the rules," I repeat. "I think Dexter was very pleased with my progress." Cortez snorts, and it comes out sounding funny since Ezra is yanking Cort's hair, wrenching his neck at an unnatural angle.

"Dexter did give me– *us* –some homework, though. I guess I'm a little too wound up, so I need to have a release before our training sessions. Dexter said something about how I'm amping up his needs. I really can't remember much of that conversation," I mutter bashfully, and Cortez tries to hold a laugh but fails.

Ezra just watches us both with calm patience, waiting for the punchline. I mutter out anxiously, "See, here's the thing. We were worked up–"

"*We?*" Pale eyebrows reach Ezra's hairline. He never breaks eye contact with me while yanking Cort's neck backward by the hair, like he's about to produce a knife out of thin air to slice Cort's throat if he doesn't like the answer he receives.

Scary motherfucker.

"We. Cort and me. *We* were worked up. Cort liked my um–fascination with Dexter. Then one thing led to another…" I trail off.

"Led to another *what*, Katya?" Ezra questions me in a creepy, calm voice.

"Cort kissed me, and then I blinked… and we'd had sex, and I can't remember a single second of it, and neither can he," I hurriedly finish.

"Is this true?" Ezra asks Cortez in an even tone.

"Yes, Master. I can't remember. It's like I blacked out on lust. I've never felt anything like that before. It's like twelve years of need exploded in a second. I came to on top of Katya after spilling myself. I don't remember, dammit!" Cort sobs into Ezra's face.

Ezra looks extremely worried yet sad. He gazes at me for a split-second, seeing if I'm all right. Clearly, it's Cort who is in obvious distress between the three of us. I'm just numb at this point.

Ezra's fingers unweave from Cortez's hair, and then he kneels on the floor next to his partner. "Why are you so distraught? You two can have each other anytime you want. We've discussed this already." Ezra says gently, with a level of patience I don't understand… and then it dawns on me.

If Ezra is manipulative, years upon years of being in Ezra Zeitler's shadow has taught Cortez Abernathy a thing or two. I have no idea if Cort is truly sorry, terrified of Ez's reaction, or if he's manipulating Ezra with his submission. Nothing fulfills Ezra like problem solving, soothing wounded psyches, and hearing his loved ones beg for help. Cort has this man pegged, and between the two of them, I can trust neither.

Cortez *and* I had sex, and here Cort is making it all about him. I was the one who was screwed and ejaculated into, not the other way around. I take full ownership of my actions, even if I can't remember it. But Cort is deflecting the truth with his theatrics to get out of trouble. How can Ezra not see this tactic for anything other than what it is? Manipulation at its finest.

"Mostly, I'm just upset over the fact that I finally had Kat, and it was obviously spectacular, but I can't remember any of it."

"That is rather perplexing," Ezra muses, showing no emotions whatsoever.

"I didn't use a condom, and you didn't give me permission to spill inside Katya." Cortez is visibly shaking by the time he finishes speaking. His bottom lip quivers and a fresh wash of tears shines in his eyes.

Cortez is good. Damn good.

"It's all right. I'm not mad. It's the wrong time of the month, anyway." Ezra pets Cort's hair in a soothing motion, while Cort looks oddly disappointed and confused by Ezra's lack of reaction.

Fed up with this Oscar-worthy performance, I snap. "Hey, how the fuck do you know my cycle?" Ezra just looks at me like I'm an idiot– no, a twit. I just shrug and sigh. Why do I even bother? "It doesn't matter anyway. Cort came on my thigh. I think. I checked."

Cortez slumps to the floor, looking guiltier by the second, and something about his demeanor forces a memory on me.

*The painful edge of pleasure as my body is violently thrust into by a cock far too large for my unprepared flesh. I gasp, causing Cortez to grunt into my ear. Shuddering, trying to adjust to a man who doesn't care that he's penetrating me over and over again before I'm ready. I fight him by clawing at his back. My fingernails scrape, furrowing his sweating flesh. I bite his chest and neck, teeth sinking in sharply. My legs spread farther apart, silently begging him to thrust deeper. I fight Cort. I fight to force him to fuck me harder– to own me with his cock. To own me with his mind, body, heart, and soul.*

*"I'm going to cum inside you, Kitten." Cortez's threat turns into a challenge. "You can't stop me. I want my own little monster, a son or daughter who will be related to Ezra's children through both their parents. Ezra and I can't make children together, but you will connect us in the only way I know how."*

*"Fuck," I snarl, turning rabid– claws and fangs coming out.*

*I hate Cortez. I hate Ezra. I hate them because I love them. I hate myself because a small part of me wants to give them exactly what they want, while the larger part of me fights for her freedom.*

*"NO!" Cort shouts in my face, never stopping the vicious onslaught of his cock owning my cunt. "You're not the only woman we could've chosen, but you're the one we both want— the one we both love. You're the one who will never cause jealousy amongst us. You're the one who loves us back as much as we love her."*

*"Lunatics!" I cry out, on the edge of climax just from hearing the insanity spewing from Cort's mouth. Dexter's devious chuckle is the perfect soundtrack to my undoing.*

*With a practiced movement of fucking countless others, Cortez circles his hips, thrusting as deeply into me as he can go, bruising my cervix with the force. The pain unleashes the torrent. I come so hard my wash of release drips down my thighs. Victorious, Cortez pours into me, grunting with the sheer force of reaching a lifelong goal.*

I snap out of the memory, snarling at the man cowering on the floor. "Coward! If you're going to do something that fucking diabolical, then the least you could do is own that shit!"

"Ah," Ez smiles to himself while humming a sound of appreciation. "Cort must love you very much, Katya, or else he wouldn't pull this bullshit. It's a special kind of torture. One that is usually only reserved for me."

"What?" I squawk. "That is *not* love. It's lunacy!"

"Word to the wise, Katya. I am not your enemy. I will *always* have your best interests in mind. However, the coward at my feet usually only has *my* best interests at heart, with horrific consequences. Cort is your worst enemy, especially now that he has placed you in his heart next to me– prepare to be tortured."

"Fuck you, Ez!" Cort snarls, abruptly pulling himself up off the floor, only to have Ezra swipe his feet out from underneath him. Cortez lands with a sharp grunt on the tile flooring, elbow smashing hard– no doubt bruising himself further.

"Only reason you're still breathing is that it's you, Cort," Ezra issues as a warning. "Let's be thankful for the small blessing that Katya menstruated while she was away from us. Otherwise, I'd castrate you on the spot."

"No, you wouldn't," Cort challenges while glaring Ezra down.

Numb, I walk backward until my ass hits the arm of the sofa, and then I topple over the side. I'm completely lost in a fog of confusion and contradiction, with my emotions warring between betrayal and excitement.

I look down at Cortez, and my voice sounds as numb as I feel. "You were faking the blackout, weren't you?"

Instead of Cortez answering me, Ezra asks me a question. "Cort's amnesia?" I nod yes. "Of course, he was lying. You, my dear, will always block out unpleasantries, at least until you're strong enough to remember. By which I mean, until you're in my comforting presence, as I lend you the strength to remember."

"That doesn't sound the least bit arrogant," I mutter sarcastically.

"Regardless, it's the truth." Ezra manages to turn a simple shrug into a patronizing gesture. "Another life lesson, if Cort tells you he can't remember, he's being a cocksucking liar."

"Why?" I gasp out, feeling betrayed.

"Why did Cort lie?" Ez asks me, but he's staring down at a felled Cort, seething his words at his partner. "Cort and I have a game we do *not* like to play. He will want me but refuses to admit it to himself, so he does childish shit to test my patience. This is where Cortez and you are one and the same, Katya."

"What? Why are you targeting me now?" I sputter out, flabbergasted.

"You don't see how your actions are parallel? Are you shitting me?" Ezra's voice bleeds incredulity. "You don't want to take responsibility for your own actions, so you force me to force you, so you can stand looking at your self-righteous face in your metaphorical mirror."

"Asshole," Cortez and I spit out in unison.

"I'm sick as fuck of having to be the bad guy," Ezra snarls. "After Cortez needles me for weeks on end, I will crack. Then we will get into an altercation, which will lead to fucking on random surfaces. Cort will then share our bed, making love while spewing endearments and forevers. When he wakes in the morning, he feigns amnesia, or simply says I manipulated him into doing what he was begging me to do in the first place. Which is what he's trying to do tonight, only this time it's against the both of us. But I won't be pushed into this bullshit again. I'm not touching you, Cort. Not now."

"Damn, I want absolutely nothing to do with your fucked up histrionics." I throw my hands up in the air and huff out a song of agitation.

"Then don't act like me," Cort accuses me, and suddenly we're all furious at each other.

"See, it's impossible for me to fuck my own ass with Cort's big dick," Ez rasps wryly, lips twisting up into a sardonic smirk. "But Cortez always finds a way to blame me. In his mind, he rewrites history, to where he didn't just fuck you, Kat. If he pretends not to remember, then it never happened. Either Cort grows up, or you get to deal with this bullshit right alongside me."

Cortez visibly winces– his entire body curling inward. "Not true," he grumbles, but his body language is screaming he's a liar.

"Not true? Not true that I refuse to play your game any longer? Not true that I've decided to move on, with or without you? Decided I want to be with an adult who accepts who he is, even if that means admitting he's in love with me *and* my cock? Or not true that you pull the dumbest shit, like skull-fucking and ninja-cum-injecting unsuspecting females who we are vetting as the mother of our future children? What about all of that is not true, Cort, because this I've got to hear?"

Crawling on his belly, on his elbows and knees again, Cort tries to supplicate to Ezra. I swear to God, the man mews like a wounded animal.

Eyes narrowed in disgust, at Cort or himself is anyone's guess, Ezra growls, "Grow the fuck up, Cort. I'm sick of the bullshit you've been pulling since Faith."

"Faith?" I gulp out.

"Don't worry about it," they say in unison, finding a common ground by lying to me. Ezra continues, "Is this really the impression you want to give to Katya? We just had to go kidnap her from her parents' home. I wanted to show Katya how life could run smoothly and pleasantly with us. I wanted her to see the benefits of raising Ava together. Instead, you're showing us in a very unfriendly light."

"I'm sorry. I was jealous," Cort admits, causing me to lose it.

Lunging off the sofa, I find myself standing over Cortez, shrieking my rage. "You have no right to be jealous of me, goddamned you! Ezra wasn't even there. Neither of you hold dominion over me. I will not be your broodmare mistress, who you hide away while you stay married and engaged. Both of you assholes can just rot in hell!"

"Calm down, Katya. You're acting like the fool you're yelling at," Ezra mutters, rolling his eyes dramatically. "I'm sure Cort didn't mean that the way it sounded."

"For once, I'd love to have sex with someone who wants to have sex with me– not use me for a purpose. Rape. Therapy. Jealousy. Just once, I want someone to love me for me." Hating how my voice breaks, I walk away toward the sofa, turning away from the Ezes to hide my head in my hands.

"Kat," Cort calls softly. "I meant I was jealous of Dexter. It had nothing to do with Ezra at all. I was jealous of the way the two of you were eye-fucking each other. Jealous because Ezra does the same goddamned thing to Dexter." Cort uses my words against me, manipulating me like a master. Sounding despondent, "I want someone to love me for me."

Ezra releases a manic laugh, so pain-filled that tears spring to my eyes. "I might as well shoot myself in the head, you cocksucker. '*I want someone to love me for me*,'" Ezra mimics Cortez and me perfectly. "Who can't say that bullshit phrase? You all say *I'm* the manipulator? You all say *I'm* the one in control? All an illusion. But I'm not going to allow your emotional extortion to derail what I'm trying to achieve."

"I'm sorry," Cort mutters again. Even though I refuse to look at either of them, he does sound genuinely repentant.

"Now that we've cleared some resentment–"

I cut Ezra off, "Who says I've said my piece?"

Hating it when I interrupt him, Ezra ignores me just like he always did when he was impersonating Dr. Jeannine. "Katya, how was your instruction?"

I turn to watch Ezra rise to his feet. He holds out a hand to Cortez, as if signaling that no harm was done and he's over it, and Cort happily accepts the affectionate gesture. Just like that, Cort is no longer enemy number one, and Ezra is perfectly content.

Oddest. Fucking. Bullshit. Ever.

"Kat definitely pushed Dexter to his limit. Heidi enjoyed Kat's company. Tonight's lesson was body language." Cortez is in helpful mode. He'd do anything to take away from the fact that a moment ago he was crawling on the floor like a dog that had shit on the carpet.

"Katya, you may go cleanup for bed," Ezra dismisses me without as much as a backward glance.

My feet walk on their own accord, or perhaps Ezra's accord, all the way to the bathroom. I want to be furious over how I was dismissed so Cort could give a play-by-play, but I'm too tired to care. Emotionally drained, fucked both mentally and physically, a bath is necessary since I'm covered in body fluids. I'm simultaneously turned off and on by the thought. Yuck and yum.

I'm fucked in the head.

# Chapter Thirteen

If I could decipher my emotions, I would put into words how I feel over the fact that while I was at work, someone had removed all of my things from my apartment. My bathroom and bedroom no longer exist. My old apartment is a construction wasteland, being transformed into whatever Ezra wants it to be, just as he does with human beings.

My personal belongings are now taking up residence in Cortez and Ezra's shared bathroom and bedroom. My dresser even materialized in the room, with my clothing hanging in the closet. My wall-hangings are on the wall. My books are shelved in the living room. My laptop and work materials are tucked in Cortez's writing lair. The room I believed to be Ezra's, now has my old bed with new linens in pale green hues to make a tween happy.

That's how terrifyingly fast Ezra works to get what he wants. That's why whatever Cortez does to upset the balance, Ezra goes with the flow, knowing nothing will ever get in his way.

If Ezra Zeitler wants, Ezra Zeitler gets. It's best to just get with the program and give in, because in the end, you'll lose no matter how hard you fight his egomaniacal pull.

Ava and I have been incorporated into Ezra and Cortez's lives– makeshift as it may be, it appears to be a permanent thing.

I thought our apartments similar, but I was wrong. My new bathroom is almost as large as my old apartment. I gaze longingly into the *ménage à trois* sized bathtub, as it fills with frothy, lemon-scented warmness. I test it with my big toe and sigh– it's perfect. I get both feet into the water and prepare to sit in the bathtub to wash my sins away.

An elegant hand hooks my waist. "Not yet," Ezra warns in a gruff voice.

"No," I assert defiantly, annoyed in the extreme over how Ezra abides by no boundaries. I'm a naked woman who deserves privacy. I *had* locked the bathroom door. "No. Absolutely not. Get out and leave me alone."

"Yes," he growls back. "Just relax."

"Go play mental gymnastics with Cortez. I'm not up for any more of your bullshit tonight." I'm exhausted, ready to sink into oblivion and leave my stress behind.

"I didn't do anything to you to warrant your censure," Ez rasps, clearly exasperated. "Last I knew, we were good. Don't punish me because Cortez threw himself like a spoiled child. And don't get all sanctimonious by pretending you didn't fuck him back. Cort would never force himself upon you."

I sigh, point taken. "What do you want? You're the one who dismissed me like I was a child, just so you could talk behind my back with Cort. Why are you bothering me? I already have nowhere for privacy, so let me bathe in peace."

I'm standing naked in the bathtub with water up to my knees, glowering at Ezra. He's definitely no longer channeling Master Ez like earlier. When he's calm and calculating, it's like he's a different person– a terrifyingly practical person. Ezra seems different now, almost as if he's finally melding into one being.

Ignoring my protests and offering me no explanations, Ezra slides his hand to my mound, fingers delving through my pubic hair, and then slipping past my lips. Yelping in shock, I try to bat him away to no avail. Two fingers invade me smoothly with expert precision, delving deep inside me.

I try to squirm away. "What are you doing?" I protest, thighs clenching as I swat at the hand assaulting me.

I push at Ezra's hand, but it gets me nowhere. He keeps up his examination, fingers probing deeper. I try not to enjoy the flicking motion, but I'm far too sensitive after what I did with Cortez earlier. It's like Cort was the foreplay and Ezra is the main event.

I look up, eyes connecting with my reflection in the mirror. I hold my own gaze steadily, realizing Karma already punished me for this same offense this morning. I might as well enjoy it before the vicious cunt turns my life into a living nightmare.

Ezra Zeitler makes me weak. He makes me insane. He has turned me into a person I don't recognize– a person I don't like. A person I stare at in the mirror, and I'm proud of her recklessness after a lifetime of being good and getting screwed for it. Fucked without the pleasure and the street cred.

Accepting my fate, I sway with the motions of Ezra's ministrations. I moan low in my throat, and he nuzzles my cheek with the tip of his nose in response.

I stare in the mirror, and an unknown, salacious woman gazes back at me with a drugged expression on her blissed out face. Mouth parted on a moan. Lips swollen and kissed with red. Cheeks flushed pink with arousal. Green eyes glowing with lust. Body beaded with condensation from the misty bathroom. Red hair a wild, tangled mass falling to her hips. Nipples engorged and pointed, begging for lips and teeth to taste them.

Turning my gaze to the man standing behind me, Ezra stares into my eyes through our reflection. As wicked as a fallen angel, Ezra is more aroused than I am. Heated. Hungry. Gray eyes so smoky, I wait for them to catch ablaze. The juxtaposition between my naked body and Ezra's clothed one is magnificent. His tall, pale body is glowing like the light from a candle, and I'm his red-headed flame.

Looking downward, I find power in watching Ezra's fingers thrust in and out of my body– lips parted by questing, unrelenting fingertips. Ezra and I literally watch his digits disappear in my depths, returning coated in a combination of my arousal and Cortez's release. It's sick. Twisted. But I find more pleasure in the knowledge that Ezra is rubbing Cortez inside and out of me, than the sensation of fingers manipulating my sex.

Abruptly, Ezra pulls his fingers from of my body, and my eyes follow the path of his hand. He squirts a gel onto the same two fingertips, and plunges back in again, penetrating me– owning me.

I try to get away, but the water weighs down my movements. In an effort to keep me immobile, Ezra drops the tube on the side of the bathtub, and then he hooks my waist again, rendering me motionless.

"It's spermicide for precaution." Ezra pants into my ear, breath tickling me, sending shivers to ripple down my spine.

"As a doctor, you do know sperm are faster than that, right? It could already be too late. Are you that worried about me producing a little monster with Cort?" I taunt Ezra, knowing how badly that would rankle him– the total loss of control. The fact that Cortez marked Ezra's unclaimed territory.

I try to push away again, but Ezra tightens his grip on my waist. He plunges his slippery fingers deep inside me, tearing a grunt from my throat– part shock, part intense pleasure.

"Katya," Ez gasps into my ear, overly excited. "I'm not against Cortez spilling inside of you. I cannot wait for it to happen. The only issue I take, is that I want to be present. I *have* to know when our children are conceived, no matter which of us is the father, so we may both take ownership of the conception."

Ezra's breathing picks up as he moves his fingers inside me in a relentless rhythm. There is no way he has to maintain this rapid pace to deliver the spermicide. I'll admit it's a nice pace if you want to climax, but it's unnecessary for what he'd trying to achieve.

"You do know that is creepy... and controlling... and fucked up... and so very you? Who talks like that?" I mutter, more annoyed by the fact that I sound like a phone-sex operator than over what Ezra just said. A part of me is celebrating, and the dominant part of me is kicking that stupid cunt's ass.

"I never said I was sane," Ezra deadpans, and then releases an evil snicker.

"Okay, I'm pretty sure you're done spreading that gunk around. Stop it!" I paw at Ezra's hand again because I'm seconds away from coming.

I enjoy my minor victory when Ezra releases me. I immediately sink into the water, knowing he can't get to my pussy underwater. I melt into the warmth, shivering with pleasure, body pricking with goose bumps. I try my damnedest to ignore Ezra's presence, but that's until he starts stripping out of his clothing.

"What are you doing?" I gasp out in a panic, scared to death of where this is going, yet secretly thrilled. My traitorous pussy is clenching like a little bitch, making her need for Ezra known.

Ezra doesn't answer me as he removes the rest of his clothing. Being anally tidy, he folds his pants and shirt before placing them on the vanity. I close my eyes, ignoring Ezra's glorious physique.

Most women lust over men who are built like Aaron and Roarke– muscular men who could bend you in half with their pinkies. Being petite, big men intimidate me. I don't care if they are tall. But when they are huge, I fear for my safety. Ezra was created in the image of a Greek statue: pure white, chiseled, with long, lean muscles, and HARD.

A highly aroused Michelangelo's David slips into the water behind me, sighing deeply as if in bliss. Ezra curls his arms around me, holding my back against his chest. Without preamble, his sneaky fingers go right back to work again– thrusting in and out of me, rubbing over my g-spot with pinpoint precision.

"I'm sure that is defeating the purpose of the spermicide," I murmur in a sluggish voice, not caring either way. "Aren't you washing it away?" My breathing picks up as I start to enjoy his invasion.

"It kills the sperm instantly. This–" Ezra moves his fingers faster and harder, splashing water over the side of the bathtub to spill to the floor. "Is just because I can. Excuse me if my pride is a bit bent tonight. You witnessed the worst of Cort– a side of him I thought he'd keep private between us. Yet again, someone else gets to have you when I cannot."

I start to protest, "Ez–" but he cuts me off.

"We both need this. The connection. The intimacy. The release. Relax. You were close to orgasming moments ago, so just enjoy it," he breathes into my ear, tickling the small hairs floating about.

My reply dies on my lips as Ezra slides me up his chest until I'm sitting in his lap. His arms are wrapped around me, one hand slipping between my parted thighs. His legs are beneath mine, holding me open to his touch. I lean my head backward, resting against his shoulder.

Ezra hums his contentment against my cheek, happy to experience this level of intimacy with me– a level I've never breached with anyone but him.

Ez shifts his hips, forcing a sharp gasp out of my throat. The sensation of his cock resting against my slit has my eyes rolling back in my head. All the while, Ezra's hand keeps up its assault, with his erection resting against his hand and my pussy. He rubs my breasts with one hand while the other is relentless on my g-spot: over and over until my eyes go sightless and I'm mewing nonsense against his neck.

Ezra tweaks my nipple hard, and I writhe from the painful pinching sensation. It's an agony just this side of pleasure. Abandoning my breast, his hand slides down my tummy, and then fists his cock, arm bending to reach its resting place between my thighs. He starts rubbing himself next to my pussy, against me, over me– teasing us both into oblivion.

Eyes squeezing shut, I try to keep the building moan at bay. Ezra's fingers are thrusting inside of me, manipulating my g-spot, while the other hand is hitting my clit with every pass over his cockhead.

"You have to stop. I've gotta pee."

My body is filling with uncomfortable pressure– bloating to the point of pain. While my mind is overcome with intense emotions I cannot release. Ezra is touching me intimately, connecting with me, and I'm loving every agonizing second of it. It hurts to know Ezra isn't mine, but it doesn't lessen the emotions rolling though my heart. I try my damnedest never to speak the words aloud.

"No, you don't," Ezra croons in my ear, fingers thrusting faster. "You've done this for me before. It won't be as messy this time since we're in the bath. Orgasm for me, Katya. I want to be the one who does it for you," he pleads in my ear, sounding desperate. "You gave this to Cortez earlier, and it kills me that I didn't get to witness the two of you come undone. Come for me," he commands.

The pressure keeps building and building, yet never cresting. When I don't think I can hold anymore, it fills me still. If I don't release the pressure and the pleasure soon, my skin will burst. My moans and groans echo throughout the bathroom. It's a keening sound of pleasure just this side of misery.

Ezra's hands move in and out and up and down like pistons, working us both to our mutual finale. From one movement to the next, I find my climax. Back arching, neck straining, I groan to the ceiling. With a burst of intense pleasure, my body releases itself into the water, pouring the pressure from my being.

Ezra shouts my name as he jerks against me in jarring, quivering eruptions. His release shoots up to land on my breasts– the contact searing me. Humming to himself in pleasure, he continues to rub his cock, pressing the waning length against my slit. Both hands slide up my slick body to play in his spendings, smearing me– marking me as his.

Within seconds, I go from overpowered by pressure, to completely drained of energy. My eyes drift shut– each blink longer than the last. Feeling more relaxed than ever, it's as if I'm floating in ecstasy.

Ezra picks me up from the bathtub, and then carries me to parts unknown. I'm so relaxed that I just don't care where. He could carry me to Hell and I would go merrily.

"You guys are soaked." I hear Cort say from a great distance as I'm swaddled in the covers of a bed that smell like my Ezes.

"Come to bed," Ezra commands huskily. I try to obey, but my body refuses.

"Are you angry with me?" Cort whispers.

"No, not anymore," Ezra replies softly, voice buzzing near my ear as he crawls onto the bed with me.

"Did you have sex with her?" Cort whispers just as softly.

Wrapping his arms around me, Ezra maneuvers me until my face is pressed against his chest. "No, I'm waiting until Kat's ready, and I will wait for you."

"I'm sorry I didn't wait for you earlier tonight. I just… You should know better than to pit me against Dexter when it comes to someone I love. I get territorial around that horse-cock motherfucker.

Sounding beyond arrogant, all Ezra says is, "I know."

Chuckling to himself, Cort mutters, "My God, you are a Machiavellian bastard, aren't you? Did you plan this?"

Chest rumbling beneath my cheek, Ezra laughs out, "No comment." Their bodies press against me from both sides, Ezra at my front and Cortez at my back. I fall into oblivion, knowing I'm safe and at home in the arms of my Ezes.

# Chapter Fourteen

Leaning back in my chair, I try to get a bit of shuteye, now that Cortez isn't pestering me relentlessly. With the threatening note, Cortez has been going to work with me, saying there is safety in numbers. I expected him to sit on the sofa with his laptop and get to writing me some chapters, but he confided in me that his writer's block is still plaguing him.

Instead of doing his job, Cortez has been helping me with mine, and he's been companionable and helpful in his efforts. The man might suck at writing right now, but he is Mr. Perfection when it comes to the work of others. He's been getting sadistic pleasure in noting plot holes, and then lording them over his fellow authors.

Earlier, I received hate texts from James Atwater, complaining over the fact that Cort was touching his manuscript. The reclusive, mute philanthropist proceeded to engage in a text war between Cortez and myself. After a series of messages— each one getting more inventive and sexually explicit than the last, bordering on torture –the erotic, BDSM writer stated an unnamed associate of his and Cortez's. James reminded Cortez that this mystery person would gladly occupy Cort's time, to the point that Cortez would be too busy to work, let alone ruin the other author's manuscript.

After twenty minutes of rolling around on the sofa compulsively laughing, where Cort would calm down, only to start right back up again, he left to go pester James Atwater.

I received a text from James minutes later, asking me to politely retrieve my missing writer from his premises, or else there would be hell to pay.

The next text I got was of an image of James and Cort sharing a pizza, both giving me a thumbs-up, clearly having no intentions of ever working again. It took me a few minutes to realize the pair was fucking with me, and they were the best of friends. I assumed it was Cort's demented way of breathing some fun into my day, and then giving me some much needed peace and quiet.

But my newest visitor is proof as to why it's stupid to assume anything with the denizens of Dominion, New York. I realize either Cort was giving Ezra and me some alone time, or James Atwater was a distraction to get Cort out of my office, so Ezra could be alone with me for the first time in weeks.

"What the hell?" Ezra enters my office, carrying the mahogany chess box. I expect him to grin at me just to piss me off, but the stoic expression never slips from his face.

With sure, unhurried movements, Ez ignores me while he sets the box down on the coffee table, types in the key-code on the lock, and then arranges the competing sides for battle. I watch Ezra with sick fascination, not knowing what to do next.

"The question is," I mutter more to myself than to him, "are you personally acquainted with James Atwater? Of course you are," I answer myself. "The next question is, is James currently distracting a witless Cort so you can make your next move? Of course he is."

I've been back in Dominion for a few weeks, long enough for the apartment to be completed and for Ava's school year to end. Kayla stays in our apartment as a babysitter until Cort and I wrap up our daily tasks at Edge Publishing. Ezra is also working a lighter load to help shoulder some of the added burden.

It's been odd for us since I returned to Dominion. Ezra and Cortez spend all of their waking hours bonding with Ava– Cort especially, wanting to know every single detail about the eleven-year-old, as if they have a connection I cannot fathom. I've witnessed a different side of Cortez Abernathy.

Never in a million years would I think the playboy would want a nuclear family life. Cortez treats Ava as if she is his daughter, going as far as to order her about with chores, to help with homework, and to assign summer reading. He's very domestic, asking us what we want for dinner and what we need. He's gone grocery shopping and picked up things Ava requested. But he's too lazy to go the extra mile and actually cook or clean. He asks us what we want, and then orders it done– sometimes I'm the one ordered to provide the service. He acts like we're all baby birds in his nest. I think if I saw Cort with a toilet brush in his hand, I'd shit a brick.

The evenings are odder than hell. We sit down to dinner like an unconventional family: Ezra, Cortez, Ava, me, Aaron, Kayla, and Roarke. After dinner, Aaron asks Ezra if he's leaving the building, and when Ezra says no, Aaron follows Kayla across the hall, where they stay until morning. Roarke says he's going home to Shadow Haven, but I know he's secretly hovering somewhere nearby, because Ezra obviously lied about staying put.

We always end the day by huddling up on the sofa before bed. With Ez, Cort, and Ava watching some boring-assed book adaptation, which is guaranteed to put my child into a coma. While they watch, I get my red pen out and punish my authors for being lazy bastards for refusing to perfect their use of the English language.

Then our nights get even odder. Ezra forces me to share a bed with him and Cortez– in the nude. I learned my lesson after protesting a second time. Ez throws these silent temper tantrums, just as Ava does, which are pure evil and scary as fuck. It's best to give in straight away for sanity's sake.

We actually sleep, with no hanky-panky to be had. Well, Cort sleeps like the dead, while I have a fitful rest. Ez disappears on his nightly rounds, not only going across the hall to check on Aaron and Kayla, but he ventures from The Edge Building to parts unknown.

The first time Ezra left and didn't come back for three hours, I was terrified. When he finally came back, he got in bed with us, wrapped himself around me, and then promptly fell right to sleep.

The next night, I got up and watched out the floor to ceiling, wall-length windows, which span the entire living room. Twenty minutes later, our black SUV exited the underground parking garage, and then drove down North Avenue toward the outskirts of town, no doubt to the Crestview gated community where Shadow Haven resides.

I stood, staring out the window, looking seven stories to the ground at the passing cars and pedestrians in the wee hours of the morning. After waiting for over an hour for Ez to return, I was just about to give up when the SUV returned. They parked outside of The Green Building, opposite of Edge, where Roarke stayed in the SUV with his tablet, and Ez entered the building, not returning for hours.

I was torn between wondering if Ez had another woman in there, or if Adelaide Whittenhower lived in The Green Building, to the point that when Ez got back in bed, I sniffed the fuck out of him when he went to sleep. He smelled like a combination of himself, Cortez and me, with traces of Ava's shampoo.

The next morning I searched for Adelaide's address, locating it as Whittenhower Estates, on the opposite side of the Crestview gated community from Shadow Haven. Nowhere near The Green Building, but definitely in the direction where Ez headed to begin with. I have no idea where he went, but I do know why.

Ezra isn't the randiest person on the planet, but he is the most anxious. If it was another affair he was having, it would be emotional more than sexual. Which hurts even more, even if we aren't together in the traditional sense.

In the weeks that have passed, I've watched Ezra perform this peculiar routine every single night, at the exact same time, with obsessive/compulsive accuracy. We're all on a learning curve, where no one wants to communicate, but our actions and body language are telling a deeper story.

I've been thankful for all the distractions of everyday life since they've kept Ezra out of my hair. Between working, raising a child, suffering through torn-up apartments being melded into one, and all of the small duties that need to be performed on a daily basis, there has been absolutely no time for uncomfortable, intimate conversations that I never want to have.

Until now.

"I felt it was time we spoke." Ezra sounds cautious, but I can tell he won't be denied. He sits down on the sofa, adjusting the board for optimum playability. His eyes flick up to mine as I sit behind my desk, frozen with indecision and fear.

I swallow thickly in response, not able to break our staring contest.

"We're not really playing chess." Ezra's lips quirk up at the corners slightly, noting how petrified I am of the chess set. "I know you. If we were to sit down on this sofa for a talk, you'd freeze me out and say nothing. I'd be talking *at* you. So, we're going to play a few rounds as a distraction to what is being said. Understood?"

I swallow again, but this time I'm able to nod my head. I quickly press CTRL + S on my laptop, completely forgetting about what I was working on before Ez walked into my office. I gingerly shut the lid to my laptop, still feeling guilty for murdering its predecessor in a fit of rage almost a month ago.

"I'm going to speak to you first. Give you a truth, and then you're going to give me one. Okay?" Ezra's eyebrows wing up in the center as he waits for my answer. Giving up, he adds, "Quid pro quo?"

"I like that." I stand from my seat, wavering on shaky legs.

"I figured you would," Ez says wryly, voice dripping with devious delight.

"Who exactly am I speaking with today?" I ask, sarcasm escaping when I wished it hadn't.

"*Me*," Ezra stresses. "I'm me. Always me."

"There are so many variants of you, I just thought I should ask." I slide into the lone chair across from the coffee table. I don't dare share the sofa with Ez. Plus, I want to be able to look him in the eye without cranking my neck to the side.

"I know I've been an ass," Ez states in an emotionless voice. "Dr. Jeannine. Kimber. The Boss. Master Ez. Dr. Ezra Zeitler," he lists off like this is sane behavior. "Even when I was playing them, I was always me. When I'm with you, Katya, I'm just Ez. Okay?"

I can't look Ezra in the eye as the words flow, just as he knew it would be. "You scare me to death for numerous reasons. You realize this, right?"

"Yes," Ez says quietly, hiding whatever emotions that lie beneath. "That's why we are sitting down to talk, no matter how long it may take. We share a child. We're building a life together– one I want very badly. I know you inside and out through nefarious acts, yet you weren't given the choice to learn about me. So I'm not going to fuck around. I'm just going to tell you the truth."

"As you see it," I blurt out.

"As I see it," Ezra agrees, tilting his chin, as if giving me a point in the game of our lives. "But, Kat, what other way matters when I'm speaking of myself? How others perceive me is how they see me. This conversation is between you and me, so the only ones who matter right now are you and me."

"Agreed," I allow, giving a point to Ezra. "Are you going to analyze me?"

"I cannot turn that part of myself off, Katya." Ezra sighs, sounding exhausted. "It's a fundamental part of me. It's not as if you aren't analyzing me as I'm analyzing you. We are more alike than you realize."

"I don't want to speak with Dr. Jeannine or Dr. Zeitler," I warn. "I just want you, but not in a professional capacity."

"I promise," Ezra breathes, meaning it. He reaches across the table to touch my hand briefly– a fleeting touch I allow. "You make the first move," he gestures to the board. "And I'll begin the conversation."

Ezra doesn't speak until I move my pawn. "You're very astute with the '*who are you right now*' bullshit. I assume Dexter spilled the beans on his theory of Ezra versus Master Ez. He's more right than he realizes. This is private, do you understand?"

"Your secrets are yours. If you share them with me, they'll still be yours. I don't trust anyone enough to speak of them in the first place," I admit, hating how lonely I sound.

"I trust you infallibly," Ezra admits, sounding surprised. "I've admitted this to no one. It's just a given in my family. Cort doesn't even know the severity. Do you understand?" he stresses that he's sharing a part of himself with me that even Cort doesn't get to touch.

"Thank you," is the only way I can reply.

"I had a psychotic break at twelve years of age. To the point that I was sedated for nearly a week– bedridden."

Silence descends because I have no idea how to respond to such a painfully deep revelation. We take turns moving our pieces about the chessboard, both losing a pawn in the process. I begin to wonder if I'm supposed to say something, but then I realize Ez is glad that I hadn't.

"It wasn't the only time," Ezra begins again. "But it was the worst. I never want our daughter to learn the truth of her conception, Katya. Ever."

I look at Ez now. Really, really look at him, and I bare my soul in return. "I'll take that bitter truth to the grave. I'd rather barefaced lie and say it was a one-night stand, and have our daughter think I'm a skank, than for her to ever learn the truth. More so, I'd rather die than ever speak those words to our daughter."

"Thank you," Ezra breathes. His slim fingers pick up a rook, as he pretends to contemplate his next move. "I'm the product of rape. I never knew this, you see. Not until I was nearly thirteen. I lived a very, very, sickeningly sweet existence. I was treated as a prince. I had everything I ever wanted, but I started to exhibit signs that were scaring my mother, and I had to visit with a therapist several times per week in my home."

I capture Ezra's knight with a pawn, and I feel vaguely bad about it because he's so distracted that he's making piss-poor moves. But I quickly come to realize he needs the distraction of playing chess more so than I do.

"I was Ezra Holden then, growing up in a home with my aunt and mother, and I was treated as the head of the family from birth– the only male in our family, the only hope to continue our line, no matter what surname I decided to use. My mother's older sister, Pearl, and my mother decided to never have any more children after Divina and me."

"Why?" I ask, interrupting whatever Ezra was going to voice. As a woman who would have a steady stream of children if she could, I can't believe someone in the position of Ezra's mother and aunt wouldn't have as many children as they wished.

"Personal reasons. Fear on my aunt's part– fear of genetic diseases being passed on." Ez never explains his mother's reasons, just keeps going on his previous line of conversation. "Pearl and Divina shared our home half of the year. During school time, my aunt stayed with us because Divina wanted to go to the same schools with Cort and me. The rest of the year they lived in California with my uncle, Richard Hastings. Our family is very small, so I never questioned why Cort and his mother lived with us. I never wondered. Not once."

"Oh," I breathe, scared at the direction this is headed.

"Celeste Hunter was my mother's best friend," Ezra mutters, causing the rook that was in my fingertips to slip from my grasp to fall to the chessboard. "As I was growing up, many rumors were circulating around Hillbrook that they were a couple, but that wasn't the case. They were life partners, similar to Cort and myself, but one hundred percent companionship, closer than sisters."

"I see," spills my lips, because I feel like I need to say something to keep Ezra talking.

"Celeste was the mother in Shadow Haven, with my mother and aunt as the father. Contrary to your observations on Adelaide," Ez says, causing my heart to burst and my blood to run cold. "An heiress is raised to rule. My aunt and mother are cold and efficient when need be, but not the most maternal souls. My aunt is a good woman, but my mother doesn't have a maternal bone in her body. Pearl and my mother were born to be the leaders of the Holdens, but I stole the position from them with my birth."

"The dynamic of the rich and influential confuses the hell out of me," I mutter, unsure how being born is stealing anything from anyone. In my world, you earn your position; you're never born into it.

"Celeste was the mother. The mother to Cort, Divina, and myself. She was the one who read us bedtime stories and baked us cookies and kissed boo-boos and taught us to ride our bikes."

"Cort," I whisper, recognizing what Cortez is doing now with Ava is exactly what his mother did for the children of Shadow Haven.

Ezra smiles fondly. "We lost Celeste less than a year after Marcus was betrothed to my mother, and after that, we all latched on to my adoptive father as our only lifeline. Ovarian cancer doesn't care whether or not you were the best human being to grace the planet, or how much money you throw at it, or how many lives it destroys when it takes someone from the lives of those who are dependent on this precious soul."

"I'm so sorry," I mumble, knowing it's too little, too late, and it will never be enough. I reach over to caress the back of Ezra's hand with a fingertip, hoping he finds comfort in the fleeting touch.

"Celeste knew she was dying, and she forced my mother's hand about the truth. As the attentive mother, she recognized something no one else noticed, not even Cortez and myself. We were nearing thirteen, and I had gone through puberty years prior, with Cort just then joining me. Things changed between us. I was seeing Cort as a man sees the person he plans on keeping for life, and Celeste had to tell me why this wasn't a good idea. But it was too late. So very late."

Ezra looks dead. Dead. His pale skin is bloodless. His gray eyes are lifeless. His voice is so listless that I fear I'm losing him as he sits before me. He's somehow stuck in the past. A wraith of misery.

I watch as the column of Ezra's throat convulses as he swallows. "I was diagnosed with a severe case of Obsessive Compulsive Disorder months prior. Cort was complaining about being chubby, so I forced us to explore the woods as exercise. *Obsessively* so. We were alone out there for hours a day, to the point that I had to have more sessions with my psychiatrist in the evenings. Being alone, hopped up on testosterone and adventuring, it led to Cort and me having sex for the first time."

"With each other," I breathe.

"With each other," Ezra breathes back. "I came home to find my mother and Celeste wanting to have a private chat with me about why my behavior was *sick*." He twists the word sick while grimacing.

Something Ezra said minutes ago rings in my mind, and I end up whimpering, "Oh, fuck," because it now makes so much sense. Too much so.

"They tainted so much for me that day. Not only my living room, but Shadow Haven as well. Worse, I realized I'd tainted the one thing I loved above all else. Cortez. I learned I was the product of rape. I learned my father was Raymond Hunter– a friend of my mother's from Hillbrook. I could live with all of that, as sick as it was. I could live with being a rapist's son."

"No, Ez," I cry out, but not for what he just said. I cry out to stop Ezra from saying what I know will undoubtedly come next. If he doesn't say it, then it can't be true.

"Yes, Kat," Ez mimics my tone. "Yes. I learned that the boy I had just made love to only hours before in the woods, was actually my blooded cousin. Celeste Hunter, the woman who raised me, was the twin of my mother's rapist. My mother and my two aunts stuck together for Cortez and me: to raise us right, to keep us safe. Yet they were too late. Way too late."

"I... I... have no idea what to say," I mutter. Shock. Actual shock rendering me speechless.

"Kat, there is nothing to say. My life was ruined from that moment on, and I promised myself I wouldn't ruin Cort in the process. I broke. I was catatonic for a week straight, sedated in my bed. If we weren't affluent, I would have been hospitalized in Wintercrest Asylum. When I woke, I wasn't who I was when I was placed under a medical-induced sleep. I was diagnosed with Dissociative Identity Disorder, and I began to lie to Cort with every breath I took."

I ignore the fact that Ezra just admitted that he himself is more than one person inside his mind, that those people Ezra portrayed are more than likely facets of his personality who are essentially Ezra. "Lie about what?"

"I was in love with Cort, and I couldn't give up the only good thing in my life when everything was so wrong. I couldn't," Ezra bites out fiercely. "Cort's mother– *my aunt* –was dying, I had a mental illness, and our mothers left us alone. Alone to be sick together. Cort was in love with me, too. He liked what we had done in the woods, and wanted it constantly, and no one could ever tell him no. So I lied with every touch, because I couldn't do to him what the truth did to me. I lied. I lied. I lied with every breath I took, and no one ever contradicted me."

"Fuck," blows out my mouth in a gust as I sit back in my chair, giving up all pretense of playing chess. I cannot fathom what must have been going through Ezra's mind– what still is.

"I never told Cortez. For years we were lovers. It didn't matter that we were children. There are people in this world who you cannot live without. We had just lost Cort's mother, leaving my mother but a shell of her former self. Shadow Haven was no longer a home but an expensive house filled with bittersweet memories. Cort discovered girls at age sixteen, and he was confused about us, so we eventually waned in our passions when jealousy infected us."

"Cort doesn't know?" I gasp out, still suffering from shock.

Ezra's bitter laughter fills my office and destroys my soul. "Oh, Cort knows, all right… I was abducted and my mother had to tell Cortez why. When your name is Cortez Julian Hunter, and you find out that the man who kidnapped your partner is Raymond Hunter, you tend to ask questions."

"I was right," I mutter in shock. "Cortez changed his name."

"Yes, afterwards he legally changed his surname to the one Aunt Celeste said belonged to Cort's father, not that we know for sure."

"My God... poor Cort."

"Poor Cort," Ezra whispers, the agony lacing his voice nearly suffocates me with its intensity. "I was missing, presumed dead, and the love of my life had to learn I'd betrayed him for years by keeping the truth from him. Then he was abducted and abused and tortured by his own uncle for my lies. My father was angry because I was gay, but more so for what I'd done to our own blood. My mother's rapist tortured me by forcing Cort to prove he was a lover of women. Ray ruined the spark inside of Cortez that wanted me– loved me."

"Cort still loves you. He still wants you," I say with absolute certainty, knowing it's not a comfort.

"I know," Ezra breathes, refusing to look at me out of shame. "We've given into temptation a few times in the years since. It was violent and raw, and left us more broken than healed afterwards. I'm not ashamed that Cortez is my cousin. I'm not ashamed that I'm in love with him. How could something so pure and innocent be wrong?"

"It's not," I say with conviction, truly feeling the righteousness of it.

"Everyone knows we're partners, but not romantically. I crave a man's touch but still find women intriguing. Cort says he's straight, but he's in denial. He touches a man other than me, so he's protesting too much. But he's definitively bent more toward women, for sure. I don't give a fuck who I have to hurt, abuse, or use, Cort will always be mine, and someday he will realize this."

I close my eyes against the tears that flood my vision. I'm one of those disposable people Ezra is using.

"Kat," Ezra commands me to look at him. When I do, he says, "Trust me. What you are thinking is wrong. You are our salvation. You are the woman who will connect us, blood bond be damned. You are the woman we both want, one who wants us back. You are the woman who loves us. The one who loves every fucked up facet of us, even if you won't admit it. That isn't being used, that is having a use."

"There is so much wrong with what you just said," I mumble, thoughts a cacophony of emotions.

"I don't give a fuck," Ezra growls. "I. Do. NOT. Give. A. Fuck." He pounds the side of his fist on the chessboard with every word he speaks, scattering the pieces to the floor.

"Cort gives a fuck," I whisper. "He gives a lot of fucks, I suspect."

"I don't care about what Cort thinks, either," Ezra snarls. "I care about what he *wants* and what he *needs*. The truth has tortured me since I was twelve years old. I'd rather be ignorant, which is why I lied to Cortez for so long."

"Which is why he hasn't forgiven you, I bet. I doubt Cort cares that you're his first cousin. It's the lies, Ezra. It's always the lies that tear people apart."

Not hearing me, Ez just keeps talking right over me. "What is so wrong with loving Cortez? What? It's not like we can have children together. I'm a doctor, for Heaven's sake. If Cortez and I could have children, our genetic ties wouldn't harm them— not even then. But yet we fight it. We lie when I want to tell the world what Cortez is to me. No one but our family knows of our blood connection."

"Have you talked to Cortez about any of this?" I ask hesitantly, wondering why I get the twisted honor of this highly uncomfortable conversation that is shredding my heart.

Laughing bitterly again, Ezra looks insane: gray eyes glossed with pain, pale face pinking, with his posture taut for attack.

"You'd think, wouldn't you? Cort and I do *not* talk. We get into bouts of physical violence, which lead to me being bent over the closest surface. Afterwards, Cort will cry and profess his undying devotion to me. When we wake from our post-coital stupor, Cortez hates my fucking guts again. He'll say I manipulated him into making love to me and saying things he didn't mean. Or worse, he pretends nothing ever happened."

"Jesus Christ," I spit out— literally spit. "Cort's selective amnesia? You fucks need professional help."

"We need you," Ezra stresses, staring at me with guileless eyes. I never thought to use that adjective with Ez, but right now, he's radiating the hope of an angel.

With the force of a tsunami, my arm sweeps the chess pieces from the board, scattering them to all four corners of my office. I'm to my feet in an instant. "I deserve more than being your goddamned Band-Aid, Ezra!" I pick the board up, chucking it at his head, but the crafty fucker ducks before he can be decapitated.

"You will not use my ass, Ezra!" I scream, vein in my forehead throbbing. "I will *not* be your goddamned pawn, not any more. I have self-respect and dignity. You fix your own shit!"

"I'm not using you!" Ezra bellows, coming to his feet. Proving he can match me tantrum to tantrum, he lobs the board right back at me, nearly slicing my arm in the process. "I told myself I'd move on from Cortez. I couldn't live in this purgatory anymore. Kat, you are the one who showed me otherwise."

Taken aback, I slump back to my chair. "How?" I breathe.

"I love you, that's how. Gay or not, I'm in love with you. In love with you in the same way I love Cort. It's not companionship, even if I could spend my life sitting in a room with you and never speaking. It's not about sex, even if the thought of you arouses me to near painful levels. It just is. But then you looked at Cort, thinking he was Master Ez, and there was a light in your eyes that gave me hope for the first time in my life."

Slumping forward, holding my head in my hands, I'm drained of all emotion except for confusion. "Hope for what?"

"Hope that I wouldn't have to move on from Cort to you. That perhaps it wouldn't be moving on or leaving someone behind, but of finding a true balance of life, love, passion, and a sense of family. You're the mother of my daughter, and my partner is looking at you with the same level of desire and longing as you're leveling at us. Balance. I'm not using you any more than I'm using Cort, and you're not using us. It's called building a life, a family, making the most of the big pile of shit fate dumped at our feet."

I breathe out why what Ezra is offering me would never work. "Divina. Adelaide. I won't be your mistress. I know I will never be someone's wife. But I've never even been someone's girlfriend. I've never been in a relationship. The only sex I've ever had, you've either witnessed or perpetrated. With Adelaide in our lives and in your heart, you make me feel badly about myself. You make me feel like a whore."

Ezra is next to me in a heartbeat, crouched down beside my chair but not touching me. "Divina is between you and Cortez, and trust me when I say it's a nonissue. Cortez told me you and he had reached a mutual agreement where Divina was concerned." Voice cold and distant, "As for Adelaide, she is nothing to any of us."

"Ez–" I try to begin, but stop myself. I just cannot get the words out. Too many emotions are tied to whatever I'm trying to say. How do you tell a man you know he's a lying bastard? How can you trust whatever comes out of his mouth after you not only witnessed but heard him profess his undying devotion to the woman he was making love to?

You can't.

"I understand," Ezra whispers, clearly *not* understanding. "I know it bothers you when I touch you. I know you want to touch me and want me to touch you, but it makes you feel badly about yourself. It's why Cortez and I have been behaving ourselves. We're not touching anyone."

"Not even each other?" I ask, eyebrow rising. I don't know why I ask, it just popped out.

"HA!" Ez makes a sound that's so pitiful it breaks my heart for him. "I can't remember the last time Cort kissed me and enjoyed it. I'm sure it was during a fight, where he called me a manipulative bastard afterwards for twisting his head. All total bullshit. No, we aren't touching anyone, not even you until you give us the greenlight."

"Ez, it's none of my business," I mutter, visions of Adelaide and Ezra dominating my thoughts.

"None of your business?" Ez asks, voice warping in pitch. "Excuse me? But I think it is. If who you are with is my business, then who I'm with is yours. Why do you think I went batshit about Dexter?"

"Because you're you," I say wryly, causing Ezra to release a real laugh– a laugh so warm my body ignites and my toes curl.

"True. See, you know me very well." Ezra grins up at me, happier than I've ever seen him, and nothing would make me take that away. "Right now we're building more than a new apartment. We're slowly building a life. I'm trying to give Ava what I never had– two attentive parents who love one another. I can't tell our daughter about her familial connection to Cortez, but I know she feels it. Perhaps someday, when I feel she will understand."

"I understand," I say, and this time, Ezra knows I truly don't.

# Chapter Fifteen

"What's Aaron doing here? I thought this was girls' night," Monica complains when she slinks into Ezra's SUV to find we have a male driver.

I shove over, allowing Monica to squeeze in next to me, bumping my elbow into Kris's boob in the process. "Ezra and Cort wouldn't let me out of the house without a chaperone. Aaron will be going home after he drops us off. He *better* be going home," I growl at Aaron, and he smirks at me through the rearview mirror.

I sigh heavily, sounding just like Ez– Aaron won't be going home. Even if it looks like he is, Kayla and I will never be out of his direct line of sight.

It's the first time I've ever gone out with a bunch of girls. It's the first time I've gone out with anyone, guy or girl. I've never been on a date, not even with Ezra or Cortez– not that either wants to take me on a date. The only person I've shared this experience with is my daughter and parents, and let's face it, that doesn't count.

Ava is at home with Ezra and Cortez, after she threw an epic temper tantrum because she wasn't invited to tag along. They invited Ezra's adoptive father, Marcus– whom I've still yet to meet –and Dexter to our apartment for dinner and games. Lord knows what antics those fools will engage in. I'd pity my daughter if she wasn't exactly like her father. Ava will have all of those dominant men doing her bidding in less than a minute.

Monica's idea for coffee expanded into a night of unadulterated female fun. Hard to believe, but I've enjoyed Monica's peculiar brand of friendship these past few weeks. She's brutally honest and takes no shit from anyone, so I know she's not manipulating me in any way, shape, or form. Not being emotionally coerced at every turn is a welcome change.

As I've been training with Dexter, the dominant side of me has been erupting in full force. But Monica brings it out of me even more. I've always been empathetic, feeling the emotions of those around me. But with dominance riding me, I can see beneath Monica's surface. She is hurting, using her smooth hair, tailored clothing, and emaciated body to strive for perfection. I want to tell Monica she has no need to be insecure. She's perfect as long as she's being her true self.

Monica called me, and I called Queen, and now we have an SUV full of giddy girls: Monica, Queen, Kayla, Fate, Kristal, Heidi, Syn, and me. Syn doesn't like any of us, but she's in the front seat, readily chatting shop with Aaron.

"Aaron?" Queen calls out from the rear seat to draw his attention. "You can go home, and then we will call you when we're finished. If you don't believe me, call Ez." Queen addresses Aaron like she is, well, a queen or some shit. Stranger yet, is that Aaron just nods his head in silent agreement and doesn't call.

"Thank God," Kristal releases, sounding relieved. "I get enough of Lurch at the club." Kristal, Fate, and Queen share a conspiratorial laugh, causing Syn to glare at all of us in the back of the SUV– not because Syn's defending Aaron, but because we breathe.

The tatted up, raven-haired, petite sadist has stared at me with loathing in her eyes since we piled into the vehicle. I've never met the woman in my life, but she took an instant dislike to me the moment she saw me across Restraint's crowded dance floor.

Aaron drops us at the front of a trendy new restaurant with a mile-long, six months in advance, reservation list. With a last name like Zeitler, Ezra called and we were issued a reserved table immediately. A valet promptly opens our door, ushering us out.

"Swanky," Monica mumbles into my ear as she slides out of the SUV. Once I'm on the sidewalk beside her, she continues. "None of the others will appreciate this like you and I will. We had more humble beginnings, while they live in their castles in the sky."

"What?" I breathe back, face scrunching up in confusion.

Softly huffing a haughty laugh, Monica rocks my world. "I'm a plumber's daughter, working my ass off for off-the-rack, clearance finds. You're a contractor's daughter, who paid her own way– only reason I liked you at first, by the way. Us blue collar girls have got to stick together."

"Damn straight," I say with more conviction than I feel. Months into my new life, and I still don't feel like I belong anywhere.

"While Queen may have been born in the slums, she has more money than Ezra– billions. Which means so does Fate and Kris. Fate grew up a princess in a mini-castle, while Kris cleaned a real castle, which is how she met Queen. Kayla and Heidi, both were spoiled, daddy's girls from rich families. Great girls, but spoiled nonetheless… you feel me, Kat?"

Yeah," I mutter. "This is a rare treat for us. But this is everyday life for them."

"Exactly," Monica says with a wide smile, proving why we get along. "Just know, I make fun of them in my head every time they speak."

"Just know, I'm not with Ez for the money. It makes me uncomfortable."

Teeth flashing white with sadistic delight, "I know," Monica states unequivocally. "That's the other reason I like you. Plus, it's fun to watch you squirm like a fish out of water."

"Sadist," I mutter with affection while grinning.

"Speaking of sadists… Syn seems to hate your fucking guts."

"No shit. I see you noticed, too."

"C'mere, baby girl," Aaron rumbles in a sexy voice, drawing Kayla into an intimate embrace. The couple shares a squee-worthy kiss that has us all cooing at the lovers. It's so damn sugary sweet, my teeth rot on the spot.

Fifty promises that we will be good, that we will call, with Queen saying that she could kick any man's ass, and Aaron still won't leave our sides. Finally, Syn just growls at Aaron and he lets us be.

"Ready, small town girl," Monica teases me as we enter a packed restaurant filled with the upper echelons of Dominion's society. "Let's order a meal that costs more than our rent, our yearly wardrobe, and our grocery bill combined."

"Jesus," I hiss, disgusted all of a sudden, and feeling inadequate and underdressed in my skirt from Kohl's, my blouse from Target, and my Payless pumps. "I would have rather ordered pizza and drank myself to sleep."

Monica just trails a devious laugh as she follows the herd through the packed restaurant, where they pile around the central-most table for optimum attention gathering. I'm last, dragging my feet, feeling eyes on me that I wish weren't there. This just reaffirms that this is my daughter's life, not mine. Never mine.

"Order anything ya want. It's on me," Queen announces. We're squeezed around the center table, which Fate proclaimed was the best in the house. They truly love the attention– I don't get it.

"Thanks, Reg," Kristal says in passing.

"Reg?" I ask the table, and no one speaks. Short for Regina, I suspect.

Kris looks like she's going to piss her pants for the gaffe she just made. Must be they don't realize I'm not a twit. After I found out half of Kimber was Queen, I Google searched her as well. Regina Regal, creator of Empowerment Internet Solutions, with her co-founders, Kristal Harris and Fate Simpson.

The waiter takes our orders and passes our drinks around the table. I instantly drain my wine glass; my discomfort getting the best of me. Kristal immediately refills my glass, whispering 'sorry, habit' underneath her breath.

I decide to test to see if these ladies will be honest with me. I love Kayla, but I could never trust her. Anything I do and say will be reported to Ezra. Heidi's a great girl, but I can't trust her either. She would more than likely keep my secrets, since Dexter isn't her actual master, but it's not a chance I'm willing to take. Queen has already proven Ezra comes first, and since Fate and Kris are her minions, I can't trust either of them. That leaves Syn– who seems to hate me for reasons unbeknownst to me – and Monica.

I trust Monica for some reason.

Instinct.

"How well do you all know each other?" I ask the table. They all shrug and nod, giving me a non-answer. "I guess I'm at a disadvantage. I bet you all know me pretty damn well, while I know nothing of you. What I do know is, there are some weird vibes being thrown around, so let's get this out of the way so we can enjoy our evening. Do you all hate me because of Cortez?"

"Why would you think that?" Queen releases an uncomfortable laugh. She reaches for her wine glass, only to drain its contents in two large swallows. Regina Regal– with her shorn blonde hair, genius mind, penetrating green stare, and a big titted, masculine body –scares the shit out of me. It's a good thing she treats me cordially.

"Just a guess, but I bet we've all fucked Cortez Abernathy. Am I right?" I eye each and every single girl around the table. "Are you all holding some kind of irrational grudge against me because of it?" No one answers me. A few girls blanch at the grudge comment, so I take matters into my own hands. "I won't ask Kayla, because I know for a fact she has. Same goes for Monica. Heidi, have you fucked Cort?"

"Yes, Mistress," Heidi replies timidly, peachy skin turning pale.

"Heidi, we're not training. I've told you to call me Kat," I chastise her gently, smiling to soften the blow. "Kristal? I'm guessing yes for you, too."

Leaning forward, with a devious glint in her hazel eyes, "All right. I'll answer," Kristal mutters with a lopsided grin.

Right here, right now, I decide I like this ballsy bitch.

"There isn't a person at this table who hasn't had Cortez inside their body. You shouldn't have asked, because you may or may not like what you find out about your guy."

"First, Cortez isn't *my* guy. Second, he's Cort. I'm not stupid. You'd be surprised at how honest he is with me." I sound defensive, but I meant every word I'd said. If I ask, Cortez answers.

Queen looks at me in a strange way, as if I've passed some test I didn't know I was taking.

"Heidi, Monica, and I were Cort's regulars," Kristal says without shame. "You know about Kayla. Cort and Syn have a history–" Syn snarls at Kris. Without missing a beat, Kris goes on like she's not terrified of the sadist. "I'd love to spill it, but Syn would gut me at this table with a broken wineglass. She's known for getting away with murder," Kris rumbles wryly. "Cort took Fate's virginity. One of us took his..." Kristal answers for everyone except for Queen.

"Don't make me do this," Queen hisses. So I stare her down until she answers. "Yes, all right! Dammit! Yes, Cort and I were together... it was torturous. We never revisited it. He is one of my best friends. Satisfied?" She flashes me a look of hurt, as if she's feeling sympathetic to my plight. "I didn't want you to know that everyone here has been with Cort, but I guess you figured that out already on your own."

"Why don't you ask who here has been with Ezra?" Kristal taunts, and I realize she is antagonistic by nature. "I've had the pleasure of his oral pleasures," she sings.

"I thought he was gay," Heidi mutters in confusion, eyes flicking around the table, looking for confirmation.

"Me too… until Kat," Monica puts her two cents into the conversation. My bitchy minion is a sweetheart compared to Kristal.

"Someone here has," Kristal taunts. "Maybe more than one someone at this table has. Maybe more than two someones."

"That's enough," Queen orders, a menacing threat in her tone. "This conversation will never be revisited. I don't want Ezra's wrath to fall upon me because I can't control my ladies. Behave or suffer my consequences, because I will not suffer Master Ez."

"Ooowww…" Kris makes a spooky sound, as if disrespectfully scoffing, *"I'm so scared."*

"Knock off the secret spilling. All of you," Queen warns. "We all know Kat is curious and sneaky, and way too smart for her own good. Kris, I will sic our master on you if you don't behave."

Sobering, Kris mutters, "Now I'm actually scared."

I know four things at once: Queen is the boss of everyone here. She's scared of Master Ez. She listed 'our master' separate from Ezra, so there is someone even more terrifying than Master Ez… and Queen has been with Ezra.

Ezra has been with four women by his own admission.

Me.

Adelaide Whittenhower.

Regina Regal.

Who else? Another person at this very table? My heart is sick, but then I remember the truth of my pitiful situation. Ezra was only with me by force. He bedded these beautiful, cultured, intelligent women because he found them intriguing, and may have even loved them. There is no competition, because I'm not even in the running.

"Well, I have no claim on Ezra," I declare to the table to lighten the mood. "Plus, once you've seen Ezra make love to a woman right before your eyes, it kind of takes the sting away from learning he has been with Queen."

Completely taken aback, "I...I... trust me, it wasn't like that. It was all about Cort and Ezra... I was just... there." Queen stammers. "Our master thought if they touched me, they'd touch each other and get over their issues."

"Sounds about right," I agree, thinking the same about the pair of idiots. "It's fine, Queen. I understand. You happened before me– after me –whichever way you want to look at it. I haven't been with Ezra since Ava was made. It's none of my business, anyway."

"Who?" At first I think Queen is wondering who told me it was her, but now I realize that Ezra having sex with a woman is a huge fucking deal because they all know he's gay.

"I'll make a deal with you, ladies. Knock off the cloak and dagger bullshit and just be honest. Hanging out is going to suck for me if I feel like you're all laughing behind my back over my ignorance."

"Fun for us, though," Syn says pointedly.

I ignore the sadist. "Each of you has to tell me who you are and how you are connected to one another– I'll know if you're lying. Queen's right about my research skills. I'll tell you my secret, *if* you're honest with me. Only Cort knows it, so if I hear it, I'll know one of you spilled. I won't care which one, I'll just kick all of your asses, and I'll bring Master Ez as backup since it's a secret about him."

"I'll start." Kristal's beyond eager, vibrating with excitement. "I'm Kristal Harris. I'm an accountant by day for Empowerment Internet Solutions, and a bartender at Restraint by night. My true master is Queen, but we say it's Pretty Boy for convenience. Since we're playing show and tell: I'm a sex addict, and that hurts my relationship with my boyfriend, Alex... and that's all I have to tell."

"I'm Fate Simpson," the blonde, prim and proper socialite begins. "I'm the chief financial analyst for a company that creates computer software and programming– Empowerment Internet Solutions. Queen is my master in all things, except for

BDSM and in the bedroom. I need the support to know my choices are sound, and Queen is that for me. I'm also scared shitless of Restraint, but I'm an adrenaline junkie, so I keep going back."

"Monica James, senior editor at Edge Publishing. We all know who my boss is." She smirks at me. "I don't have a master or a boyfriend. I'm not a gold-digger. I don't care who the guy is, as long as I feel complete with him. He could be a janitor for all I care, just so he makes me feel alive... I'm incredibly lonely." The strong emotions in Monica's voice draw tears to sting my eyes.

"Syn, and that's all *you* need to know," she states with a badass attitude.

In my nightmares, I imagine Syn's an assassin. The sadist is barely five feet tall, but she has killer curves. She is showing some flesh, and all of it's inked and pierced. I wonder who forced Syn to be here tonight. It's obvious she isn't a fan of mine. '*If looks could kill*' isn't just a saying when it involves Syn the sadist.

"Heidi Stewart. Dexter is my master of sorts. He hasn't claimed me because we can't meet all of each other's needs. But for now, it's the closest fit either of us can find. I'm an exhibitionist, and while I can tolerate a lot of pain without complaint or mental harm, I don't need it at all. I could have been anything I wanted to be, but I chose to become a nurse and a mother because of my server soul. My husband died four years ago in a car accident, and Dr. Zeitler was my grief counselor. Long story, short: I'm not ashamed to be a submissive," Heidi says with fierce pride.

"Kayla Cummings. I'm your assistant. I'm the youngest of four siblings, and the only daughter. Server soul? Where have I heard that before?" Kayla muses. "Oh, church. That also fits me. Right now, I have no clue which one of you is my true master, and it's really confusing me." She worries her bottom lip, looking about to cry. "Ezra controls us, while The Master runs all of our lives. Kat is my boss. Aaron is my boyfriend. My loyalties are divided, and I hate it."

"We'll figure it out," I promise Kayla as I reach across the table to pat her hand in comfort.

"I'm Regina Regal. But at Restraint, I am only known as Queen for my own anonymity. I'm the owner and creator of

Empowerment. If you own a digital device or a computer, my programs influence your daily lives. Kris is my accountant and Fate is my financial analyst, and they are also my housemates and my submissives. I've known Syn since she had blonde pigtails and knew how to giggle and smile while we played with Barbie dolls. I've known the guys since they were fourteen, and Ezra was just as stoic but Cort hadn't grown into his charm."

"I would have paid to see Cort as an awkward youngster," I murmur, smiling like a fool.

"It was priceless," Fate says with a laugh. "A toddler Cort hit on a grown-ass woman, and Regina squashed his ego like a bug."

Smiling fondly at Fate, Regina continues. "Kat, I know everything there is to know about you, and up until now, I believed the same was true about Ezra. Now, spill it! Who was he fucking?" she demands, leaning over the table to get into my face. She's really eager to hear the gossip.

"I wouldn't call it fucking. Ezra was making love to his fiancée right after his punishment. We were in our apartment, and Cort and I walked in and accidently saw them." I blink back tears. "Neither of them noticed us, and we've kept it a secret until now."

"Bullshit!" Queen barks. "No fucking way… Ezra doesn't see Ade like that, and I know for a fact that she doesn't see him like that. At all. Ever."

"It's true," I cry, voice breaking under the strain of my tumultuous emotions. All of the girls stare at me in utter shock. With their 'server souls', Heidi and Kayla make no move to comfort me. With her 'bitchy soul', it's Monica who reaches under the table to grip my hand, squeezing to lend me strength.

Monica's gesture of support proves my suspicions correct. Monica and I are outsiders at this table filled with people who don't allow newcomers into their inner sanctum. Therefore, I can't trust a word out of their mouths.

Kristal laughs uncomfortably. "Yeah, no doubt they were screwing. It wouldn't be the first time. But I thought it was the last time— eons ago. No way were they making love. No way." she releases a demonic snicker.

"Don't make me suffer by repeating Ezra's words of adoration as he engulfed Adelaide Whittenhower with his body. He was moaning his reverence for his fiancée in the room my daughter now sleeps in. I don't want to puke before I get my meal," I deadpan. "And as my first girls' night ever, I'd rather not spend it bawling my eyes out in the restroom."

Queen's voice is filled with pity, "Katya–" but I talk right over her.

"I know I have no right to feel as I do, but that doesn't change a damn thing. Ezra isn't mine. No matter how much Ezra would love for me to be under his control, I can't give him something he's not willing to give me in return. Whatever is between us would never be equal. I'm just an acquisition he acquired– it's as simple as that."

The ladies are stunned silent as I try to calm my emotions. I take a moment to order my words before I speak them. They fidget in their seats, staring at me. Monica exacts more pressure on my hand, lending me comfort and the strength to continue.

"I understand how having sex with Aaron means I can't bitch about walking in on Ezra and Adelaide. Logically, I know it shouldn't matter who is doing what with whom, as we aren't actually together in any sense of the word. Right now, we're just co-parents, dealing with the shit hand in life we were dealt. When I was with Aaron, it was a onetime deal, and it wasn't emotional other than out of friendship. Even though I'm in the wrong, it still hurts. Because Ezra was not only *making* love to Adelaide, but deeply *in* love with her."

Everyone is thrown by my revelation. I watch Queen's wheels spin. Emotions feverishly roll over her face: shock, surprise, anger, confusion, and finally, disbelief. I can also see that it will physically kill her not to ask Ezra what the fuck happened.

"Anyone care to explain why it's so strange for Ezra to make love to his fiancée?" I ask the table, realizing it must have been a strange occurrence, judging by their gobsmacked expressions.

"No, thank you, Kat. I'd rather not. I'd like to keep all of my appendages, and it's not Master Ez or Ezra I'm frightened of either." Fate's voice holds an ominous warning.

"Who?" I murmur.

"As I said, I want to keep my body parts. I'm not talking." Fate takes a dainty sip of wine, and then pats the corner of her lips with a napkin. I know Monica was telling the truth about Fate growing up in one of the mini-castles surrounding the city. Fate's decorum screams old money.

"I would like permission to tell this to one person. I promise he won't tell a soul." Queen's voice shakes with the need to spill the secret.

"No," I state unequivocally.

"Tell him anyway," Kris offers up, like it's her right.

"Who?" I ask again, wondering if it's the same person who will cut off arms and legs for the information.

"The big guy. The head honcho. The Master of our universe," Kris reveals, sounding sarcastic as all get out, and she gets slapped across the face for her insolence. It happened so fast that no one in the restaurant saw it. The sound was deafening and a bright red handprint is outlined on her tan face.

Hand still poised at the ready, "That was from him. Show some respect and keep your goddamned mouth shut," Queen threatens Kristal.

The waiter approaches with our food, and I have an uncontrollable urge to laugh manically. The ladies are sitting with their hands in their laps, all prim and proper. Kris, with her tits hanging out and a bunch of colorful tattoos on display, sits as if an angry handprint isn't imprinted on her face.

My sea bass disappears from my plate at a rapid rate, thanks to my ravenous appetite and my need for this disastrous night to be over. We all eat to fill the silence, but also to ensure we can't reveal secrets if our mouths are stuffed with food.

I empty my wineglass as soon as it's refilled, only to have it refilled again. Anxious, Kristal is playing bartender with everyone's glasses. I have no idea how many bottles we've drained, but it must average around one bottle each.

"Regina, you must tell him," Syn finally speaks. She takes another uninterrupted bite of her rare steak, as if words didn't just flow from her mouth. "If this is true, then Ezra is uneven again. Which could lead to a disaster."

"I agree," Queen replies to Syn, and then she turns to me. "Kat, I have to tell our master, because I must. But I promise he will keep it to himself." Queen's tone brooks no room for argument.

"Who is he?" I ask for the tenth time, my words slurring from my libations.

"I'm surprised Ezra hasn't told you about him yet, but I see that he is leaving out a lot of vital information you need. I'll have a talk with him," Queen tries to be helpful to take the sting out of her words.

I try to protest, but the look Queen flashes me screams '*back the fuck off*'. The difference between Queen and me, is the same as the difference between Kayla and me. Imagine the difference between Queen and Fate, or Syn and everyone. It's scary.

Fuck it! I drain another glass of wine– my fifth? No, my sixth glass. I'm feeling rather tipsy. I place my hands on the table, leaning forward with a painful smirk twisting my lips.

"Well, this has been a blast. So fun," I chirp acerbically. "What are we doing next? Water-boarding? Cunt-punting? Let me have at it. I'm a glutton for punishment. I guess tonight's my turn to play the masochist. I'm sure Syn is more than prepared to swing the whip."

"I want to get drunk off my ass," Kristal slurs. "And then get fucked– hard."

"I'm pretty sure you're already headed in that direction, Kris. Don't you spend every night drunk with your orifices filled with dick?" Queen chastises Kris but grins. "Kayla's loverboy is on his way from Restraint. Which means we're parting ways because I have a meeting. Aaron will take you wherever you want to go for the rest of the evening."

"Meeting?" Kristal snorts. "I'm sure it has nothing to do with our master and every word Kat spoke since we arrived."

"Do you want to be slapped again?" Syn warns. "Because the next time you say something like that, the hit is coming from me, Kristal. Beware, I'm in a bad mood."

I grab the nearest bottle of wine and drain it dry– gulp after gulp of acidic goodness washing down my throat. Setting the bottle down on the table with an audible thunk, I slur, "Well, I need some fresh air."

Queen's settling our tab within seconds of my departure. I have a trail of women following me as I weave my way through the packed restaurant. I don't even care that I'm most likely making a spectacle of myself. It's not like anyone gives two shits about who I am. It's not like Ezra and Cortez are ever going to be seen with me in public.

"I miss Vacuum Valley," I grumble as the doors eject me to the outside. I nearly trip on the uneven ground. "Why is the sidewalk so wobbly all of a sudden? Did my pumps grow taller as we dined?"

"What Ezra sees in you is beyond comprehension," Syn murmurs as she walks past me. "Cort wanting you comes as no such surprise. His taste is for trash."

"Well, smell you, Ms. My Shit Don't Stink!" I shout at Syn's retreating back, and then start giggling. "Didn't Cort fuck you, too? So what's that make you? Huh?"

"Stupid," Syn deadpans.

"Tell me something I don't already know, since I'm ignorant, white trash with a Master's Degree in English."

"We have something in common, it seems," Syn mutters dryly.

"What's that?" I call out in challenge. "English degree, or ignorant, white trash?"

"Both yet neither," Kris whispers, eyes flicking back and forth, like she's ready to break out a bucket of popcorn and be entertained.

"Our commonality? Your bed warmers," Syn replies. "Mistakes. Ignorance. Among other things."

"I'd back off," Fate warns. "Sadist. Tattoos. Piercings. Threats. All. R-E-A-L. Trust me."

"They're not threats," Queen reminds us. "Syn is giving you ample warning so you know she's coming."

"I want to know why Syn hates me." I slur, and then hiccup. "Did I shit on her shoe? Kick her puppy?"

"Something like that," Fate replies just as Kris releases an evil cackle. Kayla and Heidi look awed, yet like they are about to piss their pants with fright.

"This was– *by far* –the strangest night I've had in a long time," Monica slurs into my ear. We're standing at the curb. Well, two of us are standing, the rest of us are kind of leaning or jumping up and down with drunkenness. "And I've had some strange nights." She hiccups. "It's not a compliment. If it wasn't for the wine, free food, and disturbing gossip, I would have left."

"I agree. It was the buzz-kills." My eyes cut in the direction of Queen and Syn. "It was like partying with your grandparents and children."

"All right, everyone get into the car and behave. I have to get to a meeting." Queen points at the SUV idling at the curb, and six maniacal giggles erupt.

"Thank God, I have to go to work," Syn strings a sentence together. "Aaron, I owe you one."

"I never thought I'd see the day when someone would beg to take my job for the night." Aaron grins at Syn.

"I'd rather tame wild beasts than deal with six drunk females. You know I hate submissives unless they're screaming in pain. Happy submissives just piss me off." Syn smiles brilliantly.

"She's a crazy bitch," I whisper to Monica.

"I heard that," Syn snarls from the front seat.

"Oops!" I cover my mouth with the palm of my hand, and then shout, "Bitch!"

"I just so happen to love drunken submissives." Aaron smiles at us, as if we're the cutest things he's ever witnessed, and then he traps our asses in the car with the sadist.

# Chapter Sixteen

"More wine?" Aaron asks his gaggle of ladies. He's playing the helpful host. But what guy wouldn't love six drunk women trapped inside his apartment? Aaron's in Heaven, judging by the huge smile on his face and the even bigger bulge tenting his pants.

"I want something stronger," Kris whines for the billionth time. "If you won't give me vodka, then at least put a nip of schnapps in some soda.

"No, I'm not cleaning up puke for the rest of the night. Wine or no wine, Kris?" Aaron holds the bottle like the waiter at the restaurant did.

"Garçon!" I giggle at Aaron, and hold my wineglass out to him.

Aaron refused to take us anywhere except his apartment. He said he couldn't trust us in public, because we'd be like herding cats high on catnip. I don't blame him, since Kayla, Fate, Monica, and Heidi are dancing on the furniture and Kristal is begging for liquor. I'm just lounging on the sofa, trying to muster the energy to cross the hallway to my apartment.

Flashing me a look of understanding, Aaron hands me the bottle of wine, takes my wine glass, placing it on the counter, and then he sits next to me on the sofa.

I tip the bottle in Aaron's direction in thanks, and then take a hearty pull. I offer him a gulp, but he declines. I take another swill, and then wipe the back of my hand across my mouth.

"So," Aaron begins. "I take it your girls' night wasn't as cracked up as you thought it would be?"

I guzzle more wine in response, and Aaron chuckles deeply. "I've missed having you around," I finally admit, truly meaning it. Every day, Aaron is around less and less as he builds a life with Kayla. For the past few weeks, I've basically seen him in passing and when he's shoveling food into his gargantuan mouth during supper.

"Your baby boy had to grow up sometime," Aaron drawls out in an amused voice that manages to hold a wealth of pride.

"I've been keeping scarce so you wouldn't use me as a crutch, and you'd latch onto Ezra instead."

"That wasn't necessary," I grumble, heart quivering with ache. "I'm good at compartmentalizing. You're my friend, my only one-night-stand, and my daughter spends more time with you than I do. Call me Cortez Abernathy, for I'm feeling a wee tinge of jealousy."

Aaron's fuzzy eyebrows knit together in confusion. "Jealous of who?"

The truth spills out, words slurring together. "Just jealous. Sad. Lonely. Missing your brand of friendship. I guess, I just miss you."

"I miss you, too." Aaron leans into me, warming me with his presence, and then whispers into my ear. "In about an hour, the person who can be everything to you will be hunting your ass down, needing the same shit you need from him. While I love you and miss you, too, I'm not going to distract you. You need to see Ezra as all of those people you called friend."

"I can't get over it so easily," I stammer, voice breaking.

"You wouldn't have to miss Kimber or Dr. Jeannine if you'd just let Ezra in. You wouldn't miss me as much if you'd give Ezra what you give me."

"So," Kris sits next to me, and I could kiss her for breaking into my painful conversation with Aaron. "What's it like fucking the both of 'em?" Her eyes are bright and glazed over.

I growl deep in my throat, tired of being coerced, pushed, and manipulated by everyone. "I'm not fucking either of them," I slur belligerently.

"Bullshit!" Kris moves lightning fast and sits on my lap. The room spins and I realize she's moving at normal speed. It's just my wine consumption making everything appear to be jarring stops and starts.

"It's not bullshit," I snarl into Kris's face, only to have her grin at me in response. "The only time I've had sex with Ezra was to make our daughter. My one time with Cortez was either an accident or a trap, I haven't decided which yet. Doesn't matter anyway, since I'm still repressing portions of it." I give myself migraines while trying to concentrate on the finer details of my tryst with Cortez.

"Bull-fucking-shit," Kris drawls out. She's surprisingly sober for someone who has been drinking all night long. But she is a bartender who's begging for liquor, so maybe she has a high tolerance.

"It's true," Heidi chimes in from her position atop the coffee table, where she's swaying her hips to music only she can hear. "I saw the whole thing with Cort. Holy fuck that was hot as hell, and they didn't even know they did it." She giggles while twerking her curvy behind.

Aaron adjusts on the sofa, wiggling about, suddenly finding himself in discomfort from Heidi's provocative dance. I'd be amused by our baby boy if I wasn't experiencing my own discomfort from Kristal's line of questioning.

"Cort knew what he was doing the entire time," I interject. "He has selective amnesia when it suits his agenda."

Aaron huffs out a sharp laugh. "He also grovels like a boss. Yeah, everything is always premeditated with Cort. Don't let him tell you otherwise."

Kris leans into me, resting her forehead against mine. The alcohol running through my veins helps me tolerate the woman encroaching upon my personal space, as well as making her look like a Cyclops.

"Admit it." Kristal's breath billows against my lips, smelling like wine.

Drunk or not, I manage to mimic Ezra's stoic expression and flat tone. "I have nothing to admit, nor is it any of your business."

"Kat hasn't had sex with Ezra again. *Yet*." Aaron defends me.

"Wow…" Kris settles into my lap like she's my new bestie, snuggling in for a long conversation. She wraps a tendril of my hair around her index finger, and then smiles when it springs free in a perfect, coiled ringlet. "Why the hell not? Are you insane?"

"Cort's married," I choke out. I tip my head backward and drain the contents of the wine bottle. Aaron immediately snatches it from me, fearful I'll use it as a weapon next. He's a smart man, since when I'm inebriated, all shit hits the fan. Not only do I lose my inhibitions, I also allow myself to feel what I suppress the rest of the time. Volatile situation, that.

"So what? Cortez and Divina don't have a relationship like that. Divina's oats are well-sowed. Hell, girl, Cort stopped screwing everyone for you," Kris says without any animosity.

"Na-huh," I slur in denial. "Cort did not."

"Yes. He. Did." Kris breathes right across my parted lips, with a heavy dose of sensuality and mischievousness pouring off of her. "Cort hasn't had sex with anyone since before you got here. He dropped us all about three months or so earlier, because Ez said you're all about ethics, and right and wrong, or some such horseshit."

"I don't believe you," I mutter, eyes cutting to the side to stare at Aaron. His serious expression frightens me.

Heidi jumps down from the coffee table, coming to stand next to Monica and Kayla. The three girls stare at me with expressions just as solemn as the one Aaron's wearing.

"Why do you think we were so pissed?" Kris points over her shoulder at the rest of Cort's previous harem. "You've been here what? Three? Four months, right? Well, it's been twice as long since Cortez has had anything besides Master's cock shoved down his throat."

"What?" I bark out in shock, getting a clear picture of Cort being skull-fucked by some scary master. A master even Queen treats with deference. *"This is from him,"* she said to Kris. Less than a second afterwards, her slap echoed throughout the restaurant.

"Proceed with caution," Aaron warns Kris in a stiff voice.

"How do you know all of this?" Excited for any information I can get, my inebriated state makes me more reckless than usual. "Tell me more. Please," I beg, hands coming up to shake Kris's shoulders.

"Well, it always pays to know Regina," Kris mutters wryly. "I'm sure her meeting is only to spill everything you said at dinner tonight. You do know dinner was Ezra's idea, right?"

"No," I grumble. "But it doesn't surprise me in the least." I bite my numb lip. "I'm sure this meeting is between Queen, the elusive Master, and Ezra right as we speak."

Aaron doesn't hum like Ezra does when he's caught in a trap, but he does stare at the ceiling, eyes flitting back and forth out of guilt.

"You should give Cort some lovin' when you wander home," Kris orders me, impossibly red lips quirking up at the corners. "He deserves the attention, affection, the release, and a whole lot more. Believe me when I tell you that I know how hard it is to go without sex after using it as your only currency. I went a month without as a punishment. Cort is now going on month what? Eight?"

"Damn," the submissive trio says in unison, as if they understand the underlying meaning of Kris's words. Fate wanders in from parts unknown, looking sheepish, as if she's been snooping throughout Aaron and Kayla's apartment. "What'd I miss?" she whispers in Kayla's ear.

Kris rolls her eyes at Fate and mutters, "I'm sure their bedroom is live on the grid now," and then she turns back to me. "Kat, I know you've gone lifetimes longer, but it's pure torture for someone who is addicted to sex. Agony," Kris says, shuddering in my lap in either horror or remembrance.

"Oh. I didn't know," I mumble sadly. But then my curiosity is piqued. "What's this about a cock down Cortez's throat?"

"You weren't the first one to call him Skull-fuck. Master named him that for another reason. Cort is the skull that gets fucked," she purrs salaciously.

"Oh, no!" I cry, overcome with worry. My throat clenches as if a phantom cock is assaulting my gag reflex.

"Relax. It's their favorite pastime." Kris begins playing with my hair again, twisting a tendril around her fingertip. I don't invite her, but she does as she pleases. "In normal society, dudes grab a can of beer on their way home from work to unwind with their bros. In Dominion, dudes choke on a dick thicker than a beer can to unwind their master to save their bros."

"Um… what the fuck, Kris? I feel like the filter from your brain to your mouth is malfunctioning. I'm not *that* drunk to have misheard you."

"Welcome to Dominion, New York. Where what is normal is abnormal, and where what is hedonist, perverted, and punishable by a court of law is the norm."

"Home!" Fate shouts, startling Kayla and Heidi, while Monica flashes me a look of, "*Let's get the fuck out of here, because we sure as shit ain't in Kansas anymore.*"

"Who is this master?" I pet Kristal from her shoulders to wrists, hoping to get the information out of her. I've heard many ambiguous statements about this master this evening. I really want to know who he is, especially if he's assaulting Cortez's throat.

Hazel eyes twinkling with deviousness, Kris pets me back. "Well–"

"Kristal, stop! NO!" Aaron yells at her, vibrating the couch with his command.

Kris flinches as if struck, stumbling from my lap to go hide behind the wall of female flesh near the coffee table. Her lips tremble in fear, but her eyes are bright and eager with lust. Aaron's newfound dominant side tripped a hidden trigger within Kristal, and judging by the awestruck expressions on the rest of the girls' faces, it resonated with them too.

"You're mean," I grumble at Aaron, but all he does is laugh at me. "If Ez won't tell me, you always make sure no one else will. Please," I beg, crawling across the sofa to beseech him. I flash my Puss-in-Boots eyes, an expression that used to work on Aaron.

"You're piss-roaring drunk, Kitten," Aaron teases me, reaching a fingertip out to close my eyelids. "Kayla, get your friends over here. I need some loving before Kat forces me to do something that will result in my castration."

I watch in shock and awe as Kayla leads Heidi, Fate, and Monica over to Aaron, with Kris looking unsure over whether or not she's invited.

In the several months since Aaron and I have had sex, he's transformed. He doesn't seem to have his hang-ups anymore, for which I'm thankful. But never in a million years did I think he'd act like this.

Aaron is acting like an insatiable, horny man. A man who can have anything he wants, and he's not afraid to ask for it. Aaron just asked, and he received with great fervor.

The girls settle at Aaron's feet and start mauling him and ripping off his clothing. They work in conjunction, as if they unzip and tug jeans down thick thighs together on a constant basis. As soon as the rigid flesh is revealed, it's sucked down Kayla's throat with Heidi nursing at the nutsack. Fate works on one boot while Monica tackles the other. Kris stays on the sidelines, waiting to be invited, looking hungry yet rejected.

Aaron gazes over at me with heavy-lidded eyes and an expression of pure rapture on his face. His breath hitches in his throat at the same time I hear a gurgling noise pass Kayla's lips.

"I'd ask you to join us, Kitten, but Ezra said he'd rip my dick off if I ever touched you like that again. Worse, Cort said he'd shove my own amputated dick up my ass and fuck me with it. Sorry."

By flashing me an apologetic smile, Aaron tries to lessen the blow to my ego, and the resulting anger that the Ezes are still trying to run my life. But just then, no less than three mouths attach themselves to his cock, causing him to jerk backward into the sofa cushion.

"My Lord!" Aaron shouts. "I don't know whose tongue is licking my taint, but don't you dare fucking stop!"

All I can do is watch in wonder and laugh like a perverted little girl. Aaron is lost under a writhing mass of females. Mouths are suckling at any available patch of flesh, with hungry fingertips groping whatever they can reach. All Aaron does is lie back and enjoy as Cortez's ex-harem becomes his.

Thinking of Cortez, knowing he used to touch all of these gorgeous women, for some reason the thought doesn't make me jealous. It makes me understand the depth of his commitment to Ezra and whatever Ezra has planned. Cort has gone without for nearly a year after receiving this orgasmic treatment whenever he wanted, only to see Ezra betray his own vows with Adelaide. Now I understand why Cortez feels Ezra having sex with his own fiancée is a betrayal, after abstaining at Ezra's behest.

Cortez gave up so much, so it's no wonder he snapped by fucking me in front of Dexter and Heidi. Cortez must be beyond frustrated– night after night, sleeping naked next to the man he secretly covets but won't allow himself to have. I understand his selective amnesia and guilt now as well.

"It looks like you've got your hands full, baby boy. I'm not entirely sure how you plan on pleasuring them all. But if you do, you deserve a gold star." I shift on the sofa. "Well, since there isn't room at the trough for me…" I mutter flippantly as I stand up, earning me a deep chuckle from the budding stud.

Lust-drugged blue eyes flash me a look of understanding, and then connect with the lonely girl in the living room. "If I make room, are you willing to play, Kris?" Aaron asks the tiny antagonist who's trying her hardest not to pout.

"Was he any good?" She asks me, obviously trying to pretend she isn't dying to dive into the orgy at her feet.

"Yeah." I blush. "Very good. I'd love to take some of the credit, but Aaron's a natural."

"Well, I think I'm up for a ride. This is monumental, Aaron. I never thought I'd see you like this. I can't be left out. I'd lose my reputation when the rumors are leaked." Instead of rushing forward, Kristal's voice wavers. "You'll have to call Whitt and ask for permission. He gets angry when I... when I feed my addiction."

"I sent Pretty Boy a text before I picked you girls up at the restaurant, and he said it was okay. Regina and Syn knew that I was planning on taking advantage of a bunch of drunken submissives." Aaron's laughter is twisted with lust and filled with pride over how he premeditated his own sexual feast.

"All's good, then!" Kris dives over me, landing on the sofa cushion I was just occupying. "Sorry, Kat. No mistresses allowed. But you can watch. Or better yet, go throw Cort a bone," she teases me.

"First, I have to see how Aaron's going to coordinate this." I shake my head in awe. "Then, I may actually do as you suggested, Kris. I don't see how anyone could not end up horny as all hell after witnessing this impossible feat."

"Ladies," Aaron drawls, disengaging from the horde. "There's enough for everyone, but first you must follow me to the bedroom."

I follow the herd, surprised at how they prance and skip drunkenly after Aaron, as if he's the Pied Piper of submissives. They giggle, each sharing what they wish to do next. I detect not a single note of jealousy.

Maybe I'm not as enlightened as these ladies, but I'd feel insecure if I was competing with so many other women. But then again, I'd kill to be someone's number one.

I understand the selfless urge to share who you love with someone else you love. The thought of witnessing Cortez and Ezra coming together, even knowing I could never compete with that, it warms my heart. I'd be happy, even if I didn't get to watch.

The past is the past. But the thought of any of these women touching either of the Ezes now, makes me see violent red, even though they don't belong to me. I cannot voice the number of death fantasies I've entertained featuring Adelaide Whittenhower.

"Wow... Your bedroom is so not what I was expecting." Monica snorts at the décor. Pink, pink, and more pink, in every shade of pink, from floor to ceiling.

Aaron, with his huge build and shaven head, looks comical in this room. While aggressive when it comes to his newfound sexual needs, Aaron is obviously passive when it comes to his environment. This bedroom has Kayla's sweet signature written all over it.

"This makes me want to have a tea party, not fuck everyone in the room," Kris purrs, sounding delighted yet sarcastic.

"Is your room like this?" Monica asks me, nudging her elbow into my side.

"Hell, no," I mutter, aghast. "Our bedroom is gray. Their mutual favorite color is the fucked up shade of their own eyeballs. Ezra would never allow any pink in the apartment. Ava's bedroom is pale green, no doubt matching my irises. His OCD knows no bounds."

"Everything's gray, just like at Edge Publishing?" Incredulity is thick in Monica's voice. "Do you ever get jealous over their obsession with each other?"

"No," I answer honestly. "I just feel left out, but that's where I belong... so–"

I'm cut off by, "Katya." Aaron's mood diminishes in a second.

Refusing to ruin their nights, "What odd colors are your bedrooms?"

"Regina's room is purple." Kris snickers. "And Fate's is pink."

"And yours is such a disaster area that we can't tell what color it is," Fate burns Kris.

"Ladies," Aaron grabs his dick, fingers wrapping tightly around the shaft, and then he starts stroking in a delicious rhythm. "I don't care who has what color. I'm horny as hell."

His head hitches back as he gets into masturbating before an audience. "Get on the bed, Kayla," he growls his command.

Kayla quickly looks at me and I realize we have been putting her in a hard spot. Does she listen to Aaron, or me, or Ezra, or Cort? The poor girl is confused.

"Beauty, we aren't doing a scene. You're in your own home with your boyfriend. We will get your master figured out," I promise. Aaron looks at me in relief, silently pleading with me to tell Kayla she is his.

"Everyone but Kat has ten seconds to get naked," Aaron masters the lot of women, and they comply in record speed.

Such a wide variety of body types and Aaron loves every single one of them. His eyes rove over their bodies, as do mine. Monica is too thin, but she has a nice ass. If she'd gain a few pounds, she'd be perfectly curvy. Heidi and Kayla would be considered chubby by societal standards, but they have gorgeous, biteable, pink flesh. Fate is pale perfection, whereas Kris is a tan, curvy, inked masterpiece.

Insecurities rearing their ugly heads, I'm suddenly glad that I'm not on display. Ava left a lasting impression on my body, and no one wants to flash their stretch marks during an orgy. I fear the girls would make fun of me. Aaron would get turned off since I'd be seconds, not a first taste after waiting in anticipation for over a decade. Aaron would no longer be blind to my flaws.

"Kayla, lie on the edge of the bed. Ah, now that's a good girl," Aaron praises when she does as he asks. Voice sluggish, drugged on lust, "C'mere, Heidi. Lay on top of Kayla... Yes, just like that."

Heidi is lying directly on top of Kayla, both waiting for their next command. Aaron's heavy hand presses the small of Heidi's back. The pressure sandwiches the girls together, causing them to moan deep from their throats. Heidi and Kayla begin kissing in a voracious way only lovers do. Evidently, this isn't the first time Aaron has sandwiched them together like this.

"Girls, make sure those nubbins stay in contact while I fuck you," Aaron teases in a deep voice edged with naughty intent.

Aaron positions his engorged cockhead at Kayla's entrance. With a sharp flex of his hips, Kayla bucks as Aaron thrusts in her to the hilt. Hands fisting Heidi's hair, he gives several hard, brutal rolls of his hips, fucking Kayla while Heidi writhes above her.

Before I can register what's happening, I gasp or maybe Kris does, when Aaron jams his dick deep inside of Heidi's pussy. Relentlessly, he switches back and forth between the women every few thrusts. Just as everyone is getting into the motion, he pulls out and punches into a different cunt. Over and over again in a hypnotic cycle. Aaron's riding both Kayla and Heidi bareback, and all who witness are in awe.

Aaron's hard body beads with sweat as he flexes his hips. He fucks like a machine, muscles bunching and cording with every movement. His breathing is harsh and labored from his efforts. Both girls are moaning, groaning, and gasping for breath into each other's mouths.

This sex god is not the Aaron I know. The look on Kris, Fate, and Monica's faces mirrors my own. It's a mix of lust and shock. Aaron looks like a porn star, only better– a sex rockstar.

"Monica, you're going last because you need to make love, and I'm just the man to take the loneliness away." Aaron grunts sharply because he's switching to a different cunt again. "Kris, you're next. I'm going to pound you over the dresser. So fucking hard and rough, you won't be able to walk in an hour, let alone tomorrow. You'll be so raw, your addiction will be fed for weeks to come."

"Oh, God," the words shudder out Kristal's lips. "Please. I'll beg for it if I have to."

"Fate, sweetie, you and I will go nice and slow. I'll lie on the bed while you ride me. All the girls can caress you and make you feel oh-so nice. I know you don't like it any other way," he croons to Fate.

I slowly back out of the room, fleeing because this is too much to comprehend. This version of Aaron scares the shit out of me, and not in a way that draws physical pain. This is the Aaron I danced with at Restraint– the Aaron who fucks like a master.

I murdered innocent Aaron, and from his ashes awoke Master Aaron, with the ability to direct complicated sexual scenes with the ease of a seasoned orchestra conductor.

I walk across the hall in a daze. I had to either leave or beg to get fucked. Horny and drunk is a lethal combination.

# Chapter Seventeen

The door to our apartment smashes shut behind me. Cort looks up as I enter the living room, a quizzical expression flashing across his tan face. He's sitting on the sofa with his laptop resting on his thighs and his hand deep in a bag of Cheetos.

"What?" Cortez is no doubt asking about my wild appearance. I run a hand through my hair to smooth it down, managing to muss it up far worse than before.

"Aaron…" I swallow thickly– swallow the lust down my throat to pool between my thighs in a wash of arousal. "Aaron is not the baby boy I used to know. I don't know where he went, or who's replaced him. It's insanity. Aaron is fucking five women right now," I mutter in awe, still not believing it even though I saw it with my very own two eyes.

"No way." Cort grins at me and shakes his head no. "No, fucking way."

"Yes, fucking way. I shit you not. Aaron is over there fucking like a boss. Our night turned into a Girls' Night Out in Aaron's bed," I mutter wryly, causing Cort to snicker. "It's not the first time he's had ménage, either. Heidi and Kayla are well acquainted with our baby boy, enough so that he's riding them raw."

"No way," Cort mutters in disbelief again, eyes nearly bulging out of his skull. "No way."

"Uh-huh," I slur, and then repeat, "Yes, fucking way."

"This I have got to see." Cort snaps his laptop shut, tosses the bag of Cheetos onto the coffee table, and then licks his orange fingertips clean. "I'm gonna go have a little look-see," Cort drawls out, still sounding disbelieving. "Stumble to bed. I'll meet you there." Cort's eyes are glowing and he's grinning like a Cheshire cat.

…And stumble I do. I giggle every time I fall on my ass. I strip off my clothing, leaving a trail on our bedroom floor, and then I crawl onto the mattress. It's too much of a bother to actually get beneath the bedding.

My mind is a violent stew of contradictory thoughts. I spent the evening surrounded by beautiful, accomplished women, all of which have been with Cortez. Even harder to swallow, the fact that I've probably already met all the people Ezra has ever touched.

Ezra once told me a dominant's biggest flaw is pride, while a submissive's is insecurity. Drunk and sad, I feel closer to a submissive than I ever have before.

Staring at the ceiling while contemplating my own obvious faults, I briefly wonder how much time has passed. Maybe Cort is joining in the fun. It's not as if he hasn't previously been inside every person in that other apartment, Aaron included.

My stomach knots as a vicious wave of jealousy washes over me at the thought. It's not that Cortez is having fun– I lie to myself –it's that I wasn't invited to participate.

No matter how long I live here, I'll forever be an outsider. I can feel it to my bones, and it's not my insecurity screaming, either. Dominion is a world where everyone else comes first in all things. I'm just… here. I'm the means to an end.

An obligation.

"Ugh!" I groan while grabbing a pillow to cover my face. "Don't drink and think. Worse, don't drink and feel."

"Holy shit, Kitten!" Cort's enthusiastic voice jars me out of my self-defeatist thoughts. I ignore the warmth that infuses me because Cortez pulled himself away from an orgy to join me in our shared bed. Kris was right; Cort has been a very good boy, indeed.

I scramble to sit up. "It's wild, eh? Like a doppelganger replaced Aaron, and he's a confident, horny bastard?"

Cort runs a palm over his dark hair, clearly astonished. "Aaron was pounding Kris over the dresser when I walked in– totally banging her. Christ, that master was not the Aaron we know." Cortez chuckles deeply, affection and awe lacing the tone. "As sick as it is to say, I'm proud. I wish Ezra could have seen it."

"Oh, I've no doubt that Ezra knows. He's at a meeting with Queen and the mystery master right now, discussing my dinner date. I'm sure Queen told him what Aaron's plans were," I manage to sound exasperated even though I'm drunk as all hell.

"How do you know this?" Cort demands, sounding accusatory, as if I've been sticking my nose where it doesn't belong.

I chuck my pillow at him, growling deep from my throat. "It's a crime for Kat to know anything, is that it?"

"That's not why I was asking," Cort rumbles. He ditches his pajama bottoms, leaving on a pair of boxer briefs, and hesitates to join me on the bed. "How did you find out something I didn't even know? After Marc and Dexter left, we put Ava to bed, and then Ezra was supposedly working at Restraint for a few hours this evening. I'm annoyed that he lied to me, that's why."

I suddenly realize I'm naked and Cortez has an unobstructed view, so I tug the blankets back and slide between the sheets to cover my insecurities. "Girl talk and drinks is how I found out. All ya gotta do is ask Kris, since she's an antagonistic font of information."

Approaching hesitantly, Cortez climbs into bed next to me. "Like what?" he asks, sounding leery.

"Well, let's see," I pretend to think it over, even though it's difficult with the fog of intoxication riding me. "I had dinner with Monica, Kayla, Heidi, Kristal, Queen, Fate, and Syn. Syn hates my fucking guts for some reason, I might add. But while I was sitting there, I found out you had fucked every vagina at the table."

"Kat, I'm not exactly proud of that. Ashamed, actually," Cortez admits, and I do believe him. "If I could change my past behavior, I would in a heartbeat. I… to be completely honest, I was trying to hurt Ezra. But every girl I was with hurt me more because Ezra didn't give a flying fuck who I was with, while thoughts of him touching anyone were murdering me."

"I'm not judging, and I'm not touching anything you just said about Ezra," I add, refusing to delve too deeply into the train wreck of their relationship. "I'm saying it wasn't exactly conducive to friendship building. But neither was finding out who our gay bedmate slept with, either."

"What do you mean?" Cort questions me cautiously. He reaches out to flick the switch to lower the room-darkening shades. The man has to have absolute darkness to fall asleep. Apparently he needs it to have uncomfortable conversations as well.

"Ezra admitted to me that he's been with four women and even less men. Me," I point to myself, even though Cortez can't see me. "Adelaide Whittenhower." My voice cracks with a wealth of immense pain. "Which we have firsthand knowledge. Queen, which you also have firsthand knowledge, seeing as how the pair of you did her together. Regina Regal's words, not mine."

"That was *not* a pleasant experience. It pretty much ruined my confidence and Regina's and my friendship. It was during the initiation that crowned Regina Queen."

"It's none of my business," I mutter offhandedly, like it doesn't bother me in the least. *Liar.* "But it doesn't make it any easier on me, either. These ladies don't like me, and not because of who I am. It's because of you and Ezra. Not fair," I whimper, hugging my pillow to my chest.

"I wish life was fair. I wish they would treat you nicely. I believe that's why Ezra set up the dinner this evening in the first place. So the ladies could get to know you on a personal level, not just what Ezra tells them about you."

I try to ignore the fact that Ezra spills his guts about me to his ex-lovers while telling me jackshit about them, but I cannot. It hurts beyond belief. A deep, emotional betrayal. Is nothing sacred when it comes to Ezra?

"There's one last girl notched into Ezra's bedpost, and Kris pretty much told me that this person was at the table with us tonight. I'm not an idiot. I can do that math. Your ex-lovers are chatty bitches, while Ezra's ex-lovers are scary as fuck and serious. My deductive skills scream Syn."

"I never said you were an idiot," Cort rasps in the dark. "But I'm not going to confirm nor deny who Ezra has been with, or why. If you want to know who I've been with, I'll tell you any goddamned thing you want to know, even if it's painful."

"Anything, eh? What about like how you get skull-fucked by this mystery master? Or how you aren't having sex because of me–"

"You are never going out with them again," Cortez threatens. "If I find out you're meeting with them, I will stalk you, hunt you down, and drag your ass back home. No one understands how you feel about privacy like I do. I get it. So I think you can imagine how I must feel right now, after a group of women spilled pretty much all of my secrets, when it should have been a private, intimate conversation between the two of us."

Thoroughly chastised, "Christ," I cry out, rolling over to face Cortez. "I'm sorry. I didn't mean for it to go down that way. I just didn't like this huge elephant in the room while we were trying to be friendly."

"I get it. I do. But that doesn't take away how betrayed I feel right now. My privacy was invaded. Things I find shameful from my past were revealed. I wanted to bond with you over some of the things you learned, now that opportunity is gone."

Cort sounds so dejected, that the words stumble out of my mouth before I can stop them, "Make love to me."

"Katya, is that you? I can't see you, so I can't be too sure. But it sounds like you, even if the words aren't yours."

"Fuck me!" I demand, needing to feel anything but what I'm feeling. I crawl across the bed and kneel before Cortez. I beg by whimpering since he can't see me.

"What?" Cort laughs, but it's a disbelieving huff of a sound.

"Fuck me," I demand again, but it comes out more as a defeated pout. "I'm drunk and horny, and feeling down on myself… and you've been a very good boy."

"I'm sure this is the wine talking, not actually what you want. I don't want to be a regret you have in the morning. I've been in your position often with Ezra. Now I understand how he felt in that moment." Cortez groans as if in pain. "It's killing me to say this, but I've got to take a pass."

"Ugh!" I yelp in frustration as I flop back onto the mattress. "Why is it, when I want it, I can't have it? But when I don't want it, you and Ezra have no issue just taking it?"

"I'm going to answer your earlier question right now." Cortez successfully avoids the battlefield of landmines I've laid out. "I would tell you anything you'd ever ask if I knew it wouldn't upset Ezra." Cortez tries to soothe me with the truth. "If it's just about me, I'll be an open book. But what involves Ezra, belongs to Ezra."

"Hearing you say that, it makes me love you more," the drunk idiot in me reveals. "Because that just shows how loyal you truly are, and I respect you because of that. So don't tell me anything, or tell me everything. I'll listen to anything you wish to say, and from now on, I won't tell another soul."

"Thank you," Cortez whispers, suddenly sounding choked up. "I do want to tell you about my celibacy. That was a conversation I wanted to have with you, but wasn't sure how to broach the subject."

"Ah, Kris sure is a great icebreaker," I mutter, causing Cortez to rumble a laugh.

"She's something, all right... So, Ezra asked me to stop having sex a little over a year ago. He manipulated me into it by saying multiple partners would freak you out, and how much it hurt him to watch me be destructive."

"What do you mean?" I whisper in the dark of our bedroom, the words sounding intimate.

"At first, the celibacy was difficult after having sex daily since I was twelve years old. Sometimes several time a day. When we first started screwing, Ezra and I were insatiable. I won't lie to you, I've been in similar situations as Aaron, only it was with well over twenty writhing bodies. All girls. Dozens of girls, and just me. Restraint was a toxic place for me when we first opened."

"Holy fuck," I breathe, awed. My heart pounds out of my chest, fluttering wildly as if screaming to run back to Pennsylvania.

"Then..." Cort reaches over to grip my hand, comforting himself and restraining me at the same time. "I felt lighter. Lifted. No longer ashamed. As time went by, I felt the chains of my addiction slipping away. I realized a small touch," he squeezes my fingers, "meant so much more than a quick fuck. It should be more. Just sleeping next to you and Ezra is infinitely more than an orgy of lonely souls."

"How naïve I must look to you," I grumble, hating how selfish I sound and feel by making Cortez's admission about me.

"You know that spark you saw in Aaron, that vital piece of innocence you never felt you had? Well, Katya, that's what I saw in you– still do. I was never innocent. As a devout Catholic, I was born a sinner. The celibacy started out as being for Ezra and continued for you, but it eventually became about *me*. But I'm still no saint. I might not be getting off, but I'm still a vessel."

"Master's skull-fuckery?" I ask, curiosity thicker in my voice than judgment.

"I can't tell you who he is, but I can explain the why of it. Even this begins and ends with Ezra. The first time Master skullfucked me was when I ran to him after Ezra betrayed me so badly I didn't know how to move on. I used Master to harm Ezra. Master knew it when I did it, and he allowed me to make my own bed. As punishment for using him, Master made me lie in my own bed, too. My mouth has been his since that moment forward."

Bolting upright in bed, I shout, "Just tell him no!"

Cort laughs so loudly the bed vibrates from the force. "I can't," he rasps out breathlessly. "I don't want to tell him no," he mutters wryly. "I refuse. It's the only time I feel free, and no one else is willing to free me. Ezra is smart enough not to demand that we stop since he won't give me *that* in return."

"Isn't there anyone that demanding bastard is jealous of?" Resentment is thick in my voice. "I can't believe he willingly shares you. I've been murdering ex-submissives and ex-lovers in my head as we speak. I'd love to find Ezra's weaknesses for once."

"Jealous? Shit yeah, Ezra is a jealous bastard. He just knows better than to get between me and Master, as his betrayal put me there in the first place. He allows it as a way to punish himself. Ezra may have converted to Judaism, but he was born a sinner, just as I was."

"Forever a martyr," I whisper.

"Exactly," Cortez agrees. "Our master is everything to me: my protector, my provider, my teacher, my world," he says reverently. "What is between he and I is nothing like what is between Ezra and me, or between you and me for that matter. Ezra and I are complicated. You and I are honest and innocent– a true melding. Master and I, he treats me like a Catholic."

"What?" I gasp out. "Does this asshole have something against religion?"

More rancorous laughter fills the room. "Not a bastard, unlike most of the denizens of Dominion, and I mean that by the very definition of the word. Religious in the extreme, is our master. More than happy to punish a Catholic because he understands the guilt we are born with. The man is just pissed because nothing he did would ever convince me to give up my faith for his, which bought me a wealth of respect in his eyes."

"So he does to you what you did to me?" I ask hesitantly, an echo of that night so very long ago haunting my mind. I'm simultaneously petrified yet aroused by the events of that night, and that disturbs me beyond words.

"Exactly the same way. There are words of encouragement, soft touches to my face and hair, but otherwise he doesn't speak to me or touch me. It's about his need to control me and my need to give him my power. That's all. I feel lighter afterwards, like I just confessed to my priest. However, afterward, he feels guiltier than hell and promises never to do it again."

"But," I begin, and then have no idea how to voice what I want to ask. "You need it, though, right?"

"Yes," Cort replies instantly. "I need it. It's not about love or lust. He doesn't touch my cock. He *never* touches me sexually. He allows me to hug and kiss him on occasion, and that is it. If I could find someone– more –who could offer me what I need, while touching me in return, I would never seek him out again."

"Ezra? He would do anything you asked of him, as long as you gave yourself to him in return."

"How's that working out for ya, Kat? How much power do you feel every time you deny Ezra the last piece of you?"

"Touché, Cortez. You have me there. I can't give Ezra my all until he can give me the same in return, and that will never happen since you own his heart."

"Wrong," Cort denies me. "I may own Ezra's soul, but *you* own his heart. And until either of us can tap into his head, we can't give ourselves to him. Ezra isn't even whole himself, so how the hell can he be everything for someone? The nightmares, the fact that I'm straight, the terror I feel every time I even contemplate having sex with a man, none of that has as much influence on me as the unadulterated fear I feel over being consumed by Ezra."

"You and I are the same, my friend," I tease, but there is a lingering note of truth to my words.

"Which is why we both drive Ezra insane. Which is an impossible feat, as he is already fucking nuts as it is," Cortez declares sardonically. "Enough about that lying, betraying, frustrating assfuck."

"So…" I purr, crawling from my nest. "You've had nothing? No simple affections? No lingering touches? Nothing but your throat being brutalized in the past eight months?"

"Thirteen months, actually. But who's counting?"

"You are," I tease.

"It took the girls a few months to realize I wasn't allowing them to touch me back. In thirteen months, the only satisfaction I've received is our rage fuck in Dexter's room at Restraint and when I skull-fucked you. Prior to that, I was giving a shit-ton of oral."

"Surely you yank the exquisiteness," I taunt. My fingers take on a life of their own, fluttering against Cort's firm thigh.

"Constantly," Cort grits out between clenched teeth, voice tight all of a sudden. "If the skull-fuck is brutal enough, I pop in my pants."

"God, I'd love to witness that," I drawl, drugged on lust and drunk on wine. "So, the only person who has gotten you off in the past year is me?"

"Yes," Cortez rasps roughly. He freezes beneath my touch, understanding what my naughty intentions are as my fingertips skate up his inner thigh.

"You have no idea how turned on that makes me," I admit in a salacious voice dripping with lust and pride. "I've never been anyone's number one, and I may never be. But knowing I'm the only person who's been meeting your needs while you're meeting the needs of others… it makes me feel like a rockstar when I've felt nothing but ugly since I stepped foot on Dominion soil."

"You have no idea of your appeal, Katya. Which makes you even more desirable." Cort shifts on the mattress, forcing my fingertips to fall from his hip. I fear I'm pushing my luck as he wiggles around. Sightless, the sound of fabric zipping through the air pulses a quiver down my spine. Fingertips seek mine, and then place them on a bare-naked hip. Cort's actions silently voice his intentions.

"You're so warm," shudders out of my throat in a breathy sound.

"I'll never lie to you, Katya," Cort confesses. "If I can't tell you something, I'll explain why. But I will never lie or betray you, so please don't use my lecherous past against me."

"I'm pretty sure I'm the lone Protestant in this city. While you were taught to confess your sins and bleed guilt, we had '*Judge not lest ye be judged*' thrust down our throats. Freewill. Your actions render your consequences. I didn't do it, so it's none of my business if it doesn't outwardly affect me."

"Thank God," Cort sighs in relief. "I'm clean, by the way. My dick has always been wrapped for everyone save Ezra. So no fear, okay?"

"Okay," I mutter, voice wavering as I realize Cortez is telling me this because he plans on having sex with me. I check in with my conscience, and I realize every single part of me is good with that.

In the oppressive dark, I seek out Cort's lips, showing him how his past actions don't affect how I feel about him. Everything he did before me wasn't about me. Everything after only counts if it was about me. No one has ever been as open and honest with me as Cortez has been. He takes the time to explain the color to the blind. For weeks, he's stuck by my side, even going as far as to sit in my office, all in the name of protecting me. He's not suffocating me, stalking me, or surveying me. Cortez Abernathy is just there when I need him, because he knows I need him, and when I don't, he gives me the space to think and grow.

"You're not a consolation prize," I mutter against Cortez's lips, voicing my own thoughts aloud. He groans in response, tugging me down to his chest. "I'm not a consolation prize. Neither of us is replacing Ezra in our lives. We're charting our own course."

"Kat!" Cort cries out. A heartbeat later, his fingers are weaving through my hair, controlling our kiss. Lips sliding against one another, we both open on a moan. Our tongues dance, rolling a quiver down my spine in anticipation. My hands clench against his shoulders as his fingers yank my hair sharply, tearing a groan from my throat.

"This isn't because I'm drunk. This isn't to get back at Ezra." Cort and I think the same way. My insecurities are mirrored within him. Ezra and I share our pride, and Cortez and I share our self-doubt. I can read Cortez's needs and wants because they are my needs and wants– both of us are throbbing with ache for Ezra Zeitler.

"I won't regret this in an hour, or tomorrow morning, or next week... or ever," I promise as I move to straddle Cort's hips. The exquisiteness is as hard, throbbing, smoldering hot, and ready for anything as it rests in the cleft of my sex. I twist my hips to show Cortez exactly what I want– exactly what I'm willing to take should he deny me.

"Christ," Cort hisses, jerking upright in surprise when I swivel on him, almost impaling my cunt on his cock.

"You feel so good," I moan, luxuriating in the feel of his naked flesh gliding along mine. I bloom for him, moisture flowing from my pussy, readying itself for a good, hard fuck.

"Kitten," Cort groans, voice strained with hunger. "We can't have sex for so many reasons."

"This feels like we can," I purr salaciously as I roll my hips– the exquisiteness almost slipping inside me.

"Yet!" Cort gasps out, voice strained, body ignoring his own protests as his hips undulate beneath mine. "We can't have sex *yet*. I made a promise; don't force me to break it!"

"Please," I beg, rocking faster. I ride his hips, gliding my slit along the length of his cock. "I've never been on top before. Never in control." My neck arches as a purr of pure satisfaction pours past my lips. Mental pleasure from the power coursing through me.

Fingertips bruising my waist to halt my movements, "A compromise," Cort rasps breathlessly. "Will you take a compromise?"

"Anything," I plead, trying to rub myself on his length but to no avail. His grip is too tight, and I whimper out of frustration and need.

"I have an idea– a way we both may find our *more*. I'll give you the power you seek, if you'll allow me to feel free. Deal?"

"Fuck," I snarl, jerking my hips, trying escape his hold. "I'll do anything. I'll even make a deal with the Devil if I have to!"

"Speaking of devils. It's a pity that Master and Ezra didn't hear you say that, or else this night could have been a memory we'd never forget for lifetimes," Cort mutters wryly.

Abruptly, Cortez grips my hips, fingers biting into my flesh. He picks me up with ease, rotating me until I'm facing the other direction, and then he releases me.

I find myself sitting on Cortez's chest, staring sightlessly in the direction of his feet. His fingers seek my back, gently digging into the taut muscles of my shoulders. He sits up until his lips are brushing against my ear. The heat pouring off of him melts any insecurities and inhibitions I possess.

Rasping into my ear, "If you fuck my face, I'll fuck yours." I shudder above him, pussy grinding on the center of his chest, leaving the slickness of my arousal behind.

"Yes," I breathe hypnotically. I went years without affection and sexual release. Ezra, Cortez, and Aaron addicted me instantly, and then they ceased to touch me weeks upon weeks ago, leaving me to starve.

"Beg," Cort breathes into my ear, fluttering against my hair. "Beg me. Beg. Do it. Beg."

Whimpering, writhing, cunt clenching and protesting its emptiness, I flood Cort's chest with my arousal. "Fuck," I hiss as the hidden switch inside my psyche is pressed.

Cortez proves he's as much of a switch as I am, quickly going back and forth between dominant and submissive on a whim. I'm more dominant than submissive; which is Cortez Abernathy?

"You drive me crazy," I growl. "Forcing me to sleep between you fools. Naked. Do you have any idea the perverted images I go to sleep to at night and wake to in the morning? Logically, I realize I should be jealous of the connection and chemistry you share, but I'm not. I'm intrigued. I'm addicted. I'd kill to see you touch each other, even if it's as fleeting of a touch as a kiss."

"You suck at begging, Kitten," Cort chuckles in my ear. "But you make my cock throb with the indecent images you just projected in my head, so all is forgiven."

"Sorry. I also suck at submitting," I mutter sheepishly.

"I couldn't give a fuck less. Because in order for us to feel free, you have to be the one in charge," Cort grits out, pressing my head forward with the palm of his hand. "Suck me. Fuck me with your throat. You can be gentle with me if you find me too much to swallow. Just touch me. Love me." The longing and loneliness in his tone renders me speechless.

I lean forward on my own, lips seeking the exquisiteness. Having to hunt in the dark, I encounter Cortez's smooth hip first. With his cockhead greeting my cheek, I turn my face to nuzzle the rigid jut of flesh that knows only brutality and never kindness.

"Do whatever you want to my cock, just know I won't last for shit– my stamina is zero after so long. Grind on my face, Kitten," Cort demands, voice rolling with a husky growl. "Grind on me. Hard. Suffocate me with your cunt. Make me choke on your pussy juice…"

I yelp in surprise when Cort yanks me backward until my knees are straddling his head and my sex is poised over his lips. From one blink to the next, Cort's mouth attacks my aching pussy, tongue impaling me. His beard stubble adds to the delicious friction, abrading my labia with a slight edge of discomforting pain.

"Fuck my face, Kitten. Own it. Control it," Cort breathes against my quivering cunt, and then dives back in.

Inebriation takes every inhibition I possess and changes it into raw need. Besides a few soothing licks from Master Ez, I've never been eaten out before. I've most definitely never ridden anyone's face, and now I need it like the air I breathe.

I wantonly roll my hips against Cort's lips, his cheeks, even the tip of his nose and his chin. The friction of his stubble against my lips and the smooth slick of his tongue delving through my folds is divine ecstasy. But nothing compares to the satisfaction of being in control. Cort may be pleasuring me, but I hold the seat of power.

"You're so damn good at this," I purr, breath hitching in the back of my throat. "I should thank all of those submissives for allowing you the practice, just so you could service me perfectly."

"I love the taste of a pretty kitty." Cort chuckles, vibrating my flesh, and then he gets back to his feast, licking and sucking at my pussy lips. He expertly ravages me in a way no man ever has. His teeth sink into my labia and tug, adding a peculiar sensation to the mix. When his lips latch onto my clit and suck, I realize all I've been missing. Nothing feels as good as a man suckling at your cunt.

Absolutely nothing.

I've given exactly one blowjob, and I wasn't the one in control. I'm scared and intimidated of the exquisiteness, but I want to do it so damned badly that my insecurities mean jackshit.

I lick Cort's cock up and down in astonishment. I can't believe that he crammed most of it down my throat, or that it fit inside my pussy.

I swear for the billionth time that I wish I could remember the finer details of our first time. Maybe I'm not meant to remember because it wasn't about us: Cortez and Katya. Even though it was us coming together, it was still about jealousy and fear. I can't remember because we need a proper do-over.

I nip the plum of Cort's cock with my teeth as a test, and when he jerks underneath my tongue, I know he loves the bitter edge of pleasure. The tip of my tongue rides the groove of his glans, swirling and tasting.

"You can experiment any other time, Kitten," Cort breathlessly gasps out. "It won't take me long with you. So for the love of all that is holy, stop playing with it and get to sucking. I'm going insane," he cries.

I swallow his head and shaft down as far as my throat will allow, pressing forward forcefully. I love the sensation of his velvety cock sliding between my parted lips, and the stretch and strain of the exquisiteness's invasion. With his girth and length, he barely fits into my mouth, and I start to panic that I won't do it right.

I want Cortez to love it like our last time. As much as I protested his skull-fuckery, it turned me on so much so that it's all I can think about. I try to give him what he likes, but it's missing a vital element.

"Cort," I plead. "Yank my hair and fuck my face." Somewhere buried deep, I find the place that knows how to beg. There is a desperate edge to my tone of voice, "Skull-fuck me!"

"What?" Cort stops what he's doing between my legs and I whimper in complaint, and then he realizes what I was asking. "It's not about my dick getting skull-fucked, it's about my throat suffering. You don't have to unless you need it, too. I could pop just by you breathing on my dick, or by you riding my face and suffocating me."

"I…" I admit what I've long denied. "I need it, too. Don't stop," I firmly press my pussy on his face and grind. "Fuck my face, Cort. Skull-fuck me!"

I release a maniacal laugh. There is no way in hell I would ever say that line sober. Katya Waters does not beg. Unless she's drunk, and only because she trusts Cortez Abernathy not to penalize her for it.

"My God. I love you, Katya." Cortez pants breathlessly, sounding beyond awed.

"I love you, too, Cortez." On the heels of my adoration is a demand. "Now fuck my face before I lose my patience!"

I rock on Cort's chin, pressing the tip of his nose deep into my pussy. I lean forward farther and gulp as much of his cock down my throat as possible. After several tries to deep throat him, it's just not the same if he's not in control.

Switch: we desire the need to be in control and to submit.

Sixty-nine: the only position that is perfectly suited for a pair of confused switches. I control the pussy, and Cort controls the cock. Push and pull. Give and take. Cycling back and forth in the ultimate of power exchanges.

Cortez's fingers wrap tightly in my hair, weaving the strands in an unrelenting grip. With a sharp tug, I moan from the pain, almost coming on Cortez's face. Lunging forward, he thrust his hips, and every inch of his exquisite cock slides down my throat.

We violently brutalize each other, pouring all of our pain and frustration into our movements. Our dominant nature is being fed by the fact that I'm trying to suffocate Cortez with my cunt and he's trying to force me to choke on his cock. Our passive urges are being fed by the same, as I'm choking and he's suffocating.

In perfect harmony, we groan in unison, and then he groans again because he loved the vibrations of my throat reverberating against his throbbing cock.

Being drunk has its benefits. I'm completely relaxed, almost lethargic, and I know what to expect from the skull-fuckery this time around.

Cortez isn't as forceful as before. He's already on the edge, not needing as much from me to propel him off of the precipice.

I open my throat wide, and breathe out my nose in a rhythm synchronized with his thrusts. I bury my lips in his pubic hair and allow the contractions in my throat to massage his shaft. Not only do I revel in my ability to do this for him, I get off on it.

We counter-fuck.

Suffocate.

Choke.

Suffocate.

Choke.

I smash my hips down, smothering Cort's mouth and nostrils with my cunt: *suffocate*. Cortez jabs his hips forward, while palming the back of my skull to push me face-first into his groin: *choke*.

"I only need ten more seconds, Kitten. Hold on!" Cort pushes my head down as hard as he can. His fingers tighten in my hair to the point that strands snap off– one right after the other. It hurts so much that I moan in ecstasy. I'm starting to see stars as darkness creeps in around the edges of my vision, and my eyelids are getting heavier from the lack of oxygen.

Cort thrusts his hips up while pressing my head down farther than ever before. Not only do I accommodate his invasion, I take more, and he growls his approval against my pussy.

"Come with me, Kitten!" Cortez demands of me, and for once I do as I'm told.

I writhe on his mouth and chin as I scream around his cock. My pussy floods his face, spilling to his neck and chest. The more I scream, the more he pours fiery hot down my throat. The fit of his cock in my mouth is so tight, the overflow of his semen has no other path but to escape out my nostrils– searing me with pain.

Cortez's moans of ecstasy echo off my cunt, vibrating in a delicious rhythm I'll never forget. All energy flees my system and I lie limply on top of Cort. I may pass out from a lack of oxygen. I can't swallow anymore, and my fingernails cut into his thighs in a silent warning. My eyelids lower, but I never fear because I trust him to know what he's doing. Using the strands of hair wrapped around his fist, Cort pulls his cock free of my throat with a sharp yank to the back of my head. He continuously pours on my tongue, until we're both covered in his slick spendings.

"Katya, thank you for trusting me," Cortez breathes reverently as he slides me off his chest.

"I wanted to do it again, and I never doubted you for an instant. I cannot fathom why I liked that so much, but I did." I giggle as if high.

"Well, I have a man you need to meet if skull-fuckery gets you off." Cortez giggles, too.

"Did you just giggle like a little bitch?" I tease him, rolling to my side with a groan of pain-filled satisfaction.

"Yeah... yeah, I did." Cortez laughs deeply, more masculine this time. He reaches over to swab my face with something soft, and I realize he's cleaning me up with his pajama pants. He cleanses my face and between my thighs–taking excellent care of me.

"Sleepy time," Cortez orders. So I drag my boneless body into my usual sleeping position, with Cort curled around my back. "It wasn't just the sex talking. I love you, Katya." Cortez declares in a voice filled with pure adoration and affection, causing my eyes to prickle with tears from a wash of emotion.

"I know. It wasn't lust riding me, either." I grab his hand from where his arm is slung over my side, and grip it for dear life. "I love you, Cortez. Truly. Not because you are Ezra's partner, or because of what happened to us at the hands of your uncle. I love you for who you are right this instant."

"Just give me my pride and pretend I'm not crying," Cortez whispers against the nape of my neck.

"Ditto," I whisper as his tears and mine soak into my hair.

We're both crying for the same reason: we love each other, willing to give one another everything we have, yet we feel incomplete nonetheless.

We are both crying for the same reason...

Ezra.

I'm not sure why, but it's easier to tell Cortez that I love him than it is to tell Ezra. I think it's the brutal honesty between us, or maybe it's how we are so much alike. Cortez and I just '*get*' each other. Or perhaps it may be because Ezra keeps so many secrets from me, and how he still has a fiancée while sleeping in a bed with Cortez and me.

Ultimately, I think it boils down to respect. Cortez really does see me as his equal, and he tells me the truth because he trusts me. I don't mean he trusts me with his secrets. I mean, Cortez trusts me enough to know I can handle the truth–however painful it may be.

"Argh!" Ezra groans in the dark, waking me from half-sleep. "The intoxicating scent of sex. What have you two been doing?" I can hear the amusement in his voice.

"Did you enjoy Queen narking all of my secrets to you during your meeting?" My voice holds the bitter resentment I feel.

"We talked about Aaron and his new escapades," Ezra replies without a hint of remorse. "I didn't realize he'd been such a busy boy as of late. I've spent so much time at home that I missed this huge milestone."

"For someone who stalks everyone," Cortez mumbles in the dark, "You sure do have your head up your ass, missing the obvious."

"I'll ignore that," Ezra murmurs, never allowing Cortez to get to him. "I just learned Aaron has been running scenes in the dungeon with Kayla and Heidi. Dexter's been supervising."

"I'm sure Aaron's magnificent." The image of Aaron topping both Heidi and Kayla pops into my head.

"Katya, you don't have anything to worry about. Your secrets are safe with Regina. No matter what I threatened, she wouldn't spill, and my threats were impressive," Ezra taunts. "She only told me you had a secret, but wouldn't divulge what it was."

I roll closer to Cortez in preparation for Ezra joining us in bed. "Well, you could always just ask me yourself," I utter snidely. "Instead of using surveillance on me, stalking me, or asking others about me. You know, you could go straight to the source."

"Someone is pissed off at me, I see," Ezra mumbles as he slides into bed. "Instead of being bitter, you could always come to me when you need something, when you need to talk, when you feel I've harmed you. Just as you've said, I'm not a mind reader, either."

"Point taken," I whisper, amazed at how quickly Ezra can put me in my place. Cort vibrates against back with his silent laughter, no doubt glad he's not on the receiving end of one of Ezra's mind fucks of a lecture.

"You didn't fuck Cort to get back at me, did you? Because it's you who enacted the no sex rule. It's not me, if you remember correctly. I've been trying to obey, as I don't wish to disappoint you or earn your ire. But it seems I managed to do both somehow, anyway."

"I'm not mad at you," I admit. But I fail to voice my true feelings. *"I'm frustrated with you."* My arms wrap around Ezra's shoulders, tugging him closer to my chest.

Ezra's deep sigh of relief echoes around our bedroom as he snuggles in closer, wrapping his arms around me and Cortez. He presses me to his chest with his fingers gripping Cort's back, trying to keep us with him always– the two people who love him more than life itself, but neither is willing to be his everything.

It's all Ezra's fault, really.

"I want the name of this mystery master," I demand, "And then I won't be frustrated with you anymore."

Ezra and Cortez both freeze around me. After a heartbeat, the crazy whose heart is pounding a rapid tattoo against my cheek answers me. "You will meet him very soon. So, no, I will not tell you his name beforehand. With what you've heard of him, it wouldn't be fair to him for you to go into it with preconceived notions."

"I don't like him already," I grumble, getting more frustrated by the second. "Don't play games with me."

"I'm not," Ezra says gruffly. "You've just proven my point for me by saying you've allowed other people's impressions to cloud how you feel about an incredible person you've yet to meet."

"Excuse me if I want to make him choke on his own cock," I snarl fiercely, causing Cortez to bark a sharp laugh.

"Aww… Kitten's growing fangs for me. She's jealous of our master," Cort rasps breathlessly, while still chuckling. He snuggles in closer to my back, and whispers in my ear. "You'll love him. I promise. I don't agree with the lunatic in our bed very often, but in this I do. It's for the best that you'll meet him before you're told he's our master."

"I don't like him controlling you," I mutter, hating how protective of Cortez I've grown.

"No one controls me," Cort says firmly, the truth ringing in his words. "Even Ezra knows better than to try. Master doesn't steal my power. He gladly accepts what I have given freely. That's what makes him tick. He gets off on the knowledge that I'm kneeling at his feet on my own accord. If he has to knock a person down, then he doesn't need them because they're weak. He'll lift you up, respect you, make you more than you've ever imagined you could be, and you will bow before him out of duty and adoration."

"You sound like a goddamned zealot," I whisper, scared Cortez's words will somehow offend Ezra.

"You're so much better for him than me. It soothes me to know you're there for him, as I refuse to accept that I'm less than he. I'm either his equal or more. Aside from listening to his advice, I refuse to take it unless I deem it sound."

"Which is why you run around destroying lives just to get his attention." Cort's tone couldn't get any wryer if he tried. "Your favorite pastime is driving him to distraction as he cleans up all of your messes."

"Everybody has to have a hobby," Ezra deadpans, and then he busts out laughing.

"I don't understand either of you... not one iota." I shake my head, unable to wrap my brain around their relationship. I was raised by my parents, who have been married for forty years and only ever touched one another. This lifestyle is hard for me to envision, let alone live. I'm willing to have an open mind, but I'm unsure if my mind can be *that* open. I doubt I can compartmentalize sex versus love versus different types of love.

"Katya and I didn't have sex." Cort finally puts Ezra out of his misery. "Our boy was in his apartment, fucking five women gangbang style. Can you believe that shit? Aaron has surpassed me. I'm impressed," Cort mutters in awe. "Anyway, it got our little Kitten's motor purring. She was begging for a rough fuck or a slow screw, but I didn't want her to regret it tomorrow. So we compromised on oral."

"Ah... In that case, where's my kiss?" Ezra cuddles up to the front of me, just as we sleep every night– Cortez at my back and Ezra and me face-to-face.

Ezra kisses me tenderly, and then groans into my mouth. His kiss changes from soft and gentle to fierce hunger. He violently attacks my mouth, licking the insides of my cheeks and the roof of my mouth, even the backs of my teeth. He sucks on my tongue, drawing it into his mouth.

My alcohol-addled mind is slow. I moan in need when I figure out that Ezra tastes Cort on my tongue– a taste of a heaven Cortez has long denied Ezra.

Ezra continues to assault me, fingertips weaving into my hair, yanking me closer. Cort is curved around my back, purring his approval, luxuriating in the power he holds over his partner. In this instance, I realize Cort is the one in control of the situation. He gives himself freely, which means neither the master nor Ezra can ever take from him.

I'm sandwiched between two aroused men, and the possibilities are endless. Words spew from my mouth as I beg for things I never knew existed, things I'll never understand. I prove that Katya Waters does in fact beg. But neither will give in to me because they fear my wrath tomorrow. No matter what I say, nothing will change their minds. The harder I beg, the more they taunt me with their delighted laughter.

"You guys are meanies. You're punishing me for saying no sex before by not giving me any now," I whine.

"Right you are. Nighty night, our Kitty Kat." Ezra smiles a taunt against my lips.

# Chapter Eighteen

"Katya, for today's lesson, you will finally get to work with a submissive." Dexter begins our training for the evening, while flashing me a reassuring smile.

"I don't think I'm ready yet." My voice breaks, and I hate how weak and insecure I sound. "I'll get too into it, and I'll end up breaking Ezra's rules."

"You're ready, Kat. You need to believe in yourself more. Doubt is more debilitating than actually *not* knowing how to do something. I know you're a courageous feline; act like it," Dexter commands, and I don't even feel a spark to submit and obey.

I'll obtain confidence through educating myself with knowledge and experience. Until then, it's not a bad thing to doubt oneself. Those who don't take an objective look at themselves, end up like Ezra, who makes more mistakes than the rest of us put together– catastrophic mistakes.

Dexter and I are sitting on his Victorian settee, exactly how we begin each session. We discuss the past session, what I did right or wrong, and how I can better myself. He gives me tips about how a dominant and submissive should behave, as well as how to spot Ezra's obvious manipulations and Cort's subtler ones.

Our time together every week is something I will miss when my tutelage is complete. I feel my education has been the best '*me*' time. I've learned how to release my frustrations, as well as how to channel said frustrations into something productive and healing. Dexter is providing me with the therapy Dr. Zeitler could never produce.

It's still hard to be around Dexter during our lessons, with a potent cloud of lust weaving around us. I don't for a millisecond believe that Dexter's lust has anything to do with me. The subject matter is rather difficult to ignore. There is no way to force my libido to feel indifference when my mentor is wielding a cock the size of my forearm. I may be a moral sort, but no one on this planet wouldn't be curious about that appendage.

After a few close calls, where my hand wandered out of curiosity, I now rub one out in our private room just before I walk into Dexter's room. I'm not sure if getting off makes it better or worse, because I'm either jonesing for an orgasm or coming down from one– either way, I end up with a one-track mind.

The first time I masturbated in our private room and then made my way into Dexter's, he said he could smell sex on me. He brutally fucked Heidi the second she walked in the door. I learned a valuable lesson that day. So I now do it in the shower before I join Dexter. Worse, while he never comments that he knows I've been naughty, he stares at me as if it's written across my face.

After a few more accidental hand wanderings– not mine this time –Dexter wears a shirt, and he only lets me see his cock when it's getting sheathed up with a condom. Giving me a split-second view before he plunges into the submissive of the day.

That second glimpse is all it takes. I've resorted to masturbating the instant I leave the sessions– sometimes I only make it to the hallway before I'm jamming my hand down my pants and rubbing away at my cunny. It's embarrassing but true.

"You will be relieved with who is joining us today. Master Ez gave permission for you to enjoy her any way you wish. However, her companion is off limits," Dexter warns.

Dexter flashes me a devious smirk as he gets up from the settee. He swaggers his perfect ass across the room and opens the door.

I sigh in relief when the submissive of the day jounces in. I recognize the jiggle of Kayla's tits before my eyes light on her face. Following Kayla is Aaron. I lean back against the settee, thinking this is probably the worst idea Ezra has ever had. No doubt the rat-bastard is testing me for some reason.

"How'd you manage this?" I ask Dexter out the corner of my mouth as I smile at Kayla and Aaron in welcome.

"It's getting increasingly difficult to train you when you aren't a sadist. You like the pleasure aspect of our lifestyle, and I can't give or receive pleasure with you. So how am I to train you if I can't actually train you?"

"Ain't that the fucking truth," rumbles up my throat, my frustration leaking through.

"Kayla's fair game, but don't even think about touching Aaron," Dexter warns me. "Before we begin, we need some ground rules. Aaron, sit on the couch and don't move. Kayla, strip and show us your pretty body."

"Dexter, Kayla is off limits to you. Do *not* touch her," Aaron growls.

"I don't plan on it, big guy." Dexter pats Aaron on the shoulder. "Kayla is all yours. However, Kristal has been begging for it for the past few weeks. I finally got permission from Pretty Boy. So I've saved Kristal for when I really need a rough fuck. No doubt after tonight, I will." Dexter groans as he adjusts his bulge.

*Look away, Katya. Look away...*

"I'm just going to sit next to Aaron while you do whatever you wish," Dexter says to me as he retakes his seat. I hop up so Aaron has a place to sit.

"Beauty," my voice quivers with excitement and nervousness. "Come over here," I direct Kayla to the spanking bench.

I've always dreamed of Kayla spread out before me with her ass pinked from my hand. I know she doesn't like pain at all, so I have to be very careful. As I help her onto the bench, the poor girl is shivering like a leaf. After she is settled, I give her a massage to relax her. Kayla's soft skin glides underneath my greedy hands. I stand behind her and rub her ass until she's mewing like a kitten. I tap her lightly on the ass with the palm of my hand, and she moans in reply. I don't give her what I want yet, because she isn't ready.

I nibble a pathway down Kayla's back, and she lifts into my touch, quivering. I suck and bite to mark her skin, knowing she would deny me nothing. The satisfaction I feel at seeing my marks is unparalleled. It's a humbling experience, the amount of power Kayla transfers to me.

I understand what Dexter meant by how it was impossible for me to learn without hands-on experience. What I've been doing for the past two months was tantamount to watching instructional videos. I was learning in theory, but never in practice.

Having my hands on Kayla's skin, sensing every shift in her body and knowing I pulled the reaction out of her, is intoxicating in the extreme. Her trust in me almost brings me to my knees.

Without thought, my arm flicks back, lashing out to smack Kayla's ass. I repeat the gesture a few more times, loving the way her flesh jiggles from the hits. On the first swat, she cried out in pain. But by the fourth swat, she is begging for more.

Power rolls over me as Kayla accepts my gift. The force is so strong I could climax from it alone. It's a heady sensation, knowing that I'm causing a submissive who is afraid of pain to cry out in pleasure from my hits.

I grab a paddle and thwack Kayla's voluptuous thighs. She grunts as they turn pink, and I give them a few more swats each until they each turn red. By the time I'm finished with the paddle, Kayla is begging for more and moisture is dripping in rivulets down her red inner thighs.

I switch to something even wickeder. I want to see how far I can push Kayla's boundaries without causing her to break. I want to bend her to my will.

I grab the riding crop, understanding that this is at the top of Kayla's pain threshold, and she can endure nothing more intense. A part buried deep within me wants to find out how far I can push Kayla– just how far she trusts me not to do irreparable harm, even if it's agonizing for her.

I've seen Dexter use the riding crop often, and it's always made me long to experience it resting in my palm. My fingertips curl possessively around the leather, as if I was just awarded a royal scepter. I devour the sensation of being in control– of being strong, of not only having a choice, but of being the one who offers others a choice.

Even though Kayla is panting roughly, her muscles are lax and her pussy is drenched. I use Kayla's body language to speak for her, to inform me of her choice.

With no conscious thought on my part, I snap my wrist back. My ears register the *thwack* before my eyes adjust to the sight of the leather strap swatting Kayla's pink ass cheek. She screeches and claws the air. Her back ripples as her muscles tighten. Belying her violent reaction, her pussy becomes even more engorged. I rub Kayla's reddened flesh as I wait for her fingertips to clench the bench, signaling she's ready for me once more.

Out of reflex, I snap my wrist again. This time Kayla doesn't let out a bleating animal sound, but a very low moan from deep within her throat. She's crying steadily, unleashing a torrent of built-up emotions and pain. The tears flow down her cheeks, but not as rapidly as the moisture gushing from between her thighs.

I don't pay attention to Kayla's pleas to stop. I let her body tell me what she really feels. Her fears bubble out her mouth, but her mind controls her body. She can safe-word if it gets to be too much.

I hit Kayla time and time again. I become deaf to her cries, screams, and groans. I watch as her body beads with goose bumps. I can visibly see her pretty, pink cunny clenching with every hit.

I grab the flogger before Kayla comes up from the spell I've placed her under, knowing I have to work her down from the high we've reached. I softly skim the braids along her back, and kiss and bite in their wake. Kayla begs me to use the flogger on her, and I make her plead for several long minutes, reveling in the sensation of how powerful and alive I feel from the control I wield over Kayla.

The first hit of the flogger is soft– softer than any of the hits I've given Kayla thus far. She sighs in pleasure, relaxing. The next hit is the hardest I've dealt yet. She screams long and loud, throat opening wide to release the tortured sound.

I don't allow Kayla to get used to one gradient of pain. I alternate between light, sharp, and mid-range swats. The entire time I work her, I watch her body. Kayla isn't safe-wording because I can tell she has slipped into subspace. Her blue eyes are glazed and cloudy; their irises are eclipsed by the pupils. She is breathing softly. Her body is beaded with sweat. A gentle touch versus a rough touch elicits the same reactions from her.

As her domme, it's my responsibility to give Kayla a voice while she floats in another time and place. Since she's beyond the ability to use her safe-word, I am her only defense against irreparable harm. This is where a submissive could be taken advantage of, where the abuse of power lies. Instead of thinking of myself, I think of Kayla's needs and wants first. Instead of misusing the power Kayla so graciously offered me, I respect it and return it undamaged.

I work Kayla down by making sure each hit is lighter than the last. I kiss and massage her body while she whimpers in both agony and bliss. Her shoulders, ass, and thighs are a delicious shade of red. My teeth and suck marks blossom against her back and ass. Her thighs are drenched with her arousal.

I've never felt as proud as I do in this very moment.

My surroundings finally come into sharp focus, and I notice the room has fallen completely silent. I don't even hear Aaron or Dexter breathing. When I turn to see if they are still in the room with us, Dexter's brown eyes capture mine.

"After." Dexter clears his throat and licks his lips. "After your training is finished, you'll need to continue with me or our master. I won't tell you in what, for I fear it would terrify you as you become enlightened as to who you truly are."

"You're scaring me," I mutter, confused.

"Katya, that was… absolutely perfect. The way you took a submissive who fears pain, and by her trust in you alone, you took Kayla to places she's never been. I'm speechless," Dexter whispers, pride infusing his tone.

Dexter's eyes glow with a fiendish sort of pleasure, and I have no doubt he's envisioning the crack of his whip against virgin flesh. I don't want to admit it, but I understand what Dexter is saying. I have a bit of sadist in me, or else I wouldn't have felt so powerful in what I just did to Kayla.

It's not about causing pain. It's about being able to cause pain and knowing when to stop. It's about finding a person's limits, drawing them to the brink, and then shoving them over the other side, only to catch them before they fall.

Like Cortez's Priest, who absolves God's followers of their sins, or Ezra, who uses therapy to heal, I release the pain and guilt without the use of words. Through the release of pain is healing– the true bleeding of the soul.

Yes, I received a sick form of pleasure over the power I wielded, over the trust Kayla thrust at me. But that is such a small price I had taken compared to all I had given in exchange.

"Kayla, sweetheart? Can you come down and give your master a proper thanks?" Dexter entices Kayla from the spanking bench with soft words.

Kayla crawls to the floor, eyes flicking wildly around the room with tear-tracks marring her beautiful face. She looks between Aaron and me in confusion, not knowing which '*master*' Dexter was referring.

I know what I have to do. It's what I should have done a long time ago. We are doing to Kayla what Ezra does to me. One moment he is Master Ez, and I have to listen to him. The next he is Ezra, who won't make up his mind on Adelaide versus me. I don't know what is up or down with him, or what is left or right. The confusion is maddening. I believe Ezra thinks I understand even though I don't, and he is doing the same thing to Kayla.

I make an executive decision. Kayla has expressed her confusion over who her real master is, and she's torn from the conflict. Master Ez controls us all in a way, but that isn't the type of master I'm talking about. We all accept that Ezra will tell us what to do, and we have to do it or suffer his wrath. Ezra will just be sneaky and do it anyway. No, Kayla doesn't know if I'm her master, or if Ezra is, or if the position falls to Aaron as he is her boyfriend, or if Cortez is because he's her ex-lover. I sympathize with her plight.

"Kayla, beauty," I say to gain her attention. She raises confused, blue eyes up to me, and then looks at Aaron, and then back to me. While her loyalties are divided, I know where her heart lies.

"Kayla, from now on Aaron is your only master. You still have to respect all the other masters and you have to listen to Ezra, but you belong to Aaron from this moment forward."

"Katya, are you sure?" Aaron asks, tone a wash of utter disbelief. I can see he's fighting his need to smile in the tension surrounding his lips, because he's scared I'll shout *gotcha!*

"I'm sure. You and Kayla are lovers and you live together. I understand her confusion, and I refuse to make her suffer any longer. Am I her master? Are you? Is Ezra? Cortez? It's just wrong. If Ezra is upset about it, I'll take the blame. But regardless, Kayla is yours now, and yours alone."

Kayla mouths, "*thank you*", and then hurries to Aaron's side. She crawls into his lap and kisses him passionately. Before I can blink, the couple turns feral, tearing off Aaron's clothing as if the thinnest of barriers between them is pure torture. The scene had turned them both on, but adding to the intensity is Aaron's need to mark his territory. Within seconds, Kayla is riding Aaron's lap, with him buried deep inside of her.

"Probably not a good idea for us to watch them do that in the mood we're in," I muse to Dexter.

"Nope." Dexter pops the P in the word, all the while refusing to look at me. "Definitely not a good idea." He taps a few words out on his cellphone, texting someone. A few seconds later, the door swings opens, revealing a horny, antagonistic bartender. Kristal rushes in, peeling off her dress as she moves, and then she drops to her knees to kneel at Dexter's feet.

I rush from the room the second Dexter unleashes his monster cock. The last thing I see before I close the door behind me is Dexter palming the crown of Kristal's head, shoving her down to swallow his dick.

Outside in the hallway, I lean against Dexter's door, panting wildly. I can hear Aaron and Kayla's passions rising in pitch, but it's Dexter's deep grunt of relief that has my fingertips sliding down my pants and into my panties.

I feverishly attack my pussy. I squirm and writhe, and pant and hiss. I turn into an animal. I feel eyes on me– several sets. Three men are leaning against their doorways, hanging out in the hallway, no doubt drawn to the sounds emanating from inside Dexter's room and from my cries out here in the hallway.

I've never met these men, yet I cannot stop myself from masturbating as they act as witnesses. Something about the perversion of being watched heightens my pleasure.

The man closest to me has brown hair and looks kind of shady, like a classic, drunk, washed-up, high school math and science teacher. He sneers at me, looking as one would at a car wreck or murder scene. Even though he's giving me the stink-eye, I'm not scared of the dude. The nameplate on the door he's leaning against suggests his name is **Dalton**.

The next man is the epitome of the boy next door. I know instantly this tall, blond-haired, blue-eyed guy is the infamous Pretty Boy. He's standing watch as Dexter uses his submissive. He's impossibly young, judging by the fact that he hasn't quite grown into his height and shoulders yet. But it's the look in his brilliant, ancient eyes that is utterly terrifying.

Pretty Boy is like Ezra: affluent, poised, educated, and dominant. He doesn't ask; he expects. Entitled. Pretty Boy isn't trying to own the world; he's confident in the knowledge that he already controls it. If he's this potent as a boy, what the hell is he going to be like as a grown man?

A **II** glares blindingly from the shiny nameplate on Pretty Boy's door. No doubt a second-generation blue-blooded, entitled asshole, who just so happens to be smiling at me like he's goddamned sunshine personified while he watches me rub one out.

The third and final man is a comfort. I'm neither scared of him, nor creeped out. Hinting at a Native American ancestry, with eyes the jewel-tone shade of turquoise, tan skin, and his chin-length hair is inky black and perfectly straight. He's an impressive specimen of the male form.

While Pretty Boy II may be the rich man's boy-next-door, this fella is more like the guys I grew up around. He looks like the type who would buy underaged idiots beer and smokes, and would make no apologies as he partied with them. No doubt supplying all the medicinal libations. I'd rather be around a stoner than the hate-filled glarer or the choir boy smiler.

Occupied as I may be, I glance up to check out the nameplate on the door above his head. **Alexander**. Remembering our hellish girls' night out, Kris had said her boyfriend's name was Alex, and he had a big problem with her sex addiction, and Pretty Boy was her master because it was for the best. I assume Alexander is Alex, and he's also standing guard while Dexter fucks the living daylights out of his girlfriend.

I'm more comfortable with the death-glare on the drab, monotone Dalton than how happy Pretty Boy is. He truly is happy to see me– even as I masturbate –and I have no idea why. So I concentrate on Alex instead, especially since he is genuinely enjoying the show.

Alex rubs the heel of his palm against the growing bulge in his pants, causing brown man to snarl and Pretty Boy to laugh. I ignore those two while keeping an eye on my fellow masturbator, sinking into deviancy as my fingertips rub my clit raw.

It takes my fingernail accidently scratching my clit and causing me pain to bring my climax. I cry out and every muscle in my body seizes and ripples in delight. I clench my jaw as my eyes roll back inside my head. It takes a long time to come down from my release.

Dalton snarls derogatory comments as he stomps down the hallway toward the dungeon. Pretty Boy just looks pleased that I found my release, and I don't trust anyone who appears to be that kind-hearted. Alex is lounging against his door, looking for all the world like he wished he had a cigarette.

Confidence dwindling now that my lust has fled, my cheeks turn crimson from a killer blush. I creep soundlessly down the hallway toward the dungeon, feeling sheepish and regretful.

Kristal's men strike up a conversation as I go, chatting about a place called Transcend, making me wonder if they know James Atwater, since Transcend is his community outreach program. If I wasn't embarrassed beyond belief, I'd turn around and make friends, since these fellows are probably my kind of people.

I locate Cortez, knowing he's taunting the members in the dungeon, like a bratty child poking a lion trapped in a cage. This time he's pestering Syn, wearing his executioner's hood and a pair of ratty jeans and a t-shirt. He's running circles around Syn as she tries to snap him with her purple whip. Cort's a fast bastard, and every time Syn gets a lick too close to him, she actually smiles with sick delight.

Cortez is supposed to stay with me during my sessions, keeping watch to make sure I don't fall unto temptation, but he's my biggest temptation in the room. We both lie to Ez, who knows we're lying to him but says nothing. Cortez bothers the natives during my two-hour training sessions and never once asks me if I behaved or not. He trusts me to make my own mistakes.

I step up to the circus performers, and Syn snatches her whip up, coiling it around her palm, fighting her need to lash out at me. Cort's at my side in an instant, no doubt seeing my blush.

"I wouldn't get too close to her, Kitten," Cort warns. "Syn would love to whip my ass, but she'd take a hunk of flesh from you too."

"Seems we have something else in common," I direct at the sadist, and she nods in understanding. "After I'm a master, I suspect you and I will be spending some time together inflicting pain. You don't have to like it, but you best get used to having me around."

"No shit?" Cort croaks out, taking my arm so we can exit Restraint before Syn can respond. "Just don't take your frustrations out on me. I don't like physical pain."

"But you thrive on the emotional kind," I whisper.

Cort hears me anyway. "Anyone who loves Ezra has to."

# Chapter Nineteen

Somewhere between eating breakfast as a family every morning, spending all day working with Cortez, taking walks with Ava and Roarke, nightly chess matches with Ezra, and cooking dinner for our fucked up Norman Rockwell family, I've come to terms with the fact that I'm a mistress in more ways than one.

Our home. Our life. Our money. Our belongings. Our friends. Our family. Our businesses. The '*our*' in all of those equations is theirs– Ezra and Cortez's.

I'm just here, leeching off of them, having no way to take ownership since I'm missing the means, the know-how, and the history to get a proper foothold in our lives. I'm not naïve enough to accept any ownership in any of these things. I have a tentative grasp on my life, knowing at any second I could be tossed on my ass with nothing left to my name. I'm also under no delusions on whether or not I could fight to keep my daughter.

If I don't toe the line, then I could be back in Vacuum Valley with my parents, with absolutely no access to my daughter until she reaches the age of majority, and in the years before then, she would be indoctrinated by Ezra's way of thinking.

While this threat has never been spoken aloud, it throbs in the back of my mind continuously. I've chosen a path where I lie to myself to suffer through the day, instead of seeing my situation as it truly is.

On the same token, I realize this is where I'm safest– secure in Ezra's fortress of insanity. With the threatening notes, I don't dare run back home, dragging my living nightmares with me. If I somehow survived yet my family didn't, I'd never forgive myself.

Living in shame isn't so difficult when it's a matter of survival.

I don't recognize myself when I look in the mirror, and I don't respect who is gazing back at me. I could blame Ezra for turning me into someone I loathe, but I allowed him to put me in this position. I take full responsibility, because no one can do anything to you unless you allow it. I could have left. I could have refused to share a space while still sharing our child. But my emotions dictated how I behaved, and that is all on me. Ezra's lack of respect when it comes to me is centered on my lack of self-respect.

This isn't how I envisioned my life. After being raised by a pair of monogamous parents, it's a difficult concept to swallow. The only way I hold on to my sanity is by the fact that I withhold parts of myself from Ezra. Sometimes it's out of punishment, because I get a sick thrill out of seeing his anguish, and sometimes it's about wielding power when I feel powerless. But more often than not, it's because I'm terrified of being consumed by Ezra.

While we may live together, Ezra doesn't allow me into his personal or professional life. I've never met his family, and he keeps me apart from his friends and colleagues. Once or twice a week, Ezra will leave the bedroom looking dashing in a tux, and then he will spend the evening wining and dining Dominion's upper echelons, gaining favor for his family's endeavors. Sometimes Cortez joins him, but never Ava or myself.

We share our child. We share laughs. We share conversation. We share a home life. We also share a bed at night, but never our bodies.

While there are little intimacies between Cortez, Ezra, and I, both separately and together, I cannot go through with actual physical intimacy without feeling sick in the head, heart, and stomach.

I'm whoring myself out emotionally for the sake of love. I'm also breaking my moral code for the sake of my daughter's happiness. This might not be the life I envisioned, nor the one I truly want, but it's the one I have. The only choice I have in the matter is to make the best of it.

If I ignore the pangs of regret, heartache, and loneliness, even while in a crowded room, I find myself to be quite content in my plight. My mystery note sender has been quiet this whole time as well.

Then the mail was delivered this fine Saturday morning, removing any contentment I might feel, while highlighting how disgusting I am as a human being. I immediately swiped the offensive letter addressed to me. Numb, I'm in denial mode since the other piece of mail is at the fore of my mind.

*Diane, Pearl, & Adelaide*
*Request your presence*
*in celebration of the 30<sup>th</sup> year of Ezra's life*
*Saturday at 7 p.m.*
*Shadow Haven Estates*
*Semi-formal attire.*
*Dinner at 7:30 p.m. ~ drinks & conversation to follow.*

Just what a woman wants to read in the same day– the twelfth anniversary of her attack –a threat letter and a celebration she wasn't invited to attend.

The invitation is addressed to Cortez & Aaron, plus one. Kayla is the plus one. Logically, I know that I can't go. I understand why I'm not invited, especially when the future Mrs. Zeitler is hosting the event.

The knowledge doesn't take the pain away. My heart breaks as I realize my daughter most likely wasn't invited, either. I've never felt more like a whore than I do at this very moment. I'm the mistress that you keep out of sight, the one who isn't privy to your personal life. Our daughter would not only prove indiscretion on Ezra's part, but some simple math would equal outing him in my rape. It's funny how you can feel secure in your life and *wham!*

This isn't about me. It's Ezra's day. He loves being in control by making all of the decisions, so this is one decision I'm glad for him to make. Whether or not our daughter is a dirty little secret or something cherished is entirely up to her father. Ezra can disrespect me, but he shouldn't ever disrespect our daughter. I would love to say I'm not testing him at this moment, but that would be a lie.

*It's not about me,* I repeat to myself.

"I can't read your expression." Cort's voice startles me, breaking me free from my trance. I sit at the dining table, running my fingertip over and over the embossed writing on the expensive invitation. I look up at him as he enters the dining area.

"Nervous?" Cort joins me at the table, cranking his head to the side to reread the invitation.

"Nervous?" My voice shows my confusion. "Why would I be nervous?"

"Meeting the in-laws is always kind of scary." He shoves the offending object back into its envelope and tosses it on the table.

"In-laws?" I scrunch up my eyebrows at him. "I'm trying to think of somewhere to take Ava for the day so that she doesn't feel disappointed. She's too smart, though. It's hard to explain why she has to leave for the day when it's her father's birthday." I shrug.

"Why would you do that?" Cort's voice holds an edge— confusion laced with anger.

"Under the circumstances, I would think Ezra wouldn't want Ava to attend." I try to impart my reasoning to Cort with a look, but our minds aren't running in sync with one another as they usually are.

"What circumstances? Ava is Ezra's daughter." Cort looks and sounds as confused as I feel, but it's over entirely different things.

"I don't know if Ezra has told everyone about Ava." I close my eyes and whisper my biggest fear. "I don't know if he's told anyone how Ava came to be, and I don't want anyone ruining our daughter's life with the truth."

"Kat, Ava will be with Ezra and me, and our family would never destroy us like that."

"You're right." I might say the words, but I don't believe them. "I'm overthinking things."

"How are you today, Kat?" Cortez reaches over to caresses my cheek. The gesture is tender, and it hurts my heart more than it makes me feel warm and good inside.

"I'm good." I nod my head as I lie. "It's not just about me today. It's Ezra's birthday, but the day means different things for all of us. It was the day you, Ezra, and Aaron escaped the monster, which is bittersweet but should be celebrated. It's also the day I was attacked and Ava was conceived. I guess it's an equally painful and happy occasion."

"Today isn't an easy day for any of us," Cort admits, voice cracking.

"I know, so don't worry about me," I murmur. "I've dealt just fine with the eleven prior anniversaries. I'll try to push my own shit to the backburner and only see today as Ezra's birthday."

"Kat," Cortez groans my name, sounding exasperated. "It doesn't have to be like that. It also drives Ezra insane when you shut yourself off."

"I really didn't say that to make it about me. I'm not your typical female. I'm not passive-aggressively begging for attention. I said what I meant. There is no sense in dwelling in the past. We need to evolve this date into a day of celebration, not torment. Ezra and Ava mean too much to be discounted." Sensing Cort's need to argue, "Besides, we have more important matters at hand."

I toss my letter at Cort. Whether I'm at the bottom of the list of importance or not, I'm still on the list. No amount of emotional fortitude and physical strength could allow me to shoulder this burden all by myself. Cort's the not-so lucky bastard who was recruited to help me survive.

With my eyes squinted against the threat of tears, I watch Cortez's face pale as he reads the words and stares at the attached picture in horror.

*Katya,*

*Remember me? Remember the crunch of my fist pummeling your face, and my cock tearing your cunt? Do you remember the way it felt when I broke your eye socket? Your ribs? How did it feel to breathe with a collapsed lung? Were you terrified? Did you think you were going to die?*

*You live as if you survived, not realizing I let you get away. Your life is on borrowed time- my time. I giveth and taketh away.*

*You've never known true pain or fear, but you soon will. I will beat you within an inch of your life, and then I will fuck you while the light slowly drains from your eyes. I will disembowel your corpse, and then masturbate with your blood coating my hands.*

*I will be the last person you see, hear, feel, and touch, and that will transfer into the afterlife– I will taint your soul for all eternity.*

*Until we meet again!*

Attached to the sickening letter is a picture of the lake I cherish. Its crystalline waters beckoning me to enter serenity, with the surrounding mountainous forest providing an endless source of privacy. In the same handwriting as the threat letter is the image's caption.

*Your last moments on earth will be here, and your remains will be interred in its watery depths by my hand.*

Voice barely a breath of a sound, "When did this come?" Cort's hands shake the letter as he holds it out for me to take back. Neither of us wants to touch it, yet we can't be rid of the evidence.

"This morning. It was tucked in, hiding with the mail. After we get through today, we need to get this figured out. It could be nothing." I sound calm, but I'm lying more to myself than to Cortez.

"Or it could be that someone plans to end your life just as soon as you decided to begin living it." Cortez stands and walks from the room– just like that.

# Chapter Twenty

Knowing there is nothing to be done today, I seek out my daughter for another very painful conversation. I find Ava resting on the sofa, with her nose buried in a book. I stand, hovering nearby, just watching the young woman she is growing up to be. The thought of not seeing her transform into a woman, into a mother, kills something vital inside of me.

There is a sensation I just can't shake, like something is crawling up my spine, electrocuting me on its path. It's as if my life as I know it is teetering on a knife's edge. Be it Ezra taking my daughter from me because I finally find my self-respect and refuse to be his mistress, or by the hand of my newest stalker, when he takes me from my daughter.

"Scoot over," I order as I toss Ava's feet off the sofa cushion. I hand her the invitation, and then watch as she reads it, all the while using my newfound body language skills to tap into her emotions.

I have to have faith in my daughter to understand. I've had eleven years of experience dealing with Ava. Even at her young age, she is logical, very adult-like, and I know she will be able to deal with whatever may come our way.

"You're worried about me, aren't you?" Ava rolls her eyes at me, like I'm being ridiculous. "Don't– I won't be upset if Dad doesn't invite me. I understand most of this. I mean, I just came into his life, and I'm almost grown. It's difficult for him." She shrugs just like I do when I am lying to myself.

"It's alright to be upset, Ava." I speak as softly as possible, trying to remain calm, hoping to be a comfort to my daughter. "You have every right to be upset if you feel upset."

"Don't. Dad will either ask me, or he won't. Worrying won't change it. Besides, if Dad invites me, we can spend the night making fun of all the stuffy people." She smiles at me, enlivened by excitement. A sinister giggle slips past her lips.

"Ava, even if your father invites you, I won't be there." It takes everything in me to school my features. I try for impassive, not wanting to push my pain off onto my daughter.

God, this hurts.

"Your father's fiancée is hosting the party." I watch my daughter's face as she works through what I said. Bottom lip quivering, she huffs in a few sharp breaths, trying very hard not to bawl. I don't move to comfort her. After all, Ava is Ezra's and my daughter. One small touch and she will lose it, and then her pride will be bent. A few breaths later, Ava has regained her composure.

"I don't understand?" Ava brushes the cuff of her shirtsleeve underneath her eyes. "I don't understand Adelaide."

"Me, either. But it's not up to us, now is it? The rich have a different way of life from normal people, and none of it makes any sense to me. I'll worry when I begin to understand it."

Ava's stormy eyes narrow, and she's never looked more like her father than she does right this second. Determined. Furious. "It's my business too. If Dad plans on marrying this woman, then she's going to be my stepmother."

"I almost wish Ezra wouldn't invite you tonight, so then you wouldn't have to meet Adelaide Whittenhower. But it will only delay the inevitable." Refusing to dump Ezra's shit at our daughter's feet, I change the subject. "Where's your old man, anyway? I have a gift for him."

"Did I hear the words old man and gift in the same sentence?" Ezra's smoky voice reaches us before he does.

Ezra strolls into the living room, wearing a half-buttoned, crisp, white dress shirt with a pair of low-slung trousers resting on his hips. Even with the emotional distress, I appreciate the view. Ezra smiles at us as he pulls his fingers through his pale hair. The movement shows off a bit of skin at his waist. Even Ezra's bare feet are gorgeous.

"Ah, I do believe you heard that right, old man. Thirty is the new geriatric set. As for the gift, Ava thought we should get you a case of Depends." I wink at Ava, trying to lighten the mood.

"This said by the thirty-two-year-old?" Ezra releases a taunting laugh filled with irony. "Gimme my gift," he demands, reaching out and snapping his fingers at us.

I pull a small bag from my pocket and hand it to Ava. "Give your dad his gift before he throws a tantrum."

Ezra gingerly takes the bag from Ava. The gray velvet bag is small enough to fit in my palm. He has a hard time undoing the satin ribbon. His expression of concentration makes me smile. Ezra bites his bottom lip as he fumbles with the tie. Just as I'm about to offer to untie the bag for him, he releases a victory call. "Ah-ha! I got it!"

"It's like watching a monkey tie his shoes– all thumbs." Ava's an expert sarcasm dealer. I flash her a wicked grin, because I'm secretly proud of her attitude. I think *Atta-girl!*

Ezra sticks his tongue out at us as he pours his prize into his palm. His eyes glisten when he sees the small charm with *AVA* spelled out. It's identical to the *C, Z,* and *KW* charms on his necklace. It took me two weeks to locate the jeweler who created our charms. I used my bracelet as an example.

Ezra hurries to pull out his necklace. Excited, he fumbles at attaching the charm. All proud, he presents us the necklace with a beatific smile on his face.

The birthday boy looks like an angel, face aglow and pale hair shining as a halo. I guess that makes Cort the fallen angel. What does that make me? Worse, what does that make Ava?

"Happy birthday, Ezra!" I say brightly in a sing-song voice.

I have to look away from the emotions flowing across Ezra's face. Over the past few weeks, I've learned to read him. Sometimes it is too much to feel my own emotions, let alone know what he's feeling, especially on a day like today.

Voice clogged with intense emotions, it takes Ezra a few tries to get the words out. "I would like to invite my little one on a shopping trip– a father-daughter day. We need to get Ava something to wear for tonight."

Ezra looks at our daughter with complete and utter devotion on his face. He exudes pride, possession, respect, and love, and it's all directed at Ava. I should've never doubted Ezra's intentions when it comes to *that which is his.* Never.

I watch Ava try to rein in her feelings. She is ecstatic, nearly bursting out of her skin, yet she is emoting guilt for leaving me behind.

Ava is my baby girl, and she will never suffer the consequences of my past. I would move Heaven and Earth to obtain Ava's happiness, even if it means ruining myself.

"I think that is an excellent idea, Ezra," I say brightly, trying to assuage Ava's fears. Her answering smile takes some of my heartbreak away. She quickly bounds from the room to get ready for her date with her daddy.

Unable to help myself, I walk around the chair Ezra is sitting in. I reach up, lightly resting my palms on his shoulders, and then I begin to knead. His muscles are taut with tension beneath my hands, proving he's a consummate actor, too. He's just as upset today as I am.

I know this day is the hardest for Ezra, because it was his father and he was the one who was forced to assault me. This day– twelve years ago –Ezra was forced to make hard choices with astronomical consequences. His eighteenth birthday.

"Are you doing okay today, all things considered?" I slide my hands underneath Ezra's shirt, and begin massaging his chest. I feel his body relax beneath my palms, and his breathing picks up. I kiss the top of Ezra's head, inhaling the scent of his hair.

"I've been better, and I've been worse. This year is better than the last eleven birthdays." He sighs and leans his head back against my breasts. He rolls his eyes up and watches me from underneath the lace of his eyelashes.

"What's bothering you the most?" I lean farther forward so that I can reach his stomach. Ezra arches up into my hands, granting me greater access.

"Aaron, he's hiding from us. He's getting so much better. But I just moved down the list from superhero to leper."

I can't resist the sight of the curve of Ezra's shoulder peeking out at me from beneath his shirt– so I don't. I rub my cheek on it.

"Aaron said that today was difficult enough to get through without all of us reminding him. It's weird with him living at Kayla's. I know that Aaron is here more than anywhere, but he has lived with me for fifteen years. It's bittersweet. I feel like a father who just watched his son grow up and move on. It is a very good thing, though." Ezra smiles up at me, and I can see his pride over helping Aaron heal– pride over Aaron healing himself.

I hold Ezra's eyes, moving in slowly until we are staring at each other upside-down. I curve my neck over his head until I can reach his lips. I brush his lips softly with mine, feather-light. Tongue peeking out, I caress his bottom lip. We move our mouths leisurely against one another.

Ezra's hands travel up my arms, lingering and massaging. He reaches to palm the nape of my neck, holding me closer. Our kiss is tender and lasting, as easy as breathing. As we extend our kiss, my hands create a path from his chest, down his stomach, to press into the tops of his thighs. My love for him swells to the point of pain, heartbreak, and joy. He's gentle with me– tender as we reconnect.

"Sorry," a tiny voice echoes.

My eyes roll up, but I don't break the kiss until I meet my daughter's face, never wanting her to feel her father's and my intimacy is wrong, no matter how wrong it may be. I rise slowly in a languid movement.

I gaze down at Ezra's face. It's still tipped in my direction. His eyes are glazed over, bright, and shiny. His mouth is parted– the tip of his pink tongue visible. His chest rapidly rises and falls underneath my hands. What frightens me is the expression on his face– an expression I've never seen –an expression I have no name for.

Stepping away, I plaster a strained smile on my face. "You guys have a fun time today. Ava, behave for your dad, especially since it's his birthday."

I flee the room without looking at either of them, heart breaking inside my chest as I run. I seek the only place I have privacy and solace. My fingertips shake so badly that I can barely lock the bathroom door. As soon as I'm secure, I turn and fall backward, sliding my back down the door until my ass hits the tile.

Head buried in my hands…

Reality.

This is how low the self-righteous fall.

This is what my reality has become.

I'm my daughter's father's mistress, and that isn't even my biggest concern. Someone is stalking me with my death on their mind, but Ezra is the only thing my emotions give a fuck about.

Tears sting my eyes, burning like acid– a punishment I surely deserve. I've earned this pain. Out of nowhere, I start to weep. I'm able to stay silent until I'm positive that I'm alone in the apartment.

From one breath to the next, my silent cries turn to violent body-wracking sobs.

Like an addiction, I always feel better when I'm in Ezra or Cortez's presence. The minute that I'm parted from them, the guilt and shame slams into me. My confidence drops to the dirt. I'm confident in myself as a person and as a mother. It's the confidence in the hierarchy. The mixed signals are killing me—ruining me.

Curled up in the center of the bathroom tile, I cry harder, because the expression Ezra wore just before I fled the living room is burned into my mind.

Devotion.

Ezra looked at me just as he had Ava earlier, but it was mixed with heat and need. It terrified me. Ezra was gazing at me how he stares at Cortez when he doesn't think any of us are looking. It will trap me, imprison me, change me to the point that the Katya I honor and respect will cease to exist.

I've got to get the fuck out of here.

# Chapter Twenty-One

I lunge to my feet, destination the sink. I splash my face with cool water, and then pat it dry. I take a few minutes to blow the shit out of my nose. Bawling is not an attractive activity and it wreaks havoc on your appearance.

In a blind panic, I rush from the apartment. Not having the patience to wait for the elevator, I sprint down seven flights of stairs. Adrenaline flooding my veins, I charge across the lobby to exit the building at a flat run.

I see nothing around me except for my destination in the distance. Pedestrians step out of my way, fearful I will collide with them versus darting out of their path. Panting for breath, the few blocks go by in a blur.

The exertion helps to center me, to clear my head and dampen my emotions. I have to make time to work out again. Not because I give a shit about having a killer body, only for my mental health. It's the same reason I train with Dexter– to regain my power, to release my frustration, and to finally feel free.

Running wild is pure freedom.

I can't be in the apartment when everyone gets home. Yes, it's cowardly, and I don't give a fuck. I don't have the emotional restraint to plaster a fake smile on my face as I watch everyone strut their finery and go off to an exclusive party– one I'm excluded from. Where I'll be left behind. Alone.

I'm a selfish coward, and this is the first time I can add a horrible mother to the list. I should be there for Ava, help her dress and fix her hair. As a mother, I should support Ava as she waits to meet her new stepmother, grandmother, aunt, and cousin. But I just can't– any other day but today and I may have mustered the strength.

I find a bench at the edge of the park near the woods. I curl my knees to my chest, tucking them underneath my sweatshirt. I make myself as small as possible by tucking my chin to the top of my knees. I pull my hood up, almost covering my entire face. I view the world through a small slice of sight. I watch the sun move across the sky, waiting until it's safe to go home.

I spend my time contemplating how I've fucked up my life, where I've gone wrong, and what I need to do to fix it. I find no resolution that won't leave a trail of broken hearts.

A giggle licks across the back of my mind, almost as if it's imaginary. At first, I think it's my daughter. I almost call out to Ava until I realize it's too masculine to be her very girly giggle. It holds a sinister edge– an evilness – so much stronger than my daughter's version. My body jerks as if shocked by high voltage. I remember that sound as it cackled in my ear.

*"Fight me! Fight me back!" Smack! Blood flies from my mouth in an arc, causing loose teeth to vibrate from the force. Panting. Grunting. Rutting. Body sliding across the gravel railroad bed with every penetration, cutting my back, staining the earth with my blood. "Fight back!" Peace within my panic as my life slowly drains beneath the hands of a sociopath.*

I don't think. I react.

I don't look around. I just bolt up and try to run.

Knees tucked in my sweatshirt, my legs become tangled when I lunge. I crash to the ground, hitting my shin on the bench with enough force to seize the breath in my lung. Body and mind screaming for help, I crawl to my knees, slicing my palms on the pavement.

Leaping forward, I'm running before my feet hit the ground. I charge headlong. My only thought is of getting to Edge and locking myself in my apartment and never resurfacing again. Privacy is overrated when self-preservation is in the driver's seat.

The sensation of my Chrysalis tattoo tingling is back, as if I'm being watched and followed. A rational person tells themselves they are being paranoid. They laugh off their intuition, and then they get assaulted, raped, and left for dead, where they may or may not actually survive.

Your assailant wants you to ignore your intuition. So what if you're wrong? So what if you're being paranoid? Is your pride worth the price of your life?

Heed the tingle and live to see tomorrow.

I don't need to turn around to check and see if I'm being followed or not. I don't care if I'm being watched. Because without a shadow of a doubt, I trust my intuition.

Halfway through the park, my foot catches on an upturned tree root. I fall to my palms and knees, jarring my bones and drawing blood. But I don't stay down. Before I land to the ground, I'm already pushing back off with my hands to charge home.

Hair whipping across my face, my terror-filled breath saws out my lips, exhale clouding the air around me, I run–

Run for my life.

Hours ago, I had fled from my gilded cage, resenting its oppression. Now I fly back, terrified of the world outside of Ezra Zeitler's creation.

The sight of The Edge Building rips tears from my eyes. I huff in large gulps of air, almost hyperventilating. The doorman steps forward, trying to stop me, but one look at the insanity swirling in the depths of my eyes, has him taking a step back. I sprint across the lobby, rushing to catch the open elevator door.

I squeeze in just as the doors slide shut, forever thankful that I'm alone. Out of reflex, I quickly press *'close door'* just to make sure no one else can join me. The button to the seventh floor and our security code is typed in on autopilot.

I use the minute ride to slow my breathing and calm myself. It's hard to contain my inner-animal once the fight or flight reflex is triggered. I breathe through the adrenaline flowing in my veins, realizing nothing is going to calm my ass down any time soon.

"I can't take any more of this shit. I won't survive it," I gasp out, clutching my side. "Katya, don't be like that. You have to be strong, even if you're being a goddamned idiot." I continue to berate myself like a lunatic, mind spinning out of control. "I'm going to start carrying a weapon... and glue Roarke to my ass."

Slumping forward, I rest my bleeding palms on my knees, trying to catch my breath. I jerk forward, smashing my palm on the big, red **STOP** button. "Goddammit!"

# Chapter Twenty-Two

After a five minute panic attack, where I assaulted every available surface of the elevator, I'm radiating calm. I swear to God, if Ezra or Marcus has our elevator bugged, they are in for a real show.

I enter our apartment entryway, close the door behind me, and then make sure the security system activates. I lean against the door, trying to maintain my false calm. The potent feeling of relief by finally being inside my nest, is a high all on its own.

"Where is she? We're going to be late." Ezra's worried voice drifts in from the living room.

"I don't think Kat's coming," Cort replies.

It's wrong of me to rest here and listen in on their private conversation, but I'm too frazzled for them to see me in my current state. I pull my sleeves down over my bloody palms, hiding them from sight.

"Why isn't Katya coming?" I can hear the anxiety in Ezra's voice. I don't like it, and I don't know how to fix it.

"Did you invite her?"

"No, since when do you invite your own spouse? If one is invited so is the other, unless it's a guy or girl's night out kind of thing. I never invite you anywhere; I just expect you to show up."

"Katya is not your spouse, Ezra, and she isn't your partner. She isn't a mind reader, either. You really need to have a talk with Kat about Adelaide." Cortez sounds reasonable, which is about as frightening as what I left back at the park.

I walked into something I wish I hadn't. Whoever is stalking me is hell-bent on harming me physically. While Ezra and Cortez are unintentionally harming me mentally and emotionally. I don't know which I'm more terrified to endure.

"I don't see why. Adelaide isn't an issue." Ezra's voice rises with his panic. "I don't know why you and Kat keep bringing her up. You're confusing the hell out of me, and that's a very unwise thing to do with me."

"We've been fighting over Ade since we were sixteen fucking years old, Ezra," Cortez snarls. "We came to an impasse, where I bitch about the cunt to everyone but you, after you told me to keep my mouth shut about this topic. Hypothetically, let's just say that perhaps Katya told me to keep a secret as well. I'm toeing a fine line here, Ezra. My loyalties are divided. You need to talk to Kat. Not next week, or even tomorrow. You should have talked to Kat about Adelaide four months ago."

"You're keeping a secret from me with Katya?" As always, Ezra only heard what he wanted to hear.

I slide down the door to rest on my ass, prepared for a long wait. I rest my chin on my knee, and then I realize these fools will have to go through this door to leave me in peace, which means I'll be caught in the act. I crawl back to my feet, and slowly edge into the living room, trying to go slow enough not to be detected, but fast enough that they don't sense my presence.

I really, really don't want to get pulled into their bullshit again. Not today of all days, and not after what I just went through in the park.

"It's been you and me for a very long time, Ezra. But it's no longer just us. We're three separate people now, and we're all fighting the melding. We're guys, and we don't think like a chick, so we don't get what's going on in Kat's head."

"I think I understand Katya better than anyone." The arrogance in Ezra's voice stops me in my tracks, just outside of their periphery.

Cortez's laughter is bitter, grating like broken glass on glass. "Yeah, I don't fucking think you have a clue of what's going on inside our girl's head, says the straight guy to the gay guy."

"Sarcasm solves nothing," Ezra chastises.

"This was your idea, and I'm making the best of it. So now I'm not going to allow you to ruin it with your self-defeatist bullshit. This requires some major adjustments on all of our parts. You're too concerned with getting Katya to obey you instead of realizing she needs your support and guidance, not your totalitarianism. You're talking at her, forcing her to spill her emotions at your feet, but you're not giving her anything in return. You're suffocating her, confusing her, and it's killing her, and you can't see it. In this, I wish your ideology was more like Marc's."

"Don't go there, Cortez." Voice frigid, Ezra petrifies me with his intensity. "Ever."

"You make Katya feel weak, that's what I meant. If you want her eating out of your hand, make her feel powerful."

Radiating fury, "I'm not Marcus, and you best remember that," is a promise, not a threat.

"Fuckhead, calm yourself." Cort releases a bitter laugh. "I'm trying to help us both, and you're not hearing me. You really have to spell things out to Katya, or she doesn't see it. You can't expect her to understand what's going on with Adelaide without explaining anything. You can't expect her to show up to your birthday party when you said nothing to her. There is no being subtle or easing with Katya. We're talking capital letters here, Ezra."

"I'm not sure what you mean." Ezra's confusion is so thick, he's choking on it.

Cortez barks out a sharp laugh, finding our dynamic funny when it's torturous. "Yeah, Kat's right about one thing. She told me she possessed the traits of both of us, and that's why we're drawn to her. She said it was our best traits combined with her tits and vagina. On this subject, you are just like her– a stubborn twit."

Suddenly bewildered, Ezra voices, "Katya really didn't think she was invited?"

"No, I don't think so. I bet Kat left so it would be easier on us to go off without her. I know Kat worries about your public life, especially because you separate her from it. Plus, she believes she isn't a part of your private life. She is sad, scared, and confused, and it worries me that you don't see it."

"Katya spends most of her time freezing me out, refusing to allow me in her thoughts and emotions. This is something you do to me as well," Ezra points out.

"You're hopeless." I can hear Cortez rolling his eyes. "Earlier I found Kat trying to figure out a way to occupy Ava, so that your daughter wouldn't know about the party. Kat didn't think you'd want Ava to go, either."

"What? Why?"

"Listen, Ezra, you have to trust me on this. Talk to Kat. Resolve this so she will confide in you. Katya has a lot going on right now, more than you can imagine. I have so many secrets that I'm keeping for both of you, and it's killing me. I don't want to be in the middle anymore. I can't take it. We need your help."

The sound of Cortez's pain pulls me from my hiding spot along the wall. Ezra is sitting in his favorite chair with Cort kneeling between his legs. Cortez's head is resting on Ezra's lap, with Ezra's fingers brushing through his hair. I hear a stifled sniffle, leading me to believe Cort's crying.

"Shh… It's alright, let it out. You can talk to me, Cort." I drift toward them, watching Ezra stroke Cortez's hair in a soothing motion, trying to comfort him.

"I can't talk about it. I want to. It's the same as when you tell me to keep a confidence. I can't betray either of your trusts."

I drop to my knees to embrace Cortez from behind. "Don't cry. I'm so sorry. I didn't realize what keeping this from Ezra would mean for you. The three of us will talk about it tomorrow. I promise."

"I'm sorry," Ezra croaks out to me, his voice thick with unshed tears. "Please accompany us to my party. I want you and Ava to meet my family. I want my mother to meet my family."

Gripping the first excuse I can think of, "I don't have anything to wear," spills out my mouth before I can stop it. Even though Ezra just asked me to go with them, my fear gets the best of me.

"I wanted it to be a surprise, Katya." Ezra reaches out to touch me, but let's his hand drop before making contact. "Ava and I picked out a dress for you today. If you hurry, we won't be too late. We may make it just in time for dinner."

I cling to Cort's back, my eyes wide from fright. I bury my face against his suit jacket and pretend he's a life-sized Monkmee. I may need comfort, but I need courage more.

"Katya, I've suffered through eleven birthdays without you. I will suffer no longer. Go get dressed," Ezra commands, and I listen.

———

Cortez finds me pulling on my thigh high stockings. I ignore him while I shimmy into my new dress. I was told to hurry, but Ezra underestimated me. I'm not your typical female. In ten minutes time, I'm almost finished getting ready.

The fitted dress is tea-length with a deep V neckline. Its silver metallic fabric looks iridescent in the light. I pile my hair on top of my head, leaving a few auburn tendrils curling down to my waist. I continue to ignore Cortez as I apply kohl shadow, making my green eyes smoky and dark. I dab a bit of pale color on my lips, hoping for the appearance of a fresh kiss.

"It's Ray Hunter," I declare as I turn to face Cortez.

"How?" His tan face drains of blood before my eyes.

"I'm not sure. But it's definitely him. I'd love to say it's my imagination playing tricks on me, except I can't. I heard his cackle inches from the back of my head. I was sitting on a park bench with the woods at my back. I know he was there. I raced home, tripping along the way. He kept pace. The feeling of being watched didn't leave me until I entered the building."

I pull Cort into a hug and squeeze for dear life. I release him and step back. "It's been a hellacious day. It's the anniversary of the attack, for fuck's sake. We can wait until tomorrow to fret over this. Actually, until we make Ezra fret over this. I would protect him from this if I could. But if it really is Ray, I'm not sure there is protection for any of us."

"We need to see if the monster is still in prison. We should've been notified if he was up for parole again. That's how the system works." Cortez is practically growling as he paces the bathroom.

"And if it's Ray?" I ask.

"And if it's Ray?" he retorts.

I grab Cort's wrist, squeezing tightly. "We kill him."

"We kill him," Cort agrees.

"We kill him, not for us, but for Ezra. For Ava. For Diane. For Aaron. For every victim that monster ever took." I'm overcome with the rightness of my statement. An inner resolve infuses my soul. If the higher power is against justice via death, than why do I feel so righteous to the depths of my soul?

# Chapter Twenty-Three

We're not late. In fact, we're early, thanks to my ability to transform myself from stalked victim to high society maven in less than half an hour. I used the twenty minute ride to Shadow Haven Estates to blank my mind and shore up my courage. It was one of those times where you're happy for an SUV full of chatty people who don't realize your world is collapsing down around your ears. Cort and I were utterly silent, where Ezra simply thought I was feeling nervous and Cort was still upset with him.

The estate where Ezra and Cortez grew up, and later Aaron came to call home, comes into view as we crest the steep, mile-long drive through the woods.

I grew up in a three bedroom ranch-style house, so I am not prepared for the splendor known as Shadow Haven Estates. The Estate and its surrounding wooded area is the size of my town, and the home itself is the size of all the houses in my neighborhood combined.

Fuck.

When you fantasize about what you wish your environment could be, you usually want something bigger and better than what you already have. Shadow Haven is so much more that I didn't have the imagination to create it in my dreams. Instead, it's a nightmare because it demonstrates the chasm between me and the life the Ezes lead.

We had to go through a security checkpoint at a ten foot tall, black iron gate just to enter Crestview's gated community. Where we had to enter another gate to access the mile-long, scenic driveway.

Shadow Haven is an enormous stone manor with perfectly spaced windows and an oversized pair of medieval front doors. It's gothic and oppressive. Its appearance screams malevolence, and for some odd reason, I feel right at home.

The security around the grounds, the gate, and even at the front door is impressive. Shadow Haven is a fortress built to protect its inhabitants. Awed, I'm imprinting every detail of

Ezra and Cortez's childhood home, meanwhile no one else notices its magnificence because they are desensitized.

Ava openly gawks at her birthright, excited where I'm terrified. Everyone else acts as if dressing up in designer black tie and traipsing up to the front doors of a gargantuan estate is an everyday occurrence.

I lag at the back of the pack as we approach the house. Ezra, Cortez, and Ava are in the front, followed by Kayla and Aaron. I drag my heels up the wide, flagstone stairs, scared shitless for the night to come. I feel inadequate, and it's not an emotion I feel often, and it gives me new insight on Monica.

I'm intelligent and I know how to relate to people, so I'm not worried about interacting with Ezra's family. I don't ever want to get to a point where I'm no longer terrified of this strange new world. I feel like a country bumpkin when I see the bills resting on the desk in our home office.

Everything is exorbitant. Bloated. Disgusting.

A shirt is a shirt for the majority of us, where we spend very little to quite a bit depending on the quality. For the elite, it's making a purchase of a designer label that costs more than my first car, and the quality isn't much different than the cheapest shirt I've ever worn.

There is a part of me fighting the pull, wanting to tell Ezra he's a wasteful twit for his expenditures, but I know he will look down on me if I were to say such an asinine thing.

I don't ever want to fit in. I don't want to lose my roots, lose who I essentially am. I was born Katya Waters, and I appreciate the hard work, common sense, and ethics that were bred into me. My biggest fear is succumbing to Ezra, allowing him to digest all I am, only to reshape me in his image– a person I don't recognize, nor one I respect.

It's already infecting me.

I'm wearing a metallic flow of fabric that women across the world would kill to possess, and all I want to do is place it back on its hanger. It doesn't give me confidence. It doesn't make me look more attractive. It makes me sickened that it cost more than a family of four needs for their monthly grocery bill. It's fabric and thread, so why does it cost so much because someone named Versace put a price tag on it?

Ezra is wearing a designer, black suit with a gray pinstripe and a tie the same shade as my dress. Cortez is wearing a solid black suit with a fancy shirt the same color as my dress and no tie. The three of us are completely coordinated, and we could have purchased a house instead of three outfits.

Ava's dress is pink blush, showcasing her very pale skin. Her champagne-colored hair is held back with a silver headband. A small necklace flashes on her dainty throat. Ezra had something commissioned from a jeweler himself: a small, platinum heart embossed with *AZ*. I guess Ezra is placing his *mine* stamp on his daughter with the Z for Zeitler. I don't know why I ever doubted Ezra's need to claim Ava as his. I'm still waiting for him to start pissing on our legs.

Kayla's dress is soft pink, flowing to her ankles, with a sweetheart neckline showcasing and minimizing her ample chest. The pink dress gives the illusion that her skin is glowing. She looks absolutely beautiful as she gazes up at Aaron with adoration. Her cheeks blush and she tries to hide her satisfied smile. Aaron smiles back at her and he places a possessive hand on her waist.

I was surprised what a designer suit can do to a man. Aaron's bulk is minimized, taking him from thug, to the boy-next-door with baby blues, skull-cut fair hair, and a dimple in his cheek.

I follow the herd through the impressive front doors, pausing a moment to check out their design. If I didn't live in an apartment, I would love something like this on a smaller scale. Apartment or not, I could never afford castle doors.

I step to the side, allowing everyone to enter without me. I try to make myself invisible by blending into the walls as I take a look around me. I crank my head back, gazing at the ceiling in awe. Shadow Haven's vestibule is three stories, straight up to the roof, with a double set of staircases flanking the room.

I'm speechless.

Ezra and the gang are huddled near the center of the vestibule, engulfed by a group of partygoers. I see Adelaide's bleached head above the crowd. If I didn't already feel short, her freakishly tall, Amazonian height would do the job. She is the epitome of a blue blood, waifish, willowy, classy, and pretentious.

I want to dissolve into the walls and disappear. I do not belong here. It's not the house– I love the house. It's the people. I can almost scent their arrogance flavoring the air.

Uncomfortable, I turn away from everyone, pretending to be engrossed by a painting hanging nearby. I imprint every detail as I twist my fingers behind my back and I nibble on my bottom lip.

"It's a masterpiece, isn't it? It's a Monet." Adelaide's nasal voice chirps near my ear. She even has to bend to speak to me. I glance down and notice she's wearing flats. What a tall bitch.

"I guess if you're into that sort of thing." I shrug like I don't give a shit. In reality, the painting is a masterpiece, and I would love to stare at it for hours. Admitting I love it would be agreeing with Adelaide. I refuse to agree with her.

The last time I saw Adelaide Whittenhower, she was underneath Ezra as he sang sweet nothings into her ear. No, not nothings. They were words of reverence and adoration. The last time Adelaide saw me, she screamed bloody murder at me and called me a worthless whore. So yeah, I'm not agreeing with her, even if it's about the weather. The future is going to be ever most bright as I share my daughter's milestones with this bitch.

"You don't belong here," Adelaide hisses in my ear.

"I agree." My reply is but a whisper.

She looks at me like I'm brainless. "Then why are you standing here?"

Refusing to be baited, I just give direct answers to her questions. "I was invited."

"You could have said no." She narrows her icy, blue eyes at me.

"No, actually, I couldn't," I defend myself. "You know how Ezra is– he commands and I obey. I don't want to be here any more than you want me to be."

"Oh, somehow, I doubt that very much." Adelaide is so haughty and condescending, I could choke on it. "I would rather eat garbage than have you in my presence this very instant. You're nothing but Ezra's worthless whore. He feels nothing but pity for you. He's too good of a man to admit the truth. If I were Ezra, I would take my daughter and throw your ass on the street like the trash that you are."

"Actually, you'd love to throw my daughter and me on the street. We both complicate your life," I hiss back at Adelaide, finally being baited enough to break my false calm. "You can't throw someone on the street when they are independent of you. I can take care of my daughter just fine on my own, as I have been for the past eleven years. It was Ezra who insisted on us living as a family."

Our conversation, the equivalent of a showdown at high noon, is cut short by the appearance of an imposing, handsome man in his mid-to-late thirties. I can only see him in my peripheral, but he scares the shit out of me anyway.

Adelaide straightens up, as if she hadn't been hissing in my ear for the past few moments. I school my face with a pleasant expression and turn toward the newcomer.

"Jesus Christ," flows out my parted lips. I stare gaped-mouthed as my world tilts on its axis.

"Mmm..." Tall, dark, and deadly hums while his eyes bore through to my soul. "Jesus Christ is the Lord and Savior of Christendom. The fact that he was born a Jew is our only commonality."

"I... um..." A gargled sound trickles out of my mouth, making a total ass out of myself. "I really have no follow up to your statement."

"No, there isn't one." He smirks, trying his damnedest not to laugh. "Religion is usually a conversation ender."

"Unless you're speaking to a theologian, which I am not." I don't blush. I burn bright red from my chest to my hairline. It takes everything in me not to hide my head in my hands. I knew this day would come, and I knew meeting him would be utterly terrifying.

Intense amber eyes turn from me to pierce my antagonizer. "What are you doing, Adelaide?" His voice is smooth and deadly quiet. Terror flashes over Adelaide's pinched features, looking as if he struck her with his question.

"I was just discussing the Monet with Katya. She is extremely ignorant of art." I shake my head in agreement for some reason unbeknownst to me.

The man looks to both of us, knowing we are lying. I wouldn't have agreed with Adelaide, but he is the most intense man I've ever laid eyes upon. The power radiating off of him is frying the part of me that makes me an empath.

This man makes Ezra look like a pussycat.

Tall and athletic, with skin the same intoxicating shade of bronze as Dexter's, with short, dark hair hinting at the ringlets he's chopped off, Ezra's adoptive father is as devastating as he is frightening. I can't even find the strength to look upon him.

"I believe you are finished now. Don't talk to Katya again, Adelaide."

'*It's not a threat. It's a promise*' is not a cliché when it comes to this man. He speaks; you listen.

I take a step back from the both of them, not wanting to be in the middle, and then I take another step back, and another.

Knowing better than to argue, Adelaide replies, "Yes, Marcus," and then she disappears as quickly as she appeared.

"I apologize for anything upsetting that Adelaide may have said. She is to be on her best behavior this evening." Lips twisting up at the corners, he gives me a sad, little smile to put me at ease.

"No need to apologize. We really did talk about the Monet." I defend Adelaide and manage not to lie, if you count saying the name of the artist as talking about him.

I defended Adelaide– must be hell just froze over. This is how I'm behaving and I'm just the victim who ended up pregnant. I'm not the one with rights to Ezra. I'm acting appallingly, and I'm the one who is living, working, eating, and sleeping beside someone else's fiancé.

Mistress or not, I try to stick to my moral high ground by not having sex with Ezra. But what does that matter when you do practically everything else. I'm living someone else's life– their joys, fears, tears, and laughs. I'm sharing in all the things that should be exclusive to only Adelaide. It's no wonder she hates me. I would hate me, too. I do hate me. I hang my head in shame and cast my eyes to the floor.

"It's nice to meet you, Katya. I'm Marcus." He extends his hand into my vision since my eyes are glued to my shoes. I take his hand in mine, and then I look up. His expression changes as he takes note of what I'm emoting. The way he uses body language to read people is proof that he is a dominant.

"Nice to meet you, sir." I try for respectful, but end up sounding meek instead.

"Why are you hiding out over here in the corner, trying to blend in with the environs? Are you sticking close to the door in case you have to make a hasty escape? Fear of crowds, or just terrified of meeting the family? Because there is absolutely no reason you'd need to be afraid of a nice guy like me."

Unable to lie to this man, the truth spills forth. "I thought I'd give everyone a chance to greet each other without me being in the way."

Marcus just stares at me, looks right through me. For a good minute we stand like this– Marcus holding my hand with his eyes boring into my soul. Finally, he shakes his head and smiles, as if he's come to some foregone conclusion about me.

"Well, let me properly introduce myself. I'm Marcus Zeitler– Ezra's adoptive father."

"Katya Waters– Ezra's…" I stumble over the polite word to use. Mistress? Whore? Kept woman? Marcus's eyes narrow, reading my thoughts. I settle on, "The mother of his daughter. It truly is a pleasure to meet you. I've heard so much about you."

"Well, I'm positive it's all been complimentary. Please, come with me. I would love to introduce you to my wife." Marcus keeps my hand and places it on his forearm as he escorts me through the crowd. He continuously pats my hand as we walk, trying to put me at ease.

I find my daughter first amongst the partygoers. Ava is chatting with her father and a woman who must be her grandmother.

Diane Holden is an ethereal being with fine-spun, pale hair. She is a stunning vision in her long, gold gown. My mind conjures up an image of Ezra sitting in his favorite chair this afternoon, and I remember thinking how he looked like an angel. This woman is an angel. She is the being who created Ezra. Ezra who helped create my daughter.

I remember Monica saying, '*wait until you see her,*' and I'd asked, '*who?*' Now I know. Mother, son, and the son's daughter huddle together, and it's impossible not to see the resemblance. This is how Monica knew Ava belonged to Ezra– there is no hiding it. Diane stands in all her glory, with her son and her mini-clone at her side.

Diane turns large, gray eyes on me as if feeling my scrutiny, and I await her judgment and wrath. As I approach her with my hand on her husband's arm, she studies me, studies Ava, and then Ezra, noting our differences and likenesses.

"Diane, I would like to introduce you to Ezra's Katya." Marcus clasps my hand and extends it toward his wife, as if he's afraid I'll bolt for the medieval doors if he lets go of me.

"It's a pleasure to meet you," I say politely, unsure if I should call her Mrs. Zeitler when she might have kept her maiden name. This is all so foreign to me.

Putting me out of my misery, she answers my unspoken question. "Please, call me Diane." She takes my hand from her husband, and then pulls me into a hug.

Engulfing me in a tight embrace, Ezra's mother whispers in my ear. "I understand how this is a difficult day for you, Katya. How we all celebrate an event that brings you secret pain. It's bittersweet. I assume you feel similar on Ava's birthday."

We pull away, discretely wiping away stray tears. Diane is a woman who knows exactly how it feels to be a survivor, when the most important person in your life is a constant reminder of what you survived. We both look to our children, and they look back at us with similar expressions of confusion.

I step back and rub my daughter's back to comfort Ava as much as to center myself. Taking a deep breath, I'm secure in the knowledge that no one knows what Diane and I just bonded over, and hopefully they never will.

"Ah!" Cort materializes at my side. "There she is!" He half hugs me, wrapping an arm around my shoulders. "Kat, I want you to meet Divina." He turns me to the side before I can protest.

A fragile beauty in her early thirties is grinning at me. She isn't much taller than me, even in heels. A swingy, short, midnight blue dress brings the blue out of her gray eyes. She runs her fingers through her shoulder-length, chestnut hair in an anxious gesture. Knowing Divina is nervous helps me relax. I smile as I shake her hand.

"It's nice to finally meet you, Divina. Cort has been quite impatient for us to meet." I smirk at the man in question.

Cort has pestered me endlessly for the past two months, in the hopes I'd get annoyed and meet Divina to shut him up. He assumed that if I met his wife, I would expand the borders of my boundaries. I tried to tell him it wasn't necessary, but he really wanted me to meet her first.

"Me, too. Kat, I couldn't wait to meet you. I've driven Cortez insane." Divina pulls me into a hug. This family is very affectionate. Divina holds me tight against her chest, and her silent laughter vibrates us both. "You have no idea how crazy you're making them, do you? I don't mean to laugh, but this is entertaining as all hell. I thought Adelaide was going to yank your hair out. Everyone could see how badly you wanted the floor to swallow you up."

Divina holds me while laughing, refusing to let me go. She tries to regain her composure, hoping no one sees her making fun of this impossible situation. It's strange, hugging someone who is almost the exact same size as me. I pull away when she calms.

"That's a lovely perfume you're wearing, Divina." It really is a nice scent– lemony and fresh. I compliment her to change the subject. Plus, we seem to have attracted everyone's attention, as if the crowd is watching with bated breath.

"Stop teasing the boys and put them out of their misery," Divina mock-whispers at me, and adds a playful wink for good measure.

Cortez squeezes his wife's shoulder in a strange, brotherly manner. Then he leans down to me and whispers, "She likes you, just as I knew she would," and then he softly kisses my cheek.

I blush brilliant red. Everyone here knows exactly what our exchange meant.

"Dinner is served," Diane announces, saving me from further embarrassment.

I follow everyone into an elegant dining room. A large, oblong table dominates the space with seating for twenty. The room is decorated with chocolate brown damask wallpaper with light blue accents. I camp out near the entryway, unsure where to sit.

Palm settling on the small of my back, "Katya," Ezra commands in a soft voice, causing a spark to run up my spine.

My feet move me to Ezra's destination without conscious thought. He pulls a chair away from the table, and I sit. He takes the seat to my left with Cortez on my right, so that I am flanked by the Ezes. Ava sits next to her father in the last seat, with Diane sitting at Ava's left at the end of the table. Across from us are Marcus, Dexter, a woman I assume is Pearl, and then Divina. Slowly the table fills with the rest of the party guests.

"Kat, I'd like to introduce my mother, Pearl Hastings." Divina gestures to the older woman next to her. Pearl looks similar enough to Diane to be her identical twin. I don't dare ask and risk offending the woman, in case she's the younger sister.

Feeling awkward all of a sudden, I go for polite. "I'm pleased to meet you, Mrs. Hastings."

"As I am you, Katya," Pearl murmurs, highly amused for some reason.

Pearl may look like Diane, but her personality is mischievous like Divina. It reminds me of Ezra when he's playful, or how Ava acts when she isn't channeling her inner-grandmother. It must be a family trait– one that is comforting and welcoming.

I spend the majority of the dinner listening to the conversation flowing around me. I absorb the information as I study everyone, where I learn their personalities and note who interacts with whom. I listen to my daughter connect to the other half of her family. I watch Ezra watch Ava with a look of pride and adoration on his face. I watch Kayla and Aaron sit in a bubble of their own making, completely engrossed with each other.

Cortez picks on the couple throughout dinner, and banters with his wife and mother-in-law. I spend a lot of time trying to hide the smirk on my face because of Cort's antics.

The uncomfortable addition is sitting at the opposite end of the table, Adelaide with several of her family members and associates. I find this strange and confusing.

I sneak glances at Marcus, who continues to watch me throughout dinner as I watch everyone else. He scrutinizes me as an experiment that's at its final stages, and he's waiting for the results.

Earlier, I had asked Ezra what his father did for an occupation, only knowing it was political in nature. I wasn't shocked to learn that Marcus Zeitler is a district attorney. I would hate to be a criminal in Marc's court. While he's handsome with warm eyes and a kind voice, it's his overpowering will that has me scrunching in my seat.

"Thank you for this." Ezra brushes a tendril of hair off my bare shoulder, and then he leans forward to tenderly kiss the skin he revealed.

I stiffen but don't pull away, and Ezra takes this as the greenlight to go farther. Lips tasting of wine press against mine. I return the kiss, but keep it from turning into something more.

Our public display of affection makes me uncomfortable. It leaves me feeling ashamed of myself, because, like a constant reminder, Adelaide is at the table with us. It's fine to show simple affection, but it's an entirely different thing to be obscenely disrespectful.

What is private in our home, suddenly feels like cheating in public, especially in front of the fiancée. I sicken myself.

It's unfathomable, how this family readily accepts the mistress at the table, while still being respectful to the fiancée.

I try not to flinch as Ezra touches me. Cortez places his hand over Ezra's on my back and squeezes tightly. Cort gives Ezra a look that speaks volumes– one I don't comprehend. Ezra must read it correctly, because the pair glances at Adelaide, and then back at each other. Something passes over Ezra's face. I turn before I register its meaning, and I end up looking directly at Marcus. Marcus tips his head to the side, reading me. He gives a nod in my direction, and then turns away.

My mood plummets from comfortable amusement to awkwardness. I spend the rest of dinner looking at my plate as I swirl my food around with a fork. The Ezes keep their hands on my back, touching each other while trying to comfort me. I don't understand it. Maybe they're scared that I'll jump from my seat and run from the room without their hands restraining me.

Drinks are served in an ornate sitting room just off from the vestibule. Personally, I would rather tour the house instead of standing in a crowded room. Actually, I would rather cuddle up on my couch and watch a movie with Ava. I won't leave, though. Ava is flourishing with the attention of her father's family. A newfound confidence blazes in her eyes. My family has always doted on her to compensate for lacking half a family. Now Ava's family is complete and it agrees with her.

A few uncomfortable hours are worth the looks on Ava's and Ezra's faces. Ezra is fluttering around the room, chatting with all the guests, accepting well wishes and presenting his daughter with Cortez at their side. I feel like a voyeur peeking in the leaded-glass windows.

Strong hands grip my shoulders from behind, startling me, and then they shake me to and fro. "Relax!" is gritted out between Dexter's teeth as he teases me. "You're so damn tense I want to put a flogger in your hand and have you release your frustrations out on the guests."

"I can't help it." I plaster a strained smile on my face as I turn toward Dexter.

"You better help it, because your bullshit is feeding Marcus to the point he's bloated." Dexter's comment has my eyes seeking the man in question, who is always watching me. "Katya, you are wanted here. Everyone wants to get to know you, and they will like who they meet, but you're freezing them out with your standoffish posture and bitch-glare."

"I'm uncomfortable," I admit. "I'm also thankful that you inherited the sadist trait in your family. If your cousin had gotten all the crazy genes, Marcus Zeitler would be a world terror."

"Right now, Marc is actually trying to figure out what you're thinking so he can comfort you. Anyone in the room who can read people is experiencing your emotions right along with you. I know you understand what I'm saying. So just have a drink, chat with people who come up to you, stop acting as if Ezra is your enemy... and RELAX!"

"Yes, Master," flows sarcastically from lips that finally curve into a genuine grin.

"Ah, there's the Kat I've enjoyed mentoring!" Dexter pats me hard on the back, nearly causing me to spill my drink. "Welcome back!" He ambles away, leaving me to laugh for the first time all day.

My eyes follow Dexter because his presence is a comfort, and a small gasp is torn from my throat when I see who he joins. The boy-next-door from the hallway at Restraint gestures to me by raising his champagne flute and flashing his sunshine smile my way.

A blush stains my cheeks as I remember the first time I encountered this man. Shame slams into me, and I'm thankful that I see no censure emanating from the guy. My behavior was out of the norm for me, when I prefer to be above reproach. But my naughty display was not out of the ordinary for a member of Restraint– quite mild by comparison, actually.

I have no idea what II's actual name is as he's always referred to as Pretty Boy. Currently he's being used as a comfort object by a stocky teenager with a shock of wild, mused up ginger hair. The kid clearly doesn't want to be here any more than I do, as he keep leaning into Pretty Boy and whispering things out the corner of his mouth. The boy's eyes never leave my daughter, and as a mother, that scares the living daylights out of me. He looks like a good kid, but his body is too mature for his age. Visions of Ezra and Cort's inappropriate, youthful antics to flit though my mind.

"How ya doing, Kat?" Aaron ambles up to me. He removes my champagne flute, and then hands me a fresh glass as a peace offering. He leans against the wall next to me. I'm surprised his other half is absent. I haven't seen Aaron and Kayla separated in almost three months. With a quick scan of the room, I locate Kayla laughing at something Divina said.

"Surviving. How are you doing?" I drink half of the glass, and then grin my thanks at my usual drinking partner.

"I want to apologize to you for something," Aaron begins gruffly. "I've avoided this conversation since Ezra's punishment. I need to say my piece because it's been between us this whole time, no matter how friendly we may be."

I sigh, "Aaron. Not now. Not here. It's unnecessary."

"The anniversary has made me take a good look at myself, so I think today is the perfect time to clear the air. I've been taking a step back from everyone." Aaron finally admits something we've all noticed but have been too scared to comment on. "I've been trying to grow up. You made me see the error of my ways and how I had tunnel vision. It made me want a life of my own. I have to be the man. The grown up. I should be the one making my own decisions, not Ezra."

"Good luck with that," I murmur, not thinking for a second Aaron will get to do something Ezra disapproves of.

"Ezra still hangs the moon and stars for me. But he no longer rises and sets the sun," Aaron says wryly, mocking the words I lobbed at him so many months ago. "I told you I took a step back from you so you'd cling to Ezra, but that's only part of it. I will never regret what we…" he struggles for a party appropriate word to use. "Anyway, I recognize that it was for the wrong and right reasons, and that I was using you. Ezra allowed me to use you."

"Same here." I take a deep breath and will the tears to cease their descent. "Everything you just said. All of it. My biggest issue is that Ezra's starting to make my sun rise, and I'm hiding right now so he won't consume me to the point of setting my sun, too."

"How our roles have reversed," Aaron teases me. He clinks our flutes together, and then takes a sip of champagne.

"Lucky for you, eh? Siccing Ezra on me. I'd call you his wingman, but I think Cortez is running both offense and defense for Ezra."

"You're so fucked." Aaron releases an evil laugh, causing heads to turn and stare at us. When they look away, they all have big grins on their faces. Aaron's infectious like that, especially when he employs his dimples like he is now.

"So, I get it now. At the time of Ezra's punishment, I didn't understand what you were trying to do. I just saw you as abusing Ezra, and I was angry at you."

"Forget it, Aaron."

"No, I can't forget it. I can't have this hanging between us. After I took a step back, I saw the entire situation from your point of view, and it wasn't just wrong, it was criminal. You trusted me with your friendship and your body, and I betrayed you by acting like a spoiled rotten child, and I want to apologize for that."

Hunching my shoulders, I look away, surreptitiously wiping at my eyes.

"I'm sorry I blamed you when I wasn't able to understand. I will be here for you if you ever need me, but I still whole-heartedly believe you have to cleave to Ezra and Cortez."

I smile through the tears, suddenly happy because I recognize Aaron's growth, and I'm proud of him. "Friends?" I thrust my arm out, asking for a handshake.

"Family," Aaron rasps out in his deep voice. He grips my hand, only to pull me into a hug. "You know where to find me if you need me, but I'm taking the night off."

I squeeze Aaron tightly, feeling lighter. "Hot date tonight, eh?" I release a naughty chuckle.

"Most definitely." Aaron waggles his eyebrows as he pulls away. "But so do you," he warns, and then he's pulled back to his other half like a magnet.

I laugh to myself, part elation and part terror. I lift my flute up to take a sip when a malevolent presence makes herself known.

"I know you've fucked Aaron, too," Adelaide purrs in my ear. The sound is as potent and destructive as a chainsaw.

"I don't know who's been inside you, nor do I care. It's none of my business, same as the state of my vagina isn't yours."

"Do you enjoy being passed around like a party favor?" Adelaide twists up her face, looking sickened by the sight of me.

"I wouldn't ignore Marcus's order not to speak with me, if I were you. I'm not above becoming a tattletale," I warn, knowing the man in question hasn't taken his eyes off of me tonight for this very reason.

We're standing in Marcus Zeitler's home for his son's birthday celebration. He will not tolerate Adelaide and me making a spectacle of ourselves, because it would scream of disrespect. To disrespect someone such as he is to emasculate him in his home while surrounded by his family, friends, and colleagues.

After hearing about Ezra's adoptive father for the past few months, I know better than to do anything other than what he requests.

I behave.

Ignoring me, knowing she has a limited amount of time, Adelaide goes in for the kill. "If Ezra really cared for you, he wouldn't share you with every dick and cunt. I know you've fucked Cortez and Kayla as well. I don't have to call you a whore, because it's obvious you already know since you're acting like one."

Eyes glazing over with red, fury floods my veins. I open my mouth to say something just as nasty, but Adelaide rushes off before I can respond.

"Coward." I take a step in her direction, but a tall figure moves into my path. Eyes staring at a broad chest, I don't dare glance up, fearing there might be anger lingering in his eyes.

"No matter what she says or does, ignoring Adelaide is the best course of action," Marcus educates me. "She's not entirely stable. Any retaliation on your part will be seen as if you started it. You have no idea what that woman is capable of doing."

"Damned if you do, damned if you don't," I mouth, hating how powerless I feel right now, and knowing I'm to blame.

"Ezra and I have tried our best to calm Adelaide." Marcus shrugs one elegant shoulder. "Since she won't listen to reason, someone will have to make her listen. Who should do that, Katya?"

"Me," I mutter, feeling infinitesimal. "We need to have a woman to woman discussion."

Marcus grips my shoulder, fingers wrapping around my flesh, and then he squeezes to the point of pain. "Wrong. Ezra is the one who needs to make sure Adelaide respects you, just as he needs to make sure you respect Adelaide. My son is the common denominator, and you girls shouldn't have to enter the same space."

My eyes flick up to connect with Marcus's compassionate stare. "I deserve anything Adelaide throws my way."

"Why?" His voice is soft, the lulling tone almost makes me answer him.

My mind is spinning out of control. My heart is breaking and repairing itself, and my emotions are a tumultuous mix. I look to the ground to avoid eye contact, knowing one glance into his compassionate eyes, and I will be compelled to spill every single secret I harbor.

There is something about Marcus Zeitler that makes me want to trust him, to confide in him. But if I do and I'm wrong, it will be disastrous.

"Why aren't you with your family?" Marc tips my chin up with a fingertip, forcing his lie detector into view– my expressive eyes.

"I thought it would be easier if I stayed over here while they mingled." I'm as honest as possible while keeping so very much unsaid.

"Something is going on in this head." Marc taps a finger to my temple. "I've been trying to figure you out all night, but hell if I can solve it. How about you save us all a lot of energy and just tell me what it is?"

Marc's face screams trust, his eyes blaze honesty, and his touch offers comfort and support. I'm not afraid of Marcus because he's powerful and intense. I'm afraid because I would do anything for him, and I cannot fathom why.

My mouth spews what's been scrolling on repeat in my mind since I crossed Shadow Haven's threshold. "I belong over here, right where I am. Ezra and Cort are partners. This is their celebration, and this is their family and friends. I'm not trying to get attention by lurking in the corner; I'm trying to be respectful."

Black eyebrows hitching up to meet his closely-cropped curls, "Respectful?"

"My presence here tonight makes a lot of people feel ill-at-ease. And as nasty as Adelaide is to me, I deserve every rancid word of it. I'm trying my damnedest to respect Adelaide by not flaunting myself in her face as Ezra presents Ava to his family."

"Ava is Ezra's and your daughter. Surely you see why you should be at his side?"

"Why?" I huff, shrugging. "This isn't about me. This is Ezra and Ava's time to bond with their family. For the same reason you said Ezra is the common denominator, so therefore Adelaide and I shouldn't be in the same space, then why should I get the honor of presenting my daughter to Ezra's family?"

"I don't pity my son." Marcus rakes his hand through his hair. "Your mind is… I have no words, and that isn't a compliment. I don't appreciate you turning my words around on me, but it shows me just how intelligent you truly are."

"Marcus, I'm trying to be respectful of all parties, so I won't argue semantics with you. Even though, I can tell you would love a heated debate." I sound so damn wry that I force Marcus to laugh.

Still chuckling to himself, Marcus chants, "That I do. That I do."

"No disrespect meant to you, but it's disgusting to have a fiancée and a mistress at your birthday party. No one is that entitled, no matter how much money is in their bank account, or how they are a prince to several dying bloodlines."

I start panting wildly. All my tears dry up, and they are replaced with pure frustration, pain, and anger. I can't stop the words from spilling because I've finally found someone who might actually give a shit about what the mother of his only granddaughter thinks and feels. Dexter said Marcus was my only line of defense against Ezra, and in this, I trust him.

"This is so out of my wheelhouse. I've never felt so ignorant or small-town. But at the same time, I know this isn't right, that this isn't how people should live. I can deal with a writer who has a sexual identity crisis, a wife who he treats as his sister, and an unnamed man he blows for shits and giggles, because he respects me with the truth. I could deal with an insane psychiatrist charting my every shit if it wasn't for the mountain of violations and lack of communication. But I can't deal with Ezra humiliating me, by not only making me feel like a whore, but by turning me into one, and then rubbing it in everyone's faces– especially mine and my daughter's. I do have my dignity."

No longer laughing, Marcus grips my chin, and then stares at me for several long moments. "Shit," he hisses, dropping his hand from my chin. An expression crosses his face, as if he's finally come to some conclusion about me. "My son and you need to have a very serious discussion– like yesterday."

"No shit. That's exactly what Cort said to Ezra before we came here tonight."

"Ezra is used to commanding people, with a stance that his actions speak louder than his words. He just assumes you should know how he feels by what he does, not by what he doesn't say."

"Word," I deadpan, trying to make light of a very painful conversation. "But Ezra's lack of action and lack of words negates everything else he says and does. Being in love with someone isn't the be-all, end-all. Without something changing, I'm going to reach my breaking point."

"I'm a firm believer in saying what you mean, meaning what you say, and your actions must be consistent with your word. I am about as black and white as they come. I leave absolutely no room for interpretation, especially when emotions are involved."

"God," I cry out, turning away from Marcus. "I need that. That's what I've always needed."

"Cortez has a propensity to be childish and antagonistic, but he and I have been working on this for some time. I've tried to instill this behavior in him, especially when dealing with you.

I believe that is why you so graciously forgave him for his obvious faults. While I've done everything in my power to get Ezra to see this, we have a major hurdle in our way."

I want to tell Marcus thank you for trying to raise Cortez and Ezra right, but it seems ridiculous to say such a thing to a man no more than three or four years older than me.

So instead, I ask, "What's that?"

"How can a man be consistent in his words, actions and reactions, and his emotions, when he doesn't have a fucking clue what's going on inside his own mind? Ezra is not level, and it's a luxury to find him even. So to ask this of him is downright impossible. Which is why Cortez is trying so hard to be a balance between you and Ezra."

"I would think making the mother of your child your mistress, after she said in no uncertain terms would she abide by that, would not to be that difficult of a concept, even for a lunatic. I also don't think maintaining a relationship should be this hard."

I turn away, unable to deal with the emotions coursing through me. Marcus catches my arm, gripping tightly. "Hey, look at me," he demands. "It's going to be all right. You have to trust me on this."

"I don't know you," I whisper, but it feels like a lie. One minute with this man and you're stripped bare, with all of your wounds rubbed raw until they're clean, and then Marcus begins to heal you.

"This is the most important advice I will ever offer you, Katya. Forget Adelaide, and look to Ezra's actions. Look to who is in his daily life because he needs them to be by his side."

"I can't..." I cover my face with my upraised palms, refusing to cry in the middle of a crowded party. "I can't talk about this anymore."

"You will," Marcus demands. "You will listen, and you will hear me, and you will learn from my advice."

"Yes, sir."

"Very good," Marcus murmurs, pleased with my surrender. "You are their bridge, and they are yours. Ezra and Cortez love each other deeply, but neither believes themselves to be exclusively a lover of men. They could be content with just each other, but never truly satisfied and happy. Do you know what I mean by a bridge?"

"Yes," comes out shyly, as a blush blooms on my cheeks.

"Yes, sexually." Marcus chuckles a warm, delicious sound. "The three of you could be quite satisfied in bed, no doubt. But that's not what I meant. A bridge is integral for connecting a chasm. Neither side can connect without their bridge. Just as the bridge is nothing without solid ground."

"Three parts," I murmur, starting to get it.

"Three parts, never whole without all three parts, with each part having a specific job. If only two of the three are connected, then it's useless: the two sides never meet without the bridge, or the bridge connects to one side and hovers into nothingness, while the other side is left defenseless and alone. The three of you are connected. You need each other to feel whole. Don't fight it."

"Give and take. Know when to ask for help and when to give it."

"Precisely," Marcus praises. He reaches out to grip my wrist, gaining my undivided attention. "Your pride is going to get you killed, my dear," he warns, sounding ominous, running a shiver down my spine.

"I hope not." I release a whimper, this morning's note flashing across my mind.

"Katya, when you drive over a bridge, you don't think the bridge weak because the sides it's connecting are supporting it. Just as you don't think the side is weak, simply because the bridge is connecting it to the other side."

"No, you don't."

"Nothing is stronger than a united front, with all the pieces supporting one another. No single piece of the unit is more important than the next." Marcus gestures around his home to his family, friends, and his colleagues. "Being alone when you don't have to be isn't strength. It's selfish. It's unintelligent. Because when you are in a position to give support while being supported, and you don't join, then you are weak, a coward, and worthless."

Marcus just stares at me as mortification crosses my face and tears spring to my eyes.

"I see you gather my meaning." Marcus releases my wrist, leaving me feeling bereft without the contact. "You've forgiven

Cortez for all the faults that you're currently vilifying my son over. Maybe you should ask yourself why, and when you do, you will find out it's because you don't think yourself worthy of their support, not because you don't think you need it."

"The littlest dogs have the loudest bark," flows unbidden.

"And no bite," Marcus volleys.

"I bite."

"Which is why I want to strike you right now," Marcus states unemotionally, without an inflection of humor. "With your strength, your intelligence, and your heart... to be standing in the corner instead of sharing your thoughts, wisdom, and emotions with those around us. That is cowardly and unattractive. If you want to feel worthy, have worth. If you want to be useful, have a use. If you want to be loved, accept the love that is given freely."

Mouth gaping, I've never felt so dissected in my life, not even beneath the hands of Ezra's twisted psychiatry. I feel broken and mended simultaneously.

I've just been educated by Marcus Zeitler.

Awestruck, all I can do is babble, "Now I understand why I was so terrified to meet you."

Applause draws our attention, breaking off our uncomfortable conversation. An intricate cake is wheeled out. My face lights up when I see the cake, signaling this night is coming to close.

"Are we good?" Marcus asks me while taking my arm to escort me to where he believes I belong– at Ezra and Cortez's sides.

"I have a lot to think about, and I heard you loud and clear." I huff a laugh. "I feel like you've beaten the shit out of me, and then kissed my boo-boos... and I don't know why I feel as if I should thank you for that."

"You're under Dexter's tutelage. When you finally understand, your training will be complete."

"Thank God, Dexter is my mentor," I drawl out, still sounding awed. It was a fifty-fifty chance, and I could have ended up being educated by the terrifying Marcus Zeitler instead of the sadist.

"Welcome to the family, Katya," Marcus says in parting, and I realize this wasn't just about Ava tonight. These people wanted to meet me, and I still can't fathom why.

I stand next to my daughter, relieved for the simple comfort. "Mom! Look!" Ava giggles as she points at the cake. "Do you think they made it because you and Dad play chess every night?"

The elaborate cake is a chessboard with traditional pieces– no hedonistic figures engaged in the art of BDSM. Upon seeing the cake, I go from half in love with Ezra, to all but keeping a single thread to myself.

Ezra doesn't use words. He uses actions.

The birthday boy leans in to cut his cake, all the while holding my gaze, because he chose this cake as a message for me.

We sing a round of '*Happy Birthday, Ezra',* and my voice rises above the others– using my actions *and* words to communicate with the man I wish I didn't love.

Cortez embraces Ezra in a tight hug. I'm close enough to see Cort kiss Ezra's neck tenderly, and to hear as he whispers, "I love you. Happy birthday. I wouldn't be here today without you."

Ezra returns the sentiments, and tightens his arms around the other man. Ezra looks over at me and smiles shyly, a blush staining his pale cheeks, as if embarrassed to be caught giving and receiving such deep intimacy.

I can't help but smile at their sweet interaction, and it gives me the strength to admit defeat. Not only did I listen to Marcus, I heard him. I was allowing my own insecurities to influence how I acted around others.

Who gives a fuck if they think me a country bumpkin? If they don't like me, they can walk away. With my newfound courage, I join the party. Better late than never.

––––––––––

Three glasses of champagne later, after enduring an endless stream of small talk, I wait for the world's longest goodbyes to conclude.

My daughter dances around me out of boredom, and I join in thanks to my liquid stupid. We mock-waltz in the vestibule, waiting for our group to converge. I give up on any semblance of dance and just twirl Ava around and around, laughing at her dizziness. My heart is light since it's not often my child acts like a kid, and even rarer is that I join her.

I hear a collective *Ah!*

Aaron is down on his left knee before Kayla, concentrating with all his might to do this right. I give a little hop and clap, heart swelling to the point of pain. Ava looks at me, confused, never having seen a proposal before. I pull my daughter into a huge hug, waiting, watching for what's to come.

"Kayla, would you do me the honor of becoming my wife?" Aaron's husky, gravelly voice is unusually rough. He kneels before the beauty with his hand extended, an open ring box resting on his palm.

Kayla is stunned silent. Embarrassed and unsure, the submissive woman needs reassurance in her decision. Her eyes flick around wildly until she meets my gaze. Stark relief etches across her face when I give her an encouraging nod. Her skin flushes pink, tears stream down her cheeks, and a big smile stretches across her face.

Kayla simply says yes, because no other words were necessary.

Aaron reaches up and places an intricate knot of platinum around her delicate finger in front of all of his family and friends. Aaron stands and envelopes Kayla into a tight embrace and kisses her sweetly on the cheek. They both blush as the crowd swarms them with congratulations.

I spot Ezra leaning against the entryway, watching my reaction to the scene. He looks proud and pleased for the couple, yet sad as he watches one of his own embark on a new path in life, leaving him behind.

Lips quirking up in a sympathetic smile, I give Ezra a thumbs up, signaling that all's right with all of us. Then I resume swinging my child around, waiting my turn to offer congratulations.

I pull Aaron into a big hug and kiss his cheek when he gets within arm's reach. "So this is why you were taking the night off from solving all of our problems," I tease, squeezing him even harder.

Aaron's elated chuckle is music to my ears as he passes me his future bride.

"I'm so proud of you," I tell Kayla as I squeeze the shit out of her. Grabbing Aaron's shirt sleeve, I pull him into our embrace. "I'm so goddamned proud of you both."

# Chapter Twenty-Four

Being overly dramatic, Cortez flings open the front door to our apartment. "God, I'm so happy to be home." He charges into the living room, dropping his coat onto the floor wherever it may land, with his shoes soon to follow.

Ezra is beaming as he reaches down to pick up Cort's discarded clothing, his OCD refusing to leave the clothing where it lies. "This has been my favorite birthday, by far."

"I should hope so," Cort mumbles beneath his breath, not wanting Ava to overhear. "That's something about Aaron. The pain in the ass never told us he planned on getting hitched. Never saw it coming."

Grinning from ear to ear, my heart feels like it will burst from pure joy. "Our baby boy is growing into a fine young man."

"Kayla said I can help plan the wedding!" Ava squeals in excitement, hopping up and down, causing her dress to swirl around her. "I think everything should be pink."

"Kill me," echoes throughout the living room from several sources, one being from me. "Ava, if Kayla is nice enough to let you help, then you best let her pick out everything on her own."

Ava flashes me a look of hurt that screams, '*who, me?*', as if the eleven-year-old tyrant wouldn't railroad sweet, submissive Kayla.

"If that's the case…" Cort releases a groan. "It's guaranteed to be pink. Well, I'm done for the night. I've got to get out of this monkey suit."

"I want to sleep in my new dress! Please, Mommy, may I?"

"Sure," Cort says immediately, as Ezra and I say, "NO!" at the same time.

"You're no fun." Ava pouts better than Cortez does.

"C'mon, Monster." Cort takes Ava's hand, and then looks at Ezra and me over his shoulder, mouthing '*meanies*' at us "I'll tuck you in tonight. Your parents needn't bother."

"Cort!" I cry out, exasperated. "I better find our daughter wearing a nightgown come morning."

Cort and Ava ignore me as they leave the room, with their conversation trailing after them. "If you love pretty dresses, I'll buy you all the pretty dresses you could ever want."

"Even if they are pink?" flows my daughter's girly voice from the hallway.

"Any color you want, Monster. Anything you want."

"I think I just rolled over in my own grave, and I'm even not dead yet." I toss my purse onto the sofa, and then toe off my stilettos. "Monster is right. You guys are creating a monster out of our daughter."

Ezra snatches up my purse and shoes, stacking them on the growing pile in his arms. "Meet me in the office in five minutes?"

"We're still playing?" My voice pitches an octave higher in surprise.

"During my party, all I wanted to do was spend my time with you. But when I tried to get near you, someone would intercept me. So, yes, Katya. I want to spend the last few minutes of my birthday with you. Just us, playing chess."

"See ya in five," I mutter, briskly walking toward our home office. I brush away the tears stinging my eyes.

Ezra communicates via action, but sometimes he knows exactly what you need to hear.

Our office was designed with the three of us in mind. Cortez misses his giant library at Shadow Haven, so the entire room is wall-to-wall bookshelves. The only desk in the room belongs to Ezra, because both Cort and I would rather sit on a sofa with a laptop or a manuscript in our laps. Ezra's only prerequisite is sitting directly in the center of the room– two chairs surrounding a small table, which is holding the infamous chess set.

I settle in my seat and begin setting up tonight's battle, having yet to actually win a match but learning more and more every single time we play.

"If I could play against you every night for the rest of my life, I would die a happy man." Ezra enters, and my breath hitches in my throat. "Our daughter is wearing a nightgown, but she made Cortez hang her gown so she could see it while lying in bed."

"That girl has Cortez wrapped around her little finger." I shake my head back and forth, knowing it's a horrible thing but finding it hilarious.

Settling into his seat across from me, Ezra's lips quirk up into a sardonic grin. "Along with his other seven fingers and both of his thumbs. Our daughter will need a very strong man to survive her."

I lean forward and make the first move, just as every night. "Like her mother?"

Ezra's gray eyes swim with happiness. "Just like her mother, *and* her father."

"That's a nightmare in the making." I huff a laugh. "Ah, so that is Cort's biggest issue? He's not strong enough to survive you?"

"My woman needs to be strong enough to survive me." Ezra leans forward to make a play, managing to capture one of my pieces with his first move. "However, our man needs to be passive and patient to survive us."

"We're all too much alike." I brush off the depressing thought and use humor to deflect it. "It's a wonder we haven't killed each other yet."

"Murder is a crime of passion." Ezra winks at me, capturing another of my pieces. When he leans back, my eyes are drawn to the smooth column of his neck, and down his chest where his shirt is unbuttoned. I lick my suddenly dry lips.

"So…" Ezra glances up to pin me beneath his intense stare. "About Marcus."

"Ah!" I throw my hands up in the air, anger beginning to stir in my blood. "I knew you were waiting to lecture me."

Ezra winces, but it doesn't stop him from finishing what he wanted to say before I interrupted him. "Not a lecture. I'm glad you found succor with Marcus. You were stressed all night, refusing to let me in so I could help you. When Marcus was finished speaking with you, you looked lighter, so I felt better."

"Five minutes with that man reminded me of being spanked as a child. Where I felt disappointed in myself afterwards, but I felt better for some unknown reason."

Head cocked backward, Ezra releases a spine-tingling laugh from deep within his chest. "Apropos." His eyes roll down to meet mine. "It took me the better part of a decade before I figured out that it didn't matter what I did or didn't do, it didn't matter how disappointing I was, or if I did something worthy of praise, Marcus was going to love me unconditionally anyway. That freed me from his power."

"I couldn't imagine having that much faith in someone," I mutter, not believing I could feel that for another person.

"Marcus said he loved me unconditionally, and I didn't believe him. So I tested him in horrific ways, and he'd still hug me and tell me he loved me. I still test him on occasion, unable to help myself. So you and I do have that in common. My faith in Marcus isn't to blame; it's the faith I have in myself."

"Cortez doesn't test Marcus, does he?"

"Not in that way, no." Ezra sounds as sheepish as all hell. "The love and affection is unconditional. However, earning Marcus's respect and faith is not. Marcus trusts Cortez with all of his secrets, and me with none."

"Everyone trusts Cortez with their secrets, because he always keeps them."

"Precisely. Which is very frustrating when Cortez knows something I need to know, but he won't tell me. But it becomes a godsend when I have to confide in him and I know he won't breathe a word of it."

"It doesn't take a genius to see the parallels between the three of us. You and I love Cortez for his loyalty, but also hate and respect him because of it."

"While you and Cortez both withhold a vital part of yourselves from me," Ezra whispers so softly I barely hear him. "Not that I blame you," he says louder. "After all, Cortez knows all of the secrets, so he knows I deserve it."

Finally getting a clue, "Which is why you don't want me to know a single one."

"It's not that I don't trust you, respect you, or have faith in you. I've done horrific shit, and I'm still doing things I know I will regret in the future. I'd rather you look at me with love shining from your eyes, than with the hatred I know I will see when you finally learn all of the truth. Not telling you my secrets isn't about you; it's about me."

"That's basically what Marcus was lecturing me about earlier tonight, only about me. He said my pride and insecurities were what was forcing me to hide in the corner, not because no one wanted me to be there."

"It's true." Ezra gives up all pretenses of playing chess, which is why we play chess in the first place. He knows if we were to sit down to talk, I would clam up.

"Katya, I had kept you and Ava away from my family until I thought you were ready to meet them. It had nothing to do with me not being proud that you are in my life, and everything to do with the fact that I didn't want them to scare you away from me. Going from the only world you've known to my scary world was more than most could handle. Keeping my home life separate from my work life and my family life was because I was scared and being selfish. I wanted you and Ava all to myself– and Cortez."

Eyes pricking with tears, I have to turn away from Ezra's gaze. He has opened himself up to me, baring himself raw, even with all the secrets and lies still lying between us. He's asking me to trust him, to have faith in him.

"Even the infallible Ezra Zeitler has insecurities." Emotions too tense, I tease Ezra to lighten the mood. "Who would have thought it?"

Expression still open and honest, immense shame and pain is written across Ezra's features. "We are all human. We all have faults. We all hurt. We all cause harm, whether intentionally or not. We are all subject to the human condition."

"That's your way of saying I don't want to know why you're bleeding shame right now, that I should just have faith in you."

"In essence, yes," is pulled from his throat, as if he's choking on the words. "I also know at some point you will learn the truth, and I have to have enough faith in the both of us to know we will survive the fallout."

Our conversation is the equivalent of a verbal chess match. "You and I, we keep talking around the issues, but never admitting them."

"I'm ready and willing if you are," Ezra challenges.

My eyes seek his, connecting us. "I'm ready, honest. But not tonight. Aaron did the most selfless, beautiful thing possible. He overwrote a painful day in our histories with something that we will always cherish. Instead of thinking of today as the anniversary of our attack, we will always see it as your birthday–the day Aaron brought Kayla into our family. I won't ruin that with the conversation to come."

"Our family," Ezra muses with a smile playing along his devastating lips. "I like that. Tomorrow then?"

"Tomorrow," I promise to spill my grievances at Ezra's feet, and he promises to clean them up, even if he has to lie to make me feel better. With one glance, I know Ezra trusts me, that he respects me, and that he loves me.

I don't accuse; I state it as fact. "You and I are both prideful creatures. I know you won't tell me anything that will jeopardize that pride, but you will demand it from me as a test of my loyalty and devotion."

The evilest smirk I've ever seen twists Ezra's lips, and I know I'm going to loathe what comes out of his mouth next. "That's why I said I needed a woman who was strong enough to survive me."

Rolling my eyes, wanting to be angry but finding it impossible, I reach forward for the first black piece my fingertips encounter. I use Ezra's Bishop to flick my white King from the board, and then I place it on the square.

"Checkmate." Leaning back in my chair, I release a maniacal laugh. I cross my arms over my chest, and sing, "You win!"

Moving so fast, my mind registers it as slow, Ezra's out of his seat, body curved over the table. He cups my cheek in his palm. "Then we both win," he whispers across my parted lips. "I win you. You win me. We both win the loyal, naughty bastard lying in our bed."

Faster than a lightning strike, my lips are fused to Ezra's–and I'm the one who moved. I'm the one who kissed Ezra first.

I took what I wanted.

I had faith, and said the fuck with everything else.

*"If you want to feel worthy, have worth. If you want to be useful, have a use. If you want to be loved, accept the love that is given freely."*

I am worthy.

I am useful.

I love.

Fingers fisting Ezra's hair roughly, I yank him across the table. When the chess pieces scatter to the floor, we laugh into each other's mouths– the sound beautiful yet pained.

"Shit! Sorry!" Roarke's voice flows from the open doorway. I gaze up to catch sight of the big, burly man, looking like he's going to piss his pants because he interrupted. He raises his palms. "Don't kill me."

Smirking, Ezra looks more at peace than I've ever seen him. "Am I late?" Ezra glances at the grandfather clock. "It appears time has gotten away from me."

Roarke backs slowly out of the doorway, hands still raised to ward off Ezra. "I got worried when you didn't appear for your usual evening routine." Brown eyes flicking to light on me, "Now I see why."

I slump back down into my chair, upset but refusing to show it. I tell myself it's not about me. Ezra's issues are Ezra's issues; they are not a reflection of how he feels about me. He is not leaving me behind for all of those who come before me, because it's not as if I'm a damsel in distress. I'm in our home, with our daughter and Cortez, with Aaron and Kayla across the hall.

I have to have faith.

Ezra has prior engagements because they are important to Ezra, but that doesn't mean I'm not important to him, too.

"If it were any other night, I'd blow it off," Ezra says to comfort me, no doubt reading my expression. "For the past eleven of my birthdays, I've had a long-standing arrangement. One I will have until the day I die."

Ezra straightens up from where he was sprawled across the table. He begins buttoning his shirt. As he walks away, his hand flows down my hair in a comforting gesture.

As Ezra leaves with Roarke in tow, he calls out, "I won't be gone as long as usual, and I won't be far."

# Chapter Twenty-Five

Just call me the shit-pot stirrer. "Who's Z?" I can't leave well-enough alone, so I bother the secret keeper.

Cortez *was* lying in bed, reading a paperback, when I entered our bedroom. As soon as he comprehended my question, his tan skin turned whiter than Ezra's, and a flash of sweat beaded on his forehead.

Scuttling backward until he can't get any farther from me, Cort squawks, "What?"

"Marcus told me that Ezra's actions speak louder than words. I don't know everything he is up to, and I doubt I ever will. He's a bit of a wily bastard, our Ezra."

I walk farther into our bedroom, feeling enlivened because I've thrown Cortez for a loop. Perhaps I do have a bit of a sadist in me. I begin to undress, fingers finding the hidden zipper beneath my armpit.

"Kat, I… what?" Cortez stammers, at a loss for words because he's not allowed to speak them.

"Ezra's necklace." I jingle the bracelet on my arm. "I'd forgotten about the charms on it until I ordered one for Ava. The **C** represents you. The **KW** represents me. Ava's charm is self-explanatory. So how about you explain the **Z** to me?"

"I'd rather not." Cort shifts uncomfortably on the bed, tossing his paperback to the floor.

"Ezra and I had a good heart-to-heart while not playing chess," I explain as I strip down until I'm completely naked, feeling empowered by the way Cortez's eyes follow me. "But then he left because he had to meet someone. So, being as I'm not a moron, I put two and two together to equal Z."

"I can't," Cortez chokes on the words, voice cracking. "I can't tell you. Believe me when I say I wish I could. But I cannot."

Voice soft, I murmur as I climb onto our bed, "I know, and I understand." I reach out to wipe the sweat collecting on Cort's forehead. "You told me I wasn't to worry about Adelaide, and I didn't trust you when I probably should have. You said Ezra's actions were out of the ordinary, enough to frighten you. So in this, I want to trust you."

Swallowing hard, Cort gulps out, "In what?"

I crawl closer to him, stopping his hand when he tries to flick the switch to lower the room-darkening shades. Feeling like a seasoned dominant, I have to be able to read Cort's facial expressions, and he knows it.

"No," I breathe as I remove his fingers from the switch. "If you tell me I have nothing to worry about when it comes to Z, I will trust you."

"You. Have. Absolutely. Nothing. To. Worry. About. When. It. Comes. To. Z." Cortez says succinctly, and then he falls lax to the mattress, as if all life had just drained out of him.

"Never bring this up to Ezra," Cortez warns. "Ever. An innocent person who needed to be protected and loved nearly destroyed everything between Ezra and me. But it wasn't because of Z. It was because of secrets and lies. So I suggest you forget it all, and just trust me and Ez on this subject."

Feeling deflated and defeated, I lie down on the mattress, staring up at the ceiling. "I hate you right now." I don't mean it, and he knows it. "I trust you, though."

Defying me, Cort reaches over and flicks the switch to the shades. I'm not surprised, since I can only talk while pretending to play chess and Cort can only talk in total darkness. I stare out the wall of windows overlooking The Green Building– the building Ezra is inside this very moment. It doesn't take long until I'm staring at nothingness in the pitch-black of our bedroom.

"Do you know why I blow our master?" Cort's question shocks the hell out of me.

"He tastes scrumptious?"

Cort's laughter vibrates the mattress beneath us. "Yeah, he does. But, no, that's not why." Cort rolls over onto his side, inching toward me. "The first time I did it, I wanted to hurt Ezra in the worst way possible. I hurt, and I wanted him to hurt as much as I did– more even. But while I was doing it, while I was regretting it, it was the power I felt that kept me coming back."

Now that piqued my interests. "Power?"

"It wasn't about sex. It's never been about sex. It was about pain at first, and Master knew it. He knew I would regret it. I put him in a position that would hurt him, would make him regret. I was miserable and wanted everyone else to be, too."

Laughing without humor, "Yeah, I've been known to be a self-saboteur."

"It was a time in my life where I felt utterly powerless. I was in a position that others look down upon. When insulted, men are called cocksuckers, as if it makes them lesser men. This is always by men who have never sucked a dick but get theirs sucked. They insult both men and women with the derogatoriness."

"You felt like shit, so you wanted physical proof of it? Is that why you suck cock?"

"That's why I sucked *his* cock," Cort stresses. "I'd sucked Ez off because I loved him." A loud breath echoes throughout the darkness. "While I was on my knees, sucking the dick of a guy who didn't want me to suck him off but was giving me what I wanted, I found my power."

It's my turn to roll over onto my side, facing Cortez as if he and I are looking into each other's eyes. "Explain."

"Not only did I hurt Ezra and Master, I learned how to control them. When your lips are wrapped around a dick, you own them. Even on my knees in a subservient position, I held the seat of power. It's even more empowering if you manage to bring even the strongest of men to their knees."

"Jesus," I hiss, awed.

"You're feeling powerless right now, aren't you?" Cort sounds concerned for my well-being. He reaches out to stroke my cheek, fingertips skating across my flesh.

My breath flutters out, "Yes."

"Katya, let me help you feel empowered." Cortez cradles my face between his palms, as if the severity of what he's about to say will break me apart. "Suck. My. Dick."

"Oh, my God!" I screech. Laughter jolts through my body, and it's so jarring I almost fall off the bed. "I love you, goddamnit!" I reach out to pound the idiot in the chest.

"You think I'm jesting?" Cort wrestles me around the bed, tickling me when I giggle. "You met my wife, so we're all squared up. I know better than to ask for entrance into your sweet pussy, since you and Ezra still have unresolved issues. But your tight cocksucker is open for business."

"Oh! You've done it now, mister!" I yank Cort's hair, tugging him off of me, and then I flip him over onto his back. "I'll show you empowered."

Intuitively, my palm knows exactly where to locate what I'm seeking, even in the dark. I grip Cort's exquisiteness, squeezing to the point of pain to teach him a lesson.

"Harder," he releases breathlessly, teasing me. "If you're going to grow up to be a big, bad sadist, you better do it harder." I squeeze so dang hard I fear irreparable harm, and all Cort does is grunt and jerk his hips closer to me, seeking more friction.

"You're shameless." I give another squeeze before I let go. "But since I love you, I think I'll give you that blowjob."

"Oh!" Cort chirps happily, shifting on the mattress. "I'll be a good boy. I'll just lay here and let you do all the work, that way you're in charge. When you're done, we'll switch."

"You're such a twit," spills from my mouth as I descend on the idiot.

Cortez wanted hard and angry moments ago, so I give him whisper soft touches. Snickering to myself, I tongue his glans, edging around the flared head.

Palm landing heavily on the back of my head, Cort tries to press me forward. "Harder," he demands, getting more impatient by the second. To punish him, I lick even lighter, following the vein down his shaft.

"Sadist," Cort growls, voice thick with lust and frustration. "Why is it that Ezra always choses the sadists?" he says so quietly, as if he was thinking it and it spilled out his lips.

About ready to question Cortez, a squeak of surprise is pulled from my lips, and then I moan deep in my throat. On my elbows and knees, bent over Cortez's cock, first I receive a bite to my ass cheek, and then my spine is peppered with a fluttering of kisses. Followed by a pair of hands slipping beneath me to cup my swinging breasts.

"Took ya long enough," Cort purrs, husky and deep. "I was fluffing Kat while you were gone. How'd I do?"

"Judging from the fact that she's bent over your dick..." Ezra trails off, getting sidetracked by where the curve of my shoulder meets my neck.

My head pops up, the exquisiteness long forgotten. "Hey, how come you didn't freak out when Ezra snuck up on us?"

"Sneak?" Cort fists my hair, drawing me back down. He props up his cock, while his wingman forces my mouth open by tugging on my chin. "I felt Ezra enter the apartment. He can't sneak up on me. I just know when he's nearby."

Resisting their efforts, "Did you want Ezra to catch me sucking your dick?"

"No, I wanted you to shut up," Cort says wryly. "We were having a private conversation– one I didn't want sneaky Ezra to overhear. I thought it best to shove a cock down your throat to silence you."

"Asshole," I snarl, yanking away. I get about an inch before I'm face-planted into the mattress with my ass waving in the air. I yelp when a forceful hand swats me.

"I'd ask what you were discussing, but I bet it would be best if I didn't know." Ezra makes a soothing sound in the back of his throat while he rubs my stinging ass cheek. "We won't have sex with you tonight," he warns. "Not until you and I get out whatever is plaguing you. But all else is fair game, seeing as how I walked in on you bobbing Cort's knob, after kissing the ever-loving fuck out of me not less than an hour ago."

I hesitate for a second, with my indecision flavoring the air. I can't see them, but I can feel them. Ezra is frozen behind me, hand resting on my ass. With Cortez sprawled next to me, not as much as a muscle twitching. I don't even hear them breathing.

I ignore my morals, my codes of ethics, and all of my worries and fears and threats. I'm here with Cortez and Ezra. Me. For the past few months I've been here, where no one else has been. Actions speak louder than words. They want me here, and I want to be here, so who am I to argue?

"Okay," I breathe the word, and all life returns to Ezra and Cort.

"Kat, have you ever heard of a birthday blowjob?" Cort's voice is extra snarky, causing Ezra to bark out a laugh that's hard enough to shake the bed.

"Nope," I mutter wearily. "I can't say that I have, since I don't have a dick."

"See, the birthday boy gets a blowjob, even if he's been a bad boy." Cortez stresses that Ezra is usually misbehaving. "It's a requirement." Cort slips his thumb into my mouth, mimicking what I was just doing to his cock. "And I know for a fact that your mouth is lovely. I think Ezra would do just about anything to feel these moist lips wrapped around his pulsing cock."

Cortez leans in and kisses me, sucking my bottom lip until I squirm on the bed. "Hmm? What do you say, Kat? Does the Birthday Boy deserve his dick sucked?"

"What if I say no," I breathe against Cort's lips, challenging him because I want to know what he'll do next.

Sighing, acting put out, but you can hear the longing and excitement in Cort's voice. "Well, if you don't think Ezra deserves it, I guess I could always do it for you. I think he's been a *very*, *very*, *very* patient boy." Cortez bites my lip every time he says very.

I swallow a few times and turn to Ezra. Even though I can't see him, I can hear him breathing heavily. "Have you been a good boy?" I flip around, sensing Ezra standing at the foot of the bed. I reach out, shocked when I don't encounter any clothing besides his boxer briefs. Ezra was looking forward to some birthday attention tonight. Very presumptuous on his part.

"I might not have been a good boy, but I've been a very patient one," flows deeply from Ezra's chest.

I reach out, tracing a fingertip along the waistband of Ezra's boxer briefs. A groan, a sound of pure misery and need, echoes throughout our bedroom. Ezra flexes into my touch, begging me to touch him more.

"Would you like Cortez to reward you for your patient behavior?" Teasing, I wiggle my fingertip beneath the waistband of his boxers, dipping close to his erection. "Or would you like me to give you a birthday blowjob?"

"Pleeeeeaaaasssseeee…." Ezra cries out, with his hips jerking forward, trying to get closer to me. "Anyone. Either one of you. Preferably both of you. It's been months– *years* –since either of you have touched me like that."

Ezra's smoky voice is so rough with need, that I peel his underwear down his body. His cock nudges my cheek as he steps out of his boxers.

"So eager," I purr, nearly shaking from the strength of my need to touch Ezra. "What do you think, Cort? Should we reward our misbehaving yet patient birthday boy?"

"Yes," Cort pants out, beyond aroused at the thought of touching Ezra. "I think we should. Yes, we really, really should."

Cort half crawls over me to reach Ezra. I can't see what they're doing, but I can hear them. My imagination has them kissing, judging by their jerky movements and heady moans. I should be creeped out, but I'm not. My pussy tightens sharply like a fist, causing me to moan with them.

While they kiss, I slide from the bed to land at Ezra's feet. Needing to worship him, I nip, lick, bite, suck, and nibble my way from his toes to his thighs. His muscles spasm and thrash under my mouth, to the point that I have to hold his leg still to enjoy him. I nibble my way around Ezra's hip, avoiding the area his cock nestles in. I ache with such a fierce need to suck Ezra that I deny myself the pleasure to intensify the gratification when I finally give into temptation.

I bite Ezra in the juncture of where his leg connects to his pelvis, just shy of where his cock is resting. I can scent his arousal, and long to taste it, too. I dart my tongue out, finding a bead of arousal dripping down his hip. I moan deep from the back of my throat at Ezra's bitter taste, so silky smooth. Hungry for more of his essence, the tip of my tongue accidentally makes contact with the head of his cock. Ezra thrusts up into the air as a groan passes his lips. I freeze through the urgency to swallow him down my throat.

I feel Cortez getting nearer as I hear small sucking noises. He's kissing his way down Ezra's glorious abs. I rise up to meet him. We both lick and suck on Ezra's stomach. I seek out Cort's mouth and twine my tongue with his. He jerks against my mouth.

"Join me," Cort breathes against my mouth.

"I can't," a strangled cry pours out of my throat from the intense fear slamming into me.

"Why not?" Cort kisses me violently, lips sucking the air from my mouth, trying to change my already faltering mind. "Does it freak you out how Ez and I want to touch each other?"

"God, no! That's the hottest fucking thing," I gasp. "I've been using the thought for months as masturbation material."

I expected Cort and Ezra to chuckle at me, but instead they groan. "I'm glad you like that thought as much as we love the reality, Kitten," Cort whispers across my lips. "I think it's time you turned your fantasies into reality." He kisses me quickly but roughly.

After a second, Cortez moves lightning fast, and in result, Ezra's body jerks forward, nearly knocking both Cort and me off the edge of the bed. Joining a loud sucking sound is Ezra's exclamation of, "Cort!" at the ceiling.

Cortez's head is bobbing up and down, brushing softly against the side of my face. I kiss my way down to where Cort is cherishing Ezra's cock. I'm shocked when Cort's mouth rests on Ez's pelvis, deep-throating. Cort holds there for a few seconds as Ezra goes into a frenzy, nearly toppling to the bed. Curled fingertips bite into my shoulder for stability.

I'm awed, and I've never been as turned on as I am right now. Most women's fantasies involve two men, but those men are ravishing her as if she's a goddess. I don't think many women would be aroused by the men ravishing each other while she sat on the sidelines. But it's doing something to me. Just hearing their moans has me on the edge of release.

"Join me," Cort begs again when he comes up for air.

"I can't," I cry out. It's beyond tempting. If he asks one more time, I will undoubtedly give in to his demands.

"Kiss me, Cort. Oh God, kiss me. I need to taste Ezra on your lips," I plead, voice thready and weak as I yank the man into my arms.

Cort takes my lips in a mouth-melding kiss. I feast– I lick the inside of Cortez's cheeks, the roof of his mouth, and then suck on his lips, removing all traces of Ezra's taste that remains.

"Join me," Cort demands this time, and join him I do.

Without a thought or care, my mouth is latched onto Ezra's cock, forcing a scream out of his throat. I go from never touching him to deep-throating him. The thatch of his pubic hair tickles my nose as I hold him deep inside my mouth with the tip of his dick thrust past my gag reflex. I glorify in doing something I've long-denied us both.

I pull off his dick, saliva stringing between us. Panting for breath, I marvel over how powerful I feel after giving into what

I've wanted to do for months on end. I don't even feel guilty that I don't feel badly about it.

"Jesus Christ, Kitten! When you decide to do something, you go for broke." Cortez's awed voice is loud, coming from right next to my ear. "Watch this neat trick."

A second later, Ezra grunts as he lands heavily on the mattress, nearly bouncing me off. "Ezra is '*Mr. In Control*' in all things except for sex. Do you know how to spot a bottom?"

Intrigued, I mutter, "How?"

"By how far a dude's thighs spread when you toss him on a mattress." Cort crawls over me, moving toward Ezra, who's laughing like a lunatic.

"I'm only a bottom because that's all you'll allow," Ezra explains. "I know no other way. Cort, I've learned after eighteen years of sex with you to be patient and take whatever you're willing to give."

"You can keep on taking, assfuck, because I'm closed for business." Cort growls, but he doesn't sound angry, more frustrated that he's horny and doesn't want to admit why. He crawls around, and I reach out to find him situated between Ezra's thighs.

"Cort's scared that if anyone breaches his tight ass, he'll forever be bent over begging for it."

"You mean, like you always are?" Cort banters back, and then Ezra is arching off the mattress with a guttural moan. "Suck with me, Kitten," is the only warning I'm issued before fingertips fist my hair and yank me face-first into Ezra's crotch.

"I've never had sex with a man, and I never will, unless and until Cortez gives me the honors. He gets a bit of a high on this knowledge, lording it over me."

"Doesn't matter," Cort says around Ezra's cock, followed by a slurping noise. I decide to service the heavy sac with the tip of my tongue. "Gay, straight, bi– any guy with a prostate goes insane once he knows the pleasure. I'm never giving that power to anyone, and I like knowing that I hold the power to give you the pleasure, and to withhold both the pleasure of you receiving penetration and all access to my body. So just deal with it."

"I'm not complaining." Ezra's perfectly contented voice flows from the dark. "Just explaining why I couldn't spread my legs any farther apart if I tried. Feel free to do whatever the fuck you want to do to me. I'm ready and willing"

"You guys are nightmares," I chuckle out, the words vibrating against Ezra's nutsack. "Cort, shut him up like you did me earlier."

Ezra freezes next to me, and Cortez growls. "My dick is another thing that's off limit to Ezra's mouth."

"Jesus," I hiss, getting furious at Cortez for Ezra, understanding why the man was willing to move on rather than suffer this torture. I crawl on my elbows until I reach Ezra's face, and then I whisper into his ear. "I take that knowing Cortez loves you and wants you has to be enough."

Ezra attacks my lips in answer, yanking a surprised moan from my throat. Not wanting to live a life like Cortez has– a bitter power struggle –I curl over Ezra's chest, kissing him with a passion I've always held in check. My hands can't touch enough of him, my tongue, teeth, and lips can't taste enough of him, and Ezra gives back as good as I give.

Ezra's fingertips clench my breasts, bruising me, just as one of his hands is skating up my leg to slip between my thighs. We melt together at the mouth, with Ezra stroking my breasts and my pussy like they belong to him.

By the time I pull away, gasping for air, I'm about to spill over the edge into climax. "Slow up," I pant, clutching at Ezra's hands. "Gonna cum…"

Ezra releases a high-pitched scream, and Cort's sardonic voice weaves through it. "Did ya forget about me somehow? I'm down here with your dick in my mouth, hard to forget that… I bet you won't forget next time."

"Jesus, what'd you do?" I demand, panicking over the fact that Cortez is the most jealous creature on the planet. "Why'd you hurt him?"

"Hurt?" Cort twists out. "I bit Ez's taint. I believe he's a hairsbreadth from popping his cork. "Now flip your ass over and smother his face with your pussy, and get to sucking my dick. Three. There are three of us, not you and Ez. My dick is lonely."

"Since when did you turn into such an asshole when it comes to sex?" I accuse, but I do as I was told. Flipping around, I sit astride Ezra's chest. His hands grip my hips, fingertips dimpling my flesh, and then he yanks me up, settling me over his face.

My eyes roll back as my lids slip shut. My neck can no longer support my head. I turn into a boneless, writhing pile of bliss. Nothing is better than having a tongue laving at your slit and lips suctioned to your clit.

"So good…" heady moans pour forth.

"Kat, you like Ezra too much," Cortez snarls, but it's more of a pout. He yanks me forward, tapping his dick on my lips. I open without complaint, eagerly even, and begin softly sucking the exquisiteness.

"My need to be an asshole is contingent on whether or not I'm getting attention. Like, now, I'm the nicest guy in the world." Cort moans. I moan. Ezra moans. "Did you suddenly forget your skull-fuck? I turn into an asshole when I'm being ignored. Three. Don't forget that a ménage à trois, a triad, and a threesome involves three people. I'm not to be ignored, or used for oral services. You want me in your bed, you include me. I don't need to be touched, but you bet your ass I'll be doing some touching. I can't reach you good enough, so fucking move closer."

Hair yanked roughly, cock trying to jab my throat, "Holy shit," I garble around the intrusion, getting turned on by psycho Cortez.

"Please, fuck me. I love it when you're like this. Fuck me," Ezra begs shamelessly, voice pitching and then breaking with need. "God, I'd kill someone for you if I knew the result would be getting fucked. Please."

I flip around as if I can see the expression on Ezra's face. Shocked, I demand, "Are you serious?"

"This is the perfect example as to why no one will ever get near my ass. Which is exactly why Ezra is never allowed to suck my dick, because his tongue tends to wander. My prostate is sacred territory."

"Guilty as charged," Ezra mutters sheepishly. "I'd do as Cortez says. Sex when he's pissed is the most explosive." I'm yanked back into place. "Gimme your pussy."

"Fuck!" I grunt, torn between two lovers. Ezra is feasting at my cunt, gripping my hips so tightly I'm bruising, while Cortez is fighting the hold, trying to yank me closer to him so I can suck his dick better. Eventually, Cortez gives up and pulls away.

"What?" I mumble, wondering what he's up to.

"Thank God!" Ezra prays as his hips jack up, followed by a grunt.

"Yeah, your legs can get wider than that, assfuck." The teasing lilt in Cort's voice is accentuated by the fact that Ezra chuckles against my pussy. "Lesson number one in servicing a dude who is obsessed with his butthole: lick the fuck out of it during a blowjob."

"Jesus Christ, are you really doing that?" Intrigued and turned on, I lean forward, trying to see with my fingertips. Cort playfully nips at my fingertips and curls his tongue around the digits, and then goes back to his feast. Voice thick with wonder and arousal, I slur, "That's hot as fuck."

"Gimme that finger back," Cort demands when I go to pull away. He sucks my index finger in between his lips, wet heat enveloping it. Working his mouth, I begin to wonder what it would be like to be on the receiving end of those oral skills if I had a cock. All too soon, he pulls my finger from his mouth.

"Lesson number two in servicing a dude who is obsessed with his butthole–" Cort begins while tugging on my finger.

"Holy fuck!" Ezra and I shout in unison when Cort pushes my fingertip inside Ezra's body, with a finger of his own paving the way. Tight, feverishly hot, and the softest, pillowy flesh I've ever encounter. Not only do we ease in, Ezra's body grips us tight, sucking us in further.

"Go in slowly," Cort instructs. "Ezra's nice and relaxed, so it won't hurt at all." He eases us in further, until my hand is pressed against Ezra's body. "Where, oh, where are you?" Cort sings.

"Ugh!" Ezra grunts out, nearly toppling me off his chest.

"There we go," Cort murmurs. "Lesson number three: don't ever touch me there, but feel free to worship Ezra's prostate until your finger shrivels up and falls off. The man is completely shameless, a total slut, and will lie here for hours."

Ezra is rendered passive beneath me, just sprawled out on the bed like he took a hit of the most potent of drugs while Cortez and I manipulate him.

"How can you not fuck this man?" I shake my head back and forth in wonder. "Jesus, he's so damn warm, hotter than any pussy I've encountered, and softer too. Fucking snug. I can't imagine what it would be like to slide your–"

Finger disappearing from beside mine, "Shut up!" Cort snarls, shoving his cock down my throat. "Your voice, the fucking truth you preach, and the asshole on the bed, had me a heartbeat from losing it. I have my own reasons for not having sex with Ezra, and they are my private business. If you don't think this tempts me, then ask Ez why I never do this anymore."

"Don't fight, and don't harm Katya's throat," Ez begs, sounding close to tears.

"I'm sorry," I try to say around Cort's deflating cock. "I didn't know I was stepping on an emotional landmine. Sorry."

To prove how sorry I am, I start sucking with great vigor, causing Cortez to rock back and forth from the motion. Feeling like a consummate multitasker, I try to find Ezra's sweet spot. I know all is forgiven when not one but two fingers join mine as Cortez shows me the right way to pleasure Ezra.

And pleasured, he is. Ezra is beneath me, wiggling around, moaning and groaning, and trying to tongue my pussy but doing a half-assed job of it, not that I mind. I'm turned on enough by what I'm doing to not care what's happening to me. I know once they blow, I'll follow shortly thereafter.

"Hey!" I protest when Cortez slips from my mouth, only to fist the back of my hair. He moves around the bed, changing positions, but never releases my hair or removes his fingers from inside Ezra's body.

"I know you're a cocksucker like me," Cort praises. "Prove it. You don't have to take us to the root, but you have to get a bit of each of us in your mouth."

Fingertips prodding at the hinge of my jaw, I open wide at Cort's cue. His hand leaves my hair, only to wrap around both of their cocks. "Holy fuck," I groan, getting hot just at the thought of their cocks touching, but nowhere near as hot as Ezra is getting beneath me.

"Wider," Cort demands as he pushes their cockheads into my mouth. "Wider still. I know you can do it, Kat. You're our little cocksucker. In this, I am your mentor and you are the novice. Prove you can do it."

Making a strangled noise, part from the physical exertion, and part from how close to losing it I am, I manage to get both of their cockheads into my mouth, and maybe an inch of the shaft. My jaw hurts, my lips are pulled tight, my cheeks are puffed out as far as they will go, and I can barely breathe, but I feel victorious.

Empowered.

"Good God, Kitten!" Cort presses in farther, causing Ezra to jerk beneath me. "I'm so jealous right now. My biggest fantasy is sucking two big cocks at once. I'm so goddamned proud of you."

Something snaps inside Ezra. He begins attacking my pussy like a fiend. Rutting his face, rubbing it back and forth with his tongue impaling me. The pleasure relaxes me, and I learn to breathe through the trauma to my mouth as Cort sets a pace by moving back and forth, rubbing their dicks together while I suck them both.

My hips begin jerking roughly, riding Ezra's face, not caring if I'm hurting him since they both stopped caring about anything other than their own pleasure moments ago. Ezra's teeth latch onto my clit and bite fiercely, forcing my scream of pain to evolve into a scream of release.

Cortez does something with our fingertips, causing Ezra's grunts to vibrate against my pussy, and then he's shooting inside my mouth. Both of them are. Hot. Forceful. Jets of cum fill my mouth to spill out my lips to cling to my chin and dampen my neck and breasts.

The ecstasy is an exquisite agony I don't know if I will ever recover from. We collapse to the bed in a pile of intertwined arms and legs as the three of us gasp for breath.

"Now *that* is what you call a birthday blowjob," Cortez laughs out. "I'll expect one on mine in two months."

"Did I die? Because I thought for sure I'd go to Hell when I did. This sure feels like Heaven to me." Ezra rolls over onto his side, reaches out to yank both Cortez and me where he wants us, and then he embraces us both. "Rematch in two months."

"And again on Kat's birthday," Cort rumbles in my ear.

"Deal," I agree, and then pass the fuck out.

# Chapter Twenty-Six

I adore the sensation of half sleep: the time when you wake up and everything feels hazy and right with the world. You're neither asleep nor awake. You're in an in-between state of bliss.

"Do you think Katya regrets last night?" Ezra's voice is barely a whisper. Fingertips trail up and down my spine in a soothing motion. I lay on my tummy with my head cradled in the crook of– I inhale deeply –Cort's arm.

"Kitten loved it, and you know it." Cort's satisfied tone warms my heart.

Ezra's voice flows hesitantly, "What about you? Do you regret it?

"No, I'm not going to go postal on you this morning, Ezra. So stop looking like you're waiting for me to freak the fuck out."

"What about…" Ezra trails off, and then his long-suffering sigh echoes throughout the room. "You weren't jealous were you? Are you okay with the three of us? I know… I know how you get when you think my affections are divided from you."

"Jesus, this is one of those talks, isn't it? Can't just bask in the afterglow. The psychiatrist has to analyze every minute detail." Cort shifts beneath me, but somehow manages to keep my arm-pillow still. "I thought I would be jealous. I mean, I was a little bit. But once it was all three of us, the jealousy dissipated. I didn't like it when it was the two of you and me and you. It felt disconnected."

"Yeah, but…" Ezra clears his throat, as if uncomfortable to say what he means. "We have to be able to touch her when we're alone. I can't stop myself from wanting to hold her or kiss her when you're not in the room."

"That's not it." Cort's voice is stiff– annoyed. "If it's the three of us, it better be the three of us. It's not you and Kat, or me and you. This was your decision, so you have to make sure it works. No sitting on the sidelines for any of us. I don't want to lie in our bed, knowing you're making love to Katya, and I'm just… there. I'm not going to stop touching Kat in private just because you're not there, and I don't expect you to, either. It's when we're all together that has to be sorted out."

"Thank God," is a sigh of relief from Ezra. "This is new to us, and it will take some time to get used to. I don't want anyone's feelings getting hurt because I want you both."

"I'm doing my best, and I know Katya is too. We both want you to be happy, Ezra."

"I want the same." Ezra's laugh is light and amused. "I mean, I want you both to be happy, too, not just myself happy. Can I kiss you in private now? I know for the past few years you've avoided it."

"Yes," Cort rasps roughly.

"If you knock me on my ass and shout at me for kissing you in our living room, I will kiss you in public in retaliation." Cortez busts out laughing, causing Ezra to mutter, "That's what you do. Just warning you what I will do."

"Fair enough," Cort allows."

"Can I ask you something uncomfortable?"

"Why bother asking? We both know you're just being polite, because even if I say no, you're going to find a way to ask it anyway."

"Were you… were you going to make love to me last night? Please be honest. I need to know."

"I don't know if that answer is going to make you feel better or worse, Ez. I don't think I should answer that."

"Please," Ezra begs, voice warbling. "I need to know. Just tell me the truth."

"Fine," Cort grits out between clenched teeth. "My cock ended up slammed down Katya's throat because it was a split-second decision to keep myself from impaling you. Happy?" Cort twists nastily. "It won't happen, Ezra. The last time nearly killed me, and you know it. It's too… nightmarish."

"I'm sorry," Ezra breathes. "If I could change the past, I would. I would take your place and you could have sat in a chair and watched."

"Your fate was worse than mine. I wouldn't have survived it. So I'm okay as long as I don't have sex like that. I'm sorry that you have to go without because I can never satisfy you. Kat's with us now, and that better be enough. Because if you try to bring a guy in next, I will murder you in your sleep."

"I have no complaints. Last night will become a perfect memory as long as no one ruins it with regrets and jealousy."

"Last night would have been perfect if we were allowed to be inside Kat. You have to talk to Kat about the big elephant in the room so she'll have sex with us. You and I not having sex is bad enough. The three of us refusing to do anything but play handsy and oral would be catastrophic."

"I don't see why I have to talk to Katya about Adelaide. She's not an issue. It'll just be an uncomfortable conversation for the both of us," Ezra murmurs softly. "But we agreed we would settle our grievances today. Not looking forward to it, scared we won't survive it, but we will endure it."

"Kat's half awake, listening to us," Cort says wryly as he moves a lock of hair away from my eyes. Cort's lips twist into that fatal smile of his as he gazes down at me. "I'm going to take a long shower and work off some of my frustrations. I can't lay here and not touch you both. If you don't work this out soon, I am going to go batshit crazy."

Cortez kisses my cheek and slowly retrieves his arm. I pull a pillow under my head and cuddle into it, letting my eyelids drift shut. I don't want to wake up. I prefer this foggy state because I'm not ready to face reality yet.

"Talk," Cort orders, but it evolves into a moan. I roll my eyes up to see why his voice changed. He's pulling away from Ezra, undoubtedly from a good morning kiss.

My eyes flutter open as a hand rolls me onto my back. Ezra lowers himself on top of me, nestling between my thighs. I wrap my arms and legs around his back, basking in his warmth. I have the strongest urge to shift beneath Ezra and connect us.

We all know the score. Cortez is in love with Ezra. I'm in love with Ezra. Ezra is in love with Cortez, and his actions say he's in love with me too. Cortez and I love each other, but not the type where you dream of a happily ever after together. Ezra is the glue tying us all together. Without Ezra, Cortez and I would be best friends, sometimes lovers, and not each other's one and only. If not done with maturity, this is going to turn into a bloodbath.

"Good morning, my Kitty Kat. How are we feeling this morning?" Ezra sings while rolling his hips into me, proving just how good of a morning he's having.

"Most excellent." I release a breathy moan at the feel of his length sliding through my folds. I'm a hairsbreadth away from begging Ezra to make love to me, conversation to come be damned.

Ezra leans down to kiss my throat, lips soft and warm, and I arch up into him with a deep moan. My hands take on a mind of their own, fingertips running up and down from Ezra's perfect ass to his shoulders in a continual rhythm.

"Not to be a mood killer, but Cortez ordered us to have a conversation about Adelaide," Ezra states simply, as if he is asking whether or not I want a bagel or a smoothie for breakfast.

My lust cooled to colder than ice, I push my fists against Ezra's chest while I try to wriggle out from beneath him. "Yup, that will definitely kill a mood. I need to be clothed for this conversation." I crawl across the bed, trying to locate my nightgown, only to realize in my haze of fury that I never wore one last night.

Ezra's hand lashes out to latch onto my ankle. With a sharp yank, he drags me across the bed as I squeal and thrash and try to grip the bedding as leverage. I know Ezra's not going to harm me; I'm just furious that he would bring up his fiancée while touching me intimately. I'm not angry with him; I'm angry with myself for being too stupid to live.

"Fighting me isn't a good idea, right now, Katya." His voice is deeper– Master Ez deep. I fight harder against him, trying to get away. I kick out and clip him in the chin. He grunts from the tap, and the kick brings Master Ez to the fore.

"Master Ez isn't a good idea right now, Ezra," I warn, voice stiff with fear.

"I keep telling you that we're the same person. I'm still me, Katya."

"Yeah, you're the same person. You're still you. But Ezra and Master Ez do not share the same space at the same time, and that's what frightens me." I stifle a shiver, knowing what is going on inside Ezra's mind right now after researching it for the last three months. It's like walking around on eggshells at all times. Ezra is intense yet kind, playful, easily hurt, and then Master Ez comes out in force to protect himself.

Master Ez is brutal, pragmatic, and scary as fucking hell. It was Master Ez who was willing to kill to get Ezra fucked by

Cortez last night. Deep inside, a part of me believes him capable of it, too.

Master Ez throws me on the bed roughly, and then tackles me with the heavy weight of his body. My hands are drawn above my head, held tight in one of his fists. With an abrupt maneuver, Ez parts my thighs with his, and then mashes his hard threat of arousal against my sex.

Ezra's gone, and he's who I need to speak with. Master Ez doesn't care about anything but compliance. "Now, where were we? That's right… you tried to get away before I was ready. So, the conversation goes like this, Katya. You are mine to do with as I please. I know how badly you crave me. I crave you. End of story." He rocks his hips, cock sliding along my damp pussy, demonstrating what he and I both crave. But I don't want it like this, and not with the threat of another woman between us. I want it to mean more than that.

Fighting, struggling, fingernails biting into the back of Ez's hands, I refuse to be treated like this. "That's not the end of the story for me, dammit!" I try to get away again, but it's futile.

Ez freezes, staring down at me in confusion, not used to anyone challenging him. His facial expression warps, as if Ez and Ezra are fighting inside their shared mind. Voice soft, Ezra beats back the other half of his personality. "I will explain the entire thing, but first I want to finish our cuddle." Ezra rubs his cheek against mine in a cat-like motion.

"Ezra, I'm not in the mood to cuddle after you've thrown me around the bed and attacked me," I hiss in outrage. "Wavering back and forth between vicious Master Ez and martyr Ezra is more confusing for me than it is for you. Just let me up, and we will finish this conversation in a more appropriate location, preferably with clothing and a level head."

Master Ez descends with a vengeance, never allowing Ezra to get hurt emotionally. "This isn't an attack. I'm at the end of my leash with you, Katya. When the leash snaps, then you will know attack," Ez threatens menacingly.

The cornered rabbit versus the hungry wolf, neither of us blinks.

Ez's breathing is ragged, rasping against my ear. His whole body is strung tight with effort. I can feel his control about to snap. I try to slow my breathing and still my body's natural responses. He lays heavy and ripe, while throbbing against my core. The feel of him so close tightens things low in my body. The muscles in my pussy clench, releasing a wash of arousal.

"Oh, God... I can feel your wetness trickling down my cock," he rasps out, causing Master Ez's leash to snap.

Before I can blink, let alone issue a protest, Ez rears back and brutally enters me. The feel of Ez's cock tearing into my tight flesh, brings on an instantaneous release. Ashamed at my response to being violated, I scream his name to the ceiling and claw the sheets with my restrained hands.

Ezra freezes above me– within me. I open my eyes to meet Ezra's stormy, tortured gaze, which is staring down at me in a mix of shock and horror. "Oh, shit! I'm so sorry, Kat." His voice is no longer deep and husky. He is back to his usual smoky smooth tone. Ezra is back in control of his inner-Master Ez, and he looks like he's going to be sick.

We stare at each other, neither moving, barely breathing. I wiggle my hands and he releases them from their capture. I pull Ezra down to my chest and hold him as both of our minds wander.

Confusion slams into me. We've played on the edge since I met Master Ez at Restraint. Ezra's affections confuse me as he holds me close, only to keep me separate from his real life outside of the confines of The Edge Building.

I'm doing the same thing by allowing Ezra to touch me, and then later I always say no. My indecision created this issue. Ezra fills me for the first time in twelve years, and I can feel his guilt for taking me when I've said no over and over again.

In all things, actions speak louder than words, and my actions have screamed *take me*. Ezra's put up with Cortez's bullshit for decades, and now mine. Master Ez doesn't fuck with Cortez, but he's not going to put up with my shit. I'm in the wrong for this wishy-washy behavior, not Ezra. Master Ez is in the wrong for taking something I wasn't willing to give, and now I'm not sure how to fix it for Ezra.

We lay speechless for a few minutes, neither a willing participant in what joined us, just as it was our first time. But both of us are wanting. Ezra's cock throbs inside of me and my body clenches in response. Neither thrusts our hips to give more friction. We just feel our bodies welcome each other home. We both pant and gasp as if we're having marathon sex, not embraced and motionless with our emotions racing.

I cradle Ezra's head in my palms, whiskers pricking my skin. I try to tell him without words that I understand, and how I forgive him for something he hadn't meant to do. His stormy eyes are bleeding remorse and pain and a few stray tears.

I kiss him gently at first, just a brush of my lips against his. He presses back slightly, flesh trembling beneath mine. The kiss evolves until I'm thoroughly exploring him, and then Ezra begins matching me. Whatever I give, Ezra takes, and then he gives it right back to me with equal fervor.

Our fingertips skate across each other's skin, as if marveling that we're touching– that we're connected. I whimper into Ezra's mouth when I accidentally roll my hips up to meet his, moving his length to rock into me.

The slow build of pressure begins to knot deep inside my belly. I close my eyes and try to shut off my body, my emotions, and my heart. They don't listen– we are one, and we want to make love to Ezra. He is ours, and we want to mark him as proof.

Ezra follows my lead by rocking into me. Long, slow strokes, which allow us to feel every inch of the other. This isn't fucking, screwing, sex. It's the epitome of love making: slow, rhythmic, sensuous and full of emotion. I experience a full-body shiver from the intense sensations and emotions wracking me.

Back jackknifing off the mattress, muscles taut yet spasming, I prepare for a release that will destroy who I am, and then reform me into who I'm to become.

Ezra gazes down at me in total rapture, eyes glazed and lips parted. "Ezra, I–"

A soft knock on our bedroom door saves me from humiliation. I was about to profess something that could be detrimental to the life we've built.

"Ma... Dad..." Ava calls from the other side of the door.

Ezra doesn't move from me. He cradles me in his arms, rolling us to our sides, and then flicks the covers over us, making sure we are decent.

"You can come in," Ez summons. When Ava opens the door but doesn't enter the room, he murmurs in a coaxing tone, "Good morning, little one. Did you sleep well?"

Our daughter's eyes glue to the floor, as if something fascinating is lying on the hardwood. "Sorry, I didn't mean to interrupt. I mean... I hope I didn't interrupt anything," she stammers. "Aaron said to let you guys sleep in."

Ava lifts her eyes to us and blushes bright pink. In my ecstasy, I had forgotten that sound travels. I'm sure the household heard my cries of pleasure. I blush too, and then hide my face in the crook Ezra's neck.

Just like her father, Ava ignores embarrassment and goes straight to the heart of the matter. "Grandpa Marcus keeps calling. Both of your cells were ringing. I didn't answer either of them because I knew you wouldn't like that. But it was the same number on both. Dad's phone said *Marc calling*, so..." Ava shrugs. "I figured it was important. He called the kitchen phone, and I answered that one. Grandpa said it's an emergency, but it can wait as long as none of us leave the building." Ava's eyes glance away bashfully.

"How come you didn't get us sooner?" Ezra schools his tone, not wishing to sound demanding or impatient.

"I– um..." Ava twists side-to-side, wringing her fingers together. I smile, entertained to see my nervous trait reflected in my daughter.

"Grandpa asked why you weren't up yet." Ava blushes crimson. "I told him *why*," she breathes. "He said to call him back when you were finished. Um–Aaron said that you were... done." Ava turns around and faces the living room, hiding her embarrassment. I'm mortified for her. I'm going to skin Aaron alive for this.

"Why is Aaron here?" Ezra transforms from lover to the head of our family in an instant.

"Grandpa called Aaron. Kayla's here, too. He said we needed to stick close together. He said they weren't leaving Shadow Haven, either."

Cortez chooses that precise moment to exit the bathroom. I release a silent prayer to the Lord that he is fully dressed, and when my eyes open, Cortez is wearing a pair of ratty jeans and a vintage t-shirt.

Smirking, Cortez gazes at us while arching an eyebrow. "Ah– *that* doesn't look like much talking is happening. What's going on?"

Ava brings Cortez up to speed. In a hurry, her words stumble over each other.

Cort picks up his cellphone and frowns down at the screen. "Remind me never to silence my phone again, no matter what. I have four missed calls." He pockets his cellphone and walks through our bedroom toward Ava. "I'll take care of Marc, and see what's going on. Um– finish up here," Cortez gestures at us while wearing that evil grin of his. "I guess your talk can wait until we get this new emergency settled."

Cort escorts Ava from the room, and then firmly closes the door behind them. "Pretend the last five minutes didn't happen," Ezra rasps in my ear. "We're rewinding to the point in time where I don't feel guilty and you don't feel violated, and we're both shocked as fuck that we're finally making love."

With care, Ezra rolls me over until we're settled in the same position from earlier. He's deep inside me, as far as he can go, but he doesn't thrust.

"I'm going to need a yes this time." Ezra's voice is thick with shame, but laced with an underlying thread of need.

I lean up, pressing my lips against Ezra's. I wrap my arms around his back, fingertips venturing down to the firm globes of his ass cheeks. I hitch my thighs over his hips for leverage, and then I rock into him from below. My *yes* is spoken by my actions, by me making love to him.

"Katya," Ezra breathes out, relieved. "Thank God," is my only warning before he releases his built-up passions. Fusing his lips to mine, Ezra thrusts into me so sharply, I bite his lip to stifle my scream of shock.

Fierce yet smooth, Ezra owns my body, heart, and soul, even managing to invade my mind with his piercing eyes. Arching above me, I'm as lost in Ezra as he appears to be lost in me.

Body spasming like I'm on the verge of a seizure, I rake my nails down his back, embedding the edges into his ass. He grunts from the bite of pain, and it spurs on his thrusts. The long length of him slides deep, connecting us physically in a way we've only felt emotionally until now.

Over and over again, Ezra rocks into me, and I fracture. Mouth torn from mine, Ezra presses his palm over my lips, silencing my building song of pleasure. Gray eyes hold my green, never looking away while I delve deep into the throes of passion. His neck strains, his teeth clench beneath tautly drawn lips, but he doesn't look away, nor does he take his own pleasure.

Ezra is still firm and pulsing with need as he slides free from my body. I try not to whimper at his absence. "You didn't finish," I whine, confused. "I wanted us to go together."

Rolling out of bed, leaving me behind, I watch as the muscles in Ezra's back spasm. "I won't release inside of you until you're comfortable with us making love, and definitely not until we have our talk. I know that you worry over Adelaide, and it's holding you back. Until all that is settled, it's not a good idea for me to release inside of you."

"I've been thinking about that. Maybe I should get on birth control," I offer. "Accidents happen." I definitely have a case of the lady doth protest too much. I tell both the Ezes that I won't have sex with them, and pretty much do anyway. Now, I tell Ezra that I want protection so I can have more sex I shouldn't have. Yeah, I'm confusing myself, too.

"No birth control. If you're ever with someone else, use protection. But I'd prefer if you didn't with me or Cort." Ezra leans down to kiss my lips lightly.

"Why?" My voice warbles.

"We'll talk about that during the same conversation with the other issues. We should get up and see what Cort has found out, and then tackle that issue. But before we go to sleep tonight, we will have our conversation first," he warns.

Ezra straightens up from our kiss, and my eyes instantly latch onto his arousal. Ezra's cock stands straight out from his body, bouncing as he walks to the dresser. I stare entranced, fascinated by the sight. My mouth dries up and my breathing picks up. I clench my thighs together, trying to squash the need that surfaces in me. I whimper when my engorged flesh protests against not having its reward– Ezra's release.

Ezra looks up when I whimper. He flashes me an amused smirk as he strides back to the bed, cock bobbing cheerfully as he walks. "Is this what you want?" He clasps his cock in his fist. "Is your pussy upset that I didn't finish in it?" He teases me, voice light and playful. He's making no secret about how pleased that makes him.

Ezra starts working himself slowly by hand– stroking smoothly up and down from base to tip. When his hand makes the circuit back to the top, he twists his grip, squeezing. Every time he completes the motion, his spine bows and he throws his head back. He's biting his pouty bottom lip to stop his moans. I watch enraptured, as Ezra strokes himself to climax. He's devastating in his glory.

Gorgeous. Perfect. I want *all* of Ezra to myself– his mind, body, soul, and all of his heart– and I can never voice it because I'll lose him if I do. It hurts, but I'm willing to share with Cortez for as long as Cortez is willing to share with me. But I will never share with anyone else.

"Stop thinking bad shit," Ezra warns as he grips the nape of my neck, and then he orders, "Open." He presses his fingertips into my flesh, bruisingly so, and I comply.

I open my mouth for my reward. Ezra rests the tip of his cock on my bottom lip, and then spurts scalding, bitter liquid between my parted lips onto my tongue. He snuffs out his cries as he holds my eyes and releases into my eager mouth. I swallow all that Ezra releases, feeling a snap of connection blaze between us, knowing Ezra is going to destroy me. If not today, someday.

"There. Now *that* should satisfy you. My seed is finally in your body again. It's just what Dr. Zeitler ordered," Ezra says with a satisfied smirk. He rubs my tummy and makes an *Mmm... Mmm...* sound at the back of his throat. Then he leans down, capturing my lips in a slow, sultry kiss.

# Chapter Twenty-Seven

I showered and dressed before I dared to go see what the emergency was. My embarrassment required nothing less. I blush just thinking about entering the living room when it's full of people who just heard me scream Ezra's name in climax. I think we need the workmen to come back and soundproof our bedroom.

Upon entering a nearly vacant living room, I find Ezra in his favorite chair and Cortez pacing the space. "Where is everyone?" I curl up on the sofa, clutching a pillow to my chest as if it's my favorite teddy bear.

Cort drops onto the sofa next to me. "We sent Ava with Kayla, with Aaron watching over them." He leans forward, resting his elbows on his knees, and I don't like the serious expression marring his face.

"Why'd you send Ava away?" I look to both of them, noting Ezra's confusion as well. I guess Cort is the only one in the know.

"Kayla and Ava don't know anything, but Aaron does. So now they're watching chick flicks because Aaron told them that's what he wanted to do today."

Ezra chuckles softly. "Aaron hates those movies. What the fuck, Cort?"

Cort shifts on the sofa, getting into my direct line of sight. "Kat, we have to tell Ezra. Tell him from the beginning– everything," Cortez demands. "Then I will tell you what I just found out."

"We promised to not say anything," I whine, more frightened than ever. "Why now?"

"It's too late, Kat. It's too damned late!" Cort whisper-screams from between clenched teeth, while raking his hair with his fingertips. "I had Marcus look someone up for us, and they aren't where they're supposed to be."

I freeze when it sinks in. Ray– Ray Hunter. The monster isn't where he should be. He's not in prison anymore. He's free to terrorize anyone, especially me. It's only a matter of time before the sick bastard learns he's a grandfather. I start shaking so violently my teeth chatter, and the urge to piss myself is almost overpowering.

"What the fuck is going on? What's wrong, Katya?" Ezra's eyes dart between Cortez and me, looking more petrified than I feel.

"I got these notes," I begin, voice wavering and unsure. I pull the threat letters from my pocket. I carry them with me at all times, fearing they would fall into the wrong hands– Ezra and Ava's.

Reaching forward, I place the notes in Ezra's palm, and his fingertips curl around mine, not letting me go. "I'm sorry," I whisper, squeezing his hand before releasing it.

With a false sense of calm, I lean back against the sofa cushion. Cortez begins to nibble on his thumbnail as we watch and wait for Ezra to read the threatening notes. The muscles in his pale face tighten, and then turn red as fear and fury mix in his blood. His lips are drawn into a taut line, holding back whatever violence is threatening to spew.

"Yesterday, while you guys were shopping and getting ready for the party, I went to the park to wait you out." I swallow audibly. "Don't worry about why I was there. Marcus set me straight on that." I take a deep breath, and then release it in the form of bitter truths. "I was sitting on a bench all by myself, huddled beneath my hoodie. I was people-watching, and then I heard a laugh. A cackle we all know too well. I ran home, and I was followed every step of the way. For months, every time I leave the building alone, I'm followed. I can feel it right here," I rub the back of my neck, right over my chrysalis tattoo.

Threat letters slipping from his fingertips to fall to the floor, Ezra scrunches up his features. He's confused, frustrated, and frightened, both for me and because of me. "Why didn't you come to me, Katya?" Ezra's voice is laced with disappointment, as if he fears I don't trust him. Then he turns to the man sitting next to me, and the look of pain that warps his face springs tears to my eyes. Ezra breathes, "Cortez, why?" and it's filled with a deep vein of betrayal.

Taking ownership for our decision, "Ezra, I didn't want you to know until we were sure. I didn't want to worry you if it was just some sick prank by an ex-lover. You have so many people you have to worry about, your family and their political connections. You also have Edge and Restraint, especially with how the patrons have been behaving as of late. We were going to come to you when we knew for sure."

Mind backtracking to what I'd asked initially, Ezra repeats my question to Cortez. "Sure about what?" Ezra looks at us with suspicion, eyes flicking back and forth. "You're in mortal danger, Katya. Yet Cortez and you think it best not to rally together but to keep us apart by withholding the facts. Does this sound mature? We have a daughter at risk. You are not invincible, but you are irreplaceable."

Ezra doesn't like being left in the dark. His usual stance is in the bright light while all of us minions hang out in pitch-black darkness. His manipulation holds no bounds as he smashes us in the face with guilt.

"I've stayed in our building at all times, and Cortez always took me to Restraint to train with Dexter. Everywhere else I go, I have Roarke glued to my ass."

"I could have put preventative measures into place, such as monitoring who touched our mail to pinpoint who was delivering the threat letters. As for your always being safe, yesterday you ran off to the park for hours on end, with none of us knowing where the fuck you were," Ezra snarls, fingers curling to create fists. "That cackle you heard meant you were in mortal danger. You could have been dragged off into the woods for a repeat, Katya. A repeat you'd suffer through and perhaps not survive to tell the tale this time. Our daughter needs her mother."

Being cut down to size over my stupidity, I mutter, "I'm sorry," into my hands.

"You ought to be," Ezra utters coldly. "That was by far the dumbest fucking thing I've ever heard, and I hear a lot of bullshit from my patients. It was pathological on your part." Turning to Cortez, "I would have blamed you if anything had happened to Katya, and I would have never forgiven you. Our survival comes above all else, and anyone impeding that is dead to me."

Voice devoid of emotion, "Ray Hunter– the Monster," I blurt out to stop the fight about to erupt between Cortez and Ezra, scared half to death they will say things they can never take back– things they mean but shouldn't. "It was your birth father. There is no forgetting him, not when I see him reflected in our child."

In utter disbelief, Ezra utters my previous words, "Are you sure?"

Cortez stands up from the sofa, finding it impossible to sit still. "Yes. I asked Marcus to look into it last night. That's why he kept calling this morning." Cortez is pacing between me and the coffee table, imitating a caged tiger.

"I find this impossible." Ezra tries to cover his petrification with arrogance, but I know he's on the edge. This involves his entire family, and a few of their friends as well.

"It's possible." Cortez drops back down next to me. "Somehow we all managed to miss the last parole hearing. All of us: Katya, Aaron, you, and me. Your mother and Marcus would have been notified because we were minors when we were abducted. Aaron's parents."

My head jacks in Cortez's direction. "How the fuck? Last time, not only did I receive a phone call from the prosecutor, I had a certified letter. Even with moving, my parents would have still gotten a copy. It's our right as his victims to have a voice."

"Marcus is looking into the specifics. Either someone was championing for Ray, which we both thought was ludicrous, or that many notices went without answer. Which means, someone who had access to all of us, must have intercepted the notices. Now Raymond Hunter is a free man, walking the streets with his victims, and probably shopping for some more, knowing how he operates."

We sit in horrified silence as we digest the information. Not only is the monster straight from our living nightmares out to terrorize more victims, but he has an accomplice– someone close enough to the family to circumvent that many letters.

"What do we do?" My logical nature kicks in. It's too late to stop it, so how do we keep ourselves safe? Breaking down or throwing a tantrum won't help anything. Unwittingly, I did that yesterday, and I've since learned my lesson out of a need for self-preservation.

"Marc's already pushing through restraining orders for the entire family. For the foreseeable future, we go nowhere alone, not even if we're upset." Cortez turns to me to pierce me with a furious stare, apparently pissed that Ezra blamed him for my too stupid to live actions. "Do you understand, Kat? No running. No hiding. Be reasonable. Responsible. A goddamned adult, who just so happens to be the mother of my dying bloodline. You and Ava are as irreplaceable as Ezra and I am. Ava might have that bastard's laugh, but she also has my mother's smile."

I want to bristle under Cort's observations, but he's right. I run when I'm uncomfortable. It's a fact of life I'm willing to change. Instead of apologizing, I draw his attention to the promise we made yesterday. "Remember what we discussed last night while I was getting dressed?" Voice ringing with conviction, "If I get the chance, I'm following through with it, Cortez."

"Just don't do anything stupid, and I will agree with you. I'll help you, even under the circumstances of who I really am." Cortez reaches out to squeeze my hand, accepting my silent apology while agreeing to off his own uncle. "We can live in a constant state of fear, or we can truly live. Your way is the only way to live our lives in peace, never having to look over our shoulders or wait for parole hearings. It wasn't a life sentence. Even if we manage to re-cage him, it will be a waiting game for life."

"What are you guys talking about?" Ezra looks from Cort to me, and then back and forth several times. His mouth is twisted into an amused smirk, as if he's entertained by the fact that his lovers are blood-thirsty because we love him that fucking much, or he's simply happy that Cortez and I are working as a team, with no jealousy to behold.

"Sorry, you're not a member of the club," I shut Ezra down, adorable smirk or not. "You're our leader. Sometimes your lowly minions band together and plot against you."

"Well," Ezra leans forward in his chair, tapping his fingers impatiently on his knee. "No matter what, everywhere we go, we always go in groups. I will check on some added security since Aaron can't protect us if he's protecting himself and Kayla. Roarke will have to stick with me. Cort? What about your usual shadow? Do I ask *her* for you, or will you go straight to the source?"

"I'll take care of it," Cortez grumbles. "What you're thinking isn't happening, so don't even think of retaliating. I've already asked each and every single one of them, and you don't want to know who they suggested was the culprit. They immediately offered Katya and me protection, saying– and I quote – '*Ezra and his spawn are his family's responsibility.*'"

"Lovely how they band together, isn't it? Especially when *she* is having a fit over me at the moment." Ezra's laugh is low and dark, and Cort's twisted one joins in.

"What the fuck are you talking about?" I demand, hating being left out of the loop.

"Doesn't matter," Ezra and Cort say in unison, and then Ezra says to distract me, "We have to be careful who we trust since someone is helping that motherfucker." His voice transforms into a scary growl. "It better not be who I think it is."

"It better not be who they suggested, or why they suggested it," Cort stresses while eye-balling Ezra. "I might kill that person, should it be the truth."

"I'm always the villain of the tale," Ezra mumbles, but he looks more amused than anything. "It's a compliment, actually. I'll be sure to send the whore a thank you card."

"I don't have a goddamned idea what the fuck your cryptic bullshit means. So in plain English, who the hell is Ray's accomplice?"

"Someone who knows too much," Cort offers lamely. "That doesn't actually narrow the field at all. Hard to believe, but other than a rabid fan or a pissed off one-night-stand, I'm pretty well-liked. Now, Ezra, on the other hand. He has a very large following of people who loathe him."

Ezra just shrugs, like Cort's admission was a shining accolade. "They don't have to like me. I will accept fear and respect in its stead."

"Are you off your meds?" Cort's voice warbles with fear.

"No," Ezra drawls out, annoyed, and then issues a slow blink, which pretty much is an admission of guilt– Ezra is off his meds, or else he wouldn't have turned into Master Ez on me a few hours ago.

Cortez and I share a horror-filled look.

"Katya, you have your last lesson with Dexter tonight. I'll go with you and Cort will stay here with Ava." Ezra stands, staring down at Cortez and me. "Now that this conversation is over, Ava can come back home. Kayla and Aaron are moving their belongings over here. They will be staying in Aaron's old room until this situation is cleared up."

"Ezra?" Cortez calls out. "Why does this sound like every one of your dreams just came true? All of us under the same roof, completely under your power? Shadow Haven isn't the next step of our imprisonment, is it? So we are with Marc, Diane, Pearl, Divina, and Roarke?"

"The man who raped my mother, begetting me in the process, is out of prison. The man who tortured me, the man who forced you to rape and harm Aaron, the man who raped Katya, is a free man, walking Dominion's sidewalks beside us. Are you truly asking if I had a hand in this? Because if you are, why don't you just tear my goddamned, beating heart from my chest?"

"God, Ezra. I'm so sorry," Cortez grovels, tears dotting his cheeks.

"I have a few business-related items to deal with." Ezra releases his patented sigh. "Cort, go get the rest of our family, so we will all be together, finding comfort in the fact that we are alright."

Cortez reaches over to squeeze Ezra's hand, and then he turns and does the same to mine. He hurries across the hallway to collect the others because Ezra won't relax until he can find them at a moment's glance.

My biggest fear is realized; Ezra is putting us on house arrest, with even my imaginary freedoms taken away. "Will I get to leave this building before Ray is located? No, I don't think so," I mutter to myself.

Sounding distracted, Ezra draws my attention. "I have to call Marcus, needing more than hearsay. I'd tell you to relax, but clearly that isn't going to happen. Could I trouble you by asking you to make us all some lunch?"

"Sure thing." I'd do anything Ezra ever asked to take the lost look from his face. "Ezra," I say as I draw him into a hug. "It's not your fault," I try to reassure him, knowing it won't help.

This is why I didn't show Ezra the notes in the first place, knowing he would blame himself. He always blames himself. He is the most passive-aggressive person I know. When he's Master Ez, he is dominating and self-possessed. When he's Ezra, he's a martyr. He holds the weight of our world on his shoulders. I wasn't far off when I said how Ezra's lowly minions get together and plot against him– we're not plotting; we're protecting him. Sometimes we even protect Ezra from himself.

"Yes, it is," Ezra cries into my shoulder, gripping me tightly. "Ray's my father, even if I don't want to admit it." I squeeze him so tightly that my fingers turn white from the strain, and then I kiss him even harder.

"No!" I yank Ezra away to arm's length, shaking him a bit. "Your way of thinking would mean that your mother is responsible for what happened to you. If we play the blame game, then Diane is responsible for the guys, me, and ultimately Ava's birth. No one is to blame but that psychopathic monster, Ray Hunter, and his cowardly minion." I speak vehemently, trying to convey to Ezra the truth my words hold.

Pale face eclipsed by agony, guilt, and suffering, Ezra bares himself raw. "You're right. I know deep down that you're right. But sometimes the pressure is almost suffocating."

"Well, Dr. Zeitler. It's a good thing you know the mechanics of psychology, and that you surround yourself with people who've been there, done that, and have stock in the t-shirt company." I feel his lips quirk up into a grin against my cheek.

"You're right, as always, Katya. How lucky for me that fate placed you in my path. I just hope the feeling is mutual, as meeting me is probably your worst nightmare."

"We are all lucky to have each other. I will always be there for you, Ezra– you can come to me for anything…anytime… always." Ezra snorts at the phrase that Kimber, the virtual victim, had said to me when she outed herself as Master Ez.

"Oh, God. Katya, I lo–" Ezra is cut off by a hyper eleven-year-old tearing into the living room.

"I'm hungry. I didn't have any breakfast. You guys are neglecting me." Ava's demands warp into a pitiful pout.

I turn to my adult-sized child, and I'm thankful for her, even when she interrupts utterances of undying devotion. "Hey, you're old enough to pour a bowl of cereal or grab a Pop Tart," I point out. "Hell, you're old enough to make us breakfast in bed."

I try to hide my annoyance. I wanted– no, I needed to know what Ezra was going to say to me. I stare up into Ezra's stormy eyes, and he smiles down at me, somehow knowing the direction of my wayward thoughts.

A smiling Ezra mouths, *"Later,"* to me.

"All right, baby girl. It's just you and me. We have a meal to prepare for the gang. Kitchen," I point to the kitchen and laugh as Ava sticks her tongue out at me and drags her feet.

"I'll see you in a bit." I kiss Ezra tenderly on the lips, sipping him down.

---

We sit down to a delicious meal of enchiladas that Ava, Cortez, and I prepared, while Ezra made a dozen phone calls, showing off his prowess as The Boss, and the happy couple dragged over a few bags from their apartment.

The conversation was light and airy as we tried not to scare Kayla and Ava with the monster hidden under the bed. Not only was I nervous from Ray Hunter's reappearance, along with the knowledge that he has a helper with close access to us, Ezra informed me he wanted to have '*the talk*' just before my final exam with Dexter.

Today started off fantastic. I wish I was still lying on my stomach between the Ezes, blissed out from the haze of the in-between state of awake and dreamland.

Has today been a stressful day? Holy fuck it sure has. I just hope it doesn't get any worse.

# Chapter Twenty-Eight

"You wanted to talk– so talk," I issue grumpily. We're in our private room at Restraint, with the door barred from any interruptions.

I didn't want to have '*the talk*' before my final lesson with Dexter. I didn't think emotional distress was a good predecessor to learning about the effects of physical pain on a submissive. But Ezra was determined to hash this out once and for all.

It should make me happy to no longer be in the dark, except I'm worried that I will hear more emotionally damaging information than I can handle. There is just too much shit going on to worry about our love life. I think our *life* life is more important.

After my repeated bitching, Ezra said that the stress would make us not think clearly when it came to Ray. We needed to be a solid group to take on our victimizer and to protect ourselves. Clearly, what we needed to discuss was creating a divide between us, while stressing Cortez out.

Ezra's manipulations always win me over to his side of the argument. I'm sitting on the sofa, gazing longingly at the *Spanks for the Memories* side of our personal dungeon. I would much rather be tied down and lashed– tortured –than have this agonizing conversation.

"I don't know where to begin." Ezra is hunched over, with his elbows resting on his knees, and his head hanging in his hands. He looks defeated as he sits in the chair across from me.

It's strange that I'm the one who is on the defensive, while Ezra seems meek, considering he's the master of this domain. Interesting yet petrifying. Ezra turning bottom in the sack is hot, but not so much in life. This family needs its leader back.

"You want to tell me about Adelaide, right? That's the biggest issue we have besides Ray. So, why don't you just start at the beginning?" My words are calm, when inside I am a roiling stew of tumultuous emotions.

"That makes sense." Ezra nods his head as he speaks, voice pitching to sound hopeful. "I don't want to talk about Adelaide at all, so I'll talk about the beginning and lead up to Ade."

I hate the informal use of Adelaide Whittenhower's name from Ezra's lips. He should call her Ms. Whittenhower. If this is what it feels like to be Cortez, how jealous he gets, I pity him. It's horrific to feel so unhinged about another human being. The possessive urge to annihilate anyone who touches your person. I hope to God Cortez doesn't feel that way about me.

"When we came back home, I was a mess. It took a few years to feel normal again, to feel even within my own mind." Ezra sighs, gaining confidence by straightening his back instead of slouching. "Cortez and Divina were getting married and seemed happy about it. I know it's not a traditional marriage. But at the time, they were trying for normalcy. I was jealous. The reluctant love of my life was happily married to my cousin, and I was left to pick up all the shit my father had splattered. I'd known Adelaide my entire life, and our families wanted us to combine. I was feeling pressured from all sides. So I decided to try to have what Cort and Divina were living. I tried to force it."

"So, Adelaide wasn't *Mrs. Right*; she was *Mrs. Right Now*? Or is *Mrs. Right for the Family* more accurate?" I try to dampen the snide edge in my tone, hating how I will never be good enough in the eyes of Ezra's family because I don't have a pedigree. They made me feel welcome, but I know deep down they are thinking it. Because why wouldn't they be? "I thought Divina and Cortez weren't like that, a real couple?"

"I like that, *Mrs. Right for the Family*," Ezra muses. "That's very apt, Katya. And no, from the outside looking in, Cortez and Divina were very normal. Happily married. In less than a year, Cortez was back with me. He couldn't meet Divina's needs and she couldn't meet his. They've been happy for the last six years living separately."

"I'm relieved to learn Cortez didn't lie to me," I say beneath my breath, coming to realize I truly trust Cort.

"It was during their first year of marriage that I tried for it as well. Adelaide is the daughter of my mother's closest confidant– Daniel Whittenhower. My mother and Ade's mother, Priscilla, head several charities, including James Atwater's Transcend. So I've known Ade since I was a small child. Our inner-circles are so very small, that they intersect to incestuous levels. There were no secrets between us. She knew of my history and my sexual orientation. We dated for six months, and like a good son, I asked Adelaide to marry me. I could never go through with the marriage, and Ade has always known that."

"Why weren't you happy with Adelaide?" I scrunch up my face in confusion.

It's been six years? If Ezra wasn't happy, why prolong it? If the woman knew everything there was to know about Ezra, why would she try so hard to keep him? I have barely breached the surface, and I'm scared shitless of what else I will find. Cortez is a prerequisite. If he didn't love me, he'd probably kill me. There was no way Adelaide could conquer Ezra, not with Cortez loathing her.

"Well, Cortez came back to me." Ezra blushes at the memory. No doubt Cort manipulated Ezra in that instance. Jealousy and possession had him admitting defeat and begging his way back into Ezra's affections. If I hadn't seen it firsthand, I wouldn't believe it possible. Cortez's talent is silent, to the point you never realize you were manipulated in the first place.

"It's hard to explain my relationship with Cortez to people without outing us. Ade knew, but she was in denial the whole time. Our mutual friends kept telling her I was gay, and she would never believe it. The girl chased me through school. I don't use chased lightly, either. Which was impossible since she was grades ahead of me, graduating high school when I was entering it, even though she was only two years older than me. She managed to chase me while across the country at art school. I was her prey– a goal she would meet."

"Your kink must be smart bitches," I grumble, remembering how Regina Regal, our resident Queen, was dubbed the genius. I hope to God Ezra placed me in the smart category, too stupid to live actions aside. "Advanced placement bitches."

"Sometimes too smart leads to a lack of common sense and a drive to do anything necessary to meet your goal. Blind because the truth went against her lifelong goal, Adelaide never believed Cortez and I were together. How do you tell your fiancée that you have a male partner, and he is the love of your life? '*Oh, and by the way, wife, I don't want you, can you deal with that? I also use BDSM as a healing tool, and I get off on controlling people in all aspects of life.*' No, Adelaide and I weren't compatible, no matter how hard I tried. She's too much like me."

"A constant power struggle, with no one willing to back down, even if it means destroying you both?" I speak Ezra's and my truth. Only along the way, Cortez has taught us how to choose our battles and to give in, even if it bends our pride.

"By that time, it was too late. Our social circles run differently than mainstream America. An engagement is like a business merger mixed with celebrity gossip. If I broke it off with Adelaide for no true reason, it would ruin all of her future prospects. I wouldn't be vilified; she would be ruined."

"So, for six years, you couldn't come up with a good enough reason to bow out? I'm sorry, Ezra. But that is a pretty lame excuse."

"We have not been engaged for over three years," Ezra states unequivocally, with his eyes boring into mine.

Floored, I squawk, "What?"

Ezra's words are spoken from the heart and directed at me like a weapon. "I was lost. I didn't think I would ever find you. The records were sealed and I couldn't get Marcus to tell me the truth. Hopeless."

I reach out to hold Ezra's hand, hating how broken he looks as he speaks. His fingers weave with mine and tighten.

Voice gruff, Ezra tugs my heart strings. "I made a promise to find you, remember?"

Not breaking our connection, I repeat Ezra's words from twelve years ago back to him. "I'm sorry for what I'm about to do. If you survive, I promise I will find you. We will be together again." By the time I'm finished, my voice is thick with emotion. I brush away a stray tear slipping down my cheek. "You kept your promise."

"That was changing me back then. I was failing you, having no idea where to begin my search. I was going to marry Adelaide and live a double life, by pretending with her but secretly being with Cortez. It felt empty– meaningless. Neither part of my life was whole, even combined. When it was just Cort and me, something was missing. As it still is to this day, because he won't give himself to me as I give myself to him."

"I'm so sorry." I reach forward, taking both of Ezra's hands in mine, lending him comfort and strength. "I promise I won't do that to you anymore, especially since I can see how awful it makes you feel."

Ezra squeezes my hands back in thanks, but continues to pour out his heart. "Then one day at a parole hearing, our lives changed. I found you," he says brightly, hope shining in his eyes. "I came home and immediately broke things off with Adelaide. I gave her the length of time it took me to convince you to marry me to publicly break off our engagement, or else I threatened to do if for her. We actually signed a contract on that, stating that Ade had until I proposed to you to publicly announce that our engagement was broken. Until that moment, I still had to attend public and private functions for appearance sake."

"Getting a bit ahead of yourself, aren't you? I didn't even know your name three years ago. Yet you just expected me to marry you? You didn't even know me. At. All."

"I knew it would be work, and we'd have to soldier through it," Ezra says with great confidence. "Did you somehow forget that I'd been working you for all three of those years? After I had your name, I told the prosecutor to request that you have counseling and suggest an online victims' support group. I'd used Dr. Jeannine for information on what you remembered about the attack, and Kimber for insight into your personality."

"You are diabolical, and you sound so full of pride over invading my privacy." There is still a twinge of pain associated with the truth. But I've come to understand how Ezra operates, and why he did it.

"I won't lie– it didn't take me long to change from wanting to fix what I had broken and fulfilling a commitment, to falling in love with the person I'd found. I called you a few times, pretending to be different people, just so that I could hear your voice. I chatted with you online as different people. No one who you were close to, just impersonal chatting. I viciously stalked you for three years straight." Ezra laughs without humor, as if realizing for the first time just how insane all that sounded.

"I was obsessed. If there was information to be had, I had to have it. You did throw me a few curve balls, and it only increased my intrigue. I'd have to say, Ava was the hugest surprise. I thought she was your baby sister. I left her alone out of respect, and you were oh-so careful never to mention her to anyone. I found your online resume, and mysteriously a job appeared                        for                        you."

Ezra stops talking when I growl at him and glare. My fists latch onto a throw pillow, fingertips digging in. It's either maim the pillow, or bitch-slap Ezra. He laughs at me, and it only makes matters worse.

"Hey, it was an excellent résumé." Ezra's voice holds a mocking edge, and I have no idea which of us is the brunt of his joke. "I gave you the job that was perfectly tailored to suit you."

"My job was made up out of thin air, wasn't it?" I demand.

"No comment," Ezra says slyly while wearing a gigantic grin. "Anyway, I told Adelaide that she needed to make an out for herself, or I was going to help her do it. I have you back, and I intend to keep you."

"You are aware that you're still engaged, right? In the public eye, in private, every-fucking-where? I mean, until a few moments ago, I thought you were, too." My voice rises with my anger. "I've been beating myself up for being your goddamned mistress, for breaking my moral code by touching another woman's man. You made me feel like a whore!"

Ezra raises his hands, as if warding off my fury. "I wrongfully assumed that you knew that Adelaide and I were no more. Surely, your stunt in my office would have ended our engagement," Ezra says with great amusement. "Cort kept telling me that you thought otherwise, and I didn't believe him."

"Everywhere I looked, Adelaide's and your engagement hit me in the face. The papers. The internet. Gossip. Our mutual associates. Yesterday's goddamned birthday party invitation. When I'd ask you about her, you'd never explained, only saying it didn't matter. How the fuck was I to know, Ezra? I'm not a mind-reader!"

"I thought my actions and my words were about as concise as possible. I've been building a life with you, Katya. Why the fuck would I do that if I planned on marrying Adelaide Whittenhower?"

Voice stiff with the need to control my emotions, I grit the words out. "I don't know, but I was too terrified to ask. I don't think I could have survived it if you had confirmed that I was your mistress during that conversation. So I avoided the topic at all costs."

"Mistress?" Ezra's voice pitches, as if I'm somehow insulting him. "You thought I made you my mistress? You thought I made the woman I'd agonized over harming, spent nine years searching for and another three years stalking, and then created a home for her, that I was that big of a bastard to make her my mistress? The mother of my daughter? How poorly you must think of me."

I ignore Ezra's logic, as well as his manipulative guilt slathering, remembering four months ago when he was inside Adelaide Whittenhower, professing his undying love to the fiancée he swears she isn't.

"I spoke with Adelaide at my birthday party. I gave her a week to break off our engagement publically, or I will." Ezra sounds confident, and I hear Marcus calling him hardheaded. This is definitely one of those occasions.

"Ezra," I lean forward, placing my hand on his knee, speaking to him how you speak to someone of lesser intelligence. "You do realize that Adelaide tells me at every turn that you two are still a couple? She enjoys smearing my inadequacies in my face, and she uses the knowledge to hit me where it counts."

Ezra just looks at me in disbelief. I don't back down. I stare right back into his stormy eyes. "Seriously?" He still looks like he doesn't believe it.

"Why would I lie about this, Ezra? Why would I allow it to infect, not only how I feel about you, but how I feel about myself?" I hate how my voice breaks in pain. "Honest. Adelaide called me your whore at least three times last night. Once even saying that you share me because you think I'm a whore, too. Deep down, I agreed with her because I felt like a whore for sleeping with an engaged man. I also put up with Adelaide's bullying because I felt as if I deserved it."

"I don't understand." Ezra's eyes are clouded with confusion. "We broke our engagement three years ago when we signed the contract. If you need to see it, I'll call Roarke to grab it from my office."

"That won't be necessary." I don't doubt there is a document. But it doesn't negate what Cortez and I saw in person. That is irrefutable proof that Ezra is lying. Maybe not to me as much as to himself.

"I will take care of everything. I promise. I also want to apologize for any misunderstandings. It is my fault. I would apologize for Ade's conduct, but she isn't my responsibility. But know I hold her accountable, and will never allow her to speak to you like that again."

"Okay, just give me a few minutes to digest all of this, because I need to put something into words."

Heart breaking from Ezra's lies, I sit in silence, staring at the wall o' torture. I can feel Ezra's gaze on my face, but I ignore him. I have to tell him that no matter what he just said, it doesn't take away from the fact that I saw and heard him profess his unfaltering love for Adelaide. How can I trust what Ezra says when I saw differently with my very own eyes?

I begin again. "Just so we are very clear; you do know that you're a fucked up bastard, right?"

"Clearly," Ezra says, extremely amused.

"Good, I'm glad that's settled. Do you love her?" My voice is softer than I would have liked.

"No, I don't love Ade," Ezra sputters, like the idea is preposterous. "I don't know if I really care for her, either. Ade's personality completely clashes with mine. I'm indifferent. I wish her no ill will– I just don't care."

Feeling as if the life has drained out of me, "I saw," finally rumbles past my lips.

"Saw what?" Ezra's eyes pinch in the middle with confusion.

"Cortez and I saw." I have to swallow twice to force down the suffocating lump lodged in my throat. My eyes prickle with unshed tears. My hands shake as I become overwrought with dark emotions. I don't want to say this. I take a deep breath in, and hold it. "The night of your punishment," I exhale the words. "Cortez and I saw. We didn't mean to. It was an accident. But we saw you making love to Adelaide."

For a moment, Ezra looks confused. Then like the sun rising in the east– comprehension dawns on Ezra. "Shit," he hisses underneath his breath, like the bastard was caught red-handed.

"It's all right, Ezra. I understand." The words kill me, but I manage to put a voice to my greatest fears. "I knew from the very beginning that I've been a prize in your game. Since the moment the hunt began in the woods, you've been chasing me through life. I bring excitement by being unpredictable. I'm the ultimate prey in your predatory hunt. After everything these past few months, I know that even now, we are still playing a game. I know it was truth up until you spoke of Adelaide. I understand, Ezra. I really do. I just don't want to play a game anymore. I don't want to be your joke. I just want the truth or nothing at all."

I wring my hands in my lap and look at the floor. I don't wipe the tears away that streak down my cheeks, hoping not to draw attention to them. The agony of heartbreak is all-consuming. I'd been avoiding this conversation, knowing if I had any self-respect, it would be the end of the charade we've been living. It was a beautiful fantasy, but a harsh reality.

"I knew that one day the game would be over, and that day is today. I also know that no matter what, when Cortez is finally able to give you his all, you will forget about me. You won't need me to fulfill your needs anymore, because Cortez will make you feel complete, just as you've always longed to feel. Once that day comes, Cortez will either force you to choose, or he will push me out."

Crying so forcefully, the tears are slipping into my mouth. I swallow to clear them away while rubbing at my eyes with my sleeves. I suffocate the building sob, needing to speak my piece because I'm unable to live this lie anymore.

"I want you to know that I won't take your daughter from your life. I can't do that to Ava, or to you and Cortez. It will be difficult for me, since you now hold all the keys to my happiness– my job, my home, my friends, even my daughter... Cortez," my voice hitches on a sob.

Ezra drops to his knees in front of me, not cushioning the blow. I flinch at the loud cracking sound. He dips his head into my line of sight. "Where is this coming from?" His voice is hollow. "Why do you think me capable of all that? I thought you knew me. What you just said makes me worse than the monster himself." Ezra's voice trembles as he speaks.

"I wish– I wish I could say that I believe you, Ezra," I breathe. "Actions speak louder than words. In the case of Adelaide Whittenhower, actions and words." I stare down into

Ezra's eyes, and I pour my soul out through my words. "I saw you, Ezra. I *really* saw you, and I can't un-see or un-hear it. I wish I could. I wish I could be ignorant again. It hurts like hell. I've held this pain in for months. I want– no, I need for you to stop playing, especially with Ray back on the hunt."

"I understand your apprehension. I don't share you freely. I gave you the freedom of choice when it came to Aaron, and the choice was yours. Yes, I want you to be with Cortez, because it's for all three of us. But seeing me fuck someone else shouldn't ruin all the faith you have in me. I'm not saying it makes us even, because it's not a contest or a challenge. You and I weren't exactly together at the time, and while I can understand why it would hurt you, I don't understand why you are holding a grudge and allowing it to warp how you see me."

"If it was just the sex, I could handle it. I have no issue with you and Cort– I have hope for you both coming to terms with the past and reuniting as of old. With Adelaide, back then, I know we weren't together. If it happened now, I'd stab the cunt," I promise without mercy. "But what I saw between you and Adelaide wasn't just sex– it was making love. It was a bond. It was a connection. You truly love Adelaide, and I can't compete with that." I whisper, because to speak any louder, I fear my voice would break.

"I– What?" Ezra looks beyond confused. He shakes his head over and over, repeatedly uttering no. He looks so genuinely lost that I almost believe him. Almost. Because I know what I saw and heard.

"Cort was there, too. He saw and heard everything," I say to validate my point.

"I was crazed that night. I had to be with someone, especially after the punishment. You were touching me, and I wanted to be with you so badly. I was losing control. I worried that I would take you against your will, right on my bed. I had Cortez whisk you away so I wouldn't."

Ezra leans into me, trying to touch me without actually touching me. He stares up into my eyes, beseeching me to believe him– to believe *in* him. If I had faith in him, I'd forgive him and forget what I saw and heard.

"I don't blame you for this, and I'm not saying I was with Ade because of you. It was my choice– my decision. But I knew if I were to make love to you, you would remember your rape before you were ready. It would have been even worse if I forced myself upon you a second time, and that is not how I wanted our first true joining to be. You lying beneath me, experiencing your rape while I was trying to make love to you. I saw it play out in my mind, saw how it would taint our future, and it physically sickened me. It was like in the living room, a few months back, when I was torn between raping you and killing Dexter. Your mental health and wellness was my priority, so I chose the lesser of two evils. It just happened to be Adelaide because I had to be with someone I'd been with before, and the two others were definitely not an option. I don't even remember much from the event. I was dazed. In a frenzy inside my own mind."

"You were soft with Adelaide," I admit, remembering it as if it were happening directly before me. "You did appear to be in a daze. You kept repeating how much you loved her, that you were finally complete, and how much it meant to finally be inside her. If you don't believe me, you can ask Cort." I look away and wipe my eyes. Saying that was the hardest words I've ever uttered.

"This is what you made Cortez promise to not talk to me about, isn't it?" Ezra demands breathlessly. "This is why he's been so cold toward me? Why you've been so distant with me? Why neither of you would make love to me? This is why you left me?"

"Yes," I whisper.

"Goddamnit!" Ezra screams at the top of his lungs, a grief-stricken sound that will ring in my heart forever.

In a fit of fury, Ezra lunges from the sofa to pick up the coffee table. Arching his shoulder, he swings it against the wall. *Bang! Bang! Bang!* Repeatedly hitting the piece of furniture against the masonry until it's shards of wood. I flinch every time the table hits the wall with earth-shattering crashes, with wood flying through the air like shrapnel from an explosion.

The door flings open to bang against the wall, startling me to the point I almost piss myself. Ezra doesn't seem to notice. He picks up a side table and goes to work on it, making more kindling.

"Heel!" Dexter commands in a soft voice that manages to reach every corner of the room. Ezra drops to his knees on the hard floor and submits. I cower into the sofa cushions from the cracking noise of Ezra's bones meeting the tile. "What is the meaning of this?" Dexter demands as he walks over to the fallen man.

Dexter caresses Ezra's hair lightly in comfort. I realize this is the first time I've seen Ezra relinquish his control, or give it to someone else. Hell, it's the first time I've seen him lose control that badly. It seems to be a trend when it comes to me– causing Ezra to lose his shit.

You can see the mentor and student bond at work as Dexter rubs Ezra's back while whispering soothing words.

Ezra looks vulnerable, and I don't like it. He needs to be resilient because he's the head of our family, and we are to support him to keep him strong. I somehow manage to keep weakening him as he keeps weakening me.

I want to comfort Ezra, but I don't want to intrude. But I can't stay here, staring at what I turned Ezra into. A heavy wash of guilt descends, nearly suffocating me. I stand to start for the door, but Dexter's hand stops me from leaving the room.

"Ezra has something he wishes to say to you, and then we will have our final lesson." Dexter turns to Ezra and orders, "Tell Katya, and then meet me in my room."

Releasing my wrist, Dexter walks out, down the hall, and then enters his room, leaving the door open in invitation.

I don't turn around. I face the hallway. I can't look Ezra in the eye because he will see my shame over how I reduced him to violence, and I don't want him to misinterpret it as pity.

The heat of Ezra's body warms my back, melting into me. He makes no move to come into contact with me, just gets close enough that a hard breath would bring our bodies to a close. He leans his head down until his mouth is at my ear. I hear his breath sawing in and out. It tickles the small hairs at the nape of my neck. I smell his smoky, musky scent. I want to lean back and comfort him and myself. A heartbeat before I do, Ezra speaks.

"It was you– it was always you. I pretended Adelaide was you, pretended I was making love to you. Everything I said and did, it was to you." Ezra breathes his confession in my ear, stunning me with his revelation.

Ezra walks from the room before I can respond. I watch as the muscles in his back, thighs, and ass contract as he walks away from me to enter Dexter's private room. I breathe in and out ten times, trying to calm myself for my last lesson– pain. A condition I'm well-acquainted with enduring.

# Chapter Twenty-Nine

Ezra's head is bowed down to Dexter's, until they are almost forehead-to-forehead while deep in conversation. I enter the room as quietly as I can, trying not to disturb them. I can't hear or read a word as they whisper so fast their lips are a blur. But I do manage to make out how Ezra keeps saying, *"Yes, Master. Yes, Master,"* every time Dexter pauses in his speech.

This is the first time ever that I'm not drawn to Dexter. He still exhibits commanding power that I long to obey; I just don't want to jump him. I don't want to jump Ezra, for that matter. Stress is the anti-Viagra. One other thing is on my side; the fact that Dexter is fully clothed for once. A pity.

"Katya, please demonstrate the submissive kneeling position for your master. I believe it would make him feel better, don't you?"

I fall at Ezra's feet the second I comprehended Dexter's words. Before he is finished speaking, I'm already in position: kneeling before Ezra with my ass resting on my heels, knees spread with my palms resting on my thighs, head and eyes cast down in supplication.

"Excellent, my Kitty Kat, and so prompt, too," I can hear amusement and pride in Ezra's voice, and I can't help the smile that broadens my face. Ezra is back, no longer the broken creature annihilating the furniture in our private room.

"Master Ez is here to observe, but I am the ultimate judge on whether or not you pass to become a Mistress in Maître du Jeu."

"Yes, Master Dexter." I state clearly, not sounding submissive in the least from my position on the floor.

"First, I have an oral examination to cover all you've learned. Please answer the questions when asked, Kat." Dexter pats my head, and then walks a few feet away. I stay in position– finding it not-so pleasant –simply staring at the tips of Ezra's shoes. Proof I'm meant to pass tonight's lesson, because I'd never survive being anyone's submissive.

"Our first lesson included what, Kat?" Dexter tries to sound authoritative and fails. I try not to smile at the amusement lacing his voice. He's definitely remembering the show Cort and I put on for him. I blush bright red and cough into my hand.

"The first lesson was about body language. The importance of reading your submissive's body language in order to meet their needs. How anyone can lie with their words, but not with their body's natural responses. You watch their posture, respiration and heart rate, their muscle's reactions, perspiration or lack thereof, arousal or lack thereof. The eyes are most important when determining their emotional climate, and whether or not they have entered subspace, where their ability to consent is negated. The second part was building sensation of the skin by adding the impact of pain to the mix. A little pain will heighten the sensation of pleasure."

"Very good, Katya," Dexter praises, and I can feel Ezra's eyes boring into the top of my head. "Over the course of your training, please list the different needs a master may encounter when dealing with a submissive."

Being respectful and polite, I try to gauge what Dexter wants from me. "I will use examples, if that is all right?"

"Yes, that is fine, Katya. If it makes it easier for you to explain." A chuckle slips past Dexter's lips. I don't know why I'm being so amusing, and I don't dare ask.

"Sometimes Katya is so much like you, it's almost frightening. At other times, she is exactly like Cortez. It's an interesting combination." Dexter says to Ezra, answering my unspoken question. Dexter is such a strong dominant, he most likely read my confusion.

Ezra reaches down and smooths my hair from my face, comforting as much as connecting with me. I lean into his touch, still reeling from that horrific conversation back in our room. I take a moment to center my thoughts, soaking up Ezra's support, before I answer Dexter's question.

"Heidi's an exhibitionist. She loves being the center of attention because it makes her feel special. If she were my submissive, I would ensure the largest crowd possible. She also has a mid-to-moderate pain threshold. You can start her with stronger toys. She enjoys going from one extreme to the other, pain then pleasure. At the end of a scene, she enjoys them both simultaneously. She requires sexual stimulation to find her release."

"Very good, Katya. Go on," Dexter coaxes me with praise.

"Kayla was an interesting case. She didn't like pain but responded to it for me. After we got the *'who is Kayla's master?'* issue settled, she took to Aaron well. Surprisingly, Kayla liked hot wax. She didn't care for a crowd, and she required sexual stimuli to get off. Aaron didn't enjoy voyeurs. He wanted to be restrained to the point of no movement, and then beaten– brutally. I didn't have the stomach for it since I knew where his issues lay. I could have beaten anyone but him, though, if I knew they needed it. Aaron also loved the thought of force. Again, I knew why. He loved being bound, beaten, and then taken by Kayla. Me–"

"You?" Both Dexter and Ezra interrupt my speech.

"Yeah, I needed to know what I did and didn't like." Suddenly feeling bashful, as if I'm exposing myself bare, my eyes seek the solace of the floor.

"Who?" I notice that Master Ez's voice makes a reappearance today; must be Ezra is at risk right now. I roll my eyes up to see him glare at Dexter, who is backing away slowly with his hands out in a stop gesture.

"Master Ez?" I try to gain Ezra's attention through the fog of Master Ez. When he finally looks at me, I notice he's warring within himself. I explain to soothe his worries. "I used Kayla and Aaron, and we did nothing sexual. Hell, not even sensual. I needed to know certain limits to survive you, and they needed to cope with their burgeoning desires. It was a good fit because we trusted each other, and we knew exactly what our limitations were."

"And what did you learn?" Ezra asks, but the threat of Master Ez reappearing is evident in the tone of his voice.

I tread very carefully. "I found out that I don't like a crowd, as I'm not into attention. I enjoy bondage, and visual sensory deprivation, but not speech or hearing deprivation. I need to start off slowly with pain, but can build to stronger levels. I learned Aaron is very strong yet doesn't know how to wield such strength. I obviously love teeth– both biting and being bitten." I have to stop because I'm blushing so hard.

"What about sex?" Ezra asks softly, always intrigued to learn more.

"I don't know. I've never really explored that side of myself," I stammer. "I've only had normal sex with you guys. Before that, I'd only touched women, and they didn't reciprocate. I know force is a big thing for me."

"That you don't like it?" Ezra prompts.

"No... I... um– yeah, that totally gets me off." I want to melt into the floor from embarrassment. "You obviously remember the accidental joining this morning that evolved into actual sex. I didn't mind Cortez's abusive skull-fuck until it left lasting pain. I could have withstood the pain, but I didn't want to feel it later or have marks. Well, with the exception of teeth marks; I want those."

"Good to know," comes from Dexter. "What other types of play do submissives need?" He tries to get the lesson back on track, and Ezra growls because he wanted more of my information instead.

"How about a list from mild to wild?" I chuckle. "We have the foot fetish types, both givers and takers. The role-players: doctor/patient, teacher/student, ponies, dogs, and cats. I don't know, the babysitter? Or plushies and furries? " I bust out laughing as I imagine Ezra and Cort dressed as life-sized Monkmees.

"Then there are the babies– people who want to role-play at being a toddler, by sleeping in cribs, shitting their diapers, and drinking from a bottle. There is every form of pain imaginable, with any object imaginable. The possibilities are endless to express your independence. As I said before: sensory deprivation, voyeurism, wax, teeth, bondage, spanking, and ropes for suspension and restraint. Then there is the truly wicked shit: torture, trampling, urine, shit, and milk. Basically, if someone can think it up, it can become someone's kink."

"Very, very good, Katya," Dexter praises.

"Thank you, Master Dexter."

"Katya, I could quiz you over every single detail. But as I know I taught you well, and you soaked up the information, putting it both in application and practical use, I don't feel the need to beat a dead horse." Dexter shifts on his feet, and begins addressing Ezra. "Thoughts on proceeding to the sadism demonstration, as I believe that is the natural course for continuing Katya's education?"

"I'm curious myself," Ezra mutters.

"I have a demonstration for you on pain, on how a masochist can have needs that aren't sexual, but soul-deep. Whether shame, pain, or guilt, it needs an outlet to vent, as you've witnessed with Aaron. There are those who do not need sexual stimuli to reach a climax. When the pressure in the soul is released, the body does as well. It's cleansing, purifying."

"I've watched you work in the dungeon, but I don't think I've ever truly understood it," Ezra says to Dexter, voice very analytical. "I think it would help me with some of my patients."

"I'll tell ya, it's fascinating and rewarding for the sadist, especially watching the transformation the masochist undergoes. It's similar to the meaning of your tattoo, Kat."

"Wow." My voice sounds dreamy, sluggish, as Dexter's emotions wash over me. "I can't wait."

"After the demonstration, I will tell you about what needs the masochist fulfills for the sadist. Yes, from an outsiders' view, it looks like the masochist is brutalized while the sadist is vilified for being abusive. It is a delicate balance, one where both the sadist and the masochist need one another, and when the balance is met, it's truly extraordinary."

Ezra pulls me from the floor, helping me to my feet. He holds my hand as we cross the room. He then settles me on his lap on the ridiculous, Victorian era settee. Relaxing into each other, Ezra presses his face against the side of my neck and breathes deeply. He rubs the tip of his nose back and forth like a cat scent marking.

I close my eyes and revel in the sensation of connecting with Ezra after our horrific conversation and watching him fall apart. We both needed a moment to level each other emotionally. I pull Ezra's arms around my chest and hug him close to me. I have the strongest urge to weep because so much was said, just as so much was left unsaid. We're not even close to having our issues ironed out.

"You guys can cuddle, or whatever the hell you're doing. But pay close attention, Kat. Because this is important to who you may become." Dexter orders, and I nod my head in agreement.

Dexter opens the door, and a nude, young man walks in the room. I'm surprised that Dexter has a male submissive. He isn't a lover of men from what I've seen. The blond, blue-eyed newcomer is light-skinned, clean-cut, and glowing with good health. He even has a shy smile stretched across his face. His presence is calm-inducing.

"Tobias, apologize to Mistress Kat," Dexter orders. Confused, Ezra and I share a glance of '*what the fuck is this about?*'

The nude man approaches me hesitantly, as if afraid. He then kneels at my feet in a smooth flow of motion, so much more demure than even Heidi can pull off. Tobias gazes up at me coyly, with bright and clear, blue eyes. He is young– very young, early twenties at the oldest. He worries his lip between his teeth in a nervous gesture. His demeanor removes all sexuality from the fact that he is kneeling naked at my feet. He bleeds subservience, and all you want to do is care for him, support him, and help him.

"Please accept my humblest apologies, Mistress. I was not myself. I was an addict and I lost my way. Master has helped me find my path again, giving me a sense of purpose and a place in this world. Master has shown me my worth and led me to strive to reach my potential. I profusely apologize for any and all disrespect I caused you." Tobias's expression is one of reverent adoration every time he mentions Master Dexter.

I look from the boy, and then up to Dexter, and back again, asking for an explanation, and Ezra is doing the exact same eye-dart dance.

"You don't recognize him, do you?" Dexter asks me, and I shake my head no. "Good, that means I'm doing an excellent job of caring for Tobias. A few dominants enjoy total control, where they reshape a human being into who they should have become if the absence of nurture hadn't overpowered nature. The reward is exponential, where they see the fruits of their labor reflecting in the good deeds of their slave. I, myself, am one of these types."

"You think?" The sarcastic words are mine, but they flow from Ezra's lips. "Slave? Truly?"

"Tobias Kline hit rock bottom for me on the night of our acquaintance. Since then, I have demanded that he maintain personal hygiene, educate himself in all forms of life, retain gainful employment, eat a healthy diet and exercise, and stay away from addictive substances. I've also refused him sexual enjoyment."

"Harsh," I direct to Tobias, but he has a serene expression on his face. Evidentially it doesn't bother Tobias that Dexter is speaking of him as if he were a lesser being, or an inanimate object.

"Tonight is a graduation of sorts for Tobias. Katya, if you find him repentant, I will allow him full access to Heidi. She has been most anxiously waiting for our dear Tobias." Dexter's expression is that of a proud parent on graduation day.

"Who is he?" Dexter's face glows with pride when I ask the question he was waiting for.

Gesturing to the boy near my feet, "Katya, meet Tobias Kline, the young man who encroached upon your person. I believe he left a permanent mark of fingernail crescents on your left breast."

"Holy shit!" Tobias jumps a few inches when I shout. "Really? You're the little douchebag from the entrance of Restraint? From my first time here?"

Ezra and I both stare at the boy, both of us remembering how filthy he was, how you could smell the taint of drugs wafting from his pores. His skin was ghastly, and his hair was greasy yet brittle, and his eyes were glazed from drugs and lost from a hard life.

"Wow! Excellent job, Dexter. Are you keeping him?" I ask like Tobias is a stray puppy, not a living, breathing human being. Instantly, I feel badly over my excitement.

"Ah, yes. Tobias is a great joy for me, a comfort. He meets many of my needs as I fulfill his. As I said, it's a delicate balance. Once you find someone who complements you, and you train them properly, it is a lifetime commitment. A commitment not unlike one you would have for your children."

"Is it intimate?" Ezra treads lightly, knowing how men react when asked about homosexual acts, yet there is an odd note to Ezra's voice.

"Intimate as in a deep connection between a sadist and masochist, as well as between a dominant and slave. But not sexual, no. Now, if only Tobias was a female, preferably a Jew, who could have sex with me and make me lots of babies, I'd marry him." Dexter gives a hardy laugh. "I guess we will wait until I find my soulmate. Until then, I will split my needs between Tobias and Heidi."

"Are you saying that you will give Tobias up if you find the right one?" Ezra asks out of curiosity, no doubt wondering the same thing about himself. If Cortez finally gives Ezra his all, does that mean Ezra has to give me up?

"Oh, no. Tobias is mine for life. If I find someone who complements all my needs, I will give Heidi to another master, probably Aaron once he goes through training. I will still control Tobias, though. My wife would have to understand that I hold Tobias's leash. If I drop it, I fear he would revert to his self-destructive ways. There is great comfort in knowing you are being taken care of absolutely and unconditionally. It's a place of quiet and calm, which is what Tobias needs to survive."

"The vast majority of my patients need a keeper," Ezra mutters, still staring down at Tobias like a puzzle he longs to solve. "I hope Tobias's future bride is okay with her '*father-in-law*' controlling their lives."

"Better than my actual father, Sir," Tobias speaks, firm and with confidence.

"Dexter is my family, kid. You couldn't ask for a better champion." Ezra reaches into his pocket to pull out a business card. "If you ever want to talk, contact me– free of charge."

"Do you do family discounts and long-distant house calls to Massachusetts?" Tobias proves he has a good sense of humor while making light of a horrific situation. "How are you with faithless pastors, his wayward children who didn't realize they were siblings, and their incest survivor children because '*Pastor Sleeps with his Congregation*' kept his mouth shut? I'm the youngest sibling of three– the one who didn't marry the other – but not unique in a family of drug dealer/addict prostitute throwaways and sexual deviants."

"God," Ezra's voice wavers as a shudder rolls up his spine. "I want to delve deep inside your psyche."

Fearing for Tobias's well-being, "Katya? Ezra?" Dexter calls to gain our undivided attention. "Let me show you what I meant about how a masochist has to use physical pain as a representation to release their soul-deep guilt and shame. As you heard, Tobias is a font of shame."

Without being commanded, Tobias walks across the room to stand with his chest against a St. Andrew's cross. Working with efficiency, Dexter cuffs Tobias's wrists to the top supports and his ankles to the bottom supports. He tests the cuffs to make sure they are secure yet comfortable enough not to cut off circulation. The smaller man's shoulders, back, ass, and thighs are on display as Dexter's canvas.

Dexter picks up an actual whip– a bullwhip –bouncing the handle in his palm, weighing its balance. I've seen Dexter use the gamut of impact toys, with the exception of the whip. He's never shown me the depths of his sadism.

I don't want to feel frightened, both of the weapon and that in the future I might graduate to using it. I sink into Ezra, needing comfort and support.

"Tobias has no need for a warm up. We can go right to the end product. It won't take long, but it is completely gratifying." As he speaks, the expression on Dexter's face is beatific. He is alight with pleasure before the act even begins.

Of course, Dexter will never let Tobias go. Tobias is a lifetime commitment, but he meets every single one of Dexter's sadistic needs, plus his needs to be a good mentor and leader. After spending months with Dexter, learning from him, laughing with him, flirting with him, I had forgot that the genuinely giving and nice man was a pain-dealer.

A loud crack echoes throughout the room, breaking me from my reverie. I jump at the harsh sound, causing Ezra to grip me tighter. Frantic, I look at Tobias's back for signs of damage, and see none. The whip is cracked again, rolling as a perfect extension of Dexter's wrist. He is testing his aim on a small spot marked on the floor, but I believe he's actually building anticipation in Tobias– surprise attack.

Three more strikes, and one finally hits its target. Tobias writhes in his restraints, neck straining, muscles spasming, but he remains silent during the agonizing onslaught. A long lash mark mars his back in a diagonal line from his left shoulder to right buttock, missing the tender area of the kidneys.

It was a perfect hit. The welt is brilliant red yet not a bleeding, open wound like one would expect from a bullwhip. Dexter must be an expert with his weapon of choice, because just a fraction harder and he would have broken Tobias's skin. The thought settles me. Dexter is taking care of Tobias while feeding his own needs. I'm just not sure I can sit here and watch.

Two more strikes hit within a second of each other, as Dexter's wrist flicks out so quickly I cannot track the arc of the leather. Tobias is utterly silent as he jerks with the lashes. Dexter created a perfect **X** on Tobias's back with a third welt across the young man's ass cheeks.

The look on Dexter's face is one I thought only reserved for phenomenal sex or when gazing upon a divine being. The sadist is completely in control of himself, his masochist, and the scene. He's panting out sharp, short breaths. He's obviously aroused– the hardest I've ever seen him strain against his leathers. Dexter is more aroused now than when he takes Heidi. I don't think it is Tobias who has this effect on his libido; I think it's the pain– inflicting the pain with the purpose of doing good, not evil. No doubt if Dexter could combine sex and sadism with a masochist, he would die a happy man.

With each crack, I flinch and my eyes involuntarily snap shut. I quickly look to Ezra to gauge his reaction. He is impassive. I'm sitting in his lap and he isn't aroused. I'm pleased with that. I could never provide this level of pain for my master. I like pain, but not a beating- not torture.

The cracks come faster as Dexter builds momentum with only the flick of his wrist. So fast that I no longer flinch with the sound. I just shut my eyes and hold my body tight. The only indication of a new hit is Tobias renewed sobs. He starts to wail in a long, unending mournful tone, and then the whip ceases.

I crack my eyes open with relief that it's finally over. Dexter stands back, with his head tilted to the side as he appreciates his work like he's gazing at a masterpiece.

Tobias's back is decorated with a perfect, six-point star. The level of mastery that Dexter wields is beyond measure. It truly is a masterpiece of horrific proportions. Tobias's ass and thighs hold another intricate pattern.

Heart beating erratically, "Jesus," slips past my lips as I gaze on in wonder.

Dexter looks back at me with an expression of peace, as if he found the perfect drug. It's also obvious that he's had a release of his own– a sexual release without touch. It was simply from engaging in his greatest passion. His mind's way of providing an outlet for unfamiliar emotions in the form of sexual release.

Dexter unleashes Tobias from the cross, and then squeezes his shoulders in an affectionate, fatherly gesture. The young man turns to face us with tears drying on his cheeks, but he holds a beatific expression. He, too, looks drugged and at peace. Tobias finally found a drug he can use without the dangerous side-effects. That is if you can trust your master's control, because this drug is just as deadly if in the wrong hands.

"Katya? Ezra? Do you believe that young Tobias deserves a reward?" Even Dexter's speech is slow and soft, sluggish. We don't answer because we're both speechless. We just shake our heads like a pair of bobble headed fools.

"Very well." Dexter opens the door, gesturing for Heidi to join us. "Do your worst, son. Heidi is all yours." Dexter chuckles as he settles next to us on the settee, while Tobias and Heidi engage in a standoff.

"Toby won't last two minutes. I'm willing to take wagers." Dexter raises his eyebrows at us. The IRS agent places bets on the membership constantly, and brags about his office work pools. "What do you think, Ezra? Are you in for a minute-thirty?"

"I'll take that bet," Ezra replies slyly. "What's the wager?"

"I get Kat sometime after her initiation," Dexter negotiates. "Without your supervision. It doesn't have to be sex, just something fun. Might even let her work me over."

"Sounds good. I'll take that," Ezra agrees like I'm not sitting right here– in his lap –and it pisses me off. "Two minutes for you, and a minute and a half for me. If I win, I get to direct your reward with Katya." Ezra flashes us a wicked grin, a little bit evil and a whole helluva lot naughty.

"Deal," Dexter agrees as he reaches to shake Ezra's hand.

Furious, fuming while sitting in Ezra's lap, I watch Tobias's body language. The second Tobias sees Heidi, his young cock is instantly at attention, jutting up to his belly button.

"I want in," I rasp out, deciding they can only disrespect me if I allow it. I am Dexter and Ezra's equal, and it's about damn time I act like it. "I've got thirty seconds on Tobias. I get to choose my own submissive for this initiation bullshit."

I spoke loud enough for Heidi to hear, and she tips her chin at me in understanding. Heidi begins to undress in the most salacious manner, looking for all the world like a pinup girl. Her little dance is pumping up poor Tobias's lust. Heidi will do me proud, and Tobias is also onboard as a silent apology for disrespecting me.

"I want sex privileges for my initiation. Most submissives need sexual stimulation for release, and I don't want to look inept in front of the members of Maître du Jeu because you've stifled my choices." I sound just as sly as Ezra, more so even. I bite my tongue to keep my laugh at bay.

"Who do you have in mind, Katya?" Ezra calls me Katya with Master Ez's tone of voice. He's in protective-mode, fearful I'm trying to be unfaithful.

"Don't worry, Ezra." I squeeze his hand to comfort him. "The submissive will be female, and I've already got my sights set on her." Smiling broadly, I feel like a puppet master. "Think of the scene I will do with her, as more of an interview of sorts. I know someone who is in need of a new master, and I would like Dexter to see her in action. I think they're a perfect fit. If my intuition is correct, and it usually is, it may be the ring and a minivan kind of happily ever after."

"Deal, but you won't win," Ezra says arrogantly. "Tobias has waited too long. He'll want to go slow and make it last."

I just laugh. Tobias is a kid who hasn't had any in months, and has been under constant sexual tension. He'll get off fast, and go slow on the second round. I doubt he gets it in all the way before he blows.

Heidi bends over at the waist and touches her toes. She shows off her heart-shaped ass and peachy pussy to the room, wagging her rear end back and forth like a tail.

Tobias releases a noise that is more animal than man, and a big glob of precum splats on the floor. I laugh again. There's no freaking way Tobias will even last thirty seconds.

Heidi wiggles her ass at Tobias, and tells him to wait and enjoy the view. She is amping him up for me. She glances over her shoulder and purrs, "Come get me, big boy."

Tobias moves with lightning speed and enters Heidi in one long thrust. Before he can pull back for another plunge, he is screaming his orgasm at the ceiling. I watch him writhe against her ass, marked back spasming with bliss.

Heidi looks at me with a satisfied expression on her pretty face. She's pleased that she helped a fellow woman win, and I think she's most satisfied with Tobias. He wasn't the only one who could look but not touch for months.

*Atta Girl, Heidi!*

I don't gloat, laugh, or even smile about my win. I just sit patiently while I enjoy my silent victory. I deserve to be respected, so therefore it's up to me to grab that respect and run with it. I will never allow anyone to treat me as if I'm an inanimate object again. Both guys have a sour puss expression on their face, and that alone is worth it!

# Chapter Thirty

We had a very quiet week without any more mysterious notes, twitchy feelings on the back of my neck, or Ray sightings. The most excitement we've had is Aaron and Kayla's wedding preparations. I was shocked when the entire family got involved, especially the men. I knew that the ladies would be fanatical, but it was sweet yet strange that the men were getting into it just as much. I have a big wedding planning party scheduled for tomorrow. So while everyone else was '*oohing*' and '*aahing*' over wedding dress magazines, I've been planning a luncheon for all the ladies.

The guys won't leave the house under the circumstances, but agreed to stay in our home office. Which is a good thing, because they are being bigger divas than the bride. If I hear one more time that money isn't an object, I will scream. Just because you can afford a huge wedding, doesn't mean the bride and groom want one. I had to beg them not to attend the party so that I could find out what Kayla really wanted– not needed, as Ezra would think.

Any attached female who is coming to the party is bringing her male counterpart. I guess the office will become a daycare center. Except, instead of for kids, it's daycare for men. I have no idea what they plan on doing, or how they plan on fitting inside there. But that isn't my problem with all the other tasks I have to perform.

My entire Saturday morning has consisted of sitting at the kitchen table, making an endless stream of party favors. I don't see their appeal, but Ava and Kayla were insistent– insistent yet *not* helping.

Out of the corner of my eye, the newspaper draws my attention. I see the word Zeitler in glaring bold text. It's not a popular name, and I only know of four Zeitlers, so it's either my daughter, Ezra, or his parents. I drop the cheesy, pink tulle I'm chopping up for party favors, and then drag the paper across the table.

*Dr. Ezra Zeitler publicly announces the dissolution of his engagement to Ms. Adelaide Whittenhower. Ezra is the son of*

*Marcus Zeitler and Diane Holden, our district attorney and his philanthropic wife. Adelaide is the daughter of Daniel Whittenhower the first and Priscilla Whittenhower, the owners of more than thirty corporations. The Whittenhower, Holden, and Zeitler families have been connected for generations, and thought to be blessed to finally combine into one, highly influential powerhouse.*

*According to our records, the couple had been engaged for six years. However, Zeitler stated that the engagement was broken privately over three years ago. He cited incompatibility as the sole reason for not legalizing the union.*

*The Times quoted Zeitler from a phone interview early this morning: "I just couldn't see myself creating an everlasting life with Adelaide. We broke off our private relationship several years ago, but maintained a public relationship for business appearances, public relations, and familial obligations. My life is how I envisioned it, and I wish to no longer pretend it is otherwise."*

*When asked if he was seeing anyone romantically, Zeitler replied: "The people I share my life with wish to remain anonymous for the time being. I will say that I am happier than I've ever been. I feel comfortable to truly be myself. I look forward to a long and fruitful life with my loved ones."*

*The Times asked Zeitler if he planned on remaining a bachelor now that his engagement to Ms. Whittenhower has been broken. He replied: "The bachelor life is not for me. I see myself with a wife and a large family, and I see it in the near future. I'm sure the press will catch wind of my plans before I do."*

*Zeitler ended his phone interview with a chuckle. The Times would like to add that Ezra Zeitler was a pleasure to interview, always open and engaging. We wish him the best of luck in his romantic endeavors.*

*Our greatest sympathies go out to Ms. Adelaide Whittenhower for not tying the billionaire bachelor down.*

"Jesus," slips past my lips.

When Ezra gives you a week– you have exactly a week. No less. No more.

He didn't paint Adelaide in a bad light. The press swayed it in a way that makes her look bad, though. She really should have come up with an excuse of her own. I mean, c'mon, she had three years to think of something. Clearly, Adelaide thought she could reel Ezra back in somehow. I never thought I would feel bad for someone when their misfortune is my fortune. Well, that's not entirely true.

I have no idea where I stand with Ezra. Since our last visit to the dungeon, he has been withdrawn. Grumpy and ornery. Only to Cort and me, though. Ezra loves everyone else, seeking their constant attention and affection.

Ezra is freezing Cort and me out as punishment for not coming to him about catching him in a compromising position with Adelaide. He's dosing us with our own medicine. I miss Ezra, not for sexual reasons, just life's little intimacies. Lying in bed with his mood hovering is uncomfortable at best. None of us have been sleeping well.

Last night was the final straw when Ezra refused to allow us to kiss his cheek good night. After a string of swear words on my part, he spilled the beans. Ezra is angry that Cort and I believed him capable of loving Adelaide. He said we didn't know him or trust him, if we could believe what we saw.

Cortez had had enough at that point, and actually punched Ezra in the arm, yelling for him to snap out of it. Cortez finally got it through Ezra's head that we saw and heard him make love to Adelaide. In the end, we agreed to disagree, and then went to sleep angry– me in Cortez's arms while Ezra clung to the side of the bed. I waited for Ezra to fall asleep, and then I curled myself around him, with Cortez following.

Ezra woke in a better mood today with both Cort and me wrapped around him like giant teddy bears. He still isn't his usual self, but it's slow progress. Plus, I'm sure that Ray and his minion, the wedding preparations, and this Adelaide business is on his mind.

Ezra wouldn't allow anyone to come to the party who has access to both Shadow Haven and Edge, unless they're family members. He doesn't want Ray's accomplice in our home. I don't blame him for that.

"Oh, they printed it today," Ezra murmurs to himself as he sits across from me at the table. He lifts the article with a snap to the newspaper, and then reads.

I make more favors while I wait. I nosh on a few butter mints, avoiding the Jordan almonds. Yuck– this favor bullshit is so thirty years ago. What we endure for friends.

I sigh while snipping lengths of frilly pink ribbon for use as ties.

"Well, everything was quoted correctly, but they spun it when it came to Adelaide." Ezra sounds matter-of-fact as he folds the paper in two, hiding his cover story.

"Adelaide had three years to fix it herself. So if it bites her in the ass, that's her problem for procrastinating." I tie little bundles of tulle with the ribbon, contemplating how to proceed with caution. "I highly doubt procrastination is in Adelaide's vocabulary. I think she thought she could manipulate you over time, and when that failed, she thought you wouldn't go through with your threat. I'm sure making love to her a few months ago made her think she had won you back."

Looking around the apartment, "Where is everyone?" Ezra changes the subject because he knows I'm right, and he must feel like a dumbass for his decision to bed the woman.

I feel badly for Adelaide, and I'm still angry at Ezra for all of us. How confused that must have made Adelaide feel. How it must have made her feel used, whored out, when it didn't change Ezra's mind on marrying her.

I don't trust Adelaide, but I do understand and respect her. A woman who puts over six years into a relationship, especially one that was to solidify her family's wealth, doesn't walk away easily. Adelaide's tenacity screams of her family's influence, and her behavior shows it wasn't about love between her and Ezra. I know this isn't the last we've heard from her, even if Ezra's acting blind and deaf to that fact.

I finally give in after a few tense moments, and answer Ezra's question. "Aaron and Kayla took Ava to a movie. They should be back any second. I have no idea where Cort is hiding."

Ezra tosses the newspaper onto the kitchen island, needing it farther away from him. "Cortez is deep into a manuscript. He was very intent when I checked on him moments ago. I bet it's a masterpiece."

"I'm glad to see Cort is writing again. It will do wonders for his confidence." Voice husky, the words flow from my lips without thought. "So, we're alone, then?"

Ezra looks at me in a heated way I haven't seen in over a week. It boils my blood and flushes my face. Getting up from my chair, I straddle Ezra's legs and sit in his lap. I cradle his face between my palms, loving the slight scrape of his whisker stubble.

"I've missed you," I breathe, and then I lean into him. "I don't like being frozen out, and I've learned my lesson well. I promise I won't freeze you out ever again. I may do it by accident, but never on purpose."

Pressing our mouths together, I kiss Ezra deeply, drawing his tongue into my mouth, sucking on the succulent flesh. Rather than tell him again, I show Ezra how much I've missed him. My hands rove over his shoulders and back, luxuriating in the feel of him beneath my fingertips.

Jaw unhinging, I try to taste all of Ezra at once. My tongue is sucked deep into his mouth, as we rock together in a rhythmic motion. My fingertips bite into Ezra's shoulder muscles, refusing to let him go ever again.

"Don't ignore us ever again," I moan into Ezra's mouth. "Cortez and I are here because of you. Without you binding us together, it won't work. You have us both amenable, which might not last long if you're freezing us out. Don't throw it away out of bent pride."

"It was childish of me," Ezra breathes into my mouth. "I won't do it again. I promise."

He unleashes his passion, no longer holding it back. I'd thought I'd known the true Ezra Zeitler. I'd thought he had shown me the depths of his need, but I had been so very wrong. Ezra consumes me. His mouth, his touch, his very presence owns me. Ezra grips me and never lets me go.

I'm so caught up in the kiss that I let out a girlish meep when teeth press against the side of my neck. Ezra laughs against my mouth as Cortez snickers against my throat.

I lean back, laughing at my idiocy. "It's a good thing we aren't in enemy territory, or I'd be as good as dead right now. You distract me to no end," I admit, but it's directed at both the Ezes.

Reaching for me again, "In your defense, Cort did creep in," Ezra breathes against my parted lips.

"You saw him?" I worry that my appeal isn't as strong as I'd hoped.

"Nah." Ezra chuckles, lips curving into a huge grin against mine. "I was nibbled first. I think Cort has sexy-time radar. You must have pinged him when you slid into my lap."

"Or perhaps you both were moaning so loudly it broke into my concentration." Lips twisting into a devastating grin, Cort hitches my breath. "I thought I'd join the fun."

Cort pulls my hair abruptly, causing me to gasp in shock. He wrenches my head to the side, exposing my neck to his pleasure. Teeth piercing, he bites me hard enough to break skin. It should hurt– it does –but not in a way that makes me flinch. My muscles turn lax, but on the inside I'm imploding with the high of lust.

My gaze seeks out Ezra, and he stares back at me, emoting exactly what I'm feeling. He wears a drugged expression, and his eyes are dilated and glazed over. He captures my gaze as Cort sucks on my throat, bruising me– marking me.

I pant, whimper, and moan as my body fills with pressure. I wiggle around, needing more contact, more attention. More. No one is touching me sexually. I sit on Ezra's thighs near his knees. He isn't touching me in any other manner, just holding my gaze. Cort's hand is yanking my hair, but not touching skin. Only his mouth is making contact with my body.

I'm so close to release that I start to beg. "Please…" I don't even know what I am begging for, or why I'm saying please.

Ezra leans in slowly, his intense eyes getting closer and closer. I await his kiss, the anticipation amping up the craving. My lips ache and throb for his kiss. Ezra's lips connect with my neck instead of my mouth, where his teeth pinch sharply.

The Ezes begin kissing each other as they lick and nibble at my neck. The thought alone has me writhing in Ezra's lap, with my pussy clenching and quivering for something it isn't going to get. The three of us moan a pain-filled sound of longing and denial.

My muscles go taut. A prickling sensation starts in my toes and scalp, tightening my skin as my blood rises to the surface. The storm gathers as the sensation travels along my spine to converge in the center of my body. My body unleashes a release that is just as much mental as sexual. I writhe from the strength of an orgasm that is so much more potent than if I were brought by touch alone.

I lay completely boneless. I would've fallen if Cort hadn't pulled my back to his chest. His cheek slowly caresses mine as he murmurs his approval against my skin.

Ezra kisses me gently on the lips, as if knowing that anything stronger than a brush of a touch would be too much sensation. I close my eyes and revel in the feel of both men– *my* Ezes.

I sense them kissing each other near my ear, the vibrations causing my body to tremble. "Ah– I think we better let Kitten rest." Amusement is thick in Cort's voice.

Ezra murmurs his agreement, and I visualize him doing so against Cort's lips. Spine arching, quivering, I experience another full body spasm just from the thought.

Completely pliant, I allow Cort to pick me up and place me back in my dining chair. I slump against the backrest, with my eyelids fluttering shut and my arms falling lax to my sides.

Cort kisses me softly, and then murmurs against my lips. "Me thinks Kat likes us touching each other almost as much as we do."

"Thank God," Ezra gasps, relieved. I crack my eyelids and look at him through the slit. I don't have the energy to open my eyes fully. I draw in a huge breath and sigh it back out, feeling sleepy, like I just had the best orgasm mixed with a feel-good drug.

"Katya's got a bit of a biting fetish, I see." Ezra releases an evil laugh, and Cortez joins him. "Easily exploited, too. If we piss her off, we can always bite her into compliance."

"You just proved why I hold you at arm's length. I think I ought to talk to our girl about making promises she will regret." Cort's voice is stiff with fear, not anger.

"Cortez." Ezra sighs. "Between the two of us, Katya should be scared of *you*, not me. I love her, and I don't plan on harming her in any way. It's your volatile emotions that will fuck it all up. When I make a decision, I never deviate. As you well know, or else you and I wouldn't be where we are today, let alone on speaking terms."

"Well, let's make a few of these thingies while Kat recuperates." Cort changes the uncomfortable subject. "Ava will have a fit if she doesn't get these favors."

Distracting himself from the truth, Cortez reaches in front of me and uses his forearm to drag all the supplies to his side of the table. Ezra is right. I feel it soul-deep. In my drugged state of mind, a premonition weaves effortlessly though me. It a cold, dark blast of reality.

Nothing will force Ezra to break a promise. If he decides he wants you in his life, you're there whether you want to be or not. The only variable is Cortez. If Cortez forces Ezra's hand to choose between us, Ezra won't and it will destroy us all. One of us will have to walk away to save the others, and we all know that person isn't Cortez.

I fear the day Cortez gives Ezra all he's holding back of himself. That is the day I will finally be broken. The day Ezra's loyalties will be tested. The day I prove whose love is the purest, by walking away to give them what should have always been.

But that day may never come, as Cortez is the most stubborn person I've ever known. There is thirty years' worth of running and chasing between the pair. I understand Ezra's need to stop the insanity and move down another path.

"Kitten's gonna be wicked pissed when she looks in the mirror," Cort says as he fills a round of tulle with snacks and ties the bundle with a ribbon. I watch in fascination as he crafts favors with his large fingertips, fumbling with the ribbon. He stares proudly at the bundle nestled in his palm.

"I think that's the whole point." Ezra's reply swings my gaze back to him. He is laughing silently. I stare him down, wondering what's funny and why I'll be pissed when I look in the mirror. Upon seeing my narrow-eyed expression, Ezra's chest quakes from suppressed laughter.

I muster up enough strength to ask when Ava and the happy couple come in, effectively cutting off all conversation. Ava dominates all the attention when she sees the pile of goodies on the table.

Ava's cheeks are pinked beautifully, and her face is alight with happiness and excitement. "Oh! These are awesome!" Ava picks up handfuls of party favors while smiling ear-to-ear. "I've never been to a wedding before. I have so many ideas." Ava rambles on as my mind wanders.

I realize that this is Ava's first real experience with any of this wedding stuff. It's mine as well, but I'm not an overly excited eleven-year-old girly girl. I've never been in a wedding and I never planned on getting married, so Ava's never been a flower girl or bridesmaid. I feel badly about bitching in my head as I made the favors. This is about Kayla, and by extension, Ava. This union is about all of us coming together as a family, and I'm pissing on it, even if it's in my private thoughts.

I reach forward to grab some supplies, and diligently get back to work, deciding that if these ugly favors make my daughter and Kayla happy, then I'm make thousands of the goddamned things.

"Animal attack? Vampire? Lost control of the vacuum cleaner? A gaggle of fourteen-year-old boys experimented on Kat?" I catch the end of what Aaron is asking Ezra and Cortez.

I look a '*huh?*' at Aaron, and he releases a wicked laugh, drawing all the attention to me.

Kayla's blush creeps up her cheeks as she covers her mouth with the back of her hand. Since I haven't regained enough energy to move, I roll my head on the back of my chair, trying to take in everyone's expressions. Cort and Ez look smug. Seeming embarrassed and amused, Kayla and Aaron cover their mouths. As I squint at my daughter, she stares back at me in horror.

"What happened to your neck? Did someone hurt you?" Ava's voice is sharp, almost parental, as she studies my neck. Realization dawning, a second later she blushes bright red and stares at her dad, and then Cort. "That was not very nice. Mom won't be able to cover that up for the party tomorrow," she scolds the pair.

"That was the point," her father replies smugly.

"What?" My voice sounds drowsy and slow as I reach up to feel the side of my neck. My fingertips encounter incredibly sore wounds. "You guys didn't. Please, tell me you didn't?"

"We didn't." Ezra lies and flashes me a cocky smirk.

"Are you feeling okay, Mom?" Concerned, my daughter's fingertips hover over my skin, but don't touch the tender spot. "You look exhausted."

I smile weakly in response, refusing to explain what actually happened, and everyone snickers except for Ava and me.

Embarrassment and mortification chase away the endorphins flowing in my veins until I'm finally able to move. "Yeah, just give me a couple of minutes, and I'll be right as rain." Before anyone can say anything, I rush from the room, muttering behind me, "I'm going to take a cold shower."

I half-stumble to my bathroom, drawing to a stop at the vanity. I lean forward and stare in shock at my reflection in the mirror. I'm dumbfounded at what is reflected back at me because I don't look like myself. Not the wounds, but the glazed film over my normally vibrant green eyes, the knotted mess of my red curls, the whisker stubble burns on my cheeks, and the satisfied blush creeping up from my chest to my forehead. If I wasn't so relaxed, steam would billow out of my ears at how pissed I should be.

I poke at the bruised, ravaged skin on the side of my throat. It's so tender that I wince. Adorning my neck are two sets of intersecting bite marks, which are deep enough that they are crusted with blood. A good inch or two around the bites are suck marks and bruising.

I'm positive that it's going to scar, and for some unfathomable reason, that makes me smile at my reflection in the mirror. I should be angry by the fact that Ezra and Cortez marked me in a way I can't conceal for tomorrow's gathering, but I'm not. This wasn't Cortez marking the hell out of Ezra, and Ezra marking me, and me feeling left on the sidelines. It was both of them wanting me in their lives. However archaic, it gives me hope for our future, proving we may have longevity after all.

# Chapter Thirty-One

I return from my shower wearing comfy clothes, prepared to tackle more wedding planning party preparations. I'm in a good mood until I feel the fury emanating from the dining room.

"How could you let this happen, Aaron? Ava is my daughter for Christ's sake!" Intimidating, Ezra is leaning over the table, eyes blazing in rage, bitching rabidly at Aaron, who is appropriately cowering in his seat. Kayla's chair is overturned, and she's comforting and protecting Ava from the ensuing fight.

I've never seen Ezra like this, and I've caused him to lose his shit on many occasions. He's no longer the playful, emotional Ezra we all know, tolerate, and love. Master Ez is firmly in control, and he's overprotective and deadly. If Aaron isn't safe from this facet of Ezra's personality, is anyone?

"Whoa…" I put my hands out in a stop position. "What is going on?" Master Ez's violent gaze swings in my direction, and I don't wilt from the pressure. I just get pissed, and I give it right back to him. "Calm the hell down and don't look at me that way," I order in a composed voice belying the anger roiling inside me. "Everyone, sit in your seats like good boys and girls while we get this sorted."

Ezra blows his breath out as if he's literally blowing off steam, and then he retakes his seat with a flourish. Everyone else follows suit when Ezra is seated. Aaron rights Kayla's chair so she can sit, and then he pulls Ava's chair between him and his fiancée for safe keeping. I take my usual seat between the Ezes, with Aaron, Ava, and Kayla all staring at me, waiting for me to make it better– to control the uncontrollable.

"Cort, talk to me," I command. He's the only one who is calm, so I figure he'd be the best source of information. Like always, Cort and I work best as a team to manage Ezra.

"We were chatting about the movie they went to see." Cort's voice is distant, as if he's lost in his thoughts but answering me anyway. "Ava said she met a man, but she didn't get to finish her sentence since Ezra went batshit crazy on us."

"What man?" I ask in confusion.

"*The* man." Cort gives me a look that says he is trying to keep everyone calm while keeping his own shit together. I breathe in deeply, knowing what he's up to because now I'm in the same mode. You need to panic, but being the mother means you can't. Your freak outs come later, when you're alone and your child is safely tucked in her bed, blissfully unaware and happy in her ignorance.

"All right, there is no sense in worrying the girls," I whisper out the corner of my mouth at a despondent Ezra. "Ava, everything is perfectly fine, so why don't you start by telling me what happened from the beginning." I clasp my hands on the tabletop and smile sedately, when inside my mind is a shit-storm of fury and unadulterated terror.

"I went to get a refill of fruit punch, and a man was standing in line behind me. He just wanted to chat. He wasn't scary or anything. He seemed really nice, like how Cort is."

"Exactly like me," Cort whispers beneath his breath. "Who the fuck do you think I inherited my charisma from?" I reach out, finding his hand to lend him comfort. Not knowing if Ezra will snap my wrist or accept a comforting gesture, I reach for him as well. Both of the Ezes latch onto my hands like I'm their mother and they're lost in the dark.

"They guy said he was an old friend of the family. He asked how you guys were, calling you by name, and even asked about Cort and Aaron. He knew everybody. He knew you guys enough to ask if…" Ava's voice trails off and she flushes bright crimson. "He was curious to know if Dad and Cort were both with Mom, or if it was just Cort and Mom and Cort and Dad."

"What did you tell him?" I ask in a way that makes it sound as if I don't think it's important one way or the other. I don't want my daughter brought into this, and I don't want her feeling guilty for letting out our private business.

"The truth. I told him you guys were all together. Dad's told me about how he likes guys and Cort doesn't, but it's different between him and you and Cort and him. I kind of understand. I think." Ava sounds as confused as I feel, illuminating the fact that she doesn't truly understand. I doubt any of us do.

"I told the man the truth, and he actually looked happy about that. He said that he was glad, and that he wanted you to have a good life. He asked if Aaron was all right. He had a weird look on his face when he said it. So I told him about the wedding, and he was happy again. He said I looked like Grandma Diane, but he could tell that I act like Dad."

"That's not necessarily a good thing," Ezra murmurs. "As it means you act like *him*, too."

"The man wanted me to give you a message. He said he needed to talk to Dad. That was the message. He said it was important that he talk to Dad. I asked who he was, and he said to call him Ray, and that he was proud of all of us." Ava finishes with a confused look on her face and a shrug.

"Thanks, baby girl." I smile at Ava like nothing is wrong. I don't like how Ezra let his emotions run wild in front of Ava and Kayla. They don't need to be involved, except to be kept safe. I don't need them worrying. Ezra will just make two hysterical females who we will have to wrangle instead of getting to the heart of the matter.

"I don't feel like making dinner tonight since I have so much to prepare for the party tomorrow." I yawn loudly and stretch for added effect. "Aaron, can you help the girls pick something from the delivery menus? I think I saw them last on Ezra's desk in the office."

Aaron looks at me with hurt-filled eyes. A few seconds later, I watch as comprehension dawns. No, I am not closing him out; it's just that the girls would think something was up if he wasn't included with them. Aaron and Kayla are very sweet and innocent for their age, and my daughter is very old for her age, so the three of them get along famously.

As Aaron gets up from the table, I give him a reassuring smile and pat his hand in thanks for taking care of our girls.

"Calm, you need to be calm, Ezra." I say when I'm positive the girls and Aaron are safely tucked into the office. I lean to the side to gaze across the living room toward the hallway to be certain they aren't eavesdropping. I note Aaron was smart enough to shut the office door for added privacy.

"I can't believe this shit. You are my family, and I can't even protect you against my rapist sperm donor." Ezra groans in misery, while holding his stomach like he's going to be physically ill.

Since Ezra pulled the martyr card, I pull out my bitch shield in defense. "Hey, no! Knock it the fuck off! We need to be able to think. I don't know what Ray wants, but we know he won't hurt Ava. He never touched you, right?"

"No, Ray didn't touch me, Katya." Ezra whimpers in remembrance, while Cort just checks out, lost to his own inner miseries. "Ray never touched me. Ever. For any reason. But that isn't the point. He made me watch him rape prostitutes." Ezra's voice escalates as he recites Ray's laundry list of crimes. "Then he kidnapped Cort and Aaron. He made me sit in a chair, where he interrogated me. When I wouldn't answer his question because I was protecting someone, he tortured Cort by trying to rape the '*gay*' out of him. That's what Ray said. My father made me choose between the two people I loved more than life itself. Cort understands now why I couldn't choose him. Since I wouldn't save Cort, Ray destroyed us– destroyed Cort and me as a couple."

"My uncle said to me," Cort breathes the words, his face a mask of lifelessness. "He said to me, '*You will fuck these whores' cunts until you can no longer stand the thought of fucking your own cousin's asshole. My blood isn't gay. Hunters are men, and we bed women, and we make children. You can't make kids when you have two dicks. Since Ezra won't give me my grandson, you will continue on the Hunter bloodline.*' And when he saw how Ezra wouldn't break and give him grandkids, and how we still had an unbreakable bond, he had me rape Aaron as punishment. He ruined me, and I haven't been able to touch Ezra like that again."

I look to Ezra, knowing Cortez has had sex with Ezra in the past twelve years. Ezra's eyes narrow to slits and he shakes his head back and forth to silence my question.

"I can see you communicating," Cort mumbles, eyes cutting in our direction. He gets up from the table to pace the kitchen and dining area. "I am incapable of giving Ezra what he needs because of what happened. Like with anger, when you see red, you don't realize what you've done until it's over. That is the only way I can describe the handful of times I've had penetrative sex with Ezra since…"

"Cort," Ezra and I cry out in unison, both of us needing to comfort him.

"No pity," Cort demands. He swings around, and walks right over to stand before us. "I have a theory. My mother and Ray were twins, and my mother was an angel on Earth. There was an air about her, where you felt she was temporary. No one that good could live long with how horrific the world is. My mother got all the light, sucking it out of her twin, creating who Ray became. When she died, her twin turned evil because he couldn't deal with her loss. So even while I hate Ray, I understand him. He's not going to hurt us. He won't!"

"Did you not hear everything you just said?" Ezra grits out stiffly, holding in his need to bellow the words. "Did you not just tell Kat what Ray has done to us?"

"Ray has his grandkids." Cort looks so optimistic, so naïve. "Ray is out of prison, and he has hope for the first time since we lost my mother. He has a family."

"A family who hates his fucking guts!" Ezra shouts, fist pounding on the tabletop. "A family he raped!"

Pointing at Ezra, getting right in his face, "Ray is not stalking Kat," Cort says with conviction. "It's not him. I believe our little girl. She's not stupid. She'd feel Ray's intent, just as Kat always senses. Ray wants to talk to his son, so he's not going to harm the only family he has left. We're all right here," Cort gestures around him. "He's not going to jeopardize that."

Ezra ignores Cort, not believing a word he's saying. I have no idea who to believe, as my judgment of the monster hinges on the fact that he raped me and left me for dead.

I look back and forth between the Ezes. "What are we going to do about Ray?"

Cort looks at us with such sincerity and certainty that I want to tear up. "We need to figure out who Ray's accomplice is— the one who got him out of prison. I believe we're safe from Ray. He talked to Ava in a crowded, public place, because he wanted her to feel safe. I don't think he wanted to abduct her or harm her. He just really wanted Ezra to have that message."

Sliding into the seat across the table from us, Cort reaches over to take my hand in his right and Ezra's hand in his left. He stares at us, trying to get us to understand his point of view.

"I've been thinking. I don't think those notes are from Ray— it's not his style. Yes, it was what he said to you, Kat. But anyone who could circumvent five mailed notices for the parole hearing, they could possibly have access to the trial transcripts. I don't know if they are working together at all. I think they wanted Ray out in our world, hoping he'd fuck with us, or maybe to use his presence to cover up their crimes. If anything happened to one of us, all fingers would point at Ray, whether he did it or not, and the real perpetrator would go free."

"You're not thinking clearly," Ezra begins. "Cort, you're a storyteller. You're trying to write this out, but we are not characters. This is reality. A reality where Raymond Hunter is in Dominion with us."

Cortez ignores Ezra. "It's connected, but I don't think the stalker is actually collaborating with Ray. It just isn't his style. He always worked alone, not even allowing his partner near until it was time to clean up the messes. I was talking to… his partner. Anyway, he doesn't think Ray would do this either. Now, the movie theater is exactly how Ray would approach this. I don't know if I'm overthinking it or under-thinking it."

"I'm just going to pretend you didn't even speak," Ezra directs to Cortez, but refuses to look at him.

"Ray or no Ray, I say we go about our lives, but be extra vigilant. This was a wakeup call. I've wondered why there was such a large amount of time between notes. I think it was to give us a semblance of normalcy, so that we were always waiting, never at peace," I muse.

"Which is *not* Ray's way of hunting anyone, as you damned well remember," Cort snarls at us, championing for his uncle. "Besides, the first note came before Ray was even released." Cort drops the bombshell into our laps to make his point. "I just don't think Ray is connected to the note writer at all. I really think they are using him to fuck with us. I just hope that Ray doesn't figure it out. No. Actually, I hope he does. He would take care of them for us." Cortez gives a bitter laugh. "Then we'd only have to worry about Ray."

"I hate this– this feeling of helplessness. There is really nothing we can do until we figure out who is helping whom." I groan into my hands as I'm overcome with the largest urge to pound my forehead into the table out of pure frustration.

"You feel helpless?" Ezra twists out incredulously. "I am the leader of this family, and I can't do a thing about it. Not a damned thing. My hands are tied, and our worst nightmare is walking the streets right alongside us!"

"Hey, the derision, division, and confusion we feel between the three of us is the whole point. Whoever it is wants us to fight amongst ourselves so we don't see them coming. We have good things going on right now. We have each other to lean on. We have Ava and Katya completing our family. Aaron is healed and moving on with Kayla, going to create a new family of his own. We will not let this fucktard ruin our happy life."

Cortez squeezes my hand, but he drops Ezra's. He points across the table, getting into Ezra's face. "Ezra, if we allow this to divide us, they win. So don't act like this is a competition for who has had it worse. Katya has every right to feel helpless just as you do. It's not either/or. Hell, I even feel helpless. Let's feel helpless together, but never allow them to know they have weakened us. United front."

"You're right, Cort. You're right," Ezra murmurs, sounding sheepish. "Please accept my apology, Katya. I'm sorry." Ezra leans over and kisses my forehead.

I hear the click of the lock on the office door and peer down the hall toward the sound. Aaron sticks his head out of the doorway to see if it's clear to come out. I shake my head yes, and the three of them wander back to the table.

"Were you done?" Aaron mouths, and then says out loud, "The food should be here shortly. We ordered some calzones and wings, and I ordered Piggy a dozen cannoli."

"Fuck you, Aaron," Cort snarls while mock-punching Aaron in the arm. "Thanks, though. I need 'em."

Ava appears skittish. I look between Ava and her father, trying to give Ezra the hint to comfort her. Understanding me perfectly, he smiles at our daughter, and then stands up to greet her.

"So, Ava, do you think we have enough favors for tomorrow's party, or do we need to make some more?" Ezra pulls Ava into his side and half hugs her while they look at the mess on the table.

Ezra kisses Ava on the top of the head, his lashes shuttering his eyes. I see a look of pure terror flash across Ezra's features before he can mask it. Cortez reaches over for my hand, letting me know he saw it too. I guess Cort and I are on 'protect Ezra from himself' duty again.

The doorbell rings, signaling the arrival of our food just as we're clearing the table free of party favors. We sit in strained silence until Aaron makes it his mission to get everyone talking. I can tell that Aaron feels responsible for Ray speaking to Ava. It is and isn't his fault. But I know it weighs heavily on his mind. Ezra's chastisement didn't help matters. I try to add to the conversation to lighten the mood, but my forced enthusiasm is obvious. The conversation actually flows better when I keep my mouth shut.

# Chapter Thirty-Two

"Ma, do you wanna play a game tonight?" Ava is eating her own weight in cannoli, while Cortez pouts because he had to share. The man eyes the pastry in my daughter's hand while salivating like a begging dog. "We should do a game night like how we used to play with Grandma and Grandpa."

"Sure. That sounds fun. We'll have to pick a day of the week where we don't have much to do. Maybe Wednesdays?" I plaster a fake smile on my face. I figure out I'm not fooling anyone when Aaron cringes. Great! "What would you like to play?"

"We only have two games here, but I could run out and buy something," Ezra offers, hoping he can do something for me. Anything. Absolutely anything, so he no longer feels the guilt and has a direction to push forward, instead of this purgatory we are residing in.

"What are the choices?" This time my small smile is genuine.

"We have chess–" I burst out laughing just as Ezra had hoped. "No… no, chess isn't a good idea. That's our private time. How about Risk? There are six of us. It would be perfect."

"Risk it is!" I stand up and start to clear off the table while Ezra runs off to collect the game. I'm happy we have a distraction from Ray, scary notes, and wedding preparations. Even better because it's a distraction that bonds us together as a family.

"I want Dad as my partner!" Ava exclaims.

"You don't have partners in Risk. Allies, but never partners," I try to explain.

Ava grumbles, "Why not?"

"There are three types of Risk players: Those who play to win. Kamikazes who sacrifice themselves for another player. They are the worst, most unpredictable players, as they attack for no reason other than to mess up your game. Lastly, the crazy who doesn't know how to play but thinks they can. Sorry, baby girl, you are our designated crazy tonight."

"What kind are you?" Curiosity is strong in Ava's voice.

"Oh, I play to win. Always have. Always will." I received a wink from Cortez for that comment.

An hour into the game, Ava realizes why the game is only fun for those who play to win, for those who create chaos, or for those who truly are crazy. I feel bad as I roll to remove Ava's last piece. Yeah, I'm a bad mom for knocking my own daughter out of the game. "Sorry about that. Now I want you to watch and learn how the game is really played."

Five minutes later, our Risk student chirps, "Aaron and Kayla are kamikazes, aren't they?"

"Yeah." I chuckle beneath my breath. "But whose are they?"

"I don't know," Ava mutters in confusion.

"Just watch, and you'll see." I flash a grin.

"Hey, that's not fair, Dad!" It didn't take Ava long to notice how Aaron and Kayla never rolled against Ezra. She punches her father in the arm and he snickers at her. "How come you get both of them?"

"Just because I'm that special, little one. Watch and learn, and I will give you the keys to the kingdom." Ezra smiles at me, causing me to blush.

"Don't you care, Cort?" Ava asks.

"Nah– Ezra doesn't have a snowball's chance in hell of actually winning. He's stuck in Europe. He can cheat all he wants; it isn't gonna happen."

"You're Mom's ally, aren't you?"

"Of course. If we had fought each other, your dad would've won within the first hour." Cort turns to Ezra. "You should have figured out that Kat was smarter than that."

Another hour later, Ezra loses his helpers. I hear a giggle trail in from the living room, a giggle I know all too well. Aaron is exciting Kayla, and the pair will be locked in Aaron's old bedroom until morning.

"The game doesn't change much from this point on. It will be back and forth," Cort informs Ava. "Once you're down to three players, one will go out quickly, with the last two battling for hours on end. It may be morning before your mother overtakes your father. So you may want to go entertain yourself in your bedroom, or else you may die of boredom sitting here watching them roll dice and bicker."

"HA!" Ava jumps up from her seat as Ezra removes Cort's last piece in Russia. "Now they'll fight it out. I'm going to go watch Pretty Little Liars in my room. Night."

"Asshole," Cort taunts Ezra as he follows Ava out of the room, making sure she's doing as she said.

Ezra and I fall into the game, finally finding a challenge that requires no speaking. After months upon months of playing chess every night, but never making it through a whole game without having Dr. Zeitler using therapy on me, I've yet to beat Ezra at chess. But at Risk, we are evenly matched in wits, and tonight is my night to win.

"Just so you know…" Ezra willingly takes his tank from Madagascar, and replaces it with a Calvary and three infantry pieces. "You kicking my ass is tantamount to stripping buck-ass naked and begging me to fuck you. Every night we play chess, is another night you get better at it, which is another night I get more aroused by watching you learn. I could fuck this table and get off in five seconds flat."

"Well," I drawl out while rolling against Ezra again. "Prepare to get even hotter. Remove two infantry from Madagascar, and while you do it, I want you to rub your cock through your pants."

"Jesus!" Cortez walks into the kitchen while wearing an evil smirk. "You competitive types are fucking nuts. Getting off on Risk. That's a new kink. Next ya know, you'll be hosting Risk championships in the Dungeon of Restraint."

Ezra holds my gaze while he removes his pieces, and judging by the motion of his bicep, he's doing as I asked beneath the table.

"Fuck," I hiss, shuddering at the thought.

"Here, this will cool ya off." Cort produces a bottle of rum out of nowhere— the 151 proof kind that drops your ass in five seconds flat.

"Cool me off?" I arch a brow at Ezra, silently asking him what Cortez is up to. He shrugs in reply. "Or burst me into flame? If you light a match, we could make a Molotov cocktail."

"Now that is hot," Cort purrs. "Getting my ass kicked at Risk, not so much. Talking weapons, H-O-T!"

"Grenades. Crossbows. Sniper rifles. Dirk. Throwing star. Battle Axe. Flamethrower. Uzi. Drone. Poison."

"Katya?" Ezra gains my attention. "Are you trying to get Cortez hot and bothered, or are you warning him of the manner in which you plan on killing him? Or did we suddenly enter a First-Person Shooter, and you're calling out first dibs on your weapon selection?"

"Drone?" Cort laughs loudly, tossing his head backward. "Drink your poison, Kitten. We had a bad day, and I want you to feel good." Cort grins and tips the bottle in my direction. "I think we need to make Risk more challenging, don't you?"

"Oh, fuck no!" I cringe at the thought. "Hey, I'm winning. You're just trying to compromise me. I know Aaron told you it only takes a sip and I'm fucked up."

"Don't be such a pussy," Cortez teases. "At least take a chug."

"If you ever want inside my pussy ever again, you won't call me one," I warn Cortez while glaring daggers at him. "Could you possibly find a stronger drink, for Christ's sake?" I eye the bottle of rum that's strong enough to be rubbing alcohol.

Cort plunks the bottle in front of me and smirks. I unscrew the cap– challenge accepted. I open my mouth and take a big swill. I sputter as the fiery liquid hits the back of my throat, nearly choking me with its toxicity. In a hot line from my mouth to my stomach, I burn in hell. My nostrils scorch from the lethal vapors wafting off the liquor.

"Ha! I knew you couldn't pass a challenge." Cort taunts me, and I scrunch my face up at him.

"Do you know what this drink needs?" I take another mouthful and hiss through the pain. "We need some music." I lift to take another drink, fully invested in getting plastered– the quicker the better. Life has sucked!

A hand grabs the bottle of rum from my grasp and yanks it away, spilling a few drops to the tabletop. I scowl at Ezra as he opens his mouth and pours a steady stream down his throat.

"Dayum! Like a boss, you must have owned drinking games at the frat house in college," I mutter in appreciation.

I'm hypnotized by the sight of Ezra's throat as he swallows the liquor down. I want to lick his neck, slurp it, bite him, and mark him as mine. I'm so enthralled that I meep when the music pounds into the room. I snatch the bottle back and chug before Ezra can reclaim it.

"Mine!" I proclaim, not sure if I mean the bottle or Ezra.

"No, mine!" Cortez snatches the bottle away, only to hand it to Ezra. "By the way, I don't drink, but I like when other people do. It's your turn, Ezra. Let's get this bitch of a game finished, and never play it again. I believe we have other games to play tonight."

Just like that, Ezra declares, "I forfeit," as he pushes himself from the table.

"Hey! I wanna know who wins," I whine.

"Hmm... with Ezra's forfeit, I believe that makes you the winner, Kitten. And here is your prize." Cortez takes my hand and wraps it around the neck of the bottle of rum. He squeezes to make sure I have a good hold.

I'm already experiencing the effects of the rum. My cheeks are ruddy and numb, like fire is licking at my skin. My eyes feel like they are floating in their sockets– bubbly-eyed. When I sit still, things move. When I move, things are stationary. Bizarre.

"Bedroom?" Ezra turns to Cortez. "The little one has access to the rest of the house. Plus, we need the tools of our trade." Ezra releases a masculine laugh I've never heard from him. It's husky, smoky, and rough, and it tightens things low in my belly.

Cortez's hand reappears before I drop the bottle. He smirks at me for reacting to Ezra the way I do. "One more guzzle, Kitten, and make it worth your time." I obey by drinking a lot more than I thought possible, letting me know that I'm way past the point of no return.

"Take Kitty Kat to our room. I'll be there in a minute. I have to check on Ava," Ezra says as he moves through the room.

"You're trying to take advantage of me, aren't you?" I slur.

"Of course we are," Cortez says matter-of-factly, and then his voice turns wry. "Do you really care, Kitten?"

"Nah... right now, I guess I don't." I think for a moment or longer; I'm not sure of time at this point. "But will I regret it tomorrow?"

"Knowing you? Undoubtedly. But we both know you want to make love to us, and all you have to do is take your boundaries down. Admit it to yourself, and then to us. Tomorrow you can blame it on the rum. We'll even let you."

I allow Cort to lead me to our room. When we reach our destination without incident, I take one last pull from the bottle. I'm committed to this, bad idea that it may be. I want it more than anything. I can at least admit that to myself.

Staggering, I try to remove my socks without upending. "Did you plan this?"

"Nope," Cort admits as he watches me as if I'm the funniest thing he's ever seen. "You and Ez are the planners. I'm more of a fly by the seat of my pants type of guy."

Ezra startles me when he spanks my ass, and I lose all progress with my tricky sock.

"One more swallow for me, and the bottle is kicked," Ezra says as he reaches for the rum. I watch him swallow again, and lose my balance. I end up with my ass planted on the floor, laughing hysterically.

Big hands hook under my arms, lift, and then toss me on the bed. I bounce several times before coming to a rest. I lie sideways on the mattress, head hanging off the edge. I gaze up at Ezra, and he looks ten feet tall.

"Katya, tell us what you want," Ezra commands.

Inebriation making me stupid, "Who's asking, Master Ez or Ezra?" I challenge him.

"We're one and the same," Ezra explains for the billionth time. "But I'm not speaking of facets of myself. Us, as in Cort and I. What do you want?"

"Both of you," I simply answer.

# Chapter Thirty-Three

"Why won't you make love to us without liquid courage?" Ezra asks as he pulls me flat on my back, arranging me so my head is no longer tilted at an unnatural angle. Woozy, I think I felt clearer headed the way I was lying before.

"Nope, I'm not answering that," I slur belligerently.

"Hmm... that sounds an awful lot like disobedience." Ezra licks his lips, and I mimic the movement. "What do you think, Cort?"

"Hell, yeah. Kitten's being naughty. I think we should punish her." Cortez stares down at me with the smarmiest grin I've ever witnessed, and drunk or not, I know I'm in for it now.

"Re-education, that sounds about right. Katya's had way too much fun telling us what to do as of late. It's our turn for the night." My leather and fur cuffs materialize from Ezra's back pocket, and my eyes widen at the sight.

Shit!

"Where–" I lick my suddenly dry lips. "Where did you get those?"

"These?" Ezra's eyebrows reach his hairline, looking all innocent. "I snatched these from your jewelry box." He dangles the cuffs from their attached metal rings– taunting me.

"I don't want those," I rasp out, sounding breathy. I said I didn't want them, but my body screamed '*Hell, Y E S!*' "I mean, I want them, just not on me."

"The second you twisted the cap off the rum, you agreed to play with us. When your feet entered this room, you gave yourself to us, and you know it." Ezra arches a brow, waiting for me to argue.

Why would I argue when he's right?

I didn't give myself to Ezra when I walked into this room tonight. I gave myself to him twelve years ago in the woods of North Central Pennsylvania. Each and every day, I give Ezra and Cortez more and more of myself. Until this very moment, I hadn't realized I'd already given them my everything.

Humming to himself, Ezra straddles my waist, and then he begins buckling the cuffs around my wrists. Cort tosses Ezra a length of silk rope, while tossing me another evil smirk. Humming louder and louder, Ezra binds my wrists together with the rope, and then attaches them to the headboard. With a sharp tug, I'm repositioned on the bed, arms pulled tight above my head.

My body is throbbing with excitement, lust, and need. My muscles are quivering, readying for whatever Ezra and Cortez are willing to give me. Blood rushes to my sex, and moisture wells between my thighs. My eyes dilate and glaze over. Lungs rapidly rising and falling, I start to pant.

"Why won't you make love to me?" Ezra's face softens as he asks, and it's my undoing– I spill.

"Because I'm in love with you!" I blurt out.

Ezra gasps as he registers what I just said. "I've heard you tell Cortez you love him time and time again, but you've never told me. Not once. Why not?" Ezra stares me down, willing me to disobey. "Tell me!"

"No!" I disobey.

Ezra reaches down and tears my tank top from my body, yanking me off the bed several inches. He rents the fabric from my back with an edge of violence I've never seen him display. With jarring movements, my clothing is shredded with Ezra's bare hands. Scraps of fabric fly through the air, whipping past a stunned Cortez, who's gawking in awe at Ezra's display of lunacy.

Gazing down at me, Ezra will not be denied. "I'll ask again. Why can't you tell me you love me like you do Cortez?"

"NO!" I shout. Drunk or not, I need some semblance of control. Each time I say no, Ezra's excitement elevates. It should make him angry, but it's turning him on.

Ezra slides off of me to stand near the side of the bed. "Pants!" he orders Cortez to yank the last of my clothing from my body. I stammer a string of expletives as I'm divested of my pants with jarring pulls and fumbling fingers, until I am completely naked– exposed.

"I'll ask one more time. Why can you give Cortez the comfort of hearing you say '*I love you*', but not me? Why won't you tell me?"

Stubborn, refusing to give in, I shake my head no.

Ezra and Cortez both grab an ankle and pull until I'm stretched tight from the wrists, with my legs pulled apart, exposing my pussy. Another set of cuffs materialize from Cortez's pocket. He brandishes them with a feral grin. Fingertips tickling me, he cuffs my ankle, and then tosses the other to Ezra, who does the same routine.

Licking my lips again, "Those are some big pockets ya got there. Where the fuck is this shit coming from?"

"Last chance, Kitty Kat. I mean it. Why?" Ezra's voice is rough and husky. It's losing its smoky edge as Master Ez takes control. I still don't answer.

Eyes flicking around our bedroom, I can't see where they plan on attaching my ankles since there isn't a footboard. I stare back in defiance at the pair of Ezes.

I watch as Ezra pulls open his dresser drawer, producing a length of cord. I stare, bewildered, wondering where they will attach it. Ezra snaps the cord, causing me to jump at the sound. Then he hands Cortez a length. They move in tandem with one another as if they've done this thousands of times. They both knot their length to the metal ring on my ankle cuffs.

Ezra looks a silent question at me, raising one eyebrow in challenge. A question I don't answer. An answer I haven't admitted yet. They smirk in synchronization– lips twisting up in exactly the same manner, showing their genetic connection more so than ever. Creepy. I guess not answering is what they ultimately hoped for. Scary thought.

Without communicating, Cortez hands Ezra his length of rope, and then Ezra crawls onto the bed. Slowly he threads the length of cord through the rings on my wrist cuffs, and then pulls, raising my legs.

"Oh, shit! No. No... no... no... no. I'll answer instead." I rock my head back and forth on the bed, flinging the pillows to the side.

They don't respond to my pleas. Agonizingly slow, Ezra just continues to pull the silk rope until my knees bend and my legs spread. He doesn't stop until I'm fully open to them. My ankles are above my chest and my ass is raised off the bed.

"I said I'd answer, dammit!" I shout.

"It's too late for that particular punishment. But I will ask again, or I will get even more creative." Ezra's voice is arrogant, so sure I will obey this time. I almost deny him just for the sake of my pride. But while the tone in his voice should piss me off, it arouses me instead.

Cortez reaches back and grabs a riding crop from the open dresser drawer. My eyes pop at the sight.

"What the fuck?" I sputter. "Since when is that dresser laden with BDSM supplies?"

Cortez hands the riding crop to Ezra, while laughing sinisterly the entire time. "Ah– Kitten, you look so frightened, but we can see how very much you love this game we play." His eyes skim down my body and concentrate on my cunny.

"Shit," slips past my lips. Spread eagle, there is nothing I can do but struggle to cover up the fact that my arousal is dripping down my ass crack.

Ezra waves the riding crop back and forth in his hand, taunting me. "Are you ready to answer me? Or do you want a little pain first?" Ezra looks as if either option is fine by him, while Cortez no longer cares either way. He just wants to play with me like a fly under a magnifying glass–scorching me.

I blurt out the truth before my mind can check in with my heart. "Ezra, I haven't been able to tell you I love you because it hurts too much. Just because I haven't said it doesn't mean you aren't the center of my world. To admit it aloud, is to give you the power to destroy me."

Ezra studies me for a moment, and then he leans down to whisper into my ear, lips brushing the shell. "I love you, Katya. I've cared about you since I met you. But as I truly got to know you, I fell madly in love with the woman I found."

"I'm scared," I finally admit. "I'm scared that one day Cortez will take you away from me."

Cortez doesn't even blink, because he knows he has the power to do just that. A heady sense of power that is his favorite kind of high.

"No fear, Katya," Ezra breathes into my ear. "Cortez doesn't have anything to do with you and me. This is about us– Ezra and Katya. All three of us want it to be Ezra, Katya, and Cortez. If someday that doesn't work out, there will always be an Ezra and Katya."

"Just as there will always be an Ezra and Cortez," I whisper back, heart breaking.

"Neither is mutually exclusive. Just as you loving Cortez doesn't take your love from me." Ezra kisses my temple as he pulls away. "Unconditionally," he says to both Cortez and me.

"I'm in love with you," I admit to Ezra for the first time, and then I turn to Cortez. "I love you, too."

"As I love you, Kitten. I promise I'll do everything I can not to hurt you," is the best assurance Cortez can provide. As we all know, he doesn't have an unconditionally when it comes to anyone but Ezra.

Ezra turns to Cortez. "Ready?"

"We've waited long enough," Cort replies with obvious relief.

They strip in front of me, and my eyes feast. As clothing drops to the floor, my versions of wet dreams come to life manifest. They stand before me, and I am enthralled by the sight. So similar, yet so very unique. Both tall and shaped the same, yet Cortez has a layer of baby fat all over him that is as adorable as it is sexy and Ezra is lean with striated muscles. But the most obvious difference is that Ezra is so pale, he glows in the dark, and Cortez is so tan, he glows in the light. Standing side-by-side, the Ezes are a spectacular sight, and I don't know what I did to deserve them.

My eyes drift down the front of their bodies, loving the way their torsos taper, and the happy trail of luscious hair leading down to their arousals. Genuine fear flows over me at the sight of their size and girth. In all the excitement, I had forgotten what Cortez likes to call exquisite. A flash of memory strikes me. Cortez ramming down my throat, harming me for days to come, and then the sensation of him tearing into my unprepared flesh during my first training session.

"Don't worry. We'll fit you like a glove. It fit before, whether you want to remember it or not. You'll scream– over and over –and it won't be from pain." Cortez stalks to the bed, stride causing his hard cock to swing with his movements as a silent threat of what's to come. "I want to taste Kat first. If that's all right?" he asks Ezra, not me.

"Kitty Kat loved your tongue on her before. Plus, it will relax her," Ezra replies softly as he settles next to me on the bed.

Distracting me, Ezra takes my mouth in a tender kiss, coaxing my lips to open for him. I lose myself in his taste, in the experience. Such a small penetration has the power to render me under his ultimate control. From this moment on, I belong to Ezra.

I swallow Ezra's moans as he expertly licks the roof of my mouth, creating a sensation I've never experienced. Sparks light along my spine, a mix of bliss and anticipation. Unable to take any more, I thrash in my binds. My desire to touch them both drives me to fight my restraints.

A warm, wet line runs up my thigh, stilling me into compliance. Hot saliva turns cool when air passes over it, causing me to shiver. A deep growl vibrates against my skin, demanding all of my attention. The thrilling sensation has me breaking my kiss with Ezra to watch Cortez make his way up my inner thigh. I lift my head as high as I can, almost folding myself in two. Cort watches me from beneath his eyelashes as the tip of his tongue touches me– Soft. Wet. Silky.

Hot.

"Ah!" I gasp out in utter disbelief after fantasizing over this moment for months, yet never thinking it would become my reality.

Drawing me back from my thoughts and away from Cortez, demanding my total attention, Ezra bites my nipple. Teeth sink around the swollen bud. HARD. A scream rips from my throat from the combination of Ezra's teeth piercing my flesh and Cortez's mouth sealing around my clit while his fingers invade me.

My chest rises and falls rapidly, pressing into Ezra's teeth on the inhale, only to yank away with each exhale. The pleasurable pain is excruciating. My pussy muscles contract, drawing Cortez to penetrate me deeper, gripping him so tightly he can barely move his fingers against my lust-soaked flesh. Dark shadows spot my vision as the pressure builds within my body but refuses to ebb. My thighs quiver uncontrollably, and only the restraints keep me from dissolving into the ether.

"Holy hell. You're going to break me." Staring up at the ceiling, I lay panting as Cort climbs my body until he has access to my mouth. He devours me while forcing me to taste myself on his lips and tongue.

Another tongue joins the kiss, and I startle. Lips supple, tongue seeking, Ezra kisses both Cort and me. A three-way kiss. I didn't think it possible, not even in my private fantasies. The sensation of two sets of lips and two tongues against mine is almost criminal. I don't know if I can ever go back to normal after this.

With a single touch, I'm rendered a deviant for life.

"Unhook me," I beg, voice breaking with need and want. "I want to touch you both. God, I need to feel you. Make love to me. Please!" I cry, pleading with Ezra.

"Not yet, Katya." Ezra's husky voice soothes yet stokes the fire hotter. "Cortez wants to fuck you first, then I will unhook you."

"Please…" my voice is a mixture of begging, pleading, and crying.

"It's not what you want, but what you need." Ezra spews his psychobabble bullshit at the worst possible moment, and I snap.

"God! Fuck you, Ezra! I need and fucking want to get fucked right this second! Give me what I fucking need! Damn it!" I scream at Ezra.

Before the 'it' leaves my mouth, a sharp, stinging swat hits my erect nipple. Arching my neck, a scream flows forth from the acute pain.

"Trust me when I say, you needed it." Ezra's voice wavers from anger, riding crop still poised and at the ready in anticipation of another strike. "But more so, you asked for it and earned it."

Cortez gawks at us open-mouthed in astonishment. He lifts his head toward the ceiling and howls a laugh. "OH, MY GOD! That was fabulous. Do it again, Kitten. I've never seen Ezra lose his shit. Do it again!" He laughs more, the humorous sound edged in evil.

As I cool down, I can't believe I just said what I did, but I won't apologize. Blushing profusely, I can't contain the manic giggles from bubbling up.

"You both are too damned naughty for your own good." Ezra glares at Cortez as he tries not to laugh. "Don't encourage

Katya's bad behavior. I'll punish your sweet ass, too. Cort, I mean it!"

"In Kitten's defense, that was rather a pretentious thing to say during the height of arousal. Even for you, Dr. Zeitler," Cortez deadpans. "Now my tongue's hard work has gone to waste."

"Fine. Point taken. I will remove a few swats off of Katya's punishment." I freeze at the word punishment. "During a scene–and we can agree it's a scene, seeing as how I'm holding a riding crop and Kat is trussed up –I cannot allow her disrespect to stand."

"I'm sorry," I whimper, meaning it only because he called me on it, not because I hadn't meant what I said.

"You're only sorry because it earned you a punishment." Ezra doesn't buy my shit, and then he orders, "Count for me, Kitty Kat. Five swats instead of ten."

Cortez's face splits into an evil grin. He reaches over and tweaks my nipples. Hard. First one, and then the other. I squeak out in pain while he rasps, "Kitten's all ready for you now."

A rigid crack to my nipple has me writhing in my restraints. A profanity-filled growl spills from my mouth along with the number one. They ignore my behavior as Ezra hands Cortez the riding crop. I anticipate a hit to my other nipple. Shocked, a bloodcurdling scream is torn from between my clenched teeth when a fiery swat hits my exposed cunt, directly on my swollen clit. Cortez didn't pull his hit, either. I defiantly bitch the number two at him while my pussy bursts into flame.

"Sorry," Cort mutters, except he doesn't sound sorry at all. If anything, he looks very pleased with himself. He bends at the waist and laves a soothing lick across my tortured flesh.

Gasping, the most intense orgasm of my life flashes through my body in less than a second. I combust. I'm consumed. When I come back to myself, I lay confused.

"I think we can forget about the other three swats, Ezra. Kitten's ready for me. Right. Now," Cortez stresses, voice jittery with need.

"No, Katya gets every single one of the hits, just as she deserves. She needs to learn from it. She bellowed '*fuck you*' at me for Christ's sake." Ezra's voice is calm and calculated, devoid of any sympathy. I'd be furious if it wasn't for the fact that the second month of my tenure in Dominion, New York, was consistent with this type of treatment. If anything, it's a comfort to know Ezra is predictable. I'll always know I have to balance the consequences with every action I make.

"Hurry the hell up, assfuck! I can't wait much longer. Do you want me to twelve-year-old it and spurt on Kitten's stomach from excitement? You're killing me!"

"If either one of you says the word *fuck* in context with *me* again, I'm going to fuck you both up," Ezra seethes. "Do I make myself clear? One more swat for Katya, and two for you, Cort. We're splitting the difference." Pointing the riding crop at Cort's chest, "Don't tempt me. I'm barely holding onto myself, and Master Ez won't even feel a tinge of sympathy as he ruins any hope of a peaceful future between us all."

I look back and forth between the pair in confusion. Is Ezra really going to punish Cortez for swearing? This is a new development, since Ezra has never educated Cortez in anything.

Ezra grabs the other man by the back of the neck and inhales his lips. The force as the two meet is jarring violence– explosive. Elegant power meeting devious masculinity. Not only can you see their chemistry, you can scent it in the air.

Before I can blink, two swats ring out. They hit Cortez across the chest. *Snap… Snap…* Their lips never part as Ezra eats Cort's grunt of pain. I stare transfixed at the welts welling up on Cortez's perfect chest, directly over each of his pink nipples.

I scream before I even sense the movement. A lash connects with my thigh. I look down, shocked. I never saw the riding crop come or go. The only proof is the red mark marring my leg. Wide-eyed, I look up at the pair. Ezra looks satisfied. I follow down his arm and notice he isn't holding the crop.

Eyes flicking, I turn to Cortez. He looks smug with the crop resting in his hand. Somehow Cortez managed to swat me, and I didn't notice it. He gives me a wicked smirk as he tosses the crop over his shoulder. I watch in awe as it lands on the dresser– that took some serious skill.

"All's forgiven now," flows smoothly, soothing, as Ezra sits on the bed next to me. He hooks his hands in the crook of my knees, supporting my weight. My legs were starting to ache and tingle, falling asleep from their upright position.

Cortez stalks me on the bed. Bouncing as he moves, slapping at his belly, his cock is engorged and scary as fuck… and I ache to feel him impaling me, thrusting in me. The less foreplay, the better.

"I won't hurt you. I promise, Kitten," Cortez vows as he kneels between my upraised thighs. He reaches forward to caress my cheek tenderly with a single fingertip. He then looks to Ezra, a very soft expression on his face, and mouths *thank you.*

Something passes between my lovers, something pivotal. Ezra reaches over and takes hold of the exquisiteness in his fist. I gape at the sight of one man touching the other sexually. Ezra's pale, elegant hand is wrapped around Cort's darkly engorged cock, and the juxtaposition is breathtaking. It's shocking, thrilling, and strangely arousing. I've felt them touch, but seeing is believing.

"Don't come yet," Ezra orders, voice stiff with tumultuous emotions.

Cortez cocks his head to the side, studying his partner. He then scrunches up his face in confusion, but nods his head yes as if he understands. I don't understand, either.

Eyes bulging from shock, I watch as Ezra brings Cortez's flesh to my body. I want to ask why, but I don't want to ruin the moment. The look of deep concentration on both their faces screams there is an intense meaning to this– almost ritualistic.

It all confuses the shit out of me.

Twin gunmetal orbs hold my gaze. Lost unto them, my breath rushes out as Ezra fills me with Cortez's flesh. My channel stretches tight as Cort presses into me, almost to the point of pain. Exquisite pain. Cortez takes control of both of our bodies as Ezra settles at my side, still supporting my weight. He curls his body around mine– holding me, comforting me.

Ezra isn't inside me– penetrating me –and Cortez isn't inside Ezra. Yet the man who is doing no more than supporting us both, seems to be the conduit connecting all three of us. While I may love the man taking dominion over my body, and he may love me back, we both are in love with Ezra, and he's in love with us in return. It's a delicate balance; one that petrifies me over how life-destroying the fall will be when I tumble over the edge.

Ezra presses a kiss against my temple, murmuring his pleasure over how well Cort and I compromise for his ultimate happiness. He reaches out to trail a fingertip down Cortez's chest, lingering on the welts adorning each nipple. A sound of pure contentment bubbles up to mingle with our harsh breathing.

Cortez starts rolling his hips into me, and I whimper in delicious ecstasy. I'm relieved we aren't repeating history–ancient and recent history. My are eyes closed, with my body arcing up to meet Cort's, when fingertips begin fluttering against my wrists. My eyelids rise, revealing Ezra unhooking my restraints– giving me permission to feel what I feel.

Ezra unleashes the real Katya Waters.

"Better?" Ezra asks as I stretch my limbs to their maximum, leaving the silk rope to fall to the wayside.

"Yes, thank you," I murmur softly, thanking him for so much more than removing my cuffs. Ezra looks confused for a moment, and then a beatific smile spreads across his face.

Basking in the glow of Ezra's happiness, I wrap myself around Cortez. My arms curl around Cort's back, and my legs hook around his hips, drawing us closer together. He snuggles in deep, squeezing me tightly as if he can't believe I crave his affection as much as the man leisurely trailing fingertips across our flesh.

Wrapped in each other's arms, Cort and I find a rhythm. After a few long moments, my body stretches to accommodate his length and girth, until he's able to stroke smoothly, our combined arousal paving the way. From one thrust to the next, Cortez sinks into me until I take all of him, and the knowledge, more so than the intense sensation, takes my breath away.

"Kitten, you can fear something forever, but it doesn't change the outcome. Fuck us, make love to us as a pair or individually… it doesn't change a thing. We're in love with you and you with us. Avoiding it is only going to make us all miserable. I would know, and I don't wish you to live that type of life. As for the future, I can't make any promises other than I will do everything in my power not to hurt you."

Cort rests his palms against my cheeks, stilling me so his penetrative gaze can capture my undivided attention. Connecting us with our minds via our eyes, our souls via the man peppering kisses to our shoulders, our hearts through his honeyed-tongue words, Cort rocks his hips against me, surging forward to connect us bodily at last.

A deep moan rolls up my throat, spilling from my parted lips, as my body ignites with sparks of ecstasy. I thought Cortez had fully seated his cock within me before. I was wrong. He rotates his cock inside of me, making room to smoothly thrust his well-endowed sex. I'm rendered speechless by the most incredible sensation I've ever experienced. Cortez Abernathy may be a master of the written word, but his true passion lies in the sensual arts.

"It's too late, Kitten. I love you, and it's never going to change," Cort breathes against my lips...

... And then he kisses me tenderly, lips soft yet insistent. As I sink into the sensation of Cort's mouth ruling mine and his cock rolling inside my pussy, Ezra leans over us and joins our kiss. He engulfs us both, completing the connection. My body tightens, fills to bursting, and I'm overcome with the insane need to weep from my eyes and my cunt.

In an instant, Cortez's weight disappears and Ezra's replaces it. I start to panic, fearing the emotions I was displaying displeased one or the both of them. Shaking, a distraught cry catches in my throat.

"Shh... don't be afraid, Katya." Ezra fills my body fully in one deep stroke, never breaking eye contact. I start to cry and I don't know why. Yes, I do. I feel like I've had a glimpse of heaven and I'm waiting for them to snatch it away by realizing I'm not worthy– by realizing they don't love me as they love each other.

With a jarring thrust, yanking a grunt from low in my belly, "Tell me what you want," Ezra commands.

I simply admit, "You," as my body adjusts to his relentless invasion.

"Tell me in detail. Use your words, Katya. I want to give it to you– all of it," Ezra vows reverently. He thrusts into my body, joining us as one, and I hold him tight, never wanting to let him go.

"I want you. I want Cort. I want you both to be proud of the fact that I'm with you. I don't want to be your dirty little secret. I have to be your equal partner in life, while I need you to master me in the dungeon and make love to me in the bedroom. I want you to punish me when I break the rules and reward me when I please you, and I want that same honor in return. I want the life we've been building together– not just you and me, but all of us. I want you and Cort to be together *with* me. I want to kill Adelaide with my bare hands, and every other female who came before and after me, just because they had the pleasure of your touch, love, affection, and attention."

I look to Cortez for strength to say the last part, and he smiles reassuringly at me and nods his head yes. Courage shorn up, I finally admit my true desires– the ones I didn't even dare to voice inside my own private thoughts, as I feared the simple knowledge of them would destroy me, knowing they might never come to fruition.

"I want to be your wife," I breathe out. Gray eyes widening in shock, Ezra gazes down at me for a moment, as if unsure of what I just spoke. "I want to give my daughter a legitimate family, with little minions for her to boss around. I want to prove to you and Cort that Celeste and Raymond Hunter's beautiful traits will be reflected in our children, and not any of the bad. I want you to see hope in their eyes, knowing you are not tainted when what you created with Cort and me is so pure."

Cort's breath hitches near my ear, as if on the verge of tears. As if he had his own fantasies of a life he wished to lead, and never thought he could have it. The same fantasies he spewed while slamming into me with Dexter and Heidi as witnesses. But that union was warped, and that is why still to this day I don't remember it in great detail.

"I love you and want us to be a family– all of us. I would be proud– never ashamed –of who and what we are and how we became to be. Because when we're together, we're more than if we were apart." I swallow audibly and wait for Ezra's rejection.

"It's about time you got with the program, Mrs. Zeitler." Ezra stares down at me while reaching over to clasp Cort around the nape of his neck, drawing him down to rest his cheek against my breasts.

"I feared I would have to tie your ass down and pay a Rabbi, a Priest, anyone I could coerce to officiate a marriage that was against your will. Katya, you were always meant to be my wife."

Ezra leans forward, pressing his chest against the side of Cort's face, and then he flutters the gentlest of kisses to my lips. While still reeling from what he said, he pulls back to give Cort the exact same kiss.

"I've known only a few things to be an absolute truth. If I ever married a man, it sure as fuck was going to be you," Ezra directs to Cortez, who is dampening my breasts with his tears. "Even while I was floundering, scared shitless I'd broken the only promise I'd ever made to you, Katya, I knew with absolute certainty that I would never marry Ade. I was waiting for you, and I would have waited a lifetime."

Eyes stinging, heart throbbing, I start to cry. I'm petrified because I know Ezra meant every word he said, and I don't know if I can survive him.

Cortez pulls away, and I move to protest, but Ezra silences me by rolling onto his back with me riding his body, our sexes still connected. Wiggling about on the bed until he's comfortable, Ezra settles me against his chest with me straddling his hips. Eyes shining with unshed tears, Ezra's smile manages to be bittersweet yet nefarious.

"I have a reward for all of us. Just relax, and I promise it will be fantastic. I worry that you may never want anything else, though." Ezra releases a private laugh while his eyes twinkle with mischievousness. "Just hold still and relax."

"What are you up to, Ezra?" Cortez asks in suspicion, then his eyes widen in fright. "Oh! That would hurt Kitten's sweet ass. She's never done that before and I'm too big. We've always done it the other way around, ass-man."

I almost ask 'with who?' but Ezra's husky, lust-filled voice makes me forget the thought before it's voiced. "Not there," Ezra rasps from a voice rough with need.

"Ah!" Cort exclaims in surprise. "Are you sure you want to share Katya like that with me? I mean, I was worried about hurting her pussy with only my dick."

"I want us to make love to each other in the only way we can– the three of us together as one. Let's share each other. Please," Ezra pleads.

"I want that, too," Cort whispers. "I just don't want to hurt Kat's puss, or she may never let me inside her again."

"Trust me," Ezra stresses, and then he croons to me while rubbing the back of my neck to calm me. I'm shaking, quivering from a rush of fear and excitement. Not even in my wildest fantasies had this come to life. "Just relax and breathe."

I gasp when Cortez slides his cock along the crease of my ass, and then farther down to where Ezra impales me. Frozen in utter disbelief, I fear my muscles will tighten up or I'll jerk involuntarily. Cort nudges me with his cockhead, stretching me slowly to accommodate both of them inside my pussy. It's painful, just this side of tearing my flesh. Every few seconds, Cort waits until I get accustomed, and then pushes farther inside me, his cock sliding smoothly against Ezra's.

I lie still against Ezra's chest as both of them fill me in the same delicate spot. I don't dare breathe in fear of hurting myself. Slowly I loosen until Cortez can move freely inside of me along Ezra's length.

"My God!" Ezra prays to the ceiling, voice wavering. With a deep groan, his back bows off the bed with his abs going taut against my soft curves. "It's better than I ever thought possible. The way you feel rubbing against me," Ezra groans to Cort. "I'm at a loss for words."

"I love you both," Cortez says from above my back. Then he rolls us all onto our sides until I'm sandwiched between them in exactly the same way we sleep every night. The only difference is that we are all connected on a primal level.

They move slowly inside me and in tandem against each other. Ezra's hand reaches out to pulls Cortez down for a kiss—both mouths seek mine, lips eagerly vying for my attention. We share with each other, taking turns leading and following, giving and receiving, while waiting our turn or demanding attention.

We suspend in time: I don't know if it's minutes, hours, or a few short seconds. We maintain our kiss as our bodies make love to one another. We share our adoration, using our actions instead of our words, as it was meant to be.

Six hands rove over our flesh, never stopping to ascertain whose skin is beneath our touch, to the point we even pleasure ourselves. Lips, tongues, and teeth seek the flavor they crave, leaving me with light bruises and wounds which will take months to heal. Hands grip my breasts, fingertips both rough and punishing and playful and teasing. The louder we groan, the harder the lengths thrusting relentlessly inside of me become.

The connection is visceral, on a level most can never reach. It's not only sexual. I feel the Ezes permeate my entire being: mind, body, heart, and soul. We move toward our climax, craving it as much as avoiding it. When we reach release, it will be a dark loss. But it will also bring hope that we will do this again and again and again.

"Ezra," rolls from Cort's lips, the sound thick with need yet strained with restraint. "I have to stop if you don't want me to go inside of Katya."

"No, don't. Join us," Ezra pants. His fingertips slip from my breasts to seek out Cort's ass, not allowing him to pull away.

"That's not your gift to give, Ezra," Cort chastises through gritted teeth, still fighting the urge to seek release. "Kitten's not on birth control, and we all know you track her cycle. You've been like a Tom Cat for the past twenty-four hours, trying to figure out how to get inside Katya."

"It *is* my gift to give– Katya is mine. You are mine. I want you to join us, Cort. It wouldn't be a consequence; it would be a gift given freely from those who love you. If you don't believe me, ask Katya yourself."

"I don't think Kat is in the right state of mind to understand what you're offering," Cortez mutters incredulously, shock twisting his voice.

"Don't stop. Please," I moan, pleading. "I get it, and now isn't the time to have that very important conversation. If anything happens, it would be a miracle."

"No, not a miracle." Cort's whisper tickles along my spine. "It would be Ezra's compulsive need to plot out when you're ovulating. He's relentless in what he wants, Kitten. Never forget that. It wouldn't be a coincidence, or a miracle. I would be a well-thought-out plan of attack."

"Cortez, are you truly saying you would pass up this chance? I'm not saying this won't happen again, but this is the closest chance you'll ever get to make a child with Ezra. There are never any guarantees, and we both know what you said to me the last time we fucked," I snarl as his words from the past skate across my thoughts. "For the love of all that is holy, just orgasm. Because I'm dying to get off with two cocks pumping away in me. I'm a sick fuck, and I'd appreciate it if you'd finish feeding my sickness."

A gasp is torn from my throat when I'm nearly split in half. Cortez finally pushes all of the exquisiteness inside of me in one forceful thrust, all but tearing my cunt. My nails dig into and bleed the nearest body part they can reach– Cort's forearms.

Ezra takes Cort's howl of pleasurable agony as agreement, and his movements become jerky– rough with need. Ezra's hips flex and release, his neck arches, hitching his head backward into the pillows, and his eyes and lips are drawn tight with restraint.

Readying for the end, Cort retracts my nails from his skin. Then he grips my biceps, arching my back against his chest. The position puts that much more of his cock inside my stretched pussy.

Ezra clings closer to me, placing his neck within reach of my teeth. He shifts his head to the side, drawing his neck in a long line. I know what Ezra wishes me to do. Striking out, I bite fiercely– marking Ezra as mine. The sensation of my teeth sinking into Ezra's flesh puts me on the precipice of release. I bite hard enough to leave a scar– a mate to the one I gave Ezra on our violent, first time when our daughter was created. One lace of teeth marks for the past and one for the future– marked eternally.

The three of us make a symphony of animal noises as we reach the brink. Stillness fills the room, a collective breath before the storm, as what we are about to do is irreversible. Our bodies swell with the pressure of our pleasure. My body clenches once around the pair of them, and it's our undoing.

Unleashed. We explode, implode, and shatter. A sense of balance– rightness –overpowers me as they both pour fiery hot, filling me up with their life-giving essence. We scream our release as one.

A fleeting thought floats up to the unknown energy that we all are created from– whatever name you call it. God. Goddess. Lord. My prayer flows unbidden from my mind.

*Please give us hope by giving us life.*

We reshape, reform, and evolve into something unrecognizable, leaving ourselves behind by joining as one. The enormity of the emotions fills me until I think my spirit will burst from the pressure. Instead, it expands to encompass both Ezra and Cortez, and then our entire fucked up family.

"Those who don't understand, they may think this was wrong. Some would call us evil for the three of us joining in such a manner, especially with Cortez and I having shared blood. But if this isn't love personified, then they don't know what love is." Ezra breathes his last words against my cheek, against Cortez's parted lips.

Warm wetness drops onto my cheek, not knowing whose eyes the tears fall from, as we cease to be individuals. The three of us lay joined and weep.

# Chapter Thirty-Four

"I can't believe how crazy you guys are being over the wedding preparations. I think you're more into it than Kayla, and that's saying something." I mutter out the side of my mouth to Cortez as we enter *Naughty Baby Cake's Bakery*.

I was going to make the food for the party, but the guys kept adding more guests, and then more guests wanted to bring a plus-one, and then I gave up. No way did I have the time to make food for almost fifty people. They changed the party from a wedding planning session to a full-fledged engagement party.

"You should have seen my wedding. None of us were allowed to plan anything. It was totally up to Pearl, Divina, and Diane. I didn't care at the time since I was so young, and it wasn't like it was a true marriage or anything. Imagine how we will be when Ava gets hitched." Cort laughs, and it takes on an evil note. "Ava's a little bridesmaid monster right now. I can't imagine the bridezilla she will turn into."

"You're so bad." I grab the front of Cortez's shirt, and I pull his mouth down to mine. I nip his bottom lip playfully. "You're really cute, though."

Cort wraps his arm around my waist and lifts me while walking forward. I meet the wall of the bakery and struggle in protest. "Someone will see us. Knock it off, Cort." I wiggle to get down, and he laughs at me. I look all around, trying to see if anyone notices.

"You started it." Cort nips my lip in return. "It sucked that we had to get up early this morning. I would have loved to sleep in with my two favorite people." He gives me a lingering kiss that's so sweet it melts me on the spot. We break apart slowly, and then lean our foreheads against one another. My eyes flick up to meet Cort's stormy gaze, and a smile stretches across my face.

"I love you, Kitten. I love you so much that sometimes it hurts. I didn't think it was possible to feel this way about two people. This wedding stuff really gets you thinking about how you wish it could be. How freeing it would be to have the world accept that you, Ezra, and I love each other. It's terrifying and thrilling. But at the same time, it makes me feel alive."

I blush and look away shyly. The raw expression on Cort's face brings tears to sting my eyes. I'm overcome with emotions that I didn't think were possible to feel for more than one person. I burrow my face into his neck, moving the fabric of his shirt to the side. I feather a kiss to the dip of his throat.

"I love you, Cort. I really do," I breathe against his skin, and his body shudders from the contact.

"Mr. Abernathy? Is that you?" An excited voice breaks into our emotionally charged moment. I sigh as Cort releases his hold on my waist. I look up to see several women with huge smiles on their faces.

"I recognize you from the back cover of your books. I'm a huge fan," says a woman in her early forties. She is surrounded by a couple of kids and another woman her age. The kids look like they couldn't care less, but the women are bright-eyed and bushy-tailed.

"It's a pleasure to meet you, ladies." Cortez's smooth voice melts like butter, and it's just as fattening. I watch the kids look at Cortez in awe as their mothers liquefy just because Cort turned on his inborn charm.

I roll my eyes while moving to the side, knowing this might take a while. "I'll leave you to your fans. I'm going to go check on our confections." I step away from the crowd that is slowly filling around Cort.

Cort reaches out and tips my chin up with a fingertip, trying to gauge my expression. He's testing to see if I'm jealous. I just roll my eyes at him again and stifle a laugh. He gives me a genuine smile, one that is only reserved for our nearest and dearest, and then I watch as it changes to a devastating smirk as he returns his attention back to his fans.

I peek over my shoulder as I wait in line. Cort is in the zone, answering questions about his characters. I smile, thinking of how I'm going to have to leave him here after I get the cupcakes and pastries. No way is the illustrious Cortez Abernathy fan club going to leave him be without having to resort to rudeness.

I feel a tap on my shoulder, and I turn to see who wishes to speak with me. My world drops from beneath my feet. I am suspended in time. I slowly suck in a sharp breath when I realize

I had stopped breathing. I count in my head as I try not to hyperventilate.

*You are safe, Katya. You are safe.*

I repeat the mantra over and over again in my mind. I'm not alone. He can do nothing to me with thirty people in the shop. Too bad at least twenty of those people are entertaining my safety net.

"Wwwhat?" drags up my throat in a croak. I stare wide-eyed at the monster, and he gazes back at me with the same patient expression Ezra often wears, while painting on the same reassuring smile Cortez uses as a shield.

"I'm not going to hurt you, Katya," Ray assures me, gesturing with his hands to show he's unarmed. "I just need to speak with you for a moment. We don't even have to move. We will stay right here in front of everyone. It would probably be best if you didn't draw Cortez's attention, though. He may go crazy on us. I promise you I will not harm you. Please, this is important. Very important that you hear me out."

I study Ray's face, and I notice that the crazy look is no longer present in his eyes. He looks calm and worried. Worried about what?

"Talk fast, Ray. I hate being in your presence. For fuck's sake, you tried to kill me. I remember everything as if it happened two seconds ago. So get talking."

"In all honesty, I wanted to kill you, Katya. I tried as I had the others, but something kept stopping me. Somehow I must have sensed that you would continue on my family line. I will forever be thankful that I didn't go through with ending your life, as our precious Ava wouldn't exist today."

"Please don't speak of my child," I warn, my mother bear baring her teeth deep in my psyche.

"My apologies." Ray presses his fist to his chest, bowing his head slightly in a gesture exactly like the one his son uses on a daily basis to appear genuine. "I wasn't ready to be released. I thought that I would live out my sentence in prison, and maybe die on the inside. I knew that you guys would always show up at my hearings, and I would never be let out. I'm not safe out here, Katya. I'm not safe." I freeze up at the terror in his voice. I flinch back away from him. "No, no... no... no. Not you. I'd never harm you again," he vows with his hands in front of him, beseeching me to listen.

"Explain," I breathe, using all of my mental fortitude to keep my feet frozen in place, lest I run out of this bakery and never look back, leaving Cortez to fend for himself. My heart is beating in my ears, and my lungs burn from the force I'm exacting to keep myself from hyperventilating.

"I won't hurt you for the same reason that I never touched Diane again. You gave me family. I couldn't touch Ezra, Cortez, or Ava, either. Whatever the fuck is wrong with me, it makes it impossible to hurt you ever again."

"There are other ways to hurt someone than sexually, Ray," I mutter in exasperation.

"I know that. I got scared when my family didn't show up to my parole hearing. It's double-sided for me. It's a comfort to see you all thriving, but it also kept me safe in confinement. When no one showed, I thought something happened to all of you. I was terrified on so many levels. I'm not safe out here in the open."

Ray's eyes flick back and forth, either searching for imaginary threats or very real dangers. "I've been watching you since my release, trying to figure out what's going on. It occupies me from other pursuits that are throbbing like a toothache."

"So you stalk us– your family –so that you don't rape and murder people? That's sick, Ray, even for you."

"Don't you think I know that? I want to seek vengeance on those who ruined my life when I wasn't much older than Ava. That's all. It became a pathology for me, and now I can't control it. This is why I didn't want out of prison. I'm not safe to walk the streets. I even tried to tell this to the parole board. I knew something was amiss when no one showed up. But reality hit when I begged that I wasn't safe, my psychiatrist pleaded that I wasn't sane, and they still let me out. Someone wanted me out, hoping I'd hurt you or hurt the populous."

The terror in Ray's eyes frightens me. He knows he shouldn't be here because he's unhinged. I don't know what scares me more, the fact that he recognizes this, or the fact that I'm actually sympathizing and believing my rapist.

I'm not the same young woman I was twelve years ago. I have no issue questioning my attacker now. "Have you been sending me threat letters? You already admitted to following me. Did you chase me from the park, Ray? I was scared half to death."

"What notes?" Ray accuses, looking exactly like Cortez does when I offend him accidentally. "I haven't sent you any notes. Why would I do that? I'm trying to talk to my son, not have him murder me."

Eyes narrowed, I mull over Ray's admission. If he isn't sending me notes, who is? "What about the park?"

"I was there in the park when you were, but I wasn't anywhere near you. I saw a hooded person lean in and whisper in your ear, and then you freaked. I followed that person instead of you. I followed them following you. I then watched them enter Ezra's building directly after you. I can't get into Edge, but they can. This is serious, Katya."

I don't remember Ray being an actor. The sincerity and fright rolling off him should be impossible to duplicate. Either Ray is telling the truth, or he is in need of an Academy Award.

"I'm sorry if I frightened your daughter yesterday. I just wanted to give you a message and see my granddaughter for the first and last time. My conscience needed to see with my very own two eyes that you were okay after what I did to you. I want my family to be happy, and I see that you are. I'm blessed that I have a son, who has blessed me with grandchildren, even if all of us were made in a painful way. I mean none of you any harm. I will do everything I can to solve who was behind my release and who frightened you in the park."

I try for words, but none come. I've spent more than a decade ignoring my past, never truly coming to terms with it, only to remember that the man who I was falling in love with was my original rapist, and his father was my actual rapist. I still haven't dealt with it, and I doubt I ever will. But having Ray before me, where he's trying to be sincere versus terrifying, the moment is surreal. I think it would be easier to digest if Ray was acting as a monster, cruel and calculating.

"I'm sorry." Ray reaches out like he wishes to touch me—connect with me –but he lets his hand hang in the air. "I will leave a message specifically for you with your doorman if I find out who was behind my release, who followed you, and whoever is sending you threatening notes. I take care of my family, even if it's unconventional. Once this is taken care of, I'll leave the area. I can promise that at least."

Before I could respond, Ray abruptly turns and leaves the bakery. His large stride eats up the space between me and the door. He's gone in an instant, as if he never was even here. Only the conversation we had is proof that I'm not hallucinating.

I think calm thoughts as I wait my turn in line, while fisting my palms to keep the shakes at bay. I can hear Cort's laughter filling the air and his smooth voice answering his fans. The familiar, happy sound re-grounds me to the here and now. I'm not in the past, lying on the hard-packed ground with a rock shearing my back as a psycho ruts on me while beating me to death. I'm in a bakery, awaiting my large order of sweets. We're celebrating the start of a new life for Aaron and Kayla, and the past has to stay firmly in the past.

# Chapter Thirty-Five

"Ms. Waters? Your order has been packaged." I snap out of my reverie when the lady behind the counter calls out to me.

"Thanks," I say as I take a step forward. I hand the cashier my debit card as an arm snakes around my waist, causing me to flinch. I recognize Cort's familiar, possessive touch, and breathe a sigh of relief.

"What's the matter, Kitten?" Cort whispers in my ear. He pulls my back against his chest, and I slowly relax into the comforting warmth of his secure touch.

"I'll tell you in a minute. Let's get our order and get the hell out of here." I try not to shake. I tense my entire body, but it betrays me. Involuntarily, I shake as the shock of seeing Ray Hunter wears off.

"Are you all right?" Cort rubs his hands up and down my arms, trying to warm me with friction. It helps to relax my tense muscles, but does nothing for the chill. It's not the kind of cold that heat fixes. It is a soul-deep chill that only time can warm.

"Here ya go, guys. Tell Kayla I said congrats," the pretty girl behind the counter says as she hands us our sweets.

"Thanks, I will do that." I try to sound pleasant and manage to cover my fear. The adrenaline is evaporating from my system, leaving me exhausted, and the day has only just begun.

"What happened?" Cort asks as we walk down the block toward the Edge building.

"Ray gave me his message. The one he wanted to talk to Ezra about." I drop the bombshell with an emotionless voice. My even tone completely belies the stew of emotions brewing in my mind.

I walk listlessly down the street, while trying to carry a box of bite-sized cheesecakes and creampuffs, when every muscle in my body is betraying me. My hands are shaking compulsively, while my arms are limp like noodles. I can barely put one foot in front of the other. Only my destination keeps me going, knowing I will soon be safe and sound, with everyone under one roof.

I contemplate eating a few cheesecake bites to get my strength back. Sugar would help fight the shock; it always does. I eye Aaron's request of devil's food cupcakes that Cort is toting. Yeah, they would do a better job of chasing the shock away. I lick my lips in anticipation of chocolaty gooeyness.

"What? You saw Ray? Why didn't you call for me?" Anyone who didn't know Cortez any better than I do, would think he was angry. But I do know him better. Cortez is scared shitless.

"I could still see you. I was in a crowded bakery, and Ray couldn't hurt me. I was fine. Maybe a little scared, but physically fine."

I repeat the entire conversation I had with Ray. Verbatim.

"Do you think Ray was telling the truth?" Cort asks, hope strongly lacing his voice.

"I know you've been championing for your uncle because none of this makes any sense, and now I agree with you. Strangely enough, I believe Ray. He has no reason to lie. If he wanted to fuck with us, he would have. So why bother doing it this way?"

"That's what I've been trying to tell Ezra. Plus, the first note came while Ray was still in prison, so that removed him from the suspect list in my book. Yes, he could have an accomplice, but that's not how Ray functions. He didn't even trust his partner to watch his back, but he trusted the guy to clean up his messes. The man does not play well with others."

"Ray's eyes don't hold that crazy look anymore, either. Like his therapy and medications are working well in conjunction. Let's not tell Ezra until tomorrow morning, okay? I don't want to worry him, because he needs to be calm in order to deal with all the people invading our apartment."

"The people Ezra invited," Cort stresses.

"Exactly," I sputter, exasperated. "I won't lie, I'm scared shitless. If Ray is telling the truth, then someone at the party could be the stalker. Ray said they have access to the Edge building. But we have to find someone who has access to Edge and Shadow Haven."

We walk silently for a block, while I try to formulate a question that has been plaguing my mind. I fear history repeating itself again and again, with me left to clean up the shit I didn't splatter. Seeing Ray brought out how important it is to clear up these issues, because life is too short to dwell in the past. But I cannot accurately predict the future without a clear understanding of ancient, angst-ridden history.

"Cort, I need to ask you something, and I know that it's the total opposite of what we were just talking about. You don't have to answer if it's too uncomfortable."

"You can ask me anything, Kitten." Cort turns to look at me, and then rolls his eyes dramatically. "Anything to take Ray off my mind. Please."

"Okay, just don't get mad." My voice cracks with worry. "What was the catalyst for your separation from Ezra? I don't mean our nightmarish past. You keep saying he betrayed you, so in turn you ran off and sucked Master's cock, whoever the fuck that may be. But you've never explained, and I think I need to know."

"Of course you couldn't pick something fun to talk about, like the conflict in the Middle East, or world hunger. Not my Kat; she has to go in for the kill." Cort sighs, sounding just Ezra.

"Is it because you won't admit you like guys?" I don't bother being hesitant. You don't fall in love with a guy, while servicing another, and then claim to be straight. No way. No how.

"I don't like guys," Cortez mutters flatly, but we both can hear the denial thick in his voice. Cortez looks like he wishes he could drag his fingers through his hair out of sheer frustration, but the bakery box fills his hands. "Shit," he hisses underneath his breath.

Cortez is silent for a moment, and I just walk with him. I won't force this conversation if it's that difficult. I'll see if Ezra can make sense of it for me later during our evening chess match. He won't tell me Cort's part in anything, but he will reassure me that history won't repeat itself.

"I have no issue with touching Ezra at all. I want to very badly. It's like breathing. We were very close before Ray came into our lives. Close in the way that Ezra didn't think anyone else existed outside of me. It scared me, so I pulled away and started dating girls because they weren't Ez. Then Ray came along, and I learned the truth of who I was and how Ezra and I were related, and then he made me do horrific acts on strangers who died shortly thereafter. Aaron– I will regret for the rest of my life. I'm scared that certain acts will bring it all back in a rush, so I refuse to do them."

"I understand that more than anyone else will ever know," I say to comfort Cort, knowing it will only hurt him more because I'm one of those victims– only Ezra, Cortez, Aaron, and I survived Ray Hunter.

"The nightmares aren't why I have a difficult time letting Ezra in. He's lied to my face and betrayed me. Repeatedly. I had a girlfriend, someone I really cared about. I shared her with Ezra, not like how it is with you and us. She and I were a couple, and I shared her with Ezra because I wanted him to experience everything I did. I wanted to know whether or not he was truly gay. Then I found out Ezra was with her behind my back, just the two of them. But I understood that because they had been together before, and they were friends, too. Then Ezra cheated on me with another man."

"Christ," I breathe, heart breaking. Here I'd worried about Cort's history ruining us, and I was so stuck on Ezra's four women, that I never thought of any guys from Ezra's past coming back to haunt us.

"I can't get over it. I'm not a girl, and I can never be a girl. So Ezra being with her made sense, because she could give him things I couldn't. But a man… I'm a man, and I can't give Ezra what he needs from a man, either. After all these years, I don't even blame Ezra anymore. I blame myself. But seeing the man who fucked Ezra, both in remembrance and in actuality, hammers home how I can never fulfill my own partner's needs."

I just stare ahead in utter disbelief. Ezra is one of the most honorable people I've ever known. I just can't believe it. He may stalk, but he feels like he's doing these domineering things for our best interests. I just can't see Ezra cheating on Cortez. I can see the faith and adoration gazing out of their eyes when they look at one another. You can almost see their connection, as if the thread is a tangible thing.

"I didn't talk to Ezra for almost a year. It was the first year of my marriage to Divina, and we were playing pretend, making everyone believe we were the happy couple. When in actuality, I was sobbing in dark rooms, writing horror stories, and contemplating death, while Divina was doing her damnedest to cheer me up. I felt like Ezra sold me to his cousin– got rid of me because I couldn't touch him –and it killed me.

"It happened around the time Ezra started dating that cunt. I've always associated Adelaide with his cheating. It has nothing to do with her, but it was around that same time. So when I see Adelaide, I remember the lies, the betrayals, and the agony. Ezra tore my heart out, and he never showed a bit of remorse."

"I can see that. When I see Adelaide, I want to tear her limb-from-limb. Maybe someday we can do that together." I laugh to lighten the moment. "Who?"

"Ezra was going through a tough time and I wasn't there for him. I was wrapped up in my wedding, and then my marriage. I was trying to start a real life with Divina because I'd been pushed away. I avoided Ezra since I had a hard time not touching him when I was around him. I didn't want to admit my true feelings for him– they hurt too much. How I wanted him yet was unable to do anything about it because of night terrors.

"During that year, Ezra's life changed, and he betrayed me thrice. I could never get over it because I blamed myself. Ezra's lies and betrayals were turning my stomach. When I'd look at him, he'd lie to my face. It didn't matter if it was about his mental disorder, or because everything he did was to protect someone, I was his partner, and he shut me out."

"What did Ezra do?" My voice cracks, because if Ezra can cheat on Cort, how easy would it be for him to cheat on me?

"There was my girlfriend, the man, Adelaide, and Zane who needed to be protected, and every betrayal fed into the next. Those are the unsurmountable obstacles that can never be resolved between Ezra and me. Just as I cannot tell you about Zane for his own protection, I refuse to tell you who the girl was. It wasn't true love or anything. She was my best friend– *our* best friend. What Ezra did was disrespectful– the lying to my face. I thought we were better than that. I thought both of them were. A lot of stuff happened that I can't talk about. It's too painful. But if you think I hate Ade, then you've never seen me hate her.

"I was getting over what she and Ezra did to me, why they did it, and how they both shut me out, when Ray took Ezra. Then compounded on that, I learned the truth of who I was, and then

Ray came back for me and Aaron. Then I couldn't get over what happened to us."

"Oh, Cort," I cry, wishing I could reach out and comfort him, but the bakery boxes are filling my arms.

"It is what it is. I knew we'd eventually find our way back to one another. Afterwards, Ezra found an outlet for himself. He read about BDSM in his studies, and wanted to put the therapy into practice. We knew Marc was into the lifestyle, so Ez went to Marcus for advice. I didn't speak to Marcus even longer than Ezra after this, nearly two years of silence between us. It took me a long time to realize it wasn't their fault, and I'm still not sure if it was the other guy's fault, either. I'd love to just blame them, because it'd be a helluva lot easier than blaming myself."

"What happened? Do you blame the lifestyle because of this? Why isn't it Ezra's fault? I understand why you'd feel resentful toward him. I feel it for you. But why are you blaming yourself?" I rapid-fire question after question. Ezra is so tight-lipped and he has a gag order in place on everyone else when it pertains to him. But Cortez is his own man, and he usually answers whatever I ask.

"I'll start at the beginning," Cort mutters. "Ez and I were close, closer than brothers or lovers. We were true partners, and I thought we shared everything. Obviously I was wrong," Cort's voice breaks, causing tears to well in my eyes.

"I'm so sorry," I whisper.

"Ezra's first betrayal was keeping the most important thing from me- his mental illness. I noticed it faster than anyone else, but I was helpless to stop it. But Marc-"

"Marcus helped?" I say in shock.

"Marcus isn't much older than we are. He married Diane when we were fourteen and he was twenty." I raise my eyebrows at that, knowing the story and hearing it is different matter. "Yeah, Diane is a cradle robbing bitch," he says with a fond mien. "Anyway, Marcus came to live with us earlier than that, before he even graduated from high school. I saw Marcus as a god. He was larger than life. We could go to Marc for anything. He was like a mentor to us, our protector and teacher, which makes me feel worse for hating him for so long."

"Please tell me you aren't saying what I think you're saying," I gasp out, feeling sick to my stomach.

"No. No way." Cort's forced laughter has an uncomfortable edge, and I know I've hit on something vital Cort will refuse to talk about, even with me.

"I see Marcus as an older brother." Cort lies. I can hear it in his voice as plain as day. "Marc introduced Ezra to a man who he thought could help him. For my sake, Marc even made sure it was a man who didn't like men. I may not like men in that way, with the exception of Ezra." Again, Cort's voice breaks as if speaking the lie is physically difficult. I don't know what Cortez is hiding, but I think he's hiding it from himself.

"Marc thought he was doing the right thing for me– making sure Ezra's master didn't do men."

"Oh. My. God." I whimper, finally getting a clue. "Jesus Christ. Almighty. No."

Cort ignores my outburst, speaking over me. "As you well know, emotions and sexual chemistry are par for the course during training, and it transcends sexual orientation. One day, I decided I wanted to see what all the BDSM fuss was about, because Ezra kept inviting me as a way to reconnect during our year of no contact.

"I found Ezra bent over a bench with his new master thrusting away– giving Ezra what I'd refused him for years. I felt like I'd died. I went home and tried to make a life with Divina. But first, I punished myself by offering the unlimited use of my mouth to Master. I refused Ezra's calls, his apologies and explanations. Later, I blamed Marcus, and I cut off all contact. But he started hounding me. The more I avoided him, the more persistent he became. You can never really avoid Marcus. I didn't just lose my lover. I felt like I lost my family, my friends– my life."

"Oh, my God, Cort," I cry out, feeling the sting of betrayal as if it were happening to me right this very second. My heart constricts from the pain Cortez is emoting.

"'*Oh, my God*', doesn't quite cover how I felt. There are no words to describe how I still feel, and I'm a writer. So when we saw Ezra rutting on Adelaide the night of his punishment, I understood how you felt in that moment. Fuck, I felt every betrayal again. I wish you never saw that. I wish I never did. So I stopped touching Ezra completely after that incident, just as I had before. The first time it took me an entire year to go back to Ezra, but I still didn't give him what we both wanted. I've held myself back from truly making love to him… until last night."

"I understand you better now, Cort. I understand why you had sex with me during my first training session, why it bothered you so much to see my fascination with Dexter, and why you lied about having amnesia over the moment. I suspect Ezra knew all of this in an instant, but kept it to himself."

"Dexter," Cort snorts. "Guaranteed hot button topic. Great at family holidays, seeing as Dexter is Marc's only living relative and one of his closest friends, so he's always around. Since we're a Catholic and Jewish family, we have double the holidays."

"Awkward facing the ex at every gathering. I don't envy you."

"Really, Kat? Seeing as how if you look everywhere, you'll find either my exes or one of Ezra's, and sometimes they are the same person. So I think you'll understand that awkward isn't strong enough to describe the territorialism, the jealousy, and the need to rip Ezra's dick from his body every time you recognize someone who has touched him."

"Way to scare me off," I mutter, suddenly feeling despondent again.

"When I went back to Ezra, he was still working with Dexter. I told Dex that I would train as well, but he wasn't to touch me. When I was a good little subbie for Dexter, he had me do things I didn't want to do. You will do all sorts of things for your damned master. He made me touch Ezra again for both of our sakes, and I haven't been able to stop ever since. What Dexter made me do was mild by comparison to Master."

"Are they still lovers?" My voice is strained as my stomach tries to revolt. I've been lusting after the man who cheated with the father of my child, as he cheated on our mutual lover. I feel guilty by association.

"No," Cort says gruffly. "Seems that once your partner catches you in the act, you kind of avoid it again. Ezra confused Dexter, made him want things he couldn't understand. It was safe, they trusted each other, so they let their guard down. I don't actually blame them, but it doesn't take the hurt away. My only vengeance is that Dexter wasn't happy that the one time he decided to experiment with another guy, he was caught with his dick shoved in an asshole." Cort snickers at Dexter's expense.

"Yeah, I could see that." I snort.

"It's not an issue of sharing yourself with someone. It was cheating. I would have said yes if Ezra had asked. Even you figured this out without asking. You knew Aaron was a onetime offer. But it made me realize I would never have to doubt your faithfulness. Kat, I want to see you with other people, but only if I have a say in it, and you need to know that rule goes both ways. But seeing Dexter behind Ezra made me see red. I wanted to kill them both. There is a massive distinction."

"I think Ezra knows that now. I wonder if he was trying to hurt you for leaving him when you married Divina. It's similar to when you pulled the skull-fuck to get back at him for not sharing."

"I know that! But we're talking about feelings. Emotions are irrational. I can't just turn off the hurt and get over it!"

"My advice is talk to Ezra. You've never hashed this out with him. You must find a way to let go of the past, to forgive but never forget. Irrational or not, there is always a logical solution."

"Could you sound more like him? Next thing you'll be telling me, is that it's not what I want, but what I need, or another of Dr. Zeitler's mantras," Cortez grits out snidely.

"Hey, this conversation is over. I was just trying to understand and help because it affects me now. But I'll leave it alone, because clearly you're cruising for a fight because you feel helpless over Ray's reappearance."

Cortez doesn't agree with my last statement, but he doesn't argue with me, either. We walk into Edge, both deep in contemplation-mode, and neither of us in the mood to party.

# Chapter Thirty-Six

We push into the foyer with great difficulty since both of our hands are loaded down with pastry boxes. I hear a lot of voices drifting in from the large open room of the kitchen/dining room/living room area.

I'm already on edge, not only from seeing Ray again, but also from Cort's attitude toward my advice. I can give it, but it doesn't mean he has to take it. But this is not what gets my blood boiling. I hate it when people arrive early. When I say early, I don't mean a few minutes– I mean hours. This has happened to me in the past for Thanksgiving. Guests show up thinking they're helping, when in actuality they're just in your damned way. I already live with a big houseful of people; I don't need to add to the pandemonium. Plus, a woman isn't at her best when she's prepping for a party, and will undoubtedly need a few moments to get her emotions in check and her appearance up to par.

I paste a forced smile on my face and exit the foyer.

My eyes widen as I take in the thirty plus people milling around my home. I still have to get the food set up, do some light cleaning, and get myself presentable for the party. Now I'm being stared at by dozens of eyes, while wearing jeans and a tank top, with my hair knotted on the top of my head, looking like I've been thoroughly debauched, and my eyes are shadowed with terror.

Lovely. It's just so damned lovely. I feel sabotaged, unable to put my best foot forward for Ezra, Cortez, Aaron, and Kayla's friends and family. Now I look like I'm disorganized, messy, and slovenly, as if I'm beneath all the eyes taking in my disheveled appearance.

When I say two p.m., I mean two p.m. I do not mean eleven a.m. Now I will be forced to feed these bastards lunch while I look like shit, with food I don't have. I will have no time to myself to fortify my emotions. Then I will have to serve them the dinner I had planned in a few hours. Twice the work.

I push the boxes on the kitchen island, and then start arranging the baked goods on their elegant party trays. If I ignore the guests, maybe they aren't here yet. Yeah, it's not working. I imprint their faces into my memory. They're officially on my shit-list.

My daughter hesitantly approaches me, while wearing a dusting of powdered sugar on her chin. "Have you been eating sweets again?" I hiss at Ava, and she recoils at the venom in my voice. "You need nutrients."

"Sorry." Ava apologizes but doesn't cower away from me. "I told him you'd be mad that they were here, but he didn't believe me. He said you'd be happy for the help, and I told him that they'd be in your way."

"Who? And you didn't answer me about the sugar?" Whoever Ava is talking about it is number one on the shit-list, for multiple reasons.

"I only had an oatmeal cookie." Ava plays innocent angel, as she bats her pale eyelashes at me.

"All right, you little monster. Word of advice, if you plan on lying: first, wipe the chocolate off the corner your mouth and the sugar on your chin. Then try to get away with lying. Third, don't sell shit to the manufacturer. I know there was no chocolate chips and powdered sugar in those cookies, because I'm the one who made them in the first place."

Ava doesn't look sheepish. She looks like she's taking notes for the future. "Dad said it was all right. He gave me some Munchkins." I squint my eyes as my daughter throws her own father under the bus, as if she didn't manipulate the sweets from him. "Dad was also the one who invited everyone early– everyone is already here."

I forget all about Ava's lack of honor the instant she tells me that the entirety of the party arrived three hours early– arrived before I did. In my own home, when I'm the hostess.

"Well, if the entire party is here to set up the party, they can go right ahead and do it themselves," I threaten. "I'll come out when it's two o'clock in the afternoon like I'm just a lowly party guest, seeing as how I'm not needed anymore."

I push the boxes across the kitchen island toward my daughter, and then I walk briskly toward my bedroom, ignoring Ezra when he calls out to me. I don't look at anyone, speak to anyone, or acknowledge anyone. I'm thankful that no one intercepted me, or else I would've lost it.

I lock my bedroom door, and then slide my dresser against it as a barricade. I shove earbuds in my ears and blast hardcore rap into my eardrums to block out the fact that Ezra is knocking on the door, jiggling the doorknob, and trying to unlock it.

I don't want to fight. I refuse to fight. Not after last night, after seeing Raymond Hunter in the bakery, hearing of Cort and Ezra's past, with Cort having no intention of clearing up their bullshit, followed by being invaded by our guests hours early because the man who knows me best sabotaged me.

I block out the world by reading over a manuscript for work. My anger still hasn't subsided by one o'clock when I get up to primp in my bathroom. I'm slightly surprised that no one has bothered me or come looking for me after Ezra's initial try. A little hurt that I'm unnecessary when it comes to a party I planned. But that is mild compared to the relief of not having to attend three extra hours of a party I didn't want to attend in the first place. I'm too stressed to play the party hostess with the mostest.

At exactly two o'clock, I walk down the hallway from my room and exit into the foyer. The doorbell rings just as I walk by. It's nice that someone is considerate enough to be right on time, instead of early or late. Whoever is on the other side of my front door will become my new best friend. Even if it's Ray, he will be my newest, bestest buddy.

I open the door revealing Monica. "Hey, you're my new best friend. Thanks for being on time." I smile brightly at her as I usher her in. For some odd reason I really am happy to see her. Monica's unflinching honesty is always refreshing, even when it hits too close to home.

Blushing yet looking uncertain of her welcome, Monica stammers. "Um– hi. Yeah, I was told to come earlier. But when I asked if you knew about it, they said no. I didn't think that was very wise." Monica runs her hands down her thighs, smoothing her skirt in a nervous gesture.

Monica is dressed as she is every day for work: pencil skirt, blouse, and tightly knotted hair. For the hundredth time, I wonder what Monica would look like if she lost her restraint. I've had glimpses of the real Monica, and she is rather pretty when she lets her hair down.

"I have a proposition for you, Monica." I could seduce her, but I believe she will appreciate a no-bullshit-attitude more so. "You can say no. I don't want to embarrass you. Really, just say no if you're uncomfortable."

"Okay, what is it?" I can tell Monica is still nervous by the way she licks her lips and fidgets. Body language reading is an exceptional talent to have.

"We need privacy for this conversation." I take Monica's hand and tug her toward the guest half-bath that's positioned in the corner of the living room. I notice a few people gazing quizzically at me– Ezra being one of them –when I pull her into the bathroom. I smile innocently as I shut the door on the voyeurs, and then I lock it and lean against it. We mustn't be disturbed. I lean forward and crank the water in the sink to drown out our conversation.

Monica looks around nervously, like I'm going to attack her or something. "Relax, Monica. I just don't want them to hear our private conversation. It's a surprise of sorts. If you say yes, it will shock them." She relaxes, slumping against the sink.

The bathroom is very small– just a sink and toilet. The floor is big enough to rotate in a circle and nothing else. It's a rather intimate setting. But with what I'm proposing, it's the perfect location.

"I know you and I have had our differences. I'm going to acknowledge them, even though I believe we've moved past it into a real friendship, because I want to make it up to you. I know you blamed me at first for Cortez dropping all of his lovers. I didn't know anything about it, truly. But I've come up with a compromise that will benefit us both. If you're willing to hear me out, that is." I cross my arms over my chest and I notice Monica's eyes flash away– curious.

"Okay," Monica agrees as she moistens her lips again. "You have me intrigued now."

"You still don't have a master, correct?" She shakes her head in assent. "I have an interview of sorts set up for you with a new master. He is one of the strongest dominants I know, but you may not like the interview process."

"What do you mean? I mean, thank you. Who is he? Do you think he will like me? I'm not exactly easy to deal with." Monica's eyes are bright and a flush creeps over her skin. She is enlivened by the prospect of having all of her needs met. At last.

Chuckling beneath my breath, I hold my hands out to stop her onslaught of questions. "Let me explain first, and then I have a few questions for you. I will answer anything you need after that, okay?"

"Yes," she breathes. "Anything. I'll do anything."

I smile blindingly in response.

"I have been training as a dominant– to be a master –and I need a submissive for my final. My instructor is who I think you'd fit best with. Only masters will be present for my final, so you don't have to worry about a huge audience. I'm not a huge fan of voyeurs myself. But I do like to watch. I just don't like to be watched by those I'm uncomfortable around. So if this is an issue for you, it won't work. I don't want to force this onto you."

"I'm like you. It won't be a problem if it's not a lot of people," Monica says shyly while staring at the floor. "I think it would be easier if I didn't know who was watching, then I couldn't stress out over not being good enough, pretty enough, submissive enough."

"Lord, do I understand that," I drawl out. "I guess they're testing me, determining if I'm dominant enough to join their ranks. It's a group decision. It'll be less than ten people, I was assured."

"That's good," Monica says in obvious relief. "That's alright. I can deal with that."

"Our next issue, and this is necessary and the most important. So if you give me a no, then I can't use you as my submissive during my test." I take a deep breath, feeling odd asking such an intimate question, and then I release it in the form of words. "Unless you can reach climax without sexual contact, I'll have to have permission to touch you."

Monica's mouth opens in a big, silent O shape. I try not to laugh at the expression on her face. I smother the sound, but fail at suppressing my smile. I blush as soon as Monica realizes that I just asked for permission to make her orgasm.

"I might like that," Monica admits in a tiny voice, still refusing to look at me.

"What?" I yelp out. "Monica, you can't be that desperate for a master. I don't want you saying yes just because you need a new dominant. I don't think you understand. I have to top you, own you, and give you pleasure and pain. Your responses will impact whether or not I pass my training. But most of all, my mentor will see through you if you don't actually welcome my touch. Do you understand what I'm saying?"

"Yes," Monica rasps. "But won't he see that you don't want me in return?" Her voice quivers with sadness and insecurity, and she still won't look at me.

I have a light bulb moment.

Damn, I'm an idiot. Why didn't I see this sooner? "Monica, do you like girls?" I draw her face into my view using a single fingertip beneath her chin.

"I don't know. Being a submissive woman is confusing. I've had masters demand it of me. It gets to be an edge where you don't know what you want anymore." Monica lowers her eyelashes, shielding herself with her eyelids.

"Are you attracted to girls outside of the dungeon?" I coax.

"No– I mean, yes," Monica stumbles over her admission. "There has been one or two women I've found attractive, but no more than that."

Monica still won't look at me and my light bulb burns brighter. "Am I one of the one or two who you've found attractive?" I stroke Monica's jawline with my thumb. She leans into my touch, making her response unnecessary.

"Maybe," Monica whispers, completely submissive to my whims. Her behavior flips my switch and I want to top her in my bathroom. I draw on all of my restraint, because I need to maintain control of the situation.

"Okay, Monica. I'm going to kiss you now." She trembles against my palm. "Your response will be the deciding factor on whether or not I will top you for my final. It will determine whether or not my instructor gets to watch you perform a scene."

Beautifully broken within her own insecurities, I already know that I'm going to top Monica. I want to kiss her right now to reassure her.

So I do.

I lean in slowly to prolong Monica's anticipation. Her eyes are already closed– eyelashes creating half-moon shadows on her cheeks. Monica is rather lovely when she is relaxed and not using her bitchiness as a shield.

I kiss first one eyelid, and then the other. Monica trembles with loneliness, desperation, and need against my touch.

Hesitantly, her hands settle on my hips. I tip her face farther back with my fingertip, exposing the long line of her throat. I place feather light kisses along her neck. She slides her hands around my waist drawing our hips together. Her hands knead my ass as I nibble her throat.

"Please," pours out of her mouth.

"Please, what, Monica?" I breathe against her ear. I rub my nose against her soft skin, luxuriating in her delicate scent.

"Please, Mistress," she moans for me.

"Please, Mistress, what?" I tip Monica's head farther back, until she is looking at the ceiling. I nip the soft flesh under her chin with my front teeth. She whimpers for me, and I'm not sure I've ever been so aroused in my life. If it weren't for the fact that I love Ezra dominating me, I would wonder if I was a true domme with a taste for soft, feminine flesh, instead of the confused switch that I am.

"Please, Mistress, kiss me." Monica's hands tighten on my ass and she presses her small chest against my larger one. I want to rip her blouse from her body to see if her breasts are as perfect as they feel.

I breathe heavily, trying to regain my composure. Tenderly, I take Monica's mouth with my own, a gentle press of lips. Monica opens her lips on a blissful sigh, and I use it to my advantage to dab my tongue inside her mouth, just enough to give her a hint of my taste.

"If I didn't know any better, I'd think you wanted me, Monica." I breathe against her lips.

"Yes, dammit! I do!" I tighten my fist in Monica's hair in silent reminder to be quieter when her voice pitches to a level that could be overheard.

"I wanted you from the moment I saw you. I was confused, pissed, and hurt. I thought you wanted Kayla. Then I saw your bracelet and knew that I couldn't have you since you had a master of your own."

"I'm a switch, Monica," I purr. "I can have a master and a pet." I breathe pet into Monica's ear, and I'm rewarded when she goes lax against my hold.

"I know that now. But I didn't until we came in here and you asked me to sub for you." She giggles at that. "You have no idea how badly I want to touch you right now," she murmurs in a husky voice filled with need.

"How about I touch you instead?" I take Monica's mouth with mine and viciously kiss her– feed from her mouth like she is my last meal. Her small fists clench my ass as she mews against my mouth. I bunch her skirt up, using my fingertips until I'm underneath it. I skim my fingers up her smooth thigh and wiggle them under the seam of her panties.

"Let's see if you truly want me, Monica." My fingertips slide easily into her hairless, drenched slit. "I love a bare pussy," I purr into her ear.

"Let me touch you," Monica begs just as I slip two fingers inside her and rub my palm on her clit. I almost come when she sucks on the mark the Ezes placed on my neck.

"I'm the master here, Monica. No topping from the bottom. I won't allow it. I will punish you with great vigor if you do."

"Please," Monica pleads, and her pussy tightens around my questing fingertips. Her channel starts to contract around my fingers, milking for something I don't have. It's times like these that I wished I had a cock, because I would finally be able meet all of Ezra's cravings and needs.

"I don't allow females to touch me," I remind Monica. "I'm the master. I give the pleasure and the pain." Never once have I wanted to be touched in return. But for some undeniable reason, I do now. I'm not sure I'll be able to avoid it during my final.

"Come on my hand, Monica," I demand. "Pretend it's my big, fat cock, pumping away inside your sopping wet, tight pussy. Milk my fingers dry," I chant.

In less than a heartbeat, I have to suck Monica's kiss and eat her hungry cries of pleasure as she drenches my hand with her release. I hold her tightly while she spasms around me.

When Monica finally relaxes, I fetch a hand towel from the sink and gently wipe her dry. I settle her skirt into place as she leans against the wall. I reach up and smooth her hair from her face, putting her to rights.

"I'm very pleased with you, Monica. I would keep you if I didn't think you and your new master would complement each other so well. I think you will fulfill *all* of each other's needs."

I can't resist Monica's kiss-swollen lips, reddened from my pleasure. I brush a kiss on them, and I'm rewarded with a moan.

"Good girl. I'll let you know when the scene is. It will be soon, and it will be in Restraint's dungeon. I can't wait to enjoy you again. Perhaps your new master will allow me to play with you now and again. Knowing him, he'd enjoy that immensely."

Leaning in, I kiss Monica lingeringly.

When she can stand on her own, I turn to examine myself in the mirror. I laugh when I notice how both our lips are kiss-swollen and our eyes are glazed. Yep, there is no hiding that. I laugh as I unlock the door and step out into the living room.

I walk with my head held high as all eyes lock onto me. I glance over my shoulder as Monica follows me like a lost puppy. I chuckle as she flushes crimson from embarrassment. She veers toward Kayla, seeking comfort from another familiar submissive. I give the pair a wink, and huff a laugh when their eyes seek the floor by their feet.

"Hmm… did the Kat just eat the canary in our bathroom?" Cort teases me when I come to stand next to him. "Are you so angry with me after our conversation that you resorted to diddling one of my exes in our own home?" To show no-harm-no-foul, I rub my cheek against his shoulder like a well-contented cat.

"I needed a submissive for my final, so I was giving Monica a test drive." Being a naughty brat, I slide my fingertips into Cortez's mouth– the fingers I brought Monica with and I failed to wash.

Cort groans against my hand, and then pulls me in front of him until my back rests against his front. "That wasn't very nice, Kitten. People could see my reaction." He presses his erection against the small of my back, proving just how nice it was.

"I enjoyed it," I whisper back at him, and then I lick my fingertips clean of Cort's saliva. Being a deviant, his cock jerks behind me in anticipation.

Cort leans down to breathe into my ear, keeping our very private conversation private. "Monica is an odd yet surprising choice for your submissive. You do so love a difficult challenge."

"Overachiever." Ezra flashes us both a smirk as walks he toward us. "I think Kitty Kat is going for bonus points by getting her frenemy to submit to her will. I'm highly impressed."

Ezra shocks us when he presses his length against the front of my body, and then kisses Cortez on the lips in full view of every single one of our party guests. I lean back, trying to watch. Ezra's body tenses along mine, waiting for Cort's imminent rejection. Neither has ever displayed their affections in public.

Two sets of hands grasp the other's face as they moan quietly into each other's mouths. I'm sandwiched awkwardly between two men who are grinding their erections into the small of my back and my tummy, and they do this in front of an entire group of our friends and family. Many people in the room are unaware that the pair are lovers. Some even believe that Cort and Divina are a true married couple.

Just as I begin to panic and try to wiggle out from under their arms, Ezra detaches himself from Cortez's mouth long enough to pick me up and attack my lips. The pair descends on me like starving men, ravishing me. Before I can respond or kiss back, Ezra gently places my feet back on the floor.

"If you're going to master someone in our bathroom, the least you could do is share with your master," Ezra says with a slight tinge of Master Ez in his voice.

"I wasn't aware that I had to bring it up the hierarchy. What about your master and your master's master, as well?" I tease, trying to solve the mystery as to who is the Master of the Universe.

I watch as both men look to Dexter. His face is filled with pride as he looks to the three of us he has trained.

"Who is his master?" I tip my chin toward Dexter as I ask them both.

"You'll find out soon enough at your initiation," Ezra says as he smiles down at me. He then places a palm on my cheek and echoes the movement with Cortez. I roll my eyes to see the expression on Cort's face. He was just outed in front of everyone he knows. It must be especially difficult for someone who won't even admit they might be bisexual, let alone gay. Cort's eyes shine with unshed tears, and where I expected to see embarrassment, I see awe and relief instead.

"I've missed you both terribly since this morning. I refuse to live a lie anymore. Fuck them if they don't understand us," Ezra declares with pride.

Both Cort and I shake our heads in response, because we are rendered speechless in the face of Ezra's declaration.

# Chapter Thirty-Seven

"Well, that went better than I'd expected. But absolutely no wedding planning got done." I speak as I drag a trash bag around the room, cleaning up after the partygoers. "I guess in the end, I'll still have to be the one to do it all."

"The wedding isn't for six more weeks, so we still have plenty of time. I promise I will help more. As for the party, I wanted it to be a surprise engagement party for Aaron and Kayla. They deserved it." Ezra drops an armful of garbage as I hold the bag open for him. "Who would have thought our friends and family were such little piggies."

"You haven't hosted many parties, have you?" I chuckle as I attack a wine stain on the seat of a dining chair. "So, how are you with outing us? I know they are your family and friends, but the press will undoubtedly get wind of it. Will it affect your careers?"

Ezra discards a couple of cupcake wrappers into the trash bag. "I'm fine with it. I wouldn't have done it if I wasn't. I spoke with Marcus earlier, asking his permission, as it will shine a light on his political career. I didn't ask my mother, because if the contributions dry up, she can always diversify by starting an LGBT fund. I worry about Cort, though. My business is in the limelight, but it isn't consumer-driven like his."

"Was it a spur of the moment kind of thing because of last night, or was it premeditated?" I stop my spot-cleaning and watch Ezra as he tries to put his thoughts into words.

"I planned on doing it at the party all along. I was going to give a little speech. But when I saw the look of triumph on your face when you left the bathroom, I wanted to tell the world that you're mine– that Cortez and you are mine, and that we're each other's."

Heart bursting with happiness, I cover my emotions with humor. "Teeth marks and bracelets aren't good enough for you? I'm just waiting for you to start pissing on us," I say with a little laugh, but I'm only half joking.

"I would make you walk around with the scent of my spunk smeared all over you, if I could. You make me feel like a damned animal," Ezra growls.

I throw a cupcake at Ezra's face for that comment. He catches it midair, and then he takes a hearty bite out of it. I raise a brow at him. I'm surprised he hasn't tattooed *mine* on our foreheads during our sleep.

"You and Cort need to get something settled soon, so that we may live peacefully," I warn Ezra.

"And what would that be, Kitty Kat?" Master Ez rears his controlling head.

"I know what your issues are and why, Ezra. Cort told me about his ex-girlfriend from when you were kids, some guy named Zane, Adelaide, and Dexter. He spilled your betrayals and said he couldn't get over them."

"What?" Ezra bites out from between gritted teeth. "What did you just say? What did Cortez say?"

"Cort refused to give me details, and I didn't ask for any, nor did I expect any. What's in the past is in the past, and I want it to stay there. But it's not staying there since Cort is holding onto the animosity. I believe Cort and you feed off of one another, and I'm worried about going any farther with you guys if it will infect our relationship. So if he won't talk, you better make him listen."

"There is nothing you can do, nor can I." Ezra releases his long-suffering sigh. "I'm sure there is a lot Cortez left out of his confessional. There are also things I'm too embarrassed to tell you, but I will if you wish me to."

I slump into a dining room chair, mentally and emotionally exhausted for some reason. "What? What else I am I missing?"

Ezra sits at the table and puts his head in his hands. A deep sigh rumbles up from his chest. Eyes heavy with burden, he looks at me with an expression of years' worth of worry and stress.

"We were both doing things to hurt each other, and neither of us would back down. It's a lot better since you came back into our lives. I can ignore the little things and the big things, as long as they aren't emotionally damaging. But Cort is still with *him*," a jealous edge creeps into his voice. "What began as a way to punish all three of us, has grown into an addiction, and I don't think I can live with that for the rest of my life. So as Cort refuses to give me what we used to have, I instinctively know he'd give it to him if *he* asked. I can't forgive or forget that, and it's Cort's way of paying me back. But it's a betrayal so much more potent than I've ever dealt Cort."

"Will this master ask Cort to have sex with him?" Voice quivering, I didn't even think about how another man could destroy the life we're trying to build. I've always wanted Ezra all to myself, but not at the expense of his heart and soul being crushed. I'm trying my damnedest to heal us all, so we will have a healthy relationship.

"I watch from a distance, hoping I'm not blind to the truth. He loves us, and would never do anything to harm us. So, no, he will never ask Cort to have sex with him unless he thinks it will push us back together. He will never come between us."

"Ezra," I whisper his name while reaching across the table to hold his hand. I hate the tears swimming in his eyes. But more so, I hate the power we wield to destroy each other. I fear I'm not strong enough to live through it, even if I'm just an innocent bystander hit by the aftershocks.

"I love him," Ezra breathes, damp gray eyes flicking up to meet mine. "I love them both, and they are playing a dangerous game because emotions are involved. You believe me a martyr who will do anything for our family, but you've never known the lengths he will use to protect me from myself. So no matter how much I want to tear his cock off and force Cort to eat it, I could never harm a hair on his perfect head."

"How do you deal with it?" Both of my hands clench into fists, even the one holding Ezra's. "I could kill anyone who has ever touched you. Just the thought... it's not as bad with Cort's exes, because there are so many of them. But this even makes me see red."

"Katya," Ezra gains my undivided attention with the serious bent to his tone. "You're not going to like what I have to tell you. I hope you don't hate me for it." He stares at me for the longest time, and then abruptly takes a fortifying breath. "In the past, every time our master took Cort's mouth, I took something from him– every time. I don't want to hide anything from you, so this needs to be out in the open, especially because you agreed to become my wife. Until you moved here, this person wasn't my lover, but I was with her every time *he* took Cort's mouth as a way to punish us all."

I fall against the backrest of my chair, all the life draining out of me. I can't judge Ezra because I just got done finger-fucking Monica in our bathroom. It's the look of shame on Ezra's face that turns my stomach. My touch made Monica feel good about herself, so in turn, I felt good about myself. What Ezra and the rest of the fools are doing isn't about sex; it's about vengeance.

"This master, Cortez, and you are making it worse. You'll ruin us all," I predict, hating the feeling of premonition that overpowers me. "You guys need to grow the fuck up. If you touch each other because it feels good, great. If you feel no shame over it, then it's the right thing to do. But you're doing it to hurt each other, and that's what makes it wrong."

"I know." Ezra pulls away from me, and then slumps forward against the table, resting his cheek on the tabletop. "It's a pathology at this point, and I need your help to stop the vicious cycle. I'm behaving because I know you would never accept my erratic behavior and I'd lose you, so I haven't touched her since you came back to me. But I fear Cort will go the other way, that he'll get worse the closer he is to letting go of the past and moving forward with us. It's in his nature, and this is coming from the person closest to him and as a doctor of psychiatry."

"A.k.a. an expert in human nature," I mutter to myself. "How did being with this woman hurt the mystery master? And if you love him so much, why would you want to hurt him in the first place?"

"Because this person is the love of his life, and I could take her from him, even if for only a few minutes. I knew it would kill him. He was taking something from me, so I took something from him. Balance. I love him more than life itself, and he betrayed my trust by touching Cort. I'd tattoo my name in block letters across Cort's forehead if I could, just so that when he took Cort's mouth, all he would see is my name and recognize his betrayal."

"Jesus, you motherfuckers are lunatics," I hiss, angry with myself for falling in love with him, which makes his insane baggage mine to deal with. "I won't put up with this shit for long, just so you know. I get that whoever this guy is, he's nonnegotiable. But if either of you tries to bring some more shit down on our heads, I'm walking away and never looking back," I warn, but it's a promise. "Love can only conquer so much shit, and I don't have the history you and Cort have to overcome it."

"It's just us, and then his dick in our man's mouth," Ezra promises, but he doesn't like it any more than I do. "It's not even sexual. It's like a masochist needing a sadist. It doesn't bother me as much anymore. I was livid at first. But now I see that Master holds a different kind of love for Cort than he does for me, and both types are unconditional."

Ezra sighs deeply while I sit in stunned silence. "I kept going after his lover because I was ashamed of myself and was punishing all of us. I didn't mean to punish his partner, but at the same time, I'm jealous of her too. I'm a psychiatrist, and even I can't explain it." Ezra's voice is hollow and he's as white as a sheet. If he were bragging, I'd kick his ass. But being distraught doesn't cover Ezra's dominant temperament.

"You're being awfully calm after what I just told you," Ezra mutters, looking shamefaced. "Just so we're clear, you do understood what I just told you, right?"

"That your master still has an intimate relationship with your partner– the man who is supposed to be my partner –so you used to screw your master's girlfriend in retaliation. I get it, Ezra. You had a long-term vengeance affair with someone, but you said it's no longer going on. I even know who she is."

"Katya, no," Ezra cries. "I don't want you to know who. I don't want to make you feel uncomfortable around her."

"I'm not mad," I admit. "She was before me, so I can't bitch and I'll try not to judge. It will be hard to be around her, and that does hurt. Mostly, I'm upset that this pathology runs so deep that it will infect the longevity of our relationship if it doesn't get resolved. Ezra, you and Cort and this master, you need to fix this, sooner rather than later."

I grab Ezra's hand across the table to make a connection between us. I don't want him spiraling down where he can self-punish and play the martyr. Martyr and victim are too close for my tastes. I don't ever want to see Ezra as anything other than strong and powerful. The thought makes my stomach heave. We have too many life-threatening issues to deal with than to dwell in this emotional bullshit.

"I'm trying very hard to change for you and Ava. To say I'm ashamed of what I've done is an understatement. I used to be really bad, but I've hidden it well. Cort doesn't even know half of the shit I've done. Only our master, his partner, and a friend of ours knows the darkest parts of me, and they've protected Cortez from it. I used to be really, really *bad*," he stresses. "Ray bad. I was a monster, and sometimes I think I still am."

"So I've heard," I tease Ezra because you can't punish someone who is already punishing themselves.

"I... I can't help myself." Sounding pitiful, Ezra laughs humorlessly. "That's really lame, isn't it? I do have DID, but I won't blame my behavior on it. Right now, I have my disorder firmly in check. You've noticed, I'm sure. But when I'm not even, I do very bad things."

"Wow," I mutter breathlessly, at a loss for words. "So when you get stressed, the issues get exacerbated?" Ezra nods his head yes, so I say the obvious. "Then shouldn't you alleviate the stress?"

"Yeah, I'm working on it. It's getting a lot easier. If only I could get Cortez to forgive all the shit I've committed in the past." Ezra hides his head in his hands and shudders.

"What you need to do first, is to talk to Cort, really communicate. Put it all on the table. Then you guys need to make love, without me there as a buffer. It needn't be penetrative sex. You need to overwrite the past, and show Cortez how you feel. It's impossible to deny your true emotions during the height of passion. I know, trust me. It's what happened to me when I was with you both."

"Cort will say no," Ezra grumbles, but I see hope flare in his eyes. I give him a reassuring grin. I already have a plan set in motion. It's either their way, or mine. But they will get over their past, one way or another.

"I saw Ray at the bakery today," I say nonchalantly, as if it wasn't life-shattering news. Ezra immediately stops what he's doing and freezes mid-movement. I give Ezra a play-by-play of the entire conversation I had with his diabolical birth father. I even tell him my theories and that I think Ray is being honest. Like a switch being flipped, Ezra unfreezes.

"Come– I need to check on Ava and see that she's sleeping peacefully. You go get Cort from his writing session. I just want to lie in bed and cuddle. I need to know everyone is safe."

"Okay." I do as Ezra says by feeding into his OCD issues. I actually agree with him on this. I just want to wrap myself in the warmth of my Ezes, swaddled in blankets that smell like a combination of our scents– home –and forget the world, even if it means playing pretend.

# Chapter Thirty-Eight

"Wow! Ezra made me wait so long, I thought they'd forgotten about me," I mutter to myself as I nervously finger the purple bow topping the large garment box lying on our bed. It has been over six weeks since my last training session with Dexter, to the point he was asking if I wished to further my education by exploring sadism. I began to wonder if my induction into Maître du Jeu was dependent on whether or not I was truly a sadist.

My fingertips turn the gift tag until I can read its message.

*Wear this for your initiation.*
*Congratulations, Kitty Kat.*
*We are so very proud of you.*
*I love you. Unconditionally. Always. Forever.*
*Yours, Ezra*

I worry my bottom lip as I stare down at the gift. I should feel reassured by their confidence in me, yet it worries me. What if I fail? What if I disappoint them both in front of all the masters? It feels premature to say congratulations if I haven't passed my final test.

I pull the top off the box while wearing a naughty twist of a smirk. I experienced this same thrilling yet ambivalent feeling when I opened the hedonistic chess set at my desk while Ezra looked on. What an embarrassing moment– thoroughly titillating yet terrifying.

Behind the purple tissue paper lies a soft, black leather outfit. I pull it from the box and marvel at the size of the catsuit. There is no way my body will fit into this without being greased up like a spring pig.

"Do you like it?" Ezra asks as he pads into the room.

"It's beautiful. Thank you. I'm just not sure how I'm going to squeeze my body into something so small," I say over my shoulder as I stroke the buttery rawhide. "I feel like you're making this a bigger deal than it truly is."

"It is a big deal. I never expected you to go to Dexter and ask for training. You had asked not knowing what you were actually doing." Ezra bends down to kiss the tattoo on the nape of my neck.

Still shivering from the sparks running up and down my spine at the simple touch, I distract myself with our conversation. "Dexter told me a bit about Maître du Jeu, but he didn't know much himself. Is that what you mean?" My upward inflection betrays my confusion.

"You inadvertently trained to become a Mistress or Master of Restraint, which is a big deal. But, yes, that did pull you into something far larger, when I'd hoped to keep you separate from it."

I turn to face Ezra, catsuit clutched to my chest. "Dexter said that it didn't matter either way, because I am the mother of your child. He didn't expand more on that comment. Being a government official, he'd rather be ignorant, so his ignorance is reflected onto me. He guessed mafia, illegal activity, and that the BDSM aspects were simply a front for something larger and more nefarious. That they had chosen BDSM because it symbolized a power structure similar to their own."

"Dexter talks too much," Ezra murmurs, reaching forward to divest me of my bathrobe. His fingertips glide across my collarbone to dip down between my breasts. "I will talk and relax you, and you will listen and relax. Just like in chess, deal?"

I don't have to utter my agreement because Ezra knows all he has to do is speak and his manipulation infects me. In this case, if he speaks while touching me, I turn into a submissive creature I despise, one who forgets everything outside of Ezra Zeitler's presence.

After undressing me completely, Ezra arranges me on our bed with me lying on my belly. He straddles the backs of my thighs, and his magic fingers get to work on the knots in my lower back. That indescribable tingly feeling erupts in my scalp, making me wiggle around, and then it slowly spreads across my body, leaving gooseflesh in its wake. It's divine pleasure.

"I wished to keep you separate from the infrastructure that plagues all affluent families. Two generations ago, all the major families in Dominion came together. Close-knit friends, often times blood-tied. All were enemies. I won't go into detail, because with your nature, combined with how you were raised, you wouldn't understand, and I don't want to lose you. Just know, the rich get richer by illegal means, so Dexter is correct."

"I'm not good with that, Ezra," I whisper into our bedding. My fingertips clench when he hits a sore spot between my shoulder blades.

"I know. You're one of the most ethical people I know, as is Dexter. He grew up in this life, and decided he wanted to ignore the fact that he was born with a diamond-encrusted, silver spoon in his mouth. He gave it all to Marcus, and went about building his own life. So we leave him alone, allowing him to do what he loves– teach. Teach BDSM. We will do the same for you. You will be a Mistress, and I will not allow anything else to touch you."

"How? How could it not? Just the knowledge alone will drive me insane. What of our daughter? The scary bullshit going down at Restraint is because of this, isn't it? Does this have anything to do with my threat letters?"

"No one will dare cross me," Ezra vows in a cold voice devoid of emotion. "I said I've done bad things in the past, still am doing bad things in the present, and will undoubtedly do bad things in the future. It's a reputation that instills fear and respect in my fellow Maître du Jeu members. This will never touch you. As for Ava, the girl is my child. She is well capable of taking care of herself, even at eleven years old. I wasn't much older than her when I took over for my family."

"Ezra?" I whip my head around, pinning him with my unflinching stare. "NO!"

Sheepishness flashes over Ezra's features, but he replaces it with a calm expression. "I only meant that no one will touch our daughter, as she is my daughter. They are equally terrified by us both. All is well. Forget about the root of the group, and simply enjoy the benefits of being a member of its BDSM community, along with the rest of those hiding in the dark. Happy in the shadows of ignorance. A place I long to be. A place Cortez pretends to dwell."

Ezra's gray eyes are foggy, his expression is a blank mask, and his touch is light and automatic. It's beyond terrifying to witness Ezra fall into his own mind, and get trapped there.

I change the subject, hoping to draw Ezra back to reality. "What should I expect tonight?"

He snaps out of his haze, fingertips pressing into my muscles more firmly. "Your scene with Monica is simply for our entertainment because Dexter wanted to show off his newest student. You are already a member of Maître du Jeu, and at the completion of your training, you became a Mistress of Restraint. Do not feel any pressure to perform."

"What about the initiation? Dexter and Cortez were speaking as if I wasn't there, and it sounded scary as fuck."

Ezra shuffles back a few feet to sit on my calves, giving him better access to my body. His fingertips dig in deep, drawing a groan from my throat. "Just listen to me and follow my direction. I will keep you safe during your initiation. Yours will not follow the same pattern as the ones before. As I said, any sane person should be terrified of me. Everything you do tonight will be at my request."

"Your requests are what I'm afraid of," I murmur into the bedding as a wave of trepidation rolls up my spine.

Laughing, Ezra leans forward to flutter a kiss to my shoulder. "You compliment me." His voice is filled with pride and good humor. "Even if you didn't mean it as such." He slides from my body to stand at the foot of the bed, leaving me feeling strangely cold.

"I have more gifts for my Kitty Kat," Ezra sings, causing my muscles to clench in anticipation.

"Your gifts scare me more than anything." I bust out giggling, remembering the trail of mortifying presents Master Ez gifted me.

"Because you're intelligent, my Katya." Ezra places a heavy palm on my shoulder, rolling me over to sit on my bum. "Let's get you into your catsuit. Your gifts are accoutrements for your scene with Monica. A mistress should be well-prepared."

"So they aren't scary gifts?" My voice pitches with hope.

"No," Ezra breathes against my cheek as he draws me to my feet. "You will be very fond of your new acquisitions. Very fond."

After a few moments of awkward struggling, I stare down at the wad of black leather at my feet. "It's not humanly possible that this catsuit is ever fitting on my chubby body." I lean down, trying to tug it up my calf, only to have it get stuck.

"I measured you for this catsuit six weeks ago. You've gained a bit of weight, but we will make it fit." Ezra pushes me down onto the mattress, and then kneels by my feet.

"Thanks for making a girl feel good about herself," I grumble as he begins to work the leather up my legs. "Are you calling me fat?"

Ezra flashes me a naughty smirk, evidently pleased with himself. "I'll love you no matter what, every fleshy inch of you, especially when I'm the one who's making you fat."

"Huh?" I grunt when he yanks the leather up to my hips. "Jesus, how the hell am I supposed to breathe in this thing?"

"Think of it as armor," Ezra reminds me as he draws me to my feet. "Every inch of you will be covered, with the exception of your hands, feet, and from the neck up. If someone tries to touch you, they will encounter leather, not your flesh."

My, "Thank you," comes out wobbly as Ezra yanks the catsuit into place, covering me completely. "You think of everything. I appreciate it."

Kneeling at my feet, Ezra rolls his stormy gaze to connect with mine. "You're precious, Katya. If you want someone to touch you, do so. If I want someone to touch you, I'll ask you first. But you should never have anyone touch you against your will ever again. It is my job to ensure that never happens. Your initiation tonight is the exception, as they are highly unpredictable. Hence the catsuit that covers you like a second skin."

"You mean, I'm…" I trail off, unable to give a voice to my fears.

"Our fellow masters and mistresses will greet you, which will involve intimate touching. A few will not be respectful, as they are testing their boundaries or simply pissed at me. The majority will treat you with dignity and respect, and you will not only welcome but enjoy their attentions. Those will not overstep any boundaries."

"I'm scared," I whisper.

"Don't be." Ezra reaches up to caress my cheek. "I'll be there the entire time, as will Cortez. Dexter will be there. You've met everyone who will be in attendance, whether in passing, by introduction, or in daily life. You are safe. I promise. Just do as I say, and know everything I have you do is for a reason."

"That sounded awfully ominous, Ez." I shiver, but not from cold.

"Another gift from me." Ezra's pale white skin blushes a beautiful shade of pink. "I think this will please you greatly. It's multipurpose, as you can use it during your scene with Monica, as well as finally getting your retribution from Cortez over the skull-fuck business."

Beyond curious, I grab the large box out of Ezra's hands. Giddy with excitement, I tear into the wrapping, paper flying around our bedroom. I huff a laugh when I set sights on the object.

"Oh, my God! It's perfect. Thank you. Thank you. Thank you." I pepper Ezra's face with kisses in between giving my thanks. "See, I can appreciate a gift in the spirit in which it was given."

I pull the harness from the box, pressing it over my hips, modelling it for Ezra. "I hope it fits, seeing as how I'm chubbing up thanks to Cort's obsession with food." I drop the harness back into the box and pull out ten inches of Cyber Skin. "You naughty boy, Ez."

I wave the phallic-shaped object in Ezra's blushing face. "Ha! Ha!" he mock-laughs. "You got me. I've had a one-track mind for weeks, wanting to know what it would be like to be penetrated again, while connecting with another human being. Not a finger or tongue, but something more substantial."

I lean forward to capture Ezra's lips, needing to take the insecure, lost look from his face. "It would be my pleasure to fuck you, Dr. Zeitler. I look forward to it. But mostly, I look forward to how insanely jealous Cortez will be, which means he might actually let go of the past and meet your needs in the flesh instead of me with fake flesh."

"With you, I'll love it just the same." Ezra believes what he says, but I know nothing will ever compare to Ezra and Cortez truly connecting. Just as nothing compares to when they are inside my body.

Still kissed with a blush, Ezra turns from me to fish something out from beneath the mattress. "This gift isn't wrapped, nor is it from me. Your mentor says the moment a whip touched his palm, he found his center. He knows that is not the instrument of your passion. This gift is a test to see if you find that same sense of home. If not, he'll keep putting objects into your palm until you experience the same sensation."

Feeling overly emotional, I tear up as Ezra places the length of cane in my palm. He stares at me intently, gauging my response. Laughing through the tears, "I feel like I'm on *Say Yes to the Dress*, where I'm to experience the visceral *'bride moment'* and everyone is waiting with bated breath."

"No more bride shit for you," Ezra teases, bopping the tip of my nose with a fingertip. "Ava and Kayla are bad influences. This is a bad-ass cane, not a frilly dress. Treat it with the respect it deserves."

We laugh together as my fingers curl around the rattan cane with a no-slip, leather grip. I close my eyes, waiting for the moment of rightness to descend. I experience a moment of tingling anticipation, a fluttering in my belly and a pooling in my groin. I don't know how Dexter felt when he first held a whip, but I do know I suddenly feel alive.

"Hmm…" A satisfied sigh slips from between my parted lips. "I'll know the first time I strike out with it." With heavily hooded eyes, a smirk twists my lips. "Willing to allow me to try on your perfect behind?"

Ezra puts his hands out in front of him, while slowly walking backward toward our bedroom door. "Nah… I think I'll pass. I don't submit, nor am I a masochist. But have at it with Monica."

"Oh, I will," flows haughtily from my tongue. "If Monica bends to my will, Dexter will be very pleased."

"Sadist matchmakers, scary that." Ezra reaches out to turn the doorknob, fleeing me, and an intense sense of power descends. "Congratulations, Mistress Katya." He slips out the door, shouting as he goes. "I'll meet you in the car, and no hitting people on your way!"

# Chapter Thirty-Nine

I'm led by Ezra into the dungeon with a hood drawn over my head. Ezra told me this was part of the initiation as well, leading the blind into the dungeon. Queen had been abducted from her bed in the middle of the night, tossed into Ezra's SUV, and taken to Restraint. While I'm relieved I came here on my own volition, the blindness doesn't make me feel any better. I can't hear anything over my insanely loud breathing as it echoes inside the hood.

Startling me, the hood is drawn abruptly over my head in a *voilà* fashion. Ezra led me in here, but as soon as he removed my hood, he flashed away as if he was never here. Alone, I turn in a complete circle and see absolutely nothing.

I'm standing in a dark, hollow void of emptiness. The dungeon. I can't see, hear, smell, or feel anything. I can sense the presence of a handful of others a short distance to my right. I splay my hand in front of me– unable to see my fingers before me –and use it to feel my way around.

I'm in an abyss.

Heart pounding erratically, I try to calm my nerves by telling myself they mean me no harm. This is a test for their entertainment. As a master, if I am to lead, to be at the top of the food chain, than I must summon my inborn abilities that push me closer to animal than man. My senses sharpen to the point that I can feel a disruption in the air just over my shoulder. I turn slowly, trying not to distract myself with my own movements and the sound of my labored breath. I calm my heart to a rapid tattoo instead of the flat-line screech it was giving.

I sniff the air lightly. I smell a clean scent that I'm fond of– citrusy and soft.

Monica.

I instinctively know she is within my range. I stand still without breathing. I swear I even manage to stop my heart. In the absence of my own noise, I can hear the unmistakable sound of Monica's sharp intakes of breath as she gasps with fear. My need to comfort her overrides everything else. Knowing exactly where she is in correlation to myself, I reach out to rest my palm on her cheek, assuring her everything will be fine.

Quivering beneath my touch, "Monica," I breathe out as I caress my temporary submissive's face.

A bright light pops on. I hear the buzz of the electricity running through the wires before the light registers with my brain. I blink into the blindness, trying to see what lies beyond the light. But the light has a dual purpose: showcasing the mistress and submissive while blinding me to everything outside of the circle it casts.

I realize I passed my first test by finding my submissive in the absence of light by using my other senses. This was covered in my training with sensory deprivation. A smirk pulls at my lips because of my ingenuity.

Several muted chuckles flow from the shadows, followed by a harsh 'Shhh!' reprimand. I guess they're supposed to maintain the ominous feel of the dungeon and my initiation, but they couldn't help but release their amusement at my situation. I smile brightly with the knowledge that I passed step one and they failed their own test of staying silent.

I was able to separate the different laughs, which is exactly why they were told to remain silent. Cort's naughtiness rang loud and clear, and it flooded me with a sense of calm.

My initiation isn't life or death. This isn't even a test of my skills, but a gauge on Dexter's abilities as a mentor. I relax and decide to let my training flow through me as I work my submissive by fulfilling her needs and my own. I seek our mutual enjoyment while showcasing Monica's attributes to the watching masters. While my performance is for Dexter's pride, my true reason is to find my newfound friend someone she can trust, someone who can meet her needs, someone who will unleash the real Monica.

Eyes still fuzzy from the bright light with the halo of darkness shrouding us, I find Monica dressed in a black velvet cloak and little else. Even her chestnut hair is unbound in a frothy wave around her shoulder. She looks ethereal and lovely without her clothing and harsh hairstyle as a shield. Her silence is also a godsend, as she isn't hitting me in the face with the brutality of her words.

Fingertips unhooking the closure, "So beautiful," I murmur as I divest Monica of her cloak. Pale and as smooth as alabaster, she is beautiful. I skim my fingertips down the soft curve of her small breasts, delighted on how her nipples flush and tighten. I long to caress the splattering of freckles adorning her shoulders, chest, and belly.

"They're not as big as Kayla's," Monica whispers to me as I cup the perfect globe of her breast in my palm, squeezing gently.

Without thought, my hand flashes out in punishment, fingertips sharply pinching her erect nipple. Monica releases a silent scream, a gasp of air that wheezes out.

"Don't ever let me hear you say such a thing again. I'm your master for this evening. This breast is my breast. Don't ever compare yourself to another human being again, Monica," I chastise her severely.

"But it's true," she whines, irritating me with her insecurity.

I'm a woman, subject to the same destructive thought patterns that all women possess. I know what it's like. How debilitating it is to have no sense of self, thinking how others perceive you is the only thing that matters. I am a mother of a daughter, one who wishes her to grow up happy in her own skin. While I am just as insecure as the next person, I refuse to show it. My daughter deserves to live a life where she never second-guesses herself, especially with the things she cannot change. Monica deserves this as well. All women do. All human beings do, whether man or woman.

"I'm going to teach you a lesson, so listen closely. The only person you should ever compare yourself to is yourself. There is too much jealousy and bitterness in this world, and it's unnecessary. You will never be the prettiest person on Earth, or the smartest, thinnest, curviest, sexiest, or most interesting." Monica releases a bitter sob at my judgment, body shaking with tears rolling down her cheeks.

Monica has never looked more beautiful than she does right now with her heart bleeding from her eyes and her crushed soul written across her facial expression. This broken creature is the real Monica James.

"By the same token, someone will always be homelier, less intelligent, thinner, chubbier, more frigid, or just plain dull. These people have no bearing on you, as it's all about perception, and whatever they do or don't have will never change who you are. You're an individual. You are unique. You're an original. There is only one you, Monica."

I grip Monica's chin in my fingertips. "All of this is of little consequence, because a trained submissive knows the only opinion that matters is her master's opinion. I just called you beautiful, and you dismissed it. You called me a liar with your scoff. You showed me that you don't trust me to speak my own truth."

"I'm sorry, Mistress." Monica sobs the words, small breasts heaving with emotion. "I'm so sorry."

"Good. I can only hope you retain this lesson." I tap Monica's temple. "Inside here is negativity that has to go. It's toxic to your being. Tonight, the only thing that matters is me. Trust me. Watch me for clues. Please me. Make me proud. In doing so, know that you trust yourself, please yourself, and are worthy of pride."

Huge brown eyes cast guiltily to the floor, "Yes, Mistress," Monica submits.

"Now, where was I?" I whisper to myself. "That's right, I was inspecting my new pet." I run my fingertips softly along every inch of Monica's body, testing her responses while finding her erogenous zones and tender spots. By the time I finish my circuit, she is mewing like a kitten and following the course of my hand.

"You are so beautiful like this," I murmur just loud enough for our witnesses to overhear, but the words are solely for Monica's benefit. "Raw. Broken down to your barest form, ready to be rebuilt into who you were meant to be. You are not hidden behind a guise. No armor. No shields. No longer striving for an unobtainable level of perfection that is someone else's ideal. No longer testing those around you in hopes they will fail to prove that you are unworthy."

"Jesus Christ, Ezra," a young, male voice rings out from the shadows. "She's going to put you out of business at this rate, and she doesn't have a billion years of higher education."

"It's a good thing Katya can hold her own." The pride in Dexter's voice is a welcome comfort, as are his words. "Stop interrupting, Pretty Boy. We have a trembling, naked woman before us, and I want to watch the splendor of her tears."

Monica's eyes go wide with shock, and I realize she knows exactly who is standing outside the perimeter of our circle of light. Her lips form the shape of an **O** as understanding dawns that it's Dexter who she is performing for.

"Holy fuck," Monica mouths to me, tiny brown eyebrows knitting in the center of her forehead. "Dexter?" I laugh silently, pleased that my matchmaking seems to be a success thus far.

"There is something I love to do, and I'm going to do it to you whether you like it or not," I warn. "Whether pleasure or pain, I want you to speak encouragements to me as if you enjoy my ministrations. Tell me how much you like it, and I will be very pleased."

I stand behind Monica, affording our audience a frontal view of her slim body, tear-shaped breasts, and hairless snatch. I knot the hair at the nape of her neck in my fist, wrapping the tendrils around my fingers. I yank roughly, drawing her neck out in a smooth line for my biting pleasure. Moving with deliberate slowness, I build anticipation. I lock my stare in the general direction of the watching masters, and then I lash out, savagely biting her throat. My name is a fierce scream released from Monica's lips.

"Ah… that was definitely encouraging," purrs against the flesh resting beneath my lips, damp with a combination of my saliva and a sheen of fear-induced sweat. "I adored the sound of your pain. I may only have you for this evening, depending on your future master's whims, but I will leave a lasting impression on your pink, tender flesh."

"Oh, God," Monica moans, knees giving out.

Wrapping my arm around her waist, I stop the smaller woman from crumpling to the floor. "I love encouragement when I'm not even doing anything. Please, go on." Someone in the crowd snorts at my liberal use of sarcasm, and I can't help but smile.

I rest my hands on Monica's shoulders, making sure she will remain upright when I let go. Then I continue to nip my way down her spine, setting my teeth directly on her muscle since the woman doesn't have an ounce of fat on her.

Monica chants, "OH, GOD!" repeatedly as I nibble her flesh.

"How about we change that up a bit? Shall we, Monica? Try, '*Oh, Goddess!*' Your prayers to the divine aren't going to grow me a cock, no matter how much we both may wish me to have one."

A few chuckles erupt from the watching masters in response. I flash an evil grin their way, muttering sarcastically, "I'm such a comedian."

I go back to my feast, and Monica continues her moans by calling out my name. "No, seriously, Monica. Call me Goddess. Tonight I'm your master. Maybe a few prayers to the Wiccan Goddess, Nyx, will provide me with a cock."

The ridiculousness isn't lost on me. I'm no goddess, nor do I wish to possess anything but a vagina– Ezra might like it if I grew a cock, but Cort would murder me where I stand if that were the case. My real agenda is that I want to prove how easily Monica will slip into the submissive role, acquiescing to even the most ludicrous nonsense while maintaining a connection to the dominant.

I bite Monica's round ass cheek, teeth sinking deliciously into her flesh. The woman exercises and starves herself within an inch of her life, no doubt trying to shrink her expansive derrière. I wish Monica would come to the realization that confidence is the sexiest thing you can wear.

I lean back on my heels, gazing at Monica's ravaged flesh. A fierce surge of pride wells inside me as I marvel over the marks I left behind. Some I laid quite brutally. I used this as an indicator for Monica's pain threshold. The amount of '*Oh, Goddesses!*' erupting from her throat informed me Monica is a little pain slut.

Still nibbling, when I reach Monica's thighs, I find them glistening with her arousal. Her musky scent fogs my mind. I almost orgasm from the force of knowing that I'm leading, pleasuring, pleasing, and giving to a woman who just a few short months ago disliked me. Proof you can get more flies with honey. In this case, the honey is flowing from Monica's engorged cunt.

A smile of pure satisfaction stretches across my face, relishing the fact that I'm the reason Monica is writhing beneath my touch. No one else. *Me*. I'm mastering this bitch into submission until she resembles her true self.

Earlier I had requested a sex swing for our scene. I wanted Monica suspended and at my complete and total mercy for my pleasure and her comfort. I maneuver Monica as if she is my marionette and I'm her puppet master. I'm satisfied when she is in a slight sitting position, with her feet suspended from the floor and her thighs spread widely, showcasing her hairless cunny.

I know that Monica's biggest hang-up is her self-image. As a master, we need to fulfill our submissive's needs while meeting our own. In this case, I need to make Monica feel cherished and wanted, while I try to get over my sexual hang-up of being touched in return, with the goal of feeding my need to provide women with pleasure. I don't do this for Dexter. I don't do this for Monica. I do this for my own sexual growth.

"I must taste you, Monica." My voice is raw and husky with unsuppressed hunger. "I've dreamed of little else in the past few weeks since I touched your drenched pussy."

"Mistress," Monica pleads as she restlessly shifts in the swing.

"I know you want me to, so please relax and enjoy," I purr in a seductive tone I didn't know myself capable. I kneel in front of Monica in the perfect example of a submissive pose, with the exception that I do not bow my head. Instead, I suck the juices that coat the insides of Monica's thighs. I lap up all her glistening goodness.

Monica thrashes violently in the sex swing when the tip of my tongue grazes her bare labia. With slow deliberation, I slide my tongue up her slit, stroking her until I meet the soft, juicy flesh within.

"Oh, Goddess!" echoes around the dungeon as I inhale Monica's musky flavor.

"Men just don't appreciate the taste of a woman. Their unique bouquet, the scents and tastes from sweet to musky. But, then again, what do they know? It's the ones who love cheap, American beer who make the most pussy jokes. They just don't have the palate for a fine wine. It's an acquired taste as they say about their tinny tasting brew. Monica, you are as soft as a peach and as sweet as one, too. I could drink you down all night long as you coat my tongue and the back of my throat."

I continue to stroke, suck, lick, nibble, and bite until Monica is rocking against my face, practically weeping in pleasure. When I feel her getting close to the brink, I withdraw over and over again. The time in between is getting shorter and shorter, to where Monica has a constant need to come. It's a painful edge, where withdrawing will keep her in thrall and more pressure will shove her over the precipice.

Monica is driving me so high that I'm shamefully grinding my cunt against the heel of my foot, closing in on my own release. With an abrupt, jerky motion, I stop and stand, just before we both unleash the pressure building.

"Dexter gave me a gift he wished me to try. I thought it apropos that I should use it on you while you audition for the position of his submissive." I reach back to the nape of my neck, and extract the cane Ezra had given me earlier, where I'd hidden it in the back of my catsuit.

"Kiss it. Lick it. As it will soon be used on your flesh." I hold the cane horizontally, pressing it near Monica's lips. I move it far enough away that she has to strain to reach it with her tongue. She makes hungry, little noises as she licks the cane clean.

"Did the rattan taste good?" I try hide the wry amusement lacing my tone, not wishing everyone to know how I'm getting off on the power I wield over Monica, how she seems willing to do anything I ask.

"Yes, Mistress." Monica begs in a husky voice filled with need. "I want more."

"It's not what you want, now is it?" I mutter for Ezra's benefit, and barely stifle a laugh.

"No, Mistress. I only need what you provide," Monica murmurs breathlessly, not catching on that I'm teasing Ezra and Cortez.

"Monica, you are such an excellent submissive. You follow direction so well. How proud you make me. In reward, I think you need something tastier than rattan, don't you?"

Voice dreamy, eyes glazed, pupils blown, Monica begs, "Yes, Mistress. Please."

As a dominant, it's my job to bring Monica to the precipice of her boundaries, shove her over the edge, and then catch her before she lands. At the same time, I need to grow, to conquer my own fears. My biggest fear is accepting intimacy and touch in return from those I wish to lead.

It's time I eradicate my issue.

My catsuit is free of zippers, which posed an issue when having to use the bathroom. I located the inventive flaps that are built in the crotch area, as well as set over each breast. The panels are reminiscent of men's briefs. You slide your hand in the flap one way, turn your hand, and then slide past the opposite flap to find your goal of skin. I do this now with the handy flap at my cunny. I slide two fingers inside and collect my juice on their tips.

I've never allowed a woman to taste me, and through our unconventional friendship and her unflinching honesty, I trust Monica to be my first, and most likely my only. Anxiety floods my system, fearing she will dislike my taste, unsure if I want something so intimate to occur between us.

With shaking, wet fingertips, I stroke Monica's bottom lip. "Open up, my good, little subbie, and take your reward." She opens her mouth on a heady moan. I slide inside her warmth slowly. She sucks my taste from my fingers, and I pull them out clean of my essence. I lean down and take her mouth with my own, mingling my taste from her mouth and hers from mine.

"Mistress, please," Monica pleads. "I'm going to come." I smile against her lips in satisfaction, and she joins me.

"We can't have that, now can we?" I tease Monica by flicking my cane lightly on the bud of her breast. I do this to test Monica's pain threshold, setting a baseline.

Monica doesn't scream as I'd imagined. She moans loudly and acts like she is a heartbeat away from release. No, we can't have that yet. It would be *scene-over*, and I wouldn't get to explore the depths of my abilities, nor showcase hers.

With the flick of my wrist, I tap Monica's other nipple, and I'm reward with an immediate, shrill scream. The next is a good, heavy swat, yet Monica is still hovering on the precipice of release– curiosity, is she a closeted masochist?

"You're a little pain slut, aren't you?" I say loudly for the crowd's benefit. "I bet you were either hiding your masochism, or didn't even realize it existed."

"Yes, Mistress. It always intrigued me, but I didn't trust anyone enough to experiment," Monica replies, sounding unsure and ashamed.

Until now, we've only had two masochistic members at Restraint. Tobias Kline– Dexter's slave –and a master of unnamed origin, both being male. I flash a smile at the crowd, hoping our onsite sadist enjoyed Monica's admission. I will get them their minivan and a gaggle of kids if it's the last thing I do. They can grow into love, because on paper, they want exactly the same things out of life.

"Very well, then," I murmur as I skim the tip of the length of cane along Monica's cheek. "You will enjoy what's to come. But I warn you, do not climax until I permit, because if you do, I'll have to punish you. Your education won't be sweet, or pretty, or by your preferred method. I'm highly creative, and I will figure out your currency so that you'll learn and never forget your lesson."

I walk behind Monica to study her back for a moment. I'm transported a few weeks ago, to when Dexter displayed his craft on Tobias's flesh. I'm no expert, but Monica really is a little pain slut, so I'm safe in the knowledge that I have room to experiment and improvise without doing any harm.

I trust Monica, and unbelievably, she trusts me. That is a delicate relationship I will never fracture.

Testing, with the flick of my wrist, I swat Monica in inconsistent intervals to keep her in suspense. She jerks in her swing, grunting in pain and pleasure, while still repeating a mixture of, "*Oh, God! Oh, Goddess! Kat!*"

I'm not sure if Monica is calling me a Goddess, or if she is simply praying to God to make me stop. Monica's will is mine tonight, and I will stop when I'm good and ready, unless and until she safewords.

Leave it to control-freak Monica to choose *Antidisestablishmentarianism* as her safeword. I cannot even pronounce that on a good day, let alone when I'm entering subspace. We compromised on *Politics*– a word she doesn't utter as I lash her over and over again.

One of my biggest fears is brought to life. I come to the realization that I am a sadist from the intense pleasure I derive from Monica's pained pleas. I don't get off on harming my friend; it's because I'm giving her exactly what she needs to feel free. It doesn't have to be Dexter or me, just as long as someone Monica trusts meets her every need. I believe I'd enjoy sitting in the audience, understanding how both the sadist and masochist feel in this very moment, and I would live vicariously through them, that is how connected I am. I experience an overwhelming sense of contentment and lust as I witness Monica falling deeper and deeper into bliss, and a part of me senses my mentor mirroring my thoughts and emotions– Syn too.

If it wasn't for the leather catsuit, I'd be dripping a steady stream of arousal to my ankles. Leather isn't absorbent, so I'm uncomfortable in my stickiness. I know Ezra didn't want my body on display this evening for my own protection. In the future, when I can tell people to back the fuck off, I'm going to be naked, as it would be far more comfortable and breathable.

I step away from my work of art as Monica hangs listlessly in her swing. I gently yank her head back by using her hair for leverage, and then I stare into her face. Monica gazes at me with a drugged expression, blown pupils and eyes glazed over, with her lips are parted slightly as she pants little puffs of breath. Her flushed skin is sheened with a coating of sweat, and arousal runs in rivulets down her inner thighs.

Monica looks at me as if she is witnessing the divine firsthand. All right, perhaps Monica was calling me a goddess earlier. She truly is a pain slut. It is a sadist/masochist match made in heaven for Dexter and Monica.

Clutching a leather strap on the sex swing, I twirl my masterpiece around in view of the awaiting masters. I display Monica as the living, breathing work of art that she is. I hear a collective '*Aaaahhhh*' when they see my handiwork. Monica's back is marked with six perfectly placed letters.

*Dexter!*

"I'm just proving that I don't have to piss on or ejaculate in my submissive to prove that she is mine, even when I mark her as someone else's." I speak into the crowd, but the party it was intended for received the message loud and clear.

When Ezra said he longed to tattoo his name on Cortez's forehead, and how he wanted to splatter me with his ejaculate, I was sickened. If you're that insecure in your relationship, clearly something isn't working. Jealousy is human nature. Wishing to mark everything with a mine-stamp is not. Master knows who Cortez belongs to, even when his cock is crammed down Cort's throat. They are meeting each other's needs, and they belong to each other in that moment. It's a private experience that cannot be stolen. If Ezra has a problem with it, he should fix it.

Ezra calls me out on anything he takes an issue with, yet he lets thirty years of issues fester between him and Cortez without ever acknowledging how the fissure is ruining our lives.

I cup Monica's cheek in my palm, "She's mine right now. We both know it, so there is no sense in professing it to everyone. It's a relationship between the two of us, and it's not up for public debate. Maybe territorialism is a man thing. In which case, as you can see, Monica will belong to Dexter when I'm through. So I suggest you don't touch the man's property."

"Damn, Dexter!" A sharp whistle rents the air, and I don't recognize who releases it. "Lucky fuck."

"You've been such a good, little subbie, letting me mark your back," I croon to Monica. "I think it's time for your reward." I step away, addressing both Monica and the watching Masters. "Ezra gifted this to me for your pleasure and for Skull-fuck's punishment. I haven't had the time to educate Cortez over our first, intimate, stolen moments– albeit brutal and forced. So you will be the first one to enjoy my new toy."

I walk over to the side, where I can just make out my hood inside the edge of the circle of light. I know how Ezra operates, so I assume he placed my bag of tricks with the hood.

Let's see if everyone is right, saying Ezra and I think alike. I pick up the hood and curse when my bag isn't near it. I hate that fucking spotlight. It truly does blind all the area outside of its radius. With my hand, I fumble in the blackness until I find my satchel by the texture of its canvas strap. I drag my prize into the light while releasing a snicker of victory.

"I think we should thank the Goddess Nyx for answering your prayers, Monica." I pull a leather harness out of my bag, stepping into it. Monica's eyes widen at the sight– big brown saucers of disbelief and lust. "I know you can take this," I say as I pull a latex phallus from my bag of tricks. "Your former master prides himself on preaching the qualities of his 'exquisite' cock." I place air quotes around the word exquisite, causing the crowd to snicker and Cort to call me a bitch.

"Ezra found a dong that is roughly the same size as Cort, thinking it would be apropos that his punishment be the same as my violation."

I slide the leather up my hips and buckle the straps into place. I give a tug to make sure the fit is secure– perfect. I walk over to Monica and rearrange her in the swing. I face her toward the masters, breasts thrust out for their viewing pleasure. I adjust the straps from her thighs to her knees, until she is suspended in the doggy-style position. If the straps were flesh tone, Monica would appear as if floating in air.

I tap Monica's cheek with the toy, and I'm rewarded with a heady moan. "Moisten my cock, pet. I know that you're very excited, but I have a big, thick dick for you, and I don't want to hurt you. Lubricate it up for your own pleasure."

I watch in captivation as Monica sucks the toy until my fingers meet her lips. I gasp at the sight. Jesus, why would anyone give her up?

"Your new master will be very pleased with your deep-throating skills, pet. I hope you can take a little more, since he's bigger than this toy." I finally break Dexter of his vow of silence. I hear his sharp intake of breath when he sees his newest submissive deep-throat a ten-inch toy.

Pulling away, Monica's hot saliva slicks the Cyber Skin cock, glistening to slide down to my fingertips. I attach the phallus to the harness, and then move to stand behind Monica. My hand glides up the side of her neck with loving, lingering strokes.

Without warning, Monica gasps out in surprise when I tighten my fingers on her throat, nearly choking her, and then I thrust into her pussy to the hilt.

Body shuddering, skin beading with sweat beneath the leather, pussy contracting from the visual, mind alight from the cerebral effects, eyes held wide, I marvel over the power that courses through my veins, finally experiencing how the other half lives. Why would a man take this from a woman, when there is so much satisfaction in the power exchange? This is a sensation that can only be given freely– never taken, stolen, or violated.

Pushing in deeper, I curve around Monica's back. I press my lips to her ear, while my eyes pierce the darkness where my fellow masters lie. "Do you like that, pet? Do you like my cock deep inside of your cunt? My nerves don't extend into the dong, but I can feel your pussy clenching so hard, to the point it's vibrating the harness."

Monica's head falls backward, her cheek resting against mine. A tortured moan spills from her throat, as if she's been waiting a lifetime for this experience.

"Don't come," I warn, breath fluttering against her cheek. "Your pleasure is mine to give." My voice changes from its usual dulcet tones. I turn husky, like a chain smoker or an excellent phone sex operator.

I pick a rhythm that satisfies us both. I angle my hips so I hit Monica deeply while the base of the dong grinds against my clit. I'm close to release, but it's a matter of will not to do so. I want to prove that I am not a slave to my own body's responses– I control all aspects of self. I will display the utmost restraint possible, but it isn't without great difficulty.

I close my eyes, arching my back as I rock into Monica, and seep into the sensations wracking my body. Every nerve in my body is firing, burning to life, and thrumming with pleasure. My lower belly tightens, filling with suffocating pressure, signaling that soon, no matter how much control I may exhibit, I will release whether my mind says no or not.

The moans, whimpers, and groans echoing around the room speed my thrusts. Sweat gathers at my hairline– beads tickling and licking against my flesh like the salacious caress of a lover.

"Monica, I wish that I was inside you for real. I wonder how insane it would feel as you milked my cock dry." Breathlessly, I whisper more naughty thoughts into Monica's ear as she rocks relentlessly against my strap-on and howls her torturous pleasure at the ceiling.

"What a perfect, little submissive, you are. You know not to ask to climax. I give you permission to beg me. Beg me, Monica. Beg me," I chant in her ear. "Beg. Me."

Head thrashing from side to side, cheek pressing and releasing against mine, "Please, Mistress. I ache so badly. If I don't orgasm soon, I will explode." Monica pleads as she jerks in her swing, thrusting back onto my latex phallus. I close my eyes against the sounds of her cries and the force grinding into my clit. I bit my lip, nearly bleeding myself to stay my release.

"Trust me, pet. I understand more than you can imagine." I tighten my hold on the front of Monica's slim throat, digging my fingernails into her skin. The force I use is just this side of choking. I use the action to quiet her wails of pleasure. I test my endurance and hers as my body prickles and beads with goose bumps. The pressure builds and builds in my lower belly, balling up an explosion which will destroy me. I lean my head back and moan '*fuck*' to the ceiling while being assaulted by a full-body shudder that makes me wonder if it's possible to orgasm without release. The pressure is agonizing– pain that hurts so good.

"Come for me, Monica. Prove to me that I pleasure you like no other could." I flex my fingers around her throat, holding her in place as she writhes and thrashes in my embrace. I concentrate on the force I exert, ensuring I don't accidently choke her, and it helps me control my own need to release.

There is a part of me that refuses to relinquish its hold, refusing to share an orgasm with another female. Today is not the day I will overcome my self-imposed sexual roadblocks, and not with Monica. A high descends, much more potent than sexual release. A high because I commanded another human being while controlling my baser functions.

I hold Monica while her screams turn to cries, and then whimpers. I hold her while her spasms decrease until she is silent and still. I brush the hair from her damp forehead and place a gentle kiss on it.

"You've pleased me to no end, Monica. You will make your new master a very happy man." With care, as her muscles are still spasming and clenching around the phallus, I pull out of her pussy. With the high still riding me, my fingertips shake as I detach the dong from the harness. I walk in front of Monica and to the side, so that I don't impede the audience's viewing pleasure.

"Be a good girl and lick this clean. You were a messy, dirty, pain slut. Show me how much you appreciated all the hard work I just did."

I help Monica out of the swing, and then point to the floor, signaling that I wish her to kneel. She kneels like an expert submissive. I hand her the phallus and watch, mesmerized, as she licks and sucks it clean. I take the toy back from her as she rolls her eyes up at me. Monica looks at me through the lace of her eyelashes– the lashes have clumped together from holding unshed tears.

"I thank you, Mistress." Small breasts rising and falling, Monica sobs in relief. She abases herself to the floor, resting her chin on the cold slate. A pink tongue dabs out between her lips to lick a wet line on my bare foot. I reach down to pet her. Soothingly, I run my fingertips through the top of her hair, down to the nape of her neck, and around her jawline. I tip her chin up to me with a fingertip.

"I told you, you would be my new best friend," I mutter wryly, remembering weeks ago how Ezra pissed me off but only Monica knew better. "I didn't lie, Monica. Your only issue is your self-worth. You're an amazing human being, and I hope you can see that now." I kiss Monica lightly on the lips, just a brush of a touch.

I wait patiently while Monica kneels at my feet, awaiting the masters' next move. At a loss, I begin to count slowly in my head. When I reach a hundred, I worry that I'm missing something vitally important. When I reach a thousand, I start to sweat profusely over the fact that I'm not performing whatever is required to transition to the next step of the initiation. When I start to doubt myself, I want to cringe into the floor next to Monica.

# Chapter Forty

"Place the hood over the submissive's head, Mistress." A deep voice that sounds familiar– one I cannot place –echoes ominously throughout the cavernous dungeon.

Feeling like a total badass, all proud of myself, I smile slyly when I note the use of Mistress. It is definitely Mistress with a capital **M**. I know I've passed their tests. The voice belongs to the Master of the Universe. The man who uses Cort's mouth and throat like his cock owns it. I've heard Master's voice before, but hell if I can place it.

My feet move on their own accord, following Master's command. I don't think; I just react to the sound of Master's voice. I've never felt the need to surrender before, not to this level anyway. It's an intense, heady sensation.

Feeling like a puppet strung up to that very commanding voice, I place the hood over Monica's head, covering her face while blinding her.

"Your turn, Mistress." A piece of fabric hits me in the chest. I grab it out of reflex before it falls to the floor. "Place the hood over your head." The voice sways me into compliance, and my high keeps me from shuddering like a petrified child.

"Master Dexter, please collect your new submissive, and then escort her to your private room. Allow her to rest up for your pleasure. Promptly come back so that we may begin the next step of the initiation."

"Yes, sir." Dexter sounds wry as fuck– the use of the honorific '*sir*' is laced heavily with sarcasm, and I wait for him to get annihilated by Master. "I wouldn't want to miss the rest of the initiation," is said in a way that belies the words, causing me to shiver with trepidation. "Mmm… nice," he purrs as he helps Monica to her feet. "All mine now."

Blinded again– I make a promise to locate and destroy all of these ridiculous burlap sack hoods.

I listen as Dexter's feet whisper across the floor. He caresses my hand delicately when he passes me by, lending me comfort while praising and reassuring me. "Come, Monica. I wish you to rest up, because soon I will mark you as my own, covering all of Katya's masterful artwork."

I hear the rustle of clothing, and I imagine Dexter covering his newest acquisition with her velvet cape, no longer wishing to share with his fellow masters.

"Thank you, Master Dexter." Monica whispers, sounding uncertain. "I'm surprised you would even consider me."

"Now, there will be none of that. Remember what Katya taught you? Heed her advice. Had I known you were in need of a master and about your proclivity for pain, I would have sought you out. I think we will complement each other nicely. You *will* make me very proud." Dexter emphasizes the word *will,* as if the prospect of beating Monica until he is proud is his greatest joy. Something tells me that it is.

I go back to counting silently, changing it up by alternating every number in English, French, and Spanish– anything to distract me from what's to come.

One.

Deux.

Tres.

Four.

Cinq.

Seis.

Seven.

Hearing stronger with my sight diminished, I listen to the sounds of the sadist and masochist's footsteps until they recede down the hallway. I hear and feel movement all around me– the whisper of fabric rustling, the labored breath of my fellow masters, and the sounds of suppressed laughter. I can almost scent their excitement, arousal, and trepidation on the air.

Gradually, as if one-by-one, I feel the presence of people gathering around me. Many people. I close my eyes, even though I'm blinded by the hood. I use the clarity it brings me to pinpoint how many are surrounding me.

Nine souls shroud me.

With great efficiency, warm fingers I don't recognize clasp my wrist and flatten my hand onto a tabletop. I tense every single muscle in my body to keep from struggling, even though my mind is screaming at me.

*RUN!*

I breathe through the terror. They won't hurt me, or so I hope. My wrist is strapped down to the surface, securing it. My thumb and forefinger are wrenched apart. I try not to gasp as visions of amputations sing through my head. Are they going medieval on my ass, where you lose a finger or a hand for stealing?

The zing of electric buzzing through a machine incites me to struggle and jerk at my hand. Strong fingers pull my thumb straight out at a painful angle, and I whimper in fear.

"Katya, relax. Trust me," Ezra breathes in my ear, trying to ease me with his words and tone of voice, yet he makes no move to touch me.

"Bad shit happens when you say that," I whimper, voice warbling with fear, preparing to freak the fuck out. "Every fucking time. Without fail!"

"Trust me, then." Cort's voice is laced with amusement, barely suppressing his laughter. "If you'd pay attention, you'd recognize the sound."

"Thanks, Captain Obvious. I know it's a tattoo gun, which is why I'm about to piss my leather catsuit. Thank you very much," I snarl, readying to attack to get the fuck out of the situation they placed me in.

"Still yourself," Master orders, and I flinch, obeying him instantly.

A cold stinging radiates through the fleshy webbing between my thumb and index finger. The buzzing sound slows as a needle grinds into my flesh. I swear to God, if they tattoo something stupid on me, I will kill them all.

I don't remember seeing a tattoo on either Cort or Ezra. But then again, I've never inspected that small part of flesh on their hands.

I know the drill after having Chrysalis tattooed on the nape of my neck. I slowly inhale through my nose and exhale out my mouth as they permanently mark my flesh. It doesn't hurt. I'm just frightened of what they could possibly mark me with.

Oh, no. I hope it's not that goddamned word *mine.*

I'm so caught up in my own thoughts that I don't realize it's over until I feel something soothing massaged into my skin. I chuckle to myself when I wonder if it's something that I had in my *hall o' lube* lineup. I'm losing it.

I wait patiently as my hand is released. It takes all of my restraint not to rub the freshly inked spot. I feel movement all around me, and then I hear the table my hand was strapped to roll away on rickety casters.

Hands remove my hood, and I anticipate the alarmingly bright light of the spotlight. I'm shocked that the dungeon is pitch-black again. Hands cradle my face tenderly, and I nestle into them. "Ezra," breathes past my parted lips.

"My brave, Kitty Kat. I'm so very proud of you." Ezra's voice is soft and strangely intimate for the setting. He kisses my cheek lightly, and then rubs his forehead against mine. "Relax, Kitty Kat. The masters are now going to introduce themselves. You won't see them because of anonymity. If they wish to be known, they will tell you who they are. I gave them permission to touch you intimately, but you are not to touch back. Behave, and don't disappoint me in front of them." He whispers against my face, causing me to shiver. Whether the shiver is from anticipation, fear, or his breath tickling me is anyone's guess.

"Kat, you did damn good." I relax instantly when I hear Queen's voice.

I know there are nine people here with me. I personally know five of them: Dexter, Ezra, Cortez, Syn, and Queen, and I've seen Dalton the drab, II the pretty-boy-next-door, and Alexander the homeboy. The only mystery is Master.

"How about you tell me what's coming next, and I'll forgive you for being half of Kimber?" I try extortion because I'm that petrified, but there is good humor warping my voice.

"I wouldn't even if I could." Queen laughs huskily. "I have no idea what's in store for you. But good luck if my initiation is any gauge on yours."

"Fuck," hisses out between my clenched teeth. "That's a scary thought."

"Ezra's not looking very stable tonight, so anything that goes wrong will be his fault," Queen warns. "Not that he'll admit it."

"Well, at least this isn't life or death," I mutter as Queen walks away.

The moment his hand touches me, I go boneless. I would know those fingers even in death. Cort pulls me into a full body embrace, completely engulfing me. I melt into his body, burying my face into the crook of his neck, inhaling the scent of home.

"I look forward to that punishment, Kitten. I may even let you use it on me somewhere other than my mouth," he says in a voice gone husky with lust. I moan at the visual of dominating Cort with my strap-on.

"Hmm… I bet you'd like that," I breathe against the side of his throat. I tip my face up, waiting for my kiss. He captures my mouth, while his sneaky fingers wiggle into the flap between my thighs. His tender kiss is at complete odds with the assault he performs between my legs- for the first time ever, Cort is marking his territory.

I nip Cort's pouty bottom lip when he almost brings me to climax. I'm beyond primed and ready after denying myself with Monica. He snickers evilly as he pulls his fingers from my aching pussy.

A wet fingertip slides across my bottom lip. I move my tongue to clean my lip free of my juices, but Cort beats me to the prize. "I love you, Kitten." Cort's voice breaks with deep emotions.

"I love you, too." I'm overcome by an intense need to cry as emotions hammer me from all the masters as well as my own rampaging inside my psyche. I add, "Skull-fuck," to lighten the moment.

A petite hand wrenches my breast in a vicelike grip. No preliminaries or introductions, just a hand smaller than my own bruising me with purpose. I steel myself, allowing no pained noises to flee my mouth or emotions to flash across my face. I paste a pleasant, neutral expression to cover what I'm truly feeling.

"You think you're hot shit, don't ya? You're recyclable. Nothing new and nothing special. You're a placeholder. I was here first. In all things in your life, I was there first." Syn's voice is low and furious, warped with years of bitter resentment. "You best learn their life only fits two."

"Syn, I'm not after your spot as a sadist," I say with a voice laced heavily with sarcasm. "As far as any issue you have with either Ezra or Cortez, that's between you and them. Leave me the fuck out of it. Stop hating me because of them. I don't know you, and you sure as fuck don't know me."

Syn's fingers tighten further, which I find impossible, since I thought she was using all of her strength to begin with. Who is this bitch, the Bionic Woman? I still think she's an assassin or some shit. I just don't see her holding down a normal job. Maybe a dog catcher, and all she does is growl at them and they jump into the crate. Mortician? Butcher?

I grit my teeth as Syn twists her impossibly tight grip on my breast. I'm thankful that my breasts are larger than most. A smaller breast would have filled her palm, allowing for a better grip. Fuck! My breasts were already incredibly tender to begin with.

Holding back, the only sign I'm about to break is the bead of sweat paving its way down my cheek. When I don't whimper in pain or cower in fear, Syn releases me and steps away without a word. I guess I just passed one of her tests, but I highly doubt she will respect me after this display of dominance.

A small hand deftly slides into the flap covering my abused breast and palpitates in a soothing manner. "Thank you, sir," I moan to my mentor in relief– it's not sexual in nature. My tit is radiating fire, hot spikes of shooting pain that Dexter is massaging away.

"My pleasure, Kat." Dexter's voice contains barely leashed fury. I worry that I'm the cause and wince when he speaks. "That was not very nice of our petite sadist. Syn knows better than to abuse those who don't need it." He sounds disappointed in Syn instead of me, and we all know he's no longer speaking to me. "She knows better than to take her frustrations out on others. That is not how I trained her to behave."

Dexter continues to softly massage my aching breast. I close my eyes in relief. I pray that he will manipulate the other one, too. They are both so tender and sore– have been for weeks on end.

Dexter leans in and kisses me, tangling his tongue with mine. I'm frozen in surprise, not kissing him back. His mouth tastes of red wine, and I instantly want some to deaden whatever hell is to come. My mentor doesn't take any liberties, just thoroughly kisses me while his hand soothes my tender, achy breast.

"You and I have a date soon. It was a pleasure to train you, Kat, and I look forward to continuing your education in sadism." Dexter taps the tip of my nose while chuckling to himself. "Also, I appreciate your gift of Monica. I couldn't have asked for a more appropriate thank you present. I wish my other trainees were so thoughtful. The only thing Cortez gave me was a black eye." I can hear the smile in Dexter's deep voice, and then his presence leaves my side.

"My name's Dalton, and we've never been properly introduced. But you did give me a show in the hallway many weeks ago." Dalton's flat voice sounds like he's sneering at me. I'm thankful that I'm fully clothed, because I can picture his nasty leer. "Allow me to show you how it's really done."

The metal-on-metal grating sound of the slide of a zipper has me praying that what it contains is not meant for me. Just the sound of this man turns my stomach. In recent history, this has to be the most uncomfortable experience I've had the pleasure to live through.

My hearing increases to bat-like levels. I take air in through my nostrils so fast that I worry I will hyperventilate. The pounding of my blood through my veins overwhelms my hearing. I count as I breathe to slow both my heart and lungs. The tearing sound of a wrapper freaks me out, and if I hadn't frozen in fear, I would've ran like hell.

NO… No… no. Ezra wouldn't do this to me. Yes, he would. My only saving grace is that Cortez wouldn't allow Ezra to destroy himself by allowing this travesty. Telling myself this doesn't stop the panic from overpowering reason. I start to hyperventilate, body shaking from the force.

"I've given Dalton no permission for sex, Katya. No one will have sex with you tonight." Ezra reassures me, and I realize I was murmuring *no…no… no…* over and over again out loud. "Dalton has taken it upon himself to be the antagonist this evening, so it seems. We always have one during an initiation."

"Usually you," Cort mutters, but I can hear the fury radiating from his tone. "If you hadn't been such a dick, Dalton wouldn't be acting like an ass by abusing Kat to punish us. Dalton likes me, after all, but not you."

"Everyone likes you," Dalton mutters begrudgingly.

"Actually, it's always me who is the villain of every initiation," Master says, sounding impressively arrogant.

"Will you forever defend Ezra?" Cort accuses. If I was Master, I would have backhanded Cort for pouting.

"Shut up!" I snap. "I have shit I'm trying to deal with here. Remember me? The girl you're fighting about?"

"Now this is an initiation." Dexter laughs, sounding a bit high. "Excuse me while I get comfortable. Care to join me, Syn?"

"Fuck, yeah. I want nowhere near this shit," Syn snarls. "Regina?"

"Look, a perfectly empty piece of flooring demanding my ass inhabit it. If anyone as much as tries to get me to move from this spot, I will knock their ass out cold. I paid my dues during my initiation with a brutal blowjob, a double penetration, and a marriage proposal."

"Mine was bad, with the cocksucker's crying and secret spilling, but even I will admit yours was the worst, Regina." For the first time ever, Syn sounds respectful.

"Just get it over with, you drab asshole!" I snarl, furious yet thankful Ezra won't allow anyone to actually fuck me tonight. I don't want to recreate Queen's horrific initiation.

Clammy fingers part the flap on my catsuit with the dexterity as if he himself was the designer. Without preamble, Dalton roughly thrusts three fingers knuckle-deep, tearing at my flesh because I wasn't prepared.

Humiliation slams into me as my body flushes bright red–skin prickling at the intensity. I don't feel violated, or like a whore. All I know is mortification and fury, all directed at Ezra for placing me in this situation. But I am not without responsibility, as I placed myself in this situation, wanting to be a part of Maître du Jeu. Now I realize that was fucking stupid, as who in their right mind would want to be equal to these assholes? I shouldn't lower myself to their level. I should strive to be more than they are.

I find nothing in this situation erotic or arousing. If my body could, it would wick all of my moisture, leaving me drier than a desert. Dalton starts finger-fucking me with poor form. Even if I were aroused, it wouldn't do anything for me. I pity his bad attempt. Dalton is lacking technique. I wonder if he hasn't had much experience, or his submissives just fake their enthusiasm.

"Let's see if you can last as long as I can," Dalton mutters snidely. I want to reply that there is no contest, but then I realize what he's up to. Dalton is going to finger-fuck me while whacking off– disgusting.

I shudder in revulsion, nearly toppling to the ground from the force. I steel my muscles, becoming rigid and unyielding, refusing to show my true emotions or to allow this man to get the best of me. I can't see, but my eyes are throwing sparks of fury. I'm far from a virgin, but I've had too many men force their way between my legs, and it's taking everything in me to not feel violated.

I stand rigid, head held high with my shoulders back, exuding quiet dignity and power, as if I'm not being penetrated by a man who is punishing Ezra through me. On the inside, my psyche is a riot of darker emotions. While I cannot see, they must be able to see me in order to torture me. For all appearance, I must look like I couldn't give a shit less about what's happening to my body.

I pray that the scene with Monica turned this bastard on, to the point he pops quicker than a teenaged boy.

I flinch when Dalton moans deeply as he strokes himself, sounding like a bad actor in an amateur, online porn video. The friction of his palm rubbing against his flesh has a wave of nausea descending upon me. I swallow back bile when Dalton's fingers pick up speed inside of my body, knuckles hitting my labia in a bruising pattern. I hope the force of his jerky movements brings him closer to the brink of release.

I drop my eyes to stare down where I assume the floor is, imagining the slate tile in my mind's eye. I pretend we all suffer from the blindness the pitch-black dungeon offers. As I stand here, I develop a greater understanding of the humiliation a submissive endures. I can't imagine why they would want that need fulfilled– punishment perhaps?

I count in my head to distract and displace myself, adding Italian to the mix with the English, French, and Spanish. If this goes on any longer, I'm going to have to learn how to count in German.

I'm thankful for how aroused Monica and Cort made me, or I would be rubbed raw from Dalton's forceful assault. At a count of four-hundred-fifty-three, Dalton curses his release at the ceiling. His drawn out howl sounds rehearsed. I wonder if he stands in front of the mirror and practices his orgasm face. I'm sure it's as boring as the rest of his drab ass.

"I guess you win," Dalton sneers breathlessly as he wrenches his fingers from my body.

"Yay, me!" I mock congratulate myself, rolling my eyes but I never look back down.

The air displaces as Dalton moves toward me. I turn my face at the very last second, and his dry lips land on my cheek. I sigh out in relief as he walks away, believing neither of us enjoyed a second of it.

I'm cradled in a strong embrace. I'm so relieved that a few tears escape the corner of my eyes. I shake against Ezra, trying to contain the sob building. I don't know if I want to collapse into Ezra's arm, or shove him to the ground, sit on his chest, and bash his face in with my clenched fists.

"I'm sorry," the martyr makes an appearance, explaining away all the bad shit with a two word, meaningless phrase. We all know he'd do it again given the chance, and then act contrite once it has passed.

My mind tells my tongue to speak, but Master recognizes this before I do, and issues a warning growl for me to shut the fuck up. Proving he's a mind-reader as well as Ezra's biggest champion.

"You and I are going to have words, asshole," Cort threatens, and then he begins to cackle an evil sound that reverberates down my spine. "I'll be telling my shadow on you."

"Huh?" Dalton grunts out, but then his voice pitches higher, almost girlish, holding a thick accent. "What are you, a fucking two-year-old tattletale? What happens during an initiation stays in the initiation, that's the rules. Who are you talking about?"

"You'll find out soon enough," Cort mutters, sounding like he has a gaggle of mafia hitmen in his back pocket. "Go sit with them, and behave yourself."

Ezra massages my back and shoulders until I relax into him. After a few moments, I rebuild my confidence and shake my head against his chest, signaling that I'm ready to go on with this madness. Ezra steps back from me, but I can feel him hovering nearby.

"Hi, Katya," a pleasantly happy voice says. A warm palm slides down my right arm until he clasps my hand, and then shakes it formally.

"Nice to meet you, sir," my voice cracks from worry. He sounds pleasant enough and acts really nice, but I have no clue what's to come. I'm positive this is the pretty-boy-next-door with the blindingly bright smile that I could never trust.

"May I call you Kat?" II doesn't release my hand, as if maintaining contact during a conversation is normal behavior.

I shake my head yes, only to realize he might not be able to see me. I lick my lips a few times to moisten them. "Yes, you may call me Kat. May I call you by your given name, sir?"

He glides his thumb against the back of my hand in soothing circles as he speaks. "Call me Whitt. All my friends do. We actually met at Ezra's birthday party a few months ago, but I didn't have the pleasure of speaking with you."

"Ah, I remember you being there, holding up the ginger-haired kid who wouldn't stop staring at my daughter." My observation earns me a wide array of responses from my fellow masters, especially Ezra, who stiffens next to me.

"And the hallway," Whitt reminds me, sounding extremely amused. "Don't worry, I won't accost you." Whitt's laugh is infectious. He oozes charm and good cheer– it's disturbing to someone such as myself, who is always melancholy.

"Do you ever get sad?" blurts out before I can stop it.

"Often," Whitt answers readily. "But I'm happy to finally get to hold a conversation with you. I've been curious to see what has both Ezra and Cort so intrigued."

"I'm sure it will wear off soon," I mutter, earning me another hearty laugh from Whitt.

"Doubtful. Once Ezra latches onto someone, he never lets go." Pretty Boy proves he knows Ezra better than I do. "I won't be an asshole, but I would enjoy a simple kiss from our newest mistress." Whitt speaks formally and calmly. But I can still hear his youth beneath the surface of his deep voice.

"Okay," I whisper, feeling shy all of a sudden. Whereas Dalton skeeved me out, Whitt calms me with the power he exudes.

Whitt's mouth connects with my slightly parted lips. He kisses me with skill, not a brush of lips or a hungry feast. This is a man you could kiss for hours and still crave more. He's drinking me down, not consuming me. It's lovely and comforting, more so than arousing and sexual.

I tentatively pull Whitt's bottom lip in between mine and run the tip of my tongue along the curve of his. He rewards me with a quiet moan. He doesn't pull me any closer, or take anything I'm not willing to give. Pretty Boy proves he respects me with a kiss.

Our hands and lips are the only body parts connecting– it's sweet, almost innocent. The feel of so little is more mentally arousing than all the stimulation Dalton doled out. Whitt pulls back reluctantly, and I'm left leaning forward with my lips parted and my eyes glazed over.

"That was… I could taste both Ezra and Cort on your lips." Whitt clears his throat. "You're both lucky bastards." I feel movement to my side, and then hear a thump. I envision the man version of a hug– half handshake/half embrace.

"It must have been one hell of a kiss, Whitt. I don't think Cort or I have that effect on Katya." Ezra's affectionate laugh tells me that he isn't offended, that he found it amusing, and he and Whitt are very close friends.

"May I have a moment of your…" a heavy pause by a deep-voiced male. "Whatever Katya is to you, Ezra. I'm only asking as a courtesy, as it's paining me not to just ask the woman myself."

"No," Ezra breathes the word, yet it holds menace. "Alex." For some reason, the name flows like a verbal eye roll from Ezra's tongue. "This is your first initiation, as we were all short-changed at the lack of yours and Dalton's. It's a pity, as I wish we could schedule one now as payback. But I digress. No alone time during an initiation. This is your time with Katya, but it's done in public view."

"May we compromise by allowing me to move us to the side to speak in private? I mean Katya absolutely no harm."

"No, I trust you in that. What I don't trust you with is secrets. No doubt you're just the messenger."

"Fine," Alex allows, sounding put out. "But back up. You're crowding me. If you wouldn't stop Dalton from assaulting the mother of your child, then you should have no issue with me holding a civil conversation with the woman."

I shouldn't enjoy the judgment ringing in the man's voice. But it makes me feel vindicated somehow, like someone actually gives a shit about ethics, has a conscience, and empathy for their fellow man.

I remember when I first caught sight of Alexander, how at ease he made me feel. Even when in a mortifying position, he made me feel like what I was doing was perfectly appropriate. He enjoyed the view, and then appeared like he wanted a smoke.

The raven-haired man reminded me of the laidback guys in my hometown, which was a comfort. "If you'd walk me to the side, as I am at a disadvantage in the dark, I would speak with you as privately as possible." I reach out for Alex to take my arm, which is quickly caught in a sure grip. "Ezra, I'll sense if you follow, and I'll turn around and kick you in the nuts."

Alexander escorts me away from the crowd that is now taunting Ezra with verbal jabs. I ignore the fact that Ezra seems to be stationary yet emoting confusion, worry, and anger. I've got bigger problems than soothing his bruised ego.

"I wish I would have met you under more pleasant circumstances," I begin, hoping to find an ally. "Neither time have I been at my best. I seem to be painting myself with a whore-brush."

Chuckling, a very deep yet satisfying sound, Alex shows he's more amused than anything else. "You're lucky you're with Ezra and Cortez. Whoever kisses their asses gets a nice initiation. They played poker and ate pizza with Whitt, yet they tortured each other. Poor Regina. My God, they brutalized her as punishment for their own initiations. Thankfully I wasn't there, or else there would have been bloodshed."

"I see you know them well." My voice holds a vicious edge, annoyed with myself. "I'm not sure if I belong here."

"Exactly. The elder of my family wished to make sure *you* knew them well. That is why I asked for privacy. He didn't want you to become their pawn, even knowing your strength. I am here to warn you while offering you a safe haven from the fallout."

Ignoring the sentiment of the conversation, I go in for the jugular. "Elder? Is that like when Ezra speaks in code and calls himself the head of his family? Or is it a moniker for a crime boss?"

"Oh, my..." Alex laughs for a few minutes straight, becoming breathless. "He's going to get a big kick out of that. You'll make his night. Crime boss!" I can almost imagine Alex wiping tears of laughter from his eyes.

Calming slightly, he gasps out, "It's exactly as you surmised. Elder of the family. We'll call him a concerned friend, one who doesn't want you to be harmed by those destructive idiots."

"I'm doing my best to survive," I admit for the first time since stepping foot onto Dominion soil. "I do see Ezra and Cortez clearly. All of their faults and their good parts, and I love them anyway. I think I'm crafty enough to survive it. I also know that someday they might break my heart. But it's a chance I'm willing to take, as every day spent with them is a gift, even if they are pissing me off. Plus, I have my daughter to think about, wanting her to have her family."

"Just as he suspected," Alex rumbles. "I'm about to recite a direct quote, which I'm sure to fuck up."

"He actually wrote the message down, and forced the messenger to memorize it?" I marvel over the lunacy.

"He saved my life and gave me a reason to live, so I find it rather endearing, actually." While reverent in tone, I can almost hear the blush staining Alex's cheeks.

"Katya," Alex begins to recite in a lulling voice, so quiet I have to strain to hear. "No doubt you told my minion how you love Ezra and wish to stay with him. You need to remember who you are, never forget your roots, and never allow anyone to taint your sense of self. You are intelligent, able to work anywhere without Ezra's interference. You have the strength and wherewithal to survive anything, as your past demonstrates.

"Don't be arrogant, prideful, and a bullhead. While you don't need anyone, never forget you have friends– never forget to seek help when you need it. At the first sign of danger, go in the opposite direction as your lovers, as they are most likely the root of the destruction."

"Jesus," I interrupt. "My concerned friend doesn't like Ezra and Cortez, does he?"

"He loves them, actually," Alex answers with sincerity. "More importantly, he knows them well. He's simply here to protect you, while allowing you freewill, even if you place yourself in danger. It's your call. But he wants you to know that should you find yourself in a position where you feel alone, realize you aren't. You can come to me and I will take you to him, where you will be safe and comfortable. The offer is extended to your daughter as well, even though it's against regulations."

"Why?" I breathe, thoroughly confused as to how I obtained a benefactor.

"Let's just say he understands what it's like to be placed in a situation not of your own making, how love can turn you into someone you don't recognize, and how trusting those closest to you leads to your ultimate downfall. While there is no escape, there are concerned friends who only have your best interests at heart."

"For as long as we share the same interests," I tack on, and Alex doesn't correct me. "I'm leery of your offer."

"Understandable," Alex murmurs to me as his hand finds my forearm, ready to escort me back to Ezra. "You shouldn't trust anyone, especially those you feel you should trust the most. They are the people you should fear."

"Thanks, you ominous fucker. And here I thought you'd be a cool dude, one I could smoke with and shoot the shit."

Alex laughs as he transfers me back to a silently seething Ezra. "We can still do that. I hate the lifestyle these rich fucks live just as much as you do, as does my elder."

"Self-loathing is a real bitch, isn't it?" Ezra comments. "Are you finished with your propaganda? Did your indoctrination work its magic in turning the mother of my child away from me because I'm evil incarnate? Tell him I'll break his hands next, then he won't be able to communicate at all."

"Whoa there, killer," Alex drawls, and I can picture him raising his palms to ward off Ezra. "You must really love Kat if you're threatening the gentlest person on the planet. You can understand why he might have some concerns for Kat's welfare. He's taken an interest in her, for obvious reasons."

"Ezra is being territorial," Master interjects, calming the situation. "No one harms a hair on anyone's head without my say-so. If any harm befalls him, Ezra, so help me God, I will break you."

"I thought I was the most important person in your life." Ezra sounds like a heartbroken child.

"Jesus Christ!" Cort shouts. "I motherfucking hate initiations. It's my version of Hell. It's like a psychiatrist convention at an asylum and I'm an orderly. Ezra, M-Master is not going to allow you to hurt his best friend. Don't be a dick."

"Wait a minute!" I locate Alex by reaching out until I find his forearm. "You were sent by Master's BFF to steal me from Ezra? For what purpose?"

"Welcome to Dominion, Sweetheart!" Alex nearly sings. "The offer is open-ended. If you need help, you know where to find me. By the way, the finale of your initiation is meeting the master, so you might want to call in that favor now."

# Chapter Forty-One

"Do this for me. Please," Ez breathes in my ear so softly I'm not sure I heard him right. His voice sounds odd, not Master Ez or Ezra– foreign. "Don't think of this as me sharing you. That's not the purpose. I'm sharing him *with* you. This man has touched both Cortez and myself, and it seems befitting if you were to do the same in return. I need you to worship him."

"What?" I gasp out, realization sinking it. "You want me to do what? Get skull-fucked, you asshole?" I wrench away from Ezra, glaring in all directions, knowing they can somehow see me even though I cannot see them. "You're not my goddamned pimp! You're supposed to be the person who loves me, respects me, and treats me with dignity! I'm done!"

"NO!" Cort shouts as his heavy footfalls vibrate the floor beneath me. "Abso-fucking-lutely not!" His fingers bracket my upper arm, yanking me away from Ezra. "NO!"

"Jealous?" Ezra sneers, opening a flesh wound to the point that all three of us will bleed out.

"I hate you right now, Ez. I motherfucking hate you," Cort issues as a vow. "I love Katya, and you're going to destroy what we're building if you make her do this. She's not like me. She's like you, and this will be too heavy of a cross to bear. This haunts you, eats you alive, using Katya won't erase it."

"What's going on?" Voice cold, I whisper because if I don't I'll scream. "Answer me!"

"Don't do this, Ez. Not here. Not now. Not in front of everyone," Cort stresses. "I'm not jealous; I'm protecting you from yourself. I get why you think this is necessary. Fuck, I'll promise never to do it again as long as you let Katya walk out of this dungeon right this second."

"The past is choking me," Ezra bites out. "I need to find a balance. Right my wrongs. Erase all the evil acts I've committed. Katya will balance it."

"Ezra, all has been forgiven, even before your transgressions passed," Master breathes so softly, his words only meant for Ezra.

"That's not fair," Ezra nearly whines. "It has to be an eye for an eye."

"We're more than even," Master states loudly, voice echoing off the dungeon's walls. "I will greet Katya, give her a kiss, and call this night concluded. Katya is not Regina. She is not Cortez. She is not Faith. Get over it and move the fuck on already before you destroy our lives."

"You're hard!" Ezra bellows as an accusation. "You want this. Don't deny it."

"Don't look at my crotch!" Embarrassment rings in Master's voice, but not as heavily as the warning. "I'm a man, who was just offered a blowjob– we've all seen the skull-fuck footage. Obviously I'm not unaffected. But don't ever look at me that way again, Ezra. Boundaries."

"Ezra has no concept of boundaries," I mutter to myself, resigned to anything that's to come my way. Master's resulting laughter is amused yet pained. "Clearly, as he was passing around a video of me being violated by his partner. Thanks a fucking lot."

"Can I leave?" Dexter shouts while everyone else is either laughing or making retching noises of revulsion. "Seriously, let me fucking leave. I'm not a pervert like you, getting off on watching us get off. You've never done anything sexual in our presence, and I'd like to keep it that way. No amount of bleach will cleanse my memory."

"Dexter may leave, but the rest of you must stay," Master allows.

"The fuck! What about me?" Dalton shouts, voice sounding different.

"What about you?" Dexter, Syn, and Queen ask in unison, but Syn keeps spewing, "I don't see the connection."

"Go upstairs, Dalton," Master orders. "Regina?"

"I'm staying," Queen replies belligerently.

"You couldn't drag my ass out, if you tried," Alex purrs, tone laced heavily with arousal. "I wish I could record this for future playback." A deep grunt echoes around the dungeon, followed by a pain-filled wince. "Sorry. So sorry. Not actually sorry, but my bruised rib is."

"I want to leave, but I can't seem to get the words out to ask." Whitt's raspy voice is hoarse. "Strangely, I have a sick fascination with the thought of Katya sucking him off. It's... Jesus, Ez, are you sure about this?"

"Ezra," Cort pleads. "Don't do this. Kat keeps forgiving you. But at some point, it's all going to add up, and you'll regret it most of all. She won't hate me; she'll loathe you."

"Since Ezra sees me as his whore." I drop to the floor, not bothering to catch my fall. My knees connect with the slate tile, the sickening crunch reverberating around the dungeon. It stings, no doubt a wicked bruise will bloom by morning, but I'm numb inside and out. "Master, would you like me to suck your dick?"

"I've changed my mind. A decade of schooling won't allow me to act as a witness to something so harmful, no matter how smoking hot and hedonistic it may be." The sound of Alex getting to his feet in a hurry radiates around us. "Wait up, Dalton! I'm coming with you."

"I already explained to Katya why it was important," Ezra's voice flows to my ears. "She understands."

"Evidently not," Master breathes. "Seeing as she just called herself your whore."

"Kat is a whore," Syn snarls, causing my false calm to dissipate, replacing it with fury and shame.

"You're not sixteen anymore, Chickadee." Master's voice is cold, cutting. His words are hurled to harm everyone in their path. "I won't stop anyone from punching you, and I won't allow you to retaliate. I suggest you maintain your silence."

Movement stirs around me, but it ceases simply by Master clearing his throat. "Not you, Cort. The two of you would kill one another, and then we'd regret the loss."

"Just so we're clear." My voice rings out in the sudden silence. "I know I'm being used right now, and I realize I will not be offered an explanation. So let's just get this the fuck over with, because I'm not feeling all that great right now. I'm exhausted." I clutch my stomach as it roils, threatening to spill everything I'd consumed today.

Issuing a sigh that suspiciously sounds like Ezra's, Master gives us a way out– one not taken. "Ezra, are you positive this is what you want?"

"Yes, I have to clear my conscience," Ezra rasps, sounding sure yet terrified.

"Fine!" The sound of knees hitting the floor next to me makes me flinch. Cort wraps an arm around my waist, holding me to his side. "Moral support," he whispers into my ear. "I'll tell you what to do to make it as quick as possible." Shifting his attention upwards, "No skull-fucking," Cort warns Master. "She's been sick lately."

"Katya," a gentle command forces my face toward the sound. I tilt my head to the side, tasting the flavor of the voice in my mind. I know that voice. It's so frustrating that I can't place it. If a sound had a taste, his voice would be smooth, silky, smoky, and quiet. It's a voice you would instantly obey. A voice you would do anything to hear. A voice you pray doesn't rise against you in anger.

"Master," I reply shyly, feeling ashamed, not only because of what I'm about to do, but because it's being witnessed. Humiliated. Mortified. Heartbroken. Confused.

Not life or death. I've been raped by two men– the act witnessed. I've touched countless females. I've had sex with Aaron while Ezra and Cortez watched. The vanilla part of me– the traditional part who thought she'd get married and have children is bristling. I never thought my life would turn into this.

An odd high descends, smothering my doubts and fears, replacing it with a dominant being who takes what she wants, shows them who's boss, and doesn't give a flying fuck what someone else thinks of her.

Master's lean fingers rove over my hair, and then caress the curve of my jaw. His fingers are as soft as a female's, long and tapered– elegant. I study him as he studies me, trying to solve the puzzle of who he is. A man who works with his mind, never his hands. He's never seen a hard day's work in his life. A blunt thumb smooths across my lips, and I sigh from the satiny feel of the sensation. My scalp prickles and tingles as my body flushes hot from being seduced by an innocent touch.

"You have the right to say no," Master allows. "No one will blame you."

"Are you intimate with many people?" Blurts out as soon as I think it.

"No, I find sharing myself a sacred act after having been taken without my consent–" He is cut off by Ezra making a strangled sound deep in the back of his throat. "I will understand if you say no, Katya. Just as I understand why Ezra is asking this of the both of us. He truly means well, even if the desired outcome is not as he thinks it will be. This act will harm him, not heal him."

Cortez's fingers clench against my waist, tips digging into my flesh, as we await my answer. My mind spins a million miles a second, never coming to a conclusion. Master's last sentence is what gets me the most. If you love someone, you shouldn't wish to hurt them. But the vindictive side of me wants Ezra to feel how he's always making me feel. Tortured by his abusive brand of love.

"I'm not doing this for you, Ezra. I'm not doing this to prove I love you, or to obey you, or to right some wrong. I want no hard feelings from anyone who calls me a whore, or from any toes I'm stepping on. The only reason I'm doing this is because I have to pay my due. Those before me did as they were asked at their initiations, no matter the cost. I should be no different. I'm also doing it because I don't want to live a life with regret. I'd rather regret action than inaction."

Taking a deep breath, I shore up my nerves. On the exhale, I reach forward with shaking fingertips, trying to locate the object of my duty. Fingers clasp mine– Cort's – and navigate them to their destination, proving they can all see even though I'm blinded by the lack of light.

Thin fingers clasp both of our hands– the grip tight, almost violent –removing them from his person. "No hands," he reminds, issuing a rule that Cort must understand, as he winces as if struck. "Blowjobs are with lips, mouths, and throats, with minimal teeth usage. Hands are for handjobs, and I don't receive handjobs. Roaming hands and fingertips are meant for the intimacy with a lover– we are not lovers."

"You heard the man, keep your hands to yourself," I whisper out the side of my mouth to Cortez, and then burst out laughing at the ridiculousness of the situation. I'm sure Master's warning was meant to sound scary, but I found the seriousness of his tone to be hilarious instead. The clinical bent comforts me even more. I'm here to do a job, and that's it.

A blow job.

I fold my hands in my lap, listening to Ezra's relieved chuckles as the soundtrack to this odd moment. Ezra is no doubt relieved that I'm not going to tear his nutsack from between his legs. Ezra's probably equally relieved to learn that Cort doesn't get soft, lover-like caresses from the imposing man as thrusts his cock down Cort's throat.

Cort grunts, shifting as if uncomfortable next to me, and then I realize why. A cockhead taps against my lip, asking for admittance. Eyes held wide, I open my mouth as far as my jaw will unhinge, and yet it's not far enough.

"What the fuck?" I grumble around the intrusion, barely able to wrap my lips around the cockhead. Opening my mouth farther, another inch presses into me. As thick as a can of Coke. As smooth and hard as blown glass. As searing as a hot iron. The veins press into my tongue and scrape against the roof of my mouth, as the glans prods at the back of my throat.

Instead of worrying over what I'm doing, the bad choices I'm making, and how my lovers are watching me blow another man, I marvel over the fact that Cortez's favorite activity is skull-fucking this forearm. My eyes bulge in shock, respecting Cort more than I did before.

"Size seems to run in his family." Cort's lips brush the shell of my ear, causing me to shiver. He's quiet enough that no one can overhear. "He got the width… someone else got the length."

"Excuse me," Master interrupts, having the sonic hearing of a bat. "I am far from short. It just looks that way because of my girth. I'm just as long as you, dipshit. Now shut the fuck up."

"Make me," Cort antagonizes him, and I'd love to think it's because he's trying to save me from the throbbing appendage. But I bet he wishes our positions were reversed. Cort makes a grumbling sound, and everyone in attendance starts snickering.

"I can multitask," Master reminds Cort, who is struggling next to me. "If you promise to keep the inane chatter to a minimum, so I can concentrate on coming, I'll let go of your smug face." Cortez falls to the floor with an oath to behave, no doubt a palm forcefully shoved his face.

The cock in my mouth begins to slide back and forth slowly, informing me I'm just a passenger– the vessel of our master's pleasure. Not one who is passive, I clasp my hands behind my back and lean forward, using my knees as a fulcrum point to stabilize me as I move my neck. Rocking back and forth, my saliva finally smooths the passage of Master's mammoth cock.

"That's perfect," Cort breathes even quieter, trying not to risk Master's ire. Judging by the way the cock in my mouth flexed, Master can hear a bug's wings during flight. "Allow your spit to coat that dick. Good God, that's fucking hot."

I concentrate on Cort's breathless encouragement as I take over the blowjob, not allowing Master to find a rhythm with his hips. Finally he submits and just sways with my movement.

Getting closer to me, almost knocking me to the side, Cort leans into me. "Use your teeth a little bit. Scrape them against the underside of his cock. It'll drive him batshit. Trust me." I do as I was told, and the cock in my mouth elongates, getting impossibly larger in the cavern of my mouth, to the point I almost choke. Saliva and pre-cum stream down my chin, skeeving me out. Cort reaches forward to clean my face, knowing I hate being sticky.

"Hands," Master whispers, voice sounding more drugged than angry, and Cort shirks back as if kicked. "Very nice, Katya." A deep grunt has every inch of my body warming to volcanic temperatures and Cort tweaking out next to me. "I never allow a normal blowjob, but this is very, very nice indeed."

"Remember what I told you about how sucking him off is the best high?" Cort is being so quiet, even Master can't hear him any longer. "He's the strongest of us all. You are not a whore because you suck his cock. You're honored because he allowed it. But more so, you're stronger than him because you're about to bring him to his knees. There is nothing more empowering than weakening those who have no weaknesses."

Master shudders above me, body swaying toward me. His cock bulges, the veins beating frantically to the pace of his heart. He tries to stay silent, to maintain his restraint, but my mouth unleashes his release. Elegant fingers twist in the strands of my hair, forgetting to have a care about snapping them off painfully.

I bring our master to his knees.

Body spasming, knees thudding to the slate tile, Master howls his orgasm as he floods my mouth with his bitter essence. He doesn't relinquish my hair, using it to press my face to his abdomen, forcing me to swallow all I can hold. Nearly choking, semen pouring out of my mouth to drip from my chin, I can't help but feel accomplished for ruining the man at my feet.

"You're my hero." Cort huffs an awed laugh as if astonished.

I pull back from Master's body, his flaccid cock sliding free of my mouth. I lean over to Cortez, fisting his shirt in my grip, and scrub my face clean.

"If you kiss Ezra before you brush your teeth, I will murder everyone in this room who acted as a witness," Master warns, and his true identity hits me like an eighteen-wheeler on a freeway, and I'm driving a Kia Rio straight to Hell.

"Goddamnit!" I surge to my feet, blindness be damned. "God! Fucking! Damn! It!" Cort reaches me before I start kicking at anything that will connect with my foot. Nose flaring wildly, eyes stinging with the threat of tears, I bellow at the top of my lungs, "Ezra!" while Cortez protects everyone from my wrath.

"The initiation has met its conclusion. I suggest you all go home," Master orders in a rush to clear the dungeon.

"No, by all means, stick around to watch my humiliation," I bite out, furious. "I'm going to go scrub myself in our room. You guys can stay out here and laugh at me." I fling Cort's arm away from me, knowing the general vicinity of the back hallway. The center of the dungeon is empty, a clear shot to the hallway, so I don't fear falling and breaking a bone. Nor do I care if I look like a fool if I should fall.

Cort grips my arm before I make it ten feet, steering me in the right direction. "Ezra, you better give me time to calm her down before she sets sight on you. I fear she may actually kill you this time."

# Chapter Forty-Two

As soon as Cortez types the security code to unlock the door, I fall into our room, almost tripping over my own feet. In a rush, I reach blindly to flick the light switch. "I knew you assholes could see!"

"Night vision," Cort admits as he shuts the door by kicking it with his heel.

"No shit, Captain Obvious!" I point at the goggles he's sporting like a diabolical headband. "How could you?" I accuse, furious. "You should have told me the truth!"

I charge forward, fists meeting Cort's chest with a hollow thump. He captures my wrists, not allowing me to hurt him or myself. "Truthfully, I thought you would have figured out who Master was months ago. But I forgot how your mind protects you from unpleasant truths."

Fuming, I'm rendered speechless but not motionless. I struggle to wrench my arms free, and then I begin pacing around our mini-dungeon/apartment. I yank a paddle from the wall, needing to release my aggression. I begin smashing the hell out of the sofa cushions.

"Who is Katya Waters?" I mutter breathlessly, never relenting in my assault to the innocent furnishings. "She is nobody's whore. She is ethical, refusing to cheat on or with someone. She will not lower her standards."

"Very accurate description," Cort mutters, and it draws my attention. I lunge forward, catching the outside of his thigh with the paddle before he can get away. He shrieks, "I don't like pain! Don't!" sounding like a little girl who saw a spider.

"Ezra turns me into someone I don't recognize– someone I loathe." Without remorse, I hit the lamp as hard as possible, fascinated on how the glass explodes in a facsimile of my heart. "Knowing you are still married was hard enough."

"I'm getting a divorce!" Cort shouts, rounding the sofa to get out of my aim. "Ezra's orders. Honest. It will be finalized in less than a month."

"Not. The. God. Damn. Point." I smack whatever is nearby with every word I speak. "Ezra's phony engagement wrecked me emotionally for months! A sham! Now this!"

My eye catches a vase. Who the fuck puts a vase in a dungeon? "Rich assholes, that's who," I answer myself, causing Cort to look at me like I've lost my mind. "How the hell do I face my daughter's grandmother at Thanksgiving? Christmas? Birthdays? Ever? HOW?"

Fingertips taking on a life of their own, I watch as I grip the vase, shoulder and elbow slowly rolling back. With blinding speed, I whip it across the room, directly at Cortez's face. With a shout, "Katya!" he ducks, the vase exploding an inch above his head on the block wall, glass raining down to tinkle to the floor.

I go in for the kill since the vase missed its target. "Incestuous bunch of bastards, aren't you? I could understand Ezra's and your predicament. But this? Not only did I just blow the man who for all intents and purposes is my father-in-law, you suck his dick on a regular basis. The man who raised you as a son. And don't think I forgot what Ezra whispered in my ear, about him sucking Marcus off too!"

Not waiting for a reply, because I fear my compassion will override my self-righteous indignation, I charge into the bathroom. "Damn it! I deserve to be angry," I snarl at my reflection, hating my glazed green eyes, the ruddy flush to my cheeks, and my father-in-law's semen dried on my lips and chin.

Arm lashing out, I punch the mirror, needing to remove my reflection from the glass. But it doesn't do anything but bruise my hand, with no satisfying crash of breaking glass. I flick my eyes up, noticing Cort standing behind me with a sheepish expression and tears skating down his cheeks.

"Here," Cort offers, a toothbrush extended in his fingertips with a tube of paste in his other hand. "This will make you feel better."

I reach over my shoulder, refusing to break our staring contest, making sure every dark emotion that is assaulting my conscience is written across my facial features for Cortez to read. When his hands are empty, he breaks our contact by reaching into the cabinet to produce a bottle of mouthwash.

I brush my teeth with so much force I fear tearing my gums, but the pain clears my mind, helping me to think clearly. I spit in the sink, noting the pink-tinged cast unto the water as it swirls around the drain. I repeat with more toothpaste this time.

"Marcus and Diane are not together in the traditional sense, so there is no issue with facing her. If I can look the woman who raised me in the eyes after sucking her husband's cock, then you can. Hell, I've eaten breakfast with her minutes after doing so. If Ezra and I have the balls to look her in the face after she caught me pounding his ass over the sofa arm, then you can sit at the table and make nice."

"You all need professional mental help," I mutter around the toothbrush. "Seriously, someone Ezra didn't handpick." I spit, not caring how disgusting I look. "I was not raised this way. I was raised in a nuclear family with traditional values. I don't know if I can ever accept the kind of life you lead, no matter how much I may love you fools."

"Marcus was in love with Diane, not understanding our way of life either. He was a kid when he was dropped in our midst, after being raised by his grandmother who fiercely loved her husband. Marcus believed in the fairytale, and thought he had that with Diane."

"Idiot," I snarl, spitting into the sink, only to perform the routine again. "Diane is at least fifteen years older than Marcus."

"Thirteen years older. Diane was only eighteen when she had Ezra, and Marc is five years older than us. So obviously we saw Marc as our peer– the big brother we idolized. So as sick as whatever thoughts are running through your head, we've never had a father/son relationship, nor are we actually related by anything other than paperwork. Diane was my guardian and Marcus was my benefactor. He obviously adopted Ezra, not realizing it was because Diane would never give him children but provided him with a legal heir."

"Diane trapped Marcus somehow, I take it. Why did his grandmother allow it?" I toss the toothbrush into the sink. It clatters, and then ricochets to the floor. I grab for the mouthwash, planning on using it until it's empty.

"Rock. Hard place," is Cort's only explanation. "Diane is a lesbian, so she refused her husband any intimacy after Ray's maltreatment. She refused a religious man who didn't believe in sex outside of the confines of marriage, sentencing him to a life without touch, and then she put her son in his path."

"Obviously Marc's stance on '*outside of the confines of marriage*' has since changed. So, Marc's gay," flows from my mouth. "Why am I not surprised?" I swish the mouthwash, clearing away all traces of Marcus from my mouth, never looking away from my own disgusted reflection.

"Marc is straight," Cort admits, shocking the hell out of me. "Or at least he says he is. From personal experience, he doesn't enjoy our blowjobs. It's more like he's punishing himself. As for what happened between him and Ezra, that is their story to tell, and it haunts them both."

"I need a shower. I want to wash the filth of this night away. I wish there was a drug to erase my memory, or turn back time, while we're at it."

"Easily arranged," Cort says wryly. "The shower, not the makings of an Urban Fantasy novel." With a rough tug, my catsuit is peeled from me. It took twenty minutes to pull it on, and less than a second to rip off.

"Are you angry with me?" I whisper, finally voicing one of my greatest fears. I'm upset with Ezra for pitting Cortez and me against one another. "Did it upset you because you see Marcus as belonging to you?"

"No, Kitten." Cort caresses my cheek, his eyes bleeding sincerity. "I was trying to protect you from Ezra while protecting him from himself. Marc did and didn't want to do it, for varying reasons. As for possessiveness, I only have that for Ezra. Marc is my master, not my lover."

"I'm sorry." Whimpering, the tears that have threatened me for the past hour finally descend.

"Me too, Katya. Me too," Cort chants, never looking away from my distress. "Shower quickly. Your energy reserves are going to plummet in a few short minutes." Wary, Cortez issues a warning. "You're running on pure adrenaline, the high from dominating Monica, and your emotional distress, all of which will wear off and leave you lethargic and depressed."

Cortez picks me up to stand me in the already running shower. The warm spray tries and fails to wash away all of my sins. I look down, trying to envision their shadowy tendrils swirling around the shower drain, spilling down the pipes, and washing the evil out of my orbit. Try as I might, my conscience is still beating at me.

Only giving me two minutes of mental reflection under the therapeutic spray, Cort yanks me from the shower. Then he begins to dry me with a fluffy towel, his movements jerky and fast.

"How come you're being so rough?" I ask when I can barely stand from his ministrations.

"I'm trying to get the blood flowing. Your body and mind have had shock after shock tonight. Physically. Mentally. Emotionally. Hormonally. The fallout will be the lowest you've ever felt. I promise to be there for you every step of the way." Cort wraps me in the towel, and then pushes me toward the door. "Go snuggle up in bed. I'll be with you in a moment. I just have to get washed up."

I crawl in between the cool sheets, refusing to think over the fact that these aren't my sheets and they don't smell like home. I sigh deeply in distress. I hadn't realized how much my body hurt until I was motionless. I stretch out and groan from the hidden aches and pains.

"Drink this," Cort orders as he hands me a coffee mug adorned with Restraint's logo.

"What is it?" I eye the cup's contents with suspicion. It's a funny color. Definitely not coffee.

"Dumbass!" Cort snorts, bopping me on the tip of the nose with his finger. "It's carrot juice. It's loaded with vitamins to help with the shock and get your system back to normal once the endorphins dissipate. You have a wicked episode of Drop in your near future– both dominants and submissives can experience it if the conditions are just right. Wrong is more accurate. You'll feel hungover tomorrow, along with depression. I just hope it's not too bad for you. I've experienced this a time or two, and I felt like the world as I knew it was over. Borderline suicidal. I wouldn't wish it on my worst enemy."

I take an experimental taste of the juice, awakening my suppressed thirst, and then I down the mug in one gulp.

"Nurse this bottle of water," Cort cautions, handing me an opened bottle. "Don't take too much. I don't want you throwing up. You may feel nauseous later anyway." The worry in Cortez's voice confuses me.

"I feel fine. Just a little bit tired and achy is all," I say to assuage his fears, but my words are sluggish and slurred.

"How does your head feel?" Cort takes the bottle from my grip, setting it on the nightstand, and then he curls up to my side. "Do you have any questions?"

"My mind feels fuzzy, like I can't grasp a thought. Is that normal? I don't feel sick or anything other than that."

"It's normal, but it tells me that tomorrow is going to suck for you. I'm sorry, Kitten. I knew it would be rough. I wasn't sure if you were ready yet. Usually we train for a lot longer, take on a submissive of our own, and scene many times before we are thrust into the chaos. You went from commanding a scene as a dominant, to getting a tattoo, and then you finished off the night by submitting to not one but nine masters. Learning Marc is Master can't be helping matters, either. It's not going to be a good day tomorrow, perhaps even a week. I think this will be too much stress on your body, all things considered. I want to beat Ezra for this. I wanted to wait until after, but he wanted to do it as soon as possible."

"Why the big hurry? All things considered– what?" I sputter, sleep slowly closing in around the edges of my consciousness.

"Waiting a month or two for your initiation would have sufficed, but your body wouldn't have been up for the challenge. Then later on, you may wish to avoid that kind of play. Ezra wanted you to experience it now while you had a chance."

Mind getting foggier, as if I've been drugged, I mumble. "I still don't understand what you mean?"

"I know," Cort says, but doesn't explain. "You did wonderfully tonight, absolutely flawless. Everyone was impressed." Cort rolls me onto my side, facing him, and then snuggles up to my chest.

"Go to sleep. You'll have plenty of questions in the morning, and I want you to trust me enough to ask me anything and to tell me everything you're feeling. It will help with the Drop." My eyes flutter shut as Cortez whispers, "I love you," into the crook of my neck.

"I love you, too," tumbles out between numb lips.

I awake enough to feel Ezra cradle me from behind. "How is she?" he whispers. His cheek caresses my naked shoulder, followed by a peppering of apologetic kisses.

"I'm worried, Ezra. Kat is going to drop hard. Tonight was too much, especially with all the stress we've had lately. We've been waiting for her to get sick. I know she hasn't been feeling right lately. Now you add this on top of it. She's going to be miserable physically, not to mention mentally. I want to kill Dalton just for the look on Katya's face while he was touching her. She was humiliated, Ezra. Do you want the mother of your children to be humiliated like that? I know I don't." Cort's furious hissing is keeping me from the rest I so desperately need.

"I hated how helpless she looked and I felt. It was necessary, but now it's over. Katya will never be humiliated again," Ezra vows.

"There are never any guarantees," Cortez hisses sharply, jarring me from my sleep. "Not with you."

"Do you think I get off on this pain, Cort? Do you honestly think I enjoyed what Dalton and Faith did to Katya, knowing every bad touch and word was directed solely at me? Do you think I wanted to stand by while she sucked my father off? It was necessary, that is all. Now it's finished, and time to move on."

I drift off after a few minutes of quiet until I'm jarred awake by Cort's furious hissing again. "I don't know if I can let this go, Ezra. I don't think Katya should either. You'll just keep treating us like shit for the rest of our lives because we allow it."

"I understand the ramifications of my actions, Cortez. I was there, watching Kat's facial expressions, just as I saw the destruction of this room when I entered. I know I have a lot of explaining to do before Katya can forgive me. But I do feel lighter, feel more even now that the wrongs have been balanced."

I'm gifted with a few moments of silence before Cortez is off and running like a nagging wife again. "By the way, I love the black eye, Ezra. Is that what took you so long? While I was nursing Katya, you were off screwing someone you should leave the hell alone! You're such a jealous prick. We both know you go after her because of him and me. It's a mental *'fuck you'* every time you touch her."

"Cort," Ezra sighs heavily. "I did what I thought was right, and *I* wasn't fucking anyone tonight."

"Bullshit," Cort snarls, hand lashing out to slap Ezra across the face, reverberating straight down my spine. I struggle to breach the surface of the deadened sensation I've entered, but I cannot muster the strength.

"Marc and Katya was a way for me to forgive myself for the shit I've done to him, for what I've done to her. I won't lie–she beat the shit out of me for Kat. It wasn't because I had Kat suck Marc off. It was because she always said that if I stepped over the line with Katya, she'd kick my ass. The part of me who is Master Ez took great offense with that. I'm ashamed to admit, he retaliated."

Ezra moves away, my back cooling instantly in the night air. He sits upright, burying his head in his hands. "I don't want to do this shit, but I can't stop myself. As a psychiatrist, I can say this to make myself feel better, but it doesn't change the reality of the evil I enact."

"You didn't force her again, did you? I will never touch you again, if you did. I'm shocked Marc hasn't killed you yet."

"Marc loves me too much. You can only harm those closest to you, you know that. She's not stupid, either. She knows when I've gone off the deep end. With the way Katya looked at me when she fled the dungeon, I snapped. I vowed never to do it again, to both of them. No more retaliation. I'll turn myself into a walking zombie with antipsychotic drugs if I have to. I'm not going to ruin the future we're building."

"You need to get the shit from the past settled. It's not a matter of drug therapy. You need to come to terms with your crimes against humanity."

"Such a way with words, you have, Cortez. Prettying up rapist until it's palatable."

"I hate when you get this way. I'd rather punch myself in the face than hold a conversation with you." Cort sits up, leaving my front cold. I don't have the strength to draw the blankets around me, so I'm left shivering. "Did Marcus actually watch you get your ass handed to you tonight? I just don't see him standing by."

"Marc came in while she was kicking my ass. He hit me with a rash of brutal realities I couldn't swallow, and wouldn't stop until I was bawling like a little bitch. Then he said it was my last time with her, so I better make it count. Yeah, he watched and punished me. You have no idea what I just went through. It makes Kat's initiation look like a tea party. I wanted to be here for her, but I was detained."

"Detained– such an eloquent way of saying held against your will while being physically and sexually assaulted."

"Please, Cort," Ezra pleads. "No more. I need to be held as I sleep."

"Why won't Marcus just beat you to death, and get it over with," Cort hisses into the night like he's making a wish.

"I don't know. Why won't he just fuck you, and get it over with," Ezra hisses back.

Gathering all the strength I possess, "Hey, no more fighting. Please," I slur listlessly. "I don't want to hear anymore. You're making my brain bleed. I don't have to know what's going on to get the gist of your conversation, and I don't like any of it. I'd rather be in the dark, where ignorance is bliss. Go to sleep," I beg. "Please."

They both cuddle up to me. I feel Ezra try to touch Cort, and he flinches away. I use the rest of my strength to pull their hands against my tummy until they're touching gently. After a few tense moments, they twine their fingers together with mine. I fall into oblivion, my mind blissfully blank for once.

# Chapter Forty-Three

"Aaaahh…" I stretch my arms and legs, flexing every muscle in my body. The ache is intense. I feel bruised inside and out. But mostly, I feel confused and muddled on the inside.

"Why do I hurt so much?" I speak into the room. The bed is empty, but I assume someone is within earshot. I just can't see the over-protective fools leaving me to my own devices.

"I'll be right out!" Cort calls from the bathroom. "I warned you today would fucking suck!"

I assess my body, trying to figure out what is hurting the most. My breast is a gnarly purple, and I can just make out tiny fingertip marks. The petite sadist is getting the ass kicking of a lifetime if I ever see her in public again. Vicious cunt. The ache between my thighs makes itself known when I bring my legs together. I'm rubbed raw. Dalton– that drab asshole is added to the ass-kicking list.

I cover my face in shame when I remember why my lips are chapped and the hinge of my jaw is protesting. A whimper slips free before I can stop it.

"What's wrong, Kitten?" Cort settles at the foot of the bed– fresh from the shower and fully dressed in a pair of faded jeans and a t-shirt I bought him as a gag gift. **Writer's Block: When your imaginary friends won't talk to you.**

"Ezra keeps calling me his future wife like it's a threat. How the hell can I look myself in the mirror knowing I sucked off my father-in-law? What kind of low-rent whore behavior is that? It's too trashy for Dr. Phil. It's more Jerry Springer. Oh, how the mighty, self-righteous bitch has fallen from her pedestal of judgment."

Cortez stares at me intently while he digests everything I said. "You're going to be an emotional wreck for a good, long while." He shakes his head as if coming to a foregone conclusion. "I knew you would be. I really want to fuck Ezra up for this shit. It was not good for you to go through the initiation so soon, nor was it a brilliant fucking idea for you to touch Marcus in any way."

"I don't understand why Ezra wanted me to be with him." I cover my face in shame. "I get that he's fucking nuts, but there is no way balance can be found by doing two wrongs. That's something forced down our throats from kindergarten on."

"We can both trust Ezra not to put our safety and health at risk. But I'm now questioning his ability to keep our mental health a priority. It's damned sick considering he is a psychiatrist." Cortez snarls– last night's anger and resentment still haven't dissipated yet.

"Ezra stalked me as prey for three years, and then played a twisted game with me. I think we can safely conclude that Ezra is a shitty mental health professional. Hell, Ezra needs his own psychologist to analyze him."

"Fuck, yeah." Cortez snorts. "Ezra already has a team of psychiatrists at his disposal, and it does him no good."

Giving up on figuring out the mystery known as Ezra Zeitler, I stretch out again, only to moan in agony. "Why do I feel like shit?" I have a migraine that pounds in time with my heartbeat, and I'm slightly nauseous. Both of which are tolerable until I move.

Cort laughs at my twisted expression. "Well, genius, your body flooded with endorphins from pain, fear, excitement, and arousal. It's like you took uppers, then downers, and followed it with a bottle of liquor and a handful of sleeping pills. Combine all that with the tattoo, Syn's vise-like grip, Dalton's three finger assault, and Marc's Coke can cock, now your body feels like it was run over by a train and then shoved into a wood chipper. I can see the confusion written behind in your eyes as well. I'm so sorry, Kitten."

"My fault for agreeing." I grunt like a hog as I stretch, and then swallow back the bile that is threatening to spill from my mouth. Good Lord, I'm nauseous. "I'll live through it. I've had worse."

"How's the tattoo?" Cort arches a brow in the direction of my hand.

"Oh, shit! I forgot about it. It better not be something ridiculous," I warn as I examine my hand. The fleshy webbing between my thumb and index finger is permanently marked with an 𝕸. The capital M is written in elegant calligraphy style. "M?" I ask while I stare at the small tattoo.

"Master or Mistress, whichever you prefer," Cortez explains. He holds up his own hand, displaying his tattoo. His is exactly the same size as mine. That must be why it stayed hidden so well on his large hand. Mine looks larger in proportion to my small hand.

"In reality it means Marcus, doesn't it? You assholes are all about pissing on everything."

Laughing while nodding his head yes, Cort holds up a bottle of lotion that mysteriously manifested in his hand.

"Yes, please," I utter overenthusiastically, rolling over to expose my back to his expert touch. Cortez slowly massages all of my aching muscles, fingers rolling and biting into the painful knots. After a few minutes, I can already feel them loosening. The sigh I release is a mixture of relief and bliss.

"Just kidding, by the way. We all lie to ourselves by saying our tattoos mean Master, while Marcus gets off on the fact that it's his initial. In reality, the M is for Maître."

"So it does mean Master," I muse.

"Not in the way it sounds, though," Cort murmurs, falling into his thoughts. "Those marked have a purpose." He pauses, fingers freezing on my shoulders. "Let's change the subject."

Feeling marginally better, I start lobbing questions at Cortez. "Where's Ezra? Is he getting breakfast, or are we waiting to go home for that? Where did Ava stay last night? Man, I am a terrible mother." I hit the top of my head on the headboard a few times as punishment, or maybe I'm trying to knock some sense into myself.

Rolling me over to face him, Cort yanks me down the bed a bit so I can't assault the headboard with my thick skull. "I'll answer your questions in order." Cort winks at me as he rubs my stomach. His eyes widen in awe as he massages. I'm about to ask why he's looking at me so oddly when he finally speaks.

"Ezra is cleaning up a media shit-storm. He left around two a.m., and was back shortly thereafter. He went back to his office here at Restraint to field more calls. When he returns, he's bringing our breakfast. As for your impeccable status as the world's best mother, Ava stayed at Shadow Haven last night with her grandmother, aunt, and cousin. I think we should rename it Estrogen Haven instead."

"Poor Marcus in a house filled with ladies." My snicker is cut off when I remember how '*poor*' Marcus isn't. Shuddering, I finally register what Cort initially said. "What shit happened? It's not Ray is it?"

My voice didn't even break. Ray used to be my Boogeyman, but facing him was like facing my greatest horror head-on. It takes the fear factor out of what could happen when the worst has already happened.

"Ez will be back in a few minutes. He sent me a text while I was showering." Cort's hands grip my hips. "Roll back over. I need to work that knot out of your shoulder. But keep away from the headboard; it caused you no wrong."

I huff a laugh as I try to roll over onto my stomach. I'm hit with a wicked flash of nausea. Hand cupped over my mouth, I lunge from the bed, almost tripping on the sheets. I make it just in time to dry heave into the toilet.

Wrapped around the porcelain god, I'm thankful my body was on empty. I curl up and rest my forehead on my knee, enjoying the cold tile against my nakedness. Cort wipes my face with a washcloth, and then settles it across the back of my neck. The coolness soothes the nausea.

"That came out of nowhere. I've felt off lately. But now it's like I have the flu." My entire body feels clammy yet hot as I shiver and flush with heat.

"A symptom of Drop." Cort rubs my back in soothing circles as he speaks. "It's happens when you push too many limits, and your mind and body can't handle it. Your emotions and hormones are fucked up, and your body is adjusting to the endorphins that flooded it and then fled just as quickly. When your brain and body chemistry even out, you'll feel better."

I hear the beep signaling the security lock has disengaged all the way from the confines of the bathroom. My ears are still sensitive from last night's deprivation, allowing me to hear Ezra pad into the bathroom.

Gazing down at me, "Are you all right, Katya?" Ezra's voice is filled with concern, worry, and trepidation over the not-so welcoming reception he's anticipating.

I peek up at Ezra from beneath my lashes, doing my damnedest not to look as pitiful as I feel. "I'm not feeling very well," I rasp out. Ezra presses his lips in a flat line, as if he is trying to suppress himself. He fails miserably when a radiant smile curls his lips, looking satisfied and arrogant. "What?" I scrunch up my eyebrows. "Why are you so happy that I feel like shit? That's not very nice."

On my hands and knees, I crawl out from between the Ezes, and then stalk back into the mini-dungeon. I pull out a pair of yoga pants and a sweatshirt from the small dresser behind the sofa. I sigh when the soft fabric covers my skin. I grab a pillow from the bed as I walk by, cuddling it to my chest as I settle onto the sofa.

Ezra must have set our takeout on the new coffee table before he entered the bathroom. I start scavenging through the boxes. I'm curiously hungry after dry heaving. I select a banana nut muffin, and then pick at it as I listen to the Ezes engage in a whisper-fight. That is until the bathroom door is latched shut, effectively cutting off my eavesdropping.

I slowly nibble the top of my muffin, pretending I don't give a shit that I'm being closed out. But then again, I don't think I could handle another ounce of angst this morning. I notice the newspaper peeking out from beneath the takeout boxes. My name is in huge, bold script across the front page.

"What the fuck?" I whisper to the empty room. I snap the newspaper open, and the floor drops from my world.

*Katya Waters: from publishing maven to home-wrecker!*
*Edge Publishing's Katya Waters was the catalyst for the breakup of the Zeitler-Whittenhower union, according to Adelaide Whittenhower.*
*Ms. Whittenhower has come forward to speak her side of the story, nearly eight weeks after Dr. Zeitler publicly announced their breakup.*
*The Times quoting Ms. Adelaide Whittenhower:*
*"Ezra Zeitler is not the great man his public image portrays. The side he shows the outside world is the Humanitarian Businessman. The dark side of Zeitler is the alter ego he dubbed Master Ez. Not only is Ezra a renowned psychiatrist and the owner of Edge Publishing, he is also the warped creator of the alternative lifestyle club, Restraint. He is currently in a triad relationship with his employee, Katya Waters, and his lifelong friend, author Cortez Abernathy. The three of them engage in hedonistic, BDSM activities. Ranging*

*from 'wife swapping' to abusing people until they are bruised, to tying up unwilling victims and assaulting them.*

*"Ezra is the birth father of Katya's eleven-year-old daughter, Ava Evangeline Zeitler. I researched the time frame of the child's birth. Twelve years ago, Ezra Zeitler, Cortez Abernathy, and Aaron Frost were kidnapped by Raymond Hunter, Ezra's birth father. During the same time, Katya Waters was assaulted by Raymond Hunter, leading to his arrest and prosecution for the crimes against all four, and the resulting incarceration– all public record with the names withheld because they were minors or sexual assault victims. Nine months later, Ava was born, leading to the question, if Ava is Ezra's daughter, why was Raymond the only criminal convicted of rape? Upon meeting Ava, there is little doubt to her parentage, as she resembles the Holden lineage with her fair hair and skin.*

*"I am sickened that I spent the last six years of my life living a lie. Ezra did not break our engagement three years ago. It wasn't until Katya Waters came back into our lives, bringing her child with her, that I confronted Ezra over his infidelity. With proof in hand, I came to the realization that I couldn't spend my life with a lying, cheating rapist, no matter the familial influence."*

*The Times fact-checked Adelaide Whittenhower's accusations. Dr. Zeitler is in fact the father of Ava Zeitler, who is the daughter of Katya Waters. It is well-known that Zeitler and Abernathy were kidnapped by Raymond Hunter, along with another minor child who had remained nameless. The records are sealed in regards to the sexual assault and attempted murder conviction leveled against Hunter. He was also convicted of three counts of kidnapping at the same trial. Raymond Hunter was released from prison three months ago, and is currently on parole. We were unable to locate the owner of the club, Restraint. Tax records show a holding company as the sole proprietor. At the engagement celebration of Aaron Frost and Kayla Cummings, Zeitler, Abernathy, and Waters went public with their affair, according to several eyewitnesses.*

*The Times contacted Zeitler just before the paper went to print for a statement. Ezra Zeitler:*

*"I am deeply saddened that a six year partnership is reduced to this low level of disrespect and defamation. It is inconceivable. I will respond to every accusation. Firstly, I have signed documentation proving that Adelaide and I dissolved our engagement well over three years ago. The reason for the delay was in respect of Adelaide for public appearances.*

*"I am sickened that the past torments of my friends at the hands of Ray Hunter were exposed. It's hard enough to face myself in the mirror knowing my roots, living through the nightmares at a monster's hands, and dealing with the aftermath of our assailant being my own father. Cortez, Aaron, and myself were children, and we are being exploited yet again.*

*"Yes, Katya was assaulted and nearly murdered by my father while his other victims were present, which resulted in the conception of our precious daughter— the only saving grace that made surviving the horrific nightmare worth it. It is an unimaginable horror that we have to relive the memory that we are trying to heal. Worse is how Katya and I will have to sit our daughter down and explain to her how she was created during an act of violence— breaking a promise her mother and I made to each other for our daughter's mental health and well-being. As the product of rape, I know how detrimental learning such a thing during the fundamental years of your life can be. It reshapes you into a human being you were not meant to become. Worse, I hate how my daughter is mirroring my history, learning the truth near the tender age of twelve, when a child should remain a child.*

*"There are laws in place to protect the victims, especially minor children. Laws which should have been upheld for the anonymity and privacy of myself, Cortez Abernathy, Aaron Frost, Katya Waters, and Ava Zeitler, as well as exposing my mother— Diane Holden's secret to my conception at the hands of a rapist. The court records were sealed to protect the innocent. Now during a time of great celebration— Aaron and Kayla's wedding —we will all be suffering by the fact that our private wounds were made public, which is a violation in and of itself.*

*"As for the affair between Cortez, Katya, and myself, bonds form during traumatic experiences. In this case, we have a strong bond that I will cherish until the end of my life. I hold no shame in loving two amazing, intelligent human beings.*

*"I am the creator and owner of Restraint– a Master at Restraint. With great pride, I admit that I am a member of the BDSM lifestyle. The very lifestyle that helped me survive the aftermath of my kidnapping. I make no excuses or apologies for who I am, who I associate with, and what I do.*

*"I hope that readers realize that this is a case of a publicity seeker screaming that she is a scorned woman and victim. In reality, the true victims are being victimized. I could bring a case civilly against Ms. Whittenhower, but that would never undo the damage that has been done to my family this day. No monetary reward will ever right the wrongs, heal the wounds, and rewrite the past. We were innocent, still are innocent, yet we were besmirched."*

The newspaper slips from my numb fingertips to slowly flutter to the floor. The confusion that has been swirling in my mind since last night evaporates under a tide of pure, unadulterated fury, finally giving me a target to pinpoint. If Adelaide was standing before me at this very moment, I would rend her apart with my bare hands.

My child. My poor child. Ava didn't know. She thought she was created during an episode of lust that rendered us too stupid to use protection. We told her we were just two innocent kids who got caught up in the moment while Ezra's affluent family was visiting the Vineyards surrounding our area. After he left, I had no idea who he was, so I couldn't contact him. It was just an act of fate that I would come to work for him in Dominion. It was the type of fairytale grandkids would settle around to have a listen, and it was a lie.

Breath hitching, a sob is torn from my chest. My daughter will learn the truth. Either we tell her, or she will find out when the bullying starts, when the media starts hounding us all. Our lives are no longer our own, and my daughter's childhood– the precious years I've tried so desperately to hold onto –are all gone.

My child will suffer the consequences of my violent assault for the rest of her life, as will her children, and her children's children. Because you can't outrun the truth, even when it wasn't of your own volition. We will be assaulted by the truth until we die, until our legacy dies out.

Ezra's words haunt me. *We were innocent. We still are innocent. We* isn't Ezra– it's all of us, right down to those who haven't even been born yet. Innocence stolen again and again, even before conception. Being raped over and over again by being forced to explain the truth to your children– an experience worse than the violent act itself. The thought snaps a vital piece inside me that keeps me centered, sane, and in control.

I sweep the takeout boxes from the coffee table with the flat of my arm. I watch in bizarre fascination as food and beverage splatter on every surface. The tomato juice runs in rivulets down the slate tile, looking like freshly spilled blood from a mortal wound.

I imagine it's Adelaide's blood as I heave the new coffee table across the room with my newly acquired strength. Satisfaction roils through me as the wood smashes against the cement wall, pieces flying like shrapnel in a war zone.

But it's not enough. Everything within arm's reach finds itself a projectile of violence, an outlet for my self-loathing. A sensation of liberation takes ahold of me as my crazed scream pierces the air to echo throughout the dungeon.

Strong arms try to secure me as I fight. I struggle against the hold as my rage unleashes a monster I cannot contain. A small portion of my brain screams for me to relent– to surrender. I fight, scratch, kick, and pull against the arms that try to subdue me. I hear nothing, see nothing, feel nothing, and taste nothing but red.

The red, hot fury of being fucked without my consent yet again.

A sharp slap to my cheek whips my face to the side. It's painful enough to bring a small amount of reality into focus. But clarity doesn't seep in until minutes later as I'm standing in the shower– clothed –with freezing water cascading down around me.

Wide-eyed and frightened, I finally seek out the Ezes. I can tell by the horrified yet guilty expression on Ezra's face, that he's the one who slapped me. Their faces and arms are scored from my nails, bloody furrows that would make a cat proud.

Blood drizzles from the corner of Ezra's mouth. I must have punched him and split his lip. Both men are gasping for breath, but Ezra got the brunt of my fury.

"Are you sane?" Ezra puffs the words out with great effort. His gunmetal eyes are wide with shock and concern.

"I believe so," I gasp roughly, trying to regain my composure. "But I highly doubt an insane person realizes it." Ezra's resulting smile splits the crack in his lip wider. His tongue sneaks out to clear the blood away.

That single act makes me fall in love with Ezra all over again, knowing he will smile through the pain, even when it's a bad joke, just because I was the one who made it. I'm a glutton for punishment, who sucks up these tiny moments of Ezra at his rawest form, making the rest of the horrific bullshit worth it.

"If Katya hadn't already beaten me to the punch, I would pound you into the ground for this shit." Cortez jumps in to defend me. I love Captain Obvious because he will do anything to be my champion. "I take it you were stupid enough to bring the newspaper in here, fucktard."

"I don't have time to argue with you again for the hundredth time today." Ezra's voice is taut with frustration. "I fucked up. Again. We all know it. There is no reason to beat it like a dead horse. So quit being a self-righteous prick and help me take care of Katya."

Sick of their fighting, I stop it before it gets out of control. "No, I'll take care of myself. Just give me a minute. I'm gonna be sick again."

I try to stumble from the shower, but my body rejects the few morsels of banana nut muffin I ate before I can exit the shower. I'm thankful that I can lean out the shower door and just reach the toilet before I empty my stomach. I heave over and over until I swear my organs come up.

Feeling hot and clammy from vomiting, yet shivery from taking a cold shower with my clothing still on, I yank my sweats from my body while hovering hands try to help. I ignore them, instead concentrating on the sound of my sweatshirt splatting at their feet.

I stand under the freezing spray and allow it to continually wash the fury away. It only recedes. I can feel it simmering just beneath the surface. This is going to impact all of our lives. I thought Ray's reappearance was fatal. We will never be the same after this– none of us.

I exit the shower, ignoring the helpful hands again. I pull a towel around myself and walk into our room in search of clothing. I can feel the pair ghosting behind me, waiting for me to snap. I guess they have good reason when I see the devastation I caused.

"The next new coffee table better be made out of steel and bolted to the floor," I mutter sarcastically as I pull on a cotton dress. "I believe it's Cort's turn to explode." I don't even care that I don't have any undergarments. My body hurts too much for binding bras and panties anyway.

I pick my muffin up out of a slurry of milk and coffee, suddenly hungry again. I check it over, noticing it's only soiled on the paper wrapper. I nibble at it, marveling over how it makes the nausea better, but knowing it will bring it back with full-force in a few minutes.

"Okay, so what's the plan? What shit have you been spinning for the past few hours? How bad is this going to ruin our lives?"

"We live. That's it," is Ezra's solution. "We tell Ava the truth before she hears it from outside sources, and then we get her professional help to deal with the fallout. We love each other and our daughter. We move forward with our lives, refusing to dwell in the past. We don't respond to anything that is thrown at us by the media. If we ignore them, they will get bored without anything new to print, and then they will move on to juicier stories."

Ezra toes some of our breakfast around. With great longing, he looks at his squashed and orange-juice-drenched breakfast sandwich with hunger in his eyes. I feel sort of bad now for taking my anger and aggression out on innocent food.

"You've never ignored anything before, Ezra. Your favorite pastime is picking a scab until it's a festering wound." Cort begins wiping up the blood-red tomato juice with my towel, pausing to eat anything that isn't too gross. "What does ignoring it accomplish?"

"I stated the facts. Nothing will change them. It happened to us. It just is. Ade is slandering us, and she knows she will get away with it. To sue her is to go after Daniel, and Mom will never allow that."

"Leave the cunt to her father. He'll take care of the problem." The evil light shining in Cortez's eyes has intensified as his bitter hatred for Adelaide Whittenhower has grown. Only the donut in his path warps his expression to one of simply happiness.

I snort at the fool.

Ezra stares at Cortez as if Cort is the cutest thing he's ever witnessed, then he shares the look with me as we watch Cort eat off the floor like a street urchin. "I don't want to start a media war. I just want us to live our lives. I want our family to finally move on from this shit. This is who we are. I want to scream to the world '*take us as we are*!' If they don't– fuck 'em."

"Fuck 'em," I agree.

"Fuck 'em," Cort repeats around a mouthful of chocolate-covered donut, completely ruining the badass feel of the moment.

# Chapter Forty-Four

*...The release of the contract refutes Whittenhower's claims that she was the injured party. Ray Hunter's interview was the final nail in her coffin. The Zeitler family is all anyone can talk about, especially with the Frost-Cummings nuptials this Saturday at Shadow Haven, the Zeitler estate. An inside source informed High Society Nightly that Ezra will stand in as the best man beside Aaron Frost, and Katya Waters will act as Maid of Honor for Kayla Cummings. HSN will keep you abreast on the latest gossip surrounding our new media darlings.*

"Ava, just turn it off. Her voice is grating on my nerves." I clench my teeth and squeeze my temples against the stress-headache that's plagued me for a week.

Mysterious threatening notes long forgotten. Ray Hunter forgotten. Initiation forgotten. Wedding preparations forgotten. The only thing on our minds is our newest controversy.

Ezra and I sat our daughter down and told her our history in the fewest words possible. Instead of breaking down, Ava proved she was indeed our daughter. Calm, clinical, and pragmatic, she was furious.

For the past week, our daughter has been obsessed with the media. Intelligent mind spinning how to thwart their next moves. Angry how they stalk her at school and force us to remain locked in The Edge Building, Ava has been coming up with diversions.

"Ma, I wanted to see what else they had to say," Ava whines. "I have a birthday party next weekend, and I want to go."

Leaning forward, I grab the remote. With the press of my finger, I silence the gossip news program. "Nothing is going to change. They don't have any information we don't already know. It's pointless and unhealthy to dwell on this."

"It's Ella's birthday," Ava says as if that should mean something. "Ella and Prissy are cousins. But Ella says I can't come because her mother won't let me."

"I'm sorry, baby girl. But I haven't been feeling well for the past few weeks." I wipe the sweat beading at my forehead, feeling nauseous again. "Care to expand on that? I know the girls are your friends, but I don't see the connection to what's happening to us."

"Whitney– an older girl is trying to bully me at school. She's Prissy's sister. She's been calling Dad and Cort faggots." Ava's stormy gray eyes are filled with sorrow and silent rage. "Whitney must have convinced her aunt not to let me come to Ella's birthday party. I can't have that. She's my friend; I need to be there."

I take a sip of water, stalling. Every night after school, Ava regales us with misery during dinner. I've lost five pounds this week, unable to eat while my daughter takes great delight in ruining her bullies' lives.

"I'm so sorry, Ava. None of this is your fault, yet you have to live through it. You have to be the bigger person, no matter what your father says. You might regret your actions when you're older."

"No, I won't," Ava promises, pure evil radiating from her stormy eyes. "You don't know what Whitney's saying."

"Enlighten me, then. What is the newest bullshit she is spreading? I assume you were sent home early today for beating the shit out of this child."

I eye the healing scratch on my daughter's pale cheek, instinctively knowing the other girl looks far worse. Ava has her father's mind and height. But scarily, she also has the heart of a scrapper thanks to my father. Brains and brawn, the wherewithal to be deadly with both, and a legacy of insanity to where she won't care what happens in the aftermath.

The first thing Ezra did within minutes of telling our daughter the truth, was to arrange for unlimited sessions with a therapist for the budding terrorist.

"I broke Whitney's nose." With great pride, Ava shows me her bruised knuckles. "She kept calling Dad and Cort fags. Niel held her down for me, so did Prissy and Ella."

"What the fuck?" I hiss, eyes narrowing. "Can't you find normal friends? I've seen those tiny girls– so sweet and innocent and pink. Niel isn't that ginger kid, is he? If so, leave him alone. He's too old for you. He's got to be sixteen, at least."

"Niel is fourteen. He's Ella's brother, and their family doesn't like bigots."

With narrowed-eyes, I mutter, "But you just said Whitney-the-gay-basher is their family? No more playing with that homicidal family," I order, shuddering from the thought of homicidal befriending insane.

"Whitney is their family, and that's why I'm not invited to Ella's birthday party, even though she and Prissy are my friends. Niel is going to change his mother's mind."

"No. Abso-fucking-lutely not. You're not going anywhere near them in private. I mean it. You can be friends at school, but you will not visit your bully's house in hopes of terrorizing her on her own turf."

"They're Whittenhowers," Ava drops the bomb, smiling like an evil doll in a horror movie. "You sure I can't go to the birthday party? I've been making plans."

"Oh, my God. NO!" I shout, head pounding with the need to puke riding it. "You and your father better not be plotting destruction. I swear to God, I'll kick both your asses."

"I'll behave." Ava's radiant smile is befitting of a perfect angel. "Adelaide is their aunt, so she's guaranteed to be there. I want to humiliate her in front of her entire family. It's not enough, but at least it's something."

Head in hands, I try to press the pain away with my fingertips. "No. This conversation is over. I mean it. Drop it. Anyone in the Whittenhower family is off limits."

"You don't know what Adelaide's been saying about you, Mom. You don't have to hear Whitney spreading lies at school. I do, and I will do anything to make it stop."

"Ava, honey," I reach for her, but she flinches away. I would take offense, but I can see that my daughter is holding back tears of frustration and pain– tears I placed there.

"Whitney called you a whore, Mom. She called Dad a rapist." Ava's emotionless voice hurts my heart more so than her words. I swallow back the sobs, understanding why she so badly wants to seek vengeance. I want to find that child and punch her myself. But as the parent, I must be the bigger person, and I can't tell my daughter to act like a criminal.

I'll leave that bad advice up to Ava's father.

"She called me the bastard of a rapist and a whore. She said that you and Dad deserved what Grandpa Ray did to you, and that I'm pure evil. While I was punching Whitney, just before I broke her nose, she said you had sex with Uncle Aaron and Aunt Kayla."

Choking on rage, I channel it all inward, worried that any emotion I reveal will fuel the fire in my daughter's eyes. "If I did or didn't, it doesn't matter. It's no one's business but those involved. What worries me the most, is that if I had, no one would know except for a few close people."

"I might still be a kid, but I'm not stupid. Adelaide is telling Whitney to say this to me, and I want to make her stop. Dad won't do anything about it, so I will when I get to Ella's birthday party."

My eyes narrow against my will, revealing my innermost thoughts. For the billionth time in the past week, I envision myself beating the bitch to death. I blink away the vision of Adelaide's blood coating my hands, as if I'm experiencing a premonition.

"I want you to understand that what adults do is their private business. While you're at school, you should be focusing on your studies and your friends, not worrying about what your father and I are up to."

Ava is too pragmatic at her young age. "I will once Adelaide is stopped, so Whitney will stop."

"Ava, there are billions of people in this world, and we don't all think alike. You're never going to be friends with everyone, nor will everyone always agree with you. Some people will just rub you the wrong way, and you them– neither is right or wrong."

"Whitney is wrong!"

"I agree, but she doesn't see it that way." While I feel compassion for this child, my daughter is incapable; I can see that clearly. "The small-minded people scream the loudest when you act in a way they fear. It's their fear of judgment that creates their behavior. The girl probably bought into whatever lies her aunt fed her, and thinks she is defending her family. Just as you think you are defending yours. Both of you are fighting a fight that isn't yours to fight. Both of you are wrong for the right reasons."

"They call me a freak," Ava sputters. "Whitney's friends call me a freak."

"You're not a freak. Your dad and I may be freaks, but you most definitely are not." I smile to soften the blow. "When I was a little girl, did I dream of living this way? No, I did not. Do I want you to deal with all of this shit? No, it's killing me as I watch you cope. Who says what is normal? I will be proud of you if you grow up and want to live a traditional lifestyle, and I'll be just as proud if you choose a different path."

I reach over to cup my daughter's wounded cheek, and this time she allows the affectionate gesture of comfort. "Ava, I need you to understand something. While I could run away and dissolve the relationship the media is calling sick, I refuse to allow them to dictate my life to make yours easier. I love you with all my heart. I would kill for you. But I will not give up my life for you. I don't mean the beat of my heart kind of life. I mean the life I live on a daily basis. One day soon, you will grow up and follow your own path. If I were to drop everything and live my life for you, then when you left, what would I have but an empty life? That is not the example I wish to set for you. I want you to own your choices. I love your father and Cort, and I'm not ashamed to admit it. I wouldn't expect you to change who you are for me, or for your future children, or for anybody else for that matter. It isn't selfishness. It's reality. It's raw, and it's difficult.

"If we can't be true to ourselves, then we die a little on the inside. That's what's wrong with these judgmental people who are circling us like sharks. They need the thrill of someone else's strife to make them feel alive because they are dead on the inside– they have nothing else to live for. I won't feed their need, nor will I allow them to change who I am."

"What do I do?" Ava scrunches her tiny eyebrows in frustration. I want to smooth them out. I worry that my eleven-year-old will have wrinkles by the time she's twelve, and that's only a few weeks away.

"Ignore it. Don't feed into it. Whitney knows when she antagonizes you that you'll retaliate. When you do, she has all the power, broken nose or not. If they don't get a rise out of you, they will eventually give up. It's about boundaries. They are pushing yours, trying to get you to do something you'll regret.

You can only control yourself. People can try to control you, but only if you allow them. Don't let them."

I pull Ava into my lap, ignoring the flash of nausea that hits me. I smooth her baby-fine hair away from her forehead. "Sometimes I wish you were still a little kid, or at least acted your age. But right now, I'm so glad you're as mature as you are. But you can't go around plotting your enemy's demise."

I wipe the tears that escape the corner of my eyes. Imprinted in my memory is the broken expression on Ava's face from when her father gave her our abbreviated history. I will never forget it, and I will never forgive Adelaide for forcing us to tell Ava our private hell. My daughter has been clingy ever since. She looks at us as if she's never seen us before. It's something that happens when as an adult you realize your parents are people, not just your parents. Most children think their parents' existence began the moment they were born, that we have no life outside of their own. I didn't expect to see that expression for at least six more years. It's the expression of my daughter's childhood dissolving before my very eyes.

"Live your life with no regret, Ava. That's all I wish for you." I cuddle my daughter into my lap, even though she is taller than me, but not as heavy yet. I want to weep from the fact that Ava is allowing me to hold her like a baby. My eyes close as exhaustion waves over me.

"Hey, little one," a silky voice breaks into my nap. "Go get your stuff packed up." Ava slides off my lap, and then leaves the room without a complaint.

"What are you doing here, Marc?" I scrub at my eyes, trying to wake myself up. Marcus stands before me like an apparition. He leans down to kiss my forehead, but I flinch away, unable to stand his touch, no matter how platonic it may be. This isn't the first time I've seen him since the blowjob, but it's not getting any easier, either.

"I- uh…" Marc taps nervously from foot-to-foot. The movement looks strange on such a confident man. I tilt my head and scrutinize him. He's always doing the same to me. Turnabout is fair play. It's odd how he's only four years older than me when he feels ancient. "How are you feeling?" Marc's concern almost takes away from the fact that he didn't tell me why he is here.

"I've been better. I thought I'd feel better by now, but this is getting ridiculous." I complain, head giving another throb while my stomach roils.

"Listen, Kat." Marc sits down next to me on the sofa. "I know what we did is haunting you, and learning about what Cort and I do, as well as figuring out what Ezra and I did fifteen years ago…"

"Haunting me? That's one way of putting it," I mutter to myself. It's been odd the past few days, knowing Cort has either seen Marc or is going to see Marc, and having intimate knowledge as to why. It doesn't bother me in the faithless sense. It's just inconceivable for me to wrap my mind around it, especially how Ezra acts like it doesn't hurt him when it does.

"I want us to be family. I understand why you're feeling as you're feeling, and I want you to be able to suffer my presence, my touch, and my advice." Marc's amber eyes pierce me with his sincerity. "No more discomfort between us. It's making Ezra and Cortez upset, and Ava is feeling it. I don't want my granddaughter treating me indifferently because she thinks her mother doesn't like me."

"I *do* like you," I admit reluctantly. "It's just strange." I point between him and I. "I know I'm living an alternative lifestyle, but that doesn't change the fact that at my core I'm a very traditional soul."

Marcus leans over, pressing his lips to my forehead as if we've reached some kind of agreement and he's sealing it with a kiss. "I know," he murmurs against my forehead, and then pulls away. "It's why I'm so happy you're here. The affluent need reality shoved in their face. They need someone who knows what it's like to live in the other ninety-nine percent of the population. I wasn't raised as Cort and Ezra, and keeping them firmly in reality is difficult."

"I won't allow Ava to act as if she has no roots," I promise, ferocity warping my tone. "The minute she thinks buying a pair of thousand dollar socks is appropriate, I'm making her get a minimum-wage job."

Marcus tips his head back and releases a spine-tingling laugh. I suffer as he finds great amusement with how I am as a person. I suffer because I loathe the fact that I understand why this man draws the Ezes in like a moth to flame. I'm not unaffected either.

"Cortez must drive you fucking nuts." Marcus chuckles– the amusement and affection he has for Cort is obvious. "He spends money like water. I find it rather difficult to swallow, but that's all he knows. I'm glad you're here to ground us all."

"Oh, hey! You're here already." Ezra calls from the foyer as he walks into the living room.

"I guess I'm early." Before Ezra makes it a step into the living room, Marcus gets up from next to me to sit down in Ezra's usual chair. He makes himself at home, playing king of the hill– dominance edition.

"Yeah, Cort is doing what he's known for– avoiding me – that's why I'm late." Ezra sighs heavily in defeat while gazing at his occupied seat.

"What's up with you two? You've been fighting constantly for the past week." Marcus looks even more frustrated than Ezra. "The more you fight, the more I have to put up with Cortez."

"I don't want to talk about it," Ezra mumbles. "Kat, how are you feeling?" He sits down next to me on the sofa, being clingier than usual. "We made you a doctor's appointment in an hour. Cort will meet us there after his writers group at James Atwater's house."

"Why do I need an appointment? You said this was normal." I scowl because I hate having things planned without my knowledge, as every person who has ever met me knows.

"It is normal, but it's not Drop. You were experiencing a few side-effects from the initiation, but what's wrong with you *is* normal," Ezra stresses.

"God, I'm agreeing with Cort on this one. You're annoying as fuck lately. What the hell are you going on about?"

Marcus flashes me a look like he wants to spank my ass for Ezra. I give the challenging look right back at him. His hands tense on the arms of the chair and he starts to stand. I immediately regret my disrespect and slide down the sofa to get farther away from him. Seeing my remorse and fear, Marcus smiles broadly at me. He can be one scary motherfucker, and Ezra's champion.

"I thought you'd figure it out by now. But as Cort has brought up countless times in the past few months, you need capital letters, or perhaps a sky-writer, for you to get a clue,"

Ezra teases, but there is an edge of truth to his words. "You know how you block out unpleasantries."

"Is that what you've been arguing about, my thick skull?"

"Partly–"

I cut Ezra off, "Great, so I'm the fallout of your relationship?" I lash out like a wounded animal because I don't want to go to the doctor.

Not appreciating the tone I'm using on his adopted son, Marcus rises from his seat to sit next to me. I cling to the arm of the sofa to get away from him. He slides closer to me and rests his hand on my knee as a silent threat.

"This is a private conversation, ya know?"

"You do realize Cortez doesn't keep any secrets from me, you know?" Amusement twists Marc's arrogant voice. "There is no private when it comes to me."

"I can see who Ezra learned his lack of boundaries from." I crawl over the arm of the sofa, refusing to get anywhere near Marcus, and then sit in Ezra's chair.

Kneeling next to his chair, Ezra ignores Marc and makes me his sole focus. He weaves his fingers with mine, squeezing to lend me comfort and strength. Then he looks up to me with concern in his gunmetal eyes.

"You're late. I understand with all the stress that you wouldn't notice, or maybe the stress was the factor. When your illness didn't subside and you missed another monthly, I made you an appointment. You're going to the doctor for prenatal care." Ezra drops a bombshell, "Katya, I think you're pregnant."

All the blood drains from my body and settles at my feet. I can't be pregnant. Not with all the shit going on– it's a horrible time. We haven't had much romance lately. It was over two months ago when the three of us made love. We've had a few quickies here or there, but most of it has been oral or hands.

"Are you positive?" tumbles out from numb lips.

"I'm going to go fetch your medical records for the doctor's office," is answer enough. "I'll see if Ava is ready to go. She's staying at Shadow Haven until after the wedding. She wants to help decorate. I can't believe it's a few days away. Aaron grew up so fast." Ezra laughs as he leaves the room– leaving me alone with Marcus.

"You have to stop them from fighting. That is what a good bridge does, makes sure the two sides meet halfway. Remember?"

"One track mind, much? I just learned I could possibly be pregnant, and you're making it about Ezra and Cort. What is wrong with you?"

"What's wrong with you?" Marcus accuses me. "You know them. If they are fighting, they are going to make your life miserable. I would know, seeing as how I'm giving you the job I've held since I was seventeen years old. They turn into demons, destroying everything within a hundred mile radius around them. That is not the environment I'd want to bring a child into, not to mention they might be resentful if they aren't the father."

I break out into a cold sweat as nausea overpowers me. Grimacing and glaring, I grit out, "Way to keep my stress level down, Marc."

My personal demon strides into the living room while holding medical records I never knew existed. "Are you ready to go to the doctor?" Too bad Ezra looks so concerned yet happy and in love that I can't begrudge him anything.

"No, not really," I blurt out, but then I take Marc's advice. *'If Momma ain't happy'* is not the saying in Dominion, New York. It's *'if Ezra isn't happily even-keeled...'* "Ezra, thank you for making the appointment for me. I appreciate it."

Pleased I'm obeying him, Marcus kisses me on the forehead, and I try not to flinch for Ezra's benefit. "Good luck!" Then Marc turns and drops a kiss to Ezra's cheek.

Charging into the living room with her duffle bag dragging on the floor behind her, "I'm ready, Grandpa," Ava chirps excitedly.

"Great, little one. The house is all yours to decorate. Kayla is staying as well– something about the groom not seeing the bride before the big day."

Tugging on Marc's hand, Ava leads him to the front door. "Is Grandma okay with my friends sleeping over?"

"Sure is," Marc's melodious voice flows back into the living room as he opens the door. "Did you know that Daniel Whittenhower is your grandmother's closest friend? She's very pleased that you've befriended his grandchildren."

Shouting so loudly the vein in my forehead throbs, "Ava!" The door slams shut before I can stop her. "Goddamnit!"

# Chapter Forty-Five

Whomp…whomp… whomp… Endless and constant, the undeniable sound of a helicopter's propellers. For the past two hours, we have had to endure that annoying distraction. If I had a surface-to-air missile, I would use it. Turning evil, I find myself wishing the douche from *High Society Nightly* would fall from the open door where he is hanging with a video camera. The wedding was supposed to be a private affair, and now it's turned into a media circus.

I love Diane for her impenetrable gate and rock wall a mile from the house, and her large security team who keeps finding paparazzi sneaking through the woods.

We were all feeling rather smug after we thwarted the press, but that was until the flying nuisance showed up. I would rather have the chattering of reporters than the noise and wind the helicopter is causing. I've stopped myself countless times from flipping off the camera. It wouldn't look demure to give rude gestures while wearing a maid of honor gown.

The wedding starts in half an hour, and I wait, nerves getting the best of me. It's been nearly a year since I came to Dominion, and it still feels surreal, as if I'm living someone else's life. This is my children's birthright– my daughter and the fraternal twins sharing my womb –yet I feel like an interloper, an outside observer like the helicopter flying overhead.

It's not a matter of feeling worthy or deserving of the money, affluence, property and businesses, or the respect and love. I only feel at home when I'm in Ezra and Cortez's arms. The rest of the time, I flounder as if I only have a tentative thread tying me to their life– *their* life, not *our* life.

I stand on Shadow Haven's back veranda, staring at the wedding splendor below, thrilled that it's not me who's being married in this big production. I've never had fantasies of being a princess bride awaiting her prince. I'm a thirty-three-year-old soon-to-be mother of three, so it would be a bit exorbitant for my tastes. But I'm ecstatic for young Aaron and Kayla to be starting their lives out on a happy note.

The backyard contains row after row of white chairs, decorated with blush, pink bows, lining a flower petal aisle. A clematis-covered lattice archway sits on atop the dais, waiting for the lovely couple. Everything is soft pink and white. It screams innocence and princess, and it's flawlessly Kayla. I wanted their day to be perfect. If it wasn't for the paparazzi, it would be.

"I think they're ready for you, Katya." Marc's deep voice draws goose bumps to bead on the surface of my flesh. "You look stunning."

"Thanks." I turn to him, flashing a genuine smile. "You look very handsome yourself." Marcus and I have constantly thrown ourselves into one another's orbit to get over the awkwardness, and we've reached a pleasant plateau. We are cordial in public. But in private, he tries to manage me by ordering me about and giving me advice. He's since learned that I am a bullhead, and I will only take the advice I find sound, and I tolerate absolutely no manipulation. However, I've learned tender affection is part of the deal. I either accept it and enjoy it, or suffer and endure. I'm currently at begrudging acceptance.

Chuckling warmly, Marcus smooths his hands down the front of his tux. "I feel a little bit like the father of the groom." We share a delighted, celebratory smile.

"Katya, dear?" Diane calls from the veranda doors. "The ladies are ready to do the lineup. If you don't want your men to see you before the wedding, you better come inside, as they are about to ascend the dais now."

Marcus kisses me on the cheek in parting, and I'm surprised by the look of relief that washes across Diane's fine features. I try to wipe the confusion from my expression before either of them can see it.

Diane holds her hand out to escort me in the house, and I warily take what's offered. "I know what happened between you and my husband," she whispers to me as we enter Shadow Haven. "I'm just thankful that it hasn't disrupted the flow of our family. I'd hate for that to happen."

"I would hate me if I were you." My feet stop to allow another layer of shame to coil and wedge itself into my gut, taking root with the rest of the mistakes and regrets that dwell there.

"I understand, Katya. I understand how you feel, and how everything is difficult for you here because it's not how you were raised. So allow me to assuage your guilt. Never wanting to see another naked male for the rest of my days, I'm just relieved I don't have to service my husband. I don't care if it takes the man I've raised since birth, my son, my daughter-in-law, or that guttersnipe Marcus fancies himself in love with, just as long as I don't have to satisfy his baser urges myself."

"Jesus," I breathe, disgusted at how tainted this family is— the family my children are born unto. I finally see it clearly. Diane sacrificed her teenaged son to her equally teenaged husband, just so she wouldn't have to do her wifely duty.

Either being oblivious or sarcastic, Diane murmurs, "I pray often, too, dear," as she pats my hand. "It truly helps. You'd be amazed over how light I feel after Confession lifts the sins from my soul."

---

The tinkling of champagne flutes is almost as loud as the helicopter still hovering overhead. The only consolation is that we are indoors, and the cameraman can't zoom in close enough.

I will forever have a small-town mentality, and I don't mean ignorance. When Ezra first offered Kayla a ballroom for the reception, I wondered about transportation for the guests from Shadow Haven's back lawn to the reception venue. My comment received patient smiles, as if I was being cute yet daft. In my world, one does not have a ballroom in their home.

I'm not in my world anymore.

Hiding near a hibiscus in the corner of the ballroom, I look out over the dancing crowd. I smile as I remember how beautiful Kayla looked as she stood next to Aaron and pledged her undying devotion. I personally would have removed the '*obey*' from the vows, but Kayla is a true submissive.

The sight of my daughter dressed in her bridesmaid's gown brought tears to my eyes. Ezra and Cort's eyes weren't dry as they stood beside the man they had walked through fire with their entire lives. I could feel the sadness and happiness radiating off the pair.

I'd worried over whatever menacing retribution my daughter had cooked up for the Whittenhower grandchildren who are scattered about. But after watching with an eagle-eye, I came to the realization that Ella and Prissy were truly Ava's friends– their companionship was mutual for the three of them. Niel, the big boy with the haystack of ginger hair, stood sentry over the girls, his blonde-haired counterpart included– the bully, Whitney.

As a mother, I see my daughter clearly. I'm positive Ava is the instigator after watching the stoic Whitney for the past hour. She looks more leery than aggressive, but I can sense it wouldn't take much for her to turn a dig into a flesh wound.

I'm standing off to the side, more comfortable to be an observer than to join the fray. The dance floor is filled with family and friends. Ava and her father share their very first dance, and it's so sweet my heart melts. The happy couple is melded together and never letting go, neither allowing anyone else to dance with the other. Cort is dancing with his ex-mother-in-law, Pearl. Divina is dancing with Roarke while teasing him about Farmville. Diane looks like an angel in a pale pink gown, waltzing around the floor in Marc's arms– how disturbingly false appearances can be.

"May I have this dance?" flutters against my ear, startling me.

"Well, aren't you are as bright as a shiny new penny?" I tease Pretty Boy. I smile brilliantly, because when faced with direct sunshine, how can you not? "At least I can see you this time."

"Enjoying the view?" Whitt's blue eyes twinkle with good humor as he pulls a naughty smirk, revealing a set of swoon-worthy dimples. "Shall we?" he requests politely as he gestures to the dance floor.

I take Whitt's arm and follow him through the crowd. We dance for a few songs in a row, laughing as he regales me with stories of his youth and his hero-worship of Cort and Ezra. My favorite is when he caught Cort bending Ezra over the arm of the sofa. In retaliation, they watched Whitt lose his virginity via a security camera. Not a single boundary to be found.

I smile, laugh, and feel lighter than I have in weeks. Pretty Boy is just a delight to talk to. I look to my friends and family, hoping they are having as much fun. Niel is teaching all the girls how to waltz, leading Whitney, while the three little girls pretend they have a partner. I catch both Cort and Ezra's eyes as they attempt to dance with one another, but it turns into an awkward tangle of arms and legs. Laughing and growling out of frustration, they raise their arms in defeat before heading off to the refreshment table.

"Wow, you really are a whore," breaks into the conversation Whitt and I are having about the first time he got piss-roaring drunk thanks to the bad influence of the Ezes.

I look up in shock, standing before me is Adelaide Whittenhower. She hadn't been invited, and security was given explicit direction not to allow her on the premises. Thanks to the bloodthirsty media hounds, she's been ostracized from the elite.

Adelaide looks crazed, with her cold, blue eyes narrowed in rage. "Do you have to fuck every person in Dominion? Is that why you came here? I think you add a whole new level to the definition of a whore."

Whitt reaches out to calm and restrain the rampaging woman, but she flings his hands away. She's shouting so loudly the band cuts off. In utter silence, two-hundred-plus party guests turn to us as a unit, cutting off Ezra as he tries to reach us in time.

"Adelaide, leave." My voice is calm yet quiet, trying to defuse the situation before it escalates and ruins Kayla and Aaron's wedding reception.

"Are you trying to get back at me by screwing my baby brother? You're such a vicious cunt, no matter how dignified the media paints you." I look back and forth between my dance partner and the devil.

My face blanches when I notice all of their similarities: blue eyes, fair skin, light blonde hair, tall, lanky builds, and their suffocating sense of entitlement.

"What's your actual name, Whitt?" My tone is cold, deadly.

"Daniel Whittenhower II," he replies hesitantly, as if he's not proud of his name at the moment.

I step away from the pair of snakes in the grass, while shaking my head back and forth. "Niel? Short for Daniel Whittenhower III, I presume." My voice breaks from bitter betrayal. Attacking adults isn't acceptable. Attacking children is pure evil. "You sicced one of your own on my daughter, after your niece besmirched us all over Hillbrook Academy? You were just playing with me, weren't you, Daniel? You were doing this for your sister."

"No–" Whitt tries to reach for me but I sidestep out of his path. "Adelaide is unhinged. The family disinherited her after this last stunt. She makes us all look bad, bringing us down to her level. She's attacking our closest friends." I can sense his sincerity, frustration, and grief. "Ezra and Cortez are like my big brothers, Katya. They've known me since I was *born*," he stresses. "I was there during and after Ray, when both of our families were distraught. This shit makes me sick."

"Everything is your fault, Katya," Adelaide twists my name until it sounds like pure evil. "I had a good life. I was going to be a Zeitler wife and make Ezra lots of heirs. You're living my life as you fuck your way through the population. You begged Ray Hunter to rape you, hoping to snag Ezra, admit it. You're so sick and disgusting, I bet you have sex in front of that bastard daughter of yours."

Adelaide's head flings to the side before I can even register what happened. A small palm print blooms red against her cheek and a drizzle of blood escapes the corner of her mouth. I look around in shock, wondering who could have slapped her face. Slowly sensation returns to my body as the crowd watches me in shock. My hand begins to sting, and I know I was the one who snapped and hit her.

Shame slams into me because I ruined Kayla and Aaron's special day. I just allowed someone to take control by antagonizing me until I lost my temper. So much for living by example. I can't tell Ava to turn the other cheek, and then slap Adelaide's.

Marcus gets into Adelaide's face and stares her down until she cowers under his enraged gaze. She backs up, retreating from the ballroom. "Whitt, find Daniel and tell him to escort his spawn from my property. I was assured that Ade wouldn't try this shit."

"I'm sorry, sir. I'll go tell Father." Whitt hurries off, and then abruptly stops and turns toward me. "Kat, I apologize from our family to yours," he announces formally. "What Adelaide said is unforgivable and untrue." He rushes off into the crowd after his wayward sister.

"I'm sorry," I cry as I bolt from the room.

# Chapter Forty-Six

"Katya! Wait!" Ezra snags my arm as I run blindly through Shadow Haven with no destination in mind. My vision is warped by the wash of tears spilling from my eyes. I press my hand over my mouth, unsure if the nausea is from the twins, or from my shame and embarrassment.

"You can rest in our bedroom," Ezra murmurs a heartbeat before one arm slips behind my knees and the other across my back. I'm holstered into his arms as he strides through the impossibly large house. I press my cheek to his chest, stifling my sobs.

"I have no words to express the depth of my regret," Ezra whispers against the top of my head. "This is entirely my fault. I take complete and total ownership of it. Daniel had come to me months ago, asking for my professional opinion on Adelaide. But I was too close to see the truth."

Ezra opens a door on the second floor, to the right of a set of huge double doors– undoubtedly Diane's master bedroom. At the other end of the hallway is an identical set, either belonging to Marcus or Pearl.

"Whose room is this?" The room is lived in, not a guest bedroom. There are clothes scattered on the bed, shoes on the floor, and personal mementos on the walls and shelves.

"Our room," is Ezra's explanation as he strides into the attached bathroom, settling me on my feet. I rest my palm on the vanity, noting duplicates of all the same products in our bathroom at Edge. "It doesn't matter how much we remodel our apartment, it will never be home. Cortez and I left Shadow Haven, needing a sense of independence, not realizing you can't tear who you are from your soul."

I drop to my knees, flicking the toilet seat up as I go, readying for the surge of nausea that never comes. "I'm so humiliated," I whimper against my forearm.

Ezra smooth my hair from my forehead, and then hands me a damp washcloth. He kneels down beside me and begins removing my heels. "Katya, there wasn't a soul in the ballroom who wasn't empathizing with you, who doesn't know the absolute truth. I'm not saying they are three hundred of your biggest supporters. Jealousy, hurt pride, judgment aside, they know who you are and who Ade is."

"I shouldn't have allowed her to bait me." I scrub at my face, wanting my makeup removed. I feel as if I've been painted to resemble someone I'm not, someone everyone else wants me to be, and someone I can never become. The visage of Marcus and Diane dancing as if they love each other deeply scars my psyche. I never want to become that type of person, to live that kind of life.

"It's human nature, Katya." Ezra picks me up again, striding back into the bedroom. "You need to rest, not only for you but for the babies. The stress is killing you, and it's killing me to witness it. I know you're uncomfortable being at the reception, and Aaron and Kayla appreciate your support. But we all love you, and we'd rather have you happy and healthy than standing on the sidelines miserable."

"I don't belong," I admit the truth as I get comfortable on the bed. Ezra and Cort's scent wafts up my nose, and I begin to wonder if they stay here often, even for a few hours. I'm too scared to voice my questions, so I stay silent.

Ezra places a knee on the edge of the bed, and bends down to look me in the eye. "That's on you, Katya. Marcus explained it to you during my birthday party. You are separating yourself. Whitt danced with you because he genuinely enjoys your company. Dexter was circling, waiting for Whitt to release you. Roarke wanted to ask, but he was worried you'd reject him. Cort and I just knew better. You're the most confident person I know, except when it comes to friendships. You have friends, Katya. But you have to accept it as fact."

"Ez–"

"No, you're going to listen to me for once." Ezra's voice grits like shards of broken glass, signaling Master Ez is rising to the surface. "Divina has been trying her damnedest to befriend you, asking you to lunch, shopping, pedicures, and you avoid her because you feel guilty when you shouldn't. You've placed Kayla in the helpless box, so you refuse to connect with her as a friend. James Atwater invited you to tour Transcend with Alex, and you blew him off. The only people you've allowed to get close to you are Monica and Dexter, only because they don't put up with your bullshit."

"Monica and Dexter are like me," I mutter lamely. "They understand what it means to work. What it means to be hungry. How ridiculous it is to spend a middle class yearly salary on a wedding."

"Hungry? Then you should be speaking to Regina, who seems to fit into society despite the fact that she was starving to death at one point. Yes, Monica is working class. Dexter, are you fucking shitting me, Kat?" Ezra gray eyes throw sparks and his lips draw in a tight line as he tries to contain how frustrated he is with me. "Dexter pretends he wasn't born with a billion silver spoons in his mouth. You have a chip on your shoulder. Just as you are not the size of your bank account, neither are we. Just because we are affluent doesn't make us monsters. You're going to have to deal with the fact that our children can buy small countries. James wanted you to visit Transcend so you could teach our children that there is tremendous power to do good when you wield that much influence."

"I'm so—"

"I'm not finished," Ezra warns, but it's Master Ez glaring down at me. "I love you. I want you to be my wife. You're the mother of my children, and I want us to be a happy family, and I believe we can be. But you've dragged your feet the entire way, and I'm sick to death of coddling you. The only reason we are living at Edge instead of here at Shadow Haven is for your comfort. But I want to live in my home." Ezra gestures to the room around him. "This is my home, Kat. This is Cort's home. Our daughter already has a room here, and she's more than comfortable with it. The room adjacent is for the twins."

Ezra drops a quick kiss to my lips, but he's exuding disappointment. He draws away from me to stand near the door. "I'm finished coddling you, Katya. I'm done. I've committed countless, horrific sins to get us to where we are, and I'll only regret them if it pushes you farther away. You need to deal with the fact that you aren't a poor, small-town, young woman anymore. You are a professional, highly educated, grown woman, the mother of an heiress, and I will not allow you to be biased toward the rich blood that flows through our children's veins."

"Ezra," I plead, hating how upset he is. I crawl to the edge of the bed, trying to get closer to him.

"You don't get it," Ezra bites out, shaking his head while scrunching up his face in disgust. "There are three hundred people in *our* ballroom right this second. We control the world's economy. We make the laws by financing those who do. One is destined to become the next Vice President of the United States because *we* placed him there, for fuck's sake. And you," Ezra points at me as a silent accusation. "And you somehow manage to make us feel *beneath* you."

"That's not true," I sputter, completely taken aback.

Laughing without humor but edged with awe, "Yes, it is, Katya. You look down your nose at us like we're beneath you. It's amazing. You think you don't belong?" incredulity pours off him in waves. "Kat, if you'd get your head out of your ass, you'd realize you belong here more than we do. You're empathetic to all sides of life, and you could do great things with that knowledge."

Ezra opens the door, steps out, and then says over his shoulder, "I'll send Cort up to unruffle your feathers and to hold your hand. I can't do it right now because I have responsibilities to attend."

"I'm sorry," I shout before the door closes. I fall to my behind onto the mattress, confused and exhausted.

"For once, it's your turn to prove it." Ezra's voice flows through the door. "You make me jump through hoops. Let's see how you like it."

"Shit!" I hiss, slumping in defeat. Manic laughter bubbles up as I replay Ezra's words. My old motto was '*I won't be coddled or cuddled*,' and all along Ezra was doing just that.

I lie down on the Ezes' bed, knowing they both want it to be my bed as well. Do I get in the way of my own happiness, just as they get in the way of theirs? Should I just let all this shit go and let fate dictate my life?

I ponder the rules of the universe, where I went wrong, and what I can do to make our lives more livable, as a party rages beneath me. My eyes flutter shut, emotionally and physically drained. My number one priority is nourishing the growing human beings in my womb. They need their mother to be happy, healthy, well-rested, and fed, and I won't allow anything to get in their way– even me.

# Chapter Forty-Seven

I hear the whisper of the door opening. I snuggle deeper into the covers, relieved I have someone who might listen, understand, and then set me straight. "Cort, how pissed is Ezra? I wanted to apologize but he wouldn't let me."

Exhaustion is making it impossible for me to open my eyes. I listen as Cortez pads across the carpeting, anticipating him making me sweat it out. Blistering pain radiates across my cheek before I can register the hit.

Arm raising, I blink my eyes to clear my vision because I'm momentarily blinded by the sting of tears. Another hit comes, and another, and another, before I even realize something is wrong.

It happens so quickly. One… Two… Three… Four. I throw my arm up to shield my face before hit number five makes contact. The boney fist connects with my forearm, and the thunderous crack of a broken bone echoes throughout the room. The force of the punch stuns me, blanking my mind and freezing my body.

"What the fuck?" I moan in a daze, rolling around on the bed in agony. I try to get out of bed, but my long ball gown is wrapped around my legs and the covers are tangled around my waist.

I fall to the floor as another jab lands against my shoulder, followed by a chopping slap to the back of the neck. I've yet to see my attacker. They've taken me completely unawares, attacking when I least expected it.

My heartbeat flutters in my throat and reverberates in my ears until I hear nothing else. The rapid tattoo is that of a countdown to the end of my life. Violence and fear blanking my mind, I try to reason what's happening and how to protect myself, or else I will be dead before Cortez checks on me.

The fear of never seeing my loved ones, of never meeting my unborn children, of harm to my unborn twins, energizes me. My only job in life is to make sure my children live. Fingers reaching out, I pull the lamp off the nightstand by its cord, and then I strike out with it behind me.

A deep grunt is the only confirmation that I've made contact with my target. I swing backward again with the heavy lamp, and my attacker falls, vibrating the floor beneath us.

I struggle to my feet, only to waver and almost fall to the ground. My hand reaches out, using the nightstand to keep me upright. The brutal pounding I took hinders me. I doubt I can withstand even a few more punches of that intensity. I sway on my feet and blink to clear my vision, only to realize it's blood, not tears, obstructing my sight. My attacker is a fuzzy, red visage as I try to remain on my feet. I blink again, and she finally comes into view.

"You ruined my life!" screams from the mouth of my attacker.

"Adelaide, I swear to God, I will kill you in this room. This is not a threat." I seethe as fury floods my system. "I'm sick of your bullshit. The threat letters, the newspaper articles, I'm positive it's you ruining our lives, not the other way around!"

"I didn't post that interview in The Times!" Adelaide growls, struggling to stand, only to fall back to the ground. I freeze in shock, as my thoughts spin out of control. "If I don't marry Ezra, I'm going to spend the rest of my life in Winter Crest Asylum!"

"Because you're fucking nuts," I blurt out. I manage to make it a foot before wavering on my feet. I lean back against the nightstand for support. I wipe the blood dripping down my cheek to my chin, ignoring the pain radiating from my forearm. I have minutes before I pass out, before the threat of pain turns into a very real agony.

"Cause and effect, bitch! Cause and effect. I'm baited, and when I defend myself, I look insane. I. Did. Not. Contact. The. Media." Adelaide looks like a rabid dog, blood trickling from her mouth, with madness glowing from her eyes. "You did, so you'd look like a fucking angel."

"Wow… Why the letters? Explain that, then?" I challenge. Taking a deep breath, I decide I'm not fit enough to walk yet. "I didn't ruin your life, Adelaide. It was Ezra's decision on who he wished to marry."

I sway back and forth like a metronome, eyes fluttering shut as the need to pass out descends. I'm shocked awake when Adelaide tackles me to the ground. The air in my lungs rushes out of my body with a *harrumph* sound. The back of my head makes contact with the floor with a hollow thud. My broken forearm smashes into the floor, tearing an ear-splitting howl from my throat.

My head lolls to the side, a rush of vomit following the scream. Retching, listless, all I can think is how this is very different than when Ray attacked me. Ray didn't care if I died; Adelaide wants me dead.

I thought the two solid hits with a lamp would bring the bitch down. I should have known better. The evil force always withstands exorbitant amounts of pain– even bludgeoning with heavy, blunt objects.

Sitting astride me, Adelaide rises above me like a pissed-off lover. Her eyes are wild, her hair is mussed, and her teeth are bared. The only thing missing is froth from her mouth to mix with the blood dripping from her chin to land on my belly.

"Killing me won't make Ezra marry you," voice breathy and shallow. "Even if I die in the next minute, he won't marry you. Everyone saw you threaten me in the ballroom. You'll go from pariah to murderer."

"There is nothing I can do to change my fate. I'll live the rest of my days in Winter Crest Asylum. Killing you is to make Ezra pay for his crimes. He's the worst monster of all of us." Before I can blink, the psycho head butts me.

My skin bursts like over-ripened fruit as sharp needles of pain radiate around my skull. Dizzy, close to unconsciousness, a flow of warm blood trickles down my forehead, over my cheek, to fill my ear. The blood cools instantly, thickening in my hair to pool beneath my head.

"I will kill you in a moment. But first I will fuck with you, so I have a fond memory to last a lifetime during my incarceration." Gasping, Adelaide is out of breath as she struggles to hold me down. "Ezra is invincible, but knowing he'll feel dead inside over what happened to you, is all the vindication I need."

With a burst of energy, I kick and flail, striking out with my uninjured arm. I smash my feet to the floor for leverage and push upwards with my hips, trying to buck Adelaide off.

The freakishly tall sociopath will not back off. Adelaide pulls my wrists above my head in one of her hands, tearing a bloodcurdling scream from my throat, the sound of an animal in the throes of death.

Adelaide's free hand slaps me across the mouth, trying to silence me. A stinging sensation radiates from my split lip, the coppery saltiness of blood filling my mouth. "I'm doing you a favor," she warns as if I should feel grateful. "You have no idea what Ezra's done to you, do you?"

Wrenching my head to the side, Adelaide's hand slips from my mouth far enough for me to bite her. Teeth sinking in deeply, her bitter, tainted blood mingling with my own, I ravage her hand like an enraged animal defending its young.

Shrieking, Adelaide jumps off of me, waving her hand in the air as if that will magically heal it. "I'll kill you for this!"

"I think we've already covered that, so I might as well wound you as much as possible, to give you something to dwell on while you sit in your padded room in a straitjacket for the rest of eternity."

I'm on my feet in a heartbeat, grabbing for the fallen lamp. I do a double-hold on the base, ignoring the spike of debilitating pain that radiates up my arm. Gaining momentum, I smash the lamp into Adelaide's face with all the strength I possess.

In slow-motion, I watch in sick fascination as Adelaide falls to the ground, reverberating like a felled tree. Blood spurts like obscene fountainheads, arcing from several large gashes on her face. Pink air bubbles pop against her parted, blue-tinged lips.

The weapon falls from my numb hands, lamp shattering at my bare feet, cord tangled with my thumb. The clatter is loud and jarring, but falls upon deaf ears.

The cream carpeting turns red from the spray of blood, with a large pool growing beneath Adelaide. The duvet is tinged pink, with a white void where I used to lay. My blood is spattered on the headboard and the walls, with most of it being wicked away by my dress to drip down at my feet, painting the ceramic shards of all that remains of the lamp.

Spread before me is a scene ripped directly from an episode of CSI. With fuzzy eyes, I look down to make sure Adelaide is still unconscious. Her chest rises and falls, so at least I know I'm not a murderer. From one blink to the next, I regain clarity.

On wobbly legs, I run to the door to get help. I try to scream, but no sound releases from my throat. My fingertips are cold, an odd bloodless color, and unable to twist the knob. Knowing all that separates me from survival or certain death is a harmless doorknob, I concentrate all of my mental power into forcing my fingers to move.

A cold touch freezes me mid-motion. My eyes widen as Adelaide's acrid breath billows on the back of my neck, ominous and threatening. My eyes slowly lower until I see the object that is so cool to the touch. A knife is pressed against the side of my neck, directly over my jugular.

Fearless in the face of death, words spill without thought. "Why won't you die? You're like the terminator. How the fuck do you keep getting back up?" I barely breathe the words because I fear movement will sink the knife in deeper.

"Determination," Adelaide rasps in a voice tainted with pure evil. This is a shell of the woman I met many months ago. There is nothing sane left in Adelaide Whittenhower.

"Everything is life or death, Katya. My life was mapped out from the moment I was conceived. When my mother delivered a daughter instead of a son, I spent the rest of my life trying to make up for my gender. My only duty was to marry Ezra. If I should fail, the threat of Winter Crest has hung over my head since I was fourteen years old. Do you know what that does to a child? Marry a man you hate, or die hidden away in an asylum."

Not moving my lips or throat, my words reverberate instead of project. "I would have told my father '*fuck you*,' and then walked away and never looked back. Donating sperm doesn't make you a father, and your mother is a worthless piece of shit if she didn't protect you from him. You should have saved your own life by paving your own path." As careful as I tried to be, the edge of the blade still sliced into my flesh.

Adelaide pushes the knife against my throat until blood beads to slowly trickle down my skin. The bodice of my pink gown absorbs the flow, turning crimson. Pressing in farther, I now know the agony of metal piercing skin. You'd assume it would be fiery hot to be sliced open. Cold. Icy cold, numb, and terrifying. The less you feel, the worse you know you're injured.

"Speaking of pathological fathers who use their children as pawns, and piece of shit mothers who don't protect their young, there is a rumor going around that you're knocked up again. Who's the bastard's father this time?"

Fear has me speaking the truth against my better judgment. "I'm having fraternal twins, so it could be either Ezra or Cortez– or both." Every word moves my throat, cutting the knife's edge deeper into my skin.

"So it's true, then." My world burns to ash as the blade leaves my throat to rest against the small swell of my belly– less than an inch of vulnerable flesh is all that protects my children from certain death. "I think I will kill the bastards before I kill you. That memory will last a lifetime." Adelaide's voice takes on a maniacal note, and I know my life is hanging in the balance. She's capable of murdering three people in this room and never regretting it.

Acting on pure maternal instinct, I jab my elbow back into Adelaide's sternum, causing her to shriek as her diaphragm refuses to function, momentarily suffocating her. She doesn't move far, but it's enough to remove the blade from my belly.

Snapping, I unleash my primal nature. I do as I've dreamt for a very long time– envisioned over and over again. I attack Adelaide with my bare hands, broken arm be damned. I experience nothing but blind rage.

I ride Adelaide's willowy frame to the floor, pounding, wailing, scratching, biting, smashing and yanking, until her haughty face is unrecognizable. The bones in my hands break from the force of the beating, and the excruciating pain fuels my need to rend her apart. The skin over my knuckles bursts from the force of my hits.

Strong arms lift me, and still I scream and strike out. My death wail echoes around the room– a loud keening threatening to burst my eardrums.

"Get Katya on the bed. NOW!" Marc's booming voice pierces above the volume of my own.

I'm laid out on the bed, my arms and legs restrained. Shrieking in pain, a hand bracelets the wrist of my broken arm. My eyes seek who is torturing me, and locate both Ezra and Cortez. Their facial expressions are equally horrified and terrified.

"Let go!" I wail, back arching off the bed. "Broken. Let go!" I repeat until the hand releases my wrist, only to cradle it instead.

"Is she dead?" A grave, mournful voice flows from the hallway through the open door. "Is Ade dead?"

"Whitt, get the fuck out of here." Marc bellows the command, "NOW!"

"No, I escorted Ade from the property," Whitt cries in denial, as if Adelaide isn't lying on the floor with an ever-widening blood pool surrounding her. "It's my fault she's back here. Is she dead? Oh, God, is Kat all right?"

Momentarily lucid, my gaze lasers in across the bedroom to light on Whitt standing in the doorway, noting a horrified Regina standing behind him. "I'm so sorry. I... I didn't want to hurt her, but I had to make her stop. Adelaide was going to stab my babies."

Drawn across the room, Whitt sits on the edge of the bed. He stares in the horror at the blood covering every surface– most of it is his sister's, but the rest is mine.

"Ade's not dead. Her breathing is shallow and her heartbeat is thready." Marcus reports as he kneels next to Adelaide. "Is Faith here?"

"No," Regina mutters in a hollow voice.

"Shit," Marcus hisses with feeling. "I already called for two ambulances. Not to sound like a royal bastard, but while we wait, we need to get our stories straight. Should Ade die, Katya cannot go down for this."

As if all life drains from him, Ezra slumps to the soiled mattress. "We were downstairs making sure Adelaide's commitment papers were signed while she was up here trying to kill Katya and our unborn children. That is the definition of irony."

"We need to spin this. There is a fucking helicopter flying overhead with more than a dozen news vans parked at the gate. They will follow the ambulances up the drive. Son, you will agree to everything I say," Marcus commands, "even if it shows Adelaide in a poor light."

"Yes, sir." Whitt wipes a few stray tears from his eyes with the sleeve of his suit jacket. "This is Father's fault. If we could lock him in prison or an asylum, our lives would improve."

"I'm sure Adelaide would agree that Daniel is to blame," Marcus murmurs while staring down at the mutilated body on the floor. "But he's not up here to use as a scapegoat."

"Daniel's sitting in the hallway like the spineless coward he is." Regina offers in a cold, calculated voice, "I can drag his lifeless body in here if that will help."

"Tell them I did it," the voice that haunts my sleeping and waking hours rings through the silence. We all stare as our living nightmare solidifies from the ether. "Before you ask why I'm here, it's because I had to see that Aaron was happy and not ruined by what I did. But she's the real reason I'm here." Ray Hunter points to the Rorschach test splattered on the floor. "I've been following her since the newspaper article."

Voice thready, Ezra breathes, "Why?" while never taking his eyes off the man who equally created and destroyed him.

"Because I'm your father," is Ray's explanation. "I was making sure Cort, Aaron, Katya, and Ava were safe. Safe from *everyone*," he stresses, staring his son dead-on. "Just tell the authorities I beat both women. No one will doubt it. It's not as if I'm not a monster."

"Why are you protecting me?" Ezra's question has every eye flicking in his direction.

"I'm sick. I can't control myself. I have to go back to where I'm safe from myself, protecting everyone within my considerable reach. I was released from prison against my will by a person who wished to use me. So use me again by putting me back in my cage."

No longer wholly Ezra, "I should leave you out, just so I can torture you for the rest of my life," Master Ez seethes.

"After this, we'll be even. By taking the fall, it will ensure that Katya is safe. She's carrying children of my blood, and I always keep my family safe."

We all stare speechless– dumbfounded –as Ezra and Ray hold a conversation none of us understand.

"Time's ticking away," Marcus warns, trying to cut off their conversation before too much is said. "I need to make preparations and get our stories straight."

"Why are you doing this?" Ezra asks again.

"I may be a monster, but I'm not inhuman. I've felt as Adelaide did– powerless to stop your life from spiraling out of control. I've had people turn me into that, make me do unspeakable acts in the hope that I'd pull through to the other side. My only request is that Ms. Whittenhower be placed somewhere she is safe and can get the help she needs, somewhere far from the reach of those exploiting her. While the acts were evil, she is not evil. Adelaide was trying to survive."

I lay on the bed in a daze. Mind and body numb, no longer in pain but icy cold. Whitt is so distressed that he joins me. Together we watch as Marcus, Ezra, and Cortez negotiate with Ray, and a silently weeping Regina kneels next to Adelaide's fallen form. As it comes up the drive, the ambulance siren has everyone breaking into action.

Ray kneels down on the floor to rub his hands in Adelaide's spilt blood. He wipes it on his shirt, his pants, and even on his shoes and hair. He walks over to me, never looking me in the eye, and repeats the same procedure.

I hold in a primal scream as Raymond strikes the floor with his fists– over and over again until the bones in his hands snap. I blink, and everything goes black.

# Chapter Forty-Eight

Beep… Beep… Beep…Beep…

"Turn that racket off. It's maddening," I croak out. My mouth is so dry and pasty, I would kill for a drink. "Did I kill her?" My eyes are crusted shut, but I can sense someone is sitting nearby.

"The steady beat is a good sign, Katya. So, no, I'm glad it hasn't stopped." Ezra's voice is a relief to hear, to the point that I never want to be separated from him again.

"Is she dead?" I ask again, needing to know the truth before I go insane.

"No, Adelaide still breathes." He clears my conscience only to make me feel worse. "Physically she's just as fucked up as mentally. Adelaide flat-lined in the ambulance and died three times on the operating table. She's in a medically-induced coma. She'll also will never be in a beauty pageant after the ninety-seven stitches to the face."

An agony-fueled sob gets caught in my throat. "I'm a horrible person."

"You've been unconscious for four days, Katya. So Ade gave as good as she took. You had a concussion, and we feared swelling on the brain. But we're lucky that it wasn't the case. You have a fissure in your ulna. It isn't a clean break, just a crack, so the healing time is considerably less. None of your knuckles are broken, just fucked all to hell. You're covered in bruises, and had to have a total of thirty-four stitches on your scalp and neck. So don't feel guilty for saving your own life and the lives of our children."

"The babies are okay?" I try to reach out to cup my belly, but one hand is strapped to a board and the other is in a cast. Voice breaking as tears spill from my eyes, I admit, "I was so scared."

"I know," Ezra breathes, tears evident in his voice. "The first thing the doctors did as soon as you were stabilized was to give you an ultrasound. Cort and I saw our twins for the first time while you were sleeping. Just shy of ten weeks, their tiny heartbeats are ferocious– just like their mother."

"Thank God," I pray. "The only reason I fought so hard was because if I died, they died. In a way, the babies saved my life. I don't think I would have had the will to go on after so many hits if it wasn't for the twins."

"Our children are going to be fighters after what their mother had to endure during their conceptions and while in utero. At this rate, Ava will be the first female president." Ezra tips my chin down, and places a straw to my parched lips. "Here, drink this." I try to guzzle the tepid liquid, but the straw prohibits me. "Slowly," he cautions, no doubt cutting off my supply by squeezing the straw shut. "The last thing we need is for you to throw up because you drank too fast." Before barely wetting my mouth, the straw disappears.

"I see why you went into mental health instead of physical health, Doctor. As your bedside manner sucks, you tyrant," I tease, earning me a relieved chuckle. "Can you give me a wet tissue? I need to open my eyes."

"Sorry, no can do," Ezra denies my request.

"Tyrant," I mutter again, but my lips try to twist into a smile.

"You have ointment protecting your eyelids. They were pummeled shut, and the doctors didn't want it to affect your vision."

Ever so gently, Ezra settles on the bed and curls around me. He runs the tip of his nose against my cheek affectionately. I can barely feel him, or anything for that matter. I must be hopped up on painkillers. I breathe deeply, allowing Ezra's scent to comfort me. The scent of home– Cortez and Ezra, mixed with a bit of our daughter.

I blink about a million times, and my eyelids finally break free. I can see! It's the sweetest feeling. After years of being in the dark about my own life, then Ezra blinding me when he was Master Ez, following that up with sleeping in a pitch-black room because of Cort, and the initiation from hell, I'm so damn grateful to see the light.

"Hi!" My lips curl into a smile as I gaze at Ezra's handsome face and into his stormy eyes. "I missed you, and I'm sorry I upset you with my hesitant behavior at the reception, but especially with Adelaide."

We stare at each other for a few moments, both of us revealing our mutual pain. "I thought I lost you," Ezra croaks.

"I've always known if I lost Cort, I would soon follow. When I was holding you down on our bed, I knew I felt exactly the same about you. I don't think I'm as strong as you are, Katya. I couldn't live just to be with my children. I fear if I lose either of you, I'll never survive it."

"My name's Kat, remember?" I tease to lighten the solemn mood that has descended. "I've got seven lives left."

"I felt powerless. Helpless. It was my fault, and I knew it. It's my job to protect you, especially from the freaks I brought into your life. I failed on all accounts. I've sat here for the past four days, trying to determine where and how I went wrong because I never want do it again."

Not allowing Ezra to sink into martyr territory, I change the subject before he spirals out of control. "I think it's time to talk about one of the elephants in the room."

"There's more than one?" Happy for the reprieve, Ezra's eyes dart around the room, pretending to look for hidden elephants. I follow his gaze and notice a table full of floral arrangements. When my eyes light on the toy resting on the bed near my broken arm, I smile broadly, not caring that it pulls at my chapped lips.

"Monkmee! Who brought him?" I try to reach out with my fingertips, but Ezra helps me instead. He tucks the large, stuffed monkey between my arm and my body, snuggling it to my side.

Smiling with tears glittering in his eyes, Ezra's voice is thick with sentimentality. "Cort asked Ava if she would share Monkmee with you, because we didn't want you to be alone for a second. We even freshened up his special scent."

"Please, tell me you didn't wash him," I gasp out in horror. "Monkmee smelled like home."

"We just reactivated his scent." Ezra's eyes twinkle with happiness. "We took turns holding him so he'd smell like us– me, Ava, and Cort."

I inhale Monkmee's scent, sighing with happiness. "Smells exactly like home... Okay, time for a different animal. Elephant number one: what's going on with Adelaide?"

"While she was attacking you upstairs, Ade's family was downstairs, with Marcus as a witness, signing commitment papers for Winter Crest Asylum. She was to be remanded into their custody immediately."

"Adelaide said some weird stuff. She said her father was committing her because she didn't marry you, not because she was mentally unstable. She said she wasn't the one who sent the threat letters, nor did she contact the media with that story. She said she was being baited into acting irrationally to defend herself."

"Katya, don't believe the insane ramblings of a homicidal maniac. You're trying to solve Ade as if she is a puzzle, debating what she said to you as if it was truth. She attacked you, attempted to murder you. In doing so, she would have murdered two unborn children. Do you honestly believe a word out of her mouth?"

"I don't want to believe Adelaide after what she did, but what if she wasn't the person who sent me the notes and contacted the media? That means there is someone out there who could still harm us."

Ezra leans over me, eyes impossibly close to my own. "The notes called you a whore. Adelaide called you a whore. The notes were a threat. Ade threatened you both publicly and privately. The notes threatened your life. Adelaide tried to kill you. What more evidence do you need? Do you want me to call Marcus in here? He's out in the waiting room. He'll tell you how most criminals say they are innocent, and the majority of confessions are by innocent people who are trying to save the culprit, just as Ray did for us."

"Ray?" My voice wavers in fear. "Elephant number two: am I in trouble? It was self-defense. Ray didn't need to sacrifice himself for me."

"With Adelaide attacking us via the media, the public fight between the two of you where you slapped her, and less than an hour later both of you were half dead and nearly dead, Marcus was worried that it would look premeditated. It would have at least gone to a Grand Jury because of the publicity surrounding it, and that was not a chance any one of us was willing to take. We could have lost you to prison, or Daniel's family would have been dragged through hell with the details of Ade's mental state."

"Ah, hell," I rasp, heartrate monitor going haywire with my terror. "But, Ray? Why would he do that?"

"My father is a rapist and a murderer. But even I will never claim he doesn't love me." Ezra's stormy eyes hold a well of confusion. "He has a strange way of showing it. He loves Cortez, too. Ray respects Aaron because he survived. With you being the mother of his grandchildren and his survivor, he would do anything you asked of him. If you'd ask him to kill for you, he'd die a happy man. Going back to prison was an easy thing."

"They actually believed him?"

"In reality, the authorities know the absolute truth of what happened in our room. With Marcus being Dominion's District Attorney, he had some sway. The judge accepted Ray's confession, relieved to sweep this under the rug while putting a convicted criminal back behind bars. Neither of you women should be penalized. You're not a criminal, and Ade is getting the help she needs. The judge understood all of this. The confession, booking, and sentencing took no more than an hour, with Ray receiving five years for two counts of assault."

"I find it hard to believe that the media didn't find that bizarre. Bureaucrats do not move *that* quickly."

"As long as the story sells, they don't give a flying fuck if it's true or not. High Society Nightly's helicopter recorded everything. Somehow they had someone in the ballroom, too. The videos of the slap, the arrival of the ambulances, you and Adelaide rolled out on stretchers, and Ray's arrest have gone viral. Ava is obsessed as usual, driving Cort nuts. I think our girl has a future as a journalist. Albeit a trashy gossip rag, but a journalist nonetheless."

Laughing together at the ridiculousness, relieved to feel lighthearted even for a second, the door opening interrupts our lunacy. A fifty-something man in scrubs enters the room carrying a clipboard. The doctor says, "How's the patient doing this evening?" without ever looking up from my chart.

# Chapter Forty-Nine

"Are you completely sure about this?" Marcus asks for the tenth time as he paces my living room while Judge Kilpatrick looks at him in wry amusement. "It cannot be undone."

"Sure it can, old chap," Kilpatrick manages to halt Marc's pacing. "It's called a divorce."

Growling, amber eyes throwing sparks, Marcus is obviously envisioning what it would be like to kill his superior. "Even if you get married and manage to get a divorce later, Ezra is crazy enough to never abide by it– this is for life, no matter what the legal paperwork says."

"If you don't think I understand the inner workings and machinations of Ezra's insanity, then you've got another think coming. I've survived him for nearly thirteen years. I'm positive. I feel at peace with my decision."

Marcus strides over to where I'm seated on the sofa, and then drops down on one knee. Overly touchy, the dominant man grips my chin with two fingertips so I cannot look away. "I'm not worried over Ezra, Katya. I know he will be ecstatic. I'm worried you will regret the lack of romance, and I don't want you to resent Ezra for life because he didn't do an elaborate proposal, host an engagement party, and throw you the world's largest wedding celebration."

I raise an eyebrow at the man, showing Marcus I think he's losing his ever-loving mind. "That's not me," I admit. "At heart, I will always be a very conservative person. It's no longer about how I was raised in a small town versus the life your family leads. It's about who I am at my core. I would hate the attention and the waste. I'd rather we donated all the money to Transcend, or whatever charity Diane is championing this week."

Fuzzy black brow matching my incredulous expression, Marcus isn't hearing me. "You're a woman, surely you want some romance with a big diamond on your finger."

"Gender stereotyping again, I see," I tease Marc, earning a chuckle from the judge. I lean forward, trying to impart my sincerity. "Marcus, I've had weeks of convalescing to think over what Ezra said to me at the wedding reception. I thought about who he is as a person, and then I envisioned him as a hardworking guy from my hometown. I stripped Ezra down to his soul, and then I decided whether or not I loved what I saw and if I could deal with his flaws. I decided I would marry that version of Ezra in a heartbeat, and that proved his argument correct. I was judging him on his station in life instead of as a person."

"You can be rather haughty," Marcus allows. His devastating lips twist into a smirk when I scowl at him. "You fit in with us perfectly."

"I'll be honest. I still have reservations where Cortez is concerned. Because I believe he's lying to himself. I know he loves me, will always love me. But deep down, he's always wanted what Ezra wanted when they were kids. I also understand Ezra is not a kid anymore, and what he wants has changed. I'm willing to have my heart broken in the future to have a happy present."

"Cortez is lying to himself," Marcus agrees, hand moving to cup my cheek to comfort me because the truth is so painful. "Only time will reveal it. Maybe by then, everything will work itself out."

"Ava has been bullied a lot at Hillbrook because of our past behavior. She's almost twelve, yet she's had to deal with her father being called a rapist, her mother a whore, and being called a bastard. I don't want that for her, and I don't want that for the twins. I'm not a whore," I utter, and for once, I truly mean it. "Ezra's not the same person he used to be, either. I'm going to make damn sure my children are legal, born and protected under their father's name."

Marcus leans forward to kiss my forehead, lips curling into a smile against my skin. "Ezra has wanted to formally ask you to marry him for years, Katya. You're a tough broad, I'll give you that. But don't emasculate him by taking this rite of passage away."

"As if." I bust out laughing at the ridiculousness. "Don't you see how perfect this is for me to ask him, to have everything ready and waiting? I know he's been waiting for my cue before dropping down on one knee. I know he's been planning elaborate celebrations, worried that when I say I don't want that shit I'm lying to myself. He knew if he asked me before I was ready, I would run."

Marc falls back to sit on his heels. "Would you have?"

"Yes. Most definitely," I finally admit. "This is me taking a leap of faith into Ezra's arms, proving I want to be a part of his life. Not because he demanded it of me, but because I want to be there. He's the romantic; I'm not. Cort is especially the romantic of the three of us. I don't need grandiose gestures. I need stability, security, structure, and consistency."

"What about love?"

"That's unconditional," I whisper, getting teary-eyed. "No matter what Ezra does to me, no matter if we spend a year together in wedded bliss, or crumble to pieces less than a decade from now, that love is going to endure."

"Right answer!" Marcus hops to his feet, and then reaches into the inside pocket of his suit jacket. He produces our wedding license and hands it to the judge. "I'll make the call."

After weeks of planning, I'd arranged for Ezra and Cortez to take Ava on a father/daughter day around the city while I put everything into motion. As Marcus calls Ezra to bring him home, I stare down at my palm cupping my baby bump. I'm doing the right thing. I'm positive every bride has some reservations. If I wasn't nervous, then I'd be worried.

Most people would see the fact that I didn't invite anyone to our wedding, not even our parents, as a sign that I'm unsure. No wedding party. No expensive bridal dress. No wedding. No reception. It's not because I'm unsure, or because I don't love Ezra, or because I don't want to shout it to the rooftops that I want to be his wife. It's not even because of the media tracking our every step.

It's because I love Ezra that much, because we love Cortez just as much. The bells and whistles are a distraction from the true union. Our marriage is about Ezra, Cortez, and me, and absolutely nothing else. We need nothing but us.

"Is this the last of it?" Aaron asks as he walks into the living room carrying a box, with Roarke trailing behind him.

"For now, yes." I laugh inwardly, marveling over how Marcus was worried about romantic grandiose gestures, when I am the one who is about to rock the Ezes' worlds. They're the romantics, not me, so this is perfect. "Thanks for the help, guys."

After they get a few more feet, something hits me. "Who the hell is their bodyguard for the day?"

"They're safe," Marcus answers for them. "I promise. So… everything is ready. They're just entering Edge."

"Are you okay with the rest of this?" I ask Marc, more terrified of act two of my plan than my upcoming nuptials.

"I'm over the moon," Marc sings. I flash him a potent look, and he changes his tune. "Don't be a pervert, Katya."

"Seriously, though–" I begin, but I get cut off by the front door opening. Heart beating in my throat, palms sweating profusely, I feel like I'm going to pass the fuck out from the anticipation.

"I love shopping!" Ava shouts, dragging a bunch of bags in her wake as she charges over to me. "We got baby stuff! Lots and lots of baby stuff! Pink, blue, and green because ya never know." My daughter keeps rambling as she pulls tiny articles of clothing from her bags, not noticing my mini-melt-down. "Cort found the cutest t-shirts. See?"

Ava holds up a dinky gray t-shirt. **Evil Twin**. She drops it to pick up another. **Eviler Twin**. "Aren't they perfect for my minions?"

"Lord, save us all," I pray.

"Monster is failing to explain how most of our purchases were for her," Cort comes up behind our daughter to rest his palms on her shoulders, his bags fanning out around her like angel wings. "Ez tried to go into a museum. But instead, we had to endure hours of watching the budding fashionista try on dresses."

"Don't lie," Ezra grumbles as he joins us, completely purchase-free. "You were the one whining about the museum and suggested shopping instead." He flicks Cort in the ear. "Also the one picking out all of the purchases." Ezra looks at me as if saying, *"Save me!"* "I was tortured for the past five hours."

Commiserating with my soon-to-be husband– not that he knows that yet –I point to the bags clutched in Cort's hands. "More baby stuff?"

Ezra rolls his eyes. "More Cort stuff. We're having separate father/daughter days from now on. Cort and Ava can go shopping and watch movies, and Dad and Ava can visit museums and go to the opera."

"Mother/daughter days will be spent volunteering at Transcend, learning how to take care of oneself and the actual value of the US Dollar, and painting our toenails while watching romantic comedies," I explain to prove how vast our priorities are but how well-rounded our children will be.

"Well, hello there?" Cort ends on an upward inflection when he notices Judge Kilpatrick sitting in Ezra's favorite chair. "Marc? Kat? Why is the Honorable Kilpatrick sitting in our living room?" Tan skin tinting pink, he flushes with embarrassment. "Why is he here watching everyone pick on me?"

"Ava, can you collect all the bags, please," I order our daughter, and then I gain Ezra and Cortez's undivided attention. I hold out my palms, one for each of them. "Both of you, please c'mere."

Nearly five months pregnant with a set of twins, I'm as big as a full-term pregnant lady. There will be no bending down on one knee when I ask for Ezra's hand in marriage. So I settle for sitting on the sofa while they stand before me.

Taking their hands in mine, I look up into their confused faces. Ezra looks like he's going to be sick, his pale skin fading to lifeless. Cort twists his expression, eyebrows knitting in the center of his forehead. I grasp their hands tightly, never wanting to let go.

"I had a big ol' speech prepared, but that's not me. So, I'm just going to be blunt." I take a deep breath and release it in a gust of words. "Ezra, would you do me the honor of becoming my legal husband? Cortez, would you do us the honor of exchanging vows with us?"

Stunned, Ezra releases my hand. Knees buckling, he grips the armrest of the sofa for support. "I'm... I'm fucking speechless," he gasps, one hand clutching his chest. "Never in a million years did I expect *you* to ask *me*."

Eyes glittering with tears, Cortez stammers, "It should just be the two of you. It's not about me, ya know? So don't worry about me." He tries to back away, but my fingers clench his tighter with my nails biting into the back of his hand.

"All or nothing, Cort," I warn unflinchingly, never breaking his freaked-the-fuck-out stare. "You either stand up with us, or we don't get married at all. Our children will be born out of wedlock, and that will be on your head."

Huffing a laugh of utter shock, "Katya has learned how to manipulate us," Ezra marvels. "Well-played. I see we've been a positive influence, after all."

"You must truly mean it, or else you'd never do something so unethical." Cort continues to stare at me, testing to see if I really want this– want him.

"Cort, Ezra is in love with two people. We all realize while you and I love each other, it's not the same as what we feel for Ezra. At the same time, we need to accept that Ezra's feelings for us are equal. I love him too much to divide him. Do you love Ezra enough not to force him to choose? Because if Ezra has to choose, it will destroy him. Do you love our children enough to give them a whole family?"

"Master-level manipulator." Marcus whistles sharply. "Expert mother guilt-tripper. I think my Jewish Grandmother just sent you mad props from the grave."

I ignore Cortez's uncertainty, knowing without a shadow of a doubt that if he doesn't grow the fuck up, he's going to destroy us all. "Ezra–"

Before I can get more than a word out, I'm being suffocated by a pair of luscious lips. Ezra kisses me as if he's dying, drinking my soul in where he will keep it for the rest of eternity. When he pulls away, both of our cheeks are damp from his tears of joy.

Ezra reaches over to grip the back of Cort's neck, squeezing viciously. "Katya and I are getting married today, whether you join us or not," he warns in a cold voice. The sharp tone is reminiscent of grating broken glass, signifying Master Ez is very close to the surface.

"I want this," Ezra declares, giving a harsh shake to Cort's neck. "I've worked so hard for this moment– you have no *fucking* idea just how hard I've worked, or the things I've done –and you're not going to ruin it. I refuse to choose. Katya won't make me choose. Don't you dare *ever* ask me to choose," he threatens, squeezing harder. "This isn't about you, or me, or Katya, or the past. This is about us and our children. Right now! Grow the fuck up for five seconds, and grow a pair of balls."

Abruptly, Ezra releases Cortez, who weaves on his feet from the force. "I had bought rings, anticipating this moment for the last four years, scared to death of ever asking you, Katya." Ezra drops to his knees to kneel beside me. "I feared you would run from me and Cortez would resent me. I've wanted nothing more than for you to be my wife."

"Here," Marcus nudges Ezra with his knuckles. When Ezra turns to look over his shoulder at his adoptive father, Marc opens his hand to reveal a square jewelry box. "I found it when I was renovating your room at home. I thought you'd need it today."

Almost gingerly, Ezra takes the box in his fingertips. He runs his knuckles beneath his eyes, brushing the tears aside. "The fact that Kilpatrick is sitting in my chair says that when you make up your mind to do something, you do it."

"Tenacious, thy name is Katya Waters," I tease to lighten the mood, especially since Marc dragged Cort across the room, where he's lecturing the piss out of him.

Flicking the top of the box open, Ezra reveals three rings nestled within: an elegant but simple diamond engagement ring and two matching wedding bands: one male, one female. I make no assumptions. Instinctively, I know one of those bands is meant for Cortez.

Chuckling beneath my breath at the irony, I pluck the box that is hidden between my thigh and the armrest. I open it exactly as Ezra had, smiling when he rumbles a laugh at the contents. "While Cort is throwing himself a pity party because he thinks we forgot about him, forcing Marcus to try to calm him down, you and I both bought Cortez the same exact wedding band. The man's ring finger won't be able to bend."

Eyes downcast, looking sheepish yet happy, Cort saunters back over to us with Marcus prodding him along. "Great minds," he mutters as his arm juts out, revealing a box resting in his palm. "I guess it's meant to be, since we all managed to pick out the same wedding bands." Cort plucks the rings from the box, pressing them together. "They interlock, which is probably why it caught all of our eyes."

"I saw them when I went with Aaron to the jewelers." Ezra's biting his lip, trying not to laugh, always finding Cort and my antics entertaining.

"Kayla pointed it out to me in one of the billion wedding magazines she forced me to look at," I add.

Face scrunching, Cort narrows his eyes. "Aaron took *me* to pick out his ring. What the hell?"

"Perhaps," Marcus cuts in, "Someone influenced Aaron and Kayla to point you three idiots in the same direction. Perhaps that person would appreciate a pat on the back."

Standing from his seat, "My daughter invited me over for dinner tonight," Judge Kilpatrick interjects before we pounce on Marcus. "We definitely have the rings," he mutters with an eye roll. He holds up a piece of paper. "We have the license." Then he points at Marcus and Ava. "We have the witnesses. It's time you three parrot whatever vows I throw at you, because if you plan on creating your own vows, we'll be standing here a decade from now and my daughter's pot-roast will be burnt to a crisp."

# Chapter Fifty

Glowing like he's the blushing bride, Ezra stretches out on our bed, grinning from ear to ear. "I adore happy surprises. Knowing you, Katya, I'm not allowed to suggest an actual honeymoon, but do we at least get to have a wedding night? We haven't had any intimacy since before the initiation. A man cannot survive on oral and masturbation alone."

Winking, I walk past the bed toward the nightstand. It's been an awkward few months between the constant morning sickness, trying to heal mentally, emotionally, and physically after the beating, Cort and Ezra's constant push and pull fighting, and now motion has the babies trying to take out my lungs.

"I'm pretty sure you both woke up with your dicks in my hands this morning, and I didn't hear nary a thank you for the orgasm," I taunt. "*I* haven't had sex in months. You two," I point at a smug Ezra and a leery Cortez, "Have gotten off twice a day since my hands healed, and that doesn't count what you do in private."

"I haven't touched Ezra when you weren't around." Cort's voice is filled with sadness and longing. Dejected, shoulders turned inward, he stares at his feet. "Listen, I'll go sleep at Shadow Haven for the night and spend some time with Ava. I'll let you guys have your wedding night in peace."

Before Cort can turn to open the door, I grab something off the nightstand, throw it, and hit him upside the head with it. "Jackass, look at your ring finger. There are two bands– one from me and one from Ezra. You said the same vows as we did. Just because you didn't sign the marriage license means jackshit, and you know it. Leave the martyrdom to Ezra."

"It's our wedding night. *We* got married today," Ezra stresses. "If you take one more step away from us, I'm going to tear your ring finger off and shove it so far up your ass, you'll never shit out our wedding bands."

"I just–" at a loss for words, Cort continues to stare at his feet while he rubs the blooming welt on his forehead.

Scrambling off the bed, Ezra crosses our bedroom to press

Cort against the closed door. "You and I, we don't have to have sex if that's what you're fretting about. I've never pressured you, and I never will. If all you want to do is feel my skin against yours while we touch our wife, I'm good with that too. If you don't want any sex to happen, I'm sorry because I'm super, fucking horny right now. So just deal and watch me get off."

Cort's tear-filled, hopeful eyes flick up to connect with Ezra's. "You mean it." He sounds like he was just told Santa Claus is real. "You mean it? I don't think I will be able to–" Cort stumbles over his words. "–fuck you ever again, and that's why I was scared to get married. Who marries someone so broken?"

"Someone who's just as broken, to the point that it takes all three of us to feel whole, that's who." Leaning down to pick up what I assaulted Cort with, Ezra chuckles. "Besides, I don't think Katya plans on any fucking to be had tonight. I think she has other plans in store." With a heavy hand, Ezra slaps the ten-inch dong to Cort's chest.

"Holy fuck!" Cort huffs a laugh. "Oh, I'm game. I've been masturbating to the fantasy of this for months." Energized, the man starts shucking his clothing, letting it land wherever it lies. Surprisingly, Ezra doesn't clean up after Cort because he's too busy eye-fucking him instead.

"Negotiation time," I begin. "First, I can't do anything vigorous because to say my body is in a constant state of discomfort would be an understatement. Second, I had to make some adjustments on the harness so it rides beneath my belly. So sexy," I whisper, shuddering in revulsion. "Not at all sexy."

"Anyone else freaked the fuck out that our kids will be present during our wedding night, while their mother performs deviant acts?" Completely naked while absentmindedly stroking the dong, Cort is so erect his cock is pressed tight up against his abs.

"Mmm…" Ezra breathes, more aroused than I've ever seen him. He brushes a fingertip down Cort's length, which jumps into the touch. "You don't seem too concerned by that. But I think it's appropriate, seeing as how an evening such as tonight brought them into being."

I forget my train of thought as soon as Ezra begins undressing with the same zeal as Cortez. His clothing lands on the floor, and miraculously he doesn't bother to pick it up. Standing side-by-side, tan and pale, lean and soft and lean and toned, exactly the same height and body structure, I marvel over the fact that they are both mine. It's no wonder they've never been able to avoid each other. Their attraction is palpable as they stand shoulder to shoulder, fully aroused and ready for anything.

Deciding to follow suit, I strip out of my blouse and pants, leaving on the black tank top and shorts beneath, feeling too self-conscious with my pregnant body versus the wet dreams leaning against our bedroom door.

"Since the first time Cort touched me was to take my mouth, I thought it appropriate to return the favor."

"Yes!" Cort moves forward, cock waving back and forth like a flag. "Fuck my throat, Kitten. Skull-fuck the hell out of me." He thrusts the dong into my hands. "I want to choke on your cock."

Laughing so hard at Cort's enthusiasm, I can barely get the words out. "So eager… one condition, though."

"Uh-oh!" Ezra sings, skin flushing a gorgeous pink instead of marble white. "I like the sounds of that."

I reach over for the harness, toss it to the floor, and then step into it, knowing full and well I won't be able to bend down to pull it up to my waist. "While I'm fucking your face," I say to Cort while Ezra jumps in to fasten my harness, "Ezra's going to be sucking your dick."

Cort's eyes narrow, fury etching its way across his features. "Hey! None of that. We're all making concessions here. Tit for tat. I'm fucking your face because Ezra's doesn't like the thought of hurting you. I'm fucking Ezra's ass because you can't get over the past. Nobody's fucking me because it makes me feel like I'm in a washing machine on spin cycle, with two rabid creatures kicking my innards. The least you can do for me, is to allow Ezra to get off on you getting off on him. Got it? Get it? Get off on it!"

Lips pursing, eyelashes fluttering, "You're so bossy," Cort pouts. "Okay. I'm good with that. I can get off on that."

"I think I'm a hairsbreadth from coming," Ezra warns, and all eyes light on his throbbing cock. With a few more pulses, a drop of pre-cum drips from the tip to splatter on the floor. I snicker as Cort's eyes follow the path, tongue licking his lips like he can already taste it.

If everyone could get over their bullshit, we'd descend upon each other like ravenous wolves. But there are so many emotional landmines we're traversing, that I'm unsure where to step. For once, I'm the only one who isn't in our way.

"Maybe while I'm using the dong on Ezra, he'll allow you to suck him. If you promise to do it nicely, that is. No angry oral sex."

Still pouting but as aroused as ever, "Okay," Cort agrees with everything I say because he wants it that much. I wonder if I could coax him into penetrating Ezra. If so, this would be the best day of my husband's life.

"Logistics?" I curve my arm around my belly, hooking the dong into place. I giggle at how ridiculous I must look with a big belly and a latex phallus jutting out beneath it. "As unsexy as it is to discuss what position to use, how about Cort sits on the edge of the bed while I stand, and Ezra kneels on the floor with his head in Cort's lap. Good?"

Their only response is to scramble into position while I laugh at how eager they are. "Who starts first?" I ask, feeling beyond awkward yet excited at the same time.

"You do," Cort replies immediately. "Ezra can't put my dick in his mouth until after I'm way into it. He'll know when. If he does it too soon, I'll freak the fuck out and ruin our night."

Smirking, I point at my 'dick', expecting Cortez to get down to business. "Kat, you have to be in charge. I can't use my hands, remember?" He tucks his hands behind his back and eyes me in challenge. "Make me!"

Acting on instinct, I reach forward in the blink of an eye to yank Cort's face down to my 'dick'. "Open your goddamned mouth and get to sucking, or else I'll show you 'make me.' Do it!"

Making an ungodly sound from the back of his throat, Cort unhinges his jaw, and then I shove my 'dick' in as far as it will go. I draw back out, fearful I'm hurting him. "Lick it. Make it feel good. Get it nice and wet," I coax.

Eyelashes casting half-moons against his flushed cheeks, Cort's tongue worships the phallus, all the while moaning in bliss. I turn my face to the side to look down at Ezra, who is wearing a similar drugged expression. Blushing when he notices my attention, he leans in to nip at my thigh with his front teeth. Curling around my leg, he smiles up at me.

"Cort came a little bit when you impaled him like that. It's splattered all over his belly. He loves it rough." Ezra sighs against my thigh. "I just don't have the guts to give him what he needs. It freaks me out. But he does need it."

"Which is why you…"

"Yeah." Ezra blushes harder. "Cortez deserves to be satisfied and happy. If I can't give him that, then I'm glad Marcus has the balls to do it. It doesn't upset me anymore because I understand."

I reach down to ruffle my fingers through Ezra's hair, giving him the affection and intimacy he craves. Pulling away, I change gears from loving to violent. I cup Cort's head in both of my hands, digging my fingernails into his scalp until I almost draw blood. My fingers twist in the tendrils for leverage.

I grunt, "Skull-fuck my dick," as my hips surge forward as hard and as fast as I can thrust. Cort spasms against me, but I don't let up. With unrelenting lunges, I move in and out of Cort's mouth, going deeper with every thrust. The faster I rock, the more he grunts in ecstasy.

"Cortez isn't orgasming, but cum is pouring out of his cock. Jesus," Ezra hisses, and then matching groans echo throughout our bedroom.

Eyes held wide, I look down in utter disbelief as the exquisiteness disappears between Ezra's taut lips. Cort doesn't freak out. If anything, he starts sucking at my fake dick even harder. His thighs widen as he counterthrusts in time with Ezra's movements.

Most of the time when they touch, it's usually in the dark, so I've never seen it before. Ezra's eyes roll up to connect with mine, and I've never witnessed anything as beautiful in my entire life. Blushing harder, Cort's length slips free from his mouth, and then he nuzzles at Cort's thigh.

"You need some too," Ezra whispers, and I assume he's offering me a taste. But instead, his fingers skate up my inner thigh. He jerks the harness down a bit, settling the base of the dong lower. Then he reaches inside my shorts, parting my lips. With Cort's next hard suck on the dong, the movement presses the base against my clit.

Upon my first moan, Ezra's fingers retreat, and then Cort's

dick is slurped back into his mouth.

Surreal.

My husbands.

I'm their wife.

We knock down barriers and topple boundaries, and I've never felt closer to either of them.

I press deeply into Cort's throat. No longer thrusting, I just hold, grinding the base of the dong into my clit, using the back of his throat as leverage. A warmth descends, blanketing my whole body as my orgasm closes in around the edge. My eyes slip shut. Shuddering from the effort, I hold back my moans so I can listen to my husband's cry of pleasure instead.

Cort spasms, body jerking roughly. Coming down from my release, I make sure he rides out his climax before pulling from his mouth. I step backward, and Cort falls to the mattress, giggling like a little girl– high as fuck.

"Ah, hell!" Cort moves lightning quick, grabbing Ezra's wrist to yank him from the floor. In a perfectly executed move, Cort has Ezra flipped over onto his hands and knees with his ass in the air, and suddenly Cortez is standing next to me. "Let me prepare our naughty doctor for your pleasures, Mistress Bossy Wife."

Eyes cutting sideways, I mutter to our lazy closet-eater, "Since when are you so athletic and spry?"

Flashing me his patented grin, "Only when I'm horny."

"Ezra just sucked you dry," I sputter.

"I'm still hard, though." Cort wiggles, dick slapping one hip and then the other with his movements. "This is fun!"

"You are so high right now," I draw out, laughing. "If I ever contemplated whether or not you're a submissive, this would prove my suspicions correct."

Huffing a laugh, Ezra shimmies his hips. "Am I head down, ass up for a reason? Or are you teasing me? Unlike you lucky fucks, my dick is dripping pre-cum because it's being ignored."

Growling, "It's still going to be ignored," Cort curves into Ezra, hands gripping his hips. Cort bends down and skates his front teeth along Ezra's ass cheek. "Yummy," he purrs. Cort's fingertips dig in to open Ezra wide, revealing the pucker hidden between his ass cheeks. "Even yummier."

"Holy fuck!" Echoes around the room– Ezra's gasping exclamation of shock and my stunned outburst. Muscles clenched tight to avoid writhing, Ezra pants, "When Cort makes nice with my dick, he always does this for me."

"Does wha–" my question is cut short when Cort's tongue curls, the tip dipping to touch Ezra's pucker. "Ohhh…" Mouth held wide in the shape of an **O**, I watch in sick fascination as Cort reams Ezra's asshole. Oddly, both of them are *way* into it.

Ezra's back arches, and then dips down until his abdomen touches the mattress. With the next flick of Cort's tongue, his back arches again. Over and over, Ezra wrenches his back up and down while Cort ravages his hole.

Tongue still buried deep, Cort's eyes cut in my direction, and then he slides free. "Remember what I taught you? Get him nice and wet– the sloppier the better –and then take your finger to loosen him up." Cort draws back, and his finger replaces his tongue.

Someone snorts in disbelief– okay, it was me. "You sure are enthusiastic and eager for a man who doth protest too much," I mutter beneath my breath. Another snort– this time Ezra's. But Cort is too blissed out to notice because his tongue is reaming Ezra's asshole while a finger buried deep inside.

"C'mere," Cort orders, going from pliant submissive to impatient dominant. Perhaps Cort is a switch. He grabs my hip, moving me closer. Leaning down, this time using his hands, Cort swallows my '*dick*' whole. He bobs up and down a few times. Slurping and sucking noises fill the air. He pulls off with a '*pop*'. "This needs to be nice and wet, too. It's been years since Ez has been penetrated."

"Lube in the nightstand drawer!" Ezra calls out, voice breaking from anticipation and impatience. "I don't give a fuck if it's dry or not. I just want to feel full again."

"Ass down a bit," Cort orders, hand pressing to the small of Ezra's back. "Legs opened further apart. Yeah, just like that." He moves away to grab the lubricant so quickly I barely track the movement. "Stand right here, Kitten."

Cort places me where he wants me. Apparently it's his turn to run the show, with the one who always runs our lives lying completely pliant on the bed. I'm shifted around until I'm standing between Ezra's spread legs, with his ass cheeks brushing my big belly. Cort reaches up to press Ezra's back again. Knowing exactly what that touch meant, Ezra lowers until we're at a good angle.

I'm just a passenger as Cort takes ahold of my '*dick*', using it as if it were his own. Fisting it, he presses the head to Ezra's pucker, and begins slowly pressing in. My eyes flare wide in shock, never seeing anything like this in my entire life. "Whoa…"

When Cort turns to look at me, I gasp in awe. His pupils are blown, eyelids droopy, and his mouth is parted on a pant. "Give Ez a bit more– another inch or two. Go slowly." He instructs me, but his hand is doing all the work, slowly feeding the latex phallus into Ezra's ass.

Allowing me freedom of movement, "Gorgeous… so gorgeous," Cort chants. His hands begin running along the length of Ezra's back in a continuous wave– from shoulders to ass. "Give him more," Cort rasps out.

Pressing in another inch, Ezra turns frenetic. "Oh, God. Oh, God. Oh, God… Yes. Oh, God. Yes." Voice rough and strained, he begins begging, gyrating, hips moving up and down along my fake length.

There is no need for me to move because Ezra takes what he needs from me. Rocking back and forth on his hands and knees, he fucks himself on the dong. Instead of watching Ezra, I decide to watch Cortez instead. He's staring down at the port of entry with such longing desperation that my breath hitches in my throat.

Cort grabs the base of the dong, detaching it from the harness in record speed. "The bed. Now, Katya." Cortez never calls me Katya, so I move quickly while he begins thrusting the toy deep inside Ezra– who is so out of it, he's baying like a wounded animal. "Harness off. Shorts off. Lie on your side so you and the babies are comfortable. Prepare yourself if you're not wet enough."

Doing as I was told, the hollow thud of the toy hitting the floor confuses me. Ezra is shoved hard to the mattress, toppling sideways. "Spoon your wife." Cortez's voice takes on a husky cadence I've never heard from him before. "Slip into her but don't move. I'm the only one who moves. Neither one of you are to look at me."

Once told, I can't *not* do it. I look over my shoulder, briefly catching a view of the crazed masked painted across Cort's face.

But then Ezra is spooning me, curling up around me. "What's going on?" I breathe, heart pounding out of my chest. I'm confused and scared, yet exhilarated.

Never breaking eye contact, I can sense Ezra is feeling everything I'm feeling and then some. He reaches down between us, nudging to enter me. I wiggle around, lifting my thigh to accommodate him. Sliding in as softly as possible, trying not to jostle me or press too deeply, he fills me until we both release a contented sigh.

Cort moves, and both Ezra and I startle and freeze like spooked rabbits. Without moving a muscle other than his lips, Ezra mouths, "Cort's going to fuck me now."

Our eyes lock, neither breaking the rule of looking at Cort, and then widen at the same time. Me, because Cort releases the most mournful sound to ever grace my ears. Ezra, because Cortez is deeply rooted inside him for the first time in years.

Ezra's greatest wish.

Cortez's biggest fear.

"It's our wedding night, so this is a promise that I'll *try*." Voice thick with tears and ecstasy, Cort tells us all we could hope for. "But I make no guarantees."

Ezra clings to me, his cock growing impossibly large, moving deeper the harder Cort thrusts into him. On the retreat, Ezra's eyelashes flutter shut, mouth parting on a breathy moan. He appears drugged until Cort advances. Surging forward with immense strength, Ezra's eyes pop wide and his dick pulses deep inside me. We ride this cycle together– the three of us.

"Too much! Can't last," Ezra rasps a second before he spasms. Near convulsing, eyes rolling back in his head, he releases a primal scream. Jerking within, a hot wash flows into me.

I don't orgasm because I'm too fascinated. Ignoring Cort's edict of '*don't look at me*,' I want to imprint every single second of this historic moment into my memory bank. I have no idea how Cortez lasts through Ezra's orgasm. But every time Ezra's muscles clench around Cort's cock, he grimaces and bites his lip. But then I realize he's drawing it out, savoring something he's wanted for so long but was too terrified to experience.

Once Ezra falls lax, seeming to pass out, Cortez takes his

pleasure. He doesn't shout, or yell, or scream. He doesn't even moan. Face awash with rapture, Cortez experiences the most powerful orgasm of his life, and I know this by the flood of tears that spill from his eyes and the beatific smile curling his lips.

"I don't think I have the strength but to experience this on our anniversaries," Ezra rasps into my ear, sounding lethargic yet blissed out. "Today has been the best day of my life. So now I'm going to go to sleep. When we wake up tomorrow, I'll try to recapture it."

Rolling a bit, dislodging Ezra's spent length from my body, the babies make themselves known by kicking my bladder. "No sleeping," I order.

"What?" Cort growls. "Unlikely. We are men. We sleep after sex. Unless you're making us a sandwich. But let us nap while you fix it. I'll take a Coke, some chips, and a handful of cookies while you're at it."

I extricate myself from the tangle of arms and legs, sliding from the bed to the floor. "Nope. Shower up. Get dressed. We have somewhere we need to be. Tonight."

"Uh-huh," Ezra and Cortez ignore me. After I sigh loudly with impatience, Ezra humors me. "Where, pray tell, do we need to be at this hour on our wedding night?"

I initiate act two, proving I will put my family's needs above my own. "We're going home."

"Come back to bed." Ezra reaches out to me. "Sleep with me. It's nice and warm, and I'm snuggly."

"Home?" Proving that Ezra was worked over the most of the three of us, Cort is the first to catch on. "We are home."

"Change of address," I mutter as I walk toward the bathroom, giving into the twins' incessant need to make me piss every ten minutes. "Our new home is Shadow Haven."

# Epilogue

## *Two Years Later*

"Hi!" Ezra greets me the moment I exit to the veranda. I walk over to him. Standing behind his chair, I tilt his head backward for an upside down kiss. "I missed you today."

"Me too," I whisper against his lips, and I then pull away to take a seat next to him. "But I got a lot of work done. James's book launch is going splendidly."

"Glad to hear it." Ezra scooches his chair over so it's closer to mine. He's always a bit clingy after we've worked separate schedules for an extended period of time. His patient list is fuller than usual, and Edge Publishing had two new releases this week. Busy. Busy. Busy.

"Cort?" I pose the question because the man is distancing himself from us just as we all suspected, spending too much time in Marc's care. Plagued with writer's block but refusing to let us in, he's a stay-at-home dad now. Sometimes Cort doesn't let me be a mother, adding extra strain to our lives. Which means Ezra's mental illness is flaring with regularity. A scared and lashing out Ezra is a terrifying thing.

Ezra snorts, shaking his head back and forth as he gazes out over Shadow Haven's back lawn, where Cort is chasing the kids in circles. "After the twins went down for their nap, Cort cornered me and begged to give me a blowjob."

"Seriously?" My eyes bulge in shock. "You're shitting me, right?"

"Honest to God." Ezra places his hand over his chest. "I did it, too. Anything to make him feel connected to us again. I always feel sick afterwards. I never want to touch Cortez with anything but a kind hand."

"I'm sorry we have to go through this. I'm sorry you have to listen to all of your patients' problems, and then come home to your own. If you need me to slow down at work, I will. I'll do anything to keep Cortez content," I say of the man we're treating like the unmanageable wife, with Ezra and myself as the husband. It's like Cort lost his sense of self since the words stopped flowing onto the page.

"I think he's been better today than he was last week, so that's good. Cort needs to rediscover his identity other than being '*daddy*'. The only adult activity he does is suck dick."

"I could take a few weeks off of work, and force Cort to relinquish the kids." I sigh heavily. "Of course, last time I contradicted him in parenting, he wanted to punch me. James told me today that Cort no longer goes to their writing group."

"I don't want to talk about it anymore." Ezra reaches over to take my hand. With a tug, he pulls me out of my chair, inviting me to sit on his lap. "Over-analyzing someone who refuses help solves nothing, and it's upsetting our lives. Talk to me about anything other than our wayward husband."

I snuggle into Ezra's lap, both of us content to sit in silence while we watch Cortez tackle Ava, much to the delight of the twins. Helping our daughter to her feet, Cort stands nose-to-nose with Ava. At fourteen, the girl is the exact same height as Ezra and Cortez.

Shadow Haven is a household full of angst. Our resident teenager is rather frightening at times, to the point that she's seeing a therapist three times a week. She's dating the ginger-haired Niel, who is way too old for her, but there is nothing I can do to dissuade it. We don't get along most of the time, which is par for the course. But when Ava is with her minions, a fierce maternal instinct emerges, and the twins are her sole focus. Those rare moments erase all the negativity in a heartbeat.

Just as watching Cortez with our children erases all the angst he puts us through. I knew when I married them what I was getting myself into, and I accepted this as a fact of life. Albeit an annoying fact of life, but one I can deal with.

"Is your mother having a nice time in California with Pearl and Divina?" I try for small talk, something I am horrific at doing.

Ezra presses his lips to my temple, smiling against my skin because he knows I couldn't give a shit less. While I think Pearl is easy to chat with, with her blunt, witty personality, and Divina is a riot of chaotic happiness, I personally hate Ezra's mother's guts. But who doesn't hate their mother-in-law?

"Is this your way of trying to figure out how long of a reprieve you have? Or are you asking if my aunt and cousin will be joining my mother when she makes her return trip home, essentially acting as a buffer?"

"I pray. Often." My muttered joke has Ezra laughing soundlessly, chest heaving next to my side. A while ago, I'd told him word-for-word of the odd exchange I had with Diane. I also asked him to explain to me how confession worked, and if you were actually absolved from your sins. I almost converted to Judaism by the time he was finished, which is precisely how Marcus convinced Ezra to convert.

"Just ignore my mother. It's what I always do. I'd say she's harmless, but I promised not to lie to you anymore." Ezra laughs again– still silent –because for some reason, the sound of their father's laughter draws the twins in like we're calling their name.

"How's Restraint? Did you still need me to go in tomorrow night as a Dungeon Monitor?"

With the publicity surrounding our family, Restraint has become a warped rite of passage, leading to brawls, riots, and bursts of unexplained violence. For some odd reason, when we hire security, they up and quit with no explanation. We've been threatened by the head of Maître du Jeu. If we don't get our people under control, the organization is sending someone who can. The thought seemed to terrify Marcus, which amused Ezra.

"Yes, thank you. I'd appreciate the help." Ezra squeezes me tightly. "We had another riot last night, and this morning we lost four more security personnel. Aaron and Regina are at their wits' end. Everyone is taxed across the board. In a few months, it will get better."

"How so?"

"An old friend of mine was injured in the Middle East. He's in a military hospital in Germany right now. I've been in contact with him. When he returns home, I've offered him a job to give him a sense of purpose. He lost most of his men, and sounded despondent when I spoke to him on the phone. It's similar to what's going on with Cortez, but on a much grander scale. I want him to head our security team. Not just Restraint, but head of security for all of the members."

"Wow, what's his name?"

"Caleb Green. We were good friends when we were growing up. Of course Cort was jealous."

"AH!" I drawl out. "The kid Cort kicked in the head with

his soccer cleat. This guy being around will motivate both of them, then." I snicker, thinking of how Cort needs a fire lit under his ass.

"As I said, I will try not to lie to you. I had thought of that. Mind you, it's purely friendship on our part, and I haven't been around Caleb since he was a teenager. But I have a good feeling about this."

"Do you ever wonder if Cort resents me? Sometimes he looks at me, and it's like he's wishing I didn't exist. Now that he has our children, I'm in his way." I voice my secret fears. "Maybe Cortez would feel better if–"

"Katya," Ezra rasps, squeezing me tightly. "Don't even finish that sentence. I know you won't make me choose, and I know Cort secretly wants me to. I refuse to choose, Katya, and I refuse to let you go. Don't even think of it."

I flip around in Ezra's arms, and kiss him fiercely. Sweet yet violent. Nearly three years we've been together, and the feeling that it's temporary has never vanquished. Running my hands through Ezra's hair, I draw his eyes into my view. "I love you with all of my heart– I always will. Unconditionally. But I feel like an interloper."

"Don't." Ezra places a fingertip to my lips, silencing me. "I love you, too. We just have to wait Cortez out. Eventually he will find his footing, grow up, and find a purpose in his life. Until then, we deal."

"Deal," I agree, murmuring against his fingertip. I give it a kiss, and then ask about Cortez's pacifier. "I take it Marc's away on business?"

"Why would you think that?" Ezra's eyebrow knit in the center, and then spread out impossibly wide across his forehead. "Ah, I understand your reasoning. Nope. Marc is around. Cortez just wanted my undivided attention today. He was so relaxed when I was finished, he asked me to suck him off as a reward."

Now that is a shock. "Did you?"

"No, I was a bit distraught over the violent act I had to commit moments earlier. I gave him a quick handjob, and then played tennis against Whitt for four hours to erase how dirty I felt."

"Pretty Boy didn't drag that kid with him, did he? Any kid with hair that color is a menace."

This time Ezra's laugh isn't silent. In fact, it's so loud it calls everyone in like a damn dinner bell. "No, Whitt knows better than to bring Niel to Shadow Haven. There are too many nooks and crannies for naughty teenagers to get into trouble. As for his red hair, did you suddenly forget how yours is the color of blood?"

"That beefy, testosterone-fueled, big boy has hair like a carrot. Everyone knows gingers have no souls." By the time I'm finished speaking, Ezra and I are laughing so hard we can't catch our breath.

"Speaking of a soulless gingy," Ezra gasps out just as our toddler daughter tackles him. "You promise her hair will darken to crimson as she ages?"

"Eh," I grunt as I'm tackled by our baby boy. "I sure hope so. How's my baby boy today?" I snuggle my little fellow, and he cuddles right into my arms where he belongs.

At two and a half, Marcus Zane never speaks. He can, but he refuses. Our son is Ezra in miniature– pale of hair and skin, with a quiet, gentle refinement –an ancient soul. He is mindful, doing all he's told, an avid learner, and very compassionate. Which led to Azrael being a holy terror.

"What. Is. Funny?" Azrael tries out her words, not giving a shit that she's stepping on my boob, her brother's head, and yanking at my hair to get closer to her father's face. She pokes Ezra in the mouth, tugging at his lips, trying to get him to laugh some more.

With a nip to her fingertip, "You are," Ezra says to make Azrael giggle. "You're our funny girl."

Tan-skinned, green-eyed, flame-haired, chubby, cherub-cheeked, Azrael is a demon.

My children have taught me a lot about good and evil. If anyone is familiar with Dungeons and Dragons, they would understand. Good. Neutral. Evil. Ezra and I created children who are split down the middle. Ava is pretty much evil most of the time, but her minions turn her into a saint. Marcus Zane balances this by being the purest soul I've ever met.

Nothing good can come from the convergence of my DNA mixed with Cortez's. Azrael is consistently neutral, neither good nor evil. She's demanding, pigheaded, bossy, playful, and sarcastic. In other words, she's exactly like her parents. When I look at Azrael, I find her to be the most fascinating creature in all existence, tied with Ava and Marcus Zane.

Coming to stand before us, Cort smiles brightly. He's in a good mood for once. He blew Ezra today, so why wouldn't he be? When Cortez is in a good mood, he loves the hell out of me. When he's in a bad mood, it's my fault.

I lean forward, ignoring my daughter's foot on my shoulder and how my son is not happy with me moving, and accept the kiss Cortez is offering. I love him too, even if I want to twist his nuts on a daily basis.

Pulling away from our kiss, Cort flashes me a grin and a wink, reading my mind. I fall in love with him all over again, just as I do every single day, even knowing someday he's going to destroy my heart.

"Azrael is not soulless," Cort repeats for the billionth time, as it's a running joke we use to pick on Ava's boyfriend. "Niel is a good kid."

"No, he's not," Ava says with a naughty smirk. "What was so funny?"

"Your mother was trying to be ironic again," Ezra answers, looking blissed out.

---

This isn't the end of Katya, Ezra, and Cortez's stories. Follow their journeys as the series progresses. Cortez (**The Hunter**, M&M **#10**) | Ezra (**Integrated**, M&M **#11**) | Katya (Dual-perspective novel: **Hero & Empowered**, M&M **#12**)
Restraint's resident sadist is next in the series: **Dexter** (M&M **#3**)

The long-standing Mistress & Master of Restraint series is dark and mysterious, with a warped sense of morality. Erotic romance fans, would you prefer something just as twisted, but not as dark? Try the Blended Series, beginning with Good Girl.

# -Acknowledgements-

A lot of work goes into writing a novel, and it isn't just by the writer herself. **My parents:** for their unconditional support. **My sister:** for her patience with the cover art. **My readers**: thank you for reading my twisted words and spreading my books to the masses. For without you, no one would have ever heard of my stories. My readers are my lifeblood. A shout out to the members of the **M&M of Restraint Group on Facebook**: thanks for the endless entertainment and inspiration. Thank you to my street team: **Erica Chilson's Deviants!** You guys ROCK! **Wicked Reads**: (in all its incarnations) **Angela G.**, thank you for taking over and making Wicked Reads better than I could have done by myself. & Thank you for helping me promote my work, and the work of other authors. A huge thank you to the **Wicked Writer's Betas** for keeping me grounded and encouraging me to keep trudging along when I get frustrated. Your thoughts and observations are invaluable. ((Hugs)) Beta readers who worked on Unleashed: **Kris D, Suz A, Darcy V, Diana C, Angela G, Diane P, Lisa J, Jacki G, Linsey T, Alexis W, Tassie M, & Liz S.** Someday, I'd love to meet you all in real life- it would be the experience of a lifetime.

# About the Author

Erica Chilson does not write in the 3$^{rd}$ person, wanting her readers to *be* her characters. Therefore, writing a bio about herself, is uncomfortable in the extreme.

Born, raised, and here to stay, the Wicked Writer is a stump-jumper, a ridge-runner. Hailing from North Central Pennsylvania, directly on the New York State border; she loves the changes in seasons, the humid air, all the mountainous forest, and the gloomy atmosphere.

Introverted, but not socially awkward, Erica prides herself on thinking first and filtering her speech. There are days she doesn't speak at all. If it wasn't for the fact that she lives with her parents, giving her a sense of reality, she would be a hermit, where the delivery man finds her months after expiration.

Reading was an escape, a way to leave a not-so pleasant reality behind. Reading lent Erica the courage she gathered from the characters between the pages to long for a different life. Writing was an instrument of change, evolving Erica into the woman she is today– a better, more mature, more at peace thinker.

Erica has a wicked mind, one she pours out into her creations. Her filter doesn't allow all of it to erupt, much to her relief. Sarcastic, with a very dark, perverse sense of humor, Erica puts a bit of herself into every character she writes.

Erica Chilson loves hearing from readers. If you would like more information on release dates, works in progress, teaser chapters, and random bits of madness...

FB Fan Page: https://www.facebook.com/thewickedwriter
Website: ericachilson.com
Via email: wickedwriter.ericachilson@gmail.com
**DEVIANTS ONLY**, if you'd like to join Erica Chilson's closed Facebook group, M&M of Restraint:
https://www.facebook.com/groups/MistressandMaster/

www.ingramcontent.com/pod-product-compliance
Lightning Source LLC
Chambersburg PA
CBHW051930020726
47501CB00001B/51